A WORLD
OF
DIFFERENCE

•

Leona Blair

BANTAM BOOKS

NEW YORK • TORONTO • LONDON • SYDNEY • AUCKLAND

For

Micah Steven

Alexander Martin

and

Alexandra Seena

with love

A WORLD OF DIFFERENCE
A Bantam Book
Bantam hardcover edition / September 1989
Bantam paperback edition / September 1990

Grateful acknowledgment is made for permission to reprint the following: From "Ash Wednesday" in COLLECTED POEMS 1909–1962 by T. S. Eliot, copyright 1936 by Harcourt Brace Jovanovich, Inc. copyright © 1963, 1964 by T. S. Eliot, reprinted by permission of the publisher. Lyrics from "Do It Again" by George Gershwin and B.G. DeSylva copyright 1922 WB Music Corp. (Renewed) All rights reserved. Used by permission.

ISBN 0-553-28435-5

Published simultaneously in the United States and Canada

Bantam Books are published by Bantam Books, a division of Bantam Doubleday Dell Publishing Group, Inc. Its trademark, consisting of the words "Bantam Books" and the portrayal of a rooster, is Registered in U.S. Patent and Trademark Office and in other countries. Marca Registrada. Bantam Books, 666 Fifth Avenue, New York, New York 10103.

PRINTED IN THE UNITED STATES OF AMERICA

OPM   0 9 8 7 6 5 4 3 2 1

Teach us to care and not to care.
Teach us to sit still.

—T. S. Eliot, *Ash Wednesday*

BOOK I

◆

1904–1919

1

♦

There were two women in labor that day in Brandon's Gate, one on the flats near the river where the textile workers lived, and the other in one of the mansions on the heights overlooking the Mohawk. The doctor's carriage, pulled by a powerful pair of matched bays, was racing toward the mansion, but even in his haste he marveled at the beauty of the snow-clad countryside billowing out around him.

Dr. Phillip van Dorn, a small, slim man in his forties, had been born in one of the mansions, and the names on the neatly lettered signs he passed were familiar to him: Hendrik, Anders, van Reitjens, Cassadyne, Brandon. He was on his way to Rhys Brandon's wife, and his face betrayed both anger and concern.

"I warned him," he muttered, rubbing at the misted window to check the coach's progress. "I warned him about this." He calculated quickly. Georgianna Brandon was in labor six weeks before her baby was due. The miracle was that she had carried a child even this long after four miscarriages in as many years—all because Rhys Brandon could not master an insatiable appetite for his wife.

The doctor sighed. Sometimes he felt that the confidences his patients entrusted to him were too heavy to bear. He was a repository of the community's most intimate secrets. He had decided long ago that everyday human relationships were more shocking than any invented by fiction, and family relationships the most explosive of all. Behind the shutters of these homes were furies

3

and passions of cosmic proportions, but the world saw only
the many facades constructed to hide the wars within
Husbands and wives, parents and children, brothers and
sisters—they were all casualties of the battle in one way or
another.

The coachman had slowed the horses to turn them off
the main road and onto a private lane flanked by oaks.
Now he whipped them up again on the mile-long approach road to the house. It sat at the top of a gentle
slope, a red brick Georgian mansion with four white columns tinted russet by the frosty afternoon sun.

A quiet lay over the house. That stillness, van Dorn
knew, meant its master was not at home. Rhys had an
inner energy that galvanized everyone around him while
he himself was ever easy, always affable.

The doctor had always thought the Brandons were ill
matched, no matter what a fine-looking couple they made.
Georgianna Brandon's beauty could not disguise her essential frigidity any more than Rhys Brandon's restraint
hid his sensuality. Georgianna shone with brilliant intelligence and impeccable taste, but there was not that undercurrent of eroticism that makes some women glow, beautiful
or not.

"Where the devil is he?" Dr. van Dorn demanded
softly. He jumped down from the carriage before the
footman could pull out the steps and took the three stairs
to the portico at a bound. The front door opened for him
as he reached it.

He greeted the butler briefly and dropped his bag to let
the man help him out of his coat. Then a cry, weak but
piercing, made both men look up, and the doctor, cursing
again, retrieved his bag and climbed the broad, carpeted
stairs two at a time.

♦

By six o'clock that evening Rhys Brandon was still an hour
from home in the great Brandon coach-and-four. He poured
brandy from a silver carriage flask into a small crystal glass
and offered it to the woman who sat facing him.

"I think I will," Constance said. "It's getting colder."

Rhys smiled, pouring a healthy drink for himself. "I like a woman who enjoys fine brandy the way you do, Constance, no matter what the weather."

She smiled faintly before sipping the liquor with relish, and Rhys glanced appreciatively at his sister-in-law, enjoying the tremor of attraction between them. Constance had enormous self-assurance despite her comparative youth, but she kept a wary distance between herself and the world, a distance that, in odd moments, Rhys considered exploring. He was convinced that unlike most well-born women, she would have welcomed it.

She bore no physical resemblance to Georgianna. Constance was a handsome girl with an opulent figure, hidden at the moment under a sable cloak lined with garnet cashmere. Her hair under her sable toque was not Georgianna's shining gilt, but a more ordinary dark amber, and her eyes were a watchful, changeable hazel, neither cool nor intensely blue like her sister's. But she was sleekly healthy and there was a promise about her, all the more tantalizing because of her distance, that aroused him. He was usually careful not to show it.

She was still unmarried—a dubious distinction for a girl of nineteen—and Rhys often wondered why. It was certainly not for want of suitors. The Hendrik sisters, with little more than a year between them, had always been much sought after among the gentry of Upstate New York, and now that Rhys had reestablished the Hendrik fortune, Constance was a prize.

Yet Rhys, although vividly aware of Constance from the start, had been mesmerized by her sister. The devil himself had made Georgianna to enchant him. She was like a Botticelli, delicate as a shell. She was as tall as Constance, but her figure was slender and pliant and her coloring as breathtaking as the paintings and figurines in the Brandon art collection. He knew from the first that they would make a striking pair, both of them blond and aristocratic and fair of face, and the knowledge gratified him. He was a man who expected adulation; he had always had it. And what better wife than a girl whose physical beauty, coupled with his, would inspire it?

When they were engaged, Rhys anticipated possession of his sixteen-year-old bride with a fervor that shocked even him. He saw it as much more than the union of two of the region's first families; it would be like making love to Venus. The devastating reality was that Georgianna shrank from his embrace. After his initial astonishment—Rhys had never before been denied anything he wanted—her reluctance heightened his desire. She became an obsession: he had to make her respond to him, to make her come alive in his arms, as Pygmalion had willed warm life into his marble Galatea.

Only this latest pregnancy had kept him from her; he wanted an heir as much as he wanted her. Her intelligence made him ache all the more for a son by her. Young as she was, she could manipulate people as well as he did, using her lethal wit where charm and beauty did not suffice.

Rhys was a man of many appetites, not only for the wealth and influence to which he was born, but for beautiful objects as well. He took a deeply sensual pleasure in good food and fine wine, in luxurious apparel and furnishings, and in women. But none so compelled him as this unattainable vision, his wife, admired, adored, and coveted by every man who saw her. They all imagined, as he had done, that physical beauty, which was assumed to reflect purity of character, was a promise of sensuality too. The latter misconception, at least, was true of Rhys.

He was an impressive man, a man people trusted the moment they saw him. His height was apparent even when he was seated, as he was now in the rocking, racing carriage, but he moved with quiet grace and spoke with polite reserve. His blond beard enhanced his Jovian face. He was meticulously dressed, his frock coats tailored to lie across his broad shoulders without a wrinkle. He would have seemed a mild-mannered man except for his eyes. They were green, wide set, and absolutely inscrutable, even when he spoke to women.

"You've bought up all of Albany today," he said now to his sister-in-law, gesturing toward the boxes piled next to her.

"Most of the things are for Georgianna and the baby," she replied.

"Of course, of course," he temporized. She was uncomfortable about money because she owed almost all she had to Rhys. Only a small and dwindling fortune had remained to the Hendrik girls when Rhys and Georgianna married and Rhys had acquired the failing Hendrik textile mills along with his wife. The plant and equipment, five miles upriver, where the Hendrik farmlands were, had been rescued from the one Hendrik brother's mismanagement and made a subsidiary of Brandon Textile Mills. In addition, Georgianna's dowry included twenty percent of the Hendrik railroad shares. Constance and the incompetent brother, Adam, held equal amounts. The rest of the stock had been bought by the public.

For his part, Rhys had settled a handsome sum on Georgianna and the children she would have and had promised to restore the Hendrik fortune. He was as good as his word. In the five years since his wedding Hendrik Textiles had begun to show a profit and the railway shares continued to climb as Rhys amalgamated their holdings with his own track and added new rolling stock. His wife, with an extraordinary grasp of business, had encouraged him in all of it. Her keen judgment was shocking in a woman but she had enough breeding to keep it hidden from the world at large.

Rhys was not fond of business, as Georgianna was, but success had come easily to him from the day his father died, as it had come to all the Brandons since they settled in the Mohawk Valley before the Revolution, first to farm, then to trade, then to spin and weave. Even Rhys's aesthetic bent was profitable. Under his management the value of the Brandon art collection, started by his great-grandfather, was appreciating steadily. What he wanted now was a houseful of sons to carry on his legacy.

Georgianna had carried past her seventh month. This time, he told himself, he would have an heir.

"We've passed the mill," Constance said, peering through the window as the streetlamps of Brandon's Gate began to illuminate the darkness.

She meant the old windmill at the entrance to the town, not the great spinning mills on the flatlands near the river. The town's name derived from the gates that had ringed the Brandon estate before it grew into a township, gates that had been tended by small boys and opened, upon payment of a fee, for the farmers who used the perimeter road.

The farmers had moved west of the hill years before, surrendering their river land to the encroaching mills with their need for water power. As the mills grew, the workers' town expanded to the north and south. Only the heights remained inviolate, the preserve of wealthy families whose interests were no longer confined to farming and who had moved from their outlying estates to build fine residences on what had once been the outer fringes of Brandon land.

◆

The journey was almost at an end and Constance, who treasured every moment she managed to spend alone with Rhys, agonized at how quickly it had passed. Her composure hid a state of constant agitation whether she was near Rhys or not. She wondered what he would do if she told him she loved him. Would he take her in his arms and kiss her? Would he defy convention—she believed he would!—by seducing her? Ignorant as she was of sex, she knew he would. There was something volatile about Rhys, something behind his brotherly affability, that made her sure he desired her, whatever his apparent devotion to her sister.

He should have married *me*, Constance thought. I'm the kind of woman he needs, not Georgianna, who looks like a goddess and thinks like a banker.

Her brother, Adam, frequently observed that although

Rhys might look the part, he was not a god. When she looked at Rhys, Constance did not entirely agree.

"We'll be there none too soon for me," Rhys said, moving restlessly. He hated the confines of a carriage. Had Constance not accompanied him to Albany, he would have gone on horseback by the post road and enjoyed the expanses of virgin snow. As it was, they had started for Albany together early in the morning, she to attend to her shopping, he to his business.

His visit had been successful. He had bought out the last of the railroad's public stockholders, putting the shares in his wife's name—Georgianna would be pleased by that—and now the line was entirely his, apart from the Hendrik shares in it. Rhys and his wife virtually controlled those: Adam Hendrik would never understand business. As for Constance—but Rhys knew he could manage Constance.

Rhys glanced at her again, reviewing their early dinner at the best restaurant in Albany. He enjoyed her company. He wondered again what Constance would be like in bed, if her lush promise was as illusory as her sister's. Then he put the thought aside; a scandal like that could ruin even him. The next time he went to Albany he would go alone and spend the night at a very acceptable bordello the city offered.

"Thank you for a wonderful day," Constance said, leaning toward him as if into his thoughts.

He took her gloved hand and drew her imperceptibly forward. Her lips were parted. For a second he considered kissing her, but he only raised her hand to his mouth in a broad gesture of gallantry, released her, and leaned back, watching the glow fade from her eyes. He had not imagined it; he had seen that glow before. Yes, something had to be done about Constance, but first he must marry her off.

"Shall I take you home directly?" he asked, corking the silver flask.

"No, I'll look in and see how Georgianna is." It was impossible to tell how Constance felt about anyone. She might have adored Georgianna—or resented her—or both.

♦

There was a bustle in the entrance hall as Dr. van Dorn came down the broad, curving staircase. He could hear the snorting of the horses outside, then Rhys's boots as he stamped off the snow before he came into the foyer. Constance was at his side, and behind them were two footmen carrying piles of boxes.

"Phillip?" Rhys demanded. "Why are you here so late? Is anything wrong?"

The doctor nodded, too weary to speak, but his reddened eyes met Rhys's in angry despair.

"It's Georgianna," Constance said, coming to his side. "She's lost the baby, hasn't she?"

"No," van Dorn said, his voice so low they strained to hear him. "Not this time. This time she died." He turned toward the drawing room. "I need a drink," he said.

The other two followed him. "My God," Rhys shouted, suddenly vehement. "What did you do to her, you blundering butcher!"

Constance's eyes widened, but the doctor did not seem surprised by the uncharacteristic outburst. Van Dorn went to the sideboard, poured some whiskey, and swallowed it before he spoke again.

"What did *I* do?" he asked softly, facing Rhys and enunciating every word he said. "I warned you that another pregnancy so soon might kill her." Rhys blanched, and the doctor glanced at Constance and checked himself abruptly.

"Rhys," he said after a moment, moved by the younger man's misery, "we mustn't talk of blame. She died of a hemorrhage. There was nothing anyone could do about it." He shook his head. "You must accept that, Rhys, and mourn your wife quietly, as the rest of us will."

The doctor sat down heavily near the fire, one hand covering his eyes, and for several long moments there was no sound in the room except the crackling of the fire, no movement but the shadows it cast upon the expanses of velvet and damask and gleaming cabinetry. The portrait of

Georgianna above the fireplace gazed down upon them, exquisite and remote.

"I apologize, Phillip," Rhys said at last, turning away from the doctor. "I'm not myself. I shouldn't have . . ." His voice trembled, then faded.

The door to the drawing room opened and footsteps padded softly across the thick, deep carpets.

"I've brought the wean, sir," Georgianna's maid said to Rhys in her gentle Irish brogue. "I thought it would be a comfort to you."

Rhys turned with a distant hope. "A son?" he asked hoarsely, moving forward.

"A daughter," the woman said apologetically, and offered him the bundle. "A little Miss Georgianna."

Rhys shook his head. "Not now," he muttered. "I can't."

The maid blushed and turned to Constance with her offering. The doctor saw Constance take the child and, holding it, look intently at Rhys over the baby's head, her face unreadable. Then van Dorn rose and left the room, leaving them there together, Georgianna's stricken husband and her impassive sister and her child, poor little mite.

He wondered if the baby would survive. He sighed. He must find a wet nurse; the boiled barley water he had ordered would not keep her alive very long. He did not think she could tolerate the richness of cow's milk.

Damn Rhys, he fumed inwardly as the butler helped him on with his coat and handed him his bag. Damn Rhys and his lust. Damn all men who know nothing and care less about what a woman suffers to bear a child. The doctor shuddered. He himself had hurt Georgianna terribly, that beautiful young creature, and still he had not been able to save her.

He approached his waiting carriage and stopped as someone tugged at the hem of his overcoat. He looked down.

A small boy, obviously one of the mill workers' children, stood shivering in the wind, his cap covered with snow.

"Doctor, you must come to my mum," the child said through blue lips.

Van Dorn bent to hear him. "What is it, boy?"

"It's the babby."

"What's wrong with the baby?"

"It's been coming two nights and all this day and still it can't get born."

"Your mother won't want a doctor," van Dorn said. The mill women never let a doctor examine them, much less attend them in childbirth. "You must get the midwife."

The boy spat contemptuously in the snow. "She's a silly cow," he said. "I want you to come." His black eyes blazed like a man's, although he could not have been more than six or seven.

Van Dorn, feeling mortally weary, shook his head and put a foot on the carriage steps, but the boy clutched at the coat, his small face dark with fury. "You don't care if she dies," he said clearly. "Damn you to hell then, and if my mother dies I'll kill you and send you there, I swear it."

The man and the boy gazed at each other. A moment earlier, van Dorn said to himself, I was condemning men who were careless of a woman's suffering. Out of the mouths of babes . . .

He put a hand on the boy's shoulder. "All right, boy, I'll try to help her if she'll let me. Tell my man where we're going, then climb inside with me before you catch your death."

The carriage rattled off, away from that house so heavy with guilt and grief. But, the doctor reflected sadly, he was only abandoning one set of secrets—why had Constance not shed a tear for her sister?—for another. What manner of family, for example, had produced this furious child, already old with anger?

"What is your name?" van Dorn asked the boy sitting across from him like a Solomon in judgment.

"Connor. Connor MacKenzie."

2

◆

He crouched behind the washstand in his mother's bedroom, watching and listening.

He had streaked across the tiny kitchen-parlor and into the bedroom as soon as the coach stopped, ignoring the protests of the midwife and a neighbor woman sitting by the bed. He had pushed past them to clutch his mother's hand and beg her not to die, swearing that he would be good forever if only she would not die.

For the first time in his life she had not responded to him except with that exhausted scream and the same agonized thrashing of her swollen body that he had seen for two days. He tried not to cry but he could not help himself. His sobs mingled with tears.

Then the doctor had picked him up and put him out of the bedroom and set him to keeping the hearth fire stirred and the water boiling in the pan atop the stove. The instruments in the pan, cruel and glittering, made him shudder. Forceps, the doctor called them when he told the neighbor woman to fetch them. And Connor had slipped into the room just after her, to hide behind the washstand and pray that the three leaning over the bed would not hurt her.

"The child's dead," the doctor said softly, removing a long tube from his ear that he seemed to listen through. "I must take it with the forceps."

"Poor lass," the midwife said, "she's already suffered so much."

Connor shuddered again.

"She won't suffer anymore," the doctor said. "I have

13

chloroform in my bag." He asked for some grease and went to smooth some on Dilys MacKenzie's face. He laid a small cloth over it. "I'm going to put you to sleep, Mrs. MacKenzie," he said soothingly as he worked, and Connor adored him for his gentleness. "Don't be afraid, just breathe deeply." He put some kind of box over her mouth and nose and dripped something onto it. A heavy, sickly-sweet smell rose and mixed with the acrid body odors in the room. "Stay here," he ordered the other woman, handing her the metal flask. "I'll tell you when to use more—a drop at a time."

Then he returned to the foot of the bed and picked up one of the curved steel pieces shaped like a long flat spoon at one end. Connor stuffed a fist into his mouth to smother his sobs.

He knew, without knowing how he knew, that the baby had to come out of his mother's body from a secret place in her lap, obscured from view by the doctor and the midwife, where the forceps must be. He knew his father had put the baby in there somehow and he cursed his father silently for doing that and then deserting both of them, Dilys and Connor, to do God-knew-what, the mill-town gossips said.

He caught himself; his mother had taught him that it was wicked to take the Lord's name in vain and he didn't want to offend the Lord, not now, when she was as still as death.

"Don't listen to her prattle about God," his father had advised him, laughing fondly. "It's being a minister's daughter makes her believe such tripe. The Lord doesn't listen to the likes of us."

"Then who does He listen to?"

"Rich folk, like the Brandons up there on the heights. They're the real lords."

Honor thy father and thy mother, Dilys had taught him. And he had, he *had*! It was easy to love his mother, with her shining hair that felt so good to stroke, her skin as pink and sweet as peaches, and her soft, warm arms. And once he had loved his father, too, loved Enoch's big voice that matched his strong body and his piercing eyes, coal black like his hair. His father knew things other fathers didn't bother about, things called wealth and oppression and labor laws. Enoch cared more about those things than about anything else, including Connor.

You bastard! Connor thought, using the worst word he knew. You rotten old bastard, I'll hate you till I die.

"Here it is," the doctor said now. "Strangled by the cord, poor little thing."

"A girl!" the midwife said a second later. "And perfect too. What a pity. Still, it'll be hard enough for the poor woman to feed two mouths, let alone three."

Damn you, Connor raged silently at his father, over and over, as if rage could blot out the horror of that bloody travail and the glistening, dead little thing that was its terrible fruit, lying on a newspaper on the floor.

The two bent to their patient again. It seemed a long time to Connor before they finished whatever they were doing, and still his mother had not stirred. The doctor listened at her chest with his tube and nodded. "She'll do," he said, smiling at the waiting women, and Connor breathed again. "You might bathe her and change her linen while she's still half asleep," the doctor went on, placing his instruments in a cheesecloth sack, then in his bag. He bade the women good night and walked wearily into the kitchen, where his coachman snored in the corner.

Connor followed him, dragging a chair close to the fire for him, stirring the fire back to life. While the doctor washed and dried his hands Connor fetched a glass and the bottle of plum brandy from the shelf and proffered it silently.

The doctor drank it gratefully, studying his small host. His own son, Peter, was a little younger and, thank God, ignorant of what this child knew. He took a handkerchief from his pocket and wiped the boy's tear-stained face gently. "There, Connor, it's all over now. I'm sorry I couldn't save your sister, but your mother will be good as new in a week. You needn't be frightened anymore."

Connor drew a long, shuddery breath. "It's a fearful thing, getting born."

"You were in there? You shouldn't have been." Van Dorn shook his head. "You mustn't think about it until you're much older, Connor, until I can explain it to you." The doctor rolled down his sleeves, rose, and reached for his coat. "I gather your mother's a widow. Someone must arrange to bury the child decently."

Fury came back to the boy's face, flushing away the pallor of exhaustion. "He's not dead, but I wish he was. He went away a long time ago. He said he didn't want another baby or to work in these mills. He wants to make unions in other mills." Connor looked up, his eyes black as ink. "I don't know what unions are, but I hate him because he wants them more than me and my mother."

"I'm sorry, Connor." Van Dorn sighed and put on his greatcoat, rousing the coachman. Then a thought seemed to strike him. "Did your mother work in the mills?"

The boy looked away, shaking his head. "Never. My father's the best spinner they ever had. He made good wages." His pride struggled to the surface, then was submerged again by his rage. "She says she'll have to go to work now, but I won't let her. I'm almost seven. I can be a sweeper in the mills." He pulled his slim, sturdy body up to its full height and spoke with the absolute conviction that no longer surprised the doctor. "I'll take care of her myself."

My God, the doctor thought, what a man he'll make.

"Of course you will, Connor. But first let me see what I can do to make things easier for both of you." He turned to go and the boy tugged the cottage door open for him. "Good night, my boy. Go to bed now. Your mother will need you tomorrow. She must have some soup and tea when she wakes. I'll be by to see her before noon."

The boy gave a ragged sigh of relief that made van Dorn stop and turn back to look down into those dark eyes.

"You're a fine lad, Connor MacKenzie," he said. "I'm proud to know you." He offered his hand and Connor shook it solemnly, that touching admixture of child and man reflected as much by his dignity as it had been by his anger. Van Dorn had an impulse to clasp the child to him, to comfort him as he would have comforted his own boy, but Connor MacKenzie, almost seven, needed to feel he was a man tonight.

♦

"I don't know," Rhys said late the next morning. He rose from his chair in the book-lined study and began to pace. "I can't think clearly."

"You must decide quickly," the doctor persisted, setting down his coffee cup with a warning clatter. "This is a healthy young woman who'll have plenty of milk—and the baby needs a wet nurse soon or she'll die."

Van Dorn paused and looked at the haggard, red-eyed man before him. Rhys had been out riding in the frosty dawn but his handsome face was still pale and drawn. "Have you seen your daughter this morning?" the doctor asked.

Rhys nodded, his bleak expression unchanged. "She's delicate, like her mother." He gazed out the window, trying to control his emotions, and the doctor's heart went out to him. Rhys had loved Georgianna, even though far too well.

"I'm going to call her Georgia," Rhys said at length. "And of course we'll have the woman brought here immediately."

"What woman?" Constance spoke from the doorway. She was wearing unrelieved black but the somber dress only set off her vivid coloring. Her eyelids were slightly puffy but otherwise she seemed in complete command of herself.

"Good morning, Constance," Rhys said, going toward her, his hands outstretched to clasp hers. He bent and his cheek grazed hers. "Thank you for coming. Did you bring your things?"

"Yes, they're being brought upstairs now. What woman?"

"A wet nurse for Georgia," van Dorn said. "A woman from the flats gave birth last night, but her baby didn't survive."

Constance nodded. "We can put her in the servants' quarters."

The doctor demurred. "Too far—and connected to the house by that drafty corridor. She needs warmth and rest to recover and good food, as well, if she's going to nourish a child."

"She can live on the third floor, then. I'll tell Mrs. O'Brien to prepare a room and have the baby's things moved upstairs." Constance half turned, then looked back at Rhys. "If that's all right?" she asked, suddenly gentle.

"Certainly, Constance, whatever you say."

She nodded and moved off. "The room will be ready in an hour."

"Make it two rooms," van Dorn said. "She has a son."

Constance turned again and raised an eyebrow. "I'm not sure we want some hulking Irish boy living in this house."

"They're Scots-English," the doctor said. "And the child's not yet seven."

"Leave him with his father," Constance suggested. "Unless," she added sharply, "I'm to invite the whole family."

At least, the doctor thought a moment later, she has the grace to blush at her proprietary airs about Rhys's house. He turned to Rhys. "The father deserted them. A fellow named Enoch MacKenzie."

"Him!" Rhys said with an echo of his usual spirit. "An agitator—and the best mule spinner I had."

"Rhys," van Dorn said impatiently. "I've yet to persuade the woman to come as it is. I doubt she'd leave her only child behind. Now, what's it to be?"

"Bring him." Rhys shrugged. "There's enough room up there for a troop of little boys." His voice was strained. He had yearned for a houseful of Georgianna's sons.

The two men followed Constance out of the room and she disappeared toward the back of the house in search of the housekeeper, her hips swaying as she walked.

"I'm lucky to have her," Rhys said. "I asked her to come and see to things until the funeral's over."

The doctor glanced at him sharply but Rhys had spoken absently. Is it possible he has no idea, van Dorn won-

dered. He was convinced now of something he had long
suspected: Constance coveted her sister's husband. It had
surely been her idea to come and stay, cleverly engi-
neered to seem like his. It would undoubtedly be a pro-
tracted visit. Well, that was none of van Dorn's affair.
Rhys would be well able to look after himself once the
initial shock had passed.

The doctor climbed into his coach and set off to persuade Dilys MacKenzie to move to Brandon Hall and
bring her extraordinary son with her.

3

◆

Dilys, tucked up in the big four-poster on the third floor
of Brandon Hall that afternoon, sipped hot tea and
watched Connor anxiously, hardly daring to believe the
miracle that had come to pass on this darkest day of her
life. Bereft of her baby, she was neither wife nor widow,
with no one to help her provide for Connor. She was at
the end of the money Enoch had left . . . but she knew
she must not think of Enoch, not while she was still so
weak. She must think only of this house and these people
and of keeping the place she had been given among them.

She had been too faint when she arrived to notice the
grandeur of the house below. The footman had carried her
directly upstairs to this room, palatial by comparison with
the cottage where both her children had been born. She
herself had been raised in an English country parsonage
that was many times better. She had only a superior
education to show for that now, and memories of a better
life. The memories would have made a mill worker's cot-

tage unbearable—except for Enoch, for love of whom she
had disgraced her family to elope to America.

Now Enoch was gone forever. She had finally accepted
that. She was alone and yet, by some benign providence,
she was being cared for, she was warm and secure. She
had been put to bed between fine, soft sheets and brought
soup and fresh white bread and tea. She could rest her
battered body and regain her strength.

She was waiting now for the baby to be brought, aching
to hold a newborn in her empty arms. Her breasts were
swollen and she knew that the milk would come soon.

But Connor made her anxious. Somehow she must persuade her headstrong son to behave properly to their
benefactors. Whatever resentment he harbored against his
father now, he had been absorbing Enoch's prejudices
against the rich since the day he was born.

◆

"I won't go!" Connor had said that morning, glaring at the
doctor.

"But he wants to help you and your mother!"

"Be damned to him! We will not live under that man's
roof!"

"That man?" Dr. van Dorn had asked, astonished. "Have
you met Mr. Brandon?"

"No, but he's just like all rich men, not to be trusted."

"Come here, Connor," the doctor had said, drawing the
boy to his side. "Look at me. I'm a rich man."

"Aye, but you're different," Connor had muttered, too
embarrassed to meet the doctor's eyes.

"So is he, take my word for it. But even if he were not,
Connor, there are many things a man of honor must do to
protect his womenfolk."

And Connor, striving to be the honorable man his father
was not, had agreed to come.

◆

Dilys watched him now, adoring him even as he stood
there, planted suspiciously in the center of the room and

wearing that lowering look that darkened the beauty of his face. He had Enoch's almost-black hair and eyes, but he had her features, and the combination was strikingly beautiful whether he smiled or scowled as he was doing now, looking around the room as if it were a dungeon.

But the room was lovely! It was large and bright, with windows on two walls. The light-faded wallpaper was a pattern of pale pink trellised roses and there were pink cretonne side-drapes at the windows over white muslin curtains. A rocking chair padded with green quilted cushions faced the blazing fire; beside it was an armchair upholstered in worn but lovely tapestry. There was a small writing table and chair near one window, a chest of drawers and a wardrobe along the wall, and a folding screen in the corner beside a washstand and a rack of thick flannel towels.

The one new thing in the room was a white wicker bassinet, lined and skirted in Brandon-made pink and white gingham, that the footman had just set down near Dilys's bed. Across from it was the door to an adjoining room that would be the nursery. Connor's room was next to this one. She knew that having a room of his own had impressed him more than he would admit. He had always slept on a trundle bed in the kitchen.

There were sounds from the hallway and a heavyset, florid woman swept in wearing a black alpaca dress and a frilled bombazine apron far too formal for her manner. A large ring of keys hung from her belt. She was Mary O'Brien, the housekeeper, who had greeted Dilys and Connor when they arrived and shepherded them up the stairs along with her flock of Irish maids carrying soup and tea and hot bricks wrapped in flannel.

"There you are, Mrs. MacKenzie dear, all comfortable now, I hope. You must tell me if you need anything at all." She came to the bed and peered down at Dilys. "It's crying you've been," she clucked, her brogue broadening as it did when she was touched. "For your own little girl, to be sure."

"Yes, but also because I'm so grateful to be here."

The big woman took Dilys's hand. "And it's happy I am to welcome you. Now it's time you met Miss Georgia. Poor wee thing, she's too weak even to cry." She bustled out to the hall and returned cradling the infant. "Here she is," she said, placing the bundle in Dilys's arms.

Overcome by the feel of a baby, Dilys closed her eyes for a moment. When she opened them her son was watching her, suspicious of this new claim upon her.

She spoke softly to him. "Come and see her, Connor. She's going to live right here with us." He approached slowly and she turned back the blanket. The infant slept, tiny and fragile, her skin translucent. A pale golden fuzz covered her perfect little head.

Connor leaned on the bed to inspect her further. The other baby, his sister, had been blue and horrible; this one was as fine as white flour. But she seemed hardly to breathe.

"Will she die?"

"No, darling, not if we take good care of her." Dilys pressed her lips to the baby's head, crooning softly. The child stirred, woke, and waved a hand as delicate as a shell, grazing the boy's face.

Impulsively Connor held out a finger and the infant grasped it. His face took on an expression of delight, replacing the terror Dilys had seen while she was in labor and he dreading that she would die and leave him too.

"She's got a good grip," he said.

"Now, Master Connor," Mary O'Brien intervened, "we'll leave the ladies to get acquainted. Mr. Brandon is wanting to meet you, and after you've made your bow, Cook will give you a nice piece of gingerbread in the kitchen."

Connor turned to his mother, shaking his head decisively. "I will not meet him," he said. "What's he to me?"

"Hush, Connor," Dilys said severely. "He's taken us into his house and one of us must thank him for it."

"He only did it because he needs us."

"That will do, Connor!" Dilys admonished him, her eyes bright with sudden tears. "I will not stand for rudeness from my son."

"Don't cry, Mum," he whispered anxiously, touching her cheek. "I'll go, I'll go this minute."

"Connor," she said, her voice gentle again, "be kind to him. He's had a sad loss too."

She watched him leave in Mrs. O'Brien's ample wake, loving him as passionately for his pride as for his intelligence. He was still far too young to deal with so much heartache. His father should have thought of that before he went running off to save the workers of the new world.

The infant began to cry, a thin, thready wail. Dilys unbuttoned her gown and held her nipple to the baby's lips until they closed around it. She stroked the petal-soft cheek and the infant began to suck, easing some of the misery in Dilys's heart for her lost child, soothing her woman's pride and longing for the promise of joy Enoch had taken with him when he left. She had a job to do that was more important than he was. She had to care for this little girl and raise her son.

Now something stirred where only longing for Enoch had been. It was a resolve she had not known she possessed. Fate had offered her a way to give Connor a better life and she would make the most of it.

She lay back wearily and dozed, cradling the nursing infant, thanking God for her.

♦

"I've brought the boy," Mrs. O'Brien said, shepherding Connor into the drawing room.

"Really!" a woman's voice, cool and lofty, answered. "Can't it wait?"

"I asked for him," a man's voice replied. "It's all right, Mrs. O'Brien. You can leave him here."

The door closed and Connor waited in a vast, richly furnished room that appeared to be unoccupied except for two wing chairs before the fireplace, so positioned that one revealed only a pair of long, trousered legs stretched out and crossed at the ankles, and the other a woman's skirt. Three Irish setters, clustered around the man's chair, raised their heads momentarily. Above the fireplace loomed a life-size portrait of a blond lady wearing a white dress and diamonds in her hair who, Connor decided, must be a queen.

"Come here, boy, and let me see you," the man said, and Connor advanced across an enormous expanse of dark red carpet with a pattern that made him dizzy. He was headed for the space between the two chairs but at the last moment he turned sharply and stood to the left of the man's chair, putting a greater distance between himself and the woman who didn't want to meet him.

Even seated, it was clear the man was taller than his father. Connor raised his eyes and beheld the face of the enemy. This was the kind of man who squeezed the last drop of blood out of his workers for the least money, who kept Connor and his mother in their place. Connor had never seen a rich man before, but this one surprised him. He did not look like a slave driver.

He was fair, like the heroes in the stories Dilys told about King Arthur and his knights, and not in the least threatening, only sad. Connor's black brows relaxed a little.

"What is your name?" the rich man asked.

Connor told him and darted a look at the woman. She glanced at him briefly with large eyes, then returned to her lap desk and the papers on it. She was a pretty enough woman, but he could tell she didn't like him and Connor certainly didn't like her. He resumed his penetrating scrutiny of Mr. Brandon.

"Is your mother comfortable?" he asked.

"Yes, sir, and *she* thanks you for letting us come."

"I gather you are not as pleased."

Stand up to them, Enoch had taught him. Never let them think you're frightened by their filthy lucre and their fancy ways. "I didn't want to come," Connor said bluntly.

"Ah, I see." Mr. Brandon seemed both amused and curious. "Don't you like this house?"

Connor looked around the room again and set his shoulders firmly. "It's a nice enough house, but it isn't mine."

"There's a certain logic to that," Mr. Brandon observed to the woman.

"Impertinence, not logic," she replied.

He turned back to Connor. "You're very well spoken," he remarked.

"That I am," Connor said, wary of compliments as his father had warned him to be. He saw Mr. Brandon smile, but stiffly, as if a smile sat strangely on his lips. "My mother teaches me," Connor went on. "Her father was a minister."

"She must be proud to have a son like you," his host said, suddenly morose again, his green eyes clouded with grief.

Connor felt a rush of unbidden sympathy for his interlocutor. Whatever his faults, Mr. Brandon hadn't deserted *his* wife the way Enoch had. A silence fell as they gazed at each other. Connor's frown faded and his expression was searching, as if he could discern where the truth lay by observation alone.

"Is there something you want to tell me?" Mr. Brandon invited kindly after a moment.

A confusion of feeling made Connor mute. Then he remembered what he had decided to do. "I want to work in your mill."

"Work in the mill? Nonsense, you must go to school."

"I have to take care of my mother," Connor said, impatient at having to explain the obvious. "I can work after school."

"I see," the man said, and turned toward the woman again. "Well, van Dorn was right about this one." Again he studied Connor. "I shall have to see what work I can find for you. You may go now, Connor."

"Yes, sir." He made the bow his mother had taught him, one hand on his middle, the other at his back, and went back the way he had come, ready to claim his gingerbread from the kitchen.

◆

"Forthright little chap," Rhys said to Constance. "Handsome, too, and well mannered, all things considered, unlike the father. Have you met the mother yet?"

"No, I've been at these lists all day. I'm sure she'll do."

"She must be good with children, to judge by him." Rhys stirred restlessly in his chair, then got to his feet. The Irish setters followed suit, gaping and stretching. "I think I'll walk down to the stables."

Constance leaned forward. "Don't go, Rhys, I'll put this away. Stay and I'll ring for tea."

He shook his head. "Later, Constance. I must move around. Perhaps I'll take the boy with me. He takes me out of myself."

It was what Constance wanted to do. But she nodded and forced herself to remain quietly in her chair until he was gone, the dogs trailing after him. She sprang up when the door had closed and began to pace nervously around the room, picking up objects at random and replacing them. Then for a long moment she looked up at her sister's portrait.

"You're dead," she said venomously. "It's not my fault you're dead, but now that you are, it's my turn."

Her mouth tightened. She took a deep breath and went back to her funeral lists.

♦

Connor found the kitchen easily enough by the sounds and delicious smells coming from it. It was large and white and very clean, with polished copper pans hanging all over the walls and a great pot simmering on the enormous black range. The maids he had seen earlier sat drinking tea at a wooden table covered in yellow oilcloth. He was welcomed and introduced to the maids by a woman called Cook, who gave him gingerbread and a cup of hot cocoa and sat him at the table with the girls.

"You're tall enough to reach," Cook said kindly.

"It's a bonny boy he is," one of the maids said.

"A little thundercloud," another giggled.

"Stop your teasing, girls," Cook directed. "He'll do very well here once he gets accustomed."

Connor was beginning to think the same thing himself. He ate his cake and thought how his father would hate it, their being here in Brandon Hall. But he didn't care what his father thought anymore. His father didn't even know that his baby was dead. For all he knew, Connor was dead, too, and Mum. The bastard!

Mrs. O'Brien reappeared just as Rhys Brandon entered the kitchen. There was only a small flurry when he came in; it was his habit to wander all over his house. His black clothes made an inky contrast to the white walls and cupboards as he spoke to Connor.

"What do you know about horses?" he asked.

Connor stood up, still clutching his second piece of cake. "Not much," he said. "Sir. They're beautiful."

"If you want to work you can help feed my horses—but only after school. Would you like to do that for me?"

"And ride them?" Connor asked, testing.

Rhys smiled, aware now that he had not expected to smile for a long time and grateful to this child for giving him a reason. "And learn to ride them, yes." There was an answering smile on the boy's face now and a quick nod of agreement.

"That's settled, then. Now I must stretch my legs. We'll go down to the stables and have a look at the horses before the light's gone. Fetch your coat and meet me at the pantry door."

"Yes, *sir*." Connor left the cake and ran for the back stairs.

It was as well, Rhys thought, that Phillip van Dorn had warned him of the mark Enoch MacKenzie had left on the boy's character, but Rhys welcomed the challenge of erasing it.

Rhys now turned to the housekeeper. "Is the child getting on well with her nurse?" he asked her after refusing an offer of gingerbread from the cook.

Mary O'Brien beamed. "Very well, indeed, sir, I've just been up to see. Miss Georgia's been fed and they're sleeping like two angels, the pair of them together. There's some color in Miss Georgia's wee face already."

Rhys nodded. "Thank heaven for that." He went back to the hall to get his coat.

"The dear, lovin' man," Cook sighed.

"He is that," Mary O'Brien agreed.

"A sight too lovin' in certain ways," Georgianna's personal maid, Peggy, remarked. "But then, you can't blame him for that. It's how they are, every man jack of 'em."

The others nodded. The drawing room bell jangled and Cook's expression changed from fond to cool. "That's herself. Whatever will she be wantin' now?"

"I'll go," Mary said. "It's probably more instructions for after the funeral service. I suppose we're lucky to have her."

The cook responded with an eloquent sniff, but Mary was a practical woman, with a living to earn. When the funeral was over, God rest poor Mrs. Brandon's soul, her sister would go home and the house would settle down. It would feel empty at first, but there was the baby now. Dilys MacKenzie was a sweet little woman and her son, a bit wild though he was, had already brought a breath of fresh air to the house.

With a respectful expression already settling on her round face, the housekeeper went through the house and knocked on the library door.

♦

Rhys and Connor started down the hill to the stables, the dogs gamboling after them in the snow, Rhys looming tall and black against the whiteness as he had against the kitchen walls. Connor, looking up, saw the mourner's armband on his coat.

"I forgot to say how sorry I am for your trouble," Connor said.

Rhys nodded. "Thank you. And I for yours."

Connor was bewildered until he remembered the blue baby. But she had never been really alive. It was not as if he had known her for a long, long time the way a husband knows his wife. He searched for some comfort to offer the man. "My mother and I will take good care of Georgia," he said earnestly. "I promise."

Rhys stopped and bent to tighten the child's muffler and pull his collar up around his ears. His eyes, intensely green, met Connor's. "I know you will," he said simply. "I'm very glad you've come."

A great wave of affection swept over Connor, washing away his doubts, washing away everything Enoch had taught him about Rhys Brandon and men like him. Why should he believe anything his father said? This man wanted him and his father didn't.

"I'm glad too," he said. He took Rhys's extended hand and, bending into the wind, they walked on together down the hill to the stables.

◆

The wind screamed like a banshee, but Enoch MacKenzie had been forced awake by the fetid odor of thirty unwashed men sleeping in an airless shed. At the beginning, when he first left Brandon's Gate, he used to reach for Dilys in the morning. He missed her warm body and her innocent ardor. But that was a creature comfort. It was Connor he longed for.

He got out of his bed in his long underwear, his breath a cloud on the frosty air of the shed, and put on his boots. Then he went out to the johnny back of the shed to relieve himself, scooping a handful of clean snow on his way there and back to wash his face and freshen his mouth.

He stood a moment in the dark March morning and welcomed the sting of frigid air on his body, turning his thoughts from his son. He thought about the mills at Brandon's Gate instead, and how impossible it had been to organize the workers there.

"Faugh!" he said softly. "What did I expect?"

Brandon's Gate was not like the great textile center of Cohoes, where an active labor organization had flourished for years. The Gate was run like a paternalistic society, with Brandon playing benevolent despot, lulling them all with the crumbs from his table. And the majority of the workers were women, all of them more concerned with feeding their kids today than fighting for their futures.

He spat. Rhys Brandon was the most insidious of the textile men because he gave his workers just enough to make them love him. He paid higher wages than anyone else, so computed that they worked out to mere pennies more than others were offering. He provided a company school for the children until they were twelve—and company stores on which he turned a huge profit. He gave his workers clean, solid housing.

Didn't it matter, then, that the workers labored from six in the morning till six at night, or that children who were just getting their growth went straight into the mills to breathe that moist air, heavy with lint, and the fumes of chemicals and sizing? Or that a family, no matter how large it was, had to cram itself into two rooms?

Anger choked the breath in Enoch's throat. He was a big man, broadly built and handsome in a virile way that commanded the admiration of women and the attention of men. "My lion," Dilys called him in bed. But it was really his anger that gave him presence. It billowed up out of him so that his eyes flashed and his deep voice rumbled a call to arms wherever he went. He had a mission, and any worker who met him knew within five minutes what it was. It took the owners a little longer to find out, and when they did he was fired.

He didn't care. He had moved from job to job over the past year and widened his contacts in several industries.

He looked back at the rough shed provided for unmarried workers by this steel company in Pittsburgh and thought about what he had left behind in order to do the work he had to do. But, damn it, his mission far outweighed his responsibility to the gentle, pretty girl he had married, whose social superiority to him—she was a minister's daughter, he a miner then a laborer—sometimes rankled, no matter how much she loved him. He knew Dilys would get along. She could be a teacher or a lady's maid.

I love you, he heard her sweet voice whisper, and shook

his head briskly. Love was a woman's business, not a man's.

"She'd spend money on curtains rather than save for a strike," he said, his mouth twisting at the foolishness of females. A different expression crossed his face: he had left her pregnant.

The child was born by now. Was it a girl? Or a boy like Connor?

But there was no boy in the world like Connor, no boy with his son's courage and spirit and bright mind. If Enoch was a lion, Connor was his cub.

"I had to go!" he argued to the unheeding air. "I couldn't fight the Rhys Brandons of this world with a wife and kids hanging on my coattails, now, could I?"

Women and children held a man back, that was the long and the short of it. If a man burned to better the lot of the working class, never mind his own, he had no time for family life.

My son, he thought, with pride and anguish. My son. He'll remember everything I taught him. And as soon as he's old enough I'll fetch him away to work with me.

The wake-up siren wailed and he went back into the smelly shed, stamping snow off his boots.

"Close the goddamn door," someone shouted. "It's cold enough in here already to freeze your balls off!"

"If you had any balls, you'd strike for proper living quarters and a man's wages," Enoch bawled back.

"Keep your voice down, Scotty," the man who had the bed beside him warned. "The company'll turn you out—or worse."

"Let 'em try!" He raised a fist. "I'll speak my mind until every working sod in this country hears me."

His neighbor stopped buttoning his pants, gazed at Enoch, and nodded with reluctant admiration. "Damned if you won't," he said. "And then what?"

"Then we'll have the power! We could have it today if we'd only take it."

"He's off again," one of the men muttered.

"Barmy," agreed another.

"Yeah, but you can't help but listen to him."

Through a rough breakfast of boiled coffee, porridge, and lumpy bread, Enoch talked and the men listened, tempted but not strong enough to act. Then another blast of the siren, shrieking like a soul in torment, summoned them into the hell of a steel factory, into the incredible heat, well over one hundred degrees, the glowing pools of molten metal, the showers of sparks, and the dangerous catwalks over the open-hearth furnaces.

His great frame shining with sweat, his rage fueling the fire in his gut, Enoch labored.

4

♦

Constance hid her impatience and poured a second cup of tea for Susan Cassadyne. Susan's girlish devotion to Constance, when they were both students at the DeWitt Female Academy, had ended on the day she was engaged to Silas. Now Susan gloried in her position as matron and mother and patronized Constance for her persistent spinsterhood every time she came to call.

She had come to the Hendrik home far too often in the three months since Georgianna's death. And when Susan pecked at her teacakes like a bird with a tender beak, as she was doing now, Constance knew she was eager to impart news of still another girl's engagement.

It had long been apparent to Constance that conversations among the girls and women of her class in Brandon's Gate were largely concerned with matings—engagements, nuptials, pregnancies, births—and therefore with sex. Every girl knew, through some unspoken communication from mothers, aunts, and married sisters, that there were two kinds of respectable women in the world: those who had successfully fulfilled their destinies and been initiated into the mysteries of the marriage bed, and the failures who had not. There was an immeasurable difference between the two, and Constance did not relish belonging to the more unfortunate congregation, always pitied, often scorned.

I wish she'd lay her egg and go, Constance thought. It was already half past four and she wanted to arrive at Brandon Hall before Georgia was put down for the night. The baby was her excuse for dropping in unannounced at any time and for dining with Rhys and staying the night as often as possible. More than most men, Rhys hated dining alone, yet propriety required that he observe the seclusion of mourning for at least a year.

". . . dear Rhys last night," Susan was saying. "Flora looked absolutely lovely, if I do say it of my own little sister. I know Rhys is quite taken with her. Silas says he won't be at all surprised if something comes of it." She smiled beatifically.

Constance passed the cake tray and poured another cup of tea for herself. Her hands darted from lemon to sugar tongs to teaspoon like nervous honeybees. "It's time he saw some people, mourning or not," she made herself say calmly. My God! she thought. What can he be thinking of? Not Flora! All ringlets and giggles and breasts like little balls of dough set to rise under her frilly shirtwaists.

"Oh, I do agree," Susan said. "This was his second dinner with us, quite *intime*, of course. But Rhys is not the sort of man to live alone—he told Silas so." Rhys, her elevated brows added in the unspoken language of decent women, needs sex. "And of course he can't raise a girl child alone. The sooner he marries, the better. I said so to him straight out last night. Convention be hanged!"

And you with it, Constance thought as the wretched woman, her nasty news delivered, finally took herself off. Constance ordered a coach and ran upstairs to her bedroom, her black skirt rustling. She inspected herself carefully in the mirror.

"Damn!" she said. "I hate black!" She was satisfied with her appearance nonetheless. Her high-collared shirtwaist, made of rows of pin-tucked silk between insets of lace, was bloused loosely above a taffeta skirt piped and belted with white satin. The brim of the wide black straw hat she put on was faced with white ninon. A black mourning brooch set in diamonds was pinned to her blouse, and discreet diamond earrings dangled from her ears.

She turned to view her figure in profile. It had the fashionable Gibson girl S-curve, bottom and bosom made prominent by the cut of the clothes and the corsets and pads beneath them. Her belted waist looked tiny by comparison. Constance needed very little padding on top, but her hips were plumped out by satin-covered pads tied on between her cambric petticoat and lace-edged drawers.

Her spirits rose as she pinned on her hat. Its touch of white was as welcome as the springtime view from her window, where the trees were in full leaf and trailing arbutus and anemones blossomed in the garden. She felt almost happy despite Susan's gossip. She was going to see the man she loved.

She tucked a few things into a small reticule: a hairbrush, embroidered slippers, a blush-pink satin dressing gown and, best of all, a sheer nightdress of palest mauve chiffon. She kept it hidden at the back of her clothes press here at home, but when she lay in bed at Brandon Hall waiting for Rhys to cross the corridor from his room to hers and declare his love for her, she was arrayed to fit the fantasy. Sometimes she took the nightdress off and lay naked, stroking her breasts and belly and the warmth between her thighs. She had discovered this secret satisfaction for herself and knew it was sinful because that part of her was never mentioned except in hushed whispers and with averted eyes. But she didn't care. It comforted her while she dreamed that Rhys had come to her, drawn by a passion equal to her own.

In fact he had never so much as tapped on her door, but

tonight he would—or she would go to him. She dared not wait another day. Her hunger for him was blatantly physical; even in her ignorance she knew that. But it was not limited to romance. She wanted more of him than that. She wanted to be mistress of Brandon's Gate and the most important woman in his life.

Constance had never been first with anyone. That role had been reserved for her nonpareil sister, whose beauty and brilliance cast other females into shadow. And Georgianna, aware of her effect on men, had admitted to her charmed circle only those women, including her sister, who were willing to take second place. She was a bird of paradise who made other females dull wrens by comparison. After a meeting with Georgianna, men turned to their wives and fiancées with resignation. The women who called themselves her friends had resented her bitterly for it. Her sister hated her.

Growing up with Georgianna had been bad enough for Constance, but watching her sister receive with cool indifference the adoration of the one man Constance wanted was more than flesh and blood could bear. Constance felt free for the first time in her life when Georgianna died. She was out of her shadow at last. But it was unnatural not to mourn her sister, even if no one else knew how she felt. It was a tiny guilt, sore as a gum boil, and she worried at it in the same way.

But not today.

Constance took up her braid-trimmed jacket and her reticule and hurried down the stairs, almost colliding with her brother, Adam, as she reached the portico.

"Where are you off to in such a hurry?" he demanded cheerfully. Then he frowned. "No need to tell me. You're in pursuit of our brother-in-law again. Constance, people will talk. They're talking already."

She blushed furiously. "Let them. I go there to see Georgia."

"She'll be asleep by the time you arrive—and she has Dilys to look after her."

"I'm her aunt," Constance said with asperity, "not her nursemaid. And as it's late, I'll stay the night."

Adam removed his spectacles and with them his clerical air. He had Constance's coloring and without his glasses his face was square and pleasant, just this side of handsome. Right now it wore an expression of concern.

"Constance, Rhys Brandon is one of the most selfish men I've ever met. He cares for nothing and no one but himself, not even for Georgianna, whatever he pretends, or he'd have been more a gentleman and less a lover. I know the man! I have to work with him every day. You may think you love him but believe me, he isn't worthy of it."

She looked away. "That's not for you to decide. Georgianna wanted him."

"Not him. She wanted the Brandon fortune. We'd have been ruined without it."

"You make her sound like a sacrificial lamb! She got what she wanted, didn't she? Why shouldn't I? And I want *him*. I never expected to have him and I'm not going to miss my chance a second time."

"Your chance? For God's sake, Constance, is that what Georgianna's death represents to you?"

She bit her lip, still avoiding his eyes. "I didn't cause her death."

He shook his head. "No, you didn't, he did. But I'm worried about you. He'll make a fool of you, Constance."

She tossed her head and climbed into the waiting carriage. "When has anyone ever made a fool of me?"

And no one will, she thought as the coach bowled down the drive, least of all my darling Rhys. She relaxed against the plush upholstery, feeling the soft spring air flow over her like warm water. And most particularly not Susan Cassadyne and her doltish sister Flora. Rhys didn't want a stuffed doll for a wife!

Constance knew as well as anyone in Brandon's Gate that Rhys went often to those fancy houses in Albany and New York. But what of it? Men were expected to do that sort of thing, especially if they were married to glacial beauties like Georgianna, who had managed to convey, without ever saying a word about it, her distaste for the intimate side of marriage. From the anatomy books she had peeked at in Dr. van Dorn's office, Constance had an idea of where sexual union was achieved, but not how. She wanted to marry Rhys, whatever it entailed.

"Anything, anything," she whispered as the carriage approached Brandon Hall. Dusk was falling. She shivered, but not with cold, and greeted Mrs. O'Brien with an unusually warm smile as the butler took her things.

"Mr. Brandon is out to dinner, miss," the housekeeper said.

"I came to see my niece," Constance said, her smile congealing. "I'll go right up." Halfway up the broad staircase she stopped, aware of the housekeeper's eyes following her. "I'll be staying the night, Mrs. O'Brien," Constance said coolly. "See that my room is in order and have my supper served in the small parlor at seven o'clock."

Then she went on, taking the two flights without a pause despite her tight corset. Where is he, she worried frantically, where *is* he?

She stood outside the open door to Dilys's room to catch her breath and compose herself. She could see Dilys in the rocking chair, the baby already asleep in her arms. Connor was at the small desk near the window, clutching a pencil tightly as he bent over his copybook.

What does Rhys see in the brat? Constance railed silently. Rhys spent hours with the boy, walking with him in the woods, teaching him to ride now that the mild weather had come. Rhys even took him to the mills sometimes.

"He's bright," Rhys said when she commented on it. "He understands everything I tell him about the mills. And he's afraid of nothing. I put him up on a mare the other day and he stuck on like a cocklebur from trot to canter to gallop. This morning he rode like the wind at a tree, pretending he was charging the Black Knight to defend me from my enemy." Rhys laughed. "He amuses me."

Apparently Rhys was after a different kind of amusement tonight. But where? And with whom? Maybe Dilys knew. Constance entered the room.

♦

"Good evening, miss," Dilys said, moving as if to rise. She was always careful with Constance.

"Don't get up. I'll just take her." Dilys handed the sleeping infant up and Constance made a show of inspecting her. The baby had Georgianna's coloring. "She looks a little pale. Is she well?"

"She looks fine," Connor said from across the room, bristling at any criticism of his mother's care of Georgia—or his. "Dr. van Dorn says she's as healthy as Jericho's new foal."

"Hush, Connor," Dilys said with a warning glance at her son. She knew Constance resented the time Mr. Brandon spent with Connor as much as Dilys thanked heaven for it.

Constance sat down in the armchair, still holding the baby. "How quiet the house is," she said.

Dilys nodded. She was never talkative with either Constance or the master of the house, however kind he was. She was pleasant, neat, and industrious, all that was required of a servant. And in addition she was as meek and sober as a sparrow in her gray and white striped uniform because her instinct told her it was what Constance required of any young woman, no matter what her station, who had daily contact with Rhys Brandon. Dilys could understand that: he was not only wealthy, but manly as well, and amazingly handsome. He would not remain long alone. And Cook was right: Constance wanted him.

"She's dead scared," Cook had whispered in the kitchen last week, "that he'll get himself engaged to one of them Cassadyne girls."

"And well he might!" Peggy scowled. "The talk is he's been over to Cassadynes' far too often lately—and my poor lady not long in her grave."

Rhys came to visit his daughter once each day—although

it seemed more a duty for him than a pleasure—and when Constance accompanied him Dilys kept her eyes down and her voice low. When he came alone Dilys managed, despite her confusion, to say a few words in response to his remarks about Connor. Mr. Brandon, cool to his infant daughter, clearly hungered for a son.

Well, so much the better, Dilys thought, he has mine.

"Mr. Brandon is out to dinner so often these days," Constance observed. "I wonder how Cook keeps busy."

Dilys said nothing, taking a certain delight in Constance's devouring curiosity over Rhys's whereabouts. Even though he was in mourning, every marriageable girl from Albany to Buffalo tried to wangle invitations to the small, informal dinners his friends here in Brandon's Gate gave to keep him from sitting home alone—which was where Constance wanted him.

"I suppose he went to Albany about the railroad," Constance persisted, and there was another silence, this one more uncomfortable.

"He went to see Mr. Cassadyne," Connor said impatiently. "About the mills."

Constance was intent upon the baby. "Your son is very well informed," she remarked sourly to Dilys.

"I'm sorry, miss. He's been taught not to speak until he's spoken to."

"Here, take the baby." Dilys did, and Constance stood. "Have you everything you need for her?" It was obviously an afterthought.

"Oh, yes, miss," Dilys said. "With all the beautiful things you bring her."

"Good night, then. I'll see her again in the morning before I leave." She closed the door behind her, and Connor put his thumbs in his ears and waggled his fingers.

Dilys held up a warning hand until the footsteps died away. "She doesn't like you either. Not that I blame her, the way you look at her sometimes."

"I don't care," he said, closing his copybook. "The squire likes me." Rhys liked to be called that, Connor could tell.

"Connor, you *must* be careful with her if you want to grow up in this house."

"It's *his* house. What's she got to say about it?"

"She may marry Mr. Brandon, and then it'll be her house too."

He was shocked by that. "He never wants to marry her!"

He went to watch his mother as Dilys put Georgia down in her bassinet.

"Sleep, my little darling," she whispered, straightening the baby's gown.

Connor, stifling his dismay, pulled up the little quilt and tucked it gently around the baby. "She does too look fine," he grumbled, patting Georgia. "She'll soon be too big for this thing." Anxious, he watched Dilys move around the room as she folded the baby's freshly laundered things and put them away. "He'll never marry her, will he, Mum?"

"He might," Dilys said, privately sure that no man could escape such hot pursuit. The girl had set her cap for her brother-in-law and came to the Hall to see only him, not her niece. Constance as mistress here was not a pleasant prospect for any of the servants. It was significant that they were already resigned to it.

"Come here, Connor," Dilys said, sitting in the armchair. She put her hands on his shoulders and gave him a little shake. "You must mind what I say, son. Mr. Brandon likes you but he won't take your part against his own kind. You must be respectful to everyone, but especially to her. We have a fine place here, God forbid you make us lose it!" She shook her head with that worried expression he had not seen since they came to Brandon Hall. "Where else do you think we'd be given rooms like this—or you blooded horses to ride?"

"But he'd never send us away! He and I are good friends now, he said so."

"If you were a trouble to him he would. People in high places won't stand for any fuss from their servants, however much they like them. Do you understand me?" It hurt her to cloud Connor's relationship with Rhys. The boy needed a father as much as the man wanted a son. But she held him until he nodded his agreement.

"But I don't have to like her."

"Don't, then. The important thing is that she mustn't know it. Now, promise me."

It was Connor's first lesson in deceit. He promised, but his heart wasn't in it.

♦

Constance had two glasses of sherry before she ate supper in Georgianna's parlor, not thinking, as she usually did, of the changes she would make in the room and throughout the house when she was its mistress. Instead, she considered her situation. It was clear she had no choice but to act now.

If Rhys was going into society again, however discreetly, she must make him marry her at once. That unspoken attraction between them seemed to have waned since Georgianna's death, but Constance was sure she knew why. It was one thing to flirt with her when Georgianna was alive, but his guilt stopped him now. How foolish! People were always trying to make things up to the dead, as if it mattered to them once they were gone.

She drank a glass of wine with her dinner and had a brandy after it. Constance was never muddled by drink. It did not affect her head, only her body, and her body, by the time she went upstairs to undress, clamored for Rhys.

She lay in her bed in the blue bedroom, wide awake and perfectly sober, until she heard Rhys come in and start up the stairs. She sprang out of bed as the door to his dressing room closed and stepped into the hall just as a pencil of light appeared under the door. Ten minutes later the light went out and reappeared beneath the bedroom door. Swiftly she crossed the hall, her satin dressing gown swirling around her, and tapped on his door. He opened it and his eyes swept over her body for a moment. Then he resumed his fraternal air.

"Constance? I didn't know you were here. Is anything wrong?"

"May I come in?"

He hesitated, but the household was asleep. He stepped back. He would have left the door ajar but she closed it behind her and leaned against it, grasping the knob as if it could give her the courage she needed to speak.

"What is it?" he asked.

"It's you," she said after a long moment, her large eyes fixed on him.

"What have I done?" The reappearance of his lazy, tantalizing smile was all she needed.

"You already know I love you. I've come to show you how much."

He was silent for a moment, his face unreadable once more as he studied her intently, obviously admiring her long, loose hair and the curves of her uncorseted figure. Then he shook his head. "I'm flattered, Constance, but you don't know what you're suggesting."

"Oh, yes, I do," she said softly. "And I could make you happy."

. He sighed. "I wish it were that simple."

"Of course it is!" She was almost impatient. "I know what troubles you, but it wasn't your fault, Rhys, and you mustn't think it was. All women are meant to have children, most of all Georgianna, beautiful as she was. She just had bad luck."

His face told her that it was what he wanted to hear. Thank God no one else had had the wit or the nerve to say it to him! They all thought Rhys's lust had killed his wife, and maybe it had, but Constance didn't care. She wasn't dainty and fragile like Georgianna, and Rhys was worth whatever demands he might make on a woman. It was time she found out exactly what they were.

He crossed the room to take a cigarette from his bedside table, widening the distance between them. "It's good of you to say that, but you shouldn't be here, Constance. I have to think of your reputation if you won't."

He turned back to her, but his face changed when he

saw her. She had dropped her satin dressing gown. She knew that in the soft light of the lamp every detail of her body was clearly visible through the chiffon nightdress. She hoped the veil of silk made her all the more tempting to him. He seemed mesmerized by the sight of her, but still he hesitated, and she knew why. The seduction of his virgin sister-in-law under his own roof would ostracize him. But he was compromised already: she was in his room half naked in the middle of the night. And no one would ever know.

She walked toward him, feeling her full breasts sway, conscious that his eyes devoured her while he undid his dressing gown. With a gasp he pulled her close and kissed her deeply, his hands cupping her bottom before he moved to press her down upon the bed.

He pushed up her gown and parted her legs. She felt him touch her and was astonished that he knew about her secret vice. She waited for the familiar sensation to build, but just as it began she was startled by the hardness of his seeking body. So that was how . . . !

He went into her quickly then, but encountered a barrier inside. She sensed his frustration, his drive to go deeper, and she thrust her hips forward, shocked again by the sharp pain she felt but determined not to hinder him because of it. He was moving quickly now, his hands on her breasts, his mouth on hers. Her surprise, more than the pain, had pulled her sharply back from the brink of something. Was it the same thing that made him move even more wildly and then moan in the throes of what must be a pleasure more exquisite than the one she had discovered for herself? If there was more pleasure in this, she was greedy for it.

When he was finally still he withdrew carefully, using his nightshirt and the skirt of her gown to protect the bedclothes. "We'll have to get rid of these," he whispered.

"I don't care," she said. "I want them to know, all of them. Touch me again." She drew his hand down, pushing the gown away.

"My God, Constance, don't you know you're bleeding?"

"Will I always?"

"No, you're not a virgin anymore, you're a woman."

"I'll be a better woman after we're married. Then you can show me what to do."

"Marry? But that's impossible!"

"Why? We're not blood relations."

"Even so, I can't think of marriage now," he said. He sat up and reached for a cigarette.

"You're not the kind of man who can live alone," she said, thanking heaven for Susan Cassadyne's wagging tongue.

He said nothing, staring down at the unlit cigarette in his hand.

"Are you in love with anyone else?" she demanded.

He shook his head.

"Then you can damned well be in love with me!" When he did not reply she took the next step. "I'll give you sons, Rhys, as many as you want. For all we know, we started one tonight."

He had fallen into such an obvious trap that he almost laughed. He would, of course, have to marry her. He was neither happy nor dismayed by the prospect. She was not Georgianna, but no woman could ever be the passion of his youth, the goddess whose elusiveness had made him almost hate her and the memory of all those nights when he had tried desperately, using every technique he knew or had heard about, to awaken her while she lay there, letting him handle her, her head averted like a woman peeling onions.

Now here was Constance, anything but elusive and a highly promising bedpartner. What better mother for Georgianna's child than Georgianna's sister? It would shift the daily visits to the child away from him. He was uncomfortable every time he looked at Georgia. She was a living reminder of the woman who escaped him before he ever really possessed her.

He lit the cigarette.

"All right, I'll marry you." He put his free hand on her round breast and fondled the nipple until it was rigid. He thought idly of taking her again and dismissed the idea. "I assume you won't make me mourn alone for nine more months before I make love to you again?"

His hand on her breast aroused her, but there was something more pressing than inchoate desire. "Not nine months, Rhys," she said. "Only a week."

He turned and swung his long legs to the floor, reaching for his dressing gown. "You know I can't marry before the year is out."

"Who's to stop you? I know you, Rhys, you're no stickler for convention even if you pretend to be a pillar of the community! There'll be talk for a while, but you hate solitude a lot more than you hate talk. We'll go away until it dies down."

He said nothing, staring into the dark beyond the lamplight while he smoked. She knelt on the bed behind him and put her arms around him, her breasts crushed against his back and her lips against the curve of his neck. Instinctively she let her hand drop to his groin and was gratified by the stirring she felt under his robe.

"Very well," he said finally, standing away from her seeking hand. "Next week. But now you must go. And be certain no one sees that." He gestured toward her nightdress. "Not even we could live this down." He went to the door to retrieve her dressing gown and helped her into it. Then he turned her to him and kissed her, exploring her lips with the tip of his tongue. She pressed against him eagerly.

"Congratulations on your engagement," he said sarcastically, releasing her.

She smiled. "Next week," she murmured.

He nodded and she left. In the blue bedroom she stripped off the ruined gown and put a towel between her legs before she got into bed. She lay there, reliving what had happened. He had not said he loved her, but that was only because he was still in thrall to Georgianna's memory. But now Constance knew how to make him forget there was any other woman in the world.

5

◆

They were married in New York ten days later and sailed immediately for France. They went to Paris first, where Rhys bought a Seurat, a Renoir, and some exquisite Meissen porcelain figurines, and Constance bought gowns and shoes and hats by the dozen.

"We'll need ten trunks for all that!" Rhys said, watching Constance model a white satin Vionnet gown.

She gave him the provocative glance he had come to recognize. "Do you care?"

"No," he said, aroused by that look. "Now come here and let me take that dress off."

For the first time in years, Rhys sought no casual rendezvous with other women because Constance's appetite for sex was as robust as his. She was an anomaly: the sexual ignorance which society demanded of virtuous women had not inhibited her lusty nature.

They had traveled on to Florence, Venice, and Rome and had arrived in London before Constance told him she was three months pregnant.

"That's wonderful!" he said, a broad smile on his face.

"It must have happened that first night." She was radiant, triumphant. "I promised you sons, didn't I?"

"We'll start for home at once," Rhys said.

"No. I'm not ready to go home," Constance protested. "I prefer London to Brandon's Gate!"

"We must arrive before you begin to show," Rhys went on, consulting his calendar, as if she had not spoken. It happened more frequently than she liked. "There's been enough gossip as it is."

46

But the gossip was dying down. Rhys was the richest man in the region and his intolerance for criticism was well known. His marriage was a fait accompli that had to be accepted. News of the couple's return, however, made people wait eagerly for an invitation to Brandon Hall and a look at Constance's waistline. The consensus was that she must be pregnant; the intriguing question was how far along she was.

"She'll not be showin' yet," Cook said as the household staff lined up outside the mansion to welcome the newly-weds home.

"She may," Peggy said viciously. "The Lord knows how long it's been goin' on between those two."

"Not while Mrs. Brandon was alive!" Mary O'Brien objected. To the staff Georgianna remained Mrs. Brandon; they referred to Constance as Mrs. Rhys or herself.

"She'd never have dared," Cook agreed as they sighted the carriage turning into the long drive.

"That one'd dare anything," Peggy returned. "It's a mercy she doesn't want me for her maid."

"Stop your cackle," Jeffers, the butler, warned them. "Here's Dilys and the boy."

Connor could not contain himself, even in his stiff, starched shirt. He had worked diligently during the summer months, helping Murphy in the stables and befriending Rhys's huge black stallion, Jericho. With Murphy's help Connor had learned to ride him. It was a new sensation to be lofted high above the ground, to straddle tremendous power and make it obey his will. Someday, maybe, the squire would let him raise one of Jericho's foals. He had a name already chosen: Jupiter for a colt, Jezebel for a filly.

The carriage arrived at the door and there was a flurry among the footmen to let down the steps. Rhys descended and held out his hand to Constance. She emerged wearing a honey-colored faille traveling costume trimmed with black braid and a swooping black velvet hat and veil. With a faint smile on her lips, mocking their disappointment at her trim figure, tightly corseted for her arrival, she proceeded along the line of servants. Her hand lightly clasp-

ing her husband's arm, she looked very much the mistress
of the manor.

"Welcome home, squire!" Connor called from the end
of the line, unable to contain himself.

Rhys looked in his direction, smiling. "Connor! Come
here and let me see how you've grown!"

Connor came at a run, excited, beaming, worshipful.
Rhys caught him up and swung him high, and the watching domestics smiled at the sight of his affection for a
servant's child. A dear, good man, he was. For his sake
they would put up with Mrs. Rhys.

"I have a surprise for you!" Connor said when Rhys had
set him down. "But you must come to the stable paddock
to see it."

"Must I? Well, then, I shall change and go there straightaway. Now you must welcome Mrs. Brandon."

Connor did as his mother had instructed him. With a
little bow he wished her great happiness, and Constance,
hiding her resentment of him for usurping a place in
Rhys's affections, managed to nod graciously as she sailed
past the rest of the staff and into the house.

"You're surely not going down to the stables now!" she
said, climbing the stairs with Rhys.

"Why not?"

"It's my first day in this house as your wife!"

Rhys smiled lazily. "What shall I do, then? Hold your
embroidery hoop? I must find out what's been happening
in my absence. I'll stop at the stables to see what Connor's
up to, then go on to the mills."

They parted at the top of the stairs, each to a separate
dressing room. Constance fumed at his indifference to her
wishes. The honeymoon, apparently, was over.

"Damn that boy," she swore softly as she unpinned her
hat and threw it on a chair. She looked around the dressing room. It was papered and upholstered in Georgianna's
favorite blue, but that would soon be changed. Constance
opened several drawers and a wardrobe and was aghast to
find them full of Georgianna's clothes. Rhys had forbidden
anyone to touch them after the funeral.

But he might have ordered them cleared out before today! she thought bitterly. He might have been that considerate, at least. But it struck her that Rhys, for all his charm, was not a considerate man.

"That O'Brien bitch could have done it, with or without orders," she muttered, directing her rage elsewhere.

I'll fire all the servants, she thought, I'll send them all packing. But of course Rhys would pay no attention to her on that subject—or any other unless she found a way to make him.

Her maid, Rosemary, appeared. "Where the devil have you been?" Constance snapped. "I want these clothes out of here at once."

Then she reminded herself that she was pregnant. Once his son was born, Rhys would forget Georgianna as he appeared to have forgotten her child.

◆

Rhys changed and headed for the paddock, aware that he should first have visited the nursery but deciding that later would do well enough. He seldom mentioned Georgia.

He had never held her. "Afraid she'll break," he always said to Dilys with a winsome smile.

The child was too painful a reminder of his rejection and humiliation by her mother and of his part in her death. By passionately fathering that child, first so frail, now so flourishing, he had forfeited a dynasty of sons by Georgianna. They would have been living proof that she was his, whether she wanted him or not.

Constance seemed as discomfited in the child's presence as he. It was a secret bond between them, one they never discussed, although Constance was outspoken about everything else, sometimes distressingly so. But she was more devoted to him than he was to her, and it was better for a man to let himself be loved, even by a woman who claimed to have no illusions about his true character and motives.

Connor's unqualified devotion was a delightful balm. Connor shared Rhys's opinions of everyone, including Rhys.

The boy never mentioned his own father. In a few short months Rhys had replaced Enoch. The boy had good instincts.

And he's fearless too, Rhys thought when he reached the paddock and saw Connor, looking very small atop the great black stallion. "You're up on Jericho," he called. "Good for you."

Rhys approached the horse and stroked his silky muzzle, and the stallion whinnied a welcome.

"Shall I show you what I learned?" Connor asked eagerly.

"Yes, walk him for me," Rhys replied as Connor settled himself in the shortened stirrups and turned Jericho to the paddock rail. He handled the reins well, directing the animal with calm authority. Then, with an impish grin at Rhys, Connor clucked to Jericho and made him trot.

"Good!" Rhys called. "Excellent form." He was pleased, even proud. Only he had been astute enough to see merit in this boy, no matter that his close relationship with a mill child scandalized his wife and neighbors.

With a flush of anticipation he imagined himself instructing his own son and heir as soon as the child was able to sit a horse. In the meantime, though, he could practice fatherhood with Connor.

His expression altered when Connor took the stallion out of the paddock gate into the meadow beyond and, lying close along the horse's black mane, urged Jericho to a canter, then to a gallop, careening across the meadow at top speed.

"Why, the plucky little devil!" Rhys said.

"Aye, sir, he is that," Murphy agreed. "Sits like a lord and rides like the wind."

"That's enough," Rhys shouted after a few moments. "Come on back!"

Connor obeyed, so proud of his exploit that Rhys decided not to scold him.

"Well done," Rhys said. "You couldn't have given me a nicer homecoming present."

Connor, flushed with joy, swung his right leg over the

saddle and slid down, his eyes shining. "I sure missed you, squire," he said.

"I missed you too," Rhys returned. He had certainly thought of Connor from time to time. "I'm going to walk down to the mills. Come with me."

"Oh, yes, sir," Connor said. "After I put Jericho in his stall."

"Murphy will do that, won't you, Murphy?" Rhys nodded as the man touched his cap and came forward to take the reins. "Come along then," Rhys said to Connor.

I'd go anywhere with you, Connor thought, beside himself with love and glory. Anywhere at all.

♦

Just before Constance gave birth, the portrait of Georgianna was removed from the drawing room.

"It's for Georgia's sake," Constance told Rhys. "She's beginning to call me Mama, and I'm both her aunt and her stepmother. She's bound to ask questions about that portrait, and the relationship is too complicated to explain to a child."

To her infinite relief, Rhys agreed. Then he called the servants together, requesting their absolute discretion.

"I would, of course, have to discharge those who could not comply," he told them, smiling as if such rebellion were utterly impossible, "along with any of their relatives working in the mills."

All of them swore to keep the secret.

The Renoir Rhys had bought in Paris—a glorious young girl whose gleaming skin tones, voluptuous figure, and seductive expression were reminiscent of Constance—was hung in its place. Rhys never suggested that a portrait of Constance be commissioned to replace Georgianna's. He moved his first wife upstairs to his collection.

"Like an abduction to a harem," Constance murmured, but Rhys seemed not to hear her and she was reluctant to press the point.

The collection was housed on the third floor of the mansion's north wing, connected by a long, windowed gallery to the south wing, where Dilys and Connor lived.

Rhys was undoubtedly the collection's most talented curator. He had acquired many fine works of art on his travels and through brokers in Boston and New York. Now the paintings and watercolors, the rare porcelains and objets d'art, had been enriched by the addition of Georgianna's stunning portrait, curtained behind ruby-red velvet draw drapes.

"For discretion," Rhys said, but it looked more like a shrine to Constance. She waited impatiently for her baby's delivery.

◆

"It's a girl," Dr. van Dorn said.

"Oh, my God," Constance groaned, her long hair wet with perspiration.

The doctor knew it was disappointment, not exhaustion, but he was busy with the cord and said nothing, handing the screaming child to the midwife. He waited until the birthing process was complete, Constance sponged and changed, and her women gone before he spoke to her.

"You hardly glanced at your child," he said reprovingly. "Try to summon up some maternal feeling. What will Rhys think?"

"The same as I do! Rhys wants a son!"

"Rhys must take what God sends. He's only mortal, after all, no matter what you prefer to believe. And you're a strong, healthy woman. You'll have a son eventually."

Constance grasped at that. "How long must I wait before we can try again?"

The doctor peered at her in amazement. "After what you've just been through? If you must know, you must wait several months." Van Dorn shook his head. He had never seen a woman so voracious for a man as Constance was for Rhys. Some women loved their husbands passionately, but Constance was different. She wanted to subsume Rhys.

She's picked the wrong man, Phillip van Dorn thought. Rhys belongs to Rhys and no one else—except, in one way, to Georgianna. And he will never forgive her for not returning the compliment.

Van Dorn left Constance, still wide awake and fretful, and went downstairs to find Rhys. "You've seen your daughter?"

Rhys nodded gloomily.

"You're more disappointed than Constance. For God's sake, Rhys, your wife has given birth to a healthy child! That's no reason to mourn. Be patient. In a few months you can try again."

"You're sure?" His solicitude was clearly not for his wife but for the son he so desperately wanted.

What manner of marriage is this one, the doctor wondered.

"Absolutely sure," he said. "She's got more stamina than most men I know. Now, go up to her and try not to look as if the world had come to an end!" Impatient with the pair of them, the doctor took his leave.

Upstairs Rhys knocked and went into what once had been the blue bedroom but was now decorated in dark green. Constance had refused to give birth in the bed where her sister died, although she liked making love in it, and had chosen this guest room for the delivery. She looked up at Rhys anxiously.

He took her hand and managed a thin smile. "Was it very difficult, my dear?" he asked.

"It's so unfair!" Constance said furiously, clasping his hand as if it were a lifeline. "But the next one will be a son, I swear it."

He was obviously unconvinced. "What shall we call this one?"

"I don't know. Does it matter?"

He sighed. "We'll call her Jillian, then, after my mother. I'll go now. You must rest."

"Damn it, Rhys! The next one *will* be a son! Or the one after that, if I have to have twenty babies!"

Her assurance made him smile at last. He leaned over to kiss her cheek, but she held his face between her hands and kissed his mouth lingeringly. "Soon," she whispered.

He left her, oddly aroused by that kiss, and went upstairs to the nursery. Georgia slept in her crib. Dilys was leaning over the bassinet, crooning softly. She looked up with a bright smile.

"She's a lovely baby, Mr. Brandon."

He thought, not for the first time, that Dilys was a very pretty woman; Connor had the same radiant smile. Standing next to her, he looked down at his new daughter. "By George, she's the image of Constance," he said.

"Yes, she is."

Connor had come to stand in the doorway. "She's not as pretty as Georgia," he said philosophically. "But she's all right."

"I'm glad you approve," Rhys said. And again, as it had almost a year ago to the day, the sight of the boy brought him both comfort and pain.

"Let's go for a ride, Connor," Rhys suggested.

"But it's snowing!" Dilys said.

"Only a little. Please, Mum," Connor begged her, and Dilys agreed.

They made for the stairs and then the path to the stables. Mounted, they trotted off together, Connor on the mare named Gypsy. They rode in silence through a light swirl of snowflakes and after a time Rhys sighed.

"She's really a pretty girl," Connor said, misjudging the reason for Rhys's distress.

"All well and good, but I remain the only man in the family," Rhys said more to himself than to Connor.

"You've got me," Connor ventured, longing to comfort him.

Rhys turned his head and nodded. "Yes, my boy, I do, and I'm very glad of it. You may be the only son I'll ever have." He leaned over to touch Connor's shoulder and they looked at each other for a moment before riding on in companionable silence.

◆

Six months later Connor watched in fascination as the Irish setter puppies were born in quick succession, emerging from their mother's heaving body like little balls of wax. Then the bitch, in a corner of an empty stall in the stable, lay on the old blanket Murphy had provided, licking her progeny clean. It was at once marvelous and terrible to Connor, and he shivered, watching it.

Murphy glanced at him. "That's how all God's creatures come into the world, Connor," the groom said.

Connor nodded. "I know, but I wish He hadn't made it hurt so much."

He turned as footsteps approached and smiled when he saw Rhys with Dr. van Dorn, Mr. Cassadyne, and Mr. Anders, whose property adjoined the Brandon estate. Connor ducked his head by way of greeting to the others, then turned eagerly to Rhys. "Five puppies, squire."

"I told you it would be today," Rhys said to his friends. "You owe me ten dollars each. How did it go, Murphy?"

"Perfect, every one," the groom said. "Each with a pedigree long as your arm."

"Can I have a pedigree?" Connor asked, and the men laughed.

"No, laddie," Mr. Anders said, his voice as frosty as his manner. "It's something you must be born with."

"I'm not so sure," Silas Cassadyne put in, his carrot-colored hair shades lighter than the setter's dark copper coat. "They grow on money trees too. Look at the Astors."

"Then I'll have one when I'm rich," Connor announced, provoking new laughter from everyone but Murphy.

"May I hold a puppy?" Connor ventured when the laughter ceased.

"For a little," Murphy said. "But stay close to Queen Mab, here. Mothers are jealous of their weans."

"That's true," Connor said. "It's the fathers don't give a damn."

The men glanced at one another, then back at the little boy as, very gently, he lifted one of the puppies, first giving a reassuring pat and murmur to the bitch, Queen Mab, who rewarded him with a lick.

"You're a real beauty, you are," Connor said to the puppy. He cradled the small body, stroking it until its trembling stopped and it nestled trustingly in the curve of his neck, boy and dog rapt in an exchange of love so simple, so uninhibited, and so honest that the men watching could not fail to recognize it. Again they glanced at each other and Rhys was aware that the decision lay with him. It was at moments like this he felt most like a grand seigneur.

He had several reasons to be pleased with himself. He, like Silas Cassadyne, had served for some time on the boards of several companies in Troy and Albany, including Drummond Gas and Light and the Anders Mercantile Bank. But Rhys was beginning to think about more than industry. He was mayor of Brandon's Gate and the Republican delegate to the electoral college. He liked to speculate on what might come after that: assemblyman, state senator, congressman.

He was well known among his peers already, but this kind of thing would spread the word of his benevolence among the common people like honey. There wasn't a working family from Brandon's Gate to Troy who hadn't heard about the grand gentleman's interest in a mill boy.

"Would you like him for your own, Connor?" Rhys asked.

Connor looked up, startled, his dark eyes enormous and still lost in communion with the newborn pup. He did not smile, but nodded seriously, waiting to know if the offer was seriously meant. When Rhys confirmed it, tears of pure joy rolled down Connor's cheeks.

"There now," Murphy said. "That's right noble of you, squire."

And it was done. The story would be all over the county by tomorrow, Rhys congratulated himself. Some would disapprove of such a valuable gift to Brandon's waif, as they referred to Connor, but for the most part Rhys's kindness and generosity would carry the day. It was like storing up votes for the future.

"What do you say, Connor?" Murphy prompted.

"Thank you, sir," Connor said, animated now. "Oh,

thank you! I'll take real good care of him, you know I will." He got to his feet.

"Of course you will," Rhys said. "But you must leave him with his mother for a time. Murphy will tell you when he's weaned." He took out a snowy handkerchief and dried Connor's face. The child was trembling with emotion. "All this has exhausted you. You must go back to the house."

The men went off with Connor in tow, and Murphy, calling his master a prince of a fellow, watched them go. "What d'you suppose the master got in mind for Connor's future, your majesty?" he asked Queen Mab, but the setter only gave a great gape as her babies began to suckle.

"What will you call him?" Rhys asked of the small boy tramping along beside the men as they approached the house.

"Well, he's Irish, so I thought maybe Tyrone. Murphy said he was a great general. He beat the Earl of Essex."

"Tyrone it is, then," Rhys said. "I'll give you his papers as soon as they're ready." The small party had reached the drive and the waiting carriages. "Now go on in and tell your mother."

Connor bounded toward the pantry, then stopped and returned a few paces. "I'm very grateful to you, sir. I don't know how to show it."

"You'll find a way, Connor, when you're older. Go along now."

"A neat maneuver," John Anders said enigmatically. He handed Rhys a ten-dollar gold piece for the bet Rhys had won, and made for his carriage while Rhys smiled after him. Anders is a sharp fellow, he thought.

"You've made one small boy very happy," Silas Cassadyne said, proffering his gold eagle in turn. He studied Rhys. "It was a kind thing to do."

"I'm a kind man, Silas."

"I'm not sure it's kind to mislead Connor," Silas said.

"I beg your pardon," Rhys said, mystified.

"If you treat him like a son, he'll begin to think he is one."

Rhys grinned. "I need some comfort until Constance delivers the real thing."

"And then?"

"And then! Don't be such an old fussbudget, Silas. The boy knows his place."

Going into the house, Rhys could hear Connor shouting the news to the kitchen staff and then go pounding up the stairs to his mother. Rhys smiled. The odds were that Dilys would be grateful, too, and as soon as the opportunity arose, he would let her know how to show it.

"What's all the hullabaloo about?" Constance demanded as he joined her in the library. When he told her, she cast her eyes heavenward in a plea for deliverance from such insanity. "Are we going to have another dog wandering around the house now?" She was not fond of Rhys's setters.

"He's certain to keep it upstairs. He'll pretend it's to guard the children."

"I wish you were as attentive to Jillian as you are to that beastly boy," she said sourly.

"He's the only beastly boy around," Rhys said deliberately. He did not like his actions questioned.

Her face turned an ugly red. "Damn you, Rhys! It's not my fault! At least I can carry a child to term."

Having put her in her place, Rhys reverted to geniality. "All in the fullness of time, Constance," he said, smiling. "It's certainly not for want of trying, is it?"

She bit her lip, glaring at him, but there was nothing she could say. A woman who did not conceive a son was a sorry excuse for a wife. And what else had a wife to offer a man like Rhys, who was by nature and design unfaithful? No matter how ardent their intimate relations were, she knew he had other women when he went to New York and Albany. But he would have to respect the mother of his sons.

Constance had even taken to praying, a thing she did ungraciously.

The next thing you know, she would tell herself scornfully, I'll be going to Lourdes.

Give me a son, she entreated silently now. I can hold him that way. I'll never ask for anything else if You give me a son.

"By the way, I'll have to go to New York for a few days," Rhys said.

Her face cleared. "Wonderful!" she exclaimed. "It's just what I need."

"Sorry, my dear. This is strictly business. I'll be going alone."

She gave him a withering look, then got up and left the room. He lit his pipe, picked up his newspaper, and relaxed in his chair.

◆

He stayed in New York for a week, enjoying the city's attractions and the opportunities it gave him to meet men of wider influence and to bed the wife of a United States senator who had attracted him on his last visit. But he was glad to return to Brandon's Gate. Rhys loved space and air and the river country.

"Welcome home, Mr. Brandon," the butler said, helping him off with his coat. "We didn't expect you before tomorrow."

"It's good to be back, Jeffers. Where is everyone?" Rhys quieted the eager, leaping dogs.

Constance had gone to a dinner party in Troy, where she would spend the night. Rhys had no intention of calling her to say he had arrived home a day early. Constance had become something of a trial lately. Her frenetic social activities only partially absorbed that phenomenal energy that would have been better vented on breeding. Most of the time she exercised her wit with oblique and sarcastic criticisms of Rhys's "other loves," by which she meant his fancy women, his veneration of Georgianna's memory, his art collection, and his mills—in that order. But his wife's moods were not the reason Rhys did not want her here tonight.

"Tell Dilys I'll be up to see the children before I have dinner," Rhys instructed the butler as he started upstairs to his dressing room.

His valet was unpacking his bags and had run a bath for him. He lay in the tub thinking of Dilys and the opportunity he had been waiting for these last six months. The language of their physical attraction was necessarily mute, but she was aware that he wanted her and he had sensed her response to him, an exciting combination of denial and desire.

Rhys put on a smoking jacket for his solitary meal and went up to the nursery.

The two little girls stared at him and then Georgia smiled, while Dilys, her sweet face averted, gave all her attention to the children. She blushed painfully whenever she glanced at him.

Yes, he was thinking when he went down to supper, oh, yes.

After he had eaten, Rhys spent a restless half hour in his study trying to read his mail. At half past eight he crossed to the north wing and mounted the stairs to his collection.

He looked about him with deep satisfaction, lingering on favorites he had missed while on his travels: a dainty Fragonard lady with a lusty gleam in her eye, a Cellini bronze of a naked nymph, a rare Vermeer with fabrics so luminous, a light seemed to glow from within the canvas.

Then he went to draw aside the curtains concealing Georgianna's portrait, and raised his eyes to hers. Here was womanly perfection—but how daunting perfection was! In that relationship it was clear which one loved and which one let herself be loved, and even then only with grim resignation, because it was her duty. Sometimes he thought she died just to get away from him. Why else would she have chosen the occasion of that pregnancy, after so many others, to make her monstrous will? But this was not the moment to think about Georgianna's will.

It was ten o'clock. Connor must be fast asleep by now. He left the collection and walked softly along the third floor gallery to the opposite wing. He opened the connecting door quietly and stood a moment, listening carefully to be sure Dilys had not invited one of the maids to spend the evening with her. But there was no sound, only darkness under Connor's door and a dim light under hers.

He stepped inside without knocking and closed the door behind him. She had been sitting in the armchair in front of the fire, the only light in the room, but now she sprang to her feet, avoiding his eyes.

He crossed the room and took her hands in his. "Look at me, Dilys," he said softly. "You knew I would come. Look at me."

She did, her face lovely in its confusion.

"No," she whispered, pushing her hands against his chest. "Please, Mr. Brandon, we mustn't."

She was tense with resistance. He raked his fingers through her long, loose hair and, holding her head, kissed her cheeks and her eyelids gently. When his lips touched her mouth, she gave a little sigh and her body relaxed.

"How sweet you are," he murmured, and went on kissing her until her lips parted eagerly under his and her arms went around him. He picked her up and carried her to the bed and she lay, her eyes closed, panting slightly, while he undressed and lay down beside her.

He opened her robe and the nightdress beneath it and kissed her breasts, drawing the nipples between his lips, making them rigid with his tongue.

There was no resistance when he undressed her and caressed the length of her round body and then the softness between her thighs. The forward tilt of her hips bespoke a woman hungry for surcease. He gave her that, muffling her cries with kisses. He waited for her to touch him, but she did not and he eased into her, gliding in and out of her warm, receptive body until it trembled again and he abandoned himself with her in an enormous surge of physical release.

She did not speak until he asked, "Are you sorry, Dilys?" She shook her head. "No, oh, no. But I'm afraid."

"Of what?"

"That someone will find out." They both knew she meant Constance.

"We aren't children, to announce what's happened between us!" he said. "No one will know."

"But if someone did! What would happen to Connor and me then?"

"I will always look after you. You must trust me for that."

She gazed at him, searching his eyes. Then she nodded. "I will, I do. You're the best man I ever knew."

He was taken by that, by the poignance and the conviction. No other woman had ever said that to him, certainly not either of his wives. He was excited by her adoration and felt himself stirring inside her. He made love to her again.

He was back in the art gallery by eleven o'clock. He pulled the portrait curtains closed without looking at Georgianna and picked up a Ming vase. He caressed it lovingly, for a moment reminded of Dilys's round hips. Then he forgot about her and turned back to the priceless glaze of his porcelain.

♦

Dilys sat by the fire again, all traces of the encounter gone. Her body appeared as chaste as the newly smoothed bed, but it reverberated with the first rapture she had known since Enoch left her. She had longed for love, but where was a decent woman to find it? Could she say to a man, stay with me, I need your body? A man could do that, but not a woman with a boy to raise and a reputation to protect. So she had waited until he came to her, this aristocratic lover of her dreams.

The danger of discovery cut into her reverie.

"But I want him," she whispered, her face buried in her hands. "Heaven help me, I want him."

She had been attracted first by his good looks, as was every woman who met him. Then she was touched by his affection for Connor. And finally she had wanted him because he was a gloriously virile man and she a woman profoundly lonely in the flesh.

Want him or not, dangerous or not, she could not have refused him. She dared not risk his displeasure. He had held more than her willing body in his hands. He held her security and Connor's future, both now enhanced by this affair.

And what had she—or any other woman—but her body to offer in exchange for protection? All women sold their bodies, whether as instruments of labor or of sex. In marriage a woman offered herself in return for a home and children and a place in the social order. This was the same bargain, she thought, merely unsanctified. Then, "No," she whispered, "this bargain is a better one than I had."

She looked around the lovely room, feeling the embrace of this wealthy, gracious house. Its beautiful furnishings, its overflowing pantries and flourishing gardens and orchards, its riches, were like his own arms around her. She thought of her son, riding thoroughbred horses and given pedigreed dogs like a little prince, and with an assured future in the Brandon mills. She thought of Mary O'Brien and Cook and Peggy, all of them her good friends and companions.

She decided not to think about the outcome should the other servants discover the affair—or if Mrs. Rhys did. The risk was enormous, but so were the possible benefits for Connor, and there was nothing in the world she would not do for her son. If she continued to please Rhys, he would help Connor. Men of his class gave money and favors in exchange for a service she was all too eager to render.

And then, despite herself, she wondered what her lover would give her, for love itself. What valid token existed that did not already belong by right to his wife?

◆

In the months that followed she counted the hours between his infrequent visits, her body aching for the release he gave her. She had no fear of pregnancy; Dr. van Dorn had told her she would never conceive another child. She gave herself to Rhys freely. He was a wonderful lover, with more finesse than Enoch, although he asked her to do things that surprised her. Some of them she simply could not bring herself to do, not even when she knew she was in love with him. She was a passionate woman, but not a wanton one. They were together too seldom for him to press his case.

She wanted to watch over him in other ways, resenting Constance's offhand treatment of such a superior man, wishing she, Dilys, had the tending of him.

"You work too hard," she told him softly one day when he came out to the lawn while she supervised the little girls at play. From the house it would look like a proper greeting between master and servant, but her body swelled and tingled when she looked at him.

He smiled amiably. "It's restful to see you," he said.

She flushed, her eyes darting toward the house, as if her love for him must be visible. Her mouth trembled.

"What is it, Dilys?" he asked, assuming she knew. She was always ready for him. All he had to do was look at her and she was wet and willing. That, combined with her reticence to experiment in bed, aroused him. It titillated him to go a little further each time, to make her do the same. Eventually he would have everything he wanted from her.

"If you ever leave me, I'll die," she whispered.

He hid both gratification and a mild annoyance at such melodrama. "Nonsense," he said lazily. "How could I leave you? This is where I live."

Then the children claimed him and she sat watching him play croquet, his tall body bent over the hoop, his long, sensitive fingers curled around the mallet. She was shaking with desire, utterly obsessed, yet overcome by anguish. The girls had outgrown her, and Constance talked about hiring a governess. When that happened, Dilys and Connor would be sent away.

But no! she reminded herself. He needs Connor, Connor fills an empty place for him. And she hoped fervently that Constance would have no sons to usurp Connor's place in Rhys's heart.

6

♦

Connor galloped one of Brandon Hall's best geldings alongside Rhys, sure that in a few days his most cherished wish would be granted. A lot of his dreams had come true, but they had been baby wishes. His whole life depended on this one.

He wanted desperately to continue his education when school finished next month. His hunger to learn had not evaporated when he turned twelve, and he devoured books on all subjects. Once or twice Adam, moved by Dr. van Dorn's comments on the boy's intelligence, had lent him books from his own extensive library. The squire's annoyance over what he called Adam's interference didn't bother Connor; it was proof that Rhys wanted Connor to himself.

Rhys already had him. Connor, as if he sensed how impolitic it would be, did not mingle with the mill workers' children, although he was not accepted by the gentry either. Among people like the Anderses, van Reitjens, and Cassadynes, he had only one friend, Peter van Dorn. The two boys rode together, smoked forbidden cigars, played explorers, and confided their plans for the future.

Peter was going to be a doctor "like all the van Dorn men," he said.

"I'm going to be a textile man," Connor announced, "like all the Brandons."

Peter had been thoughtful over that. "Even though you're not a Brandon?" he asked without malice.

Connor was confident. "The squire doesn't care." He glanced at Peter. "I know some people do."

"My father says some people are fools," Peter said staunchly, "and not to pay them any mind."

But Peter had gone off to prep school a year earlier, and Rhys was once more Connor's only male companion.

Rhys had given him many proofs of the bond between them.

"You must learn how to hold your fork and knife," Rhys had told him very early on, observing Connor at table in the pantry. "Watch. Like this." It was the first of many lessons in etiquette and genteel behavior, in how a well-brought-up boy should stand—"Never slouch, and keep your hands out of your pockets"—and talk—"Don't use slang and get the brogue out of your speech"—and look— "You and your linen must be clean and your hands well tended." Some of it was hard to do, but Connor tried.

The best lesson took place when Rhys surprised Connor and Peter dancing the polka with the two little girls, while Dilys played the piano.

"No, don't stop," he had said, smiling, and remarked after a few moments that the long steps were a glide, not a leap. With Georgia to partner him, he had shown them how it was done, all of them laughing and clapping together like friends. It was a happy day for everyone, Georgia because her father had danced with her, and Jillian because she adored Peter van Dorn and followed the boy around like a puppy. Peter, patient and gentle, was kind to her even if she was only a baby.

And then just last week, when Rhys and Connor were riding together, had come the most fatherly advice of all.

"You're almost a man," the squire had begun. "You look more like fifteen than twelve"—he cast an appraising glance at Connor's face—"and a handsome one at that. There are things you should know before you get into trouble."

"Yes, sir," Connor returned, embarrassed by the praise but wondering what he had done to provoke such a warning.

"I'm talking about sex, Connor, the physical relations between men and women and how children are conceived." Rhys was looking at him soberly, suppressing a smile as Connor turned scarlet.

"I imagine you know the facts as well as any boy raised around animals?" Rhys inquired.

Almost purple now, Connor nodded. He had seen bulls mounting cows and watched Jericho, the stallion's organ immensely long and moistly, vividly vermilion, pumping and snorting as he covered the mares. He had witnessed the birth of calves and foals and lambs. But he was uncertain of human intercourse and could not imagine any female allowing him to thrust himself inside her secret place, or what the secret place was like, or how it would feel if he did. Would he bellow like the bulls did or snort and scream like Jericho?

He wished mightily that this conversation were not taking place, but he listened with burning cheeks while the squire went on, telling him how to avoid disease and pregnancies.

"Your life could be totally ruined by a casual tumble with one of the maids, Connor. I want your promise that you will resist temptation until you are much older."

"Oh, yes, sir, I will!" Sex frightened him as much as it preoccupied him. The maids would box his ears if they knew what he was thinking when he looked at them!

"Good. If you have any questions, you must come to me." The squire rode in silence for a time, and when he spoke again it was in a voice tinged with bitterness.

"You will learn eventually, Connor, that between men and women there is another factor to complicate this otherwise agreeable procedure. It is an invention of women, called love. To possess a woman, you need only convince her that you love her. But take care not to be caught in your own trap."

Connor, his face once more a normal color, glanced up at the man he so admired. "Do men never love, then?"

Rhys sighed. "Alas, yes, when they are very young."

The squire was thinking about his first wife. A great wave of compassion for his loss filled Connor's heart to bursting, but there was nothing he could say. He reached out and put a hand on the squire's arm and Rhys, meeting his glance, had covered the boy's hand with his own and nodded his acceptance of the sympathy in Connor's face

Then Rhys had urged Jericho into a canter and left th
moment behind, except in Connor's cherished list of at
tentions from his benefactor. His hopes of a higher educa
tion had increased that day.

"Study hard, Connor," Rhys had told him often enough
"It's for your future."

"There's nothing I'd rather do, squire! Nothing in th
world." And last week Connor had asked Rhys what hi
future would be.

"Why, a place here with me, Connor," Rhys had re
plied, glancing up from the papers on his desk. "I couldn'
get on without you."

Connor had swallowed hard before he went on. "Wha
place will that be, sir?"

Rhys, frowning at something in his correspondence, di
not look up again. "We'll see when the time comes. Ru
away now! I'm busy."

Closing the study door behind him, Connor had cherishe
the words. *I couldn't get on without you.* He *did* want t
work with Rhys in the mills someday—but not yet.

And when, this morning, Rhys had told him they wer
going to Troy to order a suit for Connor's graduation—"
proper outfit for the best student in his class"—Conno
could have flown to Troy without a thoroughbred geldin
to carry him.

♦

The two horses slowed from a canter to a trot as they
approached the town of Troy with its many foundries
Some of the best iron work in the country came out o
Troy, and the best stoves too. Like the textile town o
Cohoes across the river, Troy was a union town, anc
Connor knew Rhys's opinion of unions and union organiz
ers like Enoch. It was a subject to be avoided.

They picked their way through streets crowded witl
rumbling farmers' carts coming to market, a growing num
ber of automobiles, whose hard tires clattered over the
cobbled streets, and the Saturday throngs on foot.

"We'll have some hot chocolate afterward." Rhys smiled down at Connor when they reached the center of town. "By way of celebration."

Connor smiled back, too suffused by gratitude to speak. Rhys had already given him so much! The very clothes he wore today had been cut down by Dilys from one of Rhys's fine riding costumes, and the boots were Rhys's Christmas present to him. Most of all, he had given Connor his friendship and his trust. Dilys thought the squire was the best man in the world, and he was! Surely he meant to grant Connor the same education he would have given a son of his own. Why else buy him a new suit of clothes to hang in the closet while Connor put on rough denim to work in the mill?

What school has he chosen, Connor wondered, ready to go anywhere to make himself worthy of the man he so loved. One of these days, he vowed, I'll be just like him, and he'll be proud of me.

But from the bottom of his heart Connor wanted more than that. It would happen like this. Someday Rhys Brandon, with no son of his own, would adopt him.

"This is Connor," Rhys would say. "My adopted son." Or, maybe, just, "my son."

Inside the shop he stood proudly during the measuring, as straight and tall as a Brandon.

♦

Now! Connor was certain. The squire's going to tell me now!

In his new blue serge suit he felt like a grown man. He was barely aware of the merriment under the oak, of the little girls in their party dresses, or of his mother and Mrs. O'Brien and Cook and Peggy and Murphy dressed in their Sunday best to celebrate his graduation. Peter, his school already in recess for the summer, was at his side, Connor listening intently to everything his friend had to tell him about the subjects he studied.

A trestle table had been spread with a second-best cloth, but the fine white cake, with chocolate icing and

"Good Luck, Connor" written on it in whipped cream, did not tempt him. He hungered for one thing only, to hear the squire make his dream come true, and now Rhys was tapping a spoon against his glass and silence fell upon the little party.

"Ladies and gentlemen," Rhys began, elegant even with a glass of sarsaparilla in his hand, "I propose a toast to a young man who has done me proud, our own Connor MacKenzie. As he leaves the schoolroom behind to take on a man's work in the Brandon mills, I expect great things of him."

They turned to Connor, their glasses raised to drink, then lowered them untouched at the sight of his face, shock and disbelief written on it as clearly as the message on the cake.

"Connor?" Dilys said, going to him. "Are you ill?"

"You're joking!" Connor burst out, staring at Rhys. "You can't mean me to go and work in the mills now."

"I always have," said Rhys, at once baffled and amused. "We've talked about it often enough."

"Yes, squire, but don't make me go now, not until I've had my real education." His hands were clasped like a supplicant's. "You told me studying was important, that it was for my future."

"Indeed. But now you've had all the education you require. You don't need more learning, Connor. You need practical experience to become a mill foreman—and who knows what beyond that." There was nothing beyond that for any but his own sons, much as Connor diverted him from the fact that he was still without an heir. But Constance was pregnant again and this time with a son; Rhys was certain of it.

But this had all the makings of confrontation! Absurd. And unpalatable with the van Dorn boy present. Yet Rhys had to admire Connor's spirit. He had molded him, after all, made a little gentleman out of a laborer's son. Connor was tall as a soldier on parade, his body rigid with anticipation and what looked like—yes, it was—anger! It broke loose.

"Then why did you teach me all those other things, manners and riding and—all those other things?" Connor demanded stormily. "Why did you buy me this?" He pinched the fabric of his new suit contemptuously, ignoring Peter's restraining hand on his shoulder.

Rhys cast a swift glance around the circle of expectant faces awaiting his answer. By God, he told himself, the little bastard's going to start a mutiny. He glanced at Dilys. Her face was strained. I should think so, Rhys thought. She should have taught him better discipline.

"It pleased me," Rhys finally said to Connor, "as it now pleases me that you should work in my mills and learn everything about textiles so that, in time, you can move into a position of trust."

Again Connor reverted to entreaty. "I want to, sir, and I will. But please let me have a few more years at school." Tears of desperation glittered in Connor's eyes. "I'll pay you back, I swear it. And I'll work for you the rest of my life. Please, Mr. Brandon, please!"

"But this is beyond belief!" Rhys exclaimed. "I will not let a green boy dictate to me. Are you making this a condition of staying on here, Connor?"

There was absolute silence as the hope in Connor's face dimmed and was replaced by the dark suspicion of his early days here. His hands fell to his sides and he drew a deep breath. His eyes remained fixed on Rhys's face.

"Maybe I am," he said very softly.

"No, Connor, no!" Dilys warned him, thoroughly frightened now. "Not after all Mr. Brandon's done for you, not after all his kindness to both of us. You couldn't be that ungrateful!"

"I'm *not* ungrateful," Connor said, afraid the tears would roll down his cheeks. "I just want to know why."

"You don't have to know why," Dilys insisted. "You have to trust Mr. Brandon. You do trust him, don't you?"

How can I? Connor wanted to cry. Has he been playing with me all this time? His pride shouted that he should turn and walk away, yet as strong as pride was the sense of home, and deeper still were the rules on which a child of poverty is raised. Know your place and stay in it. Be grateful for favors but never ask for them. And never turn down a steady job or you might starve to death. Only Enoch spat at gratitude, and Enoch had abandoned Connor to fend for himself. And who had come to his rescue? Rhys.

Lowering his glance, Connor swallowed his pride and took a deep breath. "I'm sorry, sir. I beg your pardon."

With his head tilted back and his green eyes slightly narrowed, Rhys contemplated his unruly subject. He had no patience with scenes and no sympathy for this presumptuous boy's grandiose expectations. Constance and his neighbors would say they had warned him.

"You have it, Connor," he said with a gracious smile, then left them to their celebrations. The servants clustered around Connor at one end of the table, troubled by the scene they had just witnessed.

"I'll be blowed," Murphy said.

"I told you he was only playin'," Peggy said sourly. "There's your prince for you!"

"That's rotten luck, Connor," Peter said angrily.

"Come now, Master Peter," Dilys said. "Maybe Connor took his own hopes for Mr. Brandon's promises."

"No, Mrs. MacKenzie," Peter said, polite but firm. "My father thought the same thing Connor did. But listen, I'll send you all my books from Groton, and your mother can help you with the lessons."

Connor said nothing, too humiliated to speak. Peter meant well, but there was no comfort in the suggestion. He regretted having confided his hopes to anyone. It only made his humiliation more complete.

A hand slipped into his and he looked down at Georgia. "It isn't fair, Connor. I'm so sorry."

For a second he wanted to tell her to leave him alone, that he could not trust her any more than he could trust her father. But she was only a baby. He couldn't blame her for what her father did.

"I don't want to talk about it," he told her gruffly. "Just forget it."

She nodded, but she did not relinquish his hand and he held tight to it, needing the comfort she gave him no matter how unmanly it might be to seek it from a five-year-old girl.

"I don't know what all the fuss is about," Jillian chirped, her mouth full of cake. "I wish Papa'd let *me* stop doing lessons."

"Oh, Jilly, do be quiet," Georgia sighed. "You don't understand anything."

But Connor did not hear them. His relationship with Rhys had just altered, suddenly, irrevocably, and Connor felt mortally wounded, as if Rhys had done him a great injury instead of offering him a secure future.

Upstairs with Dilys, he was inconsolable.

"But why?" he stormed. "He knows how much it means to me! He knows! He promised me!"

"Be fair, son! He never did." She knew Rhys had led everyone to believe it, but she could not say so, not to Connor and certainly not to Rhys.

"Not exactly, maybe, but he made me think I was . . . I was more than a mill hand to him."

He mustn't carry on like this, Dilys told herself distractedly, or we'll both be sent packing. "He wants you with him in the mills," she said, clutching at straws. "*With* him, helping him, not off in some dusty school."

He considered that, his face clearing slightly, and she pressed her advantage.

"He wants the best for you, son, you know that."

His dark eyes searched hers, clinging desperately to the idea that she was still the omniscient goddess of his baby-hood. He had to believe her. He loved Rhys. He nodded and she breathed again, aghast at how her loyalties had been divided.

"But I'll show him!" Connor vowed. "I'll go to work in the mills, but I'll get my education somehow, damn me to hell if I don't!" He shook his head, confused again. "I just wish I knew why he changed his mind."

Dilys hadn't the heart to tell him why. And if what she feared came to pass, Connor's status in this house would alter even more. Constance had finally conceived again. As much as Connor, Dilys had fantasized that her child was Rhys's surrogate son and, since the start of their affair, she had dreamed impossible dreams of Connor's future. But Dilys had a foreboding that the baby would be a boy.

Mother and son sat in silence, Connor devastated, and Dilys, torn between her son and her lover, feeling as much betrayed by this pregnancy as Connor had been.

♦

Rhys Wilhelm Brandon IV was born in November and the event was duly celebrated, first by the family and several months later by a dinner dance on the evening of his christening at the Dutch Reformed Church.

"You'd think it was the Second Coming!" Peggy sniffed, arranging puff pastries on a silver tray.

Cook was filling a pastry tube with sweet whipped cream. "And why shouldn't he be happy? He's got himself a fine son."

"And what of his two fine daughters, pray, that he hardly notices, poor little things?" That was the laundress, ironing Rhys's starched dress shirt. A delicious aroma of sun-dried cotton, bluing, and starch rose from her iron.

"He notices them." It was Connor, pressed into service for the occasion. Cook handed him the tube and he began filling the puff pastries. "He sees them every day."

The women glanced at each other, not knowing what to make of this evidence of revived hero worship. But Mr. Brandon *was* a hero, aristocratic, handsome, and kind when he chose to be, as, clearly, he did since his son was born. Before that he had cast a pall on the entire household, and without ever raising his voice. As for Mrs. Rhys, she had been a bundle of nerves throughout her pregnancy and was unbearably arrogant since the birth of her son.

"Here, Connor, would you be runnin' this shirt up to himself for me, there's a love. I've still got all of the girls' petticoats to do."

Connor nodded. He didn't mind doing servants' work

when one of the servants asked him. But when *she* ordered him about, he had a hard time not telling her he wasn't a servant in this house, he was a salaried mill worker. He never would, though. It was not only for his mother's sake; it was for the squire's too. Rhys, kind and full of praise for Connor's progress at the mill, was irresistible. The rift between them seemed mended.

Connor had never seen a grown man as happy as the squire since Will was born. It cut him to the quick that he was not the reason for his joy, but he comforted himself that maybe someday he would be in another way. He was doing a man's work now, instead of helping Murphy to tend the horses and teaching the two little girls to ride. They were nice little girls and he cared for them as if they were his own sisters, but it wasn't a man's work—any more than filling pastries!

When he had finished filling them and eaten two puffs for his trouble, Connor took the shirt up to Rhys's dressing room on the second floor, where he was not allowed to go—that was *her* doing—unless he was sent there on an errand.

In the dressing room he hung up the shirt and started to leave, but he could not resist opening the closets. He looked admiringly at the rows of suits and coats and shoes, and then at the drawers full of monogrammmed shirts and underwear, most of it silk. He had never thought much about clothes until the first time he saw the squire's dressing room and knew how cheap and rough his own clothes were. And then he had started wearing Rhys's cut-down tweeds and cashmeres and felt in his true element at last—until he started working at the mill dressed in rough ticking that chafed his spirit like a hair shirt.

Always drawn by its luxury, Connor ventured now into the master bedroom. The great canopied mahogany four-poster had a gold silk damask spread and hangings, and Connor knew the hand-hemmed sheets were linen and very fine, woven in England where, the squire had told him, they spun and loomed the finest cotton in the world. Connor knew the Brandon mills could make fine cotton, but that Rhys chose not to. It was a matter of domestic demand, Rhys said. The American market wanted heavier, longer-wearing goods. The fine stuff was imported from Europe. It seemed silly to Connor when Brandon could make it here and sell it cheaper.

He walked around the room, longing to possess, someday, everything he saw: the engraved silver-backed brushes on the bureau, and the gold-tooled leather-bound book on the nightstand. He wondered again what it would be like to be the master of a house like this and own all those mills and railroads as well as the most beautiful landed estate in the world.

There was a newspaper on the leather wing chair near the window, and he opened it idly. His father's face looked back at him. "Union Organizer Threatens Two Factories," the headline said. He read part of the article, enough to discover that his father—"that rabble-rouser," Rhys and his friends called him—was trying to organize automobile workers in Detroit.

Rhys had read this paper! Rhys had seen this shame. It made Connor cringe. He was that rabble-rouser's son. Maybe Rhys thought Connor had the same bad blood. That was why he put a stop to Connor's education! Education, the squire once said, was a menace in the wrong hands.

He folded the paper, put it back, and crossed to the window to look out at the grounds, seeking comfort from the sight. Reality was too painful and he tried again to lose himself in his old, tattered fantasy of adoption, hoping the magic of it would ease his soul.

What did Will matter? He was nothing, a puling little lump who ate and slept and cried. Connor still rode and hunted and swam with Rhys on Sundays. Furthermore, after five months on the job, Connor knew he would have learned everything about the Brandon mills long before Will Brandon could sit a horse. By the time Will finished college, Connor would be running the mills!

But the magic was gone now. That little scrap of a Brandon upstairs in the nursery had made an enormous change in this family, and nothing would ever be the same for him again, not even the view from this window.

He was turning to leave just as Rhys entered the bedroom.

Connor was apologetic, where once he would have been confident. "I'm sorry, sir. I brought up your shirt for tonight and came to look out of the window."

Rhys approached and gazed out at his property. He put an arm across Connor's shoulders. "It's a beautiful place, isn't it?"

"The best in the world," Connor said hoarsely, grateful for that arm.

"Even better, now that I have a son." Rhys's arm dropped. "Do you know what that means, Connor? It changes everything." He was bursting with elation.

Connor nodded, a knot of such searing envy in his chest that he could not speak. He had to get away, but as he passed the chair he looked at the folded newspaper, then glanced at Rhys and colored.

"You saw it," Rhys said. "Well, never mind, Connor, never mind him. You shouldn't have anything to do with the likes of him."

"Yes, sir," Connor said, thinking as he left the room and his hopes behind him forever, I don't want him. I want you. I'd have been a better son to you than yours will ever be.

7

♦

Richard Rhys Brandon was born a year after his brother. "My boys," Rhys said fondly whenever he looked at them.

"I hate them," Jillian announced soon after Richard

learned to sit up and his parents made a fuss about it. Jillian hid Will's favorite toys and made fright faces at the baby. The little boys had the third floor nursery to themselves now, but Jillian had always considered her removal to a room of her own on the second floor, directly under her mother's eye, a curse brought about by her brothers. She was upstairs teasing the babies more than she was down, and the groom had to be fetched to carry her back to her own room as she sobbed loudly that her brothers were wicked spirits.

"That child's a menace to my sons," Constance announced, annoyed by the constant uproar. "She needs a good spanking."

"Don't exaggerate, my dear," Rhys said absently.

"You're away too much to know what she's like," Constance retorted. "And even when you're here you ignore her carryings-on."

"She's just spirited." Rhys smiled, preparing to leave for Albany. "Like you."

Disarmed by the compliment, Constance held her peace and Jillian continued her naughtiness.

"It's headstrong she is," Cook said when wails and screams could be heard in the kitchen.

"But she's heavy-handed about it," Peggy declared with authority. She was personal maid to both little girls now. "My Miss Georgia's got a mind of her own but she doesn't carry on about it."

"Like mother, like daughter, the pair of them," Cook murmured softly, and everyone laughed.

"But Miss Jilly's good at heart," Mary O'Brien insisted, to general agreement.

"I'm going to run away," Jillian threatened several times a day.

"But why, darling?" Dilys would ask, trying to calm her.

"Because everyone hates me."

"Jilly, don't be stupid," Georgia finally told her. "I don't hate you. Dilys doesn't, or Connor."

"Mama and Papa do."

"They don't like you much," Georgia conceded. "But they don't like me either."

"I *love* you," Jillian declared, flinging her arms around her sister. "I'll love you forever."

Georgia was the only one with any influence on Jillian, but even she failed to keep her from biting Will in the presence of company at tea one Sunday afternoon. Rhys intervened angrily and sent her away with Miss Howell, the governess. When the company had gone, Jillian was summoned to his study and Miss Howell told to wait outside.

A man with an infallibly equable disposition, Rhys communicated displeasure quietly and Jillian, facing him, was more frightened by his silky voice than she had ever been before.

"You're a disgrace to the entire family," Rhys said softly. "What do you think your punishment should be for such abominable behavior?"

Jillian shook her head. She was not certain what abominable behavior was or disgrace either, but she was clearly all bad.

"Papa," Jillian implored, her eyes brimming with tears, "I'll be good if I can sit on your lap sometimes."

"Don't be impertinent. Answer my question."

Jillian sobbed and shook her head helplessly.

"Well, then," he said, "since you have no manners, you must stay in your room until you learn some. On bread and water," he added. "Now go upstairs and wait until I find the key to lock you in."

"It isn't fair!" Jillian wailed as the governess led her away. "I only bit him once! And I'll never learn manners in time for Clarissa Cassadyne's birthday party!"

She would not promise never to bite Will again, and the punishment continued for three days. Clarissa Cassadyne's party came and went, with Georgia refusing to attend without her sister. Dilys worried about a bread and water diet for so young a child, but Constance referred her to Rhys, and Rhys would not budge.

"I will not have those girls disrupting the house," he announced. "They must be disciplined."

In the end it was Georgia who persuaded her sister, through the playroom door, to say she was sorry.

"I'm not abomal and I'm only sorry 'cause I'm locked up," Jillian wept, lonely, bored, and hungry.

"You don't have to say what you're sorry *for*," Georgia persuaded her after a moment's reflection. "Just say you're sorry and it will all be over."

And it was, to the household's vast relief.

"A long punishment for the poor little mite," Cook said.

"She's as stubborn as himself," the valet offered, drinking tea.

But Peggy did not agree. "It's Miss Georgia who's a match for him, mark my words."

"Miss Georgia's good as gold," the valet protested. "A little saint."

"She's just quiet," Peggy said with a firm nod of her head. "There's a difference."

◆

"How can I make him care about me?" Georgia asked Connor on her eighth birthday. Connor and Dilys were her rocks, but it was her father's affection she had always craved; she had given up hope of earning her mother's. All Mama cared about was Papa. Even her sons were not as important to her as he was. But Georgia could understand that: Papa was the most wonderful man in the world.

Connor considered the problem seriously. He had never been able to understand Rhys's general indifference, even aversion to his firstborn. On the other hand, Constance's veiled dislike of Georgia was not a puzzle to him or any of the servants.

"Show him you like the things he likes," Connor advised. "He liked it when you learned to jump your pony."

"What else must I like? The mills?"

"For one thing. And all his art stuff too."

Georgia nodded. "Tell me about the mills."

He told her. He had been a mill worker for two years now. He had been a picker first, going through the bales of cotton to loosen the stuff and shake out the dirt. Then he had learned to card and comb the cotton before it went to the drawing frames, where several ends of combed cotton were drawn together into one. By now he had advanced to the fly frames, where the drawn cotton was twisted and retwisted in several processes to draw it out into an even finer thread.

Soon he would be a ring spinner, in charge of over one hundred spindles on a single machine. He wanted to be a mule spinner, not because of his father, who was well remembered by the mill workers to Connor's dismay, but because the finest cotton was spun on the machine called the mule and its operators earned a top salary of twelve to twenty dollars a week.

But he had more than money in mind. "Brandon Textiles," he told Georgia, "already makes cotton almost as fine as the English do. Someday I'm going to spin cotton finer than theirs." But it would not be Brandon cotton!

Georgia nodded. "What about the art collection?"

He shook his head. "Can't help you there. I don't know anything about art. Don't care either." He had been shown the art gallery only once. Adolescent boys and porcelain, in Rhys's opinion, did not mix.

But Connor shared Georgia's sense of rejection fully now. He lived in a kind of limbo, still the recipient of special treatment—Jericho's filly, Jezebel, was virtually Connor's private mount—but aware of lines he must not cross. The blue suit, too small for Connor now, hung in his closet, a mute reminder of happier days.

He took Georgia's hand, sympathizing, and she sighed and leaned against his shoulder. They rarely needed words to express their feelings to each other. It had been that way even before Georgia could talk.

But there was a vast difference between them. Someday she would dance in the ballroom at her parents' parties, but Connor never would.

"I'll just go and sit with him when he's there," Georgia decided finally. "If he'll let me."

♦

Rhys was surprised to see her, but he let her stay, mildly gratified by her interest in his collection. After a few days of her devoted attendance he wanted her there, a pretty presence in the lofty room. She was like a porcelain shepherdess herself with her bright hair, her perfect features, her luminous blue eyes. He came to realize that what he had thought was shyness—when he had thought about her at all—was rather a gift for quiet observation unexpected in a child. It struck him that his daughter had a fine intelligence, thus far applied only to lessons in reading and writing. He began to wonder what Georgia thought about.

There was only one awkward moment, when she asked what was behind the ruby velvet curtains that covered her mother's portrait.

"Nothing," Rhys said. "It's waiting for a masterpiece. I'll know it when I see it."

"Oh, Papa!" she breathed, her eyes shining. "Maybe I can paint it for you someday!"

"Maybe you can," he said indulgently, and then asked, "Why do you come here?"

"The things are so beautiful," she said. "And you're here, Papa."

He could not help feeling a warm response to that declaration of love from Georgianna's child. And Georgia, in the sun of his approval, blossomed like a rose, displaying not only intelligence but imagination and humor as well.

Soon Rhys discovered that it was a pleasure to talk to her as he catalogued his treasures or placed them to better advantage, explaining why each one was a masterpiece, telling her where he had found it, what it had cost, and what it was worth now. The paintings and drawings attracted her most and, noticing that, he gave her a drawing pad and pencil one day and was surprised by the sketch she produced of a Meissen figurine. It had no perspective, but the detail was amazingly accurate and finely drawn.

"Why are you always smiling?" Jillian soon demanded of her sister suspiciously.

"Because I'm happy," Georgia said.

"Sitting in Papa's gallery all day?" Jillian found that no reason to rejoice.

"But Father's there, Jilly! He likes having me. You ought to come."

One day Jillian did, but she fidgeted until Rhys sent her away. Jillian was glad to go, then resentful that it was Georgia her father wanted. She was not the only one to resent it. Rhys's new relationship with his firstborn did not escape his wife's notice.

"Georgia must have art lessons," he told Constance one morning before he left on a business trip. He always rode at daybreak, then bathed and dressed for breakfast. He was served at the table near their bedroom window, Constance on a tray in bed. This morning, as usual, she lounged against a mound of lace-trimmed pillows, wearing one of her sumptuous satin negligees. Her long, luxuriant hair was loose around her shoulders.

"Then so must Jillian," she answered, determined that her offspring receive equal treatment with Georgianna's.

"Is Miss Howell qualified or shall I engage a new governess?"

"She is eminently qualified," Constance said, dismayed at the sort of woman Rhys would certainly select. "Incidentally, I have some new domestic arrangements in mind. Will must be moved downstairs from the nursery."

He looked at her curiously.

"I'm pregnant," she said.

He was delighted. At this rate, he'd have the houseful of sons he wanted.

He went to the bed and kissed her. "Good for you," he said. "Shall we make it another boy?"

"As many as you like," she replied as he returned to the table and resumed his breakfast. She hated his "business" trips, but there was nothing to be gained by letting him know it. He would simply not hear what she said. She had learned that much in eight years of marriage to him.

"I've promised to take her to the museum in Albany next time I go," he said, buttering some toast.

He was still talking about Georgia! "A little young for that, isn't she?"

"No, she's very bright." He sipped his coffee, reflecting on Georgia. Her startling resemblance to her mother no longer troubled him because she adored him as her mother never had. Her eyes, when she looked at him, had the very glow he had searched for so futilely in Georgianna's. She moved gracefully, with a serenity Jillian would never possess—or Constance either. It was the same serenity captured in the hidden portrait of Georgianna, but what was glacial in the mother was incandescent in the child. If Georgia was as brilliant as her mother—and she seemed to be—what a woman Rhys could make of her!

He finished his coffee, lit a cigarette, and rose from the table, elegant in a dark gray broadcloth coat and narrow trousers, a white silk shirt, and dark red cravat.

"Don't go," Constance said, her voice husky with desire. The mere thought of him could arouse her. The sight of him brought her to the edge of orgasm.

"I must go. The train is waiting." But he stroked his blond beard speculatively.

"It's your train. Let it wait." She turned back the covers. Her negligee fell open, baring her gleaming body. He saw that her breasts were already changed by her pregnancy, the nipples large and a slightly darker pink. She smiled at him, beckoning.

He shook his head, still stroking his beard.

Her long legs parted and she touched herself, watching his face as he watched her. "Lock the door," she said, and lay back on her pillows while he did. She had one climax watching him undress and another when he knelt by the bed and put his head between her thighs, but it was only when she was covered by him, surrounding him, that her passion reached its height, because for that moment, at least, he was hers.

◆

"Mama's making another baby," Georgia said to Connor on a Sunday afternoon a month later.

He handed her an apple and concentrated on eating his. They were in one of the orchard sheds where the apples were stored until Cook made them into apple butter and preserves and cider and pies, juicy baked apples and luscious fritters, and dried or candied slices on a string for Christmas. Jezebel and Georgia's pony, Sassafras, were munching stray apples outside.

"I don't know why she makes so many," Georgia went on. "She doesn't want to be bothered by the ones she has." She was curious, not reproachful.

"Mother says rich people never see much of their children," Connor said. He avoided any allusion to sex when he was around females, but especially with Georgia and Jillian, for whose protection he felt responsible. Sometimes, after one of those nights when he woke to humiliation and damp sheets, he was convinced he was too vile to be around innocent children. For a while he thought he was possessed by the devil. It had been a relief to hear the boys at the mill snickering over the same thing.

"But I don't care so much now," Georgia went on, smiling at him with pure joy. "I have Papa, thanks to you."

"Want another apple?" Connor asked, rubbing one on his shirt until it shone as if it had been varnished. Much as he cared for her, he envied her new relationship with her father.

Georgia declined the apple. "Connor, where do babies come from?"

"From their mothers."

"I know *that*. But how do they get inside?"

Connor shot to his feet, pocketing the apple. "We came out to go riding, not sit here nattering. Come on."

Trailing the skirt of her dark blue riding habit, she followed him out of the shed and he lifted her onto her pony's hand-tooled sidesaddle. He had taught her to ride, and their favorite time of the week was still their ride together after Sunday midday dinner. She ate her meal in the family dining room and he ate his in the kitchen. Connor was finding it increasingly difficult to accept differences like that.

"That snooty governess was *her* choice," he exclaimed to his mother.

"But, Connor, young ladies must have a proper education."

"They're still little kids, not young ladies. *She* just didn't want Georgia and Jillian to be with me so much. And she hates me because *he* still likes me. She hates anyone he likes. Sometimes I could swear she hates Georgia for the same reason, not only because Georgia isn't hers."

"Dear heaven, Connor! You mustn't ever talk about that."

"I won't, don't worry. But for Georgia's sake, not hers."

He glanced at Georgia now, ready to protect her from Constance as any brother would. No matter who taught Georgia lessons and deportment, it was to Connor that she turned first when she wanted comfort.

"Where shall we go?" he asked her. "It's your turn to choose."

"The barn in the east meadow."

They set off, Connor holding Jezebel down to a single-foot so Sassafras wouldn't burst his pony heart trying to keep up. The ground still smelled rich and loamy and Connor loved the popping sounds the twigs made under the horses' hooves. Riding was the best thing in the world and this land the most beautiful.

The autumn leaves were a riot of color against a sky as blue as Georgia's eyes. He was proud of the way she sat her pony, her back straight as he had taught her, her hands high and sure on the reins. Jillian hadn't taken Connor's advice about pleasing her father. She said horses were smelly, the mills noisy, and she didn't give a hoot about art. Jillian was a pest sometimes, but not Georgia. Connor knew exactly how hard it was to be on the outside looking in. For a girl, Georgia had been very brave all these years.

She has to be, he thought, with *her* for a mother. Constance didn't fawn over any of her children, but she left no doubt that she was their mother. She treated Georgia like a guest. Connor wondered when the squire would tell Georgia about the first Mrs. Brandon. He hoped it would be before any of the children in Brandon's Gate did. They all knew the truth; children always knew more than the grown-ups thought they did.

Then his mind turned to the new baby and another knell sounded for his vanished dream. It was hard to remember how close he and Rhys had been in those early days! It wasn't so much what they had talked about as their pleasure in being together that Connor missed. All Rhys really wanted of him now was to do a good job in the mill. In the old days he had seemed to want more—companionship, affection. They still rode together, and Rhys behaved as if they were still friends. But they no longer were.

Rhys seemed unaware that he was no longer being offered devotion of the kind Connor was still too embarrassed to call love. While Rhys waited ever more impatiently for his boys to be old enough to ride and shoot with him, he merely wanted Connor to substitute for them.

It was impossible for Connor to refuse, and part of him did not want to. Connor knew several kind and generous men—Dr. van Dorn and Adam Hendrik among them—but they were ordinary men and the squire was not.

Connor had built himself another dream: someday he would manage a mill for Rhys, maybe even a whole division. He would wear a dark suit and a white shirt and a beard like the squire's. He often practiced Rhys's manner of rubbing his jaw as if a beard had already grown on his own smooth cheeks. In his imagination it was as blond as Rhys's. He would smoke a pipe or thin cigars and have his own office with his name on the door. He would go to meetings with other company executives and be Rhys's right-hand man. But he needed a gentleman's education for that, and his had been ended by the very man he still wanted to emulate. The confusion and ambiguity of his feelings made him withdraw.

When he forced himself to face reality, it seemed that there was no way for him, no way at all. That bitter realization made him angry enough at times to break something, to hit someone.

When they reached the barn Connor and Georgia dismounted again and climbed up the ladder to the hayloft. Connor took out his apple and bit into it with a satisfying crunch.

"You're always hungry," Georgia said.

"I'm bigger than you are so I have to eat more."

She accepted that, chewing on a straw. "I forgot to tell you: next week we start dancing classes. A dancing master is coming from Albany to teach all the children in Brandon's Gate, and we have to dress up in party clothes and dancing pumps. Mama will make me wear my green and I hate green." She sighed, then brightened. "I'll teach you to dance as soon as I've learned."

"You won't either! I don't have any use for dancing."

"You used to like it! And Miss Howell says all gentlemen must know how to dance."

Connor scowled ferociously. "Bother Miss Howell! And I'm not a gentleman."

"I think you are," Georgia said with a decided lift of her chin.

"You don't even know what it means!"

"I know perfectly well. Papa is a gentleman."

"Well, I'm not," he bristled. "Mill workers can't be." It was the first time he had actually said it. The apple tasted bitter and he threw it away.

"If you can't be one then I don't care a fig for it," Georgia said imperiously. "And neither should you."

"But I *do* care!" he shouted, turning away from her. "Don't you understand, I *do* care."

They sat quietly in the hay for some minutes. The only sounds were the buzzings and rustlings of insects and small animals scuttling around in the barn.

"Connor, are you angry with me?"

He shook his head, furious with himself for having let the hurt show. It wasn't her anyway. It was something outside both of them, something so elusive that it frustrated him even to think about it. He turned to her, a little girl in a habit and a tricorne riding hat with a curled feather, waiting for an explanation. Any other child would have been in tears, yelled at by such a brute, but Georgia was not like Jillian. She had never cried much, not even when she was a few days old and weak enough to die.

"Not with you," he said. "I'll never be angry with you. Sometimes I'm just—angry. I can't explain it."

She nodded, accepting.

"Connor?"

"What?"

"Let's make a pact of friendship—in blood!"

"For Pete's sake, Georgia, are you crazy? What would the squire say if I brought you back with your finger all carved up?" He pulled her to her feet and brushed the straw off her clothes. "Come on, we'll go back along the river. Be careful going down the ladder."

"I'm not a baby," Georgia said.

He knew she was still confused by his outburst, and before they parted near the house he squatted on his heels and smiled at her.

"Do we really need a blood pact?" he asked.

Her beautiful little face glowed. She smiled and hugged him fiercely. "No. You'll always be my best friend."

That made it a little easier for him to watch her go into the front door of the mansion while he went around to the back.

8

♦

Adam Hendrik watched Rhys and Connor gallop their horses toward him from the far end of the meadow. The boy seemed to have grown again in the two short weeks since Adam had last seen him. Rhys, on the other hand, never changed. He was master of all he surveyed, often benevolent, always ruthless. But he appeared content in his marriage to Constance. The house was filled with children, and Constance was pregnant again.

Thank God, Adam thought, for Connie's constitution.

She had babies more easily than other women had parties and almost as often. Rhys, apparently, was still as demanding as ever, but Adam had to be fair. Constance was passionately in love with her husband; that was embarrassingly obvious to everyone. Adam knew people whispered about it. A nice woman didn't behave the way she did in public, seducing her own husband with her eyes, standing as close to him as she could possibly get, her breast pressing his arm, her thigh against his. Constance cared as little about the talk as Rhys did. If a baby every year or so was the price of her passion, she seemed more than willing to pay it, particularly after that barren stretch before Will arrived.

In the manner of women of her class, she turned the babies over to Dilys and a wet nurse as soon as they were born and thereafter saw them twice daily: in the morning after she had breakfasted with Rhys and in the evening before she and Rhys went in to dinner. She presided with authority over her household, with no letup until the last month of each pregnancy.

And yet Rhys still sought out other women on his frequent trips to New York and Albany! If Constance knew, she gave no indication of it, and restraint, her brother knew, was not one of Constance's virtues. Rhys had just returned from a trip this very evening and Connor, mounted on his special mare, Jezebel, had led Jericho down to the station to meet the train, as was his habit.

From across the field Rhys called up to Adam to wait and Adam watched him approach, leaving Connor behind. Rhys was at his best on horseback, Adam conceded. He was no longer jealous of his brother-in-law's undoubted physical attractiveness, only of the widespread assumption that his character was of a piece with his good looks. And Rhys, it was true, did not plot infamies for the pleasure of it. He simply could not conceive of any need other than his own. Even at home he regarded his wife and children as extensions of himself.

It looked remarkably like love.

"I'm glad you're here," Rhys said, his fair hair glinting in the setting sun. "I want your opinion on the business I've just concluded."

Adam waited. Rhys never consulted him about anything, least of all business.

"I told you months ago that John Anders was winding up his mills to move exclusively into banking. Martin van Reitjens likewise, into law. Well, I've just bought out their mills. Actually Silas Cassadyne and I divided the spoils between us."

Adam gave a low whistle. An expansion like that made Brandon Textiles a small empire. "I'm impressed," he said.

"I thought you might be. It will take careful planning to absorb the new plant and equipment into my operation in the most economical way." He paused. "I need someone who'll take a personal interest in doing that."

"They're your mills, Rhys. Put in anyone you like."

"I meant you."

Adam raised an eyebrow. "Surely not. Your opinion about my business acumen is well known. I never understood why you wanted me in the mills in the first place."

"You'll never know how to find a deal or close one,"
Rhys said loftily, "but you have a keen grasp of figures,
budgeting, cost projection. And some of the mills were
once your father's. Georgianna had very strong feelings
about family ties."

"Georgianna's been gone for eight years. Look, Rhys, I
have more than enough income to live on, thanks largely
to you. I don't need to hang on at the mills. Who knows, I
might even do something interesting with my life if you
chuck me out."

"I'm proposing to give you a share of my new acquisitions," Rhys said impatiently. "I was hoping that would
pique your interest."

Adam wondered what Rhys really wanted.

"In exchange, of course, for your railroad shares," Rhys
went on, "and your power of attorney to vote Georgia's
shares."

It was difficult for Rhys to acknowledge that Adam held
any such power. As things stood, however, Adam controlled over fifty percent of the railroad shares, his own
and Georgia's; Rhys controlled the rest, since he had
Constance's proxy. It had all been Georgianna's doing by
means of a will she had ordered to be drawn secretly by a
New York attorney when her last pregnancy began. By the
terms of the will her shares in the railroads—including the
very shares Rhys had bought in her name on the day she
died—and her interest in the mills were left to Adam in
trust for her child, should it survive, and until that child
reached twenty-one.

Rhys had been staggered by such flagrant evidence that
Georgianna did not trust him and therefore had not loved
him at all. It was a public statement, as her bedroom
rejection of him, thank heaven, was not. But the myth of
their perfect union was vital to him: he had demanded
that Adam and Constance say nothing about the will to
anyone, ever.

Georgianna's love, Adam was aware, was the one thing
Rhys had ever wanted that had been denied him. Other-

wise he had led a charmed life and still did, except for his ongoing frustration at Adam's hands.

"So that's it," Adam said. "You could have asked me outright. The answer is still no."

"Then, damn it, at least vote those shares with mine."

"No. I don't approve of all those spur lines you want to build. We've already made ugly mill flats and rail sidings out of the most beautiful countryside in America. Now you want to build more track to help destroy the forests too. You say it's for progress, but I know it's for money, and we have enough money."

"You're a fool, Adam." Rhys was visibly angry now and he rarely showed his anger. He dominated by virtue of his smiling refusal to acknowledge anything he didn't like.

"So you've always said. Well, then, when do you want me out?"

Rhys shook his head and signaled to Connor. "I can't have an open rift between us. It would cause talk. You'll stay on—unless you want to forgo all contact with my wife and children."

"You always go for the jugular, don't you, Rhys?"

But Connor was approaching and Rhys dismounted, handed the boy Jericho's reins, and headed for the house, unruffled. Adam fumed inwardly, feeling as helpless as a child, watching Connor, still mounted, walk Jericho to cool the stallion down.

It amazed Adam anew that Rhys could command the affection, admiration, and respect of a boy like Connor, who gave his trust warily when he gave it at all. Adam had long ago concluded that some people are born with a fatal charm. Rhys and Georgianna had it, although not, amazingly, for each other. Even Connor, despite his youth, had it. Constance had vitality in its place.

And I, Adam thought, must resign myself to the solitary life for lack of it.

He knew he would never marry. The kind of woman with whom he would want to share his life would never be attracted to a bookish fellow like himself. His work at the mills rarely interested him, but it filled up his days and he went home to his books and his piano the way other men went home to their families, glad to escape the constant friction between himself and Rhys.

Rhys, of course, attracted women in droves. Even the virtuous matrons of Brandon's Gate, who were shocked by Constance's open lust for him, preened themselves like peahens in his presence. And he had cast a spell over Connor MacKenzie long ago, Adam thought, glancing at the boy as he approached him.

Connor was fifteen now, almost grown into the overlong limbs of his adolescence. He would be a very tall man. His face had lost the angelic cast of childhood and had yet to settle into maturity, but indications of strength were already there. The curved brows were heavy over those brooding, near-black eyes that missed nothing. His mouth was wide but tender, like his mother's, his cheekbones high, his nose straight, his black hair thick and wavy. He was a strikingly handsome youth with a manner that was unyielding one moment and as captivating as his smile the next. The smile appeared less frequently now than in his early years at Brandon Hall.

A difficult age, Adam supposed. It occurred to him that the boy must be aware that Rhys no longer needed him in the same way since his sons were born. That was a relief to the family but it was another proof of Rhys's total insouciance about the people he charmed into loving him.

Adam was sure some Black Irish had crept into Connor's Scots ancestry, or even a royal adventurer. Connor looked the part and he rode like a highwayman. Now he was gentling Jezebel, and the two-year-old filly ambled along with her sire, Jericho, beside her. Rhys had let Connor raise the animal as if she were his own.

It was past six but still light, and Adam saw the boy put his head back and take a deep breath of the sweet Indian summer smells of evening in September, so rapt in the beauty of the place that he did not turn until Adam was alongside.

"Connor! You're dreaming."

Connor nodded. "I guess so, Mr. Hendrik. Good evening." He was respectful but not deferential in the way other servants were. But then, Adam reflected, Connor did not consider himself a servant.

"How is everything in the children's garden?" Adam asked, nodding toward the house.

"They all had a tea party today under the big oak," Connor said. "My mother let the girls dress up in old clothes from the attic—Will and Richard too. She said they looked a treat."

Adam smothered a smile. Connor's role as big brother to the children touched him; the boy was as serious about it as a paterfamilias. Still, Connor had always been older than his years and perhaps it was just as well to have an extra pair of watchful eyes around the house. Connor was another of Rhys's windfalls, unexpected and undeserved.

◆

Connor hated begging, but this was the opportunity he had been waiting for.

"Mr. Hendrik," he said, "may I ask your advice about something?"

"Of course," Adam said, mistaking Connor's strangled pride for deference and quite taken by it.

"I've been keeping up my studies with my mother, but she's taught me all she can. And there's so much more I want to learn!" Connor's voice mirrored his longing.

Pleased by this veneration for learning, Adam nodded.

"I wondered," Connor began. "That is, I thought you might know someone who could tutor me. I could pay something from my wages and I'd work to make up the rest."

Connor kept his eyes on Jezebel's mane, hoping desperately while the man beside him considered his request. Connor knew he would take his time about it. Adam Hendrik wasn't a man who made quick decisions the way the squire did.

Come on, he pleaded silently. Say you'll do it yourself!

I could do it, Adam was thinking. I could do it easily. Teaching a bright boy like Connor would be a pleasure.

It would fill Adam's solitary evenings and weekends. Rhys might object, but so much the worse for him. The boy was obviously eager enough to defy him for once.

Rhys, in fact, didn't give a damn if a fine mind like Connor's went to waste in his mills. But there were limits to Rhys's authority, and this was one of them.

Adam turned to the boy at his side. "I'll do it myself, Connor. I'll tutor you in the evenings after work. You can come directly from the mill and have your supper with me. You don't have to work for me, either, except at your books." Adam smiled. "I enjoy teaching. I should have been a professor, not a reluctant industrialist."

Connor let himself breathe deeply again, astonished that his wish had been granted. "I can't thank you enough, Mr. Hendrik! I'll work hard, you can count on that. I want to learn mathematics, chemistry, French, and German first."

"First you must learn Greek and Latin," Adam said firmly.

"They're of no use in business." Connor looked doubtful.

"That's so, but they're vital to a first-rate education and the roots of modern languages. You get enough practical training at the mills."

"Whatever you say, sir." This was no time to argue.

"Very well then, we'll start on Monday." Adam said good night and turned his horse toward the house. "I'll give you the finest education in America," he said over his shoulder.

With a little whoop of triumph Connor galloped the horses in tandem across the meadow, too excited to care that he'd have to cool them down again when he took them in.

What would Rhys say? But right now Connor didn't care!

◆

Adam waited for his sister in the drawing room. It had been redecorated, along with the rest of the house, in different colors and softer fabrics. The deep ruby velvets and garnet leathers of the room, once a perfect setting for Georgianna's fair, glittering beauty, had been replaced by the burnished gold brocades and russet satins that flattered Constance's style and coloring.

The most obvious change for Adam was the missing portrait of Georgianna. A half dozen years had gone by since it was removed, but Adam still looked for it every time he came into the room. He came often to see his nieces and nephews. His sister and her children were his sole blood relations and provided the closest experience to fatherhood that Adam expected to have.

And Rhys uses that, Adam thought now, to keep me in my place. He was filling his pipe with short, angry jabs as Constance came in, looking none the worse after a committee luncheon that had lasted until tea.

He kissed her. "Will this bother you?" he asked, holding up his pipe.

She shook her head. "Nothing bothers me when I'm pregnant except for being so bulky at the end."

"You're looking very well," he said. She had changed for dinner and wore an Empire gown of amber tussah silk, the sleeves and neckline deeply ruffled with ecru lace. The cut of the gown camouflaged her pregnancy, and the color complemented her creamy complexion. A small spray of diamonds was pinned to her bodice and another to the wide band of amber velvet that bound her lustrous hair. She was twisting one of the curls that escaped the band, a mannerism she had developed lately.

She had always been a handsome girl but now she was, if not beautiful, so striking that she seemed beautiful. She was like a tawny cat, her brother thought, sleek and lazy but certain to pounce. She and Rhys were alike in more ways than one.

"Let's have a drink," she said. "Rhys is dressing. He was late again. After three days away you'd think he'd arrive on time."

"He was riding with Connor."

She took the glass of sherry he brought her, clearly furious. "Riding with Connor! Or he's upstairs with

Georgia—when he's not in Albany on what he says is business." She drank some sherry with a stiff little tilt of her head. So Constance, along with everyone else, *did* harbor suspicions about Rhys's recreational activities when he was away from home.

"It was very important business." Adam told her about the Anders and van Reitjens mills.

"He didn't say a word about it to me." Constance sulked, looking far less pretty than when she had first appeared.

"Why would he? You have enough to do here."

But he knew it bothered her because Rhys had often discussed business with Georgianna. It wasn't enough for Constance to be his wife. She wanted to be the center of his life. But that place, Adam had tried to tell her, was already completely occupied by Rhys himself.

Rhys came in soon after and kissed his wife. He admired her gown and asked about her health like a model husband. Adam saw her glow again, her dish of cream once more within grasp of her velvet paws.

Between the two men there was no hint of their heated exchange on the slope. Rhys lounged in his chair in his characteristic attitude, long legs stretched out and crossed at the ankle, drinking whiskey and talking about his trip.

Promptly at eight o'clock the governess, a sere and slender woman, brought the two girls down to say good night, both of them fairylike in their pink wrappers. Adam was entranced by eight-year-old Georgia. Everyone was, although the child did nothing to draw attention to herself and was just becoming aware of her appearance. She was a miniature of her mother and had a similar reserve—but that was due more to this emotionally turbulent household, Adam was convinced, than to heredity.

His sister, Georgianna, had always hated to be touched, while Georgia was an affectionate and demonstrative child. Observant too. She would have seen that the woman in the banished portrait had the same face and golden hair as her own and that Constance often wore that woman's diamonds.

Jillian, if not exquisite, was pretty, noisy, and as rough

and tumble as her brother Will, not yet three. She had Constance's shining hair and hazel eyes and an echo of her mother's driving personality as well. She broke away from Miss Howell and ran to Rhys, demanding to know what he had brought her. Rhys, obviously in a good mood over his acquisitions, took both children on his lap and let them search his pockets for two small net bags of chocolates wrapped in gold paper.

"Miss Howell disapproves," Rhys said, smiling across at her. "I can tell."

"Sweets are bad for them at bedtime, Mr. Brandon," Miss Howell said, her cheeks flaming because Rhys had smiled at her.

Even a confirmed spinster like her, Adam thought. Amazing.

"Give the sweets to Miss Howell until she says you may eat them," Rhys told the children.

"Mama!" Jillian wailed.

Constance sipped her sherry. "Do as Papa says, Jillian. For heaven's sake, Miss Howell, stop their whining. Isn't it time they were in bed? Say good night to your uncle, both of you, and be quick, or Papa will take back the candies."

"She's a bit austere," Adam remarked when Miss Howell and the children had gone.

Rhys nodded, laughing. "Dry as an old stick. Constance chose her personally."

Constance tossed her head. "She's very efficient," she said. "A good teacher."

"Speaking of teaching, I'm going to tutor Connor," Adam put in.

"Why?" Rhys demanded immediately.

"Because he's bright and I want to do it. He asked me this evening about continuing his studies. He seemed to think you'd approve, Rhys. So did I. As well be served by an educated mill hand."

"Your logic is unassailable," Rhys said shortly, and Adam smiled.

"I call it foolhardy," Constance snapped. "That boy thinks too much of himself already."

"Don't be absurd," Rhys said easily, but his green eyes reflected his annoyance. "I can handle Connor." He glanced at his brother-in-law. "Just be sure this doesn't interfere with his work, Adam."

Adam, still smiling, followed them in to dinner.

9

♦

"Congratulations, Rhys," Phillip van Dorn said, coming through the open door of Rhys's study. It was just after eight on Christmas Eve. "You have another fine son."

"That's good news, Phillip." Rhys smiled, getting out of his chair to clasp the doctor's hand. "Sit down, sit down. Have a drink with me."

"Just one. They're waiting for me at home."

There were candles in the windows and a pine-scented fire blazed in the hearth while the two men talked. The new baby was to be named Malcolm George for two of his ancestors. It had been another short labor and Constance was doing very well.

"Constance always does well," Rhys said in the slightly sardonic tone he had come to use whenever he spoke of his wife. He lit a long thin cigar after van Dorn refused one and sat back, a part of his mind pursuing the appraisal he had been engaged in while waiting for the delivery.

A third son! And soon all of his mills would be running at full tilt to ensure his children's future. There was no cause in any of that for the underlying discontent that burdened him lately, although he disguised it easily enough.

He counted more blessings. His partnership with Silas Cassadyne was about to build new mills and buy cotton plantations in the American South and in Nicaragua and Haiti. They would grow their own long staple cotton where labor was cheap and docile. Financing had been immediately forthcoming from the Anders bank.

I *am* a happy man, Rhys insisted to himself.

Why shouldn't he be? He was surrounded by fortune and good friends, a network that extended far beyond Brandon's Gate. Take the van Reitjens law firm, for example: not only would Martin van Reitjens handle all the legal work for the new acquisitions, but he had excellent contacts in Washington, particularly on the Senate Finance Committee. The committee regularly voted high import duties to protect the domestic cotton market from foreign competition. When Rhys decided to expand his production of fine cotton, the duties would allow him to undersell foreign competitors and penetrate the American luxury market quickly.

Then why, even as he chatted with Phillip, did he feel such nagging discontent with his life? Constance was a good wife. She ran the house and bore healthy sons with no fuss. She was superb in bed. No man could expect to be madly in love more than once in a lifetime.

And for him there would always be Georgianna, forever out of reach and consequently more desirable as each year passed. His bitter resentment of her had faded. Once more he spent long moments gazing at her portrait in his art gallery, and she seemed more beautiful, clever, superior each time he drew aside the curtains that kept her hidden from any eyes but his.

He had her now. Time had blunted the cutting edge of that shocking will, had even blurred her revulsion for his desire, although he still wanted that mastery over her that had eluded him, still pretended it was Georgianna he possessed while her sister moaned and quivered in his arms.

"Man's reach must exceed his grasp," Robert Browning believed, "or what's a heaven for?" In Rhys's opinion heaven was for total satisfaction. Yet, with all the adulation he commanded, he wanted more.

"I looked in on Will before I came down," the doctor was saying. "He'll be good as new in a day or two. Dilys knows how to deal with croup." He laughed softly. "Connor as well. He'll be a fine father someday."

"He's going to be a good foreman first."

"I'm sure he will." The doctor paused. "But I sometimes think his prospects might have been much better."

Rhys looked his annoyance. "You sound like Adam!"

It was curious, the doctor reflected, how this family played out its rivalries through a boy unrelated to them.

"And what could be better for Connor than lifetime tenure as one of my foremen?" Rhys shook his head, dismissing any alternative. "You and Adam will oblige me by not turning his head."

"But it limits him. Any position above foreman is reserved for your sons."

"Of course—and Connor knows that. He's not a pushy fellow like that father of his, always fomenting trouble."

Van Dorn was surprised. "You have news of Enoch MacKenzie?"

Rhys nodded. "He's been all over the country, trying to organize his damned unions. Each time he's been fired, and now he can't get work in any nonunion plant. As for the unions themselves, their leaders don't welcome the kind of upstart admiral who demands sole command of the fleet. I'm told he's in Pennsylvania now, mining coal."

"Do Dilys and Connor know?"

"I doubt it. I'd never tell them. It would only bring them grief. As for Connor's future, he can do as he likes. I certainly won't interfere."

You already have, the doctor thought as he took his leave. He's still bewitched by you.

Ordinarily the future Rhys had devised for Connor would have been undreamed of for a mill boy—but this was not an ordinary mill boy.

Still, Rhys was not the only problem. The doctor and Adam, discussing the possibility of supplementing a university scholarship for Connor, had finally agreed that he would be like a fish out of water at a first-rate school. There were the barriers of class to consider. Too many doors would always be closed to him no matter how fine an education Adam was providing. It was probably more cruel than kind to give him hopes that would never materialize. Not turn his head, indeed! That was exactly what Rhys had done.

Now the doctor finished his drink and took his leave of Rhys, at ease at least about the Brandons and their new son. Rhys and Constance appeared to have reached a modus vivendi in this curious marriage, wherein husband and wife shared only a predisposition to obsession: hers was for him, his was for heaven knew what. But they were a popular couple. No one seemed to remember that theirs had been a hasty, vaguely incestuous marriage that produced a baby exactly nine months later.

With enough nerve, Phillip decided, you can live anything down, and Rhys and Constance have more nerve, individually and together, than any couple I know.

And then his thoughts turned to his own wife and children. His younger son, Peter, the light of his life, was Connor's age, a gentle, sweet-natured boy without the inner turmoil the doctor had always sensed in Connor. And there was never any doubt about a van Dorn's future, thank God. The girls were wives and the men were doctors.

♦

Rhys found Constance in the green guest room they now called the delivery room, propped up on satin pillows and drinking a brandy eggnog. Her face showed some fatigue, but her natural vitality was already reasserting itself. She waved her maid out of the room and held up her arms to her husband. He bent to kiss her. She smelled delicately of perfumed soap and dusting powder.

"Not too much the worse for your travail, I see," he said. He knew that even childbirth could not dim Constance's ardor for very long, although it barred her from full expression of it for a while. But Constance was skillful at satisfying him in other ways. Her penchant for experiment still surprised him. He often thought that under other circumstances she'd have been a famous courtesan. Then he'd have kept her. It would have been a less demanding arrangement than having her for a wife.

He wondered why he didn't love her.

Perhaps it was because there were no illusions between them. She was exciting but strangely unfulfilling. He needed a woman who adored him blindly, and Constance did not.

"I know all about you, Rhys," she told him often enough. "You're not the noble character you think you are, but what of it? You don't have to pretend with me."

All well and good, but Rhys thought of himself as an admirable man indeed. He had no shortcomings worth mentioning, while Constance, on the other hand, had quite a few.

She was strong-willed and selfish, the very things of which she accused him. She had a sharp tongue that could be maliciously amusing, but not when she turned it on him. Her children were of minor importance to her; it was Rhys she wanted. Her possessive jealousy once had aroused him as much as her sexuality, but for several years it had not been enough to keep him from the fleshpots of New York and Albany.

It was not for sexual satisfaction that he frequented deluxe bordellos, but rather for the worshipful admiration accorded him by ladies of the evening—and he was still unfulfilled because he had to pay for it. There was Dilys, to be sure, but she was a servant and her dedication to him was expected. Georgia worshipped him, but she was only a child. And Connor had begun to take himself too seriously.

"Our son picked quite a time to arrive," Constance was saying, finishing the eggnog and nestling into her pillows. "Consider him my Christmas gift to you."

"And this is mine to you." Rhys took a flat velvet box from his breast pocket.

She opened the box quickly and gasped with pleasure when she saw the necklace of topazes set in gold and diamonds. "Oh, Rhys, it's beautiful! Help me put it on."

Arrayed, she took her hand mirror from the bedside table. "Stunning," she said, and her smile flashed. "I think I'll sleep in it."

"Yes, you should get some sleep. I'm going up to see my new son." He kissed her and left.

Her smile faded as soon as the door closed. He did not love her enough, and she knew it. He did all the right things as husband, father, companion. It was as a lover that he failed her, not physically but in his feelings for her. That had been true on the night she had gone to his bedroom to seduce him into marriage and it was true still, except when passion overtook him in her arms.

She was first lady of Brandon's Gate, but she wanted more than that. She wanted something of him she had never had.

"Damn you," she screamed at her long-dead sister, muffling her voice with a pillow. "Damn you, damn you, *damn* you!"

Even now, when she had given him the sons he wanted, when she was a better mate to him than her sister had ever been, she did not command his heart. Worse, Georgianna's daughter, more like her every day, was worming her way into his affections like the crafty little bitch she was. Whatever love Rhys spent on anyone else diminished what he could give Constance. Moreover, Georgia was a constant reminder that another woman had been first with Rhys and still was.

She ripped the necklace from her throat and pulled the covers over her head.

◆

Rhys went along the corridor past the bedrooms where his four older children slept. At the back of the house he took the stairs up to the nursery and bent over the new baby's bassinet.

Children did not interest him until they were old enough to be responsive, but he was moved by the first sight of a son. Here was his mark on the future. Here was immortality. He stood looking at Malcolm George for a long moment, then touched his son's head gently with his finger before he turned to go. On an impulse he went through the half-open door to Dilys's room.

"Good evening, squire," Connor said, putting down the book he was reading. His manner was distant, as it had been for some time, more so since Adam began to tutor him, but Rhys preferred distance to familiarity now that Connor was fifteen and almost as tall as Rhys. Furthermore, when Rhys set himself to it, he could charm Connor as easily as he could everyone else.

"Congratulations, Mr. Brandon," Dilys said softly, her eyes beseeching him. It had been several months since he had made love to her.

She was not in her nursemaid's uniform at this late hour but wore the loose wrapper of cherry-colored flannel that made her cheeks glow. She was ravishing *en déshabillé*, with her hair curling around her face and tumbling over her shoulders and breasts. His appetite for the simple pleasure she gave him reawakened. He would come to her soon.

"He's the image of you," Dilys said. The other two were clearly Constance's sons. "A beautiful boy."

He nodded graciously. "I didn't bring the sherry," he said with his best rueful smile. "I wasn't sure you'd be awake. We'll drink our usual toast tomorrow, just the three of us. Good night, then, and thank you both for taking such excellent care of my children."

He could sense their response to him and thought, as he went down the stairs, that his talent to charm was being wasted.

◆

"Why isn't Jillian here?" Rhys demanded on a Sunday afternoon a few months after Malcolm's birth.

"I'll go and find her," Miss Howell said, unnerved by his tone. My stars, she thought, that man is Dr. Jekyll and Mr. Hyde without changing a hair. She glided across the library, an agitated wraith, and encountered Connor in the hall, watching from under the stairwell as the family gathered for a photograph.

"Have you seen Miss Jillian?" Miss Howell asked, her eyes darting about the entrance hall.

"No, ma'am," Connor said.

"Mercy on us," the woman murmured, and headed for the stairs.

Connor watched her go, then turned back to the little ceremony unfolding in the library. More than anything that had happened over the last few years, it made his exclusion from Rhys's charmed circle absolute.

The photographer, thin, bald, and fussy, was making his final adjustments. Constance sat in an armchair, wearing a pleated, high-necked bodice of heavy white crepe and a skirt of beige silk gabardine. Dilys hovered nearby, ready to hand baby Malcolm to her when all was ready. Rhys stood behind Constance in a snuff-colored coat, a fawn weskit, and a dark green cravat. Will and Richard, in round collars and short pants over their long stockings, were on her right; and Georgia, wearing a green dress she despised, stood on her left, with a space between them where Jillian should have been.

What's Jillian up to now, Connor wondered. I'll bet anything Georgia knows.

◆

Georgia stood silently in her place, agonizing over what was coming.

"I won't be photographed with those nasty little boys!" Jillian had announced to Georgia an hour earlier, as soon as Peggy had buttoned them both into their dresses, tied their hair ribbons, and departed. "They're nothing to me. I don't belong in this family any more than you do, even if you *are* Papa's favorite."

"I'm not his favorite." But Georgia was, and it was the most wonderful thing that had ever happened to her.

"You are too. Mama says you're a sly creature, pretending to like everything he does." Constance, in fact, had urged Jillian to follow suit.

"I *did* pretend at first," Georgia admitted, hoping a confession would mollify her sister. "But I don't anymore. I really love the collection and I like to watch the spinning and weaving in the mills. So would you, if only you'd try."

But Jillian was not to be mollified. "I did try and he sent me away. He likes you best because you're the prettiest." She sulked, her full mouth pulled into a downward curve.

Georgia wished people would stop saying she was the prettier. It was making things worse between the sisters and, after her father and Connor, Georgia loved Jillian most.

"Let's run away and hide until the picture's taken," Jillian suggested.

Georgia laughed. "Think of the fuss that would stir up. But we can't."

"*I* will!"

"No, you won't," Georgia said with more assurance than she felt.

Jillian got up, obviously determined. "I'll hide in the springhouse. Promise not to tell!"

Georgia hesitated. That would certainly anger her father, and she shrank from endangering a relationship it had taken so long to establish. She shook her head. "I'll have to tell if Papa asks me."

Jillian, aghast at such treachery, railed at her sister before she ran from the room. "If you do, I'll never forgive you. I mean it. I'll hate you till I die."

And now, just as Georgia had anticipated, her father wanted to know why Jillian wasn't here. Tattling was the lowest thing in the world, but courting her father's displeasure was worse.

"I promised not to tell," Georgia appealed to him.

"Don't be ridiculous," Constance said. "Tell us this instant."

"Georgia?" Her father's silky voice was chilly.

"She doesn't want to be in the photograph."

"Nonsense," Constance snapped. "Why wouldn't she?"

"She says you don't like her."

"Because you told her so, you little wretch."

Georgia regarded her mother intently. She hates me, she thought, Mama really hates me. "I didn't have to tell her," she said steadily.

Constance slapped her.

"That will do, Constance," Rhys said. "Georgia, go to your room. You, sir," he directed the photographer, "will make a picture of us and our sons immediately."

Georgia fled out to the foyer and up the stairs. She had never been slapped before but the malevolence on her mother's face was worse than the blow.

"Georgia!" Connor's voice whispered to her from under the stairwell.

She stopped and leaned over the rail. "Jillian's hiding in the springhouse and Mama hit me," she whispered, and went on climbing the stairs.

"I saw," Connor said, bounding up the stairs. "She has no right to touch you!"

"Papa made her stop, but he's angry at me too."

"The devil!" Connor said. "Never mind, I'll bring Jillian back and make her apologize. Don't cry," he said, peering at her anxiously. "It doesn't do any good."

"I'm not crying."

He ran down the stairs and vanished from sight. Georgia went into her room and curled up in the window seat, wondering again why, try as she would, she could not love her mother or even care very much, as long as Papa favored her, that Constance didn't love her either.

"I don't care about her at all," she whispered defiantly— and by now it was the truth.

After a while she saw the staff collecting on the lawn beneath her window, lined up by the photographer in the watery March sunlight. Rhys had generously arranged to have them photographed in a group and to offer each of them a print.

All too soon the picture-taking session was over and the photographer had packed his equipment into his carriage and was driving away.

All too soon her father would come upstairs. It was not punishment she feared; it was the loss of his love.

The sound of voices on the lawn roused Georgia, and she leaned out of the window and looked down. Connor and Jillian were coming up the gravel path.

"*Look* at her!" Constance said, her nostrils flaring in disgust at Jillian's damp, crumpled dress and wet shoes.

"I went to the springhouse to get some buttermilk for Cook and there she was," Connor said.

"Explain yourself," Rhys demanded of his daughter.

Jillian shook her head, her curls bouncing.

"Then you shall both be punished, you for running off and your sister for helping you."

"She didn't help me," Jillian protested, glaring at her father. "Nobody ever helps me. You all hate me."

"Silence! Go upstairs until I decide what to do with both of you."

Upstairs Jillian flounced into Georgia's room and flung herself into a chair. "What a fuss about nothing," she said, but she looked worried. "What happened?"

"I told Mama you didn't want to be in the picture and she slapped me." Georgia pointed to her cheek.

"She did?" Jillian was amazed. "Did it hurt?"

"Yes. You've made a real mess this time."

Jillian drew in her breath. "Do you suppose Papa will whip us?"

"I don't know."

"Were they angry?" Jillian asked.

"Furious," Georgia said, beginning to laugh. "You should have seen Mama's face!" Both girls smothered their laughter, gasping with perverse mirth while tears ran down their cheeks.

"The best part," Jillian said, holding her stomach, "is that neither of us will be in their rotten old photograph and I'm glad."

Rhys found them tear-stained, prostrate and, he supposed, properly repentant. He spanked each of them three times across the bottom with his riding crop, but they were light blows and the girls hardly felt them through their petticoats. Jillian cried; Georgia didn't. Then they were sent to bed, deprived of lunch and supper and made to do lessons all the next day. They were forbidden to speak to each other, so they communicated in sign language, totally unnerving Miss Howell. They had been denied desserts for a week, a terrible privation, but Connor smuggled cookies in at night and in a few days the incident was over.

When the picture was framed in silver and placed on the piano, not a word was said about the absence of the two girls. Constance, in fact, seemed rather pleased. There she was, she had said approvingly, surrounded by all her men.

"Those boys look terribly stupid," Jillian said when Connor and the girls stole into the drawing room for a close look at the photograph.

"Malcolm's not bad," Georgia said.

"Neither were Will and Richard when they were babies," Connor reminded her.

Through muffled laughter, as they turned to leave, Jillian said, "Connor, you're missing from your picture too. Do you mind?"

"I don't belong in that picture," he told her gruffly. "I'm not a servant."

10

♦

The bordello known as The Treasury was a favorite meeting place for Rhys and his friends when they went to New York City. It was a luxurious parlor house spread over seven attached brownstones on West 24th Street, with the atmosphere of a men's club decorated and run by Madame de Pompadour.

The ground floor rooms, where gentlemen in mandatory evening dress waited to choose girls for their pleasure, were lavishly furnished in colors and fabrics to titillate the senses and pornographic oil paintings to direct them. Upstairs the rooms had mirrored ceilings, soft beds and chaise longues, thick rugs—in some rooms laid over wall-to-wall mattresses—and atomizers that could automatically spray the air with the client's favorite perfume.

On a summer evening six months after the birth of his third son, Rhys sat in a satin-upholstered gilt chair and studied the cards in his hand. A mild Havana cigar was clamped between his lips and a glass of Veuve Cliquot sat on the table before him amid cards and chips. The man who faced him had just put up a sheaf of papers to see Rhys's cards.

On Rhys's right sat his friend and partner, Silas Cassadyne, his freckled face ruddier than usual with wine and well-being. He and Rhys had first gone upstairs with their girls, had disported themselves each in his fashion, and then, reclad in elegant evening tails and starched white shirts and weskits, had descended for supper and a friendly game of cards. They needed the relaxation after their journey to Central America to complete the purchase of two cotton plantations and a spinning mill, followed by a stop in South Carolina to buy three more mills.

"Come now, Ed," Rhys said genially to the chubby young man facing them across the card table. "We're old school friends. Your word is good enough for me. And what would I do with a lot of foundries and a steel mill?"

"Make stoves and such, the way I do," Ed Reedy replied with a booming laugh that closed his small eyes altogether. "Lots of money in forges and foundries."

"Then why lose them all at cards?" Rhys persisted.

Reedy laughed again. "I know you, Rhys. At cards you're more bluff than skill. I'm betting it's bluff tonight. Anyway, you know those foundries aren't all the Reedy holdings." He stretched lazily, lifted his arms up over his head, then lowered them and looked around the watching circle. "I'll tell you gentlemen something, though. I've had about enough of the Iron Molders International Union Number Two. I'm fed up with unions altogether."

He drank off his champagne as the other men nodded their agreement.

"The bastards are pressing the New York legislature for a fifty-four-hour work week. May get it through too. The Congress is leaning toward an eight-hour day for federal employees and in Massachusetts they're talking about a minimum wage law. They're after our profits, and something's got to be done about it."

The men nodded again. It was a dangerous trend.

"Well, I'm going into politics and do something," Ed Reedy said. "I'm going to help legislate those damned unions out of existence in this state, for a start. Hell, Rhys, I won't have time for all my foundries. Now let's get on with this game! What the devil!" He thumped the table soundly. "There's no fun without a little risk."

There were chuckles of approval around the table. Having made the gentlemanly gesture, Rhys accepted the title deeds and showed his cards.

"But I'm damned if I know what I'm going to do with forges and foundries and a rolling mill," he said to Silas later as they were walking back along Fifth Avenue to the Waldorf-Astoria on 34th Street.

Silas rubbed his chin speculatively. "You can go on making stoves, although I hear Reedy's let some of his plants run down through neglect. Maybe they could be revamped to make castings for mill machinery—ours and others."

Rhys nodded. "You have a point, Silas, the way this country's expanding. I wonder how much cash a change-over would involve."

"John and Martin deal with Reedy. They'd know. Ask them at lunch tomorrow."

"I will. I wonder what possessed Reedy to bet them."

"He was always a wild fellow and a born gambler. And he's got this bee in his bonnet about smashing the unions. Had a lot of trouble a few years back with the ironworkers." Silas glanced at Rhys. "They say your fellow MacKenzie was involved."

"*My* fellow? That brigand's got nothing to do with me. Anyway, he moved on a while back. Do you think Reedy can get into the Senate?"

"I'm sure of it. He has the right connections."

State senator. Rhys liked the ring of that. The role of parliamentarian seemed well suited to his particular talent for persuasion, and state politics was an easy, part-time occupation he had been considering for some time.

Right now he was considering tomorrow's meeting. Silas was an industrialist like Rhys, but Anders and van Reitjens were deeply involved in politics, both local and national. The lawyer and the banker seemed to communicate for the most part without speaking. They made a powerful team.

Rhys was up early the next morning to supervise the transfer to a taxi of a pair of crated Chinese vases and a small Leonardo he had been negotiating to buy for months. By half past eight he and Silas and the crates were in the Brandon private railway car and en route to Albany and lunch at the Valley Club.

◆

"I'd say you've done pretty well for yourself," Martin van Reitjens said after he had looked over the Reedy deeds. He had gray eyes, wide-set and ingenuous, as a lawyer's should be, and a very sharp mind. He smoked an expensive black cigar with his brandy. "Reedy's going to gamble away his inheritance at this rate."

"He's going into politics," Silas reminded them. "And we all know there's money to be made there!"

The four men laughed. John Anders, the former mill owner turned banker, an emaciated man with a pince-nez and a pervasive aroma of peppermint about him, said, "You must have been playing for very high stakes, Rhys. What if you'd lost?"

"It never occurred to me," Rhys said, and the men laughed again. "Now, about my winnings: I agree with

Silas that they might profitably produce a lot more than stoves."

"Castings and parts," van Reitjens suggested. "Very profitable."

"But you'd need to modernize," Anders warned. "Those foundries are not in mint condition."

"So Silas told me. I think I may have to sell them after all," Rhys said, shaking his head. "Silas and I have just made some major investments, as you know. If I took on anything of this magnitude now, I'd be overextending myself."

Van Reitjens leaned back in his chair and glanced at the banker. John Anders removed his pince-nez and, looking strangely naked without it, polished the lenses. "Suppose you offered us an interest in the operation in exchange for the capital you need to modernize or convert?" he asked with his prim smile.

"You?" Rhys asked, looking from John to Martin. He grinned broadly. "I'm flattered, but why?" He peered intently at each of them. "What do you know that I don't?"

It was the lawyer, van Reitjens, who answered him. "Rhys, the writing's on the wall. American business is acquiring commercial interests all over the world—the same as you and Silas—and those interests, along with the Americans who go out to work them, have to be protected." Martin puffed on his cigar and contemplated the smoke. "Now, we're not a bellicose nation. Our imperialism is limited to commerce and investment, but the local rulers who benefit from our presence will have to defend it—and they need the weapons to do that."

"Weapons?" Rhys raised a speculative brow. "I thought Lamartine Munitions monopolized the weapons industry here in America."

Anders nodded. "Explosives and heavy ordnance, yes. But weapons?" He shook his head. "Not quite. And it's an expanding market; there's room for one more. Moreover, I hear Lamartine's been sniffing around for small, specialized plants equipped to make prototypes of new designs and experimental weapons as well as operate under license for them. You could probably sell them those foundries, but I know what Reedy was offered for them and in the long run you stand to make a lot more selling them your services."

Anders replaced his pince-nez and picked up the title deeds to the Reedy foundries. "I'd keep these three making stoves—they're in the best shape—and convert the others." He regarded Rhys. "Well, what do you say?"

Those two are very cool customers, Rhys thought admiringly. He did not consider himself an innovator. In art he bought the tried and true. In dress he was conservative. In business he drew on the combined knowledge of friends and colleagues. It was apparent to him that such an investment must have been brewing in his friends' minds for some time, awaiting the right deal at the right price. Rhys glanced at Silas Cassadyne, who had leaned forward eagerly.

"I'd like a piece of it, too, Rhys, if John and Martin have no objections."

"None at all," said John.

"Then it's done!" Rhys said, relieved to reduce his own risk.

They had a drink on it in high spirits. "What'll we call this company?" Silas asked, his freckled face suffused with enthusiasm.

They decided on an anagram of their initials—Cassadyne, Reitjens, Anders, Brandon—and called the new consortium Crabtree Limited. A small crab apple tree would be branded onto each piece their foundries made.

"I'll draw up the papers for the legal transfers of title," Martin van Reitjens said. "Once we decide what equipment changes are needed, John can work out the capitalization and stock distribution. It'll take a little time, gentlemen, but I look forward to a tidy profit from Crabtree."

Rhys, feeling he had done a fine bit of business, shook hands as he and Silas prepared to leave, but he turned back to the two men who remained in the room, seeking a quid pro quo for what he'd just offered them.

"I've been thinking," he said.

"In your case always a fruitful occupation," John Anders said with his thin smile.

"About running for political office," Rhys went on.

Silas Cassadyne hooted. "The presidency, no doubt."

Rhys's chuckle did not even seem forced. "Something more modest for a start. State senator, perhaps."

"It's a possibility," Anders said.

Van Reitjens agreed. He considered the man before him every inch the public's image of a statesman. It would be a good thing to have another politician in his pocket. "We'll see what can be done."

"But Crabtree must be handled with the utmost discretion," Anders said, his brow puckered into a frown.

"Of course!" Rhys said. "I'll look forward to hearing from you on both matters. Come on, Silas, the car's waiting."

The two men talked animatedly about Crabtree on the drive home, but Rhys was glad to be alone after Silas had alighted at his front door. He wanted to savor the new venture by himself. Including the new mills in Central America, he had just committed almost every cent he had, and that sharpened his exhilaration. Then there was his political future and the adulation of hundreds, maybe thousands. His horizons were expanding, and that would combat his nagging discontent.

His spirits rose even higher as the car continued along the heights, and he could look down at the Brandon mills on the flats, a half hour away from closing down for the day. He was one of the most respected textile men in America and now one of the biggest.

It occurred to him that he knew nothing about stoves and weaponry, and suddenly anxiety obscured his elation, making him restless.

◆

His restlessness was difficult to hide from Constance, who, alert as a guard dog to his moods, watched him intently as he paced after dinner the following night.

"What the devil's got into you?" she demanded, lowering her book.

"Damned if I know," he said affably. He did not discuss business with his wife. "I've been indoors sorting through the mail all day. Maybe I need a good gallop."

"I thought we had one last night."

He glanced at the door lest a servant might have overheard, but he was laughing. She was incorrigible. "I meant on a horse," he said.

"On a cloudy night? You'll lame yourself as well as the horse. We'd have to shoot you both!"

He shrugged, flung himself into his chair, and lit a pipe, returning to his problem. Of course he was taking a huge risk, but that was what made it irresistible, that and the potential fortune it represented, in power as well as in money. It was a path to that inner sanctum of men who ran the world. That was where he belonged, not in this backwater, spinning cotton and raising children. He had outgrown Brandon's Gate, but he wanted proof that he could dominate anyone he chose.

He glanced at Constance, who had been ravenous for him last night, but his wife was not a woman he could dominate, in bed or out. It was why he went to Dilys.

He rose from his chair. "I think I'll have a look at my new vases," he said.

"Go ahead and play with your toys, then," she returned. "You're making me nervous." She returned to her book.

Upstairs he titillated himself by fondling the latest additions to his collection. The delicate colors and fragile painted figures on the Chinese vases stirred his sense of supremacy. He was master of this tender beauty. He owned it absolutely, to admire, to handle, even to destroy if he chose. For a moment he savored his power to crush it underfoot if he so desired.

He listened, but there was no sound from Constance

and he closed the door by which he had entered and went quietly along the gallery to Dilys. Connor, as usual, was studying at Adam's house. Rhys smiled to himself. His wretched brother-in-law had finally done something to make Rhys's life easier.

Dilys was waiting for him.

"Dear girl," he whispered, nuzzling her neck. "How I've missed you."

She put her arms around him and her full mouth opened to his kisses. He nipped lightly at her lips. She was always eager for him, but her sexual code was rigidly working class. He was going to shatter one of her rules tonight, and the prospect inflamed him. His groin throbbed.

He undid the red silk peignoir he had bought her in New York and let it drop to the floor.

"I've brought something for our pleasure," he said, showing her a flask of oil procured at The Treasury.

"How?"

"I'll show you." He uncapped the vial, poured some into his hand, and spread it on her breasts, cupping them, stroking her nipples erect. An aroma of sweet almonds mixed with the scent of her body and filled his nostrils. He poured more oil into his palm, and his hand slid down her belly, past the springing hair between her thighs.

"Come to bed," she whispered, starting to undress him. "Turn out the lights."

"No," he said. "I want to see you."

When both of them were naked on the bed, he bent to her, opening her with his fingers, moving them skillfully until she was close to climax, eager and willing. Quickly he rolled her over and made her bend her knees. His hand reached around her to continue its caresses while his penis slid back and forth between her legs, wet from her wetness, sliding farther back each time until he was between the round globes of her bottom. He reached for the oil.

"No!" she gasped when she became aware of his intent, but he was already pressing himself into her, his arms pinning her down, his excitement swelling when he penetrated the tightness between her buttocks. She moaned in pain, and he covered her face with a pillow while he thrust at her until he climaxed, panting. He pulled back, releasing her, and she collapsed in a heap at his side.

When his breath came normally, he felt for the towel she always kept ready on the night table and wiped himself, then reached for his clothes. "I must go," he said, dressing. "Constance will wonder."

She said nothing. He sensed her humiliation and her sexual frustration, but she would be all the more eager to please him the next time he wanted her. In minutes he had retraced his steps along the gallery. He washed his hands and checked his clothing and his hair in the bathroom. Then he lit his pipe and went downstairs.

"Well," Constance said after measuring his mood. "That relaxed you."

"Yes," he nodded, taking up his paper with a smile. "It always does." He felt omnipotent. There was nothing Rhys Brandon couldn't do, from the disposition of two women in the same house to the creation of a secret dynasty.

Upstairs, Dilys lay on her bed, her body aching, her heart torn between shame and the fear of losing him if she could not please him. She hated what he had done. The act had brought her neither desire nor satisfaction, nor had there been any tenderness in it. But she dared not risk his displeasure. She lived for their moments together.

"Anything," she sobbed, "I'll do anything, but don't leave me, please, Rhys, don't leave me."

◆

Connor, with Tyrone stretched out by his chair, tried to concentrate on the French Revolution, but he was concerned about Adam's cough and his feverish flush.

"You ought to go to bed," he said. "It's not the end of the world if we don't discuss this chapter tonight."

But Adam, still coughing, waved him back to his book and Connor, reluctant to vex his teacher, obliged him.

His relationship with Adam had deepened into friendship, although it was a limited friendship with certain lines neither of them would ever cross. Yet it was impossible to discuss ideas and events without a revelation of self. Connor realized that he had learned more about Adam in one year than about Rhys in eight. It was an interesting discovery, but not the only one.

The two men detested each other. They came from the same stratum of society. They were both respected in Brandon's Gate, although Rhys was influential and Adam was not. But something basic in each man made him despise the other, and Connor wanted to find out what it was.

There were differences, of course. Adam was a solitary man, for one thing, while Rhys liked to have a host of people around him to charm and manipulate. Adam worried about things like education and the effects of the industrial revolution on America, and Rhys about expanding his empire and his art collection. Adam was a contemplative man and Rhys an acquisitive one. Connor could understand Rhys, though; there was so much he wanted too.

The most glaring difference between them was that Rhys was successful and Adam was not. But for Rhys's rescue of the Hendrik family fortune, Adam would have been a poor man and would probably not have cared, provided he was left in peace with his books and music. Connor, longing for wealth and its perquisites, would never understand that.

"But even that," he said to his mother, "doesn't explain why they can't stand the sight of each other."

"It's their own affair, Connor," his mother warned, always nervous about his attitude toward Rhys. "You mustn't take sides."

But Connor championed only one cause now: his own.

A ragged snore roused him from his thoughts, and Connor smiled affectionately at Adam dozing in his chair. He went quietly to the bookcase for Ovid's *Ars Amatoria* and read the Latin treatise on love with his usual reaction. He had to return to the French Revolution to make his erection subside. By then Adam's snores had developed a steady rhythm and Connor got up and wrapped Adam's blanket more closely around his shoulders. He removed the glasses from his nose and the book from his lap. Then he put another log on the fire, replaced the screen and the Latin book and, taking his jacket, left the library with Tyrone at his heels.

He went to the butler's pantry. "He's asleep, Mr. Garth," he told Adam's man. "He needs the rest, so I'm leaving early. I hope he won't sit there too long."

"I'll see to him," the butler said, smiling. "Good night to you, Connor."

Connor let himself out and started the three-mile walk home. Sometimes he rode Jezebel between the Hall and Adam's house, but that afternoon after work he wanted a good run. The sky had cleared, and on a spring evening like this, effulgent with things mating, ripening, bursting into life, it was pure magic to walk under the moonlight with shadows all around him. He might have been anywhere—the Scottish moors, Sherwood Forest, Camelot—or anyone. He wondered who, other than Rhys, he'd have been if the choice had been his. A number of fictional figures sprang to mind, none of them Connor MacKenzie, mill worker, all of them heroes and great lovers of women.

Women like Megan O'Donal.

Connor was sixteen and looked older because of his height, but he had never yet been with a woman. At least he no longer felt clumsy everywhere but on a horse. In general his body obeyed him now—except when Mrs. O'Donal was around.

She was almost twice Connor's age and a widow, a pretty, capable woman who worked the ring frame next to his at the mill. Whenever she spoke to him in that special way of hers, Connor's penis rose up to what felt like the length of a javelin. He was sure everyone in the mill could see it. He took to wearing his shirttails out to cover his erections, and that made Megan laugh softly. Her laughter embarrassed Connor even more than his mindless shaft of flesh forever seeking a sheath. It was not that easy for a fellow his age to find one.

Women, apparently, came in two varieties: good and bad. Mothers and sisters were good and didn't like doing it. Women like Mrs. O'Donal, who talked as if she liked it very much, were supposed to be bad, but Connor didn't accept that argument. Adam had taught him to examine a premise before he accepted it. For one thing, everyone knew that all men liked to do it and all men weren't bad. Connor was always randy around Megan, but he didn't know what to do about it.

"But there, me darlin'," Megan had murmured just today, "it's a babe y'are, fer all that height and them shoulders. We'll just have to bide our time till the humor is on you."

"I have better things to do," Connor had growled, lusting for her, for her round breasts and the mystery between her thighs. It was unreasonable to be obsessed by something never seen or touched, but all the boys were.

When he wasn't thinking about sex, Connor had a great deal to do. Aside from his studies he had his job in the mill to do. He worked a ring frame now, but beyond spinning there was sizing, bleaching, dyeing, and weaving to learn, each step with a wealth of detail to be mastered.

"I want you to know every process that goes on in my mills," the squire had told him. "I want you to know as much as if they were yours."

But they would never be his.

He was still eager to learn something new. If the truth were known, ring spinning was boring once he had the hang of it. He wondered how the others could do it all day without falling asleep. The machine did the work of doubling, drawing, and twisting the thread to make it uniform; he was there to replace the spindles when they were full and keep the threads from tangling.

The same would not be true of the mule frame when the foreman let him work one. All those spindles would require attention, but now he could let a part of his mind drift. If it drifted to Megan, the result was inevitable.

To dampen his ardor he would think hard about whatever he was studying with Adam, mentally reviewing whole pages that his mind seemed to commit to memory the moment he read them. Adam said he had a mind like a sponge; it soaked up information.

"But selectively," Adam chided him frequently. "Mathematics, chemistry, languages—but not enough philosophy or literature or fine arts."

"I'm a philistine," Connor had agreed the last time with a smile.

"Indeed? Well, when we first began you didn't know what the term meant, so that, at least, is a sign of progress. You're right up to Groton levels for your age, too, and I pride myself on a job well and quickly done. Now we must go forward." Adam lit his pipe and glanced at Connor. "Has Rhys ever shown you his art collection?"

"Once, when I was very little."

"Did you like it?"

"Not much. A lot of gimcracks and crockery and pictures of men and women in fancy clothes. Georgia likes it. She's always up there with him."

Adam had nodded. Georgia's artistic bent seemed no surprise to him. "My boy, no life is complete without an appreciation of great art and literature. But we shall leave art aside for the moment and study *Hamlet* next."

Connor understood *Hamlet* because he understood the impulse to vengeance, although in his own case it was against his father, not on his father's behalf. He tried not to think about Enoch; the whispers he heard about him in the mill were painful enough. A lot of people admired his father and what he was attempting to do. Enoch would go anywhere, infiltrate any industry to help sow the seeds of union.

"There's a man who wants to help his own kind," they muttered to Connor as they worked. "Enoch MacKenzie doesn't toady to the owners."

Connor never replied.

Sometimes when he looked at his mother—the best and most beautiful woman in the world—rage choked him and he could have beaten Enoch with his fists for leaving her like that, to starve in the streets and her two children with her, for all he knew! But they hadn't starved and, much as Connor would have preferred it otherwise, they owed their privileged situation to Rhys. The obligation to repay Rhys's kindness, once so welcome, had become a burden.

What would his real father say if he saw that Dilys and Connor had been living like the gentry all these years, in rooms that had recently been redecorated, that they had enjoyed the trust and friendship of the staff and, above all, the protection of the master of the house—never mind Constance, who didn't much like anyone but her husband.

Connor came into sight of the darkened Hall, sleeping majestically under the moonlight, its white columns silvery. There was a light in the library and one upstairs in the art collection. He stopped a moment and looked at it. It was home, even if it was not his.

"Someday," he told Tyrone, "when I'm rich, I'll build a mansion of my own, just like this one."

But, standing there in the dark, it came to him that he would never succeed until he left this place. He felt the shock of loss. It was as if he had been cast out of Eden and must go far away before the leaving broke his will as well as his heart.

He had to go. He did not belong to Rhys anymore, nor with the mill hands either. It was a limbo he could not endure. He had not been Rhys's liege man since he learned the enormous difference between being loved and being used, and his resentment had gone on festering as the Brandon boys grew. If Rhys was aware of the vast change in his former acolyte, he gave no sign, but Connor couldn't go on hiding how he felt.

He went into the house by the back entrance and up the stairs, determined to tell his mother now that his mind was made up, but she had already gone to bed and her room was dark.

He told her in the morning.

◆

"No, Connor." Dilys was impatient with him, incredulous, almost in tears. "Where would we go? What sort of place could we live in on your wages?"

"My God, he's corrupted you, too, hasn't he?" Connor exclaimed.

She grew pale. "What do you mean?"

"With comfort, with all these grand things! But we live here only at his whim, and what kind of security is that? He could turn us out tomorrow if he chose, the way he dropped me when he had no use for me."

"Stop it!" she commanded him, her hands clasped to her ears. "I will not listen. And I will never leave this house."

"You don't care what I want, do you?"

"You want an education and you're getting one. Where else could you get what Mr. Hendrik gives you free of charge?"

He stalked off to work, but he knew he could not abandon her as his father had done. He had no choice but to stay on and learn faster, then find a job that earned enough to take care of her. He felt trapped by her, by Rhys, even by Adam, and he longed for the time when he need not be grateful to anyone.

♦

"The son of a bitch has got him working in the mills," Enoch groaned to his drinking partner, his words slurred by whiskey. "A puddler from Troy told me. And after making a little nob of him too!"

"Whadja expect?" Neeley Mack returned, scraping beer froth off his upper lip with his finger. The two men were in the saloon of a mining town in Pennsylvania, hunched over a scarred table. The place smelled of sweat, tobacco, and cheap spirits.

"That rotten bastard knows how to break a lad's spirit!" Enoch sneered. "First raise him up, then squash him down."

"Hell," Neeley said. "Go get yer kid, then. He's grown."

Enoch shook his large head. "Can't let him see me like this."

"What's wrong wit' ya? Yer a union organizer."

"Who still has to follow orders." Enoch wagged his head again. He looked at his hands, begrimed with coal, the dust embedded in his pores and nail ridges even though he scrubbed them raw. In secret he rubbed them with lemon the way Dilys had to keep her hands white, but it did no good. "No, I'll not see Connor till my hands are clean and I'm wearing a shirt and tie."

"Listen," Neeley said. "It's prolly the best thing fer 'im to see how the likes of us lives."

"You think so?" Enoch grabbed at it.

"I know so. Them fancy writers don't know, or them sweet-speakin' politicians neither. Mind what I say, Enoch, that boy'll be a better union man for workin' in a mill."

And Enoch, still staring at his grimy hands, grunted and finished his drink.

11

♦

"**C**ome for a ride, Connor?" Rhys asked the following week when the six o'clock whistle blew and the workers streamed out of the mill. Murphy had brought Jericho and Jezebel to meet them.

Connor mounted the mare and sat looking at Rhys with hooded eyes. "No," he said. "I'm due at Mr. Hendrik's."

"He can wait for half an hour."

You think you're God Almighty, don't you? Connor raged inside himself. That people love you no matter what you do. "You don't want me to study, do you?" he demanded, his voice harsh and very low. "You want me to be as ignorant as they are." He jerked his head in the direction of the departing workers.

"How you choose to waste your time is a matter of complete indifference to me," Rhys said softly, "unless it's the cause of your surly attitude of late."

Connor looked away. His teeth were set, Rhys saw, and his hands clenched on the reins.

"Is something troubling you, Connor?" Rhys asked after a moment, suddenly sympathetic. "Can I help?" He was startled to see sudden tears spring to Connor's eyes. The boy moved slightly forward, as if Rhys had drawn him like a magnet. Then he retreated into himself, shaking his head, and they stood gazing at each other wordlessly. Finally Connor turned Jezebel, tapped her sides with his heels, and rode away.

What the devil? Rhys thought, reverting to annoyance. Connor was becoming intolerable! I *have* spoiled him, Rhys told himself. A home, food, clothing—a horse, a dog, a job! I treated him like a son!

If this attitude continued, he would have to send Connor away, but he was reluctant to do that; it would be a public admission that Rhys's confidence in the boy had been misplaced. Besides, Dilys would have to go with him and that would throw the nursery into an uproar and deprive Rhys of her services as well.

He wondered if Connor had bedded a woman yet. Perhaps that was all he needed. Then he mounted Jericho and decided to take no action for the moment.

And Connor, riding hell-for-leather across the fields, sobbed as he had not done since his father abandoned him.

♦

Connor had always been moody, but now he became withdrawn. He spent hours alone, refusing even to answer Peter's letters, avoiding his friend when Peter came home between terms.

"What's wrong, Connor?" Peter demanded. "What is it you think I've done?"

"It's not what you've done, it's who I am," Connor said.

"Oh, damn! That doesn't make any difference to me and you know it!"

"Doesn't it? Then get Clarissa Cassadyne to invite me to her party!" He had waited for a reply from Peter, knowing there could be none.

"God damn it," Connor swore as he walked away. "Someday they'll be knocking on *my* door."

He lost his prodigious appetite and picked at his food.

"And him still growin' like a weed!" Cook clucked to Dilys. "He needs nourishment while he grows or it's the consumption'll be takin' him, mark my words."

His mother gave him sulphur and molasses and fixed him his favorite food whenever he ate at home. For her sake he forced the food down quickly and got out of the Hall—to the fields, to the stables, to Adam's house, anywhere. He saw Rhys at the mill sometimes—Rhys was away a lot these days—but it was from a safe distance, with the barriers of noise and machinery between them and, more than ever, the barriers of class.

He was not yet prepared for a life on his own. He had only one trade, and working in some other man's mill was not what he was after. Part of him loved this place and some special people in it and that made him reluctant to go, but more than that, he wanted to finish what he had begun with Adam. With mathematics, French, and German he could find a managerial job in New York City—in shipping, maybe, or banking—that earned a decent salary. Then, he would take nothing more from Rhys. More important still, he would need nothing, not even that occasional kindness that still went right to Connor's heart. Then, Dilys would have no reason to cling to Brandon's Gate.

As the year wore on he went at his books with a ferocity that gratified Adam, even while it worried him.

"You ought to take some time off, Connor, you look like a shadow."

"I don't have any time. There's too much to learn."

"Connor, if there's something you want to tell me, you can trust my discretion."

But Connor had lost the habit of trust and kept silent.

It was not only his resentment of Rhys that drove him. It was that his reprehensible father had been right about rich men. The real gods of creation, he had called them. Yes, money corrupted, but money was power and Connor now wanted power as much as he wanted wealth.

He spoke very little, but he had always been a solitary sort, and most people let him be.

Georgia did not. "You're like a thundercloud," she told him. "You never laugh anymore."

"There's nothing to laugh at," he said shortly.

"You're still angry, aren't you?"

He looked at her in amazement. He had told her briefly of his anger some time ago. But Georgia never forgot anything important. He nodded.

"I wish you'd tell me why," she said, her blue eyes beseeching.

"I can't," he muttered in great distress. Her father's seduction of him had been too personal, too subtle, for her to understand the magnitude of his betrayal. There had been so much love lost between them.

She took his hand and they sat in silence for a while. She was always a comfort to him, just by her presence. And then it was his turn to comfort her.

◆

He was lying in the loft of the east barn on a Sunday, sharing with Tyrone a picnic lunch he had begged from Cook. It had always been a favorite spot to drowse and dream, but now he came here to let his anger surface. Sometimes he pitched hay up to the loft with frantic energy, lunging with the pitchfork as if he had Rhys on the end of it.

The sound of hooves roused him, and Tyrone's ears cocked. Connor looked out of the small window of the loft. It was Georgia, her face flushed and tear-stained. She was wearing a Sunday dress, not her habit, and she was riding astride, something nice little girls didn't do, although she had insisted on learning.

"What's wrong?" he called down, but she slid from the saddle and climbed the ladder to the hayloft, sobbing too wildly to speak. She flung herself into his arms and he comforted her as he had when she was a baby, letting her cry on his shoulder. Then he dried her face with his sleeve and waited.

"Mama's not my mother," Georgia said, looking up at him.

He nodded. "I know."

"Why didn't you tell me?" She was astonished by still another betrayal. "Why didn't Dilly?"

"Your father asked us not to." He patted her gently. "He wanted to tell you himself at the right time." It stuck in his craw to defend Rhys, but he did it for Georgia.

"But he didn't tell me! *She* did—Mama—Constance. They argued at luncheon because Papa's away so much, doing God knows what, Mama—*she* said. But you know how Papa is," Georgia went on. "He pretends not to hear when she's like that. We can't pretend, though, Jillian and I. She's always in a temper at us, at me especially. Now I know why."

"Tell me what else she said."

"That she was sick of him worshipping at his shrine. What does that mean? And that she deserved more attention than she got for raising all his children—and another woman's brat into the bargain. That made Papa angry." Georgia stopped and wiped her eyes with her skirt. Connor waited.

"He told her to stop it and she got very quiet for a minute. Then Jillian said, 'What other woman's brat?' and I said, 'Mama, what do you mean?' And she told me not to call her Mama because she wasn't my mother, my mother was a horrible woman who ruined other people's lives." Georgia burst into fresh tears. "So I came to find you." He held her gently, rocking her. The setter, whimpering, came to lick her hand with his long pink tongue.

"Did you know my mother?" she asked when she could speak.

"I only saw her once, riding in her carriage."

"Was she married to my father?" Georgia whispered, and Connor knew she was thinking of an unmarried parlor maid who had been dismissed when her pregnancy was discovered. Constance didn't care what she said, even when the children were listening.

"Of course she was married to him!" Connor said. "She died when you were born."

"Oh, Connor," Georgia breathed. "Then I killed her, didn't I?"

"No," he said forcefully. "Babies can't kill anyone! They're too little and weak, you know that. She just had bad luck."

She leaned against him quietly for a few moments. "What was her name?"

"Georgianna Hendrik."

"Hendrik? Like Uncle Adam?"

"She was his sister. Constance is your aunt."

"And she called her own sister a horrible woman? *She's* horrible!" Georgia looked at him, her eyes glittering. "Now I know what it means to be angry, like you," she said. "I don't believe what she said about my mother and I'm going to find out the truth about her."

Rhys was waiting for them at the stables when Connor brought her back. Jillian, saucer-eyed, had stolen down the stairs and was standing behind him.

"I hoped she was with you," Rhys said with that earnestness that had once touched Connor's heart.

Damn you to hell for a liar, Connor thought.

"Come upstairs with me, Georgia, there's something I want you to see." Rhys held out his hand to her.

"Not without Connor and Jillian," Georgia said, refusing his hand. Rhys nodded to Jillian and Connor and they followed him upstairs. Connor had entered this house through the front door only once before, on the day he first came to it. It was his second visit to the art gallery as well, and it seemed like Aladdin's cave, the sunlight limning objects of rare beauty. He could recognize their value now because he had learned about art with Adam.

The three children followed Rhys and watched while he pulled a gold-tasseled cord. The wine-colored curtains parted to reveal the life-size portrait Connor had once supposed to be that of a queen.

She wore white satin overlaid with silver lace, and her gleaming shoulders rose out of the wide frame of the bodice like mother of pearl. Her bosom was full and her waist slender. Her hair had a golden luster and her eyes were brilliant blue. She stood with her chin high, looking beyond the viewer into some distance only she could see. Her features were harmoniously arranged in an oval face, the electric-blue eyes large and wide-set, the arched brows like silk, the nose small and straight above a full, curved mouth that seemed made to smile although she was unsmiling. A cloud of lace lay about her shoulders, as if to guard her delicate perfection.

"Oh," Georgia gasped. "How beautiful she was!"

"Yes," Rhys said. "And you are very like her. She was clever, too, and witty. She knew a great deal about art—even about business. I loved her very much."

"More than Mama?" Jillian asked, but he did not answer her.

"You should have told me," Georgia said. "You should have, Papa."

"I know that now," Rhys said. "But I was afraid to when you were so young. Can you forgive me for that?" He gathered her, unresisting, into his arms, and Connor took Jillian away and left them there together.

"He should have told me too!" Jillian said.

"It's got nothing to do with you," Connor replied.

"Yes it has! I'm sorry for Georgia, but all the same it makes Mama more mine."

"Then you ought to be happy," Connor said absently, wondering if the discovery would change Georgia.

"Except that it makes Papa more hers." Jillian, struggling with her ambivalent feelings for her sister, was uncharacteristically quiet as she went to her room.

◆

Georgia's quest for her mother began that day with Cook, Mrs. O'Brien, and Peggy. It continued over the next few Sunday afternoons, when she rode with her father to visit friends on neighboring estates. Rhys had prepared the way.

"We've told Georgia about her mother," he had confided to his neighbors. "Constance and I thought it was time. I'd be obliged if you'd say a few words to my child about Georgianna."

Constance told people the same thing, "after the devil of a rumpus with himself," Peggy reported.

They both lie, Connor thought, they deserve each other.

Adam was honest about his late sister. "She was difficult sometimes because she was so intelligent," he told Georgia. "In other times your mother might have ruled an empire, industrial or territorial."

"No one ever got the better of Georgianna," Silas Cassadyne told her. "She was as clever as she was beautiful." His wife, who had been eclipsed by Georgianna, as had every other girl in Brandon's Gate, said rather sourly that Georgianna was sweet.

"She was a fine lady," said Martin van Reitjens, who had not dared to propose to her himself. "Made a man feel like a king just by smiling at him."

"Headstrong," offered John Anders, who had tried to persuade Georgianna not to marry Rhys. "But gracious"—he recovered himself—"very gracious."

"She was more than beautiful," Dr. van Dorn told her. "She had presence."

"Will I have presence?" Georgia asked him.

"You already do."

"What is it?"

"Assurance, the kind of authority that comes with knowledge. In a great lady it is accompanied by compassion." Georgianna had been lacking in that quality, but the doctor kept that to himself.

"That's how I'm going to be," Georgia said, confiding

every detail to Connor. "Everyone says I look like her and I'm going to *be* like her."

She had always had definite opinions, but now she let them show. She became self-assured. She was respectful to her stepmother but pointedly called her Aunt Constance. She stopped romping with Jillian and her brothers and spent every spare moment with her father—the very issue that had precipitated Constance's outburst on that fateful day.

"Hoist with her own petar," Connor said, eating supper at the kitchen table.

"You and your bookish talk," Peggy scoffed. "I say it nargs the bejaysus out of herself."

"Why should it?" Jeffers asked.

"You men!" Peggy shook her head. "You don't know anything. It was always her sister he loved better—and now he's got her back, in a kind of a way, through Miss Georgia. Herself thought she had him, but she never did, nor will she."

Rhys is like that, Connor thought. You may think you have him but you never do. Constance had been as much fooled by Rhys as Connor himself, but he felt no sympathy for Constance.

It was Georgia Connor cared about and Georgia he missed, for it seemed he had lost *her* to her father, too, so intent was she on sharing her mother with Rhys. She did not ride with Connor on Sundays anymore; she rode with her father. More and more Connor felt her slipping away from him.

"Where were you all day?" he asked her.

"Watching my mother."

"I don't understand."

"In the portrait," she said. "It sounds silly, but I have this feeling that if I watch long enough and hard enough, her eyes will look down and see me."

"Georgia," he said gently, "you know that can't happen."

"I know, but I like to pretend it will. She never saw me, you know. She never knew anything about me."

"Maybe she does," he offered, anxious about her.

"You mean in heaven?" She shook her head. "I don't believe in heaven any more than you do."

And there was nothing he could say to that.

♦

He hounded the foreman at the Number One mill until he was put on a mule frame. It was exclusively a man's job—women weren't strong enough and their skirts would have been dangerous—and that patched his tattered pride a little.

The mule—so called because it was once powered by the animals—had a long carriage that moved back and forth on a five-foot iron track. The ends of cotton, taken from bobbins atop the machine, were drawn and twisted through rollers into fine threads as the carriage retreated. When it returned, at considerable speed, the thread was wound around spindles to form the cone-shaped cops. Connor's frame carried seven hundred and fifty spindles and a lot of responsibility.

He started on the mule at a salary of fifteen dollars a week, good pay for a beginner. He knew he had his supposed "friendship" with Rhys to thank for that, but he could be as good a hypocrite as any Brandon, and the more he earned the sooner he would convince his mother to come away with him.

On his first day he was tense, keeping a wary eye on the fast-moving carriage. He had supposed he was accustomed to the racket of machinery in the mill, but each time the carriage shot back, the crack of it was deafening. It was August and the heat was unbearable. In the mill the air was always humid. The machines generated static electricity, and on dry days steam was pumped in to keep the static from curling the cotton. Connor was finding it more difficult than usual to breathe the soggy air full of cotton lint, sizing chemicals, dust, and dyestuffs.

At the lunch break he went outside and waited at the pump for a drink of water. Perspiration streamed from the crown of his head down the length of his torso, trickling into his trousers and dampening his underdrawers. He

had just stripped off his shirt when Rhys appeared in the
shaded landau with Georgia next to him.

She was dressed in cool, crisp, pale blue organdy. Her
golden hair, held back by a blue taffeta ribbon, was protected
by a white straw hat trimmed with tiny velvet daisies and blue
streamers. She wore white stockings and white kid button
boots. He must have seen her dressed like that a hundred
times, but here, today, he could not bear the contrast to
himself, a stinking, sweating mill hand half naked at the pump.

She saw him and started to wave, but he shook his head
and looked away, watching from the corner of his eye as
her hand stopped, hesitated, and sank slowly into her lap.

Don't turn away from me, he shouted silently to her,
not even if I tell you to.

But when he looked at her again, his face dark and
hostile, she made no attempt to greet him. For a terrible
moment they gazed at each other, a new awareness on
both sides of the gulf that had always lain between them.

He went quickly back into Number One, conscious as
he had never been before that he was not a Brandon, that
he would never be a Brandon no matter what he did or
how hard he worked. He bent over the immobile carriage,
breathing heavily past the knot in his chest, stunned by
yet another loss, that of this girl he had so dearly cherished.

"Connor?" It was Megan, and her voice was not suggestive but worried. "Are you all right?"

He shook his head, dumb with misery.

"You've been lookin' like the wrath o' God lately. What's
wrong?"

He shook his head again.

"Listen to me, Conn. Come by tonight, just to talk."

"I can't. I have to study."

"Come after."

"It'll be late."

"I don't mind. Tomorrow's Sunday." She looked at him
kindly. "It's all right to have a friend, Connor. There are
some things a lad can't tell his mother."

He nodded. He would never tell anyone his secrets, but
he had to be with someone, and she was all he had.

12

◆

He came awake when the clock on the Presbyterian church struck two, with no clear recollection of how he had come to be lying on Megan's bed. All he remembered was that he had arrived on her doorstep exhausted by heat and despair.

He had come into the discreetly darkened cottage with no idea of what to say, half wishing he were somewhere else. Then he was glad he had come because Megan welcomed him quietly and brought him cool beer in the kitchen of a cottage exactly like the one he and his mother had left nine years before. It felt like home. It even smelled of the same yellow soap and wax, and he had sat drinking his beer and watching the candlelight glint on Megan's red hair.

Now the candles had burned out and in the dark he was aware of only two things: that she was lying next to him and that his body was swollen with need of her. He leaned over to touch her face and she stirred and raised her mouth to kiss him. No woman had ever kissed him like this, and he sighed with pleasure and reached for her. She was naked. His body shook with excitement as she took his hands and drew them to her breasts. How soft a woman's body was, softer even than it looked! A scent of lilies came from between her breasts, round and as wonderful to touch as the mound at the base of her belly. He went lower and sighed again, this time at the incredibly silky softness he encountered. He wanted to linger there, but another impulse mastered him and he sought his way insistently into that nest between her yielding thighs.

138

Warmth enveloped him now, a clasping heat unlike any he had felt before, and his one desire was for more of it, of her. He went deeper, hoping his search would last forever, but there was a force in the very center of him too powerful to resist, as if everything he thought and was and wanted had been gathered there and must be set free. He lost himself. Thought fled and he was carried away by a bliss beyond any solitary satisfaction he had ever known. He said her name again and again and shuddered with delight as the waves peaked, diminished, and died away. Her thighs enclosed him. With one hand she caressed his bottom, with the other she stroked his head. He lay upon her shoulder breathless, astounded by the miracle of woman.

"Megan?"

"Yes, darlin'."

He turned his head to kiss her. "How beautiful you are," he said.

"Not half so beautiful as you, even with that shadow on your soul."

He said nothing.

"I'll not fuss you to tell me what it is," she said, reading his thoughts. "I just want you to come here every time you can."

"I will," he murmured, kissing her neck. "How good you smell. How good you are."

She laughed softly, contentedly. "In time I'll be better still, and so will you, me bonny boy."

"You mean it can be better than that?"

She laughed again and hugged him. "Ah, Connor, you're adorable. It's a heartbreaker you'll be."

"I don't want to break anyone's heart," he said, alarmed.

She smoothed his brow. "But it's nothing to do with what you want. It's how you are."

"How am I?"

"You've had enough flattery tonight, boyo. The best of it is you still have so much to learn."

"Teach me," he said, touching her. "The humor is on me now."

They were the most healing lessons of his life. His trust had been breached and his pride shattered. Even the books he escaped into sometimes eluded or confused him. But what Megan gave him was clear and uncomplicated and totally his for the time she gave it. Sex amazed him. It ravished his senses and yet it soothed his soul. It was the deepest surcease he had ever known and the only one that did not fail him. It was what it was, and it lasted the time it lasted.

He felt he had left childhood behind him at last. In penetrating Megan's body he had penetrated an essential mystery, the one that had perplexed and tantalized him since he could think. It was an enigma of which he had been conscious long before he had decided on the getting of money and power. What he felt but could not articulate was that he had become a man, not merely because he had covered a woman's body but because they had shared a profound experience.

"Yes, yes," he whispered triumphantly each time he made her quicken, whenever her pleasure matched his own. He loved to feel those velvet ridges deep inside her press him close, close, almost close enough to obliterate his anger.

Megan asked no questions in those quiet moments after love when they lay together in the dark. He was the questioner, direct with the curiosity of youth and deadly serious because of what he knew.

"Have you ever been with a man you didn't love?"

"A few—but none I didn't like."

"Would you do this for money?"

"I might. No woman knows what she'd do in a pinch, nor any man either."

"Is it better with a rich man?"

She had laughed long at that and hugged him. "I wouldn't know, me darlin'. I suppose money'd make it easier before and after—you know, pretty clothes and all, not havin' to work—but not durin'."

"Then you wouldn't like it more with me if I was rich?"

"Oh, Connor, you young fool, don't you know I love

you, more's the pity? Love's got nothin' to do with money."

"I love you, too, Megan."

"I know you do, but not the way you're goin' to love a woman someday."

"I won't leave you. Even if I go I won't leave you behind."

"Oh, yes, you will. You must. That's the worst of it. And this," she said, stroking his groin, "this is the best."

He worked, he studied, he made love to Megan, and somehow the year passed. His face, almost set in manhood, was arresting. The straight, prominent nose and the hollows under his high cheekbones had an ascetic cast at variance with his wide, dark eyes and his sensitive mouth. His hair was as difficult to tame as he would have been, had anyone tried. But no one made the attempt. Except for Megan and his hours with Adam, he kept to himself, aloof and saturnine and brooding.

◆

Dilys worried through that year in silence. She knew how late he was coming home these nights, but she dared not question him, not even when she discovered the reason.

"A woman her age havin' dealin's with a child!" Cook said. "It's scandalous."

"Connor's not a child anymore," Peggy said. "The maids know it, if you don't. Don't you see how they flutter around him? Would you rather he took up with them? Or went to that awful place in Troy?"

"All the same, maybe Mr. Brandon should be told about her," Mary O'Brien put in. "He could send her away."

"No," Dilys said. "Why should she suffer? She's not a bad woman. Please leave Connor to me."

Rhys, Dilys thought. Rhys will help me.

◆

"I'm considering sending Connor to a military academy," Rhys said to Constance a few days later. They sat in the drawing room drinking coffee after dinner. "What do you think?"

"I don't much care what you do with Connor." Constance leaned forward to let him light her cigarette.

"The boy's been out of sorts lately. To be expected, I suppose, at his age. Growing too fast."

"He's a menace to the maids," Constance agreed. "But why a military academy? Because of the war in Europe?"

"Not at all." Rhys lit his cigar and puffed on it before he continued. "It was his mother's idea."

"Do you mean she had the nerve to ask you to send her brat away to school?"

He shook his head. "Not at all. She came to me for advice. She's worried about him—something to do with a woman on the flats."

Constance laughed heartily. "So much for your paragon! Who is it?"

"Dilys didn't say. But in my opinion he needs a different kind of education from what Adam gives him, and I said so. I said he needed discipline. She thought I meant the army—but I want him back here once he's settled down, not off fighting some war."

"Why not? If he joined the marines he could protect your property in Nicaragua." She laughed again. "For a man who says he's against foreign entanglements, you've certainly used your influence to send American troops down there."

Rhys gave her his cup. "More coffee, please." He watched her pour it. She looked very appetizing, as always. Her dinner dress was violet chiffon, pleated into a bouffant tunic over a darker shade of pleated silk. The low-cut bodice and short puffed sleeves were edged with black lace. The new fashions permitted a display of bosom, and Constance's was magnificent. Her amethysts lay upon her skin like sugared violets on cream. He decided to make love to her later tonight. It was her place to run his household and keep his bed warm, not meddle in his business affairs.

"Nicaragua is a special case," he said patiently. "It's the

federal government's responsibility to protect American industrial interests abroad."

"Nicaragua, Haiti, Cuba, China. We have a lot of industrial interests."

He glanced at her appraisingly, a faint gleam of respect in his eyes. "I didn't know you were so knowledgeable about politics."

"I'm knowledgeable about a lot of things, Rhys, particularly about what you do with our money. After all, I have my sons' future to consider."

She mentioned the boys often lately, and always in that proprietary way, although it seemed to him she was no more interested in them than she had ever been.

"They're mine too," Rhys said.

"I'm glad to hear it," she returned somewhat acidly. "I wondered if they would ever replace Connor in your affections."

"One thing's got nothing to do with the other," he said, still affable. "We owe something to people who give us loyal service. I can't think what we'd do without Dilys."

Constance shrugged. The servants were certainly not her chief concern. Rhys was—the model husband whose infidelity she must endure as best she could. But she was the mother of his sons and she intended to keep them close by her and, through them, Rhys.

Such unprepossessing children her two older sons were! They both had lank brown hair and unremarkable brown eyes. Thank heaven Malcolm looked like Rhys, but it was impossible for Constance to see any personality at all in a child so young.

Jillian, working on a ratty piece of cross-stitch embroidery while Georgia sketched a vase of flowers, had more spirit than Will and Richard put together. Jillian was pretty and lively and clever but Constance had never been interested in females. On occasion she felt a kind of sympathy for her daughter, doomed to grow up in Georgia's shadow as Constance had in Georgianna's. The two girls were still close companions, unfortunately, but more and more Jillian resented Georgia's attempts to monopolize Rhys. There

had been no stopping Georgia since Constance disclosed
who her mother was. Anyone would think she had committed a crime!

Rhys had turned on her in a cold fury, warning her
never to repeat her malicious lies "about my wife," or to
distress Georgia in any way. If she did, he would move
the household to New York without her. Weeks had passed
before he came back to her bed, and things were still not
the same between them, although she was unable to pinpoint the nature of the change. She continued to excite
him sexually, that was obvious, but there their relationship ended.

Strange, how little she and Rhys found to say to each
other out of bed. She decided to pay more attention to
politics; that appeared to raise her in his esteem.

Rhys put down his empty coffee cup and rose. He wore
dark suits to dinner lately, reserving his more formal attire
for parties. He looked almost exactly as he had the night
she went to his bedroom, except that he was clean-shaven
now and better-looking than ever with the classic lines of
his jaw uncovered and that beautiful, sensual, knowing
mouth too. He was thirty-nine, ten years her senior, but
he still had the aura of youth. He radiated sexuality.
Constance had seen women respond to it, women who,
she was certain, had never seen their husbands naked or
been seen that way themselves, who would have died
rather than do the things Constance loved to do in bed.

"Rhys, you're not going out!" she protested as he glanced
at his pocket watch and rose.

"Yes. John and Martin are up from Albany for the
weekend. We have some projects to consider because of
this war."

He stopped to bid the children good night, first leaning
over Georgia to see her sketch. "That's delightful, my
love," he said, his lips grazing her hair.

"Look, Papa," Jillian demanded. "It's a comb case for
you."

He laughed heartily. "I appreciate the thought," he
said, "but I think you'd better start again."

Jillian tossed her work to the floor with an angry look at Georgia, but Rhys was already on his way out.

Constance watched him go, wondering why he couldn't discuss business during the day like most men. But Rhys had long since turned a deaf ear to objections of any kind. He rarely went to New York with her; his business was in Troy and Albany for the most part. Now that he was in the state legislature, Silas dealt with the mills in South Carolina, and the island plantations were run by overseers. Rhys had flatly refused to go to Europe even before war was declared—he said it was dirty and uncomfortable, and she was not stupid enough to go without him. They went to Saratoga or New Orleans.

In bored desperation Constance frequently went to New York City alone. There was always shopping to do for that brood of children, but that was a pretext. Constance spent far more time and money on herself. Her dressing table was a brilliant array of crystal bottles and jars filled with French perfumes, creams, and unguents, although she wore no makeup beyond a discreet tint of rouge on her cheeks—and sometimes on her nipples to titillate Rhys.

Her closets were filled with clothes made to her measurements in Paris and London, gowns by Paquin and Doucet, by Poiret and Fortuny and Vionnet. Her bureau drawers and armoires overflowed with delicate lingerie and filmy peignoirs. She had gloves and shoes and stockings dyed to match her dresses, plumes and furs and feathers tinted to match her swooping, tilted, elegant hats. She was the best-dressed woman in Brandon's Gate, of course, and in Troy and Albany as well, and she turned heads in Saratoga and New York. Her wardrobe absorbed some of her energy. Reigning over local society in Brandon's Gate and influencing it in Troy and Albany took the rest.

But in the main she went to New York because it was exciting, and Brandon's Gate, which had once been world enough for her simply because Rhys was there, had become too stultifying to be borne. In New York she stayed with friends who took her to cabarets and music halls, to balls and operas, dinner parties and, lately, to tango parties and ragtime parties.

"If you wanted an affair," her friend Letty Pemberton whispered to her, "you'd have no trouble having one."

"Why would I want an affair, when I have Rhys?"

"Why, indeed," Letty sighed. "He's too divine. But even among the gods one wants variety, no?"

But Constance wanted only Rhys, more of him than she had, at any rate. She admitted to herself, though, that an affair would have brought some excitement to her dull provincial hours, if there had been anyone in Brandon's Gate to spark her interest when Rhys was away.

The long evening stretched before her now. She had some new French novels that were said to be madly risqué but she felt too energetic to sit in a chair and read about other women's amours. She decided to go for a walk and rang for the maid to bring her a wrap.

Ignoring Georgia, she spoke to Jillian. "Papa doesn't like you to pout," she said. "Ask Miss Howell to help you with your embroidery."

"I wanted to do it for him all by myself!" Jillian wailed.

"Not if you want him to like it, silly girl! Now, stop sniffling, I can't bear it." She turned to Georgia. "Where were you this evening after supper?"

"Riding with Connor. Uncle Adam had to go to New York."

"Riding? Are you sure that's all you were doing?" But Georgia had no idea what she meant, and Constance took another tack. "You won't have him long," she said. "He's going away."

"Going away?" Georgia's voice was anxious.

"Yes, dear." Constance smiled broadly. "To military school. It was your father's idea, and Connor certainly deserves it. You children go up to bed as soon as Miss Howell comes for you," she ordered, and left the room. In the hall her maid helped her on with a light cloak. It was August, but there was always a breeze off the river.

"I'll be glad to see the back of him," she heard Jillian say viciously.

"Why, when he's always been so good to you?"

"Not to me! You're his favorite, just the way you're Papa's. But who cares? He's only a mill hand."

"He's my friend and Peter's too—a better friend most of the time than you are."

"Don't you dare compare my Peter to Connor MacKenzie!"

Constance, satisfied by their dissension, left the house and walked along the broad flagstone terrace overlooking the lawns above the river. She heard its rush in the clear country silence and stopped to light a cigarette, her expression hostile in the flaring light of the match. Her endless suspicions of Rhys simmered.

"Damn him," she said, exhaling sharply. "What can any other woman give him that I don't?"

It was inconceivable to her that a man who was thoroughly satisfied at home should seek erotic adventures elsewhere, but she knew he did. Every instinct she possessed told her so. It was maddening! She was a good wife, mother, and companion. Brandon Hall ran like clockwork. It was grossly unfair of him to withhold any part of himself from her. He was a good husband to Constance, and generous, but she was not his sole concern, and that was what Constance would have demanded from any man—and knew by now she would never have from Rhys.

Well then, let him have his amours. All men did. It was through her sons that she could exercise the greatest influence upon her husband, and she must find a way to use them to that end.

◆

"I think we can give them what they want," Rhys told his partners in Silas Cassadyne's library, accepting another brandy. He tossed the sheaf of specification papers onto the table at his side.

"I'm sure of it." Silas smiled and settled back in his chair.

"You have the golden touch, Rhys," Martin said. "You win a game of cards in a whorehouse and a year later, who but Crabtree is invited to cast shells and make rifle and revolver parts by the biggest armaments maker in America?"

They had anticipated the invitation from Lamartine Munitions, of course. By the end of 1913 the new consortium had converted three of the foundries to weapons factories. The fact that Crabtree could cast machine tools and had its own steel mill increased the demand for its services.

"And now the orders are bound to start coming in from Europe," John Anders said. "We can make a pile on that war if it lasts long enough."

"Will others besides Lamartine call on us? Frankly I'd rather do business directly than have to rely on them as middlemen. How about Vickers?"

Anders pursed his lips, considering the big English armaments firm, once a major exporter of the steel bars used to build American railroads. When the railroad boom came to an end, Vickers had turned to making guns for the British War Office.

"They might," Anders said finally. "Their Maxim gun is a real killer—pardon the pun. It operates on its own recoil. Fires cartridges by the hundreds."

"We could make it if they granted us the license."

"I've written to say so. We should have a reply from the old boys soon. Hell, our fathers bought enough steel bars from their fathers!"

"I wonder what the chances are of our getting into that war," Rhys said.

"Nil," Silas replied. "It'll be over by the New Year, worse luck for us."

"I'm not so sure it'll be over that soon," Rhys demurred.

"Still," Martin said, "it can't do us any harm to let Washington and the army know we exist and are ready to supply them—or whatever foreign buyers they favor. That would effectively bypass Lamartine, and in any case we'll be legally free to deal independently as soon as we've filled our present contracts with them."

"I'm willing to go to Washington and talk to a few people," Rhys offered. With introductions from Anders he had made some useful friends in the capital, pressing for the invasion of Nicaragua to protect American interests there. His partners accepted his offer.

"As regards foreign sales, though, we have to be guided by our government's policy," Anders warned, his lenses glinting in the lamplight.

"Absolutely," Rhys agreed. "America's not a belligerent and we can't take sides. We'll sell to anyone who can pay the price."

Rhys drove home, wishing he'd come on horseback. Cars were well enough in the city, but a horse was the way to travel in the country. Still, he was in fine spirits. It had been a profitable evening. And a good day. It had been easy to grant Dilys's request about Connor's education, a pleasure because she asked so little and expressed her gratitude so passionately. Little by little he was stripping away every veil she clung to, and that never failed to excite him. There was still one thing she refused to do, but his generosity might help persuade her.

Furthermore, it would be a relief to rid his household of Connor until the boy outgrew his bad temper and came back to work in the mills, whipped into shape after two years of military discipline.

Finally he had forestalled Constance's suspicions by pretending to consult her about Connor. Now he was going home to keep her suspicions at bay by making ardent love to her, a prospect that hadn't lost its allure in ten years of marriage. In his mind he undressed her, baring that glossy, voluptuous body to the practiced caresses of his hands and mouth. Constance had no veils. She was as different from Dilys as a tiger from a kitten.

Variety, Rhys believed, was the spice of life.

13

♦

Three weeks after Connor arrived at Braker Military Academy, he knew he would have to fight to remain there.

In the world at large, Connor had observed, a man might prevail with brains alone: Rhys, for example, was clever and cunning and had never been physically violent in his life. But Braker was different. Brawn was the only option here.

From the beginning he kept to himself, as was his wont. His class had thirty-one cadets and he chose to room alone. The real trouble began when it became apparent that he outrode, outshot, and outdrilled his classmates in the field and outranked them in the classroom. They rewarded him for that by scrambling the contents of his locker before an inspection.

"I'm surprised at you, MacKenzie," the provost of his class said with a thin-lipped smile. Jennings was an angular boy with coarse, sandy hair and milk-white skin. He looked anemic, although he was the heir to a meat-packing fortune.

"Yes, sir," Connor replied, standing at attention. He could hear the other cadets clustered in the corridor outside his room.

"Ten demerits," Jennings said. "You'll have to stand guard duty every night this week to work them off."

That was onerous enough in the sharp November wind. It was even worse when someone threw a bucket of cold water over him from behind and disappeared into the trees before Connor could see who it was.

150

There was more. They hid his books and smeared his equipment with mud. They packed his knapsack with rocks while he drilled for hours to work off more demerits.

"Here, MacKenzie, have an apple tart," one of them would say in the mess hall, handing him an empty plate. When the commandant's eyes strayed in their direction, they offered him a dish of cold leftovers with elaborate courtesy.

He cornered Jennings in the stables one day. "What are you after?" he asked the provost roughly.

"We want you out of here," Jennings said. "We object to sharing space with a mill worker."

"I'm afraid you have no choice," Connor told him. "I'm staying."

"We'll see about that," Jennings said. And the harassment went on. It made Connor burn with a familiar sense of frustration that pervaded his every moment. Soon he stopped doing more than the bare minimum in class.

"These are shocking, MacKenzie," the commandant said a few weeks later from behind his desk. He poked at Connor's class reports with a swagger stick, as if they were too repulsive for him to touch. "I thought at first you might be officer material, even good enough for West Point. Mr. Brandon will not be pleased."

To hell with you, Connor thought, and to hell with Mr. Brandon too.

In what seemed an unspoken conspiracy, neither the commandant nor the instructors interfered with what was going on. They watched and waited to see how—or if— Connor would defend himself. They saw it as a trial by fire, a test of manly behavior. It was their idea of fair play. Connor was contemptuous of them and their code, but by mid-December he had to fight them on ground of their own choosing, the very mistake that General Clausewitz, the great military strategist, had warned against.

♦

The boy facing him inside a ring of cadets, all of them red-faced in their struggle to maintain silence or risk discovery, was not as tall as Connor, but he had the hamhock fists and thick neck of a born fighter, a fighter by choice, not necessity.

His name was Arlo Walsinger, Junior, and whatever his appearance, he came from what was called fine old southern stock. He had been the loudest and most insulting of them all, undoubtedly because of his size.

For the sake of fair play the combatants had donned boxing gloves, sneaked out of the gymnasium, and gone to a clearing in the woods out of sight of the school. Because of the gloves this secretly scheduled brawl could be called a match. It was a cold, gray day but both boys were stripped to the waist. Connor's broad shoulders narrowed to his waist, while Arlo's torso was square as a boxcar.

Connor didn't give a damn whether he won or lost for the sake of proving a point. His one concern was to avoid as much damage as he could and get on with his education. If he could beat Arlo, no one else would dare take him on.

Yet, he approached this contest with the same lethargy that had descended upon him soon after his eager arrival at Braker, hard upon the realization that he had left one untenable situation for another. He did not belong here either. No matter what he did he could never change how he had started out in life. The world was the same all over. Nothing bridged the gulf of class.

Arlo was advancing now, moving his fists in slow circles, and Connor watched him warily. For weeks he had been observing how Arlo moved. Connor had been in a few scuffles in the Brandon's Gate school yard and had learned from them to profit from an opponent's weaknesses. Arlo looked like a seed bull but he had a few soft spots. His stomach was one, his left eye another. The stomach was tender and Connor had concluded, from the way Arlo jumped hurdles and negotiated doorways, that he had poor lateral vision on his left side.

Connor blocked the first punch but was unprepared for the second. His head jerked back, his teeth slammed together, and he felt dizzy. Arlo moved in immediately, whacking methodically at Connor's ribs, and Connor backed off to the muffled jeers of the cadets.

"Stay in there and fight, you bog trotter," someone said. "What can you expect from a shanty Irishman?"

Connor uncoiled suddenly, more furious with the speakers than with the boy he was fighting, and rammed Arlo's belly with both fists and all of his strength. When Arlo doubled over momentarily, Connor smashed repeatedly at his right temple. Arlo's right eye began to swell almost immediately. He would have no lateral vision at all now. He would be vulnerable from either side. It would be awkward to throw punches at him from the side, but that strategy offered Connor his best chance.

Arlo retreated for a moment, then, breathing deeply, waded in again. It was like being rammed by the mule frame in the mill, and Connor pulled back again, waiting for a chance to attack. His nose was bleeding heavily and something had snapped in his shoulder by the time his opportunity came. He sidestepped and swung wide to hit Arlo's jaw. It was a powerful blow and Arlo spun away, pushed off balance by the force and direction of it.

There was a murmur of surprise from the spectators. "Come on, Arlo," someone said, "teach Paddy's pig a lesson."

"Show him how gentlemen fight."

To Connor, watching Arlo recover and return, the words struck a match inside his head and a sudden fire consumed the last of his defensive apathy. The anger he had bottled up exploded and he glared at his approaching adversary, not even seeing Arlo. He saw, instead, the embodiment of all his frustration and disillusion and the insufferable anguish imposed upon him by two men—not better but merely bigger and stronger than himself—and now here, again, by fools who called themselves gentlemen and him a pig.

It was not Arlo he was battering with murderous rage, but *them,* Enoch and Rhys for deserting him and humiliating him; and *it,* the way things were, the doors that would always be closed to him no matter how hard he beat on them. Megan had kept him from erupting for a while, but there was no Megan here, only cruel reality, and he attacked it blindly, ferociously, at top speed and with a vicious satisfaction he had never felt before.

He did not notice that his lip had been split and blood from his mouth had joined the rivulets pouring from his nose. He went on punching until Arlo went down and then, still ripe with rage and eager to vent it, he turned to the circle of cadets, all of them dumbstruck by the sudden speed and force of his attack.

"Who's next?" he asked.

There was no reply.

"You, Jennings?" he called to Arlo's chief hanger-on, the meat-packing heir.

Jennings blanched. "It was Arlo's fight, not mine."

"The hell it was! It was all of you, you rotten little shits." Breathing hard, Connor spat out some blood. He looked around the circle, his black eyes blazing. "You just got the dumb bastard to fight it for you. But I promise you this: if anyone gets in my way again, I'll deal with Jennings first and then with the rest of you, one by one."

He stalked away, meaning to gather up his clothes but impeded by the boxing gloves. He cursed impatiently.

"Would you like some help with those?"

Connor whirled. "Who the hell are you?"

"A new boy." He was slender and wiry, with curly blond hair and light eyes. "Name of Horace Blankenship."

Connor laughed.

"I know," the newcomer said ruefully. "Can you imagine what *they'll* do with a name like that?" He nodded toward the cadets, now occupied with reviving Arlo and hauling him to his feet. "That's why I decided to attach myself to you. I'm a devout coward. Here, let me get those gloves off."

Connor held out his arms and Horace went to work on the laces. "I think you'd better get to the infirmary," he said. "That lip looks as if it needs stitching up."

Connor nodded, aware now of the caked blood on his face and chest. He touched the corner of his mouth cautiously and winced. He used his shirt to wipe off some of the blood and shrugged into his dark blue uniform tunic, shivering. Now that the fight was over he felt cold.

Horace handed him his cap and the two boys left the clearing and walked through the woods toward the neat quadrangle of buildings that housed the commandant and his staff, the classrooms, and the academy's infirmary. The dormitories were half a mile away, across fields that were lush and green and carefully trimmed in the spring but were now covered with November rime.

"When did you get here?" Connor asked, although his lip was stiffening and it was difficult to speak.

"In time for lunch. Fortunately no one noticed me. They were all too intent on the fight coming up between you and what's-his-name."

"Arlo Walsinger. Junior. He does their fighting for them. Jennings is the point man."

"What was the fight about?"

He glanced at Horace. "Are you deaf? To them I'm an Irish mill worker. As it happens, I was born in America of Scots-English descent, but they were out for blood, no matter what its nationality." He waited a moment to see what the reaction would be. When there was none beyond a grimace of contempt clearly intended for the cadets, Connor continued. "I'm not sure you want to get mixed up with me—and I'm not sure I want you to."

"Sorry, but I'm your roommate." Horace looked apologetic.

Connor inspected Horace more closely. He was about three inches shorter than Connor but he moved with an athlete's grace and the assurance that usually went with money. His affability aroused Connor's suspicions, but Horace's pale, changeable eyes had no guile in them.

Connor shrugged, wincing again from the pain in his shoulder. "I may have to live with you, but I can't call you Horace. What did they call you at school?" It was obvious to Connor that this fellow had been to a boarding school, the kind Peter van Dorn and Timothy Cassadyne and the Anders boys attended.

"Terrible things. But my sisters call me Racey."

"This group will call you a lot worse, unless you stop them."

"I don't give a damn what I'm called by a bunch of lamebrained boys." Racey grinned. "Anyway, they won't dare pick a quarrel with your roommate. I'm no fighter."

"I didn't think I was either."

"You have a large chip on your shoulder. Add that to your size and you've got a fighter."

"Observant, aren't you? And you have no chip?"

"My trouble is that I don't give a damn about the things I'm supposed to. That seems to constitute a chip in some quarters. At any rate, it riles people up."

Connor glanced at him again as they approached the infirmary. "What school did you go to?"

"Groton. I was kicked out." Blankenship smiled happily.

"What for?"

"Sneaking off to go flying."

"Planes?"

Racey nodded. They knocked at the door of the doctor's office and went in. It took half an hour to clean Connor up, stitch his lip, and rig a sling for the broken collarbone. The doctor had accepted Connor's transparent lie—that he had been thrown from a horse—as he did the same story from Arlo, who had arrived with heavy bruises and a cracked rib. There would be a scar at the corner of Connor's mouth but it would fade in time. Right now it hurt like the devil.

The fight made life at Braker a lot smoother for Connor. He had conformed to their rotten code and beaten up another boy in a frenzy that half dismayed him. He was glad he had won, but if Arlo hadn't gone down, Connor believed he might have killed him.

Jennings, trying to hide his concern about what Connor planned for him, came to extend an olive branch. "I was mistaken about you," he said loftily. "Why not let bygones be bygones?"

"Why not go screw yourself?" Connor suggested. "Keep away from me, Jennings, and—who knows?—I might decide to keep away from you."

Things were different at Braker now. Connor was enthusiastic about his classes again, grateful for all Adam had taught him and for his ability to retain anything after he had read it once. He was ahead of his classmates in mathematics, European history, and languages, and on a par with them in engineering, military history, and other courses. He was impatient, while his collarbone mended, to resume military training because he liked riding and shooting and being outdoors.

But in one essential way he had undergone a basic change. He would have withdrawn into his habitual isolation, but in Racey he had found a friend who shared his cynicism about people and their motives. It had happened very quickly and, unlike some friendships that spring up suddenly, it flourished with time.

Racey had known Peter van Dorn and Tim Cassadyne at Groton. "They were pretty good men," he told Connor while they tramped through the snowy woods during a free period. "But Peter's an idealist and Tim's a conformist."

"And you?"

"I'm a flyer." Racey stretched his arms up to the winter-gray sky. "We're a breed apart."

They stopped to light forbidden cigarettes, cupping their hands protectively against the wind.

"What's flying like?" Connor asked.

"A little like galloping a horse, but bigger, freer. Once you've been up there the ground's a pretty dull place." Racey drew appreciatively on his cigarette. "My father wants me to be what he is, a big banker in a small city, but all I want to do is fly. I'll fly anything—mail, passengers, freight—just so I can get up there. What I'd like most would be to fly aerial reconnaissance in that war over there." He smiled. "So much for me. What do you want to do?"

Connor shook his head. "Damned if I know." He had been very blunt about his background and Rhys's patronage, neither of which moved Racey to respond with more than a nod of his head and a characteristic brief pursing of his lips.

"You sure you don't want the army? You're bound to graduate with honors, and that'll make you a candidate for West Point."

"Not on your life! I'm here because it was the only way I could get a formal education for a few years. But I'd had enough of people telling me what to do before I came here. I don't want any more of it when I leave."

He planned to stay at Braker a few more years. Adam had admitted that graduation from a military academy brought a certain cachet. Connor knew that a degree of social polish was rubbing off on him, much as he despised most of the boys whose behavior and manners he imitated so well that they were second nature to him now.

Racey, apparently unaware that Connor's manners required any polishing, suggested only one improvement. In the privacy of their room and with deadly seriousness, Racey taught him to dance.

"Don't push me around as if I were a sack of potatoes, for Pete's sake! I'm a girl, fragile and delicate."

"How can I lead without pushing you?" Connor demanded.

"Put your hand on my waist and press. Put it dead in the middle and don't let it get anywhere near my rear end. And keep your forearm well away from my bosom!"

"Oh, to hell with you and your bosom," said Connor, disgusted.

"Come on, you wretch," Racey insisted. "I'm determined to teach you to waltz by Christmas!"

14

♦

With his newly acquired assurance intact, Connor stepped off the train at Brandon's Gate to begin his Christmas holiday. He knew he looked good in his caped military greatcoat and visored cap, and he drew on his leather gloves, picked up his bag, and strode confidently out of the station.

The once-rural railroad stop was a small town now, and there was a cluster of new company stores on the main street leading from the station, among them a garage, a tearoom, and a bakery. In addition Rhys had permitted a few privately run shops to open for trade with the predominantly female workers: a milliner, a dressmaker, a yarn and trimming store.

Farther along on the flats, where the snow was a mass of gray slush, stood the mills, large, square brick buildings with small, high windows in their sloping ceilings and steam misting out of the vents. There had been five mills when Connor first went to live at the Hall. Now there were almost two dozen. He thought of Megan, working at the ring frame inside Number One, and began to wish the day away. He looked upriver at the workers' dormitories and cottages and ached for night and the bounty of her body.

He started up the road that skirted St. Joseph's Catholic Church, the Presbyterian church, and up to the heights, past the Dutch Reformed Church the gentry used. Here the snow was pristine, blanketing the rocks and draping the evergreens, clinging in little puffs to the bare oaks and elms as if to warm them until their green mantles budded in the spring. Connor had tried to forget how very beautiful Brandon's Gate was, and a rush of nostalgia overwhelmed him.

He felt his confidence ebbing little by little as he turned off the main road and made his way up the long, oak-lined drive to the Hall. He wondered if Jezebel would remember him and stopped in at the stables. Murphy was nowhere in sight and Connor stopped to stroke the mare's beautiful head and whisper, with a searing mixture of happiness and anguish, "I'm back, Jezebel, old girl, I'm back." She nickered softly back at him and nudged him with her muzzle.

Then a warm bundle of copper coat flung itself at him and he turned to embrace Tyrone as if the setter were a long-lost brother.

"Good boy," he said, fending off Ty's kisses. "Good old boy."

Dilys and the staff were watching for him at the kitchen window as he and the frolicking dog came up the path, and the pantry door flew open, faces crowding it, everyone exclaiming about how distinguished he looked in his uniform.

"You've grown again!" his mother said, kissing him. Her eyes sparkled at the sight of him, and she was more beautiful than ever. His heart tightened in his chest, just looking at her. "But what happened to you?" Tenderly she touched the scar, still bright red, that extended about an inch from the corner of his mouth toward his right ear.

"Nothing. I fell off a horse."

Peggy hooted. "The horse hasn't been foaled could throw you. You were fightin', that's what I know."

"There, it'll fade—and it makes him look like he's smilin'," Cook said, giving him a steaming cup of coffee and a slice of fruitcake.

"That'll be the day!" Peggy scoffed.

Connor's expression was forbidding. "Never mind me. How are all of you?"

He took off his coat and sat down at the table while he looked around the circle. Mary O'Brien's hair was whiter and Cook looked smaller than he remembered. He realized how little attention he had paid to anyone but himself before he went away.

Peggy looked sedate and matronly in her lady's-maid uniform of black with frilled white cap and apron. Its primness made her candor all the more refreshing by contrast. The other maids were still upstairs doing the morning cleaning, making beds, polishing mirrors and windows, gathering linen for the laundresses, scrubbing the hearths, and bringing brass scuttles of coal up from the cellar. Central heating had been installed some time ago, but the family liked its hearth fires and coal burned best in the upstairs grates. The maids were there to shine and polish and clean. They were Irish girls from the flats, every one of them counting it a rare good fortune to work here from five in the morning until nine at night instead of in the mills.

"Those girls'll swoon away when they see you," Peggy said. "How tall are you now?"

"Six feet two inches. What about the family?"

"Miss Georgia's very high spirited, though she looks like an angel," Mary said tenderly. "Just like her mother."

"And Jillian's a proper brat," Cook declared.

"Fights like a wildcat with her sister," Peggy elucidated.

"She's not bad at heart," Mary said. "She loves Georgia, if she was only let be."

"What do you mean by that?" Connor demanded, peering over the rim of his cup.

"How would you feel if everyone kept callin' your sister a beauty and made you feel like a lump?"

"If you've finished, Connor, bring your bag and come upstairs," his mother said quietly, and Connor, with a smile at the staff that made Peggy roll her eyes in mock delirium, followed her up the back stairs.

They had a few minutes before she had to return to little Malcolm. "I'm very proud of you, son," she said while Connor unpacked the few things he had brought. His room seemed very grand by comparison with the severe quarters he and Racey shared. "Mr. Brandon told me your last grades were very high."

Connor nodded.

"He wants you back to work for him when you've finished school, but Mr. Hendrik thinks you should go for a scholarship to college." She hesitated. "Would you, Connor?"

He was very decided. "No. I'd never be accepted by a top-class school, and I won't go to any other kind."

"What's to stop you?"

"Plenty!" She seemed blind to what stopped him, a monolithic social structure, massive and impenetrable. "I'd be patronized no matter where I went and I've had enough of that."

"Who's patronized you here?"

"He has. And Mr. Hendrik too."

"They're good men! They only want to help you."

"Mother, don't keep on at me. My mind's made up. As soon as I finish at Braker, I'll find a good job in New York. No more mills, either. Something managerial."

She shook her head and a strange expression crossed her face, half tender, half sad. "You're so much like your father," she said wistfully.

He frowned, his black brows bunching together. "Another good man, I suppose! My God, how can you talk about him like that, as if you still cared?"

She stiffened and her lips went white. "He was my husband and I loved him once. The memory of that time is still with me, no matter how I feel about the end of it." She turned away from him. "But you're much too young to understand what love is."

"I understand perfectly well," he snapped, but he colored furiously when she turned back to look at him.

She shook her head. "That isn't love, Connor. It's passion, and love is more than that, more than lust." Her voice was low but firm. Then she took a deep breath and without another word she left him.

Swiftly he changed from his uniform into old trousers, a sweater, and a heavy jacket that had once been Rhys's. He

streaked down the stairs and out to the stables, calling to
Cook that he wouldn't be back for lunch. Murphy, glad to
see him, helped him saddle Jezebel and he took off at a
full gallop, not caring where he went as long as he put
distance between himself and the house. He rode hard for
a long time, then slowed to let Jezebel cool off.

Left to choose her path, Jezebel wandered a while and
then took the road to the Hendrik house. Connor was in
control of himself by the time he knocked on the door.

"Connor!" the butler said with a smile. "It's good to see
you, lad. And you're in time for lunch. Mr. Hendrik's just
come in."

Adam, emerging from his study at the sound of voices,
looked older than Connor remembered and more brittle,
like a winter leaf.

"My dear boy," he said, extending his hand and shaking
Connor's warmly. "How good of you to come to me on
your first day home. Come in, come in." He led the way
into the study, still overflowing with books, smelling of ink
and paper and pipe tobacco.

"That's new," Connor said, pointing to a phonograph
sitting in the center of a mahogany table.

"Yes, but disks are hard to come by now. Germany's
producing only war matériel. Sit down, sit down." Adam
poured himself a sherry from a crystal decanter, started to
raise it to his lips, then stopped and turned to Connor. "I
forget you're no longer a boy. Here, have some of this. It's
time you developed a taste for good sherry. This is Amon-
tillado, very pale, very dry."

"The stuff in the Poe story?"

"The very same. Now tell me all about school."

Adam asked detailed questions about Connor's courses
all through lunch, finally conceding, when a rice pudding
was served for dessert, that the level of education at
Braker was acceptable. "But it's what comes after it that
concerns me." He glanced briefly at Connor, then concentrated on his pudding.

"I'll be working, sir."

Adam hesitated. If Connor gave him any encouragement at all, Adam was ready to send him to Harvard, no matter how harshly Connor would be ostracized there. But it was a delicate matter. Connor had always been a serious child, far older than his years. Then he had become a driven youth. Now he spoke as a man who had made an irrevocable decision. Nevertheless, Adam felt he had to try.

"Is that what you want?"

"I want to earn my own way. I've had enough of being grateful to last me all my life." Connor's voice shook slightly with the passion in it. He had a fragile, manly pride, different from the hotheaded temperament of his boyhood, that made Adam admire him.

Adam was not a sentimental man, but he knew from his own experience with Rhys Brandon that the still, small voice of gratitude was sweet only to those who received it, not to those who must proffer it. For the first time in his life Adam tried to imagine what it was like for Connor always to be the recipient of favor, even dependent on it. He held Connor's stormy gaze for some moments, wishing he could eradicate the bitterness he saw there, then he nodded and reached for his pipe, his appetite gone.

"I'm sorry, sir," Connor said softly. "I know how much I owe you."

"No, don't apologize, my boy, I understand. It's just that I hate to see a quick mind like yours wasted in a mill. You'll never get beyond a foreman's job there, you must know that."

"The mill? I'll never work in his damned mill again! I'd rather starve. After I graduate I won't take another penny from him!" Connor caught himself. "For the same reason I can't take any more from you," he said lamely. After a moment, he added, "I haven't told him yet."

"Nor will I," Adam said, sensing Connor's concern. Without future expectations of Connor, Rhys would not pay the Braker bills. It would put Rhys's nose considerably out of joint when Connor left, and Adam would not be the only one to relish it.

◆

It was evening before Connor saw Georgia. She came running up the stairs as soon as the car arrived, bringing her back from a shopping trip to Albany with Constance and Jillian.

"Connor! They told me you were home!"

"Hello," he said, looking up from the book he was pretending to read.

In the old days she would have rushed to embrace him, but now she smiled hesitantly from the doorway of his room, tall for a ten-year-old, a regal little figure in a burgundy velvet coat and bonnet trimmed with black sealskin, rosy color in her cheeks from the cold air and her eyes a brilliant, sparkling blue. She smiled, but her attitude was as tentative as their relationship had become.

He stood, an appropriate show of deference to the young lady of the house.

"I'm glad to see you, Connor," she said, taken aback by his formality. "I've wondered how you were." She looked at him reproachfully. "You didn't answer my letter."

"No time," he said. "I'm sorry."

There was a strained silence.

"Where's your uniform?" she asked, and waited for him to say something, but he only gestured toward the closet. "We're having a big Christmas party," she said finally. "Everyone's coming and I hope you'll wear it for that."

His smile was tight and heavy with scorn. "Miss Georgia, you know I'm not welcome as a guest in this house, not even wearing a uniform."

She gasped at his manner, then her expression turned glacial, anger displacing her hurt. "You've been angry at something all your life," she said, "but I didn't care as long as it wasn't me. All right, Connor, I withdraw the invitation and I'm not going to try anymore."

She turned quickly and left in a whirl of velvet skirts, once a member of the close little family the three of them had formed upstairs, now an imperious girl who could never be told and would not believe that her father stood between them, that her friendship with a servant's son must cease. The familiar, intolerable frustration closed in on him, and his tenuous hold on self-assurance was destroyed.

He stood where he was, listening to her retreating footsteps on the stairs, and his childhood went with her.

♦

"There, it's hungry you are," Megan whispered.

"I can't get enough of you." He kissed her fiercely, still erect inside her, and moved his body as if to burrow between her breasts. "God, I've been dreaming of this for months."

"Rest now, rest a minute." She calmed him, holding him tenderly, and he felt the urgency leave his body. Desire would flare again soon, though, and bring him the one surcease that was sure. "No girlfriends, then?" she teased him.

He made a negative sound. "There are a few women in the town who sell it, but I could never do that."

"As grand as you look in that uniform, I'd think you wouldn't have to pay."

"It isn't paying. It's the women. I don't care about them. I care about you." He had slipped out of her but his hands roamed over her, exciting them both. They stopped talking. He watched what he was doing to her by the flickering light of the candle, aroused by her abandon to the skills she had taught him, by the little cries she uttered before he could wait no longer and entered her. The only sounds they made were of lovemaking, the gasps and sighs of delight, until climax engulfed both of them and then they lay silently in each other's arms.

"I'm hungry," he said when she stirred.

"There's bread and cheese in the pantry and some beer. And I made you a pound cake."

He brought food for them both and they sat crosslegged on the bed, feeding each other. The beer made him heady and randy and they made love again.

"Tomorrow night?" he asked when he was dressed to go.

"Yes, if you want to."

"*If* I want to? You know I do."

"Maybe you won't when you hear what I have to say."

He sat down hard on the bed and waited.

"I'm gettin' married," Megan said.

"What? Why?"

She was impatient. "Why do you think? I'm not the sort of woman to live alone. I've done it long enough as it is, because of you."

He swallowed hard. "I thought you loved me."

"I do love you! I wanted to be free for you. But nothin' can ever come of it and well you know it." She peered at him in the faint light of the candle. "Don't look like that, Connor. There's been no one but you, if that's any comfort, not even him."

"Who is he?"

"It's no matter. He's a good man. He works in a foundry in Troy. He makes good money and I won't have to work at all. I can stay home and have . . . I can stay home."

He felt he could not bear to lose her even while he had no right to expect her to live alone and wait for his school holidays. He was not a fool; he was too young to marry her and would not have even if he could. He had too much to do, and where he was going she could not follow. But how he would miss her!

"When?" he asked.

"Not until after you go back. We'll have this little time together." For the first time since he had known her, her perpetual good humor deserted her. When he slipped quietly out of the cottage she seemed as miserable as he, and the holiday, which had stretched generously before him, now seemed far too short.

♦

He met Tim Cassadyne, Keith van Reitjens, and Peter van Dorn on the day before Christmas, just as he was re-mounting Jezebel after a call on the doctor.

Tim had his father's red hair and freckles but not Silas's engaging personality. He wore impeccable tweeds and a pair of highly polished riding boots and his attitude was stiffly correct, almost martial. Keith, similarly attired, was a square, blond fellow who earned varsity letters and barely passing grades.

Peter, dressed in old corduroy trousers and a heavy sweater with a long scarf wound around his neck, resembled his mother, slight and attractively fair. He had grown into a casually aristocratic young man, with kind brown eyes and a gentle manner very like his father's. He was the sort people could confide in. Connor thought he would make a fine doctor. He and Connor shook hands.

"There's a friend of yours at Braker," Connor told him. He swung himself into the saddle as the other three dismounted, Timothy and Keith barely acknowledging his presence. "Remember Racey Blankenship?"

"Oh, him," Tim said, raising his eyebrows.

"The winged menace." Keith laughed.

Connor kept his face impassive, his dislike of them deepening.

Peter smiled. "I like Racey. He's a good sort."

"He's my roommate," Connor said.

"Fascinating," Tim Cassadyne pronounced in a flat voice. He squinted at his pocket watch. "It's getting late, Peter. We'd better go in or we'll be late for lunch."

"You two go in," Peter said. "I'll catch up with you." The others, with vague gestures toward Connor, moved off, and Peter turned to him.

"Don't let them get to you," he said. "I'd apologize for them, but they aren't important enough."

"I'm the one to apologize," Connor said. "I thought you were like them, but you aren't. You're like Racey. I should have known that."

"Connor, it wasn't easy for you to know whether you were being befriended or patronized. And after you went into the mills, I couldn't get near you."

"You tried. That's enough for me."

"Damn," Peter said softly. "Why did he want to hold you back?"

"Never mind him. I'll be leaving here as soon as I've finished at Braker."

"It's for the best," Peter agreed. "I'll be leaving, too, after Groton."

"For Harvard, I know."

Peter shook his head. "If the war's still on, I'm going to France."

"Not to fight?" Connor was incredulous. Americans who fought in foreign wars could lose their citizenship.

Peter shook his head. "No, I couldn't kill anyone. To drive an ambulance."

"But college? Med school?"

"That'll have to wait."

Jezebel, as if aware of Connor's shock at such a wanton abandonment of opportunity, pranced in the snow, vapor steaming from her nostrils, and he calmed her before he asked, "What does your father say?"

Peter looked troubled. "He'd rather I didn't go, but he understands why I must. Anyway, it's a long way off. They won't take anyone under eighteen." He looked back at the house. "Connor, I have to go in now, but let's try to ride before term starts."

They shook hands and Connor watched him go up the path. The war, which was supposed to have ended by Christmas, looked as if it would drag on for some time, with both sides digging trenches on a line eastward from the Channel ports, but it would surely be over long before Peter graduated from Groton eighteen months from now.

He turned Jezebel and trotted off, wondering if he would ever be like Peter and Racey, careless of other people's opinions and prejudices, but he didn't think so. You had to be born rich to feel free.

♦

He had encountered Rhys several times during the Christmas holidays but only once at any length, in Rhys's study and by his invitation. Connor was determined that his hostility, so close to the surface before he went away to school, must remain completely hidden. He was no longer a child, unable to hide what he felt.

"Sit down, Connor. Your last report was excellent, I'm pleased to say." Rhys, of all the people at the Gate, did not seem older. He was as charming as ever, relaxed to the point of indolence, yet dressed with a consummate elegance that Connor noticed with envy, impatient for the day when he could afford tailoring like that.

"It seems you've settled down in the last few months," Rhys went on. "You look well too. Taller, but I'll bet you make another inch before you've finished. And the scar adds a Byronic touch that will appeal to the ladies." He smiled. "I'm told scars are highly prized by students in Germany."

"I don't know anything about Germans, Mr. Brandon."

"I have a feeling we're all going to know more than we'd like before too long."

"You don't think we'll get into their war, sir?" Connor was astonished that Rhys gave credence to that preposterous idea. The officers at Braker were all for it, but that was to be expected from military men.

"No, I don't. But we trade with them and will continue to do so."

"With both sides? After what the Germans did in Belgium?" Stories about what had happened in Belgium were whispered around the academy. The Germans shot civilians, cut off children's hands, raped nuns.

Rhys waved that away. "There are always atrocity stories during a war, on both sides. It helps drum up public support. President Wilson has deplored the Germans' behavior, but no one of importance really believes the reports. In any case," Rhys said, selecting a cigar from a silver humidor on his desk and clipping it with a small gold instrument attached to his watch chain, "war's no subject for us to discuss."

"No, sir."

"I've missed you, Connor," Rhys said, lighting the cigar. "I'll be glad when you graduate and come back to the mills."

"Thank you, sir," Connor said, thinking, I'll never work for you again, Rhys Brandon, not ever in my life.

Rhys rose from his desk, constrained by the hostility he sensed but of which there was no tangible evidence. Connor, handsomer than ever and with a physique any man would envy, was polite and respectful—perhaps a shade too respectful, but that was no doubt a result of military training. Connor's gaze was direct, but there was something in his eyes that Rhys found disconcerting.

Rhys took a good-size package from his desk. "This is your Christmas gift, Connor. I hope you like it."

Connor's throat tightened. "I can't accept a gift from you!" He was staggered by the gesture. It clouded his resolve that for so long had glittered with the clarity of bitterness.

"Nonsense, my boy. We're old friends, aren't we?" He walked to the door with Connor. "You go back on New Year's Day, but we'll talk again before then." But Rhys had decided they would not talk again. It was far too uncomfortable.

When Connor unwrapped the gift his emotions were even more convoluted. It was a handsome black leather briefcase, hand-sewn, with brass locks. Inside it was an envelope containing ten dollars. *Your fares and allowance for the rest of a successful school year* was written on the envelope in Rhys's distinctive slanted script.

How could a man be at once so generous and so careless of the pain he caused? Connor had wrestled with the question for a long time, and not only on his own behalf. Rhys had barely looked at Georgia and Jillian when they were little. Adam Hendrik despised him. Connor suspected that his partner, Silas Cassadyne, both envied and distrusted him. The Lord alone knew how many other people Rhys Brandon had hurt.

The child in Connor was deeply touched by a part of Rhys's nature and still loved him for it, was compelled to love him because love for this man was deeply ingrained in him, never to be forgotten. And the young man in him knew how treacherous it was to love Rhys, maybe to love anyone at all.

He was glad to leave Brandon's Gate on New Year's Day. There was nothing here for him. Megan was gone. Peter would be away for the summer holidays. He no longer had a friend in Rhys and, because of Rhys, Georgia was lost to him too. His only tie to this place was his mother, and one day she would leave to make her home with him.

If I had my way, he thought, boarding the train back to Braker, I'd never come back.

He closed his eyes as the train moved out of the station, refusing to look at the place he still loved most in the world.

15

◆

"There he is, there he is!" Jillian whispered excitedly, clutching Georgia's arm. The two girls sat at one end of the Brandon pew, separated from Miss Howell by their three brothers. The governess leaned forward with a reproving shake of her head.

"Miss Eagle-Eye is watching you," Georgia whispered back.

"He smiled!" Jillian said, careless of her sister's warning. "I think I'm going to faint."

"Shh, the service is starting. I'm sure he'll wait for you afterward."

With a grateful squeeze of Georgia's hand Jillian settled back, and her sister relaxed. What a whirlwind Jillian was! She had always been brimful of energy—like her mother, people said—and her nature seemed to intensify as she grew.

She was a year younger than Georgia but had kept pace with her in everything, even in their physical development. Now eleven, Jillian had already started her monthlies—what a drama that had been, Georgia remembered—and she had tiny breasts at which she glared every night, willing them to grow.

Jillian, wild to escape the bonds of childhood, declared herself a woman and clamored to put her hair up and her skirts down.

"Don't be ridiculous," Constance had told her daughter languidly. "You'll put your hair up when you're fourteen and not a day sooner."

Rhys, bored with disciplining children—it made him feel old—observed his younger daughter with disapproval. "Why can't you be like Georgia?" he demanded. "She doesn't carry on about everything."

"I can't be like you!" Jillian had protested yet again when the girls were alone. She brandished a hairbrush, her round face contorted and her hazel eyes, so like Constance's, abrim with tears. "I don't want to be, so there!"

"He doesn't want you to be like me!" Georgia explained with conviction. "Here, give me the brush. Your hair's all snarled."

"Then why does he always say that?"

"It's what fathers always say to little sisters. Anyway, I don't want you to be like me. I like you just the way you are."

After each of these exchanges, Jillian, repentant, would throw her arms around Georgia with protestations of devotion. They still shared everything: their treasures and their curiosity, their games and their secrets. They vied for their father's approval—along with everyone else—but despite that there was a bond between them that Georgia wanted to endure, no matter how different the two girls were.

Jillian could not be still. It would have been sheer torture for her to sit quietly for hours in the gallery, as

Georgia did, immersed in the collection. And Jillian's natural skittishness would have been exacerbated by the complicated process of spinning, dyeing, and weaving those famous Brandon cottons, muslins, ginghams, and calicos. Georgia was thoroughly beguiled by all of it.

It was hard to curb her own spirits—sometimes she felt wilder than Jillian—but it was necessary if she were to resemble, more than physically, the regal beauty who had been her mother. Surely the woman in that portrait had never screamed with laughter over a prank, or galloped a horse for the sheer pleasure of it, or taken a forbidden book from Uncle Adam's library to read in the attic while the family was at tea.

"*Aretino's Postures*," Jillian read with no enthusiasm. "You goose, you've taken a book on deportment!"

"No, I haven't," Georgia breathed, turning the pages. "It's about you-know."

Round-eyed, they had studied the pages, amazed at what they saw.

"So that's how babies get inside," Georgia said. "Men put their pee-fors into women."

"Those little things the boys have?" Jillian scoffed, having seen her brothers as infants in their baths. "How could that get inside *me*?"

"They must grow the way the people do. They get bigger. Look at this."

"How disgusting," Jillian breathed, fascinated. "But there must be another way. Mama would never do *that*"—she pointed to a particularly graphic penetration—"and all the other ladies we know have babies too."

"There must be another way for married people," Georgia had agreed.

"Of course! Only bad women and servant girls would do *this*! That's why Mama sends away the ones who get pregnant."

It was the only explanation. Georgia knew her father would never do such things.

And yet there was something between her father and his wife that made her think about those drawings. There had always been the mystery of the big bed and the closed bedroom door, of certain glances between the couple at the dinner table that made Constance color and Rhys go up to bed early. Georgia felt uncomfortable about it, but there was no one to ask, certainly not Constance.

Georgia's relationship with her stepmother was distant and wary, although Constance pretended to be affectionate and Georgia respectful. In truth they detested each other and Georgia was constantly amazed that the rest of the family didn't seem to know that.

Papa above all! He was certainly the most brilliant man in the world, not just the handsomest, and she wondered how he could be unaware of the private war going on under his own roof. But she knew better than to bother him with it. Papa liked a tranquil life at home.

Georgia adored him with a quiet fervor that she knew gratified him enormously, coming as it did from Georgianna's child. She strove mightily to be as clever as her mother was, lest Constance succeed again in coming between her and her father. It seemed Constance had given up trying. Only her resentful jealousy of her niece remained, and she was pleased when her own children were jealous of their half sister.

It was a choice Georgia had to make: her father's affection or that of her sister and brothers. Since the day of the photography session she had never hesitated.

Georgia glanced sidelong at the two older boys sitting next to Jillian. "Georgia is her father's girl," people said merrily, ignoring Jillian's dismay whenever she heard that, "but those boys are Hendriks."

Jillian couldn't bear the older brothers and Georgia didn't much like them either. Will was nearly seven and Richard almost six, "Hendriks to a hair," people said, but there their resemblance to their Uncle Adam ended. They were sturdy boys who could have been attractive, but they grew ever more sullen.

"It's pushing them forward to their father, she is," Peggy would whisper to Georgia when they were alone. Peggy doted on Georgianna's child and gave short shrift to Miss

Jillian and her moods. "They'd be like ordinary boys if she'd leave them alone!"

"That's the trouble," Georgia said. "Papa doesn't want his sons to be ordinary."

"I expect not," Peggy agreed, shaking out petticoats and hanging up dresses. "Especially after having a lad like Connor about the place."

Connor had always known, Georgia remembered, that the best way to please Rhys was to like what he liked and then to excel. Sometimes Georgia forgot how angry she was at Connor and simply missed him. He had not been home since that unhappy Christmas when they quarreled. He had spent all his holidays since then with his friend, Racey Blankenship. Papa had made light of it.

"Boys will be boys," he said. "Let him grow up and come back here a man."

The prospect of Connor's return after he graduated from Braker this June made Georgia restless, and she went back to studying her family. Did all families look so different in public? Hers seemed united and very happy and they certainly weren't.

On the other side of Will and Richard sat Malcolm, who had turned three at Christmas, in a white sailor suit. He was the only one of Constance's children who resembled Rhys, even to his personality in some ways. He was Georgia's favorite brother, a fair-haired, dreamy little boy, tall for his age, who loved stories and make-believe, would sit on none but the gentlest pony, and refused even to touch the tiny custom-made rifle Papa had given him for his birthday, much less aim it at a rabbit. He was immovable once he had made up his mind, but Malcolm never had tantrums. Young as he was, he simply prevailed, as his father did.

"We won't press him now," Papa had said, disappointed about the rifle but nonetheless indulgent toward this strong-willed little replica of himself. "But we'll have to insist when he's older." He had said that in the silky voice that made everyone in the household fidget, but Malcolm had only looked back at him with his own green eyes, totally unresponsive to the threat.

Next to Malcolm, Miss Howell sat stiffly in the pew, painfully thin in her Easter costume made of the dove-gray silk faille that had been her Christmas gift from the family. She's like old parchment, Georgia thought. In a strong wind she would crumble into little bits.

"Miss Howell doesn't know about you-know," Jillian decided with a superior air. "Spinsters don't."

"Lord, Jilly, she'd faint dead away if she knew we'd seen that book."

For a while they had considered spiriting the book out of their uncle's house and putting it under Miss Howell's pillow, but the escapade seemed too fraught with peril.

The governess was a sharp contrast to the effulgent Constance, who sat next to her. Whatever Georgia's feelings about her stepmother, she knew Constance had style. The dress she wore today was of coral silk shantung with a draped bodice caught by a velvet rose of the same color. The sleeves, gathered along the seam, extended into a fichu that richly framed her shoulders. An ankle-length skirt fell in soft gathers from a wide velvet waist band and her pale coral earrings were shaded by a broad-brimmed hat of delicate, creamy Panama straw trimmed with tiny silk flowers of coral and turquoise. The ensemble was understated, elegant, and unmistakably French.

Georgia looked down at her own dress, hated being twelve, and longed for the day when she could choose her own clothes, guided by her own aesthetic judgment rather than by the prevailing fashion and Constance's taste. She and Jillian were always dressed alike, and although frills and flounces became Jillian, Georgia detested them. Jillian's dress was coral, of course; on public occasions she was always dressed in the same color as her mother. Georgia was never offered that option and would have refused it in any case. Her dress was blue; she was forbidden to wear red, which she loved, and had flatly refused to wear green from the day she discovered Constance was not her mother.

The girls' silk dresses had square, ruffled yokes of white lace, voluminous puffed sleeves, and velvet ribbon sashes run through loops set so low on the hip that they restricted walking. Matching sacques in sheer wool were trimmed and piped in velvet braid. They wore long white lisle stockings and white kid button boots. Their hats were leghorn with ribbons to match their dresses.

"Stupid baby clothes," Jillian had scowled that morning as the girls dressed for church. "He'll think I'm still a baby."

"If you carry on like that," Peggy told her, "he certainly will."

Everyone knew who *he* was. Jillian had adored Peter van Dorn since she was six years old and he had always been patience itself with his stormy little admirer when he had accompanied his father on the doctor's house calls to the Brandon children. Jillian was bereft when he went away to school, counted the days until the holidays brought him home again, and waited impatiently for his answers to the endless notes she scrawled to him. Blotted and misspelled though her letters were, he answered her once a month. He was fond of her. "Waiting for her to grow up," Rhys joked, and Peter blushed but did not deny it.

Other people laughed at Jillian's crush, but Georgia did not. Peter van Dorn brought out the best in Jillian because she cared for him so much.

"I do love him, Georgia," Jillian had declared again this morning, her rosy face glowing with a tenderness that made her beautiful. "I really, truly do."

Peter seemed to see the same qualities in the headstrong child that her sister did. Jillian's tempers could be as quick and her tongue as biting as a winter wind, but she was loving. She was jealous and moody, but she was loyal to Georgia. Her sins were many but her repentance was always sincere.

Movement startled Georgia from her reverie. The congregation stirred and rose to sing the closing hymn, and then there was another bustle and stir as people retreated up the aisle to the door, greeting one another and talking.

"Peter!" Jillian called, racing after him despite Miss Howell's efforts to restrain her.

Georgia saw him stop and wait until Jillian reached him. He bowed slightly and offered her his arm as if she were a young lady and Jillian, beaming and decorous, walked sedately up the aisle with him.

Georgia nodded to Tim Cassadyne and Derek Anders. She liked Tim but she wished he would laugh with as much gusto as he played lawn tennis, or do something mischievous once in a while. Tim's face was attractive and not nearly as freckled as it would be in the summer. He was looking at her now with an air of surprise, probably because she had grown so tall since Christmas. Peggy had begun to make a great fuss over how beautiful Georgia was.

"A proper young lady you are too," Peggy would say at night, braiding Georgia's straight, heavy mane of blond hair. "Your sainted mother was the same, never a clumsy, gawky day did she have in her life."

When it came to young men, beauty was all-important. That was a fact Georgia seemed to have assimilated with her milk. She knew she was beautiful—Papa said so, so it must be true—but what Georgia liked most was to hear him compare her to her mother in other ways: her intelligence, her grace, her artistic talent. It was even more satisfying when Constance heard the comparisons. But none of those things mattered to young men.

Georgia smiled at Tim and Derek and continued up the aisle with her governess. Derek was nice, too, a thin young man, buff-colored and angular, very like his father, although he did not smell of peppermint or wear a pince-nez as John Anders did. His father reminded Georgia of Ichabod Crane, but Jillian said he looked more like a windmill.

Driving home with Miss Howell and Jillian and Malcolm in the Crosley, while their parents and the boys rode in the Daimler, Georgia knew that all the young men of Brandon's Gate would be at the Hall for the Brandon Easter reception this afternoon. All of them except Connor.

"What could have made him change like that, Dilly?" Georgia had asked after Connor went away that New Year's Day. She had been sitting with Dilys in the familiar room on the third floor, where she and Connor had spent so much time together. On snowy days he had read her stories in this very armchair in front of the fire. He had taught her to read.

"I don't know, my love. I wish I did." Dilys's face had been worried and wistful. "But he was always a good-hearted boy and he still is."

"It's all so stupid! I can't understand him. I told him I was going to stop trying."

She was still thinking about him as the cars turned into the drive. The lawn was spangled with daffodils, and closer to the Hall the flower beds were abloom with grape hyacinth, tulips, and forget-me-nots. Forsythia showered the oak trees with sprays of gold, and in the rock garden near the pond there were bursts of violets, ajuga, and Jacob's ladder. She remembered other springtimes, when she and Connor had wandered over the grounds of Brandon Hall, sharing a love for it.

Suddenly she felt a great wave of affection for Connor. She thought, I'm as stubborn as you are, Connor MacKenzie. You may not want me for a friend, but you've got me anyway.

She decided with that set of her head that meant her mind was made up that she would tell him so the moment she set eyes on him this summer. He would have to come home after graduation.

But that was not to be. Over an Easter dinner of roast lamb with mint jelly and new potatoes, carrots and peas, ice cream and rhubarb pie, Adam told the family that Connor was on his way to fly for the French in the European war.

"How do you know?" Rhys asked in frank surprise.

"I had a letter yesterday. He and the Blankenship boy will train in France with the other American volunteers."

"Gosh!" Richard said with a five-year-old's awe and envy. "I wish I could be a pilot in the war."

A WORLD OF DIFFERENCE

"The Pro___oved. "He might have come to tell us ___ ___ ___ ook at her sister, but Georgia's face ___ ___ the conversation.

"I always knew that boy ___ ___ with satisfaction. "He pride after a moment. "I raised him from a pup, ___ ___ with He'll make a fine pilot. With his academy training he might even be an officer."

"In which case," Adam observed, "he won't want to be a mill hand for the rest of his life."

"He'll come back to Brandon's Gate," Rhys said with a dismissive glance at Adam. "Connor will always be loyal to me."

"Unless he gets killed," Will said. He answered Georgia's angry look with a grimace.

"Will, that's not a very nice thing to say," Rhys said, frowning.

"Will's right," Constance defended her son. "French casualties have already passed two million."

"Well, he'll be safer up in the air than down in those trenches," Rhys insisted. "Does his mother know?" he asked, turning again to Adam.

"He asked me to tell her. She's worried, of course."

"That's enough about the servants!" Constance protested. "I don't want my reception spoiled by the war."

"Of course not, my dear." Rhys was benign but Constance glared at him before returning to her dessert. The way Connor and his mother kept intruding into her life was infuriating! But at least, she thought, spearing a piece of rhubarb with her fork, that odious boy was gone and with any luck he'd never come back.

I should have made him listen, Georgia told herself, a cold feeling at the pit of her stomach as the family left the table. I should have kept on trying. And now I will.

"That's very thoughtful," Adam said when she asked for Connor's address. "He'll be glad to have a letter from you."

She knew he wouldn't s. Will," Jillian said,
anyway. No matter how as. "Connor won't get killed.
keep on writing up. "Connor won't get killed.
"Don't pay as no time and poke Will in the eye." She
slipping her sister. "Forget about Connor. Let's go down
He'll comer sister. "Forget about Connor. Let's go down
the lane and wait for Peter there."

Georgia went with her, thinking that the grown-ups had
long since stopped saying the war would be over in no
time at all. It could be a very long time before she saw
Connor again.

By summer the war seemed to move closer. Peter van
Dorn was not returning to Harvard. He had volunteered
for the American Ambulance Corps and was leaving for
Paris.

"But you mustn't!" Jillian protested tearfully when he
came to say good-bye to the Brandon children. "You might
get hurt!"

"I must go," Peter said firmly, but his eyes were kind as
he calmed the frantic Jillian. "They need people to drive
the wounded to the aid stations."

"Then you won't fight at all," Will said, disappointed.

Peter shook his head. "I don't believe in killing people."

"You can't have a war without killing," Richard scoffed.
"That's what wars are for."

"I'll write to you every day," Jillian promised Peter, her
hands clasped in adoration.

Peter nodded. "I'd like that," he said, and got to his
feet. "Now I must go or I'll miss my train to New York."

"Kiss me good-bye, Peter."

He bent down and kissed her cheek, and Jillian watched
him go, tears raining down her face. "If anything happens
to him I'll die," she said, and Georgia put an arm around
her, feeling much older than she was.

16

♦

I ought to kill him, Constance thought, looking down the length of the dinner talbe at Rhys. She wondered what would happen if she took the fruit knife lying on her plate amid a curl of apple peel and sank it up to the hilt in his treacherous heart.

Instead, she smiled.

"Please don't be too long, gentlemen," she said as her guests rose from the dinner table.

"Of course not, my dear," Rhys promised with an endearing smile at the women.

Constance led the ladies into the drawing room for coffee and cordials, seating herself next to Susan Cassadyne. Susan would chatter endlessly. All she required was an occasional nod of encouragement and Constance would be free to think.

Her mind raced while her fingers played idly with her diamond necklace. She was accustomed to Rhys's infidelities, but that he should be unfaithful under her own roof was too much!

And yet it must be borne. If she confronted him she would have to insist that Dilys be dismissed and there would be talk. There could be no other reason to discharge such a paragon, and sooner or later women like Susan Cassadyne would ferret out the truth. Constance was not about to be patronized as well as cuckolded! It was one thing for a man to have an occasional fling; it was quite another for him to make love to his children's nurse-maid. My God, the next thing she knew people would start whispering that Connor was his!

Whore! she shrieked silently at Dilys while her beringed fingers toyed languidly with a translucent Royal Doulton coffee cup. Her face was frozen in a semblance of prurient interest in whatever Susan was saying while she thought, I never wanted you here, you or your miserable son. I must have known what you were, I must have sensed it from the start.

How long had they been going on, those trysts in Dilys's bed while Rhys was supposed to be rapt in his art treasures? And how utterly stupid Constance had been to advertise her total lack of interest in art—until she was driven upstairs by boredom last night only to find the collection unattended and the door to the long gallery ajar. That was the last evening Rhys would spend alone with his collection! Constance would be with him every minute.

Her taffeta-clad bosom rose and fell too rapidly, and she forced herself to breathe evenly and consider what to do. All that mattered now was to put as much distance as possible between that woman and Rhys.

"But of course they'll deny the whole thing," Susan Cassadyne said.

Constance's hazel eyes flickered. "Who?"

"Why, her husband and the governess." Susan looked around the circle of women with an acid little smile. "I always said how clever it was of Constance to hire a governess like Miss Howell. Women can't help throwing themselves at Rhys, but there's absolutely nothing to worry about with Miss Howell, is there?"

Bitch, Constance thought, but she gave a self-satisfied smirk, and lapsed into silence again as the women talked on.

She had been plaguing Rhys lately to move the family to New York City and he was beginning to come around to that idea. Now she would insist, playing upon the restlessness she sensed in him as his interests expanded and he sniffed the overwhelming musk of power that permeated the metropolis. He was far too important, she would tell him, and potentially much too influential to live in a backwater. He could be involved with state politics from the city. She would say he belonged in New York at the hub of the country's business and finance. Rhys like to be reminded of his godlike qualities.

The only way to deal with a man like Rhys, Constance thought, is to make an ally of his ego.

Then she must find some way to leave Dilys behind.

♦

"Unparalleled prosperity is all very well," John Anders said gloomily as the gentlemen sipped brandy and puffed on Rhys's fine Havana cigars in the library. "But ours has its dark side."

The men around him listened attentively to the banker, but their faces betrayed their skepticism. Nineteen sixteen had been the most prosperous year in American history. Tremendous exports of supplies and munitions to both belligerents had created shortages at home and forced prices up to start a boom that now continued into the new year with no signs of weakening.

"Explain yourself, John," one of the men said.

"It's quite clear. Britain's blockade of Germany has been very effective. As a result, neutral or not, we've made the bulk of our sales to the Allies—on credit. Now we must ask ourselves if those drafts will be worth the paper they're printed on." Anders shook his head. "What would happen if the war ended in a stalemate tomorrow, with no clear victory? Or if the Allies lost? They've had a terrible year: a slaughter at the Somme, Verdun, the French armies in mutiny. Russia is exhausted. The allies might very well lose."

"He's right," Congressman Jonah Charles said glumly. "If the war ended tomorrow, or if the Germans won, it might mean economic disaster for us."

"Might?" Anders scoffed. "It very definitely would."

"But if the war goes on until the Allies win?"

"Then we'd be all right. The Allies will demand reparations from the Germans to settle accounts with us," the congressman said. "Unless"—he stressed the word—"unless the Allies keep most of it to put their own houses back in order. But if we participate in the war, we can make it a condition that part of those reparations will come directly to us. Our economic position would be a lot brighter."

"The truth is," Martin van Reitjens said, "we're up to our necks in this war already and we'll be fighting in it before summer, mark my words." He exchanged a look with Anders, and this time Rhys knew what they were thinking. American participation in the war boded well for Crabtree. And for Brandon Textiles. America had no standing army. To fight a war she would have to raise one, train it, house it, feed it, clothe it, and arm it.

Only Silas Cassadyne was adamantly opposed. "We'll do anything short of war to ensure an Allied victory, but Americans won't send their sons to fight Europe's battles."

"They might want to," Jonah Charles countered without elaborating. There was no need. Public opinion had been mounting against the Germans ever since the first atrocity stories were splashed across the newspapers. Rhys might not have believed them, but the country did. The sinking of the British passenger ship *Lusitania* had almost precipitated the United States into the war two years earlier.

Rhys was convinced the die was cast. He was planning a trip to Washington for Crabtree, which had earned an excellent reputation for the speed and quality of its parts production and now made entire weapons under license for export to companies holding patents in America and England. But there was other business to be done in a country headed for war.

"You're very thoughtful," Constance said to him when the last guest had gone and they were climbing the wide, curving staircase.

"I heard some interesting conversation tonight."

"You'd hear a lot more if we lived in New York."

He nodded, reflecting that the congressman had come upstate by chance for the weekend and that most of his guests lived in Albany or New York City all winter long, moving their families back to the country during the heat of summer.

"I think you're right," he told Constance. "I think it's time we bought a house in New York City."

She was suspicious of his sudden capitulation. Did he have a favorite mistress in New York too? But she could not question a decision she had been fighting for.

"I'll go down to New York with you and start looking while you're in Washington," she offered.

He agreed, and they parted for their separate dressing rooms. She thought with satisfaction that at last they were engaged together in a project, they were sharing something important to both of them. He seemed very pleased to have her help, but as he came expectantly through the door of the bedroom she said she had a headache. For the first time since the day she had set eyes upon him, she did not want him to touch her. He was properly solicitous and took up his book.

This will pass, she thought, lying next to him with a cold compress on her forehead. She had urgent physical desires and Rhys knew how to satisfy them. Whatever the charms of prostitutes and servant women, she was his wife. If Dilys MacKenzie could be kept out of his sight, she would soon be out of his mind.

♦

"All I know," Silas Cassadyne stormed a few months later when he found out about Rhys's army contracts, "is that you procured contracts for Brandon Textiles and not for the mills we own in common down south—without a word to me about it. What the hell kind of partner are you?"

Adam regarded the two men silently in his office in the new administrative building on the flats, Silas red with outrage and Rhys genuinely aghast that his friend would question his integrity.

"For God's sake, Silas! I was gambling we'd get into the war and you swore we wouldn't. I had to divert some of my looms to weaving khaki cloth that might never have had a market. I had to buy knitting machinery to make the cloth they demanded for the manufacture of socks and underclothes. Would you have taken those risks?"

Silas stared back at him steadily. "I'd like to have been asked," he said. "I think you owe me that much."

Rhys put a friendly hand on the other man's shoulder. "I just didn't think you'd be interested—but let me sub-contract to you to make up for it. You'll have a piece of every contract—along with my apologies." He looked anxiously at Silas, for all the world, Adam thought, like a small boy whose good intentions had been misunderstood.

"All right," Silas said after a moment, unable to resist. "I shouldn't have blown up, Rhys." He glanced at Adam. "Sorry."

"Nonsense, it's all forgotten," Rhys said, suddenly the recipient of apologies instead of well-founded accusations. He walked out of the office with Silas and saw him to his car, and he was smiling when he came back into the office. "Well, that's all squared away," he said.

"How much of the total volume do you plan to give him?" Adam asked, virtually certain of the reply.

"No more than ten percent. I deserve some consideration for talking the quartermaster into a written commitment. And Silas can't supply any knitted cloth."

"Exactly. Does Silas know half those contracts are for knitted goods?"

"I'll tell him some other time. At the moment he's very grateful." Rhys picked up his hat and riding crop. "I'm going upriver to the Hendrik mills. Now that we're in this war, they'll all be working at full capacity."

The man leads a charmed life, Adam thought as his brother-in-law departed. He never lost a gamble—or a friend. He knew precisely whom to cheat. Rhys would never have tried that kind of thing with a man like John Anders. The banker would have done him in.

Adam set off for the Hall to lunch with his sister. Constance hadn't been herself on the few occasions he had seen her lately. She was always in New York these days, supervising the decor of her new home on Fifth Avenue. But she was too thin and he was concerned. He did not pretend that what he felt for her was deep fraternal love. In the first place, she was not a lovable woman, and if she loved anyone at all, it was herself, as was the case with Rhys. In that sense they were a perfect couple, carbon copies of each other.

Constance was in thrall to Rhys, but she did not love him as Adam understood love: caring as much for another's well-being as one's own. She had never loved Georgianna; if anything, she had detested her sister. She was jealous of Georgia. As for her own children, she was impatient with Jillian, and her main interest in her boys was using them to manipulate Rhys.

That won't be easy! Adam thought. Rhys did not consider himself lucky in his sons. All three boys were bright enough, but the two older ones, prodded by Constance, vied constantly for Rhys's favor and, failing to obtain it—possibly because they did not look like proper Brandons—sought to discredit each other. At other times they were inseparable. A pity, Adam thought. Will and Richard might have been different but for the conflicting needs of their parents.

Malcolm was another breed of cat entirely. He cared nothing for his father's favor and was deaf to his mother's machinations. He was a solitary child, preferring books to everyone's company but Georgia's, and the two often sat quietly together talking, not chattering as children do.

Adam knew it bothered Rhys to have so little influence over the only child who was the dead spit of him. Malcolm rode his pony well enough but still disdained guns and people who used them. He was precocious at lessons and learned to read at four, but he was otherwise uncommunicative and totally immune to Rhys's charm. If it were not impossible in so young a child, Adam would have said Malcolm condescended to everyone, including his own father. And yet people adored him!

"He has your charm," Constance had told Rhys recently in that arch way she had that gave another shade of meaning to her compliments. "And we all know you're irresistible."

Rhys had far better luck in his daughters. Jillian had heart. She was a terror, of course, uncontrollable and given to high dramatics, but affectionate when she wanted to be. She had been subdued since Peter van Dorn went away. It was embarrassing for a girl of twelve to declare at the top of her voice, and to anyone who would listen, that she was in love.

"But she is," Georgia had told her family. "It won't do any good to try to talk her out of it. If you insist, so will she."

Rhys always listened attentively to what Georgia said. Adam could understand why he adored her. Everyone observed that she had her mother's beauty and quick, incisive mind as well—but she had a mind of her own, too, Adam had noticed, although she took care to conceal that from her father. She had a genuine aesthetic bent and artistic talent that showed in her drawings, which were exquisitely rich and minutely detailed. But in one vital way she was different from her mother: she had the warmth that Georgianna had lacked and, as she left childhood behind, the temperament.

"We'll have to marry her off very soon at this rate," Constance had drawled last Christmas, watching the young men cluster around Georgia at a Brandon party. "Probably to Tim Cassadyne."

"Nonsense," Rhys told her with some heat. "She's only fourteen."

"Georgianna was fifteen when you asked her to marry you," Adam had observed.

"Good Lord, man!" Rhys had been visibly shocked. "Georgianna was different."

"Yes, Georgia is more—emotional," Adam returned delicately. "You'll soon have a crowd of earnest young men asking for her hand."

"Which I will certainly withhold until she's finished school!" Rhys declared. "And college," he had added, although up to that moment, Adam suspected, the man had never had the slightest intention of educating his daughters beyond finishing school. Still, there was a glow about Georgia that obviously made Rhys uneasy; Rhys could certainly recognize sensuality when he saw it. A woman who had it could become the victim of her own nature, and in anyone but Rhys, Adam had thought at the time, it would have been admirable for a father to protect his daughter from herself. In Rhys, though, moral rectitude was ridiculous.

Adam dismounted at the stables and walked up to the Hall. He would be lonely when the family moved to the city, but he was far too set in his ways to follow them.

Luncheon was a strained interlude. Constance, usually very talkative, hardly spoke and scarcely touched her food. He wondered if she was pregnant again. She was only thirty-two.

"Aren't you feeling well?" he asked her.

She shook her head and waited until the butler left the dining room, then she left her end of the table and pulled a chair up to sit close to him, whispering things that first shocked him, then made him angry.

"No!" he said. "It can't be true."

"Keep your voice down!" she ordered him. "It's true all right. That's why I've been so eager to move and leave her behind. The renovations on the house are taking forever, but it should be ready in another few weeks." She picked at her handkerchief nervously. "You must help me, Adam!"

"Of course, but how?"

"Make sure everything runs smoothly at the mills. He mustn't have any excuse to come up here and stay with her. The way he goes on about those damned government contracts, you'd think he'd discovered King Solomon's mines."

"But won't he want to take her to New York?"

"No. I got rid of Mrs. O'Brien and made Dilys housekeeper." Constance nodded with grim satisfaction. "He's already agreed she's the only one responsible enough to look after his precious house. His property means more to him than she does—or any woman." She bit her lips, methodically shredding the handkerchief with her fingernails.

"No one else knows about this?" he demanded.

"No. Those two have been very clever. But I won't be made a laughingstock, you can count on that." She peered at him shrewdly. "You really do hate him, don't you?"

He did not reply. "How long has this been going on?" he asked her.

"I don't know. Does it matter? Years, probably, but she never let on, that pious little hypocrite with her downcast eyes and rosy cheeks. Butter wouldn't melt, would it?"

His anger mounted as he rode away. Yes, he hated Rhys, and with good reason, but the main thing was to avoid a scandal. About Dilys he felt surprise and vaguely prurient curiosity. But had Dilys had any choice? It would be like Rhys to threaten her with dismissal unless she gave him what he wanted.

Yet Dilys seemed a happy woman, under no constraint at all. My God! Adam realized, she's in love with him, too, with that rotten, cheating bastard! She doesn't see that he's using her the way he uses everyone else—his wives, his children, Silas Cassadyne, Connor.

Connor! He reined in, peering at that darkly handsome young face as if it floated before him in the dark, seeing again the pain deep in those black eyes. Did Connor know? He decided not. Connor resented Rhys's treatment of him, as well he ought, but if he had found out about this, he'd have killed Rhys Brandon.

Well, he mustn't find out, Adam swore to himself. He would pay too high a price for the privilege of ridding the world of Rhys.

17

◆

A light breeze wafted along the avenue as the taxi stopped in front of Fouquet's. It was a balmy September evening in Paris and Connor's spirits rose as he paid the driver and went into the famous restaurant to meet Racey. He glanced around the dining room, but there was no sign of him.

"Bonsoir, Capitaine MacKenzie," the maître d' greeted him. *"Votre ami n'est pas encore arrivé."*

"It doesn't matter," Connor answered in fluent French. "I'll wait for him at the bar."

Connor lit a cigarette and paced slowly up and down, sipping his sherry and thinking about a table he had just glimpsed in the dining room. It was set for eight, but one of its places bore a single red rose like a flaming reproach. It was in memory of a pilot who had been killed in combat the day before, a tradition among some of the flyers.

Romantic, Connor thought. For some reason war inspires romance.

Not in him. Not a war like this, for which there was no better reason, he had decided, than that a spoiled kaiser had wanted a little blood sport and a bigger navy than his British cousin, King George. The rest of the world had followed, willy-nilly, hell-bent on territorial expansion, never supposing that the war would drag on so long at such a cost. It was like Sinbad's genie, let out of the bottle and now uncontrollable.

Connor had fled to France in search of adventure. He was at war because it was more exciting than hunting for work and because he could not tolerate autocrats, whether they were German kaisers or American textile barons. But as death crept closer to him, he was not sure the fight had been worth the staggering casualties.

His own squadron had buried two more men the past week. They had been very different, one a professional dancer who had turned into a fearless, reckless pilot; the other a Phi Beta Kappa from Yale who hated war but had volunteered to fight out of idealism. In Connor's opinion there was nothing romantic about those deaths.

"It's no good brooding about them," Racey had told him last week. "Come and have a drink instead."

But Connor still felt what he felt: threatened because those two men were dead, and elated because he was not.

It still amazed every man in the squadron when a pilot was killed. They felt invincible in the open biplanes they flew, although none of them could explain why. Some sixteen square yards of fabric-covered wing surface kept aloft by a one-hundred-fifty-horsepower engine did not offer much protection from the hostile machine guns on the German Fokker Eindeckers. Before some clever fellow had synchronized machine guns to fire between the prop blades, the pilots had shot at each other with revolvers.

"In a gentlemanly fashion," Connor had said cynically. "Like duelists."

"And a lot less lethal," Racey reminded him.

But for the moment Connor was safe at Fouquet's, their favorite restaurant, which had consistently managed to rise above the severe food shortages afflicting France. The elegant diners had turned to look at Connor with that curiously personal affection a uniform inspires during a war, and now they watched him pace, a tall figure in his crisply pressed tunic, breeches, and polished boots, a young man electric with the energy that had always emanated from him.

By now Connor was accustomed to having people turn to look at him and he no longer reacted with suspicious hostility. He knew they were not judging him and finding him wanting. For the first time in his life he belonged to an elite group. Fighter pilots were the popular heroes of this war, and Connor was an ace, a member in good standing of a charmed circle. His American captain's insignia said so.

"The women wouldn't care if you wore a canvas sack and flew a barrel," Racey often told him.

Connor stood six feet three inches tall, his father's height, had he known it. His memories of Enoch were simply of an explosive man who had soared above him like an eagle only to withdraw the protection of his wings. But reports of Enoch's unionizing efforts, surfacing regularly, still made him wince.

"Why?" Racey had asked him once. "Because he represents the wrong class?"

"No. Because he had what your class would call prior obligations which he chose to ignore."

The fact was that every mention of Enoch, whether by the press or the workers at Brandon's Gate, had kept the wound of his desertion raw. Even now Connor never knew when a color, a scent, a sound would catapult him back to that man-forsaken cottage and the chilling fear he and his mother had tried vainly to hide from each other. Even here, half a world away, Enoch was in his blood and his bones and there was no escape from him, try as Connor might.

Two years of war had expunged the last traces of adolescence from his face and body, but the changes in his personality were far more subtle. He was not so much withdrawn now as restrained, a man who was clearly conscious of his strengths but chose to keep them under tight control.

Death had a monopoly on his days and sex on his nights, whether he was confronting either situation or merely thinking about it. He had become addicted to living on the edge, as had most of the men he flew with. Their actions were strictly disciplined, but not their emotions, which they kept hidden, and Connor felt at ease among them. For years before he went to France he had been behaving one way and feeling another. Once he arrived to start his training, though, he began to relax, to brood less and to laugh more. The brilliant smile of his childhood had returned, dazzling to women, disarming to men.

He and Racey had been together since Connor finished his pilot training with the French Armée de l'Air. From the time Connor joined the squadron there was very little about his life that Connor did not share with his friend, things he had never been able to say to anyone, not even Peter.

"A favored member of a wealthy household," Racey had exclaimed, "who rode its thoroughbreds and tended its children but was obliged to use the back door! How the hell did you know who you were?"

"I didn't," Connor told him. "But I'm beginning to find out."

"Who are you, then?"

"I'm prepared to deal with the world as it is, for one thing."

"Even Brandon?"

"The world is full of Brandons."

They were an oddly assorted pair, Connor tall, dark, and intense, Racey of average height, slight, and debonair.

"I befriended this Adonis at Braker for the services he offered," Racey told the other pilots when Connor joined the squadron. "He's still my protector in case of bar brawls, and my ticket to the only pearly gates I crave to enter. Women can't resist him. When he chooses one, the others turn to me for comfort."

They had two special girls from the corps de ballet of the Paris Opéra to take to bed when they were on leave in the capital, and two alternates from the Folies in case of emergency. Lately their leaves were few and far between and they turned to the village women near whatever billet they were assigned to, with varying degrees of success. Life was sweet. Danger made it sweeter.

Now Major Blankenship had a squadron under his command and Captain MacKenzie led a flight of six airplanes.

◆

"Connor!" Racey breezed into Fouquet's and clapped him on the back. "Sorry I'm late. The meeting dragged on, but we still have time for a drink before dinner." Racey had been to a staff meeting at First Army headquarters. American pilots, released by the French after the American declaration of war, were now part of the United States Army.

They sat down in the bar and ordered Veuve Cliquot. "What's the word?" Connor asked.

"We're going to be very busy for a while, and in my informed opinion we'd better get laid tonight."

"It's all arranged," Connor said. "I stopped in to see the girls after I left the officers' club."

"A friendly act in a hostile world! Did you pick up any mail?" Racey took the two letters Connor handed him. "My father and Belinda," he said, looking at the writing. Belinda was almost his fiancée. He smiled at the letters. "I'll save them to read back at the base. Anything for you?"

"One from Georgia, one from my mother."

"Ah?" Racey leaned back, his left ankle resting on his right knee, and lit a cigarette. "Everything all right?"

"Everything's fine." His mother had been made housekeeper at the Hall when the family moved to New York. Connor and Georgia were friends again. He was remorseful for having behaved so badly to her, and he wrote to her frequently. Georgia's letters sparkled with fascinating details about New York City and comical stories about the fashionable school she and Jillian attended. They always ended with blotted postscripts from Jillian asking about Peter.

The two young men had met soon after Connor arrived in France. Connor found Peter edgy and very thin, although he insisted he was fit, only homesick. They had spent a few evenings together, far different from the ones he spent with Racey. Peter was obsessed by the war; it was as if he left half of himself up on the line where the fighting was. When he wasn't worrying about the war, he was back in Brandon's Gate.

"All I want," Peter said, "is to go home and be a country doctor."

"And marry Jillian as soon as she's grown. You'll have no peace unless you do."

And Peter, with his sweet smile, had nodded. "I'm perfectly willing to wait until she grows up. I like the idea of marrying the girl next door."

They hadn't met often; their paths kept diverging in the confusion of the war.

Connor and Racey went in to dinner and talked about planes, as usual, over asparagus vinaigrette, poached turbot, *poulet forestière*, and brandied pears with Brie. They chose a Pouilly Fumé with the meal and a VSOP cognac with their coffee. Replete, they took a long walk along the Seine in the city that still retained its special charm, even though it had been shelled and rationed and twice had narrowly escaped enemy occupation. When it was time to pick up their girls at the Opéra, good manners required that they offer the ballerinas a champagne supper before taking them home to the tiny apartment they shared. Tonight it was Racey's turn to make do on the narrow couch while Connor took the double bed.

The girls, lithe and slender, were interchangeable. They were both brown-eyed brunettes with firm bodies, long legs, and tiny breasts. They moved beautifully, especially in bed, where they were totally without inhibition. Connor was with Marie France tonight, and he lay naked on the bed, watching while she undressed. It excited him to see a woman disrobe with such exquisite grace.

"*Dépêche-toi,*" he said. "Hurry."

She smiled and came to the bed, walking with her toes turned out, as if she were still wearing her ballet slippers.

"*Quelle jolie fleur,*" she said, her eyes widening in mock surprise at the size of his erection. One of her graceful hands closed around it while the other trailed slowly up and down his body. "*Tu es merveilleux,*" she said. "You should have been a dancer."

He laughed softly. "Lie down," he invited her, "and let me show you I'm no dancer and that is no flower."

She lay down but first she feasted on him, slowly and delicately, knowing exactly when to stop. Then she moved languorously to offer herself to him and he reciprocated, building passion and retreating from it to prolong the pleasure until they could wait no longer and her arms and legs came up like graceful wings to enfold him.

Megan had given him comfort. This girl gave him the pure eroticism of the impersonal. They were two bodies moving through space. It was like flying.

◆

Connor listened to the engine of the SPAD VII and nodded, satisfied that all was well. He climbed smoothly, then dipped his right wing to check the position of the plane he was escorting. The struts between the upper and lower wings interrupted his line of vision when the plane was level, and he could not see over his machine gun unless he dipped the nose, something he preferred to avoid. He signaled to the supply plane and followed the pilot as he pulled away west.

They were bound for some units of the 308th, cut off in the Argonne forest. The squadron's mission was to drop supplies to them until they could be reached and rescued. "We'll show them what an air force can do in addition to reconnaissance and aerial combat!" Racey had told the squadron with satisfaction.

"Have you ever flown over a forest?" one of the men asked. "We'll have to find those men first!" But no one paid him any attention. They had taken off at dawn.

The weather was glorious, the sky a pellucid October blue with some creamy cloud banks to the east. Each time Connor looked down it was a shock to see the thick fleece of the Argonne. He had become accustomed to expanses of gray mud punctuated by charred trees reaching up for him like claws. The Western Front was a grotesque terrain, pocked with craters and scarred by the meandering line of trenches that snaked from the English Channel to the Swiss border, where men lived like maggots in mud, amid putrefying bodies and their own filth. Out of this combat by suicidal frontal charge and stalemate had come a new fashion, the trench coat—and new diseases: trench foot, trench mouth, trench fever.

Connor had never been in the trenches, but he had flown low enough over them to know that the air was a better place to fight a war and a plane crash a better way to die if your luck ran out.

He kept the supply plane in sight while his eyes moved back and forth constantly, sweeping the sky for German fighter planes. For the moment he was alone in his little piece of space.

Flying gave him the same feeling of power he had experienced the first time he galloped Jericho, but it was infinitely more exalting. He was as addicted to flight now as he was to danger, and knew that he could never give up either completely, no matter what else he did after the war. The sky made him feel free and the silence, whenever he cut his engine to relish it, was both pure and exciting, like a beautiful woman.

"Jesus!" Connor yelled. The German Albatros had come on him without warning, and bullets whined around him like a cloud of gnats. Connor pulled back on the throttle and his plane dropped, but his attacker had anticipated the maneuver and dropped with him.

He pushed the throttle forward and shot up again to dodge the spray of fire. Then a bullet cut the left aileron control and sliced through Connor's leather helmet. Blood cascaded from his head as the plane floated down. He slumped against the edge of the cockpit, stunned but alive and aware that the Albatros had overtaken him and was flying level on his right to get a closer look at him.

He stayed very still until the German, apparently convinced by Connor's bloody head that he was dead and not worth the waste of more ammunition, peeled off and headed away without spotting the supply plane.

Connor felt the aircraft drifting, gradually losing altitude. After a few moments that seemed agonizingly long, he opened his eyes and looked around. He reduced his speed and listened intently for the sound of another engine, but he heard nothing. He had lost the German and the supply plane too.

His head pounded but he made himself reach forward to grab the severed ends of the control rod and hold them together. He felt the plane stop fluttering and respond to direction, but he knew he could not hold the rod together long enough to return to base. He was dizzy, on the verge of blacking out. He would have to land—if he could find a clearing in that luxuriant forest—and take his chances on the ground.

He spotted a small opening among the trees and eased the throttle back to begin his descent. He was fifty feet above the treetops when he jettisoned his fuel tank.

♦

An hour later he struggled back to consciousness as if he were emerging from oily water and groaned with pain the moment he moved. He rested a minute and tried again. This time he managed to push himself upright and move his head to look around. The wings of his plane had been neatly sheared off by two huge trees and the nose had crumpled like tissue paper against the trunk of a third, but the cockpit was intact, hanging five feet above the ground. He felt over his body carefully. He was badly bruised, but there were no bones broken.

He felt his head. The blood had congealed under his helmet so that he could not remove it, although he took his goggles off. They were covered with a film of oil; the engine always threw some grease, and the unprotected lower half of his face was black with it. The forest around him was absolutely silent.

After another rest he checked to see if he had his revolver and the flask of cognac he always carried, before he pulled himself out of the cockpit with a mighty effort, painfully aware of his chest and ribs. He slid down to the ground, landing with a jolt that made him dizzy again. He stayed where he fell, resting.

The light had changed by the time he moved off in what he thought was the general direction of his original objective, although he had little real hope of reaching the stranded men through a forest swarming with Germans. For all he knew, the Germans had seen him come down and would be watching for him. He moved as silently as he could through the trees.

He had gone about a mile when he heard a man moan and he froze, thinking at the same time what a universal language pain was: it had no accent.

He found an American major with no apparent injury but a small, blood-caked hole in his side where the bullet had gone in. He was burning with fever. The man was about Racey's size but it was still an effort for Connor to kneel, hoist him up, and drape him across his shoulders. He went on, still dizzy but only slightly stooped under the weight, judging his direction by the slanting rays of the sun.

The major regained his senses at intervals but lapsed almost immediately into unconsciousness. Just as well, Connor thought. The man's moans could give them away.

Just before night fell, while Connor was forcing himself to put one foot in front of the other as long as he could still see the ground, he froze again, leaning his head against a tree with his burden on his back, trying not to gasp for breath. He heard German voices not more than a hundred yards away and turned back in the direction from which he had come, hoping fervently that the major would not come to and start moaning again.

When he splashed into a stream he knew he had mistaken his direction in the dusk, but he could go no farther. Carefully he lowered the major to the mossy ground at the water's edge, his knotted neck and shoulder muscles protesting as he bent down. His head spun and he stayed for a while on all fours, gathering what remained of his strength. After a while he made a pillow of leaves for the major's head. The man was shivering pitifully and Connor covered him with his jacket. He sat down beside him, opened his flask of cognac, and took a deep swallow.

"I'm Petrie, Major, United States Army," the major said, suddenly lucid in the dark. "Who are you?"

"Speak softly, sir, there are Germans all over the place." Connor identified himself and held the flask to the major's lips. "Here, have some of this, it'll help the pain."

"No," the major whispered, his hands moving over his legs. "There isn't any. I have no feeling in my legs at all."

"Drink!" Connor commanded, and the man swallowed twice more. Connor closed the flask regretfully. Petrie would need the brandy if the feeling in his legs came back.

He got up and went the few steps to the stream, cupping his hands to drink the cold, fresh water that hit his empty stomach like a stone. He splashed some on his throbbing head, but the leather helmet stuck and he was reluctant to start the bleeding again by tearing it off. He carried water to the major in his cupped hands, making a dozen trips so he could drink his fill. Petrie's lips felt hot and soft against Connor's hands, like Jezebel taking sugar. He drank enormously, then lay back.

"Why in hell didn't you leave me where I was?" Petrie demanded. His tone was accusatory, hostile. He sounded slightly drunk.

"You'd have died!"

"D'you think I want to live like this, you damned fool? My legs are paralyzed! They have been since I was hit." He drew a breath that became a sob. "I dragged myself under a fallen tree so my men couldn't find me when they pulled out. I'd have been dead by now except for you, you son of a bitch hero!"

"I'm no hero," Connor said. "And I don't intend to be taken prisoner either, so lower your goddamned voice." His head throbbed painfully. A new kind of anxiety possessed him, as if he were about to face something far more difficult than the Germans or the Argonne forest. When you save a life, the legend had it, that life belongs to you. He didn't believe in legends. He simply had to save this man.

They lay in silence like feuding lovers, stretched out side by side beneath the trees.

"Captain," the major whispered after a while. "I apologize for what I said. But I want you to leave me here in the morning."

"No," Connor whispered back. "No."

"Listen, you stubborn bastard, this is *my* life! I'm not going to live it as a freak."

"You may not have to," Connor said, putting a hard edge on his voice. "Maybe they can fix you up. Or maybe we won't get out of here alive."

"Damn you," the major moaned. "What gives you the right to decide my future for me?"

Was he really guilty of ordering another man's destiny? The thought cut through Connor like a knife. It was what Rhys had tried to do to him.

"Where's my revolver?" Petrie demanded suddenly.

"You didn't have one." In fact, the major's revolver was jammed into Connor's belt. His own was in a holster on his hip.

"You're a rotten liar, MacKenzie," Petrie said desperately, on the verge of tears. "I order you to give it to me!"

"I think we're beyond orders," Connor said, torn by the man's pain and frustration, knowing he must not yield to it. "You can't shoot yourself tonight, anyway, not with the Germans so close. I'm not ready to die yet, even if you are."

"Go to hell." Suddenly Petrie began to weep.

Connor sat there dumbly for a while, drawn into the man's desperation, becoming part of it. When he could bear the sobs no longer he put a hand on Petrie's shaking shoulder. "Listen, Major. I'll make a deal with you. I'll give you five years back home. If you haven't changed your mind I'll help you . . . do what you want to do."

"Two years."

"Three."

There were several moments of taut silence before Petrie turned his head toward Connor and said, "Done." His hand, hot with fever, found Connor's and clasped it. "Swear, on your honor as an officer and a gentleman."

"I swear it, on my honor."

Petrie sighed, then whispered into the mysterious depths

of the forest. "I'll look for you in October 1921. I'm Oliver
Preston Petrie and I live in Preston City, Ohio."

"In a big house on a hill," Connor said, relieved that
one struggle, at least, was over.

"Yes. How did you know?"

"I know a man who has a town named after him. He
lives in a big house on a hill. I admired him very much."
He wondered why he was talking about Rhys here in the
cold, inky night, to a man whose suicide he had just sworn
to assist.

"But you don't anymore?"

"He's a Judas," Connor said with no particular emotion.
"I wish I'd never set eyes on the bastard!"

"Your father?"

"Hell, no, but how I used to wish he was!"

A pause. Then Petrie said desolately, "That's what comes
of seeing people as you want them to be, not as they are,"
and Connor was moved anew by him. There was something else they shared besides a conspiracy of death. "But
it's our fault, you know, mine and yours, not theirs."

"Here," Connor said, handing him the brandy flask.
Then he took a swallow himself and lay down again. "We
might as well talk about it, Major," Connor said. "It's
going to be a long night."

After a moment Petrie began to speak about his wife, as
a painter might who was profoundly in love with his
subject. He told Connor in detail about the day he met
her. He described his wedding day and the radiant woman
who came down the aisle to him like a vision of delight, a
woman to whom he had pledged himself long before he
took his vows.

He was intoxicated by his memories, his inhibitions
blunted by fever and brandy, by darkness and the strange
intimacy that had sprung up between the two men. It was
as if, he told Connor, he were talking to himself.

"I know," Connor said. "Go on."

Petrie sighed. "There's nothing more beautiful than a
woman's body, is there? Especially hers. She has breasts
as smooth as satin. She was very shy on our wedding

night, not responsive, but I didn't expect that so soon."
Again he sighed deeply. "She was a virgin, of course.
Have you ever been with a virgin?"

"No," Connor said.

"It gives a man the most colossal sense of possession to
be the first. I knew she belonged to me and always would
in the most elemental way. I'll never forget that moment.
It was beyond mere physical ecstasy. That night all I
thought of was the years of love we would have together
when marriage wasn't so new and frightening for her."

Petrie stopped for a while, and when he went on his
voice had changed, no longer touched by the sublime. "I
was so blinded by love that it took me two years to see
what she's really like. My wife is a vain and selfish woman,
even with our son. She has no passion. Gossip and finery
excite her far more than I do. She lets me sleep with her
because it's her duty. And that was when I was whole.
She'll never let me touch her now." His voice trembled.
"But it isn't her fault, you see. The fault is mine, for
seeing something in her that was never there, the way you
did in your Judas. It's our expectations of people that
destroy us, not the people themselves."

"I have no expectations of anyone," Connor said.

"You did once."

"Not anymore. And I could never love a woman in the
way you do." To his surprise, the knowledge saddened
him as much as Oliver Petrie did, Oliver with his heart in
his hands and no one to receive it.

Connor lay without speaking until Oliver was asleep.
He shivered in the frosty darkness, trying to conjure up
something pleasant. His first day at Brandon Hall flared in
his memory. His mother, pale, young Dilys, in the big
bed. Georgia, fragile as a snowflake, in her arms. Cook
and Peggy and Mrs. O'Brien in the warm white kitchen
redolent of hot chocolate and gingerbread and rich soup
simmering on the range. But most of all Rhys, tightening
Connor's muffler against the cold and saying, *I'm very
glad you came*.

My expectations? Connor thought. Was it all my fault,

then, not his? And do I care anymore? He was ready to
surrender his anger and with it the ties that bound him to
Brandon's Gate. He would put Rhys aside and go on with
his life in another place.

He fell asleep.

♦

In the morning, aching and stiff from the cold, he drank as
much water as he could hold. He gave the major the last
of the brandy before he filled the flask from the stream
and poured water down Petrie's throat. The sick man's
skin was still dry and parched, and he muttered as his
fever began to rise again.

Connor took off his bloodied white scarf, rinsed it in the
stream, and gagged Oliver with it to muffle the sound he
made. He wound the wet ends around Petrie's forehead,
feeling its heat. He was dizzy and nauseated and it took
him several minutes to reshoulder his burden. By then he
was burning himself, but inside, with frustration and pity
and stubborn determination to save them both.

When the sun's rays were vertical, he rested, drank
some water, and gave the rest to Oliver, studying his face
closely for the first time. He was neither plain nor handsome. No one could have guessed what depths of passion
stirred in this pleasant-looking young man. What sort of
woman could inspire love like that and be immune to it?

"Don't die on me, buddy," Connor muttered, cradling
Oliver in his arms. "Don't die before they can fix you up."
He stroked Oliver's face. "It'll be all right, just wait and
see." He was sure of it. He realized he didn't know the
color of Oliver's eyes.

He hadn't the heart to gag him again. Picking him up,
Connor went on, unmindful now of his direction, only
fleeing death as it trailed them through the forest and
tapped with a bony finger on the major's back. His head
was down as he staggered up a small rise, on the lookout
for deep ravines and fallen trees treacherously camouflaged by leaves and moss.

He thought he was hallucinating when, near the top of

the rise, a soldier's muddy boots stepped from behind the trees and into his blurred line of vision. He peered up out of a face blackened with dried blood and engine grease, white as chalk where his goggles had been. He was a wild apparition and the stranger, as dirty and unshaven as he, looked fierce and held his rifle at the ready.

"Who the fuck are you?" the soldier asked, and then he caught the major as Connor's knees buckled and he pitched forward into pillowy blackness.

♦

The same face was above him when he woke. It was morning again, but the atmosphere was curiously flat and without the hope of a new day. A susurrus of strange sounds assailed him: curses, sporadic machine-gun fire, and, amazingly, the cooing of doves. But the screams were what jarred him awake, the screams and a fetid, gamy smell.

He looked around. He was on a ledge at the side of the hill he had struggled up the night before. He could not see above the protective overhang, but some fifty yards below was a stream gushing freshets of cool, clear, delicious water. His mouth was like the red felt that covered the emery in his mother's workbasket.

He sat up.

"Hello, flyboy!" the soldier said. "Welcome to the real war."

"Where's the major?" Connor asked, his words as thick as the coating on his tongue.

"The one you carried in?" The man gestured toward the other side of the ledge. It was from there that the smell came, borne to them undiluted by the brisk autumn breeze. The wounded lay behind fallen trees and in hastily dug foxholes. Some of the men Connor could see were ominously still; from the others, like a fingernail scratching on slate, came the shrieks of pain.

The soldier answered Connor's accusatory look with a shrug. "Got no medicine for the poor bastids," he said, "not even the ones with gangrene. Got nowheres to bury them when they croak neither. Got hardly no food left. And we're runnin' out of ammo. The next time the Heinies attack, they could take us like Grant took Richmond."

Connor tried to wet his lips. Failing, he got to his feet.

"Sit down," his companion said, divining his intent. "You ain't goin' nowheres. The stream's off limits." He pointed upward with his rifle. "The Germans drew a bead on it two days ago. And if they don't shoot you, one of us will. Major's orders."

"Where the hell am I?" Connor demanded. "And what outfit is this?"

It was the center thrust of a three-pronged drive on the German line in the Argonne, a line that had to be broken at all costs. The plan had failed when the Germans beat back the two flanking columns fiercely, then turned and closed that one hole in their lines through which the center had penetrated. The closure had surrounded units of three American battalions, some six hundred men, cutting them off.

"You're the guys I was looking for," Connor said.

"No shit? Well, you found us. You better get yourself a rifle," the soldier said, looking at the two pistols in Connor's belt. "You can't do much against Germans with them pop guns."

"Where's the supply depot?" Connor asked sourly.

"Over there." The man butted his head toward the farthest point on the ledge where the dead lay, covered with autumn leaves, looking like bloated, obscene cigars.

"Jesus," Connor muttered.

"The men already been over them with a fine-tooth comb, lookin' for food. They won't wake up if you take a rifle from the stack."

"You're a real ray of sunshine," Connor said.

"Let's see how you turn out when you been livin' on coffee grounds and seeds for a few days."

Both men crouched suddenly as heavy fire from the German regiment on the crest of the hill began, and Connor sprinted to the makeshift morgue and grabbed the first rifle he saw, avoiding the bodies, breathing shallowly against the miasma. Checking the rifle for ammunition, he joined the ragged line of men huddled in the center, protected by the overhang, while trench mortars and potato-masher grenades rained down on the perimeter of the ledge.

He lay flat on the earth. He would have burrowed into it if he could.

"You'll get used to it," a cultured voice on his left said in the first lull. It was the commanding officer, the major who had placed the stream off limits.

"Never," Connor said.

"No, I suppose not. Anyway, thank you for trying to make it in."

"I never intended to get this close. Major, have no airborne supplies reached you at all?"

The major shook his head. "The packages fall behind the German lines. They amuse themselves by shouting a list of the contents to us: ham, chocolate, biscuits, butter. It annihilates what little morale we have left. The dead and wounded are piling up." He shook his head. "I don't know why we persist. And now they're using flamethrowers."

"Flamethrowers?"

"They don't do much damage. The overhang protects us, and this ledge is so defoliated by now there's nothing left to catch fire. But they terrify the men."

"And you, sir? Don't they terrify you?"

"You haven't read your army regs, Captain. Officers are not permitted such cleansing emotions."

Connor felt a wave of admiration for the man. "Any chance of reinforcements?"

"The Germans have captured every one of the runners from both directions, in and out. Our men will have to break through a stubborn line."

"Do you know where you are?"

"We know. Found a map on one of your buddies who didn't make it. I'm glad you did."

Connor shrugged. "What happens now?"

"We hold on as long as we can, hoping for reinforcements and supplies. When we get to the end of our tether, we'll notify them by carrier pigeon. We have two left."

The major's eyes narrowed suddenly and he sprang to his feet. "Over there!" he shouted. "They're attacking over there."

It was a familiar impulse that made Connor charge after the major, but he did not identify it until the assault was over and the Germans had been beaten back again. He fought savagely, using the butt of his rifle when he ran out of bullets. He fought for himself and for Oliver and for the glum, resigned soldier he had spoken to that morning who now lay crumpled like a used rag four yards to his right, for the soft-spoken major and for the two carrier pigeons he had mistaken for doves. He fought for them all because they were his. It was a primitive impulse, a need to protect what was his mixed with a primordial rage to live, very like what he'd felt when he was fighting Arlo Walsinger.

In the course of that one assault he became one with the beleaguered men trapped in this pocket, and in the long hours that followed he shared their hunger and thirst, breathed with them the stink of the putrefying dead and the gangrenous living, and became inured to the screams of the wounded. He watched while the soldiers wrote farewell notes to their kin, scrawling on old bandages and pieces of uniform, using mud for ink, or sometimes their own blood.

He defied the major's orders and went several times to the stream under cover of darkness, sliding past the pickets like a snake, gobbling water like a drunkard gobbling wine. Every night he filled his flask with water for Oliver and poured it down the unconscious man's throat in the inky blackness, shutting his ears to the delirious pleas for water from the men around him. It was the hardest thing he had ever had to do—deny so many in order to save one—and he had no idea why he was obsessed with saving Oliver Petrie. He knew only that he had to save him.

He took his turn at guarding the last two carrier pigeons, even while he lusted to rend them apart and devour their bloody flesh.

At the end of the second day he stood with a group of desperate men while the pigeon keeper prepared to send one of the two pigeons off with word that they would be forced to surrender in twenty-four hours. The circle of men was silent, all of them mesmerized by the fluttering gray feathers, the jut of the bird's head, and its beady, demented eyes.

He gave a shout of outraged anger when the nervous pigeon keeper released the bird before its message was secured.

"What've you done, you stupid bastard?" the men raged. "Are you crazy?"

"Quiet," the major commanded, gesturing to the keeper to give him the last bird. "I'll hold it while you attach the message." His hands, filthy but long-fingered and graceful, stilled the bird while the metal circlet was attached to its scaly leg.

They watched the pigeon, thrown upward by the major, rise, circle—and perch stubbornly atop a burned-out tree.

"Dirty fucker!" the men yelled. "Fly, God curse you, move your ass and fly!"

"Stones," the major ordered. "But throw them gently. Don't kill him, just make him move!"

Later it would be comical. At the moment, the stoning was a deadly serious mission, and a cheer arose when at last the bird took flight.

Connor helped beat off another attack that morning, howling like a maniac, shooting, hacking, stabbing to defend this enclave. At the end of an hour the major made his way to him. "You can stop, MacKenzie. It's over for the moment. They've fallen back." He put a hand on Connor's shoulder. "If someone had to wander into this hellhole, I'm glad it was you."

"Thanks," Connor said. "You're the only one who is."

"I'm not so sure," the major returned.

It was late afternoon when the Germans finally withdrew from the sector and a patrol from the 307th Infantry crossed their deserted line and entered the pocket. Of the more than six hundred men who had entered and defended it, one hundred ninety-four marched out on October eighth. One hundred and seventy were dead. The rest, Oliver Petrie among them, were carried out on stretchers.

18

♦

"**A**nd although wounded himself, and at the risk of his own life . . ."

Minutes after his arrival from France, Connor sat on a bunting-draped platform on the pier in New York City and wondered what in hell he was doing here. Coming down the ship's gangway, he had been met by Rhys and several bumptious men, all of them well dressed and immaculately barbered, and whisked onto the platform. Now he listened while the United States senator from New York read the citation Connor had already heard when the medal was presented to him in France the day after the armistice.

Rhys and his colleagues had insisted that Connor wear the medal, and under those peremptory stares he had acquiesced, feeling more the child he was when he went away than the man he had become. Around his neck was the Medal of Honor, an inverted five-pointed star suspended from a sky-blue ribbon by an eagle and a bar that read VALOR.

He didn't listen to the senator describing his exploits in the Argonne. Connor knew he was not a hero. He admired the men who wore the medal, but he was not like them. He had gone to France for escape and adventure and he had rescued the major for reasons of his own.

"Don't tell that to anyone else," Racey had advised in

his offhand way. "They'll point out that you didn't have to carry the man for two days through a forest swarming with Germans."

"I couldn't leave him there, could I?"

"I'd have surrendered. *You* delivered him to the Lost Battalion and fought on with them against impossible odds— for all of which you've been awarded the Medal of Honor. That makes you a hero whether you like it or not!"

Oliver had been rushed to a field hospital and then to Paris while Connor rejoined his squadron through the last days of the war. By the time the armistice came, Oliver was en route to America.

I'll write to him, Connor promised himself, as soon as I find out where he is. He inquired a few times, but in the joyful confusion of the armistice, no one could tell him. And then he drowned the memory of that travail and of the impossible promise he had made, in a long, wild spree with Racey in Paris, pushing death and danger far away. Yet the date, October 1921, was never completely absent from his mind.

Nor was his last sight of Peter van Dorn in the American Hospital at Neuilly.

♦

"Septicemia from his wound," the doctor said wearily, shaking his head. "We've tried everything we know. Nothing works. My ignorance appalls me." He pinched the bridge of his nose, his hand trembling with fatigue. "He's been waiting for a friend called Connor. Is that you?"

Connor nodded.

The doctor looked at him sadly. "You'd better go in now. He's delirious with fever, but they sometimes have lucid moments toward the end."

Peter's eyelids fluttered when Connor came in and crossed to the bed. He took one of Peter's hands and was shocked by its heat, by the patches of purple mottling his skin and the hectic flush of fever in his cheeks.

He leaned over and said softly, "Peter, it's Connor. I'm here."

The eyes opened, and a flicker of recognition flared before they closed again.

"My father," Peter said, and tried to wet his dry lips with a furred tongue. Connor found a glass of water on the bedside tray and raised Peter's head to let him drink. He sipped. "Tell him I'm sorry," he said.

"Jesus, Peter, he isn't angry at you."

After a moment Peter clutched Connor's hand weakly. "Talk to me about home," he said.

And Connor rambled on about Brandon's Gate, about the riding trails through the woods and the sunsets on the river, sledding parties in the winter and bonfires in the snow and Georgia and Jillian, while Peter began to turn his head from side to side as delirium took him again.

"Sweet little Jilly," Peter mumbled.

"She knows you're waiting for her to grow up."

"I'm dying," Peter gasped, terrified.

Connor clasped the burning hand desperately, and tears coursed down his cheeks. "You promised to wait for her, Peter. Try, please try."

"I'm falling," Peter said. "Don't let me go!" And then he spoke in the whimper of a frightened child. "Mother, is that you?"

"Oh, God," Connor moaned, and stroked Peter's hair gently.

"Mother?"

"I'm here, Peter," Connor whispered and, frantic to comfort him, put his arms around the feebly thrashing body and held Peter close, rocking him until his movements stilled.

"Hush," he soothed him, "hush now." Without thinking, he began to hum a lullaby he used to sing to Georgia and Jillian, and pressed his cheek to Peter's burning forehead. He did not stop when the nurse came in and stood watching before she came to the bed, found Peter's wrist, and felt for his pulse.

"He's gone, Captain," she said. "I think he was only waiting for you."

"I didn't know what else to do," Connor said, weeping. "He wanted his mother."

The nurse handed him a towel to dry his face. "They all do, Captain. They think they want war and bugles and glory, but in the end they all want their mothers. It was a kind thing to sing him to sleep. They all deserve that, even the Germans."

◆

Sitting on the platform now, Connor reflected that he had no particular grudge against the Germans, either the nation or the soldiers he had captured, a group of dirty, hungry, demoralized young men sick of killing other young men.

No, his grudges were not on an international level; they were very particular, and the moment he set foot on American soil he knew they were still with him. He had packed them up carefully to carry wherever he went. He no longer remembered that moment in the forest when he was ready to put them down.

He glanced at Rhys, sitting on the platform with him, and resented him all the more for arranging this circus. It served Rhys somehow, that much was certain. For that matter, every man on the platform would derive some advantage from it. They were not there for Connor's sake, but to bask in the reflected glory of the medal. He wondered if it would open any doors for him—but doors to what? He had no clear idea of what he would do once he and Dilys left Brandon's Gate. It was because of her that he had not stayed in France with Racey in the first place, waiting for some new adventure that was bound to arise.

Rhys had not aged. If anything, he was more youthful without his beard, though less Olympian. Connor was the same height as Rhys now, but part of him would always be a boy, dominated and manipulated by emotions he could not control. He should have refused to take part in this charade. Why hadn't he? He knew well enough that once he took off the medal and the uniform he would not be welcomed by the men who honored him today—with the exception of two staunch friends, Adam and the doctor.

Adam, standing in the front row of a curious crowd that had gathered on the pier, looked much older to Connor, as if he had retreated early to the harbor of age. And Dr. van Dorn's face, pinched and white, betrayed his anguish at his loss. He would want to talk to Connor about his son. It weighed upon Connor that he and Peter hadn't managed to meet more often, as if he should have tried harder, as if one more meeting might have saved Peter's life.

Dilys had not come. She was busy preparing for a ball at Brandon's Gate, Rhys had explained quickly, "that will start about an hour after our arrival. I'm glad you came home in time to attend it."

Connor had made no reply. Go to a Brandon ball? "Through which door?" Racey would have asked. Connor, with an interior grimace of skepticism, decided he would go. He had more than earned the right, and if Rhys was currying favor with him for a change, so much the better. Besides, he owed Rhys something for the good times, for Tyrone and Jezebel and Braker.

He had planned to go to Brandon's Gate anyway, to see his mother and make arrangements for her to leave with him. He had one hundred dollars in his pocket, a captain's insignia on his uniform, and the most coveted medal in the nation on his chest. That should convince her she would be secure with him.

". . . And the great state of New York is proud to welcome our hero home."

Confronted by the senator's hand, Connor rose to shake it amid generous applause, and the ceremony was over. Rhys shepherded him down the steps, where photographers and reporters waited.

"Planning on running for the state Senate, are you, Mr. Brandon?" a reporter asked when the photographers had finished.

"Gentlemen, I'm an industrialist," Rhys replied with a broad smile, "not a politician."

"You look like a senator to me," the other said with a cynical smile.

So that's what this is all about, Connor thought. Vote for Rhys Brandon, friend of the working man, benefactor of humble heroes! Rhys, the benefactor, was as much a fraud as Connor, the hero. They could scratch each other's backs.

They were joined by Adam and Dr. van Dorn and, together with several other men who were bound for Brandon's Gate in Rhys's private railway car, they moved off the pier and climbed into the automobiles waiting outside. Connor was about to get into Rhys's car when someone called him. He turned.

♦

"Hello, son," Enoch MacKenzie said, his white teeth flashing in a broad smile as he bore down on Connor.

Connor stood by the open door of the car and stared at the man he hadn't seen for fifteen years. Was this the god of his infancy and the devil of his boyhood, this man whose cheap suit could not lessen the impact of his massive build and impressive head? Those penetrating black eyes had once been able to read Connor's heart, whether it was filled with joy or fear or love. He had been Connor's universe—and he had destroyed it without a second thought, not once but again and again, with every mention of his name.

"I read in the papers you were coming home today," Enoch said, a Scottish burr still lingering in his speech. "I'm proud of you, son." He put his hands on Connor's shoulders.

"Take your hands off me, you bastard," Connor said in a strangled voice, his face contorted.

Enoch's face changed as his arms dropped. "Mind your tongue, boy. I'm still your father."

"My father deserted me. I'm my mother's son, not yours."

Enoch shook his head impatiently. "Ah, Conn, you're a man now, you've been to war. You've seen for yourself the better part of a man's life has no room for women and sentiment."

"Shut up," Connor said. "And keep away from me or I'll kill you, I swear it."

From behind him Rhys said, "MacKenzie, you aren't welcome here," and he put a proprietary hand on Connor's shoulder.

Connor pulled away from it. "Stay out of this," he said, still glaring at his father.

"Yes, stay out of it, you money-grubbing son of a bitch," Enoch roared at Rhys. "Who gave you the right to parade my boy like a pet monkey? He's *my* son, not yours."

"But I've been a father to him, and you haven't," Rhys said disdainfully. "It's his choice. I think he's already made it." He stepped back to the open door of the car. "Connor?"

Connor stood between them, despising one, hating the other. He shot another lowering look at his father and got into the car.

"Don't let him corrupt you with his blood money," Enoch shouted as Rhys got in and closed the door, and his words went straight to Connor's heart. "His kind preys on people like us. Be your own man, Conn, not his!"

Mute with shock, Connor sat next to Rhys as the car picked up speed and headed for the station. Adam and the doctor faced him silently on the folding seats. In a moment the three older men began to talk among themselves and Connor, his fists clenched, made himself sit there, enraged and ashamed, hearing little Connor crying, in that corner of himself that would always be a child, Why, why, why did you leave me?

◆

Enoch stood on the deserted pier, clutching at his belly as if his vitals had been pierced.

"Jesus, God," he groaned. "He hates me." He twisted from side to side as the conviction penetrated.

It was all the more unbearable because Enoch had known it might happen. He had chosen to ignore it, hoping that a bond as basic as blood would bind his son to him, no matter that he, the father, had hacked those ties asunder.

"But what did I do so bad?" Enoch muttered, clenching his fists. He had left enough money to keep them until the child was born and Dilys could find work. *She* had the education to go for a teacher or a lady's maid. She had always been far above him—except in bed.

But she had never shared his anger at the rotten fate he had been dealt at birth: to be poor, disenfranchised, despoiled by men like Rhys Brandon. How could he live with a woman who was content with things as they were?

"I had a *reason,* Conn," he muttered, straightening up and brushing his sleeve across his eyes. "I didn't leave you for a whim or a woman. I had a *reason.*"

He walked off the pier, large hands thrust deep into his pockets, head bent, great shoulders curved inward. He should have explained to the boy before he left—but how would a child comprehend how rage can be a sharper spur than love or duty? There were the masters, like Brandon, whom Enoch hated worse than death. And there were the workers, ignorant of their own power. They needed someone to lead them, someone like Enoch, obsessed, fearless, and with something in him that galvanized the meek to follow him and the helpless to trust him.

But Connor hated him, his own father! In that agonized look there had been not the merest hint of the love that was now lost between them, still less a hint of respect for his growing eminence in the union movement. It was in the papers. Connor must have seen it. But Connor was loyal to no one but Brandon. He was ashamed of his father.

"I canna bear it," Enoch groaned, the accent of his youth dredged up by his anguish. "I canna bear it."

He walked blindly until he reached a shabby but respectable building on Third Avenue and again he mopped his eyes, this time with a handkerchief. Then he climbed two flights of stairs heavy with the odors of thousands of meals, and let himself into the door of apartment S.

It was a railroad flat: one room led to the other like cars

on a train. Dim daylight came through the windows to fall upon the scant furnishings: a bed and a chest of drawers in the back room and, in the parlor, some leather armchairs belching stuffing here and there.

Enoch never paid much attention to where he lived or what he wore, but now he looked down at his cheap suit and worn shoes, at his chapped, callused hands, and frowned. Even though the United Mine Workers counted four hundred thousand members and had become a force capable of paralyzing the American economy, workingmen still distrusted swells in tailor-made suits.

Enoch had already attached himself to another popular union leader of Scots descent, but Enoch never ran for office. He was a negotiator who used his influence to garner strength. He was a wily, clever politician, a lobbyist for the UMW in Washington, where his shabby suits and worn heels were a slap in the face to the mine owners.

"First the power," he always reminded himself. "Then the money."

Now he flung his cap aside and sat down heavily in one of the armchairs to light a cigarette. He watched the smoke rise and, because he was a man who could neither admit nor accept defeat, he began planning how to win his son back when Connor wasn't surrounded by hypocrites like Brandon who turned his head, sucked up to him like leeches for the publicity they could get from him. Blood would tell in the end.

"I'll get him back, by God I will," Enoch said softly, raising his head. By the time a knock sounded on the door, he was convinced of it.

He admitted four men whose names and faces were familiar to workers in textiles, steel, automobiles, and coal—and to major industrialists as well. They were David Delaney, Karel Winowski, Aaron Weiss, and Neeley Mack.

Like most union men, they had made great advances during the war. But the war was over and reaction had set in. They had been fired from many jobs, blacklisted in certain cities, sometimes beaten by thugs hired by the mine and mill owners to intimidate union organizers.

Now they lived in the shadows while they urged
workingmen that their only hope lay in union. Now they
took any kind of unskilled job they could get by day—
dishwasher, road worker, itinerant farmer—and preached
the gospel of union by night.

The men took seats, saying little, waiting for Enoch to
begin. They looked to him because he never lost hope.

"All right," Enoch said, "let's remind our people that
the armistice works both ways: they won't be screwing our
fighting men if they strike. Now we begin in earnest. The
Establishment thinks it's got us by the balls, but they're
going to fear us again by the time we're through."

The deep voice that galvanized every man who heard
him rang with conviction. Enoch was fighting again.

♦

"Connor!" Dilys said, her arms around him. "My dearest
boy."

She had been waiting when the car stopped in the
driveway, and Connor sprang out to embrace her, released from conversation with Rhys, which had become
increasingly strained after Adam and the doctor had been
deposited at their own homes. Rhys had watched the
reunion of mother and son for a second, a gratified smile
on his face—the boy was worth his weight in publicity—
before he went inside. Connor, spared from refusing the
front door his mother could not use, walked with her to
the servants' entrance and into the pantry.

Dilys kept him there for a moment, her eyes shining as
her fingers moved over his face, and he saw again how
lovely his mother was, how young and elegant in a simple
crepe dress of navy blue ruched with white organdy, and a
flush of happiness freshening her cheeks. He hugged her,
catching the delicate floral scent she wore.

He followed Dilys into the bustling kitchen. His old
friends came to welcome him home, then scurried to
complete the party preparations, still calling to him as
they worked.

"Go upstairs, darling," Dilys said. "Have a hot bath if

you like. There are fresh towels in your bathroom. I'll be up in a minute. If you need anything pressed, leave it out."

Apart from a second bathroom, their apartment seemed the same until he noticed the changes in his mother's room. The lampshades were new and they were silk, like the bedspread and its lace-trimmed cushions. A small oil painting, very fine, hung over the bed, and there were some handsome leatherbound books on the shelves, things too rich for a housekeeper's salary. They were obviously presents from Rhys to make it up to Dilys for staying on here all alone.

His own room seemed smaller than the last time he had seen it. The bed was much too short for him, but he had learned to sleep on the diagonal. He opened his suitcase and took out his dress uniform as his mother came up the stairs.

♦

"No, Connor!" Dilys said firmly from her rocker while she sewed a button on his jacket. "I will not leave this house tomorrow. Where would we go? We have no home. You have no job."

"I'll get one. Do you want to be a servant for the rest of your life?" he demanded. "In this house, that's all we can be."

So that was it! she thought. Dilys had begged Rhys not to invite him to the ball. Connor understood that, hero or not, his presence tonight would be resented by some people. Her heart ached for her son and his terrible pride that was as much a curse as a blessing.

"It's honest work," she said more gently. "I'm not ashamed of it."

And Connor knew it was hopeless. He had nothing firm to offer her yet, not even a clear ambition about what he wanted to do, not even a plan. All he had was the hundred dollars he had borrowed from Racey after that last spree in Paris, and rent for decent lodgings would be high. On his own, he could live anywhere.

Dilys got up from her chair and came toward him. "Connor, what do you want that you can't have here? You've always loved this place. And we're safe."

"Safe is not enough! I want to be free. Don't you?"

"But I am! I've loved every minute of my life here."

Fast upon her words came the shattering realization that they were true! She *loved* the Brandons. Out of loyalty to Rhys, she was willing to live up here alone most of the year, guarding his precious property. But Rhys had always been a master at making people love him. Connor had loved him from that first day.

"Connor!" Dilys saw the anger in his face, in the rigidity of his body. "Connor?"

He took a deep breath. "Then stay," he said, turning away from her. "But I can't."

"Yes," she said, "I know that now." She said it sadly, as if he were deserting her as heartlessly as his father had. He could not bear for her to believe that.

He went to put his arms around her, flinching from the memory of Enoch's hands touching him that morning. "I'm not like him," he said. "I'll never desert you. It's by your own choice you stay, not mine."

But the appalling truth was that her decision was a relief to him. He needed to be on his own to accomplish anything at all. It would be as difficult for him to take her with him as it was demeaning to leave her.

"I'm not comparing you, son," she assured him. But comparison was inevitable. There was not only the physical resemblance, although Connor was taller, slimmer, and far better-looking than his father, with education and polish. But he had Enoch's hot temper, his pent-up passions, his towering ambition. At least Connor's ambition was for himself and her. Enoch wanted to lead multitudes.

She loved her son dearly, but she loved Rhys too. He had his faults, but he was good to her, generous as a man, and demanding as a lover. The winters in this huge house were terribly lonely with only a small staff to keep her company, but after he was elected to the state senate he would spend almost as much time in Albany as he did in

New York. From Albany it was only a short motor trip to Brandon's Gate. The knowledge warmed her, filling her with both anticipation and apprehension at some of the things he liked to do in bed, evil, erotic things she could no longer resist.

"Don't worry about me, Connor," she said, preparing to go downstairs. "I'll be fine here."

"I'll send for you as soon as I can."

"I know you will."

But she would never leave this house or the man who held her in thrall, not even for her son.

♦

"What is she doing to your dress?" Jillian demanded, coming into Georgia's room. She ignored Peggy, who returned the favor; Peggy was impervious to Miss Jillian's bad manners.

"Taking the bertha off," Georgia said. She stood in her lace-trimmed sheer linen camisole and drawers, watching Peggy snip carefully at the wide pleated-chiffon flounce that had bordered the neckline of her white gown. "It's too fussy for me."

"Mama will have a fit." But Jillian said it idly; she had been saying it for years. Georgia paid no attention to Constance, and that usually inspired Jillian's envy, although on occasion she resented such cavalier treatment of her mother.

Jillian looked at herself in the oval pier glass. Her gown was white crepe de Chine, looped and tasseled with braided silk, the skirt embroidered with tiny flowers. It flattered her figure and her lustrous hair, but she shrugged at her reflection. "It doesn't matter how I look."

Georgia looked up quickly and studied her sister. "Jillian! You promised me."

"All right, all right," Jillian said, pouting. "I won't ruin this stupid party, but I don't really care about it either, not without Peter." Jillian's gloved fingers touched the single strand of pearls around her neck, then patted her hair, while she complained that it wasn't straight and smooth like Georgia's. It was dressed high at the back of her head with one long, burnished curl lying on her shoulder, but no amount of brushing could keep it from waving and curling around her face. She was a striking girl, mature at fourteen and very like Constance, but she was really pretty only when she smiled.

"There," Georgia said, and stepped into her dress. Denuded of its flounce, the chiffon velvet bodice curved in from tiny puffed sleeves and ended at a wide blue taffeta cummerbund set in just below the bosom. Twenty-five yards of white silk chiffon skirt belled out from the cummerbund in extravagant profusion, ending just above Georgia's ankles. Her white silk stockings, like Jillian's, had lace clocks; her shoes were white kid with Louis heels and silver buckles.

She was a head taller than her sister, as long-waisted as her mother had been and with the same regal carriage. Her only jewelry was a strand of pearls and pearl earrings exactly like Jillian's. Her hair, sparkling blond in the lamplight, had been pulled back and wound into a thick coil at the nape of her neck. The simplicity of it accentuated the fine features of her face, the high cheekbones, the intense blue eyes, the patrician nose. She was a woman, not a girl.

"Holy saints," Peggy said, doing up the tiny buttons at the back. "It's marvelous you are."

"Thank you, Peggy." Georgia put on her white kid gloves. "I'll take Mother's lace now." Peggy brought the cloud of lace Georgianna had worn for her portrait and put it across her daughter's shoulders. Georgia nodded, satisfied.

"Do you like it, Jillian?" she asked when Peggy had left the room.

"Why ask me? You're the beauty." Jillian's expression had soured as she watched. "There's no reason for me to go downstairs at all."

"I can think of two. It's your first real party and you want to see Connor."

"He won't know I'm there. No one will, not even Papa. They'll all be gaping at you."

Georgia grew very still. Deep inside her calm was something her sister had come to recognize, a fury that burned like dry ice. Her blue eyes glittered with it now and Jillian looked away.

"I won't listen to it," Georgia said. "You parrot everything she says. You're *letting* her come between us. All right, then. If that's what you want, I'll oblige you."

Jillian, aghast, shook her head. "No! Oh, Georgia, don't be angry! I'm sorry, truly I am." Jillian clasped her gloved hands, then let them fall. "I'm afraid you won't listen to that either, someday."

The two girls looked at each other for a long moment.

"Jillian," Georgia said gently. "I can't hide myself from sight and I certainly won't make Papa hate me so he'll love you better. You'll have to take me as I am."

"I know," Jillian said. "It's because Connor came back and Peter didn't."

Georgia held out her hand and they left the bedroom together. Music rose to greet them from the ground floor of the mansion.

◆

Connor had gone down the front stairs and into the foyer. The house was ablaze with light, and the sound of music drew him across the flower-decked hall and into the drawing room. The guests' eyes followed him as he entered the room, and he was glad of his dress uniform, an armor he would be reluctant to part with. He was conscious of the sky-blue bar on his breast that signified the Medal of Honor, although he did not wear the medal itself.

He would have to best these people on their own terms, without the paraphernalia of war and rank and heroism, but for the moment he was walking on air.

He nodded to some of the faces he had seen often, when he did chores around the house and helped his mother with the children. Now he was a guest, but their expressions, as he had expected, were less than welcoming.

What do they expect me to do, he wondered, grunt and spit on the floor?

He did not speak to any of the women, although he

shook hands with Silas Cassadyne and John Anders. He looked for Adam but he had not arrived yet. And the van Dorns, still in mourning, were not expected.

He crossed the drawing room, cleared for dancing and already filled with men in formal evening clothes, bejeweled women in gorgeous gowns, and girls adrift like butterflies in pastel summer dresses. Georgia and Jillian were not among them.

Constance was standing near a flower-banked fireplace, and he went toward her, wondering, just as Constance caught sight of him, which of them was more surprised by the sight of the other. She had never seen him as a flying officer, and he had never seen her as a woman before, only as the bane of his boyhood. But he was a man now and Constance was ineluctably female, her hair and skin gleaming softly against gossamer champagne lace and row upon row of lustrous pearls.

He looked appraisingly at the glossy woman as he made his way slowly through the throng. With Constance in his bed, what need had Rhys of all those other women?

He greeted Constance with the suggestion of a bow.

Her hand rose but, retrieving her aplomb, she did not offer it. "I might have known you'd come back alive," she said sardonically.

"I appreciate your concern for my safety, ma'am." His smile matched the sting in his voice.

She scrutinized him from head to toe, then raised a silky eyebrow. "The war hasn't sweetened your nature at all," she said.

"Nor yours," he replied.

She regarded him coldly, then turned away and Connor, clearly dismissed, looked around the vast room, relishing his presence in it. His father's last words to him that morning flashed into his mind, but he shook them off and went to get a drink.

"Where's the medal?" Timothy Cassadyne asked, arching a supercilious brow. He handed Connor a cup of punch, but the two young men did not shake hands. Silas Cassadyne had arranged to keep his son out of the war, as had John Anders and Martin van Reitjens. The fathers were untroubled by that, but apparently the sons were not, to judge by Tim's bravado.

"I wear it only on state occasions," Connor said.

"But you're still in uniform."

"By request. It pleases the ladies." He enjoyed Tim's hostility as he had enjoyed Constance's surprise. But Tim had turned away.

"There she is," Connor heard Tim say, and he turned as Georgia and Jillian came into the room.

He had last seen Georgia when she was ten years old, a child in a velvet coat and bonnet. It was, foolishly, how he had thought of her when he answered her letters. The change amazed him.

She had always been a lovely child, but she had become a beautiful young woman, ravishing in billowing white, a stranger to him as they stood looking at each other across the room. Then she smiled and he walked toward her eagerly.

◆

My God, Rhys thought the moment Georgia entered the room, she's the image of Georgianna.

He was transfixed by her. She had always been a beautiful child, but there was something about his daughter tonight that staggered him. It was the one quality her mother had lacked, the true promise of joy that makes a woman, beautiful or plain, irresistible to men. It was the lushness Rhys had sought vainly in Georgianna. This girl, young as she was, was brimful of sensuality. She was ravishing. She was at once his and absolutely forbidden to him.

He swallowed, smothering a passion that must not be, that he could not admit he harbored, not even to himself.

It was a comfort to know that Georgia loved him. Georgianna never had; she had merely shared his interests. Constance's jealousy was flattering, but not fulfilling. And Dilys's worship gratified but did not exalt him. But Georgia loved him and he could monopolize her affections, keep her by his side, guard her from her own temperament, and protect her from other men.

Rhys knew what a sculptor must experience when, his creation emerged from its marble chrysalis, he could polish it to perfection. What a woman he would make of her!

She was smiling radiantly, but not at him, and Rhys followed her glance and saw Connor through her eyes, every inch the rogue male, virile, heroic, seductive. He watched, revolted, as the handsome captain approached his daughter and she held out her hands to him as if she would take him in her arms.

"There's a charming trio for you," Constance said, following her husband's gaze. "Georgia's overjoyed to see him, wouldn't you say? And he's barely noticed Jillian. Ah, now they're a quartet. Timothy looks madder than a wet hen."

Rhys's eyes flicked to Tim. The young man's interest in Georgia was as obvious as his red hair. Timothy wanted to marry her. It infuriated Rhys that he had the right. He was overcome by jealousy, and the nature of his jealousy, monstrous and inadmissible, shook him from his trance.

"Good Lord, I do believe she's turning Timothy down to dance with your protégé, the dashing Captain MacKenzie," Constance said with distaste.

Rhys felt his gorge rise and made no reply. Surely Georgia had more sense! It had been politically desirable for Rhys to welcome a worker hero home from the wars, and a brilliant touch to permit him to attend a party under the very roof that had nurtured him. But it was unthinkable for a mill worker to dance with the daughter of the house—particularly when the mill worker was Connor MacKenzie. The change in Connor—his physique, his manners, his incredible good looks—were no longer proof of Rhys's good judgment in favoring the boy. The boy had become a threat.

What utter nonsense, Rhys told himself. I can handle Connor.

Yet he stood motionless at Constance's side, masking his outrage as Connor led Georgia out among the dancers. He saw Connor's arm encircle Georgia's waist and rest against the warm, pliant flesh beneath her velvet bodice. Would his arm brush against that delectable bosom? Did Connor feel what any man would feel with Georgia in his arms?

"For God's sake," Constance hissed. "*Do* something!"

The couples on the floor went on dancing, but the other guests whispered among themselves about the scene unfolding across the room.

Rhys started forward. He had to get Connor away from her.

♦

Connor had not expected to dance with Georgia or anyone else. He had come to add a final picture to his album of memories, good and bad, about this place. He had come because he was of use to Rhys again—and it was exactly the right moment to tell Rhys he was leaving him forever.

But to dance with this girl in this house before these people was a triumph he had never even considered.

They danced as if they always had, her white chiffon skirt enfolding them in a mist. She smiled at him dreamily.

"I'm proud of you, Connor."

"I'm proud of you too," he said, looking at her with a particular kind of warmth he had never felt for her before.

"Why?" She was delighted, but curious.

"I brought you up," he said. "And that makes you mine." He had not intended to say it.

She looked at him intently, but he was not certain she understood what he meant or the nature of his sudden intoxicating desire for her.

"Thank heaven you came home safely," she said.

"I'm not here to stay."

"I know that." Her prescience startled him until he remembered how well they had always understood each other. "But what will you do?"

"Make my fortune," he said. And come back for you, he thought, but he couldn't say it, not with so many people watching. She was not yet sixteen, too young for such a declaration in public. Throughout her life he had loved

her in many, many ways, but never like this. He had
wanted many women, but she was the first he *had* to
have. He knew what he had to do before he could come
back to claim her, but it was very clear to him. If he had
Georgia, he would have everything.

The quality of the silence between them had altered,
and he thought, *She knows!* She seemed bathed in sensuality, sharing his intense physical awareness and the electricity between them. He could sense the woman in her,
striving to get free, to join him, and he was bewitched by
her passion and the power of his claim upon it, upon her
womanhood, her life. He wanted her. He had to tell her
so. He leaned toward her.

Rhys tapped his shoulder and Connor drew back. He
and Georgia stopped dancing and he became aware of the
people watching them intently. Their outrage was almost
palpable behind a gossamer veil of polite behavior.

To hell with you, he thought. She's worth more than all
of you put together, and *she* wants *me*.

"Georgia," Rhys said with authority, "Constance needs
you for a moment and I have things to discuss with Connor."

"Now, Papa?"

"Georgia, please do as I tell you!" he said. With a last
glance at Connor she walked away, and the two men faced
each other, Rhys slightly flushed, Connor attentive.

"You have something to say to me?" he asked. Again he
savored the prospect of refusing whatever Rhys offered
him.

"Not here!" Rhys replied shortly, but with a pleasant
smile for the onlookers' benefit. "Come with me." He
stretched a friendly arm across Connor's shoulders, careful
not to touch him as they walked out of the drawing room
and down the hall to his study.

◆

Rhys crossed to his desk and rounded on Connor the
moment the door was closed.

"Who gave you permission to dance?" he demanded.
"Who the hell do you think you are?"

Connor's eyes widened in surprise. "Your guest," he shot back. "You invited me."

"I didn't ask you here to dance with my daughter. But a man with breeding would have known that."

Connor stiffened, regarding Rhys as if he had an enemy plane in his sights. "A gentleman does not set limits on his invitations."

"MacKenzie, I want you out of this town tonight, do you hear me? You are to stay away from Brandon property wherever it may be. And you are to keep your filthy paws off my daughter."

"This is about Georgia, isn't it?" Connor said slowly, his fists clenching. "Well, why shouldn't I dance with her? I took care of her from the day she was born."

"Do you suppose that gives you any rights in this house?"

Connor leaned forward, his hands on the desk between them. "You gave me rights when you wanted a boy to play God to. You needed me until after Will was born. Then you treated me like a peasant with house privileges and that's what you want me to be for the rest of my life. But I have other plans."

"Don't take your war record seriously, MacKenzie. No one else will." Rhys hooked his thumbs into his white weskit, his green eyes hard. "You're finished here. And how far do you think you'll go anyplace else? Try getting above yourself and I'll crush you like the vermin you are."

"The worst of you, Rhys," Connor said, using that name for the first time with the impact of a slap, "isn't what you do, even though that's bad enough. What's so contemptible is your monumental indifference to the people you've used as soon as your need for them is over."

"You insolent bastard! Get out of my house or I'll have you horsewhipped."

"No you won't," Connor said. "The publicity would ruin your senate campaign."

"Don't threaten me, boy," Rhys said, instinctively seizing the offensive. "Do you think the press would take the word of a common laborer over mine? Or that I'd hold back out of sentiment? You're nothing to me. You were always nothing. You were expendable from the start. This superficial gloss you've acquired doesn't go deep. We know whose bad seed you are."

I've got to get away from him, Connor thought. He lunged for the door, then stopped and looked back at Rhys. "I'm going now, but I'll be back for Georgia," he said.

She was his ultimate weapon; he knew that now.

"I'll kill you if you come anywhere near her," Rhys shouted.

"I won't have to. She'll find me! She loves me, you fool. She always has and there's not a damned thing you can do about it!"

He slammed the door behind him and strode down the corridor, past the shocked faces of those near the drawing room doors who had heard the sound of furious voices. Careless of the others, he looked swiftly around for Georgia, but she was not in sight, and he heaved open the heavy front door and went out. Tenacious as his memories, the long shaft of light tied him to the house until he disappeared into the shadows.

BOOK II

◆

1920–1924

19

♦

Connor knew that he would be hired by the man on the other side of the desk in this small, neat office near New York's Union Square. Whitelaw was a portly man with thinning hair and deceptively mild blue eyes behind wire-framed spectacles. He looked like a professor; in fact, he was a recruiter of mercenaries to fight in foreign wars.

He was very shrewd as he drew out Connor about his experience as an officer, trying to discern whether Connor was not only discreet but a good judge of men. Anyone in this line of work would have to be.

By now Connor knew he could win over people, men as well as women, if he played to their image of themselves. The man facing him did not consider himself a flesh merchant. That was why he dressed soberly and spoke like a captain of industry, using terms like supply and demand, capital, orders, and commissions. Connor would follow suit when he had something to say. For the moment he just listened, having heard most of it already from Teacher, the casual bar acquaintance who had sent him here.

♦

"You mean you supply mercenaries?" Connor had asked Teacher, amazed. They were drinking scotch whiskey surreptitiously from a flask Teacher carried. The glasses before them held root beer as a sop to Prohibition.

"Me, I just find the bodies," Teacher said with a shrug. "Trouble is, I don't like the work. What I mean, it's okay, but I'd rather be in the fight myself." Teacher, a ruddy, baby-faced ex-pilot in his early twenties, sighed. "There's a lotta guys just like me, so bored they'll bet on whether two flies'll fuck just to liven up the day."

Connor nodded. He could pick them out in any bar, the men who loved war, who were addicted to living on the edge. They were always reminiscing about the war as if it had been a wondrous experience. Their nostalgia for battle had mystified him until he realized that for them life held no other prospect of excitement. Connor craved excitement, too, but of a vastly different kind.

Teacher took a quick pull from his flask. "Hey, MacKenzie, if you don't wanna fight, would you be interested in takin' over my job?" He leaned forward eagerly. "It's easy. The only thing you gotta do is fill whatever orders you contract for. That's why I can't get out yet. This guy I work for is not a guy to cross. Looks like a swell. Talks like one, too, but he's cold as a witch's tit and very smart. He's okay, though, pays well, cash on the barrelhead. What do you think?"

♦

Connor was thinking rapidly as his moment of decision neared. He had nothing to lose—except pride in what he did for a living, and at this point in his life pride was only an obstruction.

The ten dollars in his pocket was all the money he had. His medals had proved as useless as Rhys Brandon said they would, and, when Racey's loan ran out, he had worked at a few poorly paid, futureless jobs—driving a milk van, delivering parcels for a big department store. But starting at the bottom of another ladder was not what Connor wanted. He had been waiting for an opportunity and he was convinced it had just arrived.

He hungered for money. For one thing, he was accustomed to living in the midst of all it bought, and he knew exactly how it would feel to be rich in his own right. In addition to power he wanted a magnificent home, beautiful clothes, gorgeous women, luxurious cars, thoroughbred horses, and a plane of his own.

Futile desires, he had begun to think, until today, when the promise of fast money appeared out of the blue.

Last night, heating his supper of baked beans over a gas ring, he had looked around the shabby room he loathed and at himself, a gaunt and threadbare reflection in the splotched mirror, acknowledging for the first time that Georgia might not be his for the taking, that his sublime scheme for settling his account with Rhys might be as fictitious as that moment with her in the ballroom.

But money could change that.

♦

"You'll get a healthy commission," Jerome Whitelaw was saying, "for every man you sign who reports for departure."

"What's the demand these days?"

"More than adequate. There are always little wars going on around the globe. Now the Russkis and the Poles are going at each other and there's a squadron being organized—the Koskiusko Squadron—to fly against the Bolsheviks." Whitelaw folded his small, well-tended hands. "There are risks, of course. Our business has gone out of fashion in America since the war. An American who sells his services to a foreign army can lose his citizenship, and so can the man who recruits him. You have to be careful whom you approach and what you say."

"I'm not much of a talker, but I listen well," Connor said. "I learn a lot about people that way." The other man was studying him carefully, and he took the scrutiny for a while, then nodded slowly. "I know I'm your man, Mr. Whitelaw," he said with just the right combination of respect and assurance.

The other extended his hand. "I agree. You can take over from Teacher right away."

♦

New York City was his richest hunting ground. A steady stream of disgruntled young men, bored with country life after the glamour of France and Paris, headed for the metropolis and adventure. But as time went on Connor began to travel to neighboring states and beyond at his own expense, concentrating on the larger cities but willing to go to smaller towns as well.

"Come on and have a drink," his new recruits invariably said once their business was concluded, but their company depressed him. The odds were that half of them would be dead within a year.

Still he worked incessantly to fill as many "orders" as Whitelaw offered rather than let other recruiters get the commissions for them.

It wasn't hard to find out where veterans congregated. The clergy usually knew. One group led him to others. In each town he rented a room and spent a few evenings in neighborhood bars, talking or playing cards before he approached anyone. He never divulged his name or his address, and when he returned to a big town he usually found men waiting eagerly for him. Some were running from marriage or family responsibility, some from boredom, some from the law. Most of them just liked to fight.

Their motives were not Connor's concern. If he didn't accommodate them, someone else would.

He had bought some decent, unobtrusive clothes and moved to a more comfortable rooming house that provided breakfast and dinner when he was in New York. He was sending money to his mother every month, despite her protests that she had more than enough. And he was able, at last, to save for a future of which he was still uncertain, except that he *would* do what he had set out to do: make a fortune and take Georgia away from Rhys.

♦

"Be there no later than Friday," Connor told the man he had just signed up in a seedy pool hall in Philadelphia. He passed him a neatly printed card. "There's the address. Use the name I gave you. And don't try to pass that on to a friend, it won't work."

"What do you take me for?" the recruit protested. "But I do know another guy who wants to go, if you're interested."

"Sure thing. What's his name and where do I find him?"

"It'll cost you a fin," the man said belligerently.

Connor studied him, deciding whether or not it was a real lead.

"Would I con a veteran?" the man demanded. "One as big as you?"

Connor gave him five dollars and in the late afternoon took a bus to a small town called Chester. The intense heat of the August day was beginning to abate, and it was pleasant to walk along the quiet, elm-shaded streets. He asked directions of a man watering his lawn and in a few minutes found the street he was looking for.

It was flanked by modest but comfortable clapboard houses with gables, turrets, and wide, screened verandas bordered by flowers, some of them wilted from the heat. It was the kind of town he had not seen before he began traveling. In Brandon's Gate there were either company cottages or mansions, nothing in between.

He turned in at the third house, went up the walk, and knocked at the screen door.

"Harry? Is that you?" a woman's voice called as she came running down the stairs. She was obviously just out of the bath. There was a towel around her hair and she wore a cotton robe. Her face, when she saw Connor, fell instantly from expectation to profound disappointment. "Oh," she said, "I thought you were my husband."

"It's your husband I came to see."

Now she was anxious. "Is anything wrong?"

"No, Mrs. Ritter, I just wanted to talk to him. Could I leave a message for him?"

She stood looking at him for a few seconds, then became conscious of her appearance and began rubbing her pale hair dry with the towel. She must have been pretty once, but she was drab and faded now, like the flowers outside. Connor had seen many women like her on the flats, women whose men had left them. They were not like his mother.

But he was reluctant to add to this woman's misery and

was about to say good-bye and leave when she opened the screen door and motioned him to come in. It was somewhat more appealing than sitting in his sweltering hotel room until train time.

He nodded and went in.

She gave him a cool bottle of soda pop in the kitchen and, quite suddenly, began to talk, as if she had to unburden herself to someone who wouldn't be around to gossip about it later.

Harry Ritter, it turned out, had not stayed at home longer than a month at a stretch since he returned from the war. This time he had been gone for six weeks. He was a good man, a good worker, but he didn't want to hold a job. He didn't want the quiet life they'd led before he went to war.

"If you ask me," his wife said, twisting the belt of her robe, "he didn't want that awful war to end. He liked it."

Connor nodded. "He's not the only one, ma'am. There are a lot of men like that."

"Are there?" It seemed to surprise her. "Are you like that about war?"

"No, I'm like that about money." He surprised himself. He never discussed himself with anyone, but he was sorry for her. The Harry Ritter she had married would never come back, but still she went on hoping, trying to make herself attractive in case he did.

Wasn't that what everyone did, one way or another? She restyled her hair. He was trying to paper himself with money. He felt as miserable as she did.

"I don't understand men," she said dejectedly, and stared into her glass.

"Neither do I sometimes," he agreed. When he came right down to it, Hamlet was the only man he had ever understood—Hamlet and his need to avenge himself against a smiling, damned villain.

A moment later she asked, "What did you want with Harry?"

"To offer him a job—out of the country, I'm afraid. I didn't know about you, or I wouldn't have come."

She looked at him angrily and their rapport, so briefly sparked, vanished. "I suppose you'll ask him anyway when he comes back."

He felt as if he had stepped into the kind of emotional quagmire he had disciplined himself to avoid. He got to his feet. "No, I won't. I'd better go now. Thanks for the drink, Mrs. Ritter."

Suddenly her eyes filled with tears that streaked silently down her cheeks as she gazed up at him. At that moment he felt a kinship with her. Her life was as solitary as his. On an impulse he put his hand over hers for a moment, then left the kitchen. She followed him along the narrow hall toward the front of the house.

"Oh, God," her muffled voice said behind him. "I'm so lonely I could die."

He turned and, moved to compassion by her desolation, he held her for a moment, rocking her gently as she wept. He would have released her, but her arms tightened around his neck and she pressed herself closer to him. He could feel her body through the cotton robe.

"Don't go," she whispered. "Stay with me." Her meaning was unmistakable.

He wasn't sure why he nodded his agreement. Physically she was not the sort of woman who attracted him.

But he had been a long time without a woman. He had not come across one who remotely resembled Megan or any of the girls in Paris, and prostitutes did not attract him. After one experience of fast, mechanical sex, he preferred to do without.

But this woman was different. She was as lonely as he for someone to hold.

They went upstairs to a bedroom at the back of the house and she lay down on the bed. When he was almost naked, she closed her eyes, waiting, and lay perfectly still when he lay down beside her and opened her robe. She had a slim, boyish body, with small breasts and narrow hips. Her hair and skin smelled of dime-store soap, lily of the valley, he thought, and that moved him even more, that pathetic attempt to lure Harry back and keep him.

He kissed her with sympathy for her and Harry and their ruined lives. He stroked her back and her breasts, but when his hand moved between her legs she stiffened in his arms and he realized with surprise that all women were not as adventurous or as knowledgeable as the ones he had known, from blessed Megan to the French dancers. Then she relaxed and let him touch her, and soon she was moist and moaning in his arms and he was aroused and took her. It was a strange experience, more poignant than passionate, but it was a sexual release for both of them and he felt a grateful tenderness toward her. They lay quietly together for a while, then he got up and found the bathroom.

She was still on the bed, her robe chastely closed about her, when he came back and started to dress. He almost accepted her wistful invitation to stay for dinner, but he could not let himself become involved with her—with anyone.

"I have business in Philly," he said.

"Will you come back sometime?" she asked, flushing.

"If I can." He knew he wouldn't. "I don't like to make a promise I'm not sure I can keep."

She smiled sadly at him. "You're a kind man. Most good-looking men aren't."

Kind? He wondered if he was. He used to be, once.

He bent and touched her cheek briefly before he left her, still lying there on the bed, alone in her desolation. He looked for a way to ease her hurt pride. It was much harder than easing her body.

"Your Harry is a lucky man," he said. It was only after he had let himself out and was walking down the twilit street that he realized he didn't know her first name.

It was the first of many encounters he had with women who waited hopelessly for their men to settle down again. The women were sometimes wildly responsive, sometimes passive, always desperately lonely. It had become apparent to him that he was lonely, too, and sometimes he wondered if any woman could banish the sense of isolation that sex only deepened.

◆

"You don't look well," he told his mother anxiously. "Have you seen the doctor?"

"He stops in regularly to have tea. I'm perfectly well, son." She rocked placidly, intent on her embroidery.

He had waited until after Thanksgiving, when Rhys and Constance and the boys were back in their limestone mansion in New York, before he went to Brandon's Gate to see his mother. It disturbed him to be here, although the fire in the grate was cheerful and everything in her rooms new.

Her apartment had been expanded and completely refurnished. His room was now an office where she kept her household accounts and gave orders to the servants, and both old nurseries had been joined to make a separate sitting room for her. The suite was attractive, even luxurious, and cozy, but he had a sense of something missing when he looked at her, as if a light had gone out within her.

"You're too thin," he insisted. "And you must be lonely, rattling around in this great place all by yourself. You could easily find a housekeeping job somewhere else, even in New York City. I never understood why they didn't take you to New York with them in the first place."

"Mr. Brandon wanted someone he could trust to take care of the estate," she said quietly. "And Brandon's Gate is my home, dear."

Her reluctance to discuss her situation was obvious, and he let it go, unwilling to argue when he saw her so seldom.

"How's Georgia?"

"She and Jillian are still in finishing school in Switzerland." Dilys beamed whenever she mentioned her nurslings. She took an envelope from her pocket. "Here's the last photograph they sent me."

He looked at the two girls wrapped in furs in their horse-drawn sleigh like two czarinas. Georgia was dazzling, her long blond hair glinting in the alpine sun. He remembered that she had promised Rhys never to cut it.

"Finishing school!" he said mockingly. "Prison is a better description." Rhys had whisked Georgia off to Switzerland a few weeks after the ball, a clear indication to Connor that the man was anxious.

"But she doesn't answer my letters." Connor frowned, shaking his head. "I'm sure he intercepts them."

Dilys said nothing. He wondered how much she knew about his last argument with Rhys.

"Mother," he said impulsively, "will you enclose my letters to her with yours?"

She recoiled as if he had touched her with a hot iron. "Connor! Don't ask me to do such an underhand thing."

He was startled. "Damn it, what do you think I'm planning to write to her? You can read the letters if you like before you send them."

"It isn't that," she began, then stopped, shaking her head. Her hands were clasped so tightly together that her knuckles were white.

"I see," he said. "He's given orders that there's to be no communication between us."

She was silent.

"And when she asks you for news of me, you tell her nothing—or something vague."

She nodded.

He knelt by her chair, disengaged her hands, and held them to his face. "Mother, please! There'll always be a bond between us, no matter what happens between her father and me! Where's the harm in that?" It was true. Contact was all he wanted now.

Dilys gazed at him, wanting to help him, terrified to help him. Oh, God, she pleaded, what am I going to do? It was not the first time she had been torn between her son and her lover. But how could she risk Rhys's anger? She saw him so seldom these days as it was. That was what was making her shrivel up, outside and in, and she was frantic that Rhys would find her withered and undesirable the next time he came. It made her so anxious that she couldn't sleep without Veronal. That was why Dr. van Dorn came to see her so often.

But this was her son, whom she loved so much and knew so well. She had never believed Rhys's implication that Connor was planning to seduce Georgia. The boy loved Georgia. He could never bring himself to hurt her.

"All right," she told him. "Send your letters to me."

He hugged her fiercely, as he had when he was a boy, and she let him go back to the city with the photograph of the two girls and a promise she was not sure she could keep.

◆

Connor worked harder still after he returned to New York. He traveled almost constantly. He had no time to make new friends, women or men. He worked and watched his money accumulate like a miser. He read. Books were his one extravagance and his room in New York was stacked with them. He lost himself in history, biography, fiction. And he waited for the next opportunity—and a letter from Georgia that never came.

20

◆

"One of our best bachelor flats," said the rotund little man. "Only gentlemen tenants here and a porter," he went on, and added, with a wink, "No ladies except the ones you care to invite yourself. You'll have no complaints from any moralizing matrons."

The apartment was on the second floor of a corner brownstone at Fifteenth Street and Fifth Avenue. It had a large living room, two bedrooms connected by a bathroom, a study, a kitchen, and a small dining room. It was furnished in masculine good taste and with a minimum of bric-a-brac. The color scheme, beige and burgundy against cream walls and Turkish carpets, was consistent throughout, and he liked the feeling of uninterrupted flow it produced.

There were fireplaces in the living room, the master bedroom, and the study. The furniture was man-sized and comfortable, and there were plenty of bookshelves for his growing collection.

He walked through the place a few times, debating whether to spend that much on rent. But he could certainly afford it and, with a little nod of decision, he returned to the living room to tell the agent he would take the place.

"Mind if I put in a bigger bed?"

"Not a bit! The height you are, you need one. We can store this. Anything else, Mr. MacKenzie?"

It was the first time anyone had called him that, and he liked the way it sounded. He had been either Connor or MacKenzie in school and the army, and he was anonymous in his present work.

"Only a cleaning woman once a week."

"I can arrange that for you, sir."

Sir. That, too, fell sweetly on the ear.

Connor knew he looked like a successful young businessman, never mind that he bartered bodies. He had already been to a good tailor for two winter suits, one gray, one dark blue, and an overcoat to add to the corduroy pants and tweed jackets he wore when he was working. Evening clothes and a riding habit were on order; he was impatient to gallop a horse through the park. The store for whom he had delivered parcels during his first year in New York had furnished a supply of linen, shirts, gloves, and hats. His room at the boardinghouse was bulging with new clothes.

All right, then, he *looked* like a businessman. But he did not feel like one and would not until he was in a legitimate profession. Only Whitelaw and Racey, with whom he corresponded regularly, knew what he was doing.

"It sounds as if you hate it," Racey had written in his last letter. "And it's a solitary life. Why not do some flying, even if it's only to deliver the mail?"

"Every veteran pilot," Connor wrote back, "has signed up for a flying job—and they pay next to nothing."

It *was* a solitary life, but he had never had any close friends except Racey and Peter and, during one extraordinary hour in the Argonne, Oliver Petrie.

Peter was gone. Racey was in the Middle East, flying for some Arab sheikh named Faisal, and Connor did not want to know what had become of Oliver Petrie, not with their October 1921 rendezvous only months away.

Maybe Oliver was dead, but somehow Connor did not believe that their odyssey through the forest would end as simply as that. The pledge he had made hung over his head, a promise he could never keep. As he had done many times before, he resolved that Preston City was one place he would never go.

He moved to his new apartment the next day.

◆

"I wonder about you," Whitelaw said.

"Why? I fill every order you give me!"

"Not about that. About you."

Connor eyed him warily.

"I've never met a man," Whitelaw said, "as—what is the word?—as removed as you are."

"Ever consider yourself?" Connor said, relieved to hear that his job was not in jeopardy.

The older man chuckled. "But I'm twice your age. Youth is more gregarious—and more forgiving."

Connor said nothing, and Whitelaw took another tack.

"Well, if you're in the mood for a little diversion, there's a speakeasy in Harlem that calls itself a supper club. The food and liquor are good, the jazz is better. You see lots of show people there."

"I'll consider it," Connor said politely.

The perceptive bastard knows I'm in need of female companionship, Connor thought that evening as he knotted his tie. His evening clothes were not ready, but a speakeasy would accept him in a dark suit. He gave his hair a final brush, eschewing both a center part and brilliantine, then picked up his hat, overcoat, and gloves and went out.

In the taxi he pondered Whitelaw's attempt to personalize their relationship by implying that they might go out to listen to jazz together. They had been working together for two years and neither knew very much about the other, but that was how Connor wanted it. Whitelaw was not the sort of man he could afford to befriend.

The cab stopped at the Dixie Club, an almost elegant establishment with a small, round canopy and a handsome black varnished door lit by two carriage lamps. He went in. There was a second door, and he waited while someone peered at him through the peephole. The door opened and the sound of Dixieland jazz ushered him inside. He had heard that music first on a trip to New Orleans and it was in his blood now.

"Ya'll by your lonesome?" the checkroom girl asked him, cradling his coat as if he were still inside it.

"Yes. Is that allowed?" He took the number she offered him.

Her laugh showed dazzling white teeth against her gleaming black skin. "Sure, honey, but I'll bet ya'll won't be alone for long."

"Good," he told her. "That's the object of the exercise."

"What exercise you have in mind?"

But he was already following the captain to a small table in the front ring next to a tiny dance floor. He ordered whiskey and water. The scotch came in a coffee cup and the water in a carafe. He lit a cigarette and sipped his drink while he ordered dinner from a typical American menu—roast beef, mashed potatoes, peas and carrots, apple pie—and thought about the food at Fouquet's.

He looked around curiously while he waited, encountering the glances directed at him, the men's brief, the women's sometimes lingering. The club was larger than its exterior suggested. It was after nine, and the tables were filling rapidly with well-dressed people, the men in dark suits or evening clothes and most of the women in calf-length sheaths with sheer overdresses that reached the floor. Connor liked fashionable women, and in New York they had a flair he had seen in no other American city. Their hair was cut short and waved close to their heads, and they wore miniature cartwheel hats of feathers, or wide forehead bands of ribbon swagged with beads. The crowd was a cheerful lot, intent on the music. Feet tapped, hands kept time, bodies swayed in the red plush chairs.

The club offered a fair Bordeaux to go with the beef and Connor rolled it gratefully on his tongue. By the time he had finished dinner he was relaxed, warmed by the wine and the music, and very glad he had come out. He ordered a brandy and lit a cigarette.

The lights dimmed and there was a fanfare from the band.

"And now," a voice said, "the Dixie Club is proud to present its latest attraction, that wonderful singer of songs, Miss Tirzah Kent."

A spotlight appeared on the darkened dance floor and a

girl moved into it. She was young, with dark red hair and
slanted, intensely green eyes, the color enhanced by heavy
mascara and green shadow. She wore a long green gown
fringed with crystal beads. Under the spotlight it released
shards of color when she moved. The bodice, held up by
tiny straps, did not restrict her ample breasts. They swayed
seductively as she straightened from her bow. She was
luscious, if not really beautiful, Connor decided, but that
was before she started to sing.

He had never heard a voice like hers. It was like
velvet—no, like the best cognac, smooth but intensely
rich and hot in effect. It had body and strength and a
languor that was overwhelmingly sensual, no matter what
words she sang. She could have sung the national anthem
and it would have made Connor want to put her on a bed
and get as far inside her as his demanding body could go.

She sang five songs, but she had noticed him before the
second one ended and she sang the rest in part to him.
Most of the time she closed her eyes and sang for herself.
He was embarrassingly aroused, and when she raised her
arms—breasts lifting and rounding, hips thrusting forward
to the beat—and begged him to give her what she cried
for, he knew he wouldn't rest until he did.

She disappeared into the wings when the set was over,
and as soon as the wild applause gave way to more jazz he
signaled for the waiter. "Will you ask Miss Kent to join
me?"

"You don't have to ask me," her husky voice said. "I'm
already here." She had an accent he could not place.

He rose and held a chair for her. "What would you like
to drink?"

"Champagne," she said with a one-sided smile that raised
the right corner of her full mouth. "Is there anything
else?"

He ordered it. "I've never heard anyone like you," he
said.

"I've never seen anyone like you."

"What time do you finish?"

"About four in the morning."

He lit her cigarette. "I may not survive until then," he said; it was a clear invitation.

She accepted. "The waiting's the best part."

He shook his head. "Not this time."

Her eyelids closed and she licked her lips briefly. "I think maybe you're right."

They said very little after that. Conversation between them was superfluous at this point and impossible over the music that was as rhythmic as the sex they were both anticipating. She sang three more sets, disappearing backstage after each one, before she joined him again, wrapped in her long cloak, and they left the club and got into a taxi. As if by mutual consent, his hand on her arm was the only contact they had until they were standing in his bedroom. Then he turned her to him and kissed her mouth. Her lips parted and she put her arms around him, blending her body into his. He had never been kissed with such ferocity or such abandon. After a while his hands undid her cloak and tossed it aside, then slid the straps from her shoulders and bared her breasts. Her skin had a glossy, golden cast, like honey.

"My God," he whispered, and sucked her nipples in a sexual frenzy that seemed to feed upon her body. No matter what he did, he wanted more.

They undressed each other, their hands stopping to touch, to tease in a delirious, prolonged frustration until they lay together on the bed. Then the erotic messages they had been sending each other for hours took shape and were played out, syllable by syllable. She lay with her thighs spread wide and now she was like brandy again, soft and wet and fiery until, finally, he could wait no longer and plunged inside her.

She was a strong woman and she gripped him with her thighs and her hands while they climbed violently toward a peak and cried out sharply together when they reached the top and went over it. He was submerged in pleasure and he heard her and felt her and knew she was too.

Still inside her, he kissed her bruised mouth gently. "Stay with me tonight," he said. "Don't go."

She tensed the muscles inside her, gripping him. "Does that feel like I'm ready to go?"

At the end of the week he asked her to live with him, but although she stayed several nights a week she refused a permanent arrangement.

"I want a place of my own," she told him. "I have a lot to do."

If anyone had a prior claim upon her, he was unaware of it. If she slept with any other men when he was out of town, he did not want to know about it. She was sexually volcanic. She wanted him often and in every conceivable way, and it was that powerful lust in her that people sensed when she sang, that made them beg for more. Just to watch her made Connor wild, and when she sang to him he thought he would explode.

"You have skin the color of honey," he told her, his head cradled between her breasts.

"Gypsy father," she said.

"Real Gypsy?"

"Romany. And a Swedish mother."

"Where in hell did they find each other?"

"In a barn in Minnesota."

He stretched out at her side. "I never would have guessed Gypsy."

"Try orphanage. Would you have guessed orphanage?"

He looked at her compassionately. "Bad?"

"The worst—especially for a dark-skinned little bastard." She shrugged. "But it made me tough."

"Tell me."

It was a tale of neglect and abuse from the day she was born. "Until they discovered I had a voice. They had me singing in the church choir! Then I ran away. I hitched a ride to Chicago."

"With a man?"

"Yeah. But all of a sudden I got lucky. He was one of those men who likes women. Sex, of course, but women, too, for themselves. Like you. Anyway, we fucked our way to Chicago, him taking precautions like I was a real lady, and he gave me ten bucks before he left me. I got myself a job as a singing waitress in a bar—and here I am."

"Just like that," he said. "Clover all the way." He put an arm around her. He was achingly sad for her. He could guess some of what had happened to her between then and now. The incredible thing was that despite it all she hadn't turned out cold and careful, as he had.

He turned to her again, seeking her female scent under the bath oil she used, trying to find in her lush body what he had lost in himself.

Tirzah was musk. She was round breasts rising under him, satin thighs yielding to his mouth or straining to encircle him, hands pulling him deep inside her, out of himself. She was a throaty laugh, a dancing tongue, teeth that nipped him, lips that tantalized him. She was joyful.

She was voluptuous and vulgar and untidy. Chairs and sofas were festooned with the things she left at his apartment, a petticoat, a silk stocking, an odd glove. She was lazy about everything but her work, and in that she was as driven as he was. Her goal, after she reached the prime nightclub circuit, was to star in her own revue, with her own musicians. She wanted fame more than money.

"But to perform in the class clubs I need some gorgeous outfits to impress the owners."

"I can help out some," he offered, but she refused. She wanted to do it on her own, to rely solely on herself. He was the same way, and he was relieved by her independence. They both understood ambition; it was as exciting to them as sex.

"You can be as rich as you want," she whispered one night against his mouth, her full breasts pressed to his chest, her hand between his thighs, arousing him by what she did and herself by what she said, "but I'm gonna be famous. I'm the best goddamn singer in this whole fuckin' country and someday everyone's gonna know it."

"You're the most goddamn woman in this country," he replied. "Who else knows that?"

"Do you really care?" She climbed on top of him and slid down onto him, her hips circling slowly.

He shook his head, deaf to her words, consumed by his desire for her.

Later, he reflected that he would have preferred to have her to himself, but that the idea of her coupling with another man did not make him murderously jealous. She was not the kind of woman who thought of sex as anything but pleasure. It was neither a pledge nor a guarantee against loneliness to her, only a sensation, an appetite to be satisfied. It meant no more to her to sleep with a man than to share a thick, juicy steak with him.

When he thought about it again, en route to Baltimore to find men who would put down the anticipated rising in Brazil, he realized that he had never been jealous of a woman and never would be.

He was making money, he was making love. For the moment, it was enough.

◆

Connor slowed his horse to a jaunting trot and then to a walk.

The park was at its best in May, a vast cloud of pale green leaves and early blossoms rippling in the breeze. But he was catapulted by cruel memory back to Jezebel and Brandon's Gate, the sweep of green lawn from the driveway to the house, the majestic trees splashed by forsythia, Dilys under the big oak with three small boys, and Connor reading a story to Georgia and Jillian.

What would happen when the girls had been "finished" in Switzerland? Rhys had total control over his children until they reached majority at twenty-one, and he would certainly exercise it as long as he could. How would Georgia feel about her childhood hero by then?

He remembered the exquisite girl he had held in his arms for the too brief moments of a waltz, a girl he desired because she was lovely and wanted because she was the surest way to punish Rhys.

His spirits plummeted again. She had probably believed her father's version of events, whatever it was, or she would have answered Connor's letters long before this.

Her devotion to Rhys might be stronger than passion—if passion was what she had felt for Connor that night. Each day that passed made it seem more unlikely. What would a sheltered fifteen-year-old girl know of passion?

He shook his head and concentrated on Rhys again.

"I wonder why he's not a state senator yet," he had written to Racey. "The business boom has come to an end, but that doesn't seem to have affected Brandon Textiles. Of course, I mustn't forget that Rhys is immune to the afflictions of ordinary men."

"I wish to hell you'd forget about Rhys!" Racey wrote back.

Connor had always known that Rhys's comeuppance, beyond his loss of Georgia to the man Rhys despised most, had to be plotted. It would not simply come to pass, arranged by a just fate.

A tall blond girl came toward him on the bridle path, the sight of her jostling him from his thoughts, and for a moment Connor's breath caught in his throat. But she was not Georgia.

She cantered past him with a brief sidelong glance, and Connor was alone again, this time with a different memory of Georgia's face, that beautiful face he had watched from infancy to girlhood. It was suffused by the perfect trust that had been the pride of his childhood and the comfort of his youth.

He saw Georgia as a baby, a toddler, a little girl, and, for the first time since he had stalked away from Brandon's Gate, the impulse to possess her—was it because she was Rhys's or because she was his?—struggled with his impulse to protect her.

Frustrated by the contradiction, he cantered his horse back to the stables and took a taxi home.

"Tirzah?" he called.

"I just got out of the tub. I'm about to get dressed."

He was half out of his clothes. "No, you're not. Not yet." He strode into the bathroom, naked and hot, and swept her onto the bed, enveloping her, trying to hide himself in her lushness, to bury in her what he could not confront in himself, that intensity of lust and love, of wanting so much more than he had—and Georgia too.

"Holy shit," she breathed when they both lay panting on the bed. "What got into you?"

He looked down at her, his eyes as black as night. "Do you care?"

"Hell, no." She stretched. "But I'd love a cup of coffee."

She dressed and went into the living room to read the paper while she drank her coffee.

"He's the one who calls every now and then, isn't he?" she asked, waving the front-page photograph of Enoch at him.

"Since he suddenly remembered I was his son," Connor said cynically. "I don't know him very well."

"He's doing a great job for working folks, according to this article."

Connor poured himself a cup of coffee and sat down opposite her, pausing to light a cigarette. He took little satisfaction in the astonishing fact that his father was more widely recognized by the public than any labor organizers except John L. Lewis and Samuel Gompers.

"Why wouldn't he?" Connor said finally. "He always cared more about working folks than he did about my mother and me."

"Men do rotten things," Tirzah said with an expression of disgust. "And the mean ones do them on purpose. He's got guts, though. He gets what he goes after, the same as you and me. You have to give him credit."

"I don't have to give him anything." Connor finished his coffee and got up. "What I have to do is pack a bag. I'm going to Ohio tonight."

"Okay, I get the picture," Tirzah said, turning the page of the newspaper. "The subject of Daddy is closed."

But for Connor the subject was never closed. Wherever there were workingmen, there was Enoch, exhorting them to organize. He hung over Connor's life like a dark cloud and, as if that were not enough, he persisted in telephoning at odd intervals, even though Connor invariably hung up on him.

On the train Connor sat in the club car with a whiskey and water, taking stock of the past year. It had been a prosperous one for him. The country was in an economic slump, but his business didn't suffer because of it—or anything else. War was always in style somewhere in the world.

But the money he had accumulated gave him the same kind of satisfaction Tirzah did: it was an attribute of triumph, not triumph itself. For that he needed millions, and he watched the slow growth of his bank account with impatience, feeling that he was in a race against time.

When he finally got into the berth of his Pullman drawing room, he forgot everything but his destination and the man he was going to see.

◆

Connor paced nervously in the library of Oliver Petrie's house in Preston City. The room was very like the library at Brandon's Gate, and he wondered if the homes of the wealthy were all alike and why he had lacked the will to stay away from this one.

When the door opened he was prepared to see the wheelchair; he had heard about it from the taxi driver who brought him up from the station and would return for him in an hour. What shocked him was Oliver's white-streaked hair, his stony face—and the absolute despair in his thickly lashed brown eyes, as beautiful as a woman's. Connor had never seen this man in daylight with his eyes open.

The sight made his throat ache, and he pushed back the gasp that almost escaped him.

Oliver dismissed the butler and rolled himself across the room toward Connor. The two men studied each other.

"So that's what Captain MacKenzie looks like," Oliver said.

"Connor."

"Talk to me, will you? I know you better as a voice in the dark." Oliver closed his eyes momentarily.

"I wasn't going to come," Connor said in a hollow voice. "You must have known that."

"No. I had your word of honor." Petrie opened his eyes.

"My honor?" Connor shook his head. What had honor to do with him?

"But you *are* here, aren't you? Have a drink." Oliver rolled his chair to an open bar near the window and poured two drinks from a crystal decanter. "Armagnac," he said. "The only drink for us, I think. Sit down."

In his wheelchair he seemed a much taller man than he actually was. There was an authority about him that was not at all military but sprang, Connor suddenly perceived, from having nothing more to lose.

"I haven't come for a chat," Connor said, needing to know what he was in for.

"As you wish," Oliver said, handing him a glass. "I've abandoned the idea of suicide for the present. If I should change my mind, I won't need you to help me."

Connor sat down and took a deep swallow of the brandy. "I wish I'd known that."

"You would have if you'd telephoned."

"I was afraid to. Tell me what happened."

"There isn't much to tell. There's a piece of shrapnel still lodged in my spine. Removing it could either cure me or paralyze me completely. I won't chance paralysis. I'd be completely at my family's mercy then."

"What in hell do you mean by that?" Connor demanded.

"Their cheerfulness is appalling. They pretend I sit in this chair on a whim. If I were paralyzed, they'd pretend I'd chosen to lie still." The desolate brown eyes looked steadily at Connor. "*They* are very grateful to you for saving my life."

"Christ," Connor whispered. "Jesus Christ."

"Yes." Petrie sipped his drink. "But I have a son who's too young for hypocrisy. Children are refreshingly honest. He's horrified by my condition, but he loves me. He needs me. I've stayed for his sake." He took Connor's empty glass, held it between his knees, and rolled his chair to the bar to pour more Armagnac. "I'm a lot better off than the wounded who had their limbs chopped off or their eyes blown out or their faces ripped away. They try to tell me I'm a lot better off than the dead."

For a searing moment Connor was in a hospital room in France holding Peter in his arms. *I'm here*, he heard himself whispering to Peter. *I'm here*. But he was as useless now as he had been then.

"We've been more or less forgotten, haven't we?" Petrie was saying. "I plan to do something about that."

"What, exactly?" Connor could not have managed another word.

"I'm not sure yet. I have to find out where the power is." He drank, studying Connor over his glass.

"Remember the man I told you about that night?" Connor said, recovering himself. "He thinks power lies in political office."

Oliver looked into his glass. "I don't recall having talked about anything but our agreement that night."

"No, you were out of your head with fever," Connor said. You damned fool, he cursed himself. In the clear light of day, what man would say the things Major Petrie had, plunging them both into an intimacy that went far beyond friendship? "But you're a natural for politics."

"You mean that even if the voters hated my politics they'd have to elect my legs."

"Obviously," Connor said steadily. Pity was not what Oliver wanted. "You'd be a fool not to make the most of them. What *are* your politics anyway?"

Oliver smiled as if he welcomed a conversation without pretense. "I'll make them up as I go along," he said. "For the moment I want to get something done for our veterans. The way people ignore it, you'd think a war that killed over one hundred thousand Americans never happened."

"That many?"

"Yes, that many, in battle or otherwise." He shook his head. "There's nothing I can do for our dead, but maybe I can help the living. I sit somewhere between them."

There was a silence.

"And I put you there," Connor said hoarsely. "With my goddamned good intentions!"

There were voices from the hall, one of them a woman's. The two men gazed at each other without a word as the door opened and Oliver's wife came in.

She was a slim, shapely brunette with a heart-shaped face. She wore a dark wool jersey dress with a white collar and cuffs. A perpetual virgin, Connor thought, the kind who makes love with her teeth clenched. Placing a hand on Oliver's shoulder as if she were posing for a Victorian photograph, she said how happy she was to welcome the man who had saved her husband's life.

"He couldn't tell us what you looked like," she said, at once demure and flirtatious, a dove among eagles.

Connor disliked her intensely, but Oliver covered her dainty hand with his in what Connor saw was a perverse pride of ownership. The man was still in love with her, clutching the chains that bound him! Did they make love? Could he? Would she? Did she even care?

"You must stay for dinner," she said, but Connor shook his head, glancing at his watch.

"I have to be in Columbus tonight on business."

"What business are you in?" Mrs. Petrie chirped.

"Real estate," Connor said. He had written the same lie to Georgia in one of the letters she had never answered. Georgia was worth ten of this woman. He held out a hand to Oliver.

"Thanks for coming," Oliver said.

"Good luck, whatever you decide to do."

"You must come again soon," the woman said.

The two men looked at each other, Oliver's eyes blank, Connor's despairing, before he murmured an excuse and walked quickly from the room and out of that house, shaken by his part in the tragedy it harbored. He would not see Oliver again. He could not bear to see his guilt objectified.

Never again! he swore as the taxi rolled away. No more benevolent tinkering with other people's lives! Whatever the intent, it always ended in disaster. Rhys was the only exception: in his case disaster *was* the intent. But Oliver had vindicated Connor's resolve to stay at a safe remove from everyone else.

As the train sped on to Chicago, he contemplated the irony of his having saved one man only to send so many others away to fight. With distance, though, he was able to separate the two issues, and he flatly rejected any moral judgment of the mercenaries or himself. War was what they wanted. He wanted something else, and not all the moralizing in the world was going to keep him from getting it.

21

♦

"**C**heckmate," Jerome Whitelaw said, and relit his cigar. The ceiling light glistened on his bald pate as he contemplated the board. "You're a crack chess player, MacKenzie. That's because you have an analytical mind and an incredible memory. But sometimes you're impetuous. Restraint is the secret of success, in chess as in life."

Connor, accustomed to these little homilies, tabled his king and leaned back in the wooden chair in Whitelaw's office, where they always played. His own apartment would have been far more comfortable, but it was littered with bits of Tirzah's wardrobe, with her dog-eared novels, half-eaten boxes of chocolate, and whatever sheet music she was working on at the moment.

He glanced at his watch. It was time to go home, change into evening clothes, and make the first show at

ValRae's, the swank nightclub where Tirzah headed the bill. She was right on schedule in her climb to the top.

But another year had gone by and time was slipping away from him. The distance between what he had and what he wanted never seemed to narrow. Connor had accumulated twenty thousand dollars, a small fortune in a country where a family lived comfortably on two thousand a year, but he could not bring himself to risk it on anything that wasn't absolutely sure.

Fool! he berated himself regularly. Sure things don't make big money fast. And still he hesitated.

"What's your position on armaments?" Whitelaw said, scrutinizing Connor closely.

"How do you mean?"

"This country is violently pacifist, if I may use two mutually exclusive terms. Would you object to selling guns?"

"Not if it pays well."

"It pays extremely well."

"I assume you have the buyers, but where do we find the merchandise?"

Whitelaw emptied his glass and got up to refill it, pouring a second drink for Connor. "Sometimes from the manufacturers, more often from people who buy up second-hand goods and warehouse them, waiting for people like us."

Connor nodded. "There must have been a lot of warehousing after the armistice."

"And more since we brought our last troops back from Germany."

"I thought the bootleggers had a corner on the market."

"Far from it. The international market is much bigger than they are, and we already have an inside track to foreign buyers. The whole thing makes good business sense for us." Whitelaw rubbed his hands together in a rare display of enthusiasm. "Do you know there are countries that'll pay well for Civil War muskets?"

He went on to outline the terms and conditions of the trade. He would find the buyers and take seventy percent of the profits at the outset. When Connor had built up a reliable string of suppliers, they would split sixty-forty. "Well, what do you say?" he finished.

"When do I start?"

Whitelaw permitted himself a bleak smile. "Not tonight. Next week will be soon enough. You can start with a supplier in Boston."

"Fair enough." Connor got to his feet. "Now, I have a few things to do before seeing the New Year in." He held out his hand. "Thanks for cutting me in on the new deal."

"I hesitated for a while," Whitelaw said with his swift, dry handshake. "I know you'll leave as soon as you have a big enough stake."

"I never pretended otherwise," Connor said, waving as he went out the door.

He had to do something soon, no matter how much these arms sales might bring in. He wanted control, not a share of someone else's business. He thought about it while he bathed and dressed in white tie and tails, a shiny top hat, and a fur-collared overcoat, then caught a taxi to ValRae's.

◆

He was shown to his usual table a few minutes before Tirzah's first set began. A moisture-beaded bottle of Dom Pérignon lolled in a bucket and Russian caviar was heaped in a cut-glass bowl surrounded by shaved ice and garnished with triangles of toasted bread and dishes of finely chopped egg and onions. It would see him through the set. Then he would have dinner with Tirzah in her dressing room.

Before he had finished the first glass of champagne the lights went down and Tirzah, her entrance heralded by a blare of trumpets, walked into the spotlight. She wore a red satin sheath so tight it strained across her crotch. Rows of rippling silk fringe spilled from the bodice to the hem. A pouf of red chiffon sat on one shoulder, and a wide swathe of the airy fabric billowed from it and cascaded to the floor, moving when she did. There was a wide, glittering gold band around her forehead, and she wore long, narrow marcasite earrings that brushed her shoulders.

When the applause subsided she held out her arms. "Do it again," she invited in her husky, suggestive voice, and there wasn't a man in that room who didn't want to. "I may say no," she sang slowly, then, sliding down the scale, "but do it again." She sang from the pit of her stomach with all she had, the way she did everything.

He was lucky to have found her.

Connor gave himself to the crisp, dry champagne, the tangy caviar, and Tirzah's performance. When the set was over he went back to her dressing room, followed by a waiter wheeling a table with their dinner.

"Leave the covers on," Tirzah told the waiter, kicking off her shoes. "I'm not ready to eat yet." When the man had departed she grinned at Connor. "Well?" she asked, coming to put her arms around his neck. "How was that for a top-of-the-bill opening?"

"Fantastic." He kissed her and her hands moved swiftly to her back to open her dress. It made petals of red on the floor, and she stood at their center, naked except for her black silk stockings and round red garters.

"Success makes me horny," she said, unbuttoning his trousers and stroking him erect. "Ummm," she murmured with satisfaction at his arousal. She moved her hips hard against him. "Lock the door," she said.

He did and took off his clothes. She lay voluptuously on the couch, stroking her triangle of russet hair, waiting for him. He knelt by her side, parting her secret inner lips with his mouth, seeking and stroking her soft flesh with his tongue.

"Oh, yes," she said, her hand tight around him, "oh, yes, yes, now."

They made love quickly and violently. Her fingers raked his back and he was glad she bit her nails. The sound of the jazz in the nightclub covered their sounds of delight. Then they washed, dressed—Tirzah in a green gown this time—unlocked the door, and sat down to dinner like two sober citizens.

He reached into his breast pocket. "I brought this to celebrate your opening," he said, handing her a rectangular velvet box.

She opened it and looked up questioningly from the rope of pearls he had selected that afternoon at Tiffany's. "Hey," she said, "these are gorgeous. But what's the occasion?"

"I just told you." He was suddenly nervous, as if he had just taken an irrevocable step.

She dangled the pearls in one hand and put down her fork, appraising him. "I've had other openings. So why tonight? Hey, Conn, you're not getting serious, are you?"

Was he? It took him by surprise that he might be. Maybe he had had enough of living alone, year in, year out. Tirzah was the best company in the world, as a lover and as a friend, but Tirzah wasn't always there when he wanted company. He drank some champagne before he answered, venturing nearer the brink of marriage with every word he said, like a man flirting with fate, leaving the final decision to something extrinsic to himself, letting her decide.

"I don't know," he said. "But I'd never have made it through the past few years without you, and no one else could live with either of us. What if I were serious?"

She shook her head decidedly, but her voice was gentle. "No, Connor. You're a great guy, but I can't marry anyone until I get where I'm going, not even you."

He sat looking at her, his relief equaled by his astonishment at what he had almost done. *Why* had he done it? He wasn't that lonely! Tirzah was not the kind of wife he had to have to do what he had set out to do. Or was he beginning to think she was the only kind of wife he could get, a woman with a murky past and no social standing at all?

And what of Georgia?

"Okay," he said lightly. "I just thought I'd ask."

She picked up her fork and speared a piece of steak. "You want the pearls back—or will you take it out in trade?"

He smiled wickedly. "Eat your dinner, woman," he said. "You're going to need your strength."

♦

He liked Jack Dickinson, the square, apple-cheeked man who met him at the Boston station with a neat little Marmon roadster and drove him to a warehouse on the outskirts of the city. It was lined with bins containing weapons of every kind: pistols, revolvers, muskets, rifles, grenades, even gas masks.

"But this," Dickinson said, cradling a Thompson submachine gun tenderly, "is the star of the show."

Connor recognized it. They had called it a trench broom during the war. It was a Tommy gun now. The weapon was accurate and easy to fire with a .45 caliber automatic pistol round.

"The stock is removable," Dickinson said. "Very convenient for firing out of car windows. Makes it popular with the mob."

"Do you sell to the mob?"

"Are you crazy? Anyone gets mixed up with those guys can get his nuts shot off. No, I deal strictly with foreigners itching to take over each other's countries. More power to 'em, I say. The Thompson's the top of the line, but if you want cheaper merchandise, I have that too."

Connor made his selection, settled on a price, and arranged for delivery to a cargo ship in Boston harbor that was headed for the Middle East.

"Where do you find this stuff?" Connor asked.

"Around and about. Some of it's foreign made, some grown in America. Some secondhand, some new from people like Winchester, Remington, Lamartine, or Crabtree out of Troy. Small stuff but some of the best when we can get our hands on it."

"I didn't know there were any munitions factories in Troy," Connor said. "But these days they don't advertise, do they?"

"I like doing business with a guy like you," Dickinson said on the way back to town. "You don't fool around.

Now, how about some of the best lobster you ever ate for lunch?"

They went to a place near the Charles River, picked out two enormous lobsters from the tank, and had a drink at the bar while they waited. It was an open bar, with bottles of imported liquor ranged behind it.

"Hasn't this town heard of Prohibition?" Connor asked.

Dickinson beamed. "Sure, but we don't pay any attention to it and neither do the police. Anyway, you and me got nothing to worry about. It's a crime to sell the stuff, not to drink it."

Connor knew it was the same in Harlem, in San Francisco, in Rhode Island, places where Prohibition did not seem to exist, where the liquor was authentic and reasonably priced. In those places the Volstead Act had virtually been repealed.

The lobsters were succulent and they had brandy with their coffee. "It's a shame you can't stay tonight," Jack said. "I know some girls as juicy as those lobsters."

"Sorry," Connor said. "Maybe next time."

"You got two hours before your train," Jack said, looking at his watch. "Want to stop by a bucket shop on the way?"

"What's a bucket shop?"

"Some places sell stocks, but in this place you can bet on them. You know, a wire from the New York Stock Exchange."

Connor was curious. "Bet on stocks—or buy them?"

"Bet on them. If you bet a stock'll go up and it does, you win. Or you can bet it'll go down. It pays even better if you say how many points."

"But how can you figure the odds?"

"Some guys try to. I just play it like a game. Come on, I'll show you."

It was a busy place in a second-rate hotel. The walls were completely covered with columned blackboards. Clerks in gray smocks stood on ladders, chalking prices in frantically as the exchange moved to its three o'clock closing.

The columns were divided into categories of stock traded,

among them railroads, utilities, mining, automobiles, and banks. Every entry on the board represented the offering price of a share in American industry and Connor, who had never seen the economic heart of the country displayed this way, was fascinated.

"The prices change so fast," he said to Dickinson.

"Yeah. Faster every day lately—and mostly up. I tell you, this market beats horse racing." Dickinson's round face was flushed. "If my Radio stock stays up, I'll have won me fifty bucks."

"Hell, Jack, you made a lot more than that on our deal this morning."

"Sure, but I had to work for it. This is play money."

Connor made no bets but he watched the board, concentrating on several stocks that seemed most volatile.

"If a man had enough money to buy those shares of stock," he said to Jack, "he could make a fortune in a few months."

"Or lose one. Me, I like this. I have to buy a form to dope out the horses, but this"—he waved a hand expansively—"is plain fun. And there's the bell!" He clapped Connor on the shoulder. "What'd I tell ya?"

Jack collected his winnings and they went back to the Marmon and headed for the railroad station, Connor talking about the rises and falls in various stocks.

"Hey," Jack said. "You write down all those figures?"

"No. I have that kind of memory. I have to see something only once and it's there for as long as I want it. For example, the serial number on that Thompson you showed me is C25489—and it had a tree on the barrel."

"I'll be damned! You sure?"

"Check on it when you get back. I suppose that was made by Crabtree."

"Yeah," Jack said. At the station he extended a large, warm hand. "Nice knowing you, Connor. And keep your eyes open. A memory like yours must be worth something."

On the train heading south, Connor decided he was right. That panorama of American business, charted with its amazing rises and falls, had sparked something in him.

He knew he had found what he was looking for, although he was not certain in precisely what way. It was too important a discovery to take lightly—or to bet on in a bucket shop. The next day, he decided, he would go down to Wall Street to take a look at the New York Stock Exchange. Then he would go to the library.

Almost everything that was known, Adam had always taught him, could be found in a book.

◆

It took him only a short time to understand how the market worked. Daily attendance in the Visitors' Gallery became his habit when he was in New York, and by summer the sixteen thousand square feet of the Exchange were familiar to him.

He knew which stocks were traded at each of the counters around the Exchange—United Aircraft at One, Chrysler and General Motors at Two and Four respectively, and RCA Radio, the one that most fascinated him, at Post Twelve. He knew the closing prices of all of the stocks he had followed over the past thirty days.

Among them, Brandon Textiles was still doing well, although cotton had plunged last year from forty cents a pound to ten, which meant that Rhys's mills were supporting his plantations. The price of Brandon stock was down as a result.

Soon Connor shared the conviction, dear to Wall Street regulars, that business in America did not begin until the gavel hit the gong at 10 A.M., and that business stopped dead at 3 P.M. on weekdays and noon on Saturdays. Connor always arrived in time to watch the superintendent of the Exchange make his way to the pulpit and stand with watch in hand before he struck the gong. As if by magic, scores of telephonists, tube attendants, clerks, and page boys sprang to life and the floor began to fill with paper— buy-and-sell orders, notes, memos, ticker tape.

"I recognize some of the members already," he told Tirzah. "They're the only people permitted to trade on the floor."

"And you want to be one of them?"

He nodded. "It's the big wheelers among them who fascinate me, men like Michael J. Meehan, who organizes pools. When they start buying, the price of a stock rises, and when the public gets on the bandwagon, prices go through the roof. He's making a fortune in Radio shares."

"It sounds crooked to me," Tirzah said.

"But it's perfectly legal!" Connor said excitedly. "All it takes is plenty of working capital."

"And a little madness," Tirzah protested. "A fella could lose his shirt."

"Not if he knows what he's doing."

His conviction grew that he had found his Mecca. He liked to walk through the financial district. The narrow streets bulged with energy. Here were housed the headquarters of the country's largest corporations, trusts, and banks, reaching steadily outward to world commerce and finance. But it was the Stock Exchange itself that was better than a shot in the arm to him. Beyond the commotion and din, the excitement of power was palpable, incredible, infectious.

The only thing that eased the tension inside him was flying. Whenever he could he went to a Long Island field and hired a plane for a few hours. He dreamed that one day he could buy his own plane. He knew just what he wanted: a Handley-Page four-seater.

In March he opened an account with a small brokerage house and began to make cautious investments.

"You have a keen instinct for the market, Mr. MacKenzie," his broker told him after the first month.

"When it follows the laws of supply and demand, all you need is logic."

"True. But there are—other forces at work, aren't there?" the man said with a wink. "The trick is to find out what they are this week."

Connor nodded. There were trends—and then there were men who created them. There were pools to manipulate stock prices—the bulls buying them up or the bears selling them down as their stock positions dictated—and they made millions in a week, sometimes in a day. It was what Connor had decided to do, but it took a small fortune to make a big one and it would take time for him to earn a fortune.

He was jealous of the time he spent filling orders for Whitelaw. On the other hand, he was gratified by his burgeoning bank account. He put his books aside and spent every spare moment studying the industries that interested him most and everything that affected them.

"Everything matters," he told Tirzah, determined to interest her in his other passion. "Behind each major industry are the natural resources it depends on. Behind the resources are the workers who get the minerals—coal, iron, whatever—out of the ground. Behind the workers are the unions. You have to watch everything from strikes to the weather to be able to call the shots."

"The only shot I want comes in a glass," Tirzah said. "I never thought I'd live to see the day you'd sit stark naked on this settee with me and talk about stocks!"

"Any complaints?" he asked.

"Listen, honey, if you get a kick out of watching numbers, go right ahead." She eyed him speculatively. "It isn't what you're doing that baffles me. It's how you've changed."

"How do you mean?"

"Ever since I met you, you've been looking back. Now you're looking ahead—some."

He knew it was true the moment she said it. Rhys was still the negative force that drove him, but there was something new: a positive force that pulled him forward, a quest for power not measured against Rhys Brandon.

♦

His obsession with the market accelerated. He could smell success, like a ripe apple hanging just beyond his reach.

He had hit upon a way to get the investment capital he needed. He would buy direct from a manufacturer of light arms without paying commissions to middlemen like Jack. A few big orders was all he needed to put this behind him forever.

The big arms manufacturers were pretty well married to their dealers. What Connor needed was a smaller, more independent outfit. He had a list of several possible suppliers, among them Capitol Industries in Detroit and Crabtree in Troy. He decided to try Crabtree first, and went up to Troy at the next opportunity to introduce himself—under one of the names he used for arms deals—to the executive vice president in charge of "small sales," a euphemism for discreet sales to political factions of which the federal government did not officially approve.

"Expecting something big?" Edwin Trask inquired genially after Connor had made some preliminary inquiries.

"Several things," Connor said, persuading himself that the really big deal could not fail to materialize soon.

"We take a twenty-percent deposit on order, balance on delivery. No credit, no exceptions. That all right with you?"

Connor placed an order then and there, with his own funds, to build up a rating with Trask—and moved the arms two weeks later. He was in a state of feverish activity, filling orders by day and charting market trends by night. He gambled carefully, judiciously, and he waited, researching companies, small and large, that caught his eye.

His research was always to his benefit—but sometimes it led to dismay. Wherever there was industry, there was Enoch.

◆

Enoch roared with laughter when Neeley Mack told him about Connor and his latest sideline.

"Made himself a couple thousand in one hour playing the market," Neeley said glumly. But Neeley was always glum.

"Now, that's what I call class," Enoch declared with satisfaction, feeling he had attained a modicum of class himself. He glanced at his clean, manicured hands and noted with particular pleasure the quality of his suit fabric. That his garments invariably looked rumpled two minutes after he put them on, that his shirt collars seemed to curl up no matter where he had them made, was something of a trial. Still, he earned five thousand a year as ambassador-at-large to any union who needed him, and workingmen were not interested in fashion.

In point of fact, Enoch's real reason for pursuing sartorial splendor was the son he never saw. Connor had fiercely repulsed the few attempts his father made to establish even a limited relationship between them. It would take time, Enoch convinced himself, and he kept on trying because that was his nature.

This office in Philadelphia was where he held court and where his faithful retainers came with whatever information they had been sent out to gather about a given industry: how many workers, at what wage, for how many hours of labor, for what age of worker, and under what conditions. Was there compulsory company housing and a compulsory company store? Most important of all, what was the degree of worker discontent?

There was one kind of information gathering, though, that Enoch entrusted only to Neeley Mack. It concerned Connor and, lately, Dilys too.

He became aware of his companion's discomfort and looked sharply at Neeley. "What else?" he demanded.

"You ain't gonna like this," Neeley warned.

"Speak."

"Yer missus is still there at the Hall," Neeley said.

Enoch's heavy brows curled into a frown of surprise. A few months back Neeley had finally found the courage to tell him what had been common knowledge at the Gate for years: his wife was Brandon's mistress. If the man had been anyone else but Brandon, Enoch might have let the matter slide. But Brandon? The father Connor preferred to his own flesh and blood?

Enoch's rage against the man was not on his wife's account—Dilys had certainly had no choice—but on his son's.

Connor must have found out about it. That must be why he had abandoned his former idol, why Connor had walked away from Brandon's Gate and all it offered, to live like a beggar before he got into supplying mercenaries and guns.

Dilys's situation offered Enoch a way to ingratiate himself with Connor while soothing his own conscience. Two months earlier Enoch had sent Dilys enough money to escape her bondage—only to discover today that she had not considered it bondage at all!

"Jesus!" Enoch muttered, working his jaw like an English bulldog. So, not content with Connor's worship, Brandon had appropriated Dilys's too!

"My wife!" he barked, an irrational jealousy seizing him, fueling the fire of his animosity toward Rhys. "That son of a bitch seduced my wife," he rumbled.

"Hell, Enoch, ya ain't seen 'er in near on twenty years."

"She's still my wife!" Enoch said, his face a dangerous red. "When you marry a woman and get a son by her, by God, she's part of you for life."

"Yeah," Neeley said, watching the big man seethe. "I guess so."

Enoch sat hunched in his chair, staring at the leaden sky outside his office window.

"What about the Brandon mill workers?" he asked after an extended silence.

Neeley shrugged. "He wanted them to vote him state senator, so he raised wages and made things real cushy before the election. His workers wouldn't unionize for nothin'."

"Then we'll go for his southern mills."

"Now yer tawkin'," Neeley said with one of his rare, gap-toothed smiles. "It'll take time," he warned. "He's in thick with the police down there, and he's got guards and dogs of his own, like the resta them owners."

"Fuck him and the owners together with him," Enoch said. "I don't care how long it takes. I'm going down there to get it started. Meantime, keep an eye on my kid. I wish to God he'd stop flying around in those bloody machines. It's unnatural! He must like gambling with his life. Some of those gun runners he deals with are bad people."

"You'd think he had enough money by now," Neeley said.

"No. He wants something he thinks only a fortune of money can buy."

"What?"

"I wish I knew," Enoch said. "I'd get it for him."

22

♦

Connor came back from Baltimore to find a taxi in front of the brownstone and Tirzah just leaving his apartment. She was working at the most exclusive speakeasy in town, the Club El Fey on West 40th Street. Its hostess, Texas Guinan, brayed a loud "Hello, suckers!" to members who crowded in eagerly to be insulted and fleeced. They drank watered Scotch at $1.50 a shot and gladly paid $25.00 for a bottle of aerated cider with a dash of alcohol that was billed as "champagne."

"I'm glad I caught you," Tirzah said in her husky voice. "I just stopped by to welcome you back."

She held his face between her hands but did not kiss him. She never smeared her makeup after she put it on.

She was wearing a black satin cocoon coat trimmed in ostrich and a spray of black osprey feathers in her hair band. Only the rope of pearls he had given her was real; the other two were good imitations. He knew it killed her to spend money on clothes and jewelry when she was trying to save for a club of her own, but people were beginning to recognize her in restaurants and speakeasies and department stores, and she had to dress the part—

without any help from him. She wouldn't take his money and he needed it too much to insist.

"God, I'm glad to be here," he said. "You look sensational."

"*You* don't look so hot. You coming down with something?"

"I'm fine. I wish you didn't have to work."

"Come with me," she invited.

"Not tonight. It's been a rough trip."

She studied his expression. "A ride on a choo-choo couldn't tire you, MacKenzie. What happened?"

He shrugged. "Let's just say I haven't been mingling with the best people."

She hooted. "Neither have I! Listen, I'm late. I'll drop in after the last show to see if you learned anything exciting while you were away. Okay?"

He nodded, thinking that theirs was the perfect arrangement. He was both aroused and soothed by her volcanic sexuality, but he was no longer consumed by it. He could tell her anything—and usually did. He was in control of his emotional life and that, after the pain that had been dealt him for caring too much and doubting too little, was how he wanted it.

The telephone was ringing as he stepped into the apartment. He was not surprised to hear Enoch's voice.

"I thought I told you to stay out of my life," Connor said, more weary than irate.

"Don't hang up, Conn! This is important."

Connor waited.

"These people you just went to see, they're dangerous."

"Jesus, are you having me followed?"

"I have a lot of contacts," Enoch began hastily. "Sometimes—"

"I can take care of myself!" Connor shouted. "I had to learn how because of you! Now, keep the hell away from me, do you hear?" He slammed down the telephone and turned away, flabbergasted. It was tempting to think Enoch was motivated by fatherly concern, but Connor had not been that naive for years. What did he want?

It seemed to Connor that he would never be rid of the two men he most detested. During this last big coal strike,

Enoch had been all over the papers, fighting for the strikers; and Rhys had also been in evidence, decrying all union organizers and labor laws as Bolshevik plots.

It was unsettling to think that, in Rhys, he and his father had a common enemy.

Connor wondered if his mother had seen all those stories about Enoch, all those photographs of him. Or the press coverage of State Senator Rhys Brandon? A captain of industry, the columnists said, who could lead the state in the right direction. Dilys never mentioned either man in her letters, and Connor followed suit. They were difficult letters to write: there was so much neither could say to the other about the men who loomed large in both their lives.

He sighed, got up, and went to the icebox. He chipped some ice from the block in the top compartment, poured himself a large whiskey, and settled down to think about the deal he had just made.

His meeting in Baltimore had taken place in a seedy dockside tavern with a pockmarked, tobacco-colored man about five feet tall and skinny as a krait. He called himself José and had sought Connor out to buy a staggering supply of sidearms, Thompsons, and rifles.

"But no garbage," José cautioned. "Only the bes' you got."

Connor did some rapid calculations and named a target price to be confirmed before delivery.

José chewed on a dead cigar and considered, his arms crossed, his head tilted back as he looked up at Connor with black eyes as hard as shoe buttons. The soft voice and the singsong Spanish accent did not mask the brutality of the man. Finally he spoke.

"Is talk the Yankees make a law soon for no selling guns to rebels in Cuba and Honduras, *sí*? Jus' like in Nicaragua?"

Connor nodded.

"Then is bes' I buy now," José concluded, "before is costin' *muchos pesos más.*" His voice dropped even lower. "Señor, I come to you because they tell me you are *hombre de confianza*, you deliver when and where we say." He glanced at a nearby table, where three men sat watching Connor, one of them paring his nails with a lethal-looking knife, and Connor felt a prickle of apprehension. He could handle José easily enough, but not a gang of desperadoes. He almost told José to go to the devil, but he had waited too long for a deal like this.

"Delivery is guaranteed," Connor said.

"*Seguro?*" The button eyes regarded Connor with menace for another long moment, then José shrugged. "Is your life," he said.

"Don't threaten me, mister," Connor replied quietly. "I offered you a fair price. Take it or leave it."

José had handed over a brown paper bag stuffed with money to secure the deal, and Connor left the café. The dank odors of sweat and cheap wine lingered in his nostrils long after he boarded the train for New York.

He was revolted by the meeting. He had always managed to keep what he did for a living apart from his inner self, but now he felt tainted by it, as by something alien to his nature.

♦

Edgar Trask gave a low whistle the next day when Connor phoned his order in. "That's a big one, even for you," he said. "Nice work."

"This one *must* be delivered on time, Mr. Trask. If there's any question, tell me now. I'm dealing with an unusually ugly customer."

"Have we ever failed to deliver?" Trask countered with lofty assurance. "We have our reputation to consider. Just send me the usual deposit of twenty percent and don't worry about a thing."

"Who was that?" Rhys Brandon asked as Trask put down the telephone.

"A fairly recent account, but one of our best. He gave me a false name, but that's not unusual in this business. I've had him checked out thoroughly. It's all in the file." He handed it to Rhys.

Rhys studied it, his expression unchanged except for a

slight movement of his lips that might have been a smile. "Connor MacKenzie," he said.

"Do you know him?"

Rhys shook his head. "I've heard he's related to Enoch MacKenzie."

"That renegade," Trask said, pursing his lips in disgust. "He's driving our costs sky high with his wage demands. The man needs to be taught a lesson."

Rhys nodded and handed back the folder. "When does he want these guns?" he asked.

"In three weeks."

"Wait until two days before delivery, then tell him he can't have them. Tell him we've had a bad run or an accident."

Trask looked up, startled. "Mr. Brandon! He'll know better. And you don't want to do a thing like that!"

Rhys raised his brows and waited, increasing the other man's agitation.

"I don't think you understand, sir," Trask explained. "The people he sells to are brigands, not merchants. They don't take cancellations lightly. God knows what could happen to him if he didn't deliver."

"Nonsense. He can buy them elsewhere at a premium price."

Trask swallowed uneasily and tried again. "It won't enhance our reputation with the other independent dealers," he said.

"Don't tell them about it, Mr. Trask. You can be sure *he* won't. It would cast doubts on his credit." Rhys gazed at him steadily. "You must remember that a good part of the traffic you deal in is illegal and you know it—or why would you be keeping a separate set of books?"

Trask spluttered indignantly, but fear silenced both indignation and his conscience as he registered the full implication of what Brandon had just said. Trask kept separate books at Brandon's request! Trask sold to traffickers with Brandon's full knowledge and approval! It made a good profit for both men, one that the Crabtree partners didn't share.

But Trask had no proof, and who would believe him if State Senator Rhys Brandon, as punishment for not following orders, accused him of illegal traffic to line his own pockets? It wouldn't be the first time a poor man took the blame for a rich man's sins.

"Think of it this way, Trask," Rhys said as he rose to go. "He probably wants the guns for his father's union thugs. It's a chance to teach MacKenzie Senior that lesson you agree he needs. I wouldn't lose any sleep over it." Rhys smiled expansively.

"No, sir," Trask said. He shivered when Rhys had gone.

♦

Rhys left the building and got into his waiting car. "Brandon Hall," he instructed the chauffeur. He sat back and lit a pipe. After two months in Europe, he was going to Brandon's Gate to make love to Dilys.

Sometimes he wondered why he bothered taking her to bed, except that he relied on her to manage his estate, and an occasional orgasm kept her content to live alone at Brandon's Gate. And then, too, she was a nice little woman and sweet-natured. Living with a wife like Constance, he appreciated that, even though Dilys was well past youth and still passive in bed unless he insisted.

Her son was not, Rhys had decided, and the thought always made his expression darken. Connor was a womanizer; it took one to know one. Rhys always shuddered when he imagined Connor and Georgia together—and he imagined it often and in exquisitely painful detail. He could see it clearly right now, Georgia's round thighs and ripe breasts plundered by Connor's powerful body.

"Never!" he said softly. "I'll kill him first."

Perhaps he had just solved the problem in Trask's office. Connor would certainly be horsewhipped by those thugs. That might lead to a police inquiry and jail, where Master MacKenzie belonged. And if the "brigands" killed him, no one would know Rhys had anything to do with it.

The Hall came into view, spacious and serene on its heights, set like a jewel amid well-tended orchards, fields, and meadows. The dairy farm and the stables of the Mohawk Stud, out of sight beyond the crest of the hill, showed a consistent profit. He had to give Dilys credit for her management, and he decided to be gentle with her today, although her very abjectness sometimes excited him to erotic variations—that and the fact that she was Connor's mother.

It was sad to recall how much genuine pleasure he had taken in being her lover when Connor was a boy. The MacKenzies had made a second, more affectionate family for him than Constance and his two—at the time—unwelcome daughters. It was Connor who had shattered that idyll, Connor who had changed, who had threatened to use Georgia. He deserved whatever he got.

◆

"Darling," Dilys whispered, curving her body into his.

"Mmm?" he said, drowsing by her side in the bed.

"Nothing. I just like to hear you answer when I say it." She kissed his shoulder and lapsed into contented silence.

"I must go," he said presently.

"Oh, Rhys, no," she pleaded. "Not so soon. After so many weeks away!"

"I'm sorry, my dear, but there is trouble in the Carolina mills and Silas and I are taking the train down tonight. When the senate's in session, we'll be together more."

"Yes, I know," she said, watching his tall, slim body disappear into the bathroom. When he came out, she watched him dress, filling her eyes with him as he had just filled her soul and body.

He took an envelope from his breast pocket and handed it to her. "A little gift," he said. "To celebrate my election." He sat down on the edge of the bed and kissed her tenderly.

"I'm sorry," he said gently, "but I'll stay a few days next time, I promise." He turned her face up to his. "Do you forgive me?"

"Oh, my darling," she whispered, "I would forgive you anything."

◆

Dilys basked in that final embrace, even as she listened to
Rhys's footsteps fade away along the gallery. There were
only two maids and a footman in the house, all of them too
well trained to venture above stairs when the master came
to visit, but he always used the old, stealthy route by way
of the collection. Rhys had moved the collection to his
mansion in New York, along with everything else he valued, everything but her. But in their moments together,
here in the safe harbor of this house, he was completely
and utterly hers.

She pulled the quilt up over her, listening to the sound
of his car's departure and then to the absence of sound he
always left behind him, as if the world went deaf and
dumb and colorless without him.

She held the envelope to her cheek, imagining his
touch still lingered on it, before she opened it. It was a
receipt for a deposit made with the firm of Harper and
Harte, Attorneys, of New York City. They were trustees
for the account Rhys had opened for her years before, an
irrevocable trust into which gifts like this were deposited
from time to time. It was to that account she sent Connor's monthly check—her son was her sole beneficiary
under the will Mr. Harte had drawn for her—as well as a
good part of her salary and the money that had arrived
once from Enoch, bearing no return address and for what
purpose she never knew.

It was not money she wanted from any of the three men
who gave it to her! It was a different kind of security she
yearned for, the kind that came from being held, cherished, *required* by a man as something vital and precious
to him. Rhys gave her that assurance of need. Once she
had guarded his children. Now she watched over his house
and his land.

"It's in thrall to him you are," Peggy had told her
worriedly just before she and the girls were whisked off to
Switzerland four years earlier. "It's madness to stay on

here all by yourself, just waitin' for the sight of 'im. He'll be in Europe half the time, seein' to Miss Georgia."

"I can wait," Dilys had replied. "I love him."

"Ay, but he doesn't love you—nor nobody but his own self."

Dilys refused to believe that. Rhys was generous to a fault. And he always apologized ruefully after any indignities he demanded of her in bed.

"Carried away by you," he always said, a compliment to her womanhood she could not reject—and wasn't a woman meant to pleasure her man?

When he was with her she was alive again, and young, and in love. Sometimes, when he stayed a night or two and they rode over the estate before they dined together, she could believe that she, not Constance, was the true chatelaine of Brandon Hall.

Dilys had been mortified when Enoch tried to start a groundswell among the Brandon workers to block Rhys's election to the state Senate, and relieved when Enoch failed. She was grateful that Connor had stopped writing to Georgia many months before and she no longer had to pretend to be forwarding the letters. Rhys, tactful as always, never troubled her by mentioning her son or her husband.

What an extraordinary man he was! Of course she could forgive him anything. There was never anything to forgive.

♦

Connor had not felt so close to death since the German machine gun had spat bullets at him in the sky. Over the Argonne forest he hadn't even seen his attacker, but now he could smell José's breath and his greasy clothes, and he could see the bore of the cocked revolver José held.

Behind him were the other three men, one of them with a knife blade poised below Connor's right ear, ready to slice it off if José gave the sign. There was no one else in the alley where he had been directed with jerks of José's revolver.

My God, Connor thought, they're crazy enough to kill

me! These filthy little turds could kill me over a shipment of guns.

But dying was preposterous! There was too much he had to do, too much he wanted and was within a hair's breadth of getting! First he must master his panic.

"Would I have come if I wanted to cheat you?" he said, trying to keep the tremor out of his voice.

"Because you know I will find *you*, señor."

"You didn't even have to look. And you'll have your order tomorrow. Come on, José, you're too smart to wait another month for prime merchandise instead of one lousy day."

"*Y los camiones? Y mi equipo a pagar?*"

José jerked his head and the knife point sliced upward, detaching a small portion of Connor's earlobe. He jerked his head away and drove back his elbows hard into the belly of the man behind him. He heard a grunt as the man fell to his knees and whirled to grab the throats of the other two, pressing their Adam's apples so furiously with his thumbs that he lifted them off the ground.

"That's enough," he warned José over his shoulder. "Shoot if you're going to. Then you can whistle for your guns." He thrust the two men away contemptuously and turned back. He became aware that his neck was damp and pulled the handkerchief from his breast pocket to mop his bleeding ear. "I'll pay for the trucks and the men you brought tonight. If you're smart, you can make more on the deal than you bargained for."

José, waving his men back, resumed his ruminatory stance, one arm athwart his snake-slim body while the other circled the revolver as if choosing its target at leisure: heart or belly or genitals. "You pay *ahora mismo?*"

"Right now. I brought the money."

Connor jerked his chin toward his inside pocket and José extricated his wallet, removed the ten hundred-dollar bills Connor had placed there, counted them, and smiled. He pocketed the revolver and proffered the empty billfold with an exaggerated bow, then swept off his cap and waved Connor out of the alley.

"Tomorrow, same time, same place," Connor said, aware of the knots in his stomach.

"*Si Dios quiere*," José said.

God's will, Connor thought, walking out of the alley with his handkerchief pressed to his ear, had nothing to do with this. He sensed four pairs of eyes following him, and the tiny hairs on his lower back rose. The muscles of his thighs felt like jelly, and he had to force himself to put one leg in front of the other until he was out of range.

If he had been disgusted by his first meeting with José, he felt utterly degraded tonight, incredulous that in the pursuit of money he had become as low as Rhys said he was. It hit him harder than the financial loss: Crabtree's default had cost him several thousand dollars.

"Bad luck," Trask had called it, his voice shaking as he babbled about a mechanical error at the Crabtree plant that might cost him his job and promised that Connor's deposit would be returned.

"Jesus Christ!" Connor had shouted into the telephone. "Don't talk to me about your job! My life is on the line!"

"I'm sorry, MacKenzie. I tried, but there was nothing I could do."

Connor, too frantic to pursue it, had turned to Jack Dickinson to supply the arms, grateful that Dickinson showed no smugness—Connor, after all, had done Jack out of commissions by dealing directly with a manufacturer. Jack didn't even ask which one. He simply moved quickly to help.

"You make me feel like more of a shit than I already did," Connor told Jack.

"C'mon, Connor, all's fair in love and gunrunning."

But Connor didn't think so. A man had to know who his friends were and treat them accordingly, or he wasn't a man. He was Rhys Brandon.

Now he kept walking until he had reached a better section of Baltimore and found a speakeasy he had frequented before. Glad of the darkness, he ordered a double brandy. He bolted the liquor, oblivious of the noise, the smoke, and the sound of a jazz piano, and went to the men's room to bathe his cut ear and daub at the blood on his collar.

He gripped the edge of the basin, staring at himself in the mirror. The enormity of what he had risked came home to him. José might have shot him dead after those jackals had sliced off both his ears and God alone knew what else. But for a long time he had been at risk of losing something else, the one thing he had to have to make his life worthwhile. What if he had been discovered? Imprisoned? What kind of status would he have then? For years he had been skirting degradation in his frenzied pursuit of money.

The magnitude of that gamble made his stomach heave, and he splashed cold water on his face until the wave of nausea passed.

I'm getting out of this game, he swore silently to his haggard image in the mirror. Right now. Tonight.

He dried his face, combed his hair, and returned to the bar for another drink.

He would make this delivery and then tell Whitelaw it was his last. Someone else could complete the few remaining deals he had set up. The losses meant he would have only fifty thousand to plunge on the right stock when he found it.

But fifty thousand was a nice number. Round. Better than a hole in his head. Better than ruin.

♦

"What'll you do when you find this magic stock?" Tirzah asked him.

"Dress up like Astor's pet horse and take my money to an influential brokerage house to buy the shares for me."

"Why influential?"

He smiled. "It'll be my first step inside the Establishment."

"From what I've heard about those sharks in the Establishment," she said, "you were probably safer running guns." But he refused to talk about Baltimore, and she let it pass. "You could lose fifty thousand simoleons, Conn!"

"But I won't! I'll double it to one hundred thousand in

an hour, maybe to five hundred thousand in a few days." He looked at her eagerly, as if he needed her to believe that. "If I'm sharp enough and fast enough, I'll get in near the bottom and out near the top, over and over again. That's how fortunes are being made these days."

She studied him carefully, glad to see the change in him after the last few days. His enthusiasm was infectious and his conviction too strong to resist.

"What the hell," she said. "If you can't do it, then God didn't make little green apples. I'm in for two thousand five."

"You mean it?" he shouted, swooping her up. If he were a man to believe in signs, she had just given him one. "You won't regret it, lady. You're going to have your own club long before you expected to."

"And you? What will you have?"

"A Park Avenue duplex to start with. Then a fast car, a plane, probably a black stallion!"

"Crazy!" She laughed. "You're absolutely crazy!"

◆

Dilys came to New York to see him not long after, as she did periodically. He always booked a room for her at the Waldorf-Astoria, and this time they had dinner at Luchow's and went to the latest Broadway revue before he brought her back to the hotel for a nightcap.

A wave of tenderness swept over him when they were seated in a quiet corner of Peacock Alley. She seemed so delicate, so fragile in her sober, elegant, black crepe dress and pearls that must have been a Christmas gift from the family, since she could not have afforded them on a housekeeper's salary. She looked every inch a lady, but the sweet glow of youth had vanished from her eyes and he realized, with a shock, that his mother was profoundly sad.

The realization galled him. "Why do you stay there?" he demanded abruptly.

"Please, Connor, not again."

"How can you choose him over me?" he persisted, suddenly as agonized as a child.

Her face crumpled into abject misery. "Oh, Connor, don't say that!"

"But it's true! I earn enough now for you to live here in the city, in your own apartment. You won't have to work unless you want to. But for some reason you'd rather stay buried alive up there looking after his house! How can you be loyal to him after the way he treated me?"

She was speechless, and the dark smudges under her eyes were very apparent in her shocked, white face. Then she covered her face with hands that trembled.

"Leave me alone, Connor," she entreated him.

"No! He's only your employer. I'm your son and I want you here!"

Her voice was muffled behind her hands. "This city upsets me," she told him, because it was a partial truth and she could never tell him the whole truth. Even while it excited her to be in the same city with Rhys, to drive by his mansion as often as she could, she knew she could not see him there. And it had become increasingly difficult for her to leave Brandon's Gate, even to venture far from the Hall when Rhys was in America, in case he should come or telephone.

"I'm not alone," she insisted, her voice rising. "Malcolm comes for most of his school holidays and Will and Richard in the summer." Her hands dropped and a gleam of anger showed in her face. "It's my home! I feel safe there! Why should I leave it just to suit you?"

"It isn't for me!"

"Yes, it is! You want me to turn my life upside down so I can be your go-between with Georgia when she comes back here to live."

He was speechless. If once he had wanted Dilys to smooth his path to Georgia, for some time he had known he mustn't ask it of her. He loved his mother! He would have died for her when Enoch left. He wanted to take care of her!

But Rhys had come between them, Rhys and his insidious charm and the crumbs he tossed to Dilys: the gifts at Christmas, the redecoration of her living quarters, his sentimental gratitude for her services to his children. She could never be adequately paid for her services! She loved those children as her own, especially Georgia. She had been as much Georgia's mother as his.

"I despise that man," he said venomously. "I'd like to kill him!"

The look on her face was one he had never seen there, and it chilled him to his marrow. "That's enough, Connor," she said hoarsely, getting swiftly to her feet. "I won't hear another word against him. No," she warned him, holding up her hand, "don't come with me." She left him and walked to the elevator and he stared after her in confusion until the truth crashed in upon him.

She was in love with Rhys! She was his mistress!

For how long, he asked himself, his mind racing as he tried to remember words, attitudes, incidents. When had her rooms first been redone? When he went away to Braker! How long had she been wearing those pearls? For years! For years she had fought every suggestion that she leave Brandon's Gate. Ever since he was a boy, a stupid, trusting boy! Or a man who did not dare to ask what he did not want to know.

He thought he was going to be sick.

My God, he agonized, swallowing hard, my God! Will that man stop at nothing?

He already knew the answer. Rhys would go on until Connor stopped him.

But until that day came, Connor's bondage to the Brandons had to end, he knew that now, before that sick thing between his mother and Rhys poisoned him too! Hadn't he contemplated using Georgia in the same way?

He gulped down the rest of his brandy, shivered, and left the hotel. He walked for a long time before he turned homeward, and when he got there he told Tirzah what had happened. He had no one else to tell and he felt that he must talk or explode.

"It's not that she sleeps with him," he said, aware that

he flinched at the words. "It's her self-abnegation. He's broken her will. She's become pathetic."

"She's obsessed," Tirzah said. "It happens, mostly to women."

"She's let him use her," he said, unhearing. "She prefers him to me. She can't see that he doesn't care a damn for her, that he wants her up there only to take care of his bloody house!"

"Maybe he does care for her, honey. From what you've told me about his wife, you can't blame him for looking elsewhere!"

He scowled blackly. "Him? He's had almost every woman on the East Coast for consolation. No, he's using her the way he did me. He uses his children, Georgia more than the others. He uses everyone who trusts him."

"It's what most people do," Tirzah said.

"Not you!" he said, horrified. "Not me!"

"I've been known," she said. "And you're human too."

He felt himself flush at her implication.

"All right," he said. "But that's over. I'm letting go."

"Of Brandon's Gate," she said. "And him. Senator Brandon."

"Not him."

"Just your fairy princess?"

He wished he had not told her quite so much. "Yes," he said, and, getting up, made for the shower.

"You're only fooling yourself," Tirzah said.

He turned back. "What do you mean by that?"

"How can you let her go? She's part of your plan to get into the Establishment through the front door. And all of a fucking sudden you're not going to do it. Why?"

He did not meet her eyes. "I could never use her the way that bastard uses my mother."

"Of course you can't! Because you're in love with her!"

"Because she's not responsible for what her father does!"

"To hell with that! If she doesn't get you through that golden door they slammed in your face, some other woman will. It's just this one you can't use."

"She trusts me, damn it! She always has! Now, drop it, will you?"

"Just tell me one thing," Tirzah insisted, a sting in her voice. "Is it always her inside your head when we're together?"

"No!" he exclaimed hotly. "That isn't true."

"I don't mind a little star-gazing once in a while, but, damn it, there's more to me than this!" One hand touched her pubis, the other her breasts.

"Tirzah, for God's sake, you know what I feel for you."

The torment in his face made her believe him. "Yeah. The question is, do you know what you feel for *her*?"

"It doesn't matter anymore," he said. "It's over now. It's finished." He came to put his arms around her. "I *do* love you," he said, ignoring her halfhearted attempt to free herself. "I always will, all my life, whatever happens. You're my friend, the only one I have, except for Racey. But there's something I have to have that you can't give me—and I *must* have it, even if it means losing a friend."

She relaxed and leaned against him, understanding his drive because she shared it. It was not for her to judge his dream less worthy than her own.

"Okay, okay," she said. "You're not going to lose me so fast." She turned to look at him. "But when you pick out your next guide to the winner's circle, I want to know who she is."

"You will. I swear it. But don't hold your breath."

He went into the bathroom and Tirzah watched the door close. With a little sigh she shook her head.

Connor turned the shower on full force and stood under the tingling spray, dealing with a decision he must have made months before, or he would have worked harder, been richer, gone after Georgia and pulled her into an impossible triangle in his battle with Rhys.

Oliver would have called it an honorable impulse, but Connor was not on close terms with honor.

The impulse was fear. He was afraid to interfere in her life after what he had done to Oliver's. He was afraid to venture upon a love he might not be able to control, for Georgia held the key to him as no one else ever would.

With another woman he could strike a bargain on more equal terms. He would offer a mountain of money in return for social status, with no memories to cloud the issue and no love to burden it.

When he called his mother the next morning, she had already checked out of the hotel.

He wrote to apologize to her, not for what he had said but for how he had said it. He did not mention his shattering discovery. How could he? She was his mother! She would die of mortification if he alluded to her sexual life. She was not a "modern" woman.

Her letter crossed his; she had written in much the same way.

He had sent the monthly money order with his letter and although in the past she had always protested that she did not need it, now she accepted it without comment as if she knew it was something he had to do.

◆

"Welcome home, you flying fool!" Connor beamed when, out of the blue, Racey came home.

He seized Racey in a bear hug, then held him at arm's length and looked him over. "You haven't changed a bit. Come on in and have a drink. What tempts your palate?"

"Champagne," Racey said. He glanced around the apartment. "From the looks of this place I'm sure you have champagne—and," he added, picking up one of Tirzah's silk teddies by a narrow strap, "all the other comforts too."

Connor was uncorking a bottle of Dom Pérignon. "What brings you back home so suddenly?"

Racey smiled. "I'm getting married."

"Belinda, of course."

"Belinda. She said if I wasn't home by day after tomorrow, I needn't ever come on her account. Anyway, I've had enough of being shot at to last me a lifetime."

"Amen to that. Sit down. What will you do? Go into business with your father?"

Racey shook his head. "I'll never give up flying. Don't tell me you have."

"I don't have much time, but whenever I'm near an airfield I take one up."

"I tell you, Connor," Racey said enthusiastically, "the West Coast is the place to start a local air service—freight and passenger transport—and that's what I'm going to do. Those movie people do things in a big way. Short hops to Frisco and Mexico, big money—and all kinds of gorgeous women looking for handsome bachelors like you. Come in with me, Connor. It's a lot safer than putting everything you have in the stock market."

"Not necessarily—and it certainly won't pay as much."

"Maybe not for the first few years, but you can bank on the future of flight, and that's more than I'd say about the market. When you come right down to it, Wall Street is just a classy way to gamble."

"I see it differently," Connor said. "For example, I think radio has as much of a future as flight, now that technology's gone beyond the crystal set and earphones. Sears, Roebuck has finally put a loudspeaker radio on the market for a hundred and fifty dollars. High, but the price is bound to come down. When it does, they'll sell like hotcakes. You can't lose on radio stocks."

Racey lit a cigarette and surveyed his friend intently. "Are you still after Rhys Brandon?"

"Yes, but there are other things I want just as much. More, in fact."

"Such as?"

"What you have, things you don't even think about because you've always had them. Money. Position. The right kind of wife. You know what I've had to do to get this far. It isn't a profession I'd want my bride to know about."

Racey sighed. "But there's more than one way to get what you're after. Come out to the Coast with me and we'll build something for other people to buy stock in. You might even be happy for a change, the way you were in France!"

The two men looked at each other. "I'm tempted," Connor said, feeling the pull of this special friendship, remembering their good times together. He would be flying again. And Racey was right: there was a great future in aviation.

But that would take time and he had no time. He was under a compulsion to follow his plan.

He straightened up and shook his head. "Sorry, Racey, but I'm in too much of a hurry. Now let me take you over to the club to hear Tirzah. You won't know what hit you."

"Not this trip," Racey said. "My train leaves at midnight, and Belinda's waiting for me in Chicago. Don't forget, you're my best man when the great day arrives."

Watching Racey's train pull out was like watching a cork being drawn on emotions he had kept securely bottled up. In a sudden agonized rush of yearning, he ran after the train and what it was taking with it: friendship, happiness, a new business he and Racey could build together around the exhilaration of flight.

He ran, his legs pumping like pistons, until the platform ended. Then he stood, panting, while the train dwindled out of sight. What he had to do must be done alone. He would have great wealth and the power that went with it. He would marry well and attain the social prominence he hungered for. He would be a gentleman. And then he would destroy Rhys Brandon.

23

♦

"It's the big fish," the young woman said. "Always out to swallow the little ones."

She was about twenty-five, petite, and very attractive in a small-town way, with curly brown hair and wide brown eyes. The Eton collar she wore with her black pullover was a failed attempt to make a sexy girl look like the company owner's staid secretary.

"Big fish?"

She shook her head, and her smile confirmed his impression of her. "Company secret. I shouldn't have let it slip."

He smiled back at her. "Never mind the company," he said, the conviction growing that he might be onto something. "Would you let anything else slip?"

"I might." Her wide eyes traveled up and down his body knowledgeably.

"Shall we talk about it over dinner?" he suggested, determined to coax the information out of her.

"I think we should," she said. Her name was Rhoda Bonner. She wrote it on a slip of paper with her address. "I'll be ready at seven."

She worked for Capitol Industries, a large and very efficient maker of automobile parts with a sideline in small arms, which was how Connor had come across it. He knew it increased its profit annually and raised its dividend accordingly—and it was clearly undervalued even at the top of its trading curve. There was no reason whatever for the recent gradual slide in Capitol stock—except manipulation by the "big fish" to set up a cheap takeover.

Precisely at seven o'clock Connor rang Rhoda Bonner's door and she came down to let him in. She lived in a well-furnished attic apartment on the third floor of a pretty frame house. He followed her swaying hips up two flights of stairs.

"Charming," he said when he was inside her door. "But the only place I can stand up is in the middle of the room."

"Then sit down," she said. "I've made some dry martinis. We can have a drink before we go."

He sat on the overstuffed chintz sofa she indicated and sipped the cocktail she handed him. It had far too much vermouth in it.

"Perfect," he said.

She sat down beside him. She wore a black crepe sheath dress that slid up over her knees when she sat, exposing four inches of flesh above her rolled stockings, flesh as firm and white as the skin of her bare arms.

"What do you like to do besides buy guns?" she asked, and let her hand rest lightly on his thigh.

He turned to look at her, and she leaned toward him with an invitation that was not to be refused if he wanted to learn anything. He kissed her. She drew a deep, ragged breath, as if she had been long deprived of air. Her lips parted and her hand moved to his crotch, her fingers finding and pressing the tip of his penis. She took his drink and placed it beside hers on the coffee table, then she moved to lie back on the couch, drawing him down on top of her.

"Come to mama," she said. She took his hand and pulled it between her legs. "Please. Oh, please, please."

Her skirt was bunched up around her waist and she wore nothing under it. She had a great bush of black pubic hair, somehow surprising on such a compact person, and a velvety black mole on one thigh. She let one leg slide to the floor, opening herself to him. He stroked her, first slowly, then swiftly until she shook and gave a sharp little scream of pleasure when he slid two fingers into her. He was aroused but still fully clothed when she stopped moaning.

"Come into the bedroom," she whispered, and he followed her, keeping his head down to avoid the sloping roof while he dropped his clothes.

It was an astonishing performance. She was generous in bed, skilled at everything she did, but she was more avid than passionate and that kept him aloof from her. Or maybe it was the real object of the encounter that disturbed him. It was the first time he had made love to a woman for something other than mutual comfort or pleasure.

"I'm glad you needed more guns," she said when they were eating scrambled eggs in her kitchen.

"I'm glad too," he told her, but he had not come for guns. "Maybe next time we'll get out to dinner." He realized at once that he had said exactly the right thing. Before they finished the eggs she had told him what he needed to know.

"I.M.," she said, naming one of the country's biggest automobile makers. "They're looking to buy us out so they can make everything themselves, soup to nuts. But my boss has a perfectly viable business here and he likes his independence."

"Can he hold out?" Connor asked, munching toast and feeling again that visceral excitement that always meant he had found what he was looking for.

She shrugged. "I don't see how, but he's the kind of guy who would rather go under than give in."

"You realize," he said, "that a takeover offer would raise the value of Capitol stock."

"Yes, I do." She watched him carefully. "So does I.M. So they're playing it cagey. They're fooling around with Capitol stock, too, pushing it down."

"It could mean a lot of money," Connor persisted, "for anyone who knew in advance when the offer was going to be made."

Her eyes were shrewd. "Do you play the market?"

He shook his head. "Not in a big way. But I don't mind taking an occasional flyer. How about you?"

She nodded, her gaze steady. "I'll call you," she said.

He shook his head, unwilling to tell her too much. "I'm always on the road. I'll call you." He put down his coffee cup and took her hand. "How about a nightcap before I go?" They went back to the bedroom.

He called her every night in the month that followed and once he sent her flowers. During that time Capitol stock moved up and down. "A baby step up," Rhoda commented, "a giant step down."

The manipulation was carefully managed and rumors about Capitol's slide toward bankruptcy were circulated to the public. Connor knew he was not the only one watching the drama, but he would be among the few to know exactly when it was going to reach its denouement.

Capitol stood at two dollars a share when Rhoda Bonner told Connor that I.M. would offer to buy in two days and Capitol would refuse to sell.

"Can Capitol hold out?"

"No," she said. "It's David and Goliath without the slingshot."

◆

"Mr. Torrance," the young man said into the tube on his desk. "There is a Mr. MacKenzie to see you." He put the tube to his ear and listened for a moment, said, "Yes, I think so," listened again, then rose and said, "This way, please," opening the oak door with a flourish. It was the most impressive of several oak doors Connor had passed on his way to see the president of Torrance, DeVries, and Deventer, Brokers.

Guthrie Torrance did not come forward to greet Connor. Instead, he rose and extended a hand across his desk, somewhat reluctantly, Connor perceived. Torrance did not often grant interviews with persons of unknown origin. Connor had been insistent—pushy, Torrance would have said—although at the sight of Connor he relaxed somewhat.

It's my gray homburg, Connor thought, and my pearl stickpin and my gloves and walking stick. Amazing, the importance of appearance. The devil has power to assume a pleasing shape, he thought, remembering *Hamlet*. Torrance had probably been expecting someone in ill-fitting clothes, with bad teeth and no manners. In his judgment, all of that could be assumed in people without the proper connections.

"Please sit down, Mr. MacKenzie," Torrance said. He was of medium height and build, and wore his gray-flecked brown hair parted in the center and slicked back from the temples. His brows swirled over his eyes like horizontal question marks, giving him a look of perpetual doubt and suspicion. His mouth was wide, with a thin upper lip whose bow was so deep it divided his mouth in two, making it seem delicate, almost girlish. His eyes, light brown and narrow, belied that impression.

"How may I help you?" he inquired.

"I'm in need of a broker," Connor said. "I've chosen you."

"Ah," Torrance said, pursing his mouth and supporting his chin on two fingers. "May I ask who made the recommendation?"

"I never rely on anyone's judgment but my own," Connor replied, purposely misunderstanding the question. He knew any number of men who could have provided an introduction to Torrance—men he'd seen innumerable times at Brandon Hall—but not for him. "Your firm has the best reputation on the Street," he assured Torrance.

Torrance smiled, accepting the compliment with lordly grace. In a minute the man would offer his ring to be kissed!

Connor sat in the armchair as Rhys would have, long legs lazily crossed. Occasionally he surveyed his manicured nails. When he looked at Torrance, Connor's attitude was almost insolent.

Before Torrance could speak, he said, "I'm sure your time is as valuable as mine." He took out a black alligator billfold and extracted a bank draft for fifty thousand dollars. "This will serve to open my account."

By this firm's standards it was a moderate amount, but an acceptable beginning for a new client.

"It is my intention to increase my account with you,"
Connor said, "after we've established a working relationship."

Torrance nodded and, taking up his speaking tube, instructed his secretary to open an account and prepare a
receipt. "Any market instructions?" he inquired.

Connor nodded. "Buy fifty thousand shares of Capitol
Industries—on margin."

Torrance cleared his throat. "I'm afraid the firm's policy
precludes investments on margin until the working relationship you mentioned has been established."

Connor fixed his dark eyes on Torrance with the indul-
gence a parent accords a naughty child. Bastard, he thought.
"As you wish, Mr. Torrance. Buy twenty-five thousand
shares at market." Connor rose to go.

"It is not an investment I would recommend," Torrance
said. "Capitol is a small company, rather unstable lately,
and while there are rumors, there will be no takeover.
The word is that I.M. will buy elsewhere."

Connor drew on his gloves. "I appreciate your advice,
but I prefer to trust my intuition. Good day, Mr. Torrance."

He felt a cold sweat start between his shoulder blades at
parting with all that money based solely on Rhoda Bonner's appreciation of the situation, but he could not resist.
He gave the secretary his address and telephone number
and picked up his receipt, then went down in the elevator
and hailed a taxicab on Water Street.

There wasn't a chance in a hundred that anything could
go wrong, but the remote possibility still made him pace
around the apartment chain-smoking when he got home
from Torrance's office. He called Rhoda three times and
was assured that matters were proceeding, but there was
no change in the price of Capitol stock that day.

Tirzah called him from the club before her first set.
"Did your fancy broker take us on?"

Connor nodded. "I behaved like a gentleman so he took
me for one."

"Then it's going to be all right."

"How do you know that?" he demanded belligerently.

"Because you said so! Do you think I'd have given you

all that money if I had any doubts? Look how lucky we've been since we got together! It's been smooth sailing. Whatever we go for, we get."

"That's what worries me," he said.

"Me too," she said gloomily, and hung up.

◆

He spent the next day from nine till three in the Visitors' Gallery of the Stock Exchange and smoked himself dry at home that night. He was in that rare torment that comes when a person has done all that can be done and then must leave the outcome in the hands of others.

Capitol stock opened up the next morning. Obviously there had been more than one leak. At noon the offer was announced and refused and Capitol stock jumped to six. Everyone knew a pygmy could not hold out against a giant.

"Sell," Tirzah pleaded. "You've done what you wanted to do. For God's sake, sell!"

"One more day," he said. "But I'll sell out your share if you want me to." He was going to unload Rhoda Bonner's shares as well.

Tirzah looked at him closely. "I hope this Capitol guy is as stubborn as you. Okay, one more day."

"It's nice to know you trust me!"

"Shit, honey, it's 'cause you're so goddamn smart. And who wouldn't trust that face?"

He called Rhoda that night. "How's your boss holding out?"

"He isn't. The writing's on the wall."

"I have your money," he said. "I'll wire it."

There was a brief silence. "Why not bring it?"

"All right, I will," he said. But he wired it that night.

The stock went to ten the next day and again he convinced Tirzah to hang on until the market opened Monday. In twenty minutes Capitol climbed to twelve and he called Torrance, DeVries, and Deventer and told them to sell.

Tirzah's twenty-five hundred dollars had become thirty

thousand. Connor had made over a quarter million. He took a check from Torrance for hers and left the bulk of his with the broker.

"A tidy little coup, Mr. MacKenzie," Torrance said when he handed Connor the check, wondering how his client had been privy to a schedule of events other people had failed to acquire. "Any more split-second timing like this one?"

"Not today," Connor said, concealing his exultation behind a mask of urbanity. "But I have a few things in mind and you'll be the first to know what I decide." He glanced briefly at a photograph of Torrance's predebutante daughter, Audrey. Why not, when she was old enough? After today, anything was possible.

He walked toward 15th Street, unable to believe his sudden wealth or to decide how he felt about it—elated, certainly, and so jubilant that he could not stop smiling even though people turned to look at him and several women smiled back.

He was sure this was only the beginning, that he was on the brink of power, real power. He felt it in his bones. The money would give him influence, and with the right connections he would wield it from inside the Establishment.

He cashed Tirzah's check at his bank and when he got home he spread the money on the bed. He closed the curtains, lit some candles, and put a record on the Victrola—it was Tirzah, singing "After You've Gone." When she came home and saw his face she gave a little scream of delight and threw her arms over her head. He picked her up and carried her to the bedroom. She lay on her back, laughing with pleasure while he covered her with bills.

"Do you know what this means?" she asked him. "My own club! It'll be my Christmas present to myself." She kissed him gleefully. "What'll you do?"

He began to undress her. "After I do this, I'm going to make more money," he said, pulling her dress over her head.

"But what will you buy right away?"

"I told you. A black stallion and an airplane."

She whooped. "Connor MacKenzie, I'll never understand you!"

"I know." He pulled off her panties. The bills crackled under them.

"Hurry," she whispered, "or the sound of that money is gonna make me come without you."

"Wanna bet?" he said.

♦

Constance Brandon and Letty Pemberton came into the chic little speakeasy in the West Fifties at about four o'clock, after shopping themselves to a frazzle.

"Tea time, Marco," Letty said to the hovering waiter in her creamiest Southern tones. "Make mine straight bourbon, no cream, no sugar." Her long, hollow-cheeked face, the fine skin strikingly white against her black hair, turned to Constance, and she peered at her with large, myopic eyes. "What about you?"

"Sherry," Constance said, glancing around the room. Its small square tables were set with white cloths and napkins and small vases of dark red carnations that matched the plush on the gilt-framed chairs.

"This place looks for all the world like a *salon de thé*," Constance said.

"Or the waiting room in a Venetian whorehouse," Letty suggested.

There was a curving mahogany bar upholstered in tufted red leather on the other side of the room, where several men were talking quietly.

"Anyone interesting at the bar?" Letty inquired. She never wore her glasses in public.

"I thought you were exhausted."

"Not *there*," Letty smirked. "I do wish my Lester was as athletic in bed as your Rhys."

"How do you know what Rhys is like in bed?" Constance demanded.

"Don't get your dander up, Connie," Letty said languidly, mentally biting her tongue for the slip. If Constance knew about her affair with Rhys, there'd be hell to pay from both Brandons!

"You told me so yourself," she went on. "I quite envy you all these honeymoons you've been having in Paris." When Constance made no reply, she smiled angelically. "How are the girls?"

"Still studying art."

"Stars above! Are they all that talented?"

"Georgia thinks she is and Rhys, of course, agrees. She's dropped fine arts entirely for textile design. She's got a bee in her bonnet about Rhys using her designs on sheer cotton, if you please."

"But what a bore for the poor things, rattling around alone in that great house."

"Paris is hardly boring. And we need the space. Rhys insists on dragging the boys along for every holiday. Anyway, it keeps the girls out of my hair. Rhys is determined to keep them there until Georgia marries a title."

"He does dote on her," Letty said, and was rewarded by a frigid stare from Constance. She changed the subject. "Why isn't Rhys coming to my little do tonight?" She considered it a clever ploy to ask a question to which she knew the answer perfectly well.

"He's gone to South Carolina with Silas. They're having some union troubles," Constance said. "Then they're off to Nicaragua and Haiti to look at the plantations. He'll be away for weeks."

Letty clucked sympathetically, although the sympathy was for herself. She had spent many an afternoon in bed with Rhys and wondered how she would endure his absence. "You poor darling. How ever will you manage?" Now you must excuse me while I stagger to the loo. When I come back I want to hear everything you know about Cecily Anders's adventures in Paris. They say she surrendered her maidenhead to a Senegalese, and we know they're colossally endowed! You'd think she'd have chosen something more modest for her debut."

Letty glided away and Constance twirled the stem of her sherry glass, furious with Rhys for deserting her the minute their ship docked, and rushing away—first to Brandon's Gate and a tryst with his mealy-mouthed mistress, and then to that pesthole in the South where Plantation cotton was grown for DonCasster Mills to spin. From there he and Silas would journey to their Nica Sugar and Centro Coffee plantations in Nicaragua. Thank God Rhys wasn't planning a trip to his ChinaTex mills in the Orient!

And yet she could not object. All of Rhys's companies would come to her sons in due course, and it was because of his sons that Rhys protected his image as a faithful family man. His sons would carry on his name and he would not tarnish it with impunity. Constance had lost patience with Jillian a long time before, and she detested Georgia as much as ever, but the boys were her insurance.

The boys—and Rhys's political ambition! Constance prayed passionately that Rhys would soon be a United States senator. Financiers and industrialists could get away with casual adultery, but not members of Congress. Of course, a politician's wife was supposed to be a model of propriety, and Constance, more out of spite than passion, had not been since they moved to New York. What was good for the goose, she told herself. But in a way, her sexual adventures were hollow triumphs. She still wanted Rhys to love her, and it enraged her that he did not.

Why the hell didn't he? She had turned into a stunning woman, after all! Even her women friends said so, and the jealousy of women was the surest form of flattery. Constance knew she looked fully ten years less than her thirty-nine years and her lovers were almost always younger men. When she was with them it diluted the horror of turning forty—but they always turned around and married girls their own age! It was so unfair! What had she ever done to deserve it, except love her husband to distraction?

Her vision now fully adjusted to the gloom, Constance examined the men at the bar as if they were a rack of coats among which she could choose, scanning them until she came to the last one on the side nearest her. He was alone and he was looking at her.

The idea hit her the moment she recognized Connor.
What a way to punish Rhys! It was positively Machiavellian.

And whyever not? Connor was not the millboy-cum-
pilot who had made a scandal at the Gate. This man was
an elegant stranger. Constance knew expensive clothes
when she saw them, and his had been hand-tailored to
perfection. He wore a dark suit and gray spats, a French-
cuffed white shirt with heavy gold links, and a striped silk
tie. There was a gold signet ring on his left hand and a
heavy gold chain across his vest.

He stood with one foot on the bar rail in an attitude of
relaxed authority that intrigued her. She had never been
to bed with one of the lower classes before—nor he with a
woman whose horses he once had groomed.

She nodded to Connor, and he left the bar and walked
over to the table. The graceful way his tall body moved
made heat flare suddenly at the base of her belly. She
moistened her lips. He was one of the best-looking men
she had ever seen.

♦

Watching her from the bar, he had seen her as in a
three-way mirror: his boyhood nemesis, Georgia's callous
stepmother, Rhys's wife. When she summoned him with
an imperious nod, he wondered what she wanted of him,
but he was damned if he'd behave like a supplicant.

"Mrs. Brandon," he said in what was almost a parody of
good manners. "You haven't changed at all."

She took it as a compliment and acknowledged it with a
majestic nod, a queen to a peasant. "And you look very
prosperous," she said. "Have you murdered some doting
widow for her money?"

He did not react to the barb. "No, I came by it as all the
best people do: by manipulations in the stock market."

She smiled and put a cigarette in her holder. He leaned
down to light it and her eyes met his. "Aside from manip-
ulating, what do you do?" she asked softly.

"I ride, out on Long Island, where I'm building a house.
I fly my plane whenever I can find the time."

"I've always wondered what it would be like up there," she said.

He felt as if he were standing off in the distance, watching her seduce him, for surely that was what she was doing.

"Would you like me to take you up sometime?"

"I might," she said. "How would I let you know?"

Now he was sure! She was a woman he thoroughly despised, but what a way to begin the revenge he had anticipated for so long! The fact that she was a gorgeous-looking woman gave the plan an added fillip.

He took a card from a silver case and handed it to her. "Call me there any morning before nine and tell me where to pick you up."

"What would I wear?"

"Jodhpurs and a warm jacket. I can provide whatever else you'd need."

"I'm sure you could," she said, her luminous eyes fixed on him.

With a little bow he left her. He paused to drop a bill on the bar before leaving the restaurant, wondering if she knew about Rhys and Dilys.

◆

Constance watched him disappear, as pleased with herself as she had been the night she seduced Rhys into marriage, but with the added tang of pure malice. She drank some sherry and did a quick calculation. He must be about twenty-seven now, the perfect age for a lover. She wondered if he had really made his money in the market and if his last argument with Rhys had been over Georgia or Dilys.

Dilys! What a divine retribution to go to bed with her son! Rhys still did not realize Constance knew about his disgusting affair with the housekeeper. What kind of fool did he take her for?

"Who was that tall person?" Letty demanded, sliding back into her chair.

"Someone we met in Europe." Constance lit a cigarette and inhaled with relish. "Rhys hates him."

"How delicious," Letty crowed. "To have an affair with a man one's husband hates."

"Really, Letty, I hardly know the man."

"I was only speculating."

Constance shrugged and Letty clapped her hands delightedly. "Now, tell me all about him. What's his name?"

"Frank," Constance said. "Frank Millman." She told an imaginative story about a casual meeting in the casino at Deauville the previous year. It would give Letty something to talk about and put Rhys off the track.

On her way home in the chauffeured Packard, Constance thought how insulting it was that Rhys still made love to her as energetically as if he never touched another woman—which only proved that all females were interchangeable to him. Except, of course, for his precious daughter, and he couldn't go to bed with Georgia, thank God! It galled Constance, too, that even if Rhys knew about his wife's affairs he probably wouldn't care enough to be outraged.

Except for this one! The very mention of Connor's name infuriated Rhys! They would have to be careful.

She decided to let Connor stew for a while before she called him. It was good strategy to make a man wait.

◆

"Ah'm sorry, Mr. Brandon, Mr. Cassadyne," the mill manager said in his slow southern drawl. "If you want these mills to start *pro*ducin' again, you'll have to talk to Enoch MacKenzie."

Rhys and Silas looked at each other in amazement. They were in the sweltering office of the DonCasster Mills manager in South Carolina. The ceiling fan did little to move the soggy air, and Rhys, fastidious to a fault even in his shirt-sleeves, flared his nostrils at his surroundings.

"Explain yourself, Hilliard," he demanded.

"Well, sir, I never did see the like. The workers down here didn't want to hear union until MacKenzie showed

up. Now they say they're going to form an 'organization'
—not a union, mind. They want MacKenzie to explain it
to you. As he's an influential man in the labor movement,
I thought it was prudent to let you decide."

Silas shook his head, mopping his red face. "Damn the
man! We lose thousands of dollars every hour these mills
are idle."

"We'll lose thousands more if MacKenzie organizes a
union," Rhys said.

"Ah'm tellin' you, Mr. Brandon, the workers say they
don't want a union."

"Yet," Rhys scoffed.

"Well, I guess there's always that chance," Hilliard said.

"Let's see him," Silas said. "Better a devil you know
than a devil you don't."

Rhys nodded. Hilliard went to the door and in a few
minutes Enoch MacKenzie walked into the office, making
it seem smaller by his very presence. He seemed unaware
of anyone but Rhys and stood, bulky and disheveled,
studying his former employer from under his heavy brows.

"Say your piece, MacKenzie," Rhys commanded, "and
then get off my property."

"Don't give me orders, Brandon," Enoch returned. "I
don't work for you anymore."

Silas removed his jacket impatiently. "Let's' get on with
it, MacKenzie. If the workers don't want you and your
union, what in hell do they want?"

"A higher wage, for one thing."

"We pay the going rate in these parts," Hilliard said.

"That's why so many of them are moving north," Enoch
said, his eyes still fixed on Rhys's face. "In a few years you
won't have enough skilled workers in the South to spin
your cotton at any wage. Where's the sense in that?" He
sat down on a corner of Hilliard's desk, still looking down
at Rhys.

"Is that all they want?" Rhys snapped.

"They want shorter hours for kids under eleven," Enoch
said.

"Hell, Rhys!" Silas spluttered. "I didn't know we hired them under eleven."

"I'm sure you don't know about a lot of things he does, Mr. Cassadyne," Enoch said, turning to Silas.

"That'll do, MacKenzie," Silas snapped. "Mr. Brandon has reasons for what he does." He glanced at Rhys.

Rhys shrugged. "These people insist on sending their children to work. It's their choice, not mine. Don't hold me responsible for their greed."

"Greed?" Enoch roared, rising to his feet. "You ought to see how they live!"

"And you ought to learn some manners," Rhys said softly. "You're no better than he is."

"He's the best thing ever happened to you, Brandon."

"Who are they talkin' about?" Hilliard demanded as Rhys rose abruptly and went to the window, turning his back on all of them.

"Jesus Christ!" Silas exclaimed. "This is a business discussion, not the Hatfields and the McCoys. Listen, MacKenzie. The workers wanted us to hear you, and we have. We won't employ children under eleven, and we'll authorize a wage raise of five cents an hour. But no union and no 'organization.' They can appoint a man to speak for them, provided it isn't you. I don't know what you're doing here in the first place. You have bigger fish to fry in coal and automobiles. So keep away. That's the deal, take it or leave it."

"As you say, Mr. Cassadyne," Enoch said, once more calm if not conciliatory. "I'll tell them what you said. The rest is their decision."

"The hell it is," Rhys said, still facing the window. "This meeting was your idea, not theirs."

Enoch sent him a mirthless smile before he left the office.

"That," Hilliard said, "is a very dangerous man."

"Don't exaggerate, Mr. Hilliard," Rhys said. "He can be managed. I know because he used to work for me."

Hilliard nodded. "If you say so, Mr. Brandon. But he's

got a lot of power among the working people of this country."

"He's betraying them," Rhys said. "The workers of this country are patriotic Americans. He's a Bolshevik infiltrator and he'll be exposed as one."

"How are you going to manage that?" Silas asked.

"Legally. We're fighting some ridiculous new labor demands in the New York State legislature already—minimum wages, maximum hours, coverage for injuries, and worse. I want the same fight waged in Washington."

"Well, Mr. Brandon," Hilliard said, extending his hand, "I sure hope you get sent there to do the job."

Rhys shook the manager's hand, gravely portentous, while Silas raised his eyes to heaven.

"Come on, Rhys," he urged impatiently. "Washington's a long way off and so is Nicaragua."

The two men avoided mention of Enoch MacKenzie until they were approaching New York two months later, on the return trip, catching up on back newspapers full of Enoch and labor's grumblings.

"He must be stopped," Rhys insisted, rattling his paper angrily.

"And you're the one to do it, I suppose," Silas said.

"Yes, I am. I could be elected to the United States Senate without half trying. John Anders and Martin van Reitjens have been promising their support long enough. Now they have to deliver. I cabled them to arrange a meeting next week. I want you to be there."

"They're the political back-room boys, not me."

"You're an industrialist, Silas, and I must have business on my side. I need you to plead my cause with my friends and colleagues. Who knows a man better than his partner?"

Silas, looking harried, asked, "What do you want me to say about you, Rhys?"

"I'll do the talking, Silas. All you have to do is nod. You can start at the dinner dance Constance has arranged for this weekend, to welcome us home."

Letty Pemberton would be at that party, Rhys reminded himself. There was something intriguing about Letty's myopic sloth. For a year he had been jolting her out of her lethargy in bed.

"What will you promise the voters, Rhys? A new Eden?"

"I'll promise not to hand this country over to a lot of Communists."

"You mean not to one in particular. Enoch MacKenzie."

"You're a wise man, Silas. In a riot, the thing to do is shoot the ringleader."

"Shoot?" Silas demanded in alarm.

"I didn't mean it literally," Rhys said, shaking his head with infinite patience.

"Thank God for small mercies," Silas said.

◆

"What naughty things were you doin' in the islands?" drawled Letty Pemberton. She danced with Rhys as if they were welded together from the waist down. Letty could be a Southern belle whenever it suited her, and now she patted Rhys's cheek and let her fingers linger there too long. He placed her hand on his shoulder and glanced briefly around the room to see if anyone was watching them.

It annoyed Letty that even after their year-long affair he was still so concerned about what Constance might do if she found out. Especially since Constance didn't have a thought in her head these days except for Frank Millman, also known, to those who took the trouble to read the columns, as Connor MacKenzie. Letty pondered that often enough. MacKenzie was a handsome bastard, but Rhys was good enough in bed to satisfy any woman—except, of course, a nymphomaniac like Constance. He was good enough to make Letty dream of divorcing Lester and marrying him. Constance certainly wouldn't care, not now.

"Rhys," Letty whispered, warmed by the memory of their recent reunion. "We're good together, aren't we?"

"Splendid," he said.

"I've been thinkin' we ought to make it permanent. I've been thinkin' we ought to get married."

She had rehearsed a number of probable reactions from him, but not laughter. It made her so furious that she lost her head completely.

"How dare you laugh at me?"

He was still chuckling. "Forgive me, my dear, but that was a very funny suggestion. What would Lester say? What would Constance do?"

"Constance? She'd just go on sleepin' with Connor MacKenzie."

She could tell by his face that she had surprised him. Well, what of it? He deserved it. Laugh at her, would he?

"Didn't know about him, did you?"

He made no reply and, without waiting for the music to stop, he took her back to Lester.

"Thanks for lending me your wife," Rhys said smoothly, his face still pale. "I just remembered I have an important call to make."

"What ails him?" Lester asked his wife.

"Why, honey lamb, how should I know?" Letty warbled, watching Rhys stalk toward the library.

♦

In the library Rhys lowered himself into a chair and stared blankly at his trembling hands.

Connor! His wife and Connor! It was unbelievable. Constance had always hated Connor. What possible motive, even including her enormous sexual appetite, could she have for demeaning herself by bedding a servant, *that* servant in particular?

Unless . . . Rhys put his head back and closed his eyes. Unless she had found out about Dilys.

His hands were shaking and he closed them into fists.

"I'll kill the bitch! I'll break her bloody neck! I'll divorce her!"

But he couldn't divorce her, not if he wanted to be a senator—and more, one day. It was easier for a camel to go through the eye of a needle than for a divorced man to get elected to public office, much less the highest office of them all.

His body was rigid as he thought wildly, looking for a solution. Finally one occurred to him, one he could live with.

Maybe she hoped, through this intimacy, to discover something Rhys could use to put an end to MacKenzie's meteoric rise on Wall Street, to get Connor out of the way once and for all.

Rhys sat up and took out his cigar case with hands that had suddenly relaxed. He cut one end of a thin cigar with the gold clipper in his pocket, lit the aromatic cigar, and blew the smoke out slowly.

That had to be it! It was the only credible explanation. Constance always said he didn't appreciate the lengths to which she was prepared to go on his behalf. And for all he knew, it was only a flirtation, not an affair. Letty was capable of saying anything when she was angry. He shouldn't have laughed at her. Not that he cared what Constance did with her body when he wasn't using it, but she was, after all, his wife, and Caesar's wife must be above reproach.

If those so-called friends of his gave him the nomination, she would have to be as chaste as a nun.

Damn women! They were more trouble than they were worth. He'd never had any real joy from a single one of them in all his life, and God knew he had searched far and wide.

He finished his cigar and, once more calm and in possession of himself now that he had correctly assessed Letty's vicious slander, he smoothed his hair, rearranged the handkerchief in his breast pocket, and left the library. Constance was in his direct line of vision as he came through the door, in the center of an admiring circle of men, the skin of her throat and shoulders satin smooth against her black velvet dress.

He would know for certain how far she had gone when he took her to bed tonight. He knew women too well to be fooled by his own wife!

24

♦

"These utilities," Connor said to Guthrie Torrance. He handed Torrance a list.

Torrance nodded and put the list in a folder on his desk.

"And these six companies," Connor went on.

Torrance riffled through the pages. "I haven't heard great things about any of them."

"You will," Connor said confidently. "They're all infant companies utilizing new technologies. They'll pay off in time."

Privately he decided he would turn the utilities over quickly. As for Radio, he bounced in and out of the volatile stock like a rubber ball.

He waited while Torrance studied the lists. TD&D would profit hugely from them, but Connor knew that no invitation to join the firm would be forthcoming as a result.

In the months since his first visit to TD&D, Connor had made over a million dollars, some of it still on paper. He bought on margin, putting up only ten percent of the total amount he wanted to invest, while the firm provided the rest. Buying on margin meant paying interest to TD&D as well as commission, but it gave him the chance to invest heavily in stocks that were high and going higher.

Torrance always welcomed him personally now. More and more, he followed Connor's leads with his own money and the clients' accounts. Even so, there had not been the slightest show of gratitude, just respect for his market savvy. Partnership! Torrance had not invited him to have so much as a drink!

"Maybe it's too soon," he grumbled to Tirzah. "But what more do they want? I have money. I have manners. I'm presentable."

"The problem is what *you* want," she told him. "You want to be one of them. Why can't you enjoy being young, handsome, and rich as plain old Connor MacKenzie?"

"Why can't you enjoy being gorgeous and talented as plain old Tirzah Kent? You want to be a star. Well, so do I!"

He chewed on it all the time. After all, his manners were impeccable. His education equaled or surpassed that of men like Guthrie Torrance, and he was easily as cultured as any of them—with polish far beyond that of the limited circles in which he moved with Tirzah. It was true that he was most comfortable alone or with men like himself, to whom the getting of money was aphrodisiac, but it was not enough.

Furious with Torrance, he decided to broker his own investments. A month later, Hemisphere Investments rented space on Water Street. The offices were ample, if not vast, equipped with the latest in telephone and telex wires. He hired five clerks for their discretion and their ability to keep a board of fifty stocks absolutely up to the minute. He hired two secretaries and five statisticians whose job it was to research every stock he followed.

"This is a surprise!" Guthrie Torrance said testily when Connor told him he would be handling his own account.

"Yes, I suppose it is," Connor said, barely concealing his satisfaction at Torrance's dismay.

"I assume you have a client list?" Guthrie said, a frown curling his peculiar eyebrows.

"For the moment, I'm my only client," Connor said.

"Mmm," Guthrie said gloomily. "Well, I hope we can still do business together, one way or another."

"Certainly, Mr. Torrance," Connor assured him, knowing the man mourned the loss of his advice as much as his business.

He cherished his instinct for the market as other men did possessions or fame or women. Tirzah, busy redecorating the nightclub she'd bought on Fifty-second Street, satisfied his sexual needs. Lately they rarely met except in bed.

He spent long hours in his office, and those hours never palled. Even after he acquired a seven-seater Handley-Page plane and had its cabin fitted out like a drawing room, even when he drove out to Long Island in his Hispano-Suiza car to fly it, his mind was reviewing facts and figures. It was the same when he went riding, even when he finally owned the horse he wanted.

"A horse is a horse," Tirzah told him, stretching out beside him and shaking her head.

"Woman," he said, "you know nothing about horseflesh."

"Manflesh is enough for me."

"This is one of Jericho's colts from the Mohawk Stud."

"Who's Jericho?"

"A black stallion I once rode."

Connor had bought Jupiter under an assumed name. Rhys would never knowingly have sold him one of Jericho's get.

"You're *rich!*" she shouted. "And all you've got to show's a plane, a car, a horse, and an apartment. Although I admit it's gonna be some swell apartment if that constipated decorator ever finishes it."

"What else should I have to show for it?"

"Satisfaction, honey, satisfaction!"

He crossed his arms under his head and looked up at the ceiling. "Being rich is like breaking in a pair of new riding boots. I have to get used to it gradually."

"No one would guess you weren't born with a silver spoon, looking at you."

"Looking rich is easy. It's the inner man who has to adapt."

"Thank God you're adaptable," she said, gnawing at a fingernail.

He pulled her hand away from her mouth. "Why?"

"I'm moving to California," she said, the words tumbling out quickly. "I have an offer I can't pass up."

"What offer?" he demanded, a hollowness beginning to

spread through his vitals at the prospect of life without her.

She got out of bed and went into the bathroom, calling to him over the splashing water. "It's a syndicate of picture people. They're going to bankroll me in a huge nightclub, ten times the size of mine, one of those California palaces."

"But it won't be yours!"

"The club is mine."

"But the club is what you've always wanted."

"And now I've got it. And I want more—and better—and bigger. Just like you."

"For God's sake, Tirzah, you hate working for other people."

"Half of it will be mine," she said, emerging from the bathroom and beginning to dress. "Half of me will be working for myself. And California's where show people are really going places. There'll be publicity and tie-ins. Sheet music, recordings, maybe movies too."

"Great!" he said derisively. "A singer with no sound!"

"So I'll act! I'll get to be famous all over this country, not just New York City."

They looked at each other in explosive silence.

"Why the hell didn't you ask me?" he demanded.

"No! We'd never make it as business partners. We'd fight like cats and dogs." She shook her head. "I'm not going to the end of the world, Connor," she said finally. "We'll still see each other."

"When? Twice a year?" He shook his head angrily. "All right, tell me what I have to do to make you stay!"

"Damn you!" she retorted. "I'm not trying to con you into anything."

"Aren't you? If I asked you to marry me, would you stay in New York?"

"Why don't you ask me and see?" she said tightly. She turned away to gather her hat and gloves and he watched her, thinking that he was not ready for marriage, not now—when what he wanted was within sight, if not yet within reach.

"I can't ask you," he said hotly. "Not now."

"I figure not ever," she said.

"Christ, Tirzah, I asked you once and you turned me down!"

"Your heart wasn't in it."

"What about yours?"

"So mine wasn't either! Oh, shit, anyway. I never knew what the hell I wanted when it came to you and I still don't. But I know what *you* want!"

"Oh, sure! I'm an open book."

"Yeah, with Brandon written all over the title page."

"That's none of your business," he warned her.

"Georgia Brandon," she persisted.

"Not anymore."

She fixed him mercilessly for a long moment with her green cat's eyes and then she shrugged and turned to put on her hat.

"When will you leave?" he asked her.

"Not until I open my club and get it rolling. That'll take a few months." She slung her coat over her shoulders and left the bedroom. "I'll see you later," she called back from the hall, but a few days passed before they saw each other again and neither of them mentioned their conversation or her imminent departure. The hours they spent together now were charged with what they did not say.

A vagrant hope rose in him as the reservations for the opening of Tirzah's, as the new club was called, poured in, along with capacity bookings for many weeks after that. If, in addition to that kind of success, he could match what the syndicate had offered her, she might change her mind about going to California.

There was a way to turn a large profit very quickly, and he decided to take the risk.

◆

On Wall Street it was called a pool, a group of men pooling their resources to manipulate the price of a given stock, buying it at the bottom, forcing it up, selling it at the top.

There were other places for investment where profits emanated from real growth, not the trading of paper. Germany, at that time, for example, was making a spectacular recovery thanks to a $2.5 billion loan from America to revive its industry.

But a pool was quicker and far more exciting to the men known on the Street as "players."

Connor put half a million dollars into a Radio pool just starting up, but he had to watch the action from the Visitors' Gallery. His next step would have to be the purchase of a seat on the Exchange, now priced in the neighborhood of one hundred and fifty thousand dollars.

"I'd feel safer if I were managing this pool myself," he told Torrance uneasily on the eve of the action. He had thought it politic to give TD&D an inside tip.

"I'm not in favor of pools," Guthrie Torrance said, bleak with anxiety. "They're entirely too risky. If the timing is off, or word gets out, the whole thing can collapse like a house of cards."

"That's what makes it exciting."

"Youth," sighed Torrance. "Where's Radio now?"

It was at 81 when the pool was confidentially announced to the customary participants, who then began to buy in small lots through widely scattered brokerage firms. The pool managers kept a healthy distance from Post 12 to make interest in the stock appear completely spontaneous.

The next day Radio closed at 89.

It continued gathering momentum the following day when the small investors, sniffing a winner, climbed aboard.

By the end of the week it stood at 109; the pool sold and Connor racked up a fat little fortune. RCA stock, having been dumped back on the market in quantity, sank back to 87¼.

"One more deal like that," he told Tirzah, "and I'll build you a goddamn palace right here in New York!"

"Connor, please don't let's talk about it anymore."

Her club opening had been the most successful and widely reviewed in years, but it hadn't changed her mind.

If she wanted something more from him, she did not say so.

◆

"I tell you, Mr. MacKenzie," the captain at Tirzah's greeted him on the night of her last appearance, "people are really riding the crest."

Connor agreed with him. The feeling of cheer in the country was more than holiday spirit. It sprang from a prosperity that was expanding day by day. The new year, 1925, promised to be even better, and the boom would go on well beyond that, Connor thought, sitting down at his table directly opposite the bandstand.

America was getting rich enough to do as it pleased. It was a creditor nation for the first time in its history, flexing its muscles like a newly wakened giant, beginning to influence international policy.

Unlike Europe, wrung dry of young men and beggared by the war, America was awash in energy and capital. A rash of new magazines reported a stream of consumer goods waiting to be bought, along with wondrous developments in technology and medicine, flight and communications, and the scandalous new art, literature, and music that titillated the senses and tempted people to find out that freedom really meant money and booze and sex.

"The world's been made safe for capitalism," Guthrie Torrance was fond of saying, "but Europe's too decimated to take advantage of it."

It was in America that factories were mushrooming and working at full tilt, that workers earned enough to buy what other workers produced. The roar of the mid-twenties was fueled as much by a sense of well-being as by bootleg gin.

So the country enjoyed itself with zest, all the more so in a place like Tirzah's, decorated with swags of satin the color of new money that hung from the ceiling in rich folds. There were mirrors everywhere else to reflect women in short, skimpy, tubular dresses, garnished at the hip with floor-length panels of tulle or feathers.

Connor lit a cigarette and looked appreciatively at the women. Hair cropped like a man's, breasts flattened, they were nevertheless women. They were bolder and more tantalizing than ever before. Ignoring Prohibition and the old rules governing ladylike behavior, they had graduated from corsets and sherry to skimpy step-ins and the cocktails now in vogue: dry martinis, sidecars, Manhattans, between-the-sheets. Warmed by alcohol and jazz, they danced the Side Step, the Charleston, and the Black Bottom in a display of female flesh not seen in the west since the Bacchanalia of ancient Rome. Sex was fun. Sex was healthy. Dr. Freud said so, didn't he?

Connor ordered a dry martini and sipped it as music ushered Tirzah into the spotlight to a roar of applause. He felt the applause was for him, too, for his success as well as that of the woman who stood in the spotlight, wearing sequined white and singing in that voice that made every man in the room want her.

She was leaving him, and the prospect filled him with a sense of deprivation familiar from his youth. But there was something he wanted more than her, and he was getting close enough to grab it.

He sensed someone watching him and turned his head.

It was Constance.

The affair had been going on for months. They saw each other regularly; the combination of his revenge and her sensuality was as addictive to him as a drug. She was Rhys Brandon's wife, and Rhys was jealous of his property, whether he loved it or not.

Who could love Constance, anyway? The fly in the ointment of this affair was that Connor actively disliked her.

She was with a group of her friends and there was no sign of Rhys. She was looking sidelong at Connor, and after a moment she dipped a finger into her drink and sucked it suggestively. Then, with a little smile, she folded her napkin to represent a plane and waggled its wings.

Her mouth formed the word *tomorrow*. He shook his head and said *Saturday*, and she nodded imperceptibly as the applause exploded and she turned back to her friends.

"Who's the lady?" Tirzah asked him in the taxi that night.

"You *do* have cat's eyes! How do you manage to sing and watch the action at the same time?"

"Who is she?"

"Constance Brandon."

"You're kidding!" She turned to see if he was serious. "Well, it's obvious what she wants with you, but what do you want with her?"

"Not much," he said.

"But you're going to see her."

"I'm taking her flying on Saturday."

"A flying fuck?"

He frowned. They had never questioned each other about the lovers each occasionally took, Tirzah far more often than Connor, but the anticipated separation had made both of them touchy.

"Okay, okay," she said impatiently. "I know it's none of my business. But I thought you detested the Brandons, her as much as him."

He said nothing.

"I get it," Tirzah said softly. "It's him you'll be screwing!"

"I don't know that I'll screw anyone at all," he said. "Now let's drop it."

"I wish you *could* drop it," she said. "The whole lot of them."

But he turned his head to look out of the window and they finished the drive to her apartment in silence.

"Tirzah, what's happening to us?" he asked her before she could get out of the cab.

"I don't know, but we sure as hell need to be apart for a while."

"Does it have to start on your last night?"

She leaned back into his arms and he gave the driver his address. They made love very tenderly that night, saying good-bye, and she left for California two days later.

♦

"I'm well aware of the shift in public opinion," Rhys said, puffing rapidly on his cigar in the library of his New York mansion.

"It's more than a shift, Rhys, it's a total turnabout," Martin van Reitjens insisted. "This country is categorically opposed to war in general and arms manufacturers in particular. New scandals surface every day."

A furor had been mounting on both sides of the Atlantic since the end of the war because of those scandals. British guns, sold to the Turks, had killed British soldiers at the Dardanelles. German Krupp guns, bought by Russia, had been fired on German troops. In America, Carnegie's average annual profit had jumped by more than one hundred and thirty million dollars during the war years. Munitions makers and arms merchants had been accused by the Federal Trade Commission of "inordinate greed and barefaced fraud."

"Now they're saying we planned and prolonged the damn war!" Silas added.

"I know that," Rhys said. "But Crabtree has always operated discreetly and can continue to do so. It's far too profitable to sell! You don't see other munitions makers beating their castings into plowshares."

"They're not running for political office, either," John Anders reminded him.

"It's my risk, not yours." Rhys picked up the brandy decanter and refilled the four glasses. "You boys are influential in politics but from well behind the scenes. You can't be hurt politically by your connection to Crabtree."

There was a silence.

"He's right," van Reitjens said. "Let's not confuse the issues. But that doesn't alter our decision. Look here, Rhys, we're determined to get out of the arms business and we've had a damned good offer for Crabtree. You're holding up the sale."

Rhys glanced at Silas. "*Et tu, Brute?*" he asked, and Silas nodded.

It was clear to Rhys that this time he could not win. It happened to him only rarely and he always found a way around it. "All right," he conceded. "If you're so afraid of being tarred and feathered, I'll buy you out."

Silas whistled. "Buy Crabtree? You know what we've been offered for it, Rhys!"

"That, too, is my concern." But Rhys had a plan he had been working on since the armistice. He had already formed Republic Industries, a holding company for everything he owned: Brandon Textiles; his share of the cotton, sugar, and coffee plantations he held with Silas; his privately owned distributorships in China, which imported large amounts of Brandon coarse cotton goods to be wadded into traditional peasant pants and jackets; and his new linen and hemp mills in Tientsin. Crabtree would be safely tucked away behind them, far from the madding crowd until this antiwar hysteria was over.

"It strikes me," Anders said, "that this comes at an unfortunate time for you. The wartime boom's over. Business is bound to be depressed."

"Not the arms business," Rhys said, goading them. "My offer stands." He would have to sell off the last of his railroad lines and a large block of Brandon Textiles shares in order to come up with the down payment on Crabtree. But Rhys had gambled before and won. He had faith in his star.

There were still fat profits to be made from the manufacture of small arms, not only for the minor wars erupting all over the globe but for the defense of America's interests abroad. American troops were stationed in Haiti and Nicaragua to protect property and guarantee political stability. Washington had to protect free access to the Panama Canal as well, and something would eventually have to be done to guarantee free trade with China. That meant by force of arms.

He would be temporarily short of cash, but no slump lasted forever, and America, undespoiled by the war and able to profit from the new technologies the war had spawned, was on the upward slope of an unparalleled expansion. He could feel it in his bones.

But more seductive still was the power complex consti- tuted by the munitions industry. Rhys wanted a hand in running the world.

"What terms do you suggest?" Anders now asked.

"Once we've agreed on the price, I propose to take over your shares immediately with a down payment of, say, ten percent. I'll pay out the rest, at an annual current interest, over a ten-year period. I think that's eminently fair. You'll be safely out of armaments and I"—he smiled engagingly— "will not be ruined."

The others were quiet.

"Think it over, gentlemen. If Lamartine Munitions buys your shares, they're gone forever. If *I* do, there's always a chance you can buy them back. The price must, of course, reflect that unusual option."

After a pause Anders nodded. "Who knows what the future holds?"

"Not another war for this country." Silas was adamant.

Rhys raised his shoulders, indifferent on that score. "Let me know what you decide." He sipped his drink. "Now to politics. As a state senator I'm doing everything you require and I'm gathering favorable press. By 1926 I'll be ready to make a run for the U.S. Senate. Are you with me?"

Martin van Reitjens, clearly more relaxed than he had been half an hour before, sat back in his capacious leather chair and crossed his legs. "Nineteen twenty-six it is," he said.

"Good!" Rhys smiled broadly. "I'll do my best."

"Oh, you'll be elected. You even look the part," Martin said with that hint of rancor a homely man harbors for a blatantly handsome one. "Now that women have the vote, you'll win in a landslide."

Silas was still standing, his brows drawn into a deep frown. "It's Rhys's women I'm worried about."

Martin stared at him. "What do you mean by that?"

"Rhys knows," Silas muttered. "You two have lived in Washington too long."

Anders clasped his thin, pale hands. "Not really. I've heard the talk."

A faint sneer crossed Rhys's face. They were as jealous as schoolboys! "If you mean I must be more circumspect in my adventures . . ."

"Only the one with your housekeeper." Van Reitjens's shock kept Anders silent for a few moments. "Maybe the men won't mind your kicking up your heels, but the women will. And they'll sure as hell object to your doing it under your own roof, Rhys."

Rhys said nothing.

"We're not sitting in judgment," Anders said smugly. "But you can't go to the Gate to check on your mills as long as she's there."

"But I need her there to run the estate!"

"Find someone else. Or keep her, if you must, but let Silas or Adam see to the mills."

The silence was very thick. The clock on the mantel, ticking unnoticed, was suddenly audible. Anders shifted noisily in his leather chair, removed his pince-nez, and polished the lenses. When he had replaced them on his nose and folded his handkerchief, the banker summed up.

"As long as you're discreet, you can have every woman from here to Haiti as far as we're concerned. But if you want to be elected to the United States Senate, you can't have that one. It would be impossible to hide."

"What do you say, Rhys?" Martin inquired softly.

"All right," Rhys replied. "All right."

♦

He told Constance that night and watched her nostrils flare, as if she could smell the power within his grasp.

"My God!" she exulted. "The parties I'll give in Washington! The people I'll meet!"

"You'll have to stop your private parties," he said, scrutinizing her closely. "The least breath of scandal would kill my chances."

"Really?" She put her hands on her hips. "And what about you?"

"Don't play games with me, Constance," Rhys said, his voice softly menacing.

Her eyes flashed with scorn. "Then *you* stop screwing every woman you see! Maybe I wouldn't mind an occasional fling, Rhys, if you stuck to your own class, but sometimes your taste is absolutely degrading!"

He said nothing. Her arrogance was comforting. It meant she had only been toying with Connor.

"As for me," she went on, "you have nothing to worry about." She faced him with unabashed candor. "I want that Senate seat as much as you do. I'll do anything to help you get it."

He smiled, aroused by her fervor. "As long as we understand each other," he said.

"Of course we do. We always have. Now, stop lecturing and come to bed. That's where we understand each other best."

But tonight, while he made love to her, she pretended he was Connor.

◆

"Rhys!" Guthrie Torrance said. "This is an unexpected pleasure."

"Hello, Guthrie."

Rhys's host nodded and went on to talk to some other men while Rhys stopped at Torrance's table in the Stock Exchange Luncheon Club. It was a large, pleasant, and very private dining room on the seventh floor of the building. A seat on the Exchange was the requirement for membership, and members' guests were assumed to be gentlemen.

It was almost two o'clock, the time for table-hopping before the market claimed the financiers' attention in its closing hour.

Rhys extended a hand. "How are you? But I needn't ask, when the market's on a rise. Hudson was telling me all about it over lunch."

Rhys gestured toward his host, a J. P. Morgan partner, who had gone on ahead.

"Sit down for a moment," Torrance said. "I haven't seen you in months."

Rhys obliged. He was pressed for time, but a politician needed every friend he had, and Guthrie Torrance knew many of the people Rhys had no time to cultivate.

"Who's your guest today?" Rhys asked, looking at the second place on Guthrie's table. "Anyone I know?"

"I don't think so. He's a client, most extraordinary young fellow. Had a major stake in that Radio pool a while back. Most uncanny instinct for the market. I've made millions for my clients since I met him. You should let me do the same for you."

"Who is this paragon?" Rhys asked, lighting a cigarette.

"His name is Connor MacKenzie."

Rhys snapped his lighter shut and returned it to his pocket. "Never heard of him."

"I know very little about him myself, although he's already made a name for himself on the Street. Well-educated chap, but never mentions where he went to school. Lives like a lord but doesn't mix with our kind of people."

"That's as it should be," Rhys said. "Money doesn't care whom it goes to these days."

Torrance glanced up. "Here he comes now. I'm sure Harris, Forbes has been trying to milk him for information, but he's loyal to me. Rhys, may I present Mr. MacKenzie of Hemisphere Investments. MacKenzie, this is Senator Brandon."

Torrance was busy signaling the waiter for more coffee and did not notice that neither man offered his hand. They had barely acknowledged each other as Connor sat down.

Connor turned the conversation to the market—very smoothly, Rhys noticed, but then Connor *was* smooth, in speech, in dress, in manner. His looks had always been striking and now, in the prime of his twenties, Connor was the kind of man over whom women like Constance lost their heads. But Constance was too clever to succumb; Georgia might not be.

Rhys was somewhat unsettled, too, by the change in Connor's attitude, a cool self-assurance that Rhys himself had always used to his own advantage and rarely encountered in other men.

It was demeaning to sit at table with Connor—he never had before, not in all the years they had lived under the same roof—but the opportunity to observe an enemy at close range was too good to be missed. Guthrie, that fool, hung on Connor's every word until someone from Dillon, Read came by and took him away.

♦

For the first time in five years they confronted each other, Rhys disdainful, Connor impregnable behind his armor of success. At the very least, Rhys had to acknowledge that Connor was here, in the Stock Exchange Luncheon Club, the matrix of the Establishment.

"I'm surprised they let you in here, MacKenzie," Rhys said. "You belong in the kitchen."

"Not anymore," Connor returned, feeling a crack in his armor.

Rhys smiled thinly. "Your sort always believes a social metamorphosis comes with money. You were born a mill worker and you'll die a mill worker."

"I could buy Brandon Hall tomorrow," Connor said, his control slipping further.

"Over my dead body!"

"Preferably." Connor got hold of himself. "How's Georgia?" he jabbed, and was rewarded when Rhys's cool hauteur deserted him.

"Well out of your reach, you presumptuous bastard."

"A mere ship's crossing away," Connor persisted.

"I'll have you arrested if you come within a mile of her!"

Connor smiled enigmatically. "You've made an expatriate of her, but I wonder how the voters will feel about that. Americans like their politicians' families home grown and on display."

Torrance reappeared, rubbing his hands over a deal well made. "Glad to see you two getting on so well. Stay on if you like, but I must get back to my office."

"So must I," Rhys said. "Good-bye, Guthrie. A pleasure to see you." He turned away from the table and Torrance, signing the bill, missed the lethal looks the two men exchanged.

But, Rhys reflected as he collected his hat and coat and left the club, one point was well taken: if Rhys wanted to further his political career, he must soon bring his daughters home and make his entire family a part of his campaign for the United States Senate.

That was not a problem. Until they came of age, he controlled his children absolutely; subsequently he would control them with money. Georgia, it was true, would soon come into her mother's estate and, with it, legal independence. But Georgia was devoted to Rhys, and should her freedom temporarily go to her head, no executor, not even that pious hypocrite, Adam, would give a green girl control of such a fortune.

She would be a great heiress. She was already a great beauty. Rhys would arrange a splendid match for her—but not yet. He loved her too dearly to let her go so soon. First he must bring her back home to help him win the election. His beautiful darling. He could protect her from Connor no matter where she was.

◆

Connor opened the door to his new Park Avenue duplex at five o'clock that afternoon, not surprised to hear the telephone ringing as he walked in. He knew it was Constance.

"MacKenzie," he said.

"Half an hour," she replied, and hung up.

His three servants—Mills the valet, the housekeeper, and the maid—were ordered to take off the first Friday in every month and they were too well paid to question their employer's vagaries.

He stood for a moment, looking at his living room with

satisfaction. It had been decorated by Syrie Maugham in white and glass, mirrors and chrome. Spotlights sunk into the ceiling cast pools of light on the glass vitrines that housed the beginnings of his three collections: Nyphenburg porcelain, celadon vases, and bronze horses.

He opened a case and picked up his favorite bronze, a mare with her nursing filly. The filly might have been Jezebel the day she was born.

She's in your care, Connor, he could hear Rhys saying, and he remembered, more than the thrill of ownership, his pride in the trust and favor those words had conveyed. He felt betrayed again by Rhys, newly humiliated by his total contempt for his accomplishments, infuriated by Rhys's relationship with his mother.

It amazed Connor that Rhys could revive in him the boy Connor had thought forever gone, could open old wounds with a look, a phrase. What more did he have to do to make Rhys acknowledge him?

And why did he still want acknowledgment from a man he loathed?

He went upstairs, showered quickly, and changed into slacks and a velvet smoking jacket. He turned back the bed before he went downstairs. A few minutes later Constance rang the bell.

He let her in, feeling a bitter kind of lust as he surveyed her. She was a voluptuous woman, hot and uninhibited. He might have enjoyed going to bed with her if he hadn't known her so well. In his mind's eye he saw her at Brandon Hall, baiting the girls and ordering his mother around. She didn't dare give Connor orders anymore.

"Hello, Constance," he said with especially mixed feelings about her today.

"Hello, Connor," she replied with one of her slow smiles.

He never kissed her when she arrived or when she left. He never touched her at all while they were downstairs. They usually went into the living room for a drink and some desultory conversation before going up to his bedroom, where he always watched her undress. Hers was a vaguely vicious eroticism that aroused him. She had long legs, slim hips, and full breasts that drooped provocatively, as if waiting for a man's hands to contain their weight.

She liked to make love in every conceivable position, but when they finished he was always on top of her.

"Do you want a drink?" he asked while they still stood in the foyer of his apartment. His dark eyes were fixed on her mouth because he could not bring himself to look her in the eye.

"You know what I want," Constance said.

"Then let's get on with it."

She preceded him up the stairs and he put his hands under her skirt and felt the motion of her hips. She never wore a corset when she came to him. She didn't need one. Once inside the bedroom, she tossed her hat, purse, and gloves on one of the armchairs and unbuttoned her jacket. Watching him watch her, she placed the jacket neatly on the chair, then took off her skirt.

Her lingerie was black silk trimmed with lace, and against it her creamy skin had the luster of the enormous pearls she now removed. She unhooked her brassiere, liberating her breasts. Her nipples were already rigid, the aureoles around them large, pink, and velvety. She pushed down her step-ins, moving her hips until they dropped to the floor and were kicked aside. Her garter belt and stockings followed, and she stood there naked for a moment, legs apart, hands on her hips, before she walked to the bed and sat down at the edge of it.

He followed her, shedding his clothes as he went. She reached for him and he knelt, sliding his hand between her legs, brushing her nipples with his lips before he pushed her back on the bed and pressed her thighs apart. He bent and teased her with his tongue, a prolonged performance that ended with her muffled scream of pleasure. Then she pulled him onto the bed.

She was a woman who gave as good as she got. Today, though, he did not let her prolong the blandishments of her eager mouth. He knelt, raised her legs to rest against his shoulders, and sank himself inside her.

"Oh, God," she said. "Oh, yes!"

He said nothing. He moved savagely until she began to shudder in a deep, drawn-out climax. He fell forward against her, her long legs enclosed him, and he let himself go.

It had been an encounter of unadulterated lust, but for all its eroticism, he had felt no ardor. With her he never had. He felt empty, hollowed out, and utterly depressed.

"Oh, Connor," she whispered when they both lay panting and wet with perspiration. "Oh, Connor." She kissed him, holding his face between her hands.

He was dismayed. The way she held him was too personal, as if some tie other than carnality existed between them. He got up to find his cigarettes and she stretched out on the bed, drying her body with the sheet. She accepted a cigarette, and when he lit it for her she drew on it, eyeing him as if she would inhale him with the smoke.

Uneasy, he searched for something to say. "How did you manage to stay out so late last time?"

He had persuaded her to have dinner with him, although she would agree only to an out-of-the-way place in Greenwich Village, where no one she knew was likely to go. He had never cared if they were seen together—he half hoped they would be—but Constance cared. She wanted that Senate seat as much as Rhys did.

"I say I'm with a friend. I'm hardly missed. He's campaigning as if the election were only two months away, not almost two years. But I'd rather talk about us." She glanced at him expectantly.

"What about us?" He was newly alarmed.

"You were unusually ardent today."

She was as coy as a schoolgirl, making a lovers' tryst out of a mutual vendetta!

It had never occurred to him that, having started from the same premise, they might arrive at different conclusions. He felt nothing for her but that most basic physical lechery he had felt for any number of women, yet it was obvious she believed he was fond of her! Worse, she behaved as if she were more than fond of him! The last thing he wanted was Constance fawning over him. She had only one redeeming quality: she belonged to Rhys.

Suddenly he felt demeaned by that.

Constance stroked his thigh. "Tell me what you're thinking about."

"Getting married," he said.

Her hand stilled. "To whom?"

He shrugged. "Someone suitable." But Audrey Torrance, sixteen, blond, blue-eyed, and very social, was the kind of girl he had in mind. He had glimpsed her several times in Guthrie Torrance's office before she forced her father to introduce them. Connor's behavior had been absolutely correct, but Audrey had flirted outrageously, and her smile had reinforced his scheme for the future.

"Well, that's sensible," Constance agreed after a moment, resuming her caresses. "It's the only way for someone like you to get into society. Maybe I can help. I know all the available debutantes. What sort of wife do you want?"

"What sorts are there?" he asked, furious at her patronizing "someone like you."

"You can have a bedroom companion, a Madonna with child, or a social dragon."

"Not all of the above?" Audrey was obviously a virgin, but she had a gleam in her eye that was promising and, given time, would certainly become a social dragon.

Constance shook her head. "How many well-brought-up young girls do you know who're all three?"

"None," he conceded. "But I don't spend much time with well-brought-up young girls."

"They're extremely boring, let me assure you. I'll make a list of likely candidates," she promised, patting his cheek.

"Thanks," he said. He felt claustrophobic. In a moment she would spread herself over him like a giant phagocyte, and he knew he could never make love to her again.

"I have to dress," he said, getting out of bed. "I have a dinner engagement."

"You wouldn't be throwing me out of bed, would you?"
Her eyes matched the edge in her voice.

"Business waits for no woman. We could have a drink at
the Plaza if you like." He knew the Plaza was off limits.

"Another time," she said, not concealing her displeasure. She had recovered by the time they left the apartment.

"In four weeks," she said before they parted. "It will
feel like forever."

Alone again, he was furious with himself for having
let the affair begin in the first place. Why had he?
It had seemed the kind of low maneuver perfectly suited
to Rhys; now it only seemed as despicable as Rhys
was.

He went upstairs to his study and surveyed the piles of
research folders he had brought home from his office.
Work had always been a solace to him and now he made a
decision. He had a seat on the Stock Exchange and Hemisphere Investments to administer his personal fortune. He
was about to take the next step in making himself a force
to be reckoned with on Wall Street.

◆

The telephone rang and he let it jar the silence twice
before he picked it up.

"MacKenzie," he said.

"At last! I'd know that voice anywhere!"

"Oliver?" Connor was incredulous. "Oliver Petrie!"

"I've been trying to find you. I didn't know what city
you lived in until I read a gossip column in the *New York
Journal*."

"Where are you? Are you all right?"

"I am now. I called to tell you something."

"What, for Christ's sake, what?"

"Connor, listen to me. You didn't put me in this wheelchair. I let you say it and I let you think it because I
wanted someone to share my pain and you were the only
one strong enough to do that. But I can deal with it myself
now. You didn't put me here, Connor. A war and a stray
bullet did."

"Oh, my God," Connor said, tears stinging his eyes.
"You don't know how much I needed to hear that."

"I'm sorry it took me so long to say it."

"Never mind, you've said it now. Where are you?"

"Home. The family's gone to Palm Beach, but I stayed
on to meet with a few political hacks. I'm running for
Congress in '26. Why do you ask?"

"I thought I'd fly out to see you."

For the first time Connor heard Oliver laugh. "God,
yes. Come for New Year's. Stay as long as you like. I'll
tell you all about this political gambit. I finally figured
out what it was you saved me for. Let me know the time
and I'll meet you at the airfield. And this time, don't
crash."

"Not this time," Connor said. "Not ever again."

But he was not so certain of that. He put down the
telephone and leaned forward, his head in his hands,
grateful for the breadth of Oliver's spirit, for the fraternity
between them that had begun so strangely and survived so
much—and for a place to go after he found out whether he
was a multimillionaire—or headed right back where he
started from.

◆

He was setting up an investment trust, more precisely a
company that managed a portfolio consisting of other companies' securities, and invited clients to participate. But in
addition, as some investment trusts were beginning to do,
Connor planned to sell stock in the Hemisphere Investment Trust itself.

He knew the single essential factor in making a success
of it was the public's faith in the genius of the trust's
manager. Connor had a growing reputation for genius.
The "players" on Wall Street were beginning to acquire
the celebrity of matinee idols, and after the Radio pool,
Connor had been christened a "Wall Street Wunderkind"
by the press.

He turned to TD&D to sponsor the offering in exchange
for warrants entitling them to buy shares at the issue

price. TD&D, in turn, could either keep the shares or sell them to its clients at a premium.

"I don't know," Linton DeVries rumbled when Guthrie Torrance and his senior partners met to consider Connor's proposal. "It's like owning stock in thin air! An investment trust is no more than a transaction masquerading as a corporation."

"Precisely," Walter Deventer agreed. "An investment trust is a function. It has no plant, no product, no inventory, and therefore no equity, except the brains and luck of its managers."

"But expertise is what people want to buy," Connor said. "It's why they pay you commissions for your advice." He did not add that some of the advice had been his, given to the firm for no compensation of any kind.

"But just one serious mistake in judgment"—DeVries held up a warning hand—"or a break in the market, and the trust collapses—to say nothing of the trust directors' reputations. And the sponsors'."

"I don't plan to make any mistakes, Mr. DeVries," Connor said with a cool confidence he always felt when the bargaining was hot.

The partners glanced at each other.

"My dear fellow," Guthrie said, his delicate mouth aquiver. "No one is infallible."

"And pride goeth before a fall," Connor agreed. "But not if you cover your bets, as I fully intend to do. Very well, gentlemen, I won't embarrass you by persisting."

"You're not going to do it on your own?" DeVries demanded, shocked.

"No. I'll have to get another sponsor, but that won't be a problem. I'm a broker now, and a member of the Exchange. I've acquired a reputation for making money in the market. That's the prime requirement for inspiring confidence in any investment trust."

"Ah, yes, gentlemen," Guthrie said. "He'll inspire confidence, all right."

Deventer examined his signet ring attentively. "Unless his father's reputation stands in his way."

The room grew still as the partners waited.

"He has nothing to do with this," Connor said furiously with a sudden urge to defend his father.

"You have to admit it could be a problem."

"I admit nothing of the kind," Connor retorted. "I have no interest in what he does, but at least he does it openly—which is more than can be said of some people in high places."

There was another pause. Guthrie looked pained. DeVries coughed.

"I'm prepared," Connor went on then, as if Enoch had never been mentioned, "to guarantee that shares in Hemisphere Investment Trust will rise by ten percent within three months of the offering."

"Guarantee?" Deventer pressed softly. "To what extent?"

It was an out-and-out bribe. "Two million," Connor said, vowing that he would never be dependent on a sponsor again. When the trust paid off, he'd buy a bank and sponsor himself!

The three men glanced at one another. "All right," DeVries said, "subject to our approval of the portfolio."

"Of course," Connor said. "*After* you announce your sponsorship." He had given these men free investment advice for the last time.

After another tense moment they agreed.

When he had gone, DeVries cut himself a fresh cigar and lit it before he said, "Cocky bastard. That young man will go ass over teakettle one of these days, mark my words."

"I don't think so, Linton," Torrance replied. "Not, at least, until he's made a few fortunes."

"Stolen them, more like!" Deventer exploded. "You know what these investment trusts do. They take money for stocks they never even buy. It's out-and-out robbery."

"I doubt he'll do anything illegal," Guthrie said. "He's too intelligent."

"He will if he stands to lose two million!"

"Does MacKenzie *have* two million?"

"If he doesn't have it now, he will within days of our

announcement. His Hemisphere shares are bound to be oversubscribed."

"If they aren't, we'll send him to jail," DeVries said. "Guthrie, what's this MacKenzie after, aside from money?"

"Power," Guthrie suggested, pursing his lips. "Social status. I think he wants to join our club."

"When hell freezes over!" DeVries snapped, and his jowls wobbled as he shook his head. "Damned impudence!"

♦

Connor returned to his office, tossed back two cognacs, and waited for his interior trembling to stop. It was not only from the risk he had just taken, it was from the humiliation of having to bribe them into backing a sure thing—and their effrontery in bringing Enoch into it!

It was too quiet. The voices of his staff were barely audible through the heavy door and he got up to open it a crack. The sound of telephones and tickers and typewriters, of clerks calling out quotes, were more reassuring than cognac.

He tried counting his blessings.

Despite what Tirzah thought, he enjoyed his spacious apartment, his car, his plane, and Jupiter, virtually a carbon copy of Jericho. He was excited about the house he was building at Sands Point. And it excited him that he had just gambled everything he owned and all he might possibly borrow.

The same publicity that was vital to his success made him uncomfortable. It was unlikely that the people he knew from his association with Whitelaw would expose him: they were as intent upon secrecy as he was. No one knew where he had grown up. A large donation to Braker Military Academy had destroyed the records linking him to Rhys Brandon.

But he was still on the outside looking in. He needed a label more acceptable to Guthrie Torrance's circle than that of Wall Street speculator. "Financier" would be a lot better—or even "industrialist." As soon as Hemisphere paid off, that was what he would go for. The prospect of a hostile takeover of Brandon Textiles beckoned. It would require a real fortune, but soon he would have a real fortune.

♦

There was a knock at the door. "A Mr. Abbott to see you," his secretary said. "About the post of confidential assistant."

Connor smiled when he recognized Barney Abbott, one of TD&D's brilliant young analysts.

"Why me," Connor asked after the preliminaries, "when you have a guaranteed future at TD&D?"

"Because they'll never make me a partner," Abbott said. "I haven't got the right pedigree."

They looked at each other. Abbott was slim, fair, bespectacled, and very, very shrewd, Connor thought.

"I don't have any plans for creating a partnership," he said.

"There's a difference between that and deliberate exclusion, isn't there?"

"Yes, there is. Have you spoken to Mr. Torrance?"

"I gave him my notice this morning."

Connor laughed. "Pretty sure of me, weren't you?"

Abbott smiled, looking far less forbidding for a moment. "I had to get out of there, no matter what. And I've been watching you for some time, Mr. MacKenzie. You're very good. This trust is going to make a fortune."

"DeVries thinks I'll lose my shirt."

"DeVries doesn't move with the times," Abbott said. "He has no imagination, but he's been following your every lead."

"The amusing thing is that, with luck, a lot of men just like him will be following my lead," Connor said.

"What's amusing about that?"

"Most of them wouldn't invite me to tea."

Abbott grimaced. "Their loss," he said. "They wouldn't invite me either."

"We haven't discussed salary."

"I'll leave that to you," Abbott said.

♦

Connor had refused Constance's calls for several weeks, but she was not a woman to be shaken off so easily and he finally agreed to meet her before she and Rhys sailed to France for the Christmas holidays. Connor was in no mood for a scene, not on the eve of TD&D's announcing its sponsorship of Hemisphere, but Constance had never been perceptive. His attitude made no impression on her. He would have to spell it out.

They met at his apartment. Too late he realized a public place might have been wiser, given her ferocious temper.

"What the hell have you been playing at?" she demanded as soon as she was inside the door. "I don't care what you're doing, you can't be that busy!"

"Come into the living room," he said. "I have something to tell you."

"You can bet your Nellie you have, and it had better be good!" She flung herself into a chair and crossed her long, slim legs.

He offered her a drink but she refused, glowering up at him. "Well?"

"Constance, we won't be seeing each other anymore."

"Why not?"

"It's pretty clear, isn't it? We had an affair and now it's over."

Her eyes shot daggers at him, and her bosom rose and fell as she glared.

"Just an affair?" she said, seething.

He made a gesture of acquiescence. "All right, not just an affair. You're not stupid, Constance. You knew we were both in it to punish Rhys."

"Rhys?" she shouted. "I was only a way for you to get back at Rhys?"

"What else?" he said impatiently. "It was the same for you. We never could stand the sight of each other. The affair served its purpose, but there isn't any future in it."

"How *dare* you?" she screamed, springing to her feet

and approaching him. "Do you think you can use people and throw them away when it suits you?"

"*You* always have." He was enjoying this.

She slapped him hard enough to leave marks on his cheek.

He regarded her impassively. "You'd better go," he said. "We have nothing more to say to each other."

"I'll have plenty to say to anyone who'll listen!"

"And compromise yourself? And finish Rhys in politics? Stop it, Constance. I'm not a child."

"No, damn your black heart, you're not! You never were. You were an evil little brute and you grew up to be a low-down, rotten, miserable, scheming bastard."

She walked back to the couch for her things, picked up a heavy crystal ashtray from the cocktail table, and hurled it at his head with all her strength. He ducked and the crystal shattered against the wall as she made for the door, turning to deliver one last salvo.

"I know what you're really after," she said. "Georgia. But you'll never get her. You're up against *me* now as well as Rhys."

He heard the door slam with relief—and revulsion, as much for himself as for her. If he had not realized years before that he could never bring himself to use Georgia as a weapon in this fight, he would have known it now.

♦

The silence in the apartment after she had gone soon turned gloomy. He was too much on edge to put on a record and read, and there was no one in town he wanted to meet for dinner or a drink. The market was closed for the weekend and the people he lunched and dined with had gone home to their families. Tirzah and Racey were in California, Racey about to become a father.

He missed Tirzah even more than he had anticipated, maybe because, much as he deplored sentimentality, Christmas was coming and it was no time to be alone. For years he had spent it with happy people in convivial surroundings, listening to Tirzah sing. This year he would spend it in that anxious solitude that always revived his memories of Brandon's Gate—the house full of children and Christmas stockings hung on the mantel, Connor's among them until he started working at the mill and had to hang his stocking in the kitchen.

For a moment he smelled that wonderful kitchen, a blend of fresh bread and stove blacking, soup and roast lamb and cinnamon apples, soap and starch and blueing on laundry day, and the blissful odor of sun-dried linen sizzling under the laundress's iron.

It struck him that he had lost most of the people he cared about by death or deceit or desertion: Enoch, his mother, Peter—and Georgia. He would have liked to talk to Georgia. Better than anyone, Georgia knew who he was and how he was driven to be better, even as a child.

And he had lost Rhys—or his vision of him as a friend and mentor. The man was still his constant companion, the perverse inspiration for his success and the reason why Connor was about to risk all he had for higher stakes.

The possibility of failure—and there was always that possibility from a moment's inattention, one inaccurate projection, a sudden fall in the market—made him shiver, but he could not stay where he was. He had to move on.

BOOK III

◆

1924–1929

25

♦

Georgia lay on the chaise longue the wrong way around, her long legs raised and resting on its back and her naked body stretched to its full length against the crimson velvet upholstery. Her hands were clasped over her head and the curve of one arm hid her face.

Samson Breen, his expression intense, worked at his canvas with quick, sure strokes.

He never spoke when he worked, and although she could not see the painting, she could see the painter from beneath her shielding arm. Breen's left hand held the palette, and the muscles of his arm bulged. His chest strained against the old unbuttoned nightshirt he used as an artist's smock. His shoulders were square, and he stood with his columnar legs planted firmly before the easel, like a colossus bestriding the earth.

Breen, she thought affectionately, you have genius, intelligence, and strength, but absolutely no grace.

It was incredible to her that a man so devoid of charm could be an artist of skill and sensitivity. He did not dress; he threw himself together in rough workmen's blues. He behaved like a peasant, although he described himself as a fugitive from a respectable middle-class Iowa family. But what he said, even though it was crudely phrased, usually made sense.

He stopped painting now and looked at her, then at his painting, then back at her again. The expression in his blue eyes altered slowly from deep, inward-looking concentration to satisfaction.

"Oh, baby!" he exclaimed. "I've really got you now."

"You've had me repeatedly," she said, her soft laughter muffled by her arm.

He threw his head back and laughed loudly, then cast his palette onto a table cluttered with oil paints, pots, and rags, and approached her, tossing aside the nightshirt and stepping out of his paint-splotched trousers. He stood over her, his eyes traveling the length of the body he had painted so often, and she looked up, watching his penis rise from a tangle of pubic hair as dark as the hair of his head and beard.

"There isn't a man alive won't get a hard-on when he looks at that painting," he said. "I deserve to have the real thing as my reward."

She smiled and reached out to touch his penis, running her fingers from the base to the tip as it grew harder in her hand. She held out her other hand, palm up, curling her fingers expectantly, and he laughed again and bent to take a condom from the pocket of his discarded trousers.

"A princess in any situation," he said, handing it to her. "There's only one place you really let down your hair and that's bed."

She put the contraceptive on him, rolling it on slowly. When it was secure he bent, swooped her up, and carried her to the unmade bed in a dim corner of his studio.

Her breasts tingled when his hands touched them. His mouth came down hard on hers, and for an instant she smelled tobacco and turpentine. Then she gave herself over to the delights of sex, relishing the eddies of sensation hands could summon up, without dwelling on whose hands these were. Her eyes were closed and her head thrown back, her legs flung wide apart. She felt his beard brush her belly, then her thighs, and she was unaware of their sounds of desire and response, aware only that this act made her feel like a woman with an identity apart from the one she had worn for twenty years.

Then he came into her, driving hard against her churning hips, and she lost all perception of him and escaped into the fantasy that he was Connor, dancing with her, lying with her, loving her, that it was his warm breath panting, his mouth pressed against her hair.

"Jesus H. Christ!" Breen said when they were both breathing quietly. He rose on his elbows to look down at her. "You live up to my paintings of you."

She said nothing, reluctant to return to reality.

He rolled over onto his back and searched the floor near the bed for cigarettes, offering her one and lighting them both. The match flared close to his face, breaking the spell. He was not Connor. He was a tall man with dark hair, but there the physical resemblance to Connor ended.

"What I don't understand," Samson said, sucking in the smoke, "is why, with that bonfire inside you, you hung on to your cherry for so long."

"The Social Register," she said, citing it because it was one of his pet peeves, "considers it essential for a girl to hang on to her cherry until she marries."

"Baloney!" he said. "I've lit up more debutantes than I have cigarettes." Breen got out of bed, retrieved his pants, and went behind the battered screen that hid the lavabos from view. She heard him splashing.

Samson was her first and only lover and had been for more than a year, but after the first few months she knew she was not in love with him. His earthy virility had attracted her at a time when she was bursting with untapped sexuality, but there were other things too. He was American and she was homesick. She was a connoisseur of art and had enormous respect for his talent. He was proud but abjectly poor, and she enjoyed bringing him daintily wrapped packages from Fauchon, as if she were coming to take tea rather than to be his nude model and mistress. Once a month she paid his bill at the art supply shop and left five hundred francs under his pillow, which he perceived as fair since the idle rich could justify their existence only by becoming patrons of the arts.

But his brooding, driving temperament reminded her of Connor. He combined Connor's intensity with her father's indifference to anyone's wishes but his own.

He came out from behind the screen, naked and still

carrying his pants, and dropped them when he looked at the canvas. A beatific smile formed on his face.

"I've done it again!" he said. "Goddamn if I haven't! Any hack can paint the shell of a beautiful woman, but I paint you the way you are. Soft and strong and sensual. Look!"

He swung the easel around toward her and she studied it, careful to separate Georgia the model cum lover from Georgia the critically astute director of the Brandon Art Collection. There was an urgency about the woman lying there, not in repose but in erotic expectation. Her face was hidden—Georgia had insisted on that for all the paintings he had done of her—but mystery only enhanced the sensuality of the piece. Anonymous, she was every man's dream of passion. And she was eager for passion. It was in the insinuating curve of her hips, raised against the back of the chaise, in the fullness of her breasts pulled high by her upraised arms like twin offerings, in the temptation of her slightly parted thighs.

She nodded. "God, Sam, you're really good! I wish I could buy them for the collection."

He was hauling a stack of canvases to the easel, carefully putting aside the painting of her he was working on and lifting the finished oils to the easel one by one. There were six of her in all, standing, sitting, lying by sun, moon, and candlelight.

"My Georgias!" he said excitedly when the last was on the easel. "My gallery of naked Georgias!" He beamed at her in triumph. "This series is going to make my fortune!"

"Rechristened," she reminded him.

He nodded, pulling on his pants and a bulky sweater. "Your father would murder you."

"Any father would."

Breen folded his arms, still gazing at the easel where his first painting of her rested: a seated Georgia, her knees drawn up to graze the nipples of her breasts, was brushing the cascade of golden hair that fell from her bent head to shower down between her parted legs. The composition was a constant curve that carried the eye to that fall of hair

and what it veiled. There was an almost palpable warmth
in the satiny skin, a near detectable scent of perfumed
flesh.

"No," he said, his keen blue eyes returning to her.
"Any father would murder *me*! Yours is different. I tell
you, the bastard's in love with you."

"Don't exaggerate, Sam," Georgia said, sitting up and
wrapping a shawl around her shoulders. "I love him too.
We have a unique relationship."

"I'll say! He hovers over you like a lover! What man
squires his daughter around more than his wife? What
father chooses every stitch his daughter wears, from her
bloomers to her furs? He's taught you more about the
textile industry than he's taught his sons. You buy and sell
for his art collection. He's braided your life into his! When
are you going to get the hell away from him?"

"As soon as I turn twenty-one."

"Inconsistency, thy name is woman! You love him, but
you're gonna leave him. After twenty years of playing
handmaiden to this demigod, you're gonna walk out in two
months, just like that!" Breen snapped his fingers.

"In six weeks—and I won't be walking out," Georgia
said, beginning to dress. "I'll be going back to the States."

"To do what? Marry some horse's ass and become a
society matron?"

"No! To design textiles." She crossed to the far wall,
where a series of her designs had been framed and hung.
She studied them for a moment. The colors were brilliant
and their combinations exciting. The designs varied, from
delicately traced patterns to bold geometrics, cubist in
feeling. She turned back to Breen.

"*You're* the one who convinced me these were good
enough."

"They are."

"*You* made me patent all my designs. Were you telling
the truth? Or was it flattery to ensure a steady supply of
food and money?" She spoke quietly, but the anger was
there in her face, in her eyes.

"It's the truth, goddammit! You're too smart for flat-

tery." He began wiping his brushes. "Why can't you design textiles in Paris? Or are you going to New York to be
closer to your father?"

She dropped her ivory silk chemise dress over her
head. "No. He spends most of his time in Washington.
Sam, you know as well as I do that the French think only
the French are good enough to design couture fabrics. As
a novice, I don't have a chance here." She pinned her hair
into a knot, pulled a cloche hat down to her eyebrows, and
reached for her lynx-trimmed cashmere coat. "When I've
made a success of it at home, I'll be back."

"I hope so," he said gruffly. "I'm going to miss you."
His keen eyes surveyed her. "You look like a million
bucks."

"Why, Sam, you old grizzly bear," she said, batting her
lashes at him. "I'm beginning to think you care for me."

"Yeah. When's the next sitting? There's still work to be
done on number six."

"It's hard to say exactly, with the whole family descending. We're going to Cap d'Antibes right after Christmas,
but I don't know how long we'll stay. I'll write to you. In
the meantime, look under your pillow." She blew him a
kiss. "Au revoir, Sam. Merry Christmas!"

◆

Driving along the boulevard in a taxi, Georgia looked out
at the cobbled streets of Montmartre, watching the lights
of the shops and cafés wink on in the December dusk.
There were signs of Christmas, especially in the *pâtisserie*
windows with their displays of cakes and sugared almonds
and *bûches de Noël*, the traditional Christmas cake shaped
like a Yule log. But Christmas tended to be a devotional
day in Catholic France; the noisier celebrations came on
New Year's Day and Twelfth Night.

She remembered what New York was like at Christmas:
exuberant, friendly, truly merry. For her, at this distance,
New York had assumed the allure of Kubla Khan's pleasure dome! If it was not stately, if it lacked the spacious-
ness of Paris and the elegance of her parks and boulevards,

New York had a lustiness that was similar to Georgia's own.

"Paris is a feminine city," she had once told Breen. "New York's more virile."

"Any town you're in would be virile. Any man worth his salt can sniff what's going on behind your princess facade. I bet you don't let it show at home."

"No. My father would find it vulgar—and Constance has an uncanny intuition when it comes to matters sexual. She's eternally suspicious of Jillian—with absolutely no reason to be." Georgia had smiled fondly. "Jillian has no talent for dissimulation. When she loses her virginity, everyone will know it! I envy her her spontaneity."

"You can be pretty spontaneous yourself."

"That's sex. Sex is different."

"Vive la différence!"

She knew it was time to go back to America and start living her life, establishing herself in an atmosphere more open to change than Europe was. One of the Brandon mills could be set up to print her designs on their finest cotton and test them for fastness. There was no such facility at her disposal in Paris.

Once she had dreamed of going back to Connor. Now she knew that, whatever her fantasies when Samson Breen made love to her, she would be no match for Connor's anger. It had never been directed at her, but it had come between them time and time again and always would.

"Hush now," Peggy had tried to comfort her when months had become years without a word from Connor. "You're still so young. You don't understand these things."

"He loved me once, Peggy. That night I could have sworn he loved me just as much, and more besides—the way a man loves a woman."

"A woman who swears by Connor is askin' for trouble. His own mother says Connor has the devil's own anger in him. He can't see beyond it to any woman, not even to you."

Georgia had no answer to that. Connor had obviously not been shaken to the depths by that powerful surge of feeling between them, or he would have come to her. At the very least, he would have written! He would not have deserted her, as he had done several times before, without a word.

No, she couldn't rely on Connor or anyone else. She had to make a life of her own, for her own sake and to be true to her mother and—yes—to escape her father's smothering love, the love she had struggled so hard to earn and in which she had gloried for so long.

"Never mind, my darling," Rhys had told her the night of the ball, when he and Connor argued so violently. "We have each other and that's all we need."

He had whisked her off to finishing school in Switzerland, with Jillian as a reluctant companion, and had insisted they stay on in Paris afterward in the large, luxurious house he rented in the Avenue d'Iena, "a setting," he had said at the time, "befitting a rare jewel."

He was an indulgent father. He let her drop her studies in fine arts for courses in textile design and was lavish in his praise for the patterns she produced, but he would not let her return to New York, and New York offered the best chance to break into commercial textile design. She would convince him this time! She knew how. She had made a study of pleasing him all her life.

She shivered. Damn Breen and his theories! She shook her head, rejecting them, recoiling from them.

But Rhys *did* still believe he was all she needed. It astounded her that he regarded her as a sexual neuter, something like an angel. He spoke about her eventual marriage, but he objected to any man in whom she displayed the slightest interest. She often wondered what he would do when she met someone she wanted to marry.

"I tell you, the man's in love with you." Breen had said it the first time a few months after they had become lovers.

"Oh, Breen, that's ridiculous! For you everything comes down to sex."

"Do you have a better explanation for him—and

your recent 'discomfort' with him, to use one of your euphemisms?"

"Yes. I don't object to his loving me. I resent his wanting me to *be* my mother."

"I thought that's what you wanted too."

"I want to be worthy of her. I adore her. I admire her. I want to be what she'd have been if she'd lived in my time instead of hers. But he wants me to *be* Georgianna, bound by the same conventions, eternally under his protection."

"I rest my case" was Samson's reply.

Breen disturbed her, but Georgia had much to thank him for. Sex *was* a catalyst, the single area of her life that was beyond her father's power to control. It had made her perceive herself as a woman, not solely a daughter, whether Rhys's or Georgianna's. And Breen's encouragement of her artistic talent had given her purpose. He convinced her that there was a commercial market for her designs.

"Don't listen to all that romantic crap about art for art's sake," Breen had insisted in one of his post-coital sermons. "Art has no meaning unless someone beholds it. Even the cavemen had an audience for their bison paintings."

"Your paintings would be art even if no one saw them!"

"Not nowadays. Once it was enough to create for the glory of God or a sovereign. Now we need broad public recognition, and the best way to get it is to be extravagantly well paid for it. Someday you'll be able to sell your designs to any textile manufacturer in the world, starting right here in France, at top fees. That ought to appeal to your capitalistic heart!"

It appealed more to her need for independence, for separation.

Surely Rhys would approve her plans when he heard them! Why else had he taught her so much about the textile industry? She had been a dutiful daughter, but now she was a woman, excited by her talent and eager to use it. Her father, of all people, would encourage her. It was their lack of talent that he deplored in his other children.

The taxi stopped in front of the house in the Avenue

d'Iena, unable to pull inside the gates. There were three Rolls-Royces parked in the drive. The family had arrived from America for the holidays.

A familiar smothering sensation descended upon her.

♦

Georgia and Jillian, waiting for the others in the drawing room before dinner, sipped sherry in an atmosphere of comradely gloom.

"I sometimes wonder," Georgia said, "why you don't hate me."

"Be comforted," Jillian returned. "I sometimes do. But why should I, in particular?"

"Because Father made you my companion in exile."

Jillian shrugged. "I prefer Paris, with Miss Howell as a duenna, to living in New York with Mama."

"That's because you *like* going to parties with effete young men and blasé young women, going to the races, to teas and luncheons and dinner parties. I feel as if I've been moving backward ever since we started finishing school. I want to *do* something!"

"Don't I know it! You'd rather mope around a textile mill, having epiphanies over dye lots."

"But soon I *will* do something! Why else has Father taught me so much about the industry?"

Jillian shrugged. "Who knows why he does anything? But I'm not as serious about life as you are. What I hate is Papa's decree that *you* must marry before I can. I'll die if I don't get away from this family soon, even if I have to marry some fool of a man to do it."

She ticked the family off on her fingers. "Mama's always plotting. Papa doesn't care about anything but politics and business—and you, of course. Will and Richard are hateful, and Malcolm likes books better than people! What would Dr. Freud make of us?" Jillian subsided for a moment, then said explosively, "Why *don't* you get married anyway? You've been asked often enough."

Georgia shook her head. "Not by anyone I love."

"Love has nothing to do with marriage. Look at Mama and Papa."

"I'd rather not."

Jillian scowled and relapsed into silence.

The sisters were still complete opposites, in appearance as well as in character—Georgia a mystery, Jillian an open book. Jillian resented Georgia's discretion and was certain that her sister was no longer chaste, as Jillian continued to be. Jillian said she was being faithful to Peter's memory, but she was also affronted by the mechanics of sex, or what little she knew of them. Her ignorance, too, was a source of discontent.

"I tell you everything I do!" Jillian would complain. "Why are you so secretive?"

"I only seem that way," Georgia would equivocate. "It comes of battling Constance. You should stand up to her more."

"It's easy for you! She's not *your* mother."

"Constance may be your burden. Papa is mine."

"You'll get no sympathy from me. He dotes on you."

"I don't want to be doted on."

"Then you'll have to move out," had been Jillian's impossible advice—until now.

♦

There was a rustle at the door and Constance swept in, splendid in turquoise taffeta and diamonds.

"Hello, you two," she said to the girls. "What mischief have you been up to while we were away?"

Clearly uninterested in a reply, she snapped her fingers at the footman, who poured her a dry martini from the frosty shaker he had just brought in.

The three boys had followed in her wake. Will and Richard, still inseparable rivals in their early teens, were sturdy but unprepossessing boys with Adam's square build and coloring. They slouched over to the damask divan near the French windows, but Malcolm joined his sisters.

"Hello, Rapunzel," he greeted Georgia, noticing she still deferred to Rhys's wishes by not bobbing her hair.

But the mockery could not conceal the deep affection between them.

"Glad to be here?" she asked him.

"Only to see you," Malcolm said, turning to include Jillian. He was always considerate of Jillian, because, he had told Georgia, Jillian had been bruised enough. "But I'll be glad to get home at Easter."

Malcolm lived most of the year away at school, but he spent his summers at Brandon's Gate, reading literature and philosophy with his uncle Adam.

"Unhealthy!" Rhys called it. "Ridiculous for a boy."

But Malcolm had never been boyish. At twelve he was the image of Rhys, blond, green-eyed, and just as handsome. The differences between them were fundamental, though: Malcolm never tried to charm anyone, and he was almost eerily perceptive of other people's feelings, whether or not he admired them. He never feigned admiration, and in fact patronized his father. Yet Rhys preferred Malcolm to his other sons, who strove mightily to please him.

"Have you heard the news about Connor?" Malcolm asked now.

Georgia sat very still, but Jillian demanded to hear everything.

"He's making a fortune in the stock market. Gets his name in the financial pages every other day. Father says he's in over his head this time, though, with something called an investment trust that Connor has put together. That's all I know." Malcolm glanced at Georgia.

"Well!" Jillian said. "That must really rattle Papa."

"He never mentions Connor, you know that," Georgia said, finding her voice.

"Do those dreadful boys know?" Jillian asked, getting up. "The way they hate Connor, I can't wait to tell them!"

Georgia and Malcolm remained alone on the couch.

"You're not still waiting for him, are you, Georgia?" Malcolm asked worriedly.

Georgia shook her head. "I used to think love was always reciprocal, that love would generate love. It doesn't, you know."

"Any man who doesn't love you is a fool," Malcolm said. Georgia put an arm around him. "Thanks, darling."

"I wonder what his fight with Father was about." He glanced at his sister, baffled. "I liked him a lot when I was little. I pretended he was my brother."

"When I was little, so did I."

◆

"Georgia!"

It was Rhys, his hands outstretched as he approached his daughter. He drew her up and put his arms around her, kissing her cheeks and her hair, with only a nod to Jillian, who looked on from across the room. The embrace finally terminated, Rhys held Georgia at arm's length, noting her dress, her hair, and her jewelry. "Lovely," he said. "You're lovelier than ever. Come and tell me what you've been doing without me."

The rest of the family, exuding both confusion and hostility, observed the two in silence as Rhys sat down next to Georgia, his arm encircling her waist, and questioned her in minute detail about everything she had seen and done since his last trip to Paris.

Constrained by the family's scrutiny, Georgia took refuge in business.

"I hope you haven't abandoned the high-count cotton," she told Rhys. "I'm about to create a huge demand for it."

He smiled fatuously. "Are you, my little industrialist?"

God, she thought, he treats me like a baby!

"Father, there's a lot of money in America. More people will buy fine domestic cotton if it's—"

"Must you talk business tonight?" Constance demanded. "It's Christmas Eve!"

Georgia was spared a reply when the butler appeared to announce dinner.

"We must talk after dinner," Rhys told Georgia. "I have a very important matter to discuss with you."

"It will have to wait until tomorrow," Constance said. "We're going to the theater." She looked at Georgia with a smug little smile. "Tim made the voyage with us. He'll be over to see you after dinner."

"Lovey-dovey," Will sneered.

"Mush," Richard chimed in.

"Be quiet, both of you," Rhys snapped. "Speak when you're spoken to."

Constance shook her head at her sons and reclaimed her husband's arm to go in to dinner, only to be separated from him again by the long dining table glittering with crystal and china around a centerpiece of holly.

"Holly!" Jillian said, delighted. "Where did it come from?"

"Uncle Adam brought it from the Gate especially for you and Georgia," Malcolm told her. "The ship's florist kept it for me on the crossing."

"How is everyone at home?" Georgia asked eagerly. "How's my Dilys?"

Constance rang the silver dinner bell in front of her, summoning the first course. She glanced at her husband from under her lashes.

"Everyone is well," Rhys said, careless or unaware that Will and Richard were suddenly absorbed in their empty service plates. "Malcolm goes up there so often that I no longer have to. He'll be running those mills before I know it."

"I have no interest in running the Brandon mills," Malcolm said calmly.

"Indeed?" Rhys smiled indulgently. "And what will you do when you're a man?"

"Teach history and write novels."

"You won't get far in the world doing that," Will said with great contempt.

Throughout dinner there was a growing tension in the room, and Georgia attributed it, inevitably, to her father. He was a shade too convivial, a hair too affable, and that made everyone nervous. It was not, she decided, due to an argument with Constance. Those two no longer argued. They coexisted in separate bubbles of discontent, bound together by ambition—which was amplified, on Constance's side, by her eternal craving to possess him utterly.

"That was a dreary dinner," Will complained when his parents had gone out.

"Where was your scintillating conversation?" Jillian asked, yawning.

"I could tell you a thing or two about what goes on at home," Richard said slyly.

"Shut up, Rich," Will commanded him.

"Mama's in a stinking mood," Jillian observed. "As if something bit her."

"I wonder what was on *his* mind?" Malcolm said.

Richard was immediately attentive. "What do you think?"

"Politics?" Will offered hopefully.

"No, it was more than that," Malcolm said. "Maybe it's the 'something important' he wants to discuss with Georgia."

"Oh, well," Will said, relieved. "As long as it's got nothing to do with me."

"Nothing you do could possibly interest Papa," Jillian said.

"Silly bitch," Will shot back.

"Darling," Jillian said. "You're such a darling boy."

"I'm going up to my room to read," Malcolm said abruptly.

Richard watched him go with exaggerated disgust. "Pantywaist!" he called after him. "Come on, Will, let's play billiards."

"I'm going up too," Jillian said. "Georgia's the one Tim wants to see. What a miserable Christmas Eve!"

Georgia waited alone for Timothy Cassadyne, puzzling over her father's behavior. She was still thinking about it later that evening when Tim, red-headed, freckled, and terribly nervous, asked her to marry him and she refused.

♦

Remorse overcame her when Tim had gone and she was in her room. She had handled a delicate situation clumsily. She had hurt his feelings. She was half tempted to call him and apologize.

But for what? Declining to marry a man she had never loved, no matter how he felt about her? She was not responsible for Timothy Cassadyne's assumptions.

Jillian came in, wielding a hairbrush.

"Why did Tim leave so early?"

"He asked me to marry him and I said no."

"Oh, for God's sake, Georgia! You've refused half the men we know! I really can't see you as an old-maid artist. You'll have to marry someone eventually."

"But not Tim. And not now. Jilly, listen. I'm not going to stay in Paris. I'm going back to New York."

"You're crazy! Papa will never let you."

"In February he won't be able to stop me."

"You *are* mad! He'll find a way. And what'll you use for money? Or didn't you think about that?"

Georgia shook her head. "Frankly, no. But when I'm twenty-one I'll own my Brandon stock outright. I can sell that if I have to."

"He'd disown you! You know how he is about keeping those shares in the family."

Georgia said nothing, and Jillian's eyes began to glitter with tears of hurt frustration. "You *will* do it, won't you? You'll go and leave me here alone."

"Only for a year. Then you'll be free too. You can live on the income from your shares."

"I'd have to live in a slum! So will you if you're counting on your silly designs to support yourself. You should have accepted Tim. You'll never get away from home until you're married, and neither will I." Jillian, her face sullen, began to brush her hair again in short, angry strokes.

"Was Tim angry?" she asked after a while.

"Very."

"He had a right to be! You've been leading him on for years. He was your first lover, I know that much!"

"That isn't true," Georgia said patiently. "We've never been anything but friends."

"I don't believe you. And I know just how he feels. Tossed aside, that's how. I ought to call and comfort him."

"I wish you would," Georgia said absently. She was wondering what Rhys had to tell her.

♦

Jillian dialed the Ritz and asked for Tim. "It's Jillian," she said when he answered. "I called to tell you how sorry I am about what happened tonight."

"Oh," he said.

"Tim, take me to dinner tomorrow night."

"Why?"

"Just to talk," she said, and added, "I think my sister's crazy."

There was a brief pause before he said, "All right, but I'd rather not come to the house. I'll send a car for you at eight."

"Perfect," Jillian said.

She replaced the receiver and lay back on her pillows. She could sympathize with Timothy because she understood frustration and rejection. Georgia didn't. Georgia had never been denied anything she wanted, or anyone, except maybe Connor for a while, and that was just a crush left over from childhood.

"She thinks Tim will hang around waiting," Jillian muttered, "and come running when she calls."

Maybe he would. Sex was supposed to be a powerful bond and no matter what Georgia said, Jillian was certain Tim had been her lover. All those cozy little evenings à deux whenever Tim came to Paris! All those summers on the Riviera while Tim undressed Georgia with his eyes! Papa loathed Tim because of the way he looked at Georgia.

What a coup it would be to take faithful Tim away from Georgia!

Jillian turned out the light and stared into the dark. What did it matter whom she married, since she couldn't have Peter?

26

♦

"So you see, my darling," Rhys finished in his private sitting room the next morning, "your mother's estate has expanded considerably since she bequeathed it to you. Added to your Brandon inheritance, it comes to a sizable fortune for you."

He looked at her sitting opposite him and thought she had never been more beautiful. She transformed any room she entered merely by her presence.

"I had no idea, Father, not the slightest!" she said delightedly. "And I know exactly how I'm going to use Mother's legacy."

Rhys felt a distant warning stir. "Georgia, considering the dangers that beset an heiress as beautiful as you are, I trust you don't propose to manage your money yourself."

She hesitated. "Not until I'm as good at it as you've been," she said, regretting that she hadn't taken a course in economics at the Sorbonne.

"Your uncle Adam is your executor," Rhys said stiffly.

"Uncle Adam? Not you?"

"Those were your mother's wishes."

She was astounded, but his manner warned her away from the subject. She would have to ask Adam—or Peggy! Peggy told her things about this family that no one else did.

"Father, I already have a project in mind for some of it." She sprang up, excitement making her incautious, and told him her plans, her eyes sparkling, her voice eager.

Her animation disturbed him. He preferred her usual cool patrician demeanor, so like her mother's. When she had finished, he regarded her for a long moment which became longer while he lit a fresh cigar.

Never! he was thinking. Live alone in New York, within easy reach of Connor MacKenzie? Was it Connor she was really after, with all this poppycock about designing prints for cotton?

"That's preposterous," he said finally.

"Not at all. I'm good enough—several experts have told me so—and there's no reason why cotton—"

"Cotton be damned!" he said, his voice taking on the quality that his children dreaded, that he almost never turned on her. "You will not go about peddling your designs and you will not live alone. You will remain under my roof and behave like a lady until you marry."

A flat dull feeling possessed her, but no surprise. Breen had warned her that her faith in Rhys's encouragement was misplaced. Perhaps she had known it herself.

She turned away from her father, steeling herself for a moment that had been a long time coming. She must free herself, for he would never let her go! She turned back to him, her face pale and still again, and forced herself to be calm.

"Father, I'm sorry you disapprove, but in February I'll be twenty-one and legally free to do as I like. You've just told me Mother gave me the means, and I intend to use them."

His expression was one of cool hauteur. "No, Georgia, you will not have the means. There are ways for a father to keep a headstrong girl from ruining her reputation and squandering her fortune."

She stared at him, as resolute as he, and he saw an obduracy in her he had never marked before. Her lissome body was tense and her head slightly averted. She was Georgianna to the life, denying him what he wanted! It came to him that he would never dominate Georgia by force, any more than he had her mother. He would have to persuade her or, at least, bargain for time until he could devise another plan of action. He thought swiftly and got to his feet.

"I simply can't believe you want to ruin me!"

"Of course not, Father! I don't know what you mean."

"Georgia, times have changed, perhaps, for shopgirls and secretaries, but not for you, not for a politician's daughter! Unmarried women who live alone are grist for the scandal mills. I would lose the election because of you."

He leaned toward her, careful to show only hurt and anxiety, not the angry panic that he felt.

"I beg you not to stand in my way just now," he pleaded. "The Senate is only a first step on a much longer road, but I *must* win the twenty-six election and win overwhelmingly."

"I fail to see—"

"Because you've been away too long! American voters don't allow their political leaders the same latitude in their private lives as the French do—or their families either. They would resent an heiress who took a workingman's job away from him. They would gossip about a beautiful, wealthy young woman who lived alone. Georgia, be fair! They would gossip about that here too. It just isn't done!"

He waited. She said nothing, but he sensed that she was struggling with herself.

"Go back if you must," he offered, "but live with the family in Washington and New York. You can have anything you need to experiment with designs for cotton, but do it discreetly for the moment. Let our own mills sell it without calling attention to you. Isn't that a fair offer? Georgia, I beseech you, give me a little more time. Don't blight my hopes for the presidency."

"The presidency?" She looked up at him.

He nodded.

She felt wrenched between her own desires and his. Breen had said it: she was so braided into his life that she could not tear herself away without hurting him. How could she deny him a few short years after all he had given her? And yet she must. She *must*.

"Try to understand," she began again, feeling like a fly trapped in honey. "You must know that Mother's legacy is more to me than money. It's a trust, a kind of handing over, so that I can do what she couldn't. If you loved her, don't stand in my way."

Rhys looked at her lovely face, her attitude of supplication, and sank back into his chair, his manner totally changed. His hands were clasped between his knees and his head was bent. "*If* I loved her? You know how I worshipped her. She was the only woman I ever wanted, not Constance, never Constance. I should not have remarried but, God help me, I was so lonely, so bereft. And I thought her sister . . . But they are no more alike than you and Jillian. And for a long time I was too ridden with guilt to love you, my own daughter."

"Guilt?" She felt slightly dizzy as one revelation followed so swiftly on the heels of another.

He nodded. His head sank into his hands in a posture of utter despair. "Your mother was too delicate to have children, but she wanted desperately to give me a son and I—"

He paused for a moment, aroused by the prospect of her reaction to what he was about to say, wanted to say, as if by telling her about this ultimate intimacy he could make her part of it. He spoke now in a hoarse whisper, watching her embarrassment grow with every word he said, every act he implied.

"We were very much in love," he said, and now his voice trembled of itself. "And I . . . how could I resist her? I had only to look at her to shake with desire. To touch her was paradise, and to lie . . ."

"Father, please! I don't want to hear any more!"

He made himself stop. After a while he said in a low voice, "Forgive me, you're still a girl. You can't understand these things. No wonder you judge me harshly."

But those muffled words had explained to her his womanizing, a fact of life the family lived with and conspired to ignore. With a wife like Constance, who could blame him for seeking comfort elsewhere?

Her heart went out to him in his anguish, his remorse, but she could not tell him how very well she understood that passion now, or why she had no right to judge him at all.

She was just like him! If it had not been Breen, it would have been some other man, maybe several. And there would be others after Breen. Maybe love was selective, but desire and passion were not.

"And you, my beautiful darling," her father's muffled voice went on, "were living proof that I had killed her."

"No, Father, no!" She went to his side.

"Oh, yes. The sight of you made me ashamed—of myself and of my marriage to Constance." He uncovered his face and looked at her. His cheeks were wet. "Can you understand that? Can you forgive me for it and help me make my life meaningful again?"

"Hush," she said, taking the handkerchief from his breast pocket and reaching up to pat his face dry. "I understand now, and there's nothing to forgive."

"Then will you stay with me, Georgia?"

"Yes, Father, of course I will," she said. There was too much at stake for him. It would only be until after the election for the U.S. Senate seat—but how very long the next two years would seem! Resentment came rushing up to crowd in beside love and duty. She handed him the handkerchief and walked quickly to the door.

"Georgia," he said. "Your mother left you something else. Her portrait and all her jewelry."

She nodded, then leaned against the door. "Including the things Constance has been wearing all these years?"

"Some of them."

"Tell her I want them," Georgia said, and went out, closing the door behind her.

◆

Rhys refolded his damp handkerchief so the embroidered initials would show and tucked it carefully into his breast pocket. Then he stood at the window, staring out of it with his lips compressed and his hands clenched in his pockets. He was mortified by his outburst and furious with her for pushing him to it.

"Where's her loyalty?" he muttered. "Where's her love?"
His head jerked around as the door opened.

"Oh, it's you," he said to Constance, disappointed.

"Yes, your loving wife. What did she say? By the look of
you, nothing good."

"She wanted to move into an apartment in New York
and make a career of designing textiles! Did you ever hear
the like?"

"I've warned you often enough, Rhys! She's not as saintly
as she looks. What did you tell her?"

"Everything I could think of."

"And?"

"She'll go on designing but she'll remain at home until
I've won the election."

"And then?" Constance said, spreading her hands in
dismay. "There'll be other elections! I've been telling you
for years to marry off that girl. She'll ruin everything for
us. You've let her wind you around her little finger long
enough."

He gave her a withering glance. "That's rubbish. I was
indulgent, yes, but mainly in order to protect her."

"Well, you failed!" Constance said, her eyes sliding
away from his. She put a cigarette into her jade holder and
lit it. "It's time you knew she's been sleeping with some
grubby artist in Montmartre for over a year." She waited
in one of the more ominous silences of her marriage.

"That's a lie," he said finally, his voice strangled in his
throat.

"I assure you it is not," she told him, flushing with
malicious pleasure. "His name is Samson Breen and she's
been very clever about him, I'll grant her that. Even
Jillian doesn't know. But I do."

His face went white. "Someday I'll kill you," he said
between his teeth.

"Kill *me*?" Her voice rose in outrage. "Can I help it if
your precious princess likes to wallow in the mud?"

"You're the one for mud!" he countered swiftly. "For
manure!" He waited for her to deny it and suddenly

knew she would not. "What else would you call your performance with that stable boy?"

She gasped in surprise, then recovered herself and shouted at him triumphantly. "I'm glad you know, you son of a bitch! What better way to pay you back for *your* performance with his mother?"

"When did you find out about Dilys?" he demanded, as if she were guilty of a gross invasion of his privacy.

"Soon enough! I had years to think about it. That's why I had an affair with Connor, and I'd do it again!"

But it was Georgia's perfidy that shook him more. Revulsion overcame him. He could feel the veins in his head throbbing with his wrath.

"You disgust me," he muttered.

"Then we're even. Do you think he meant anything to me? The irony is that no man ever has, not since the first day I met you. But did that matter to you? No! You preferred to chase your harlots like a stag in rut—and pretend Georgia was Georgianna come back to life! I tell you, she must be married soon, whether you like the idea or not. You can't have her, Rhys, no matter what you do!"

"Shut up!" he warned her, his face flushed. "Just shut up!"

She subsided. If she had no hope of him, she had herself and her children to protect, and in her view there was only one way to do that before Rhys's unnatural worship of his daughter got out of hand.

"Listen to me, Rhys," she said quietly. "Marriage is the only solution. How do you know it isn't Connor she still wants? I always thought there was a lot more than friendship between those two." She put up a placating hand as he rounded on her. "All right, even if there wasn't! But there might be, once February comes and she's free and back in America, where he is. Remember how she was the last time they were together? She moped over him for months! She couldn't get him out of her mind! Why else has she been yearning for New York all this time, if not because it's where he is?"

At last Rhys was listening to her, and she pressed the point home.

"I know him! He's like you: he hangs on until he gets what he wants. And Georgia's like you too, Rhys! If you want to protect her and your political ambitions, get her married."

He was revolted by the prospect of another man having rights over his daughter, in particular those he could never exercise himself, but he knew that it was the lesser of several other evils. Georgia might take more lovers, God forbid, MacKenzie among them. Worst of all, she could become a threat to his own political aspirations.

"If fornicate she must," he muttered with a grimace, "it will be with a husband of my choice."

"Just don't let her know that," Constance advised. "She wouldn't marry God Himself if she knew you'd chosen Him for her—and why."

"Get out of here," he rasped suddenly. "Leave me alone. And get her mother's jewels together. She wants them."

"She can have them with my blessings!" Constance snapped. "They'll be part of her dowry."

Alone again, Rhys smoked, shaken. Georgia was not only disloyal, but unchaste. The nightmare of his beloved daughter naked in a man's arms had become fact. If she had been in the room, he would have struck her, not once but again and again, for being unfaithful to him, to his trust in her.

He paced, grinding his teeth and thinking furiously. First he would get rid of this artist—Samson Breen, that was the name—with an anonymous gift of money conditional upon the brute's immediate departure for Tahiti.

Then he would find a proper consort for Georgia, titled and preferably French. They were easier to deal with than the British, although just as hungry for fortunes in the aftermath of the war that had crippled Europe.

He took out his book of social acquaintances and went through the pages. Etienne Archaix? No, he would not appeal to Georgia. That handsome duke he had met in

Monte Carlo? Rhys shook his head; he didn't want a pederast for a son-in-law. The Marquis de Sevignac?

Rhys leaned back in his chair, rubbing his earlobe between his thumb and forefinger. He had first met Antoine de Sevignac through their mutual interest in art. The marquis was a widower of about forty-five with three grown sons. He was attractive, too, in the slim, elegant fashion of the French aristocracy, with properties in the Loire and the most prestigious silk mills in France which, by all reports, he was running into the ground with his poor management.

A man in financial straits must be in the market for an heiress, certainly one like Georgia. He must be prevented from getting control of Georgia's money, but a marriage contract would guarantee that.

He picked up the telephone and called de Sevignac's office in Lyons. He was told that Monsieur le Marquis was at the Ritz in Paris.

No wonder his mills are in trouble, Rhys thought as he called the hotel.

"Delighted to hear from you, my dear sir," de Sevignac said. "Have you changed your mind about buying that Manet?"

"Not quite," Rhys replied, glad to hear that the man still needed money. "There's another matter I'd like to discuss with you, something that requires the utmost discretion, even as regards our meeting."

"I am intrigued," said the marquis. "And at your disposal this afternoon or tomorrow morning. After that I'm off to Monte Carlo for the New Year celebrations."

Better and better, Rhys thought. Georgia will meet him on the Riviera.

He chose tomorrow morning—today he had to deal with Breen—and they arranged to meet in one of the private rooms of an obscure art gallery on the Île St. Louis.

♦

"It is vital," Rhys said, stretching his long legs and crossing them at the ankle, "that she know nothing of our understanding. She's a child of her time." He smiled indulgently.

"As we are children of ours," Antoine de Sevignac said, smiling back. His almond-shaped eyes danced and his teeth gleamed, white and even under his narrow mustache. "My first marriage was arranged in exactly this way."

"Yes, well, if this one's to happen at all . . ."

"I quite understand." But Tony was not sure he did. Rhys Brandon was something of an enigma. Not because he wanted to marry his daughter to Tony—every father in France wanted to do that—but because he wanted the engagement arranged so quickly. Could the girl be pregnant?

Tony dismissed that idea. If that were the case, Brandon would be talking about an immediate wedding, otherwise she would be too scandalously large with child. Was Mademoiselle Brandon in love with an unacceptable man? Even if she was, Tony was sure he could charm her into an engagement in a matter of days. He had a way with women.

Heaven knows, he thought, I've had enough practice!

She was certainly attractive. Tony had glimpsed her once or twice at Deauville and the opera, and had heard about the ravishing *Américaine* long before that. She was a blonde and he preferred brunettes with fulsome breasts and juicy thighs, but marriage would not stop him having mistresses.

But the girl must have had dozens of offers by now! Why hadn't she accepted anyone? Headstrong, was she? That could be titillating in a wife.

So it was not the girl who disturbed him. It was Brandon.

"There is another matter," Rhys said. "The pre-nuptial agreement."

Antoine nodded.

"I understand your mills are in trouble," Rhys observed.

"Only temporarily—and they are not the extent of de Sevignac assets. There is prime real estate in Lyons, as well as the house and extensive farmlands and orchards at

Charet-le-Roi, the family seat. There is the château de Sevignac and its vineyards on the Loire and, as you know, a collection of Impressionist paintings that rivals the Louvre's—all of it entailed for my sons."

"None of which you can eat and all of which is mortgaged to the hilt."

Well, what else had he expected from an American? Tony thought. In that benighted country even a man who inherited money was expected to increase his fortune, not enjoy it. Americans were drunk on work; that was why they had no culture beyond what they imported from Europe along with their furniture and their fashions.

He sat back, scrutinizing his companion carefully, and lit another gold-tipped Turkish cigarette. It was clear that, regardless of his own financial difficulties, Brandon wanted this marriage. He wanted a famous name for his daughter, a title that went back to the Sun King, a place among the cream of European nobility. A dowry would therefore be forthcoming.

"A very generous settlement will go with my daughter," Brandon said, reading his mind, "but you will not control her estate."

"Who will?"

"I will, for the present, although eventually Georgia might take it over."

Fine! Tony thought; once in her hands, it's as good as in mine. Again, he nodded. "Is that all?"

"Broadly speaking, yes," Rhys said. "I have another project in mind that will almost certainly interest you, but it is contingent upon my daughter's agreement to marry you."

Bastard, de Sevignac thought. Am I a donkey, to be shown a carrot on a stick! But he had been right: Brandon wanted something more for his money.

Tony smiled. "I shall do my best to obtain it," he said, privately deciding that he would have to meet the girl before he committed himself. "When shall I meet her?"

"Next week, at the Villa Ivoire on Cap d'Antibes, if that is agreeable. I hold a large open house on New Year's

Day, wherever we are. I'll have a card sent to you at your hotel."

The two men stood up, shook hands, and parted, Tony persuaded that he would emerge victorious and put an end to his staggering debts; and Rhys torn between jealousy and his determination that Georgia should marry the man.

♦

"You'll have to have the settings changed," Jillian said, looking through the jewelry Constance had bundled into a silk scarf and deposited on Georgia's bed.

"Why? They're perfect as they are."

"Some of them are passé," Jillian said, wrinkling her nose. "Mama never wore those pieces."

"I refuse to change something beautiful just to keep up with fashion."

"Who am I to dispute an heiress?" Jillian shrugged. "But if I found out I had just inherited a fortune of my own, I wouldn't look as miserable as you do."

"What's the difference? I've agreed to live at home until the election."

"But he's given you a free hand for your designing! And we're both going home. I'm glad you're not leaving me, even if you aren't." Jillian held a pair of Georgianna's diamond earrings to her ears and turned her head from side to side in front of the mirror. "You have such crazy ideas! Aren't these gorgeous? Cheer up, Georgia, you may meet your Prince Charming long before you become wrinkled and bent from slaving over a dye press. Now I'm off to tell the maids what to pack for the Riviera."

Georgia went on sorting the jewelry and puzzling over her father's attitude toward her. It had altered in an indefinable way since yesterday, as if he wanted to keep her at arm's length. But perhaps he was ill at ease over his emotional outburst.

She certainly was. And she would be ashamed to tell Breen that she had acceded, even temporarily, to her father's wishes. She had been so sure of herself, so determined to be what her mother wanted her to be, all the more because of the legacy that she could see only as a trust.

No wonder her mother had chosen Uncle Adam! She had known Rhys well enough to anticipate his possessiveness.

She began to put the jewelry away in the jewel box he had given her for Christmas, along with a sable coat and the gold keys to a new car waiting for her in New York. She looked up when Peggy put her head in and then came to stand behind her at the dressing table.

"Lovely, aren't they?" Georgia said.

"That they are. It brings her back to see them with you, where they belong." Peggy pointed to the spray of diamonds Georgianna had worn for her portrait. "I mind the day that picture was finished. It's a wonder, but it doesn't do her justice."

"They were very happy together, weren't they, Peggy?"

Peggy pursed her lips, polishing a brooch on her sleeve. "They got what each of 'em wanted. I suppose that's happiness."

"What did each of them want?"

"She had to marry well—your uncle Adam's got no head for business and he'd lost almost everything—and there came Mr. Rhys, handsome as a prince and rich as Croesus."

"And what did Father want?"

"He wanted *her*. He fell in love with her at her first ball, when she was only fifteen. Like an enchantment on him, it was."

"So they fell in love with each other at first sight." It was a story Georgia had listened to rapturously since childhood.

"Men and women have different ways of lovin', Miss Georgia." Peggy went to the closet and began sorting through Georgia's dresses. "Shall I pack the red gown or the white satin? Or both?"

"Both. Peggy, why didn't my mother want Father to look after my inheritance for me?"

There was silence from the depths of the closet until Peggy emerged with an armful of dresses.

"She was expectin' and she didn't want him to know she was thinkin' about such things as a will. So she asked Mr. Adam."

"Of course," Georgia said softly. "It was to spare him. I should have guessed."

"The pale blue or the coral?" Peggy asked.

27

♦

The Villa Ivoire, behind its modest entrance gate, was a large, low, rambling stone building. Its roofs were the lovely terra-cotta *tuiles* of Provence, and its flower-spangled lawns stretched lushly from the villa terraces down to the Mediterranean, with a swimming pool sparkling like a jewel in between.

On New Year's Day the Riviera sun was strong, the air clear and mild, and the gardens resplendent with cyclamen, lilies, carnations, and azaleas. The low terrace walls, covered with bougainvillea, echoed the rise and fall of conversation and the laughter of the fashionable couples who drifted from the house to the gardens amid tables stacked with delicacies and jeroboams of champagne. A gramophone played tunes from Tin Pan Alley: "Ain't We Got Fun?," "The Sheik of Araby," "Carolina in the Morning." As Georgia walked down the rolling lawn toward the sea, the scandalous words of "Do It Again," seductively sung by Tirzah Kent, seemed to follow her.

Her promise to Rhys—or, more accurately, the way it had been wrung out of her—still rankled, as if she must be a perpetual child, forever subject to his demands. She was disinclined to chat with the guests, and was in search of a few moments of solitude, only to discover that solitude was not what she wanted.

Breen's right, she thought. Sex permeates everything.

She felt the warmth of the sun on her face and smelled the grass and flowers mingling with the crisp odor of the sea and knew she wanted the impossible: to love someone totally.

"What a marvelous voice," a man's voice said in English but with an attractive French accent.

She turned, hiding her annoyance at the speaker who approached her. "Yes," she said politely. "She's Tirzah Kent, one of my favorite singers."

"May I introduce myself? Antoine de Sevignac."

"Georgia Brandon." She offered her hand and he bowed over it, kissing the air a quarter inch above it.

"Georgia Brandon," he murmured. "But, of course, you're the senator's artistic daughter."

She nodded. "I've bought and sold for his collection."

"Cigarette?"

She accepted one of his gold-tipped Turkish cigarettes, and they stood looking out to sea, smoking quietly. She was grateful for his quietness, although he was an attractive man, somewhat taller than she, with a slender body well suited to his elegant style of dress. He was too muscular to be foppish, even with a white rose in his buttonhole. She glanced at the dusting of gray at his temples and his wide-set, honey-colored eyes and wondered what sort of man he was. His face was almost ascetic, with slightly hollow cheeks and a narrow nose, but his mouth, under that thin mustache, was sensual.

He turned to summon a waiter, snapping his fingers. "Champagne?" he asked her when the waiter reached them, and handed her a glass before he took one for himself, sipped it, and nodded. "Veuve Cliquot," he said. "Trust the senator to choose the best."

"Do you know my father well?"

"Only through our mutual interest in art. I can't think why you and I have never met before. Tell me, what do young American ladies do with their time?"

"I've been studying textile design."

"Really? Then we have a great deal in common already. Have you heard of the Soieries Sevignac?"

"The Marquis de Sevignac! Of course! I hadn't made the connection!" Her sudden animation was not lost on him. "Your silks are works of art, monsieur. And Sevignac designs are the best I've ever seen."

He acknowledged the compliment with a quiet pride that charmed her. He was really a very charming man, she decided. She had heard somewhere that he had a reputation for collecting women as well as art, but she knew of no man who didn't, save stuffy old bachelors like her uncle Adam.

She went on speaking knowledgeably about trends in fabric design, and he listened as if the subject fascinated him, but he was thinking how exquisite she was. She was unusually tall and unmistakably patrician, even imperial, in manner and posture. That was rare in American girls, those loping, braying, brash young women whose speech alone was so offputting.

Her face was ravishing, her blue eyes fringed with heavy lashes, her mouth made to be kissed. And her figure, long-legged and deep-bosomed, was perfect. He felt desire stir within him.

Ah, yes, he thought. Yes, indeed.

She was smiling ruefully. "I know you think only the French can create designs worthy of your silks, but someday my designs will persuade you otherwise."

"Why wait until someday?" he said. "If you came to see the mills in Lyons, we could have a few of your designs loomed straightaway. Would you like that?"

"I would be ecstatic," she said, her smile radiant now.

"Then we shall arrange it."

She remembered suddenly where she had heard those stories about him.

"Do you know," she said, wondering what his reaction would be, "your name came up just before Christmas when I was at Varnet for a fitting."

He glanced at her quickly. "Ah, yes, Marie-Véronique. We have been doing business together for a long time."

"So she said."

He studied her, a faint gleam of mischief in his eyes. "What else did she say?"

"That you are a true hedonist."

"You disapprove of my devotion to pleasure?"

"Not at all! Why should I?"

"A serious connoisseur of art like yourself? A textile designer?"

"Now you're mocking me," she said pleasantly.

He shrugged. "A little. Art and design were never *my* chief sources of pleasure." His extraordinary eyes dropped momentarily to her breasts, then traveled slowly upward to her mouth.

A glow, unmistakably sexual, enveloped her. Why not flirt? she thought. She had nothing else to do for the moment.

"But I like all the things women like, Monsieur le Marquis."

"Tony," he said, raising his glass to her. "I look forward to providing you with them, mademoiselle."

"Georgia," she answered, and spent the rest of the afternoon talking to him. She accepted an invitation to dine and go to a new nightclub with him that evening and studied herself carefully after Peggy had helped her dress.

"There," Peggy said, clasping Georgianna's diamond necklace around Georgia's neck. "It's lovely as you are, just like the Ice Queen in the fairy tale."

The Varnet gown was ice blue, a backless sheath of Sevignac satin that rippled to the floor under a sheer chiffon overdress. Georgia's hair fell from a center part to frame her face.

An ice queen, she reflected as she drew on long white kid gloves and let Peggy drape a white fox cape over her shoulders. She wondered if she gave a frosty impression to every man she met—except Breen, of course.

She felt trapped inside walls of her own making and knew they were the hardest kind to breach. With men of

her class, she had always been distant because she knew
Rhys wanted her to be without his having to say so.

He demands too much of me, she thought resentfully.
Everything, in fact.

She had fled to Montparnasse to be herself, but she
would not flee anymore.

It was an evening of fine food and sparkling conversation, followed by good music at a nightclub with a fashion-
ably tiny, very crowded floor. Their conversation stopped
when they got up to dance.

Her body curved readily against his. His hand was
warm against her back, and she regretted even the thin
veil of chiffon between his skin and hers. His mustache
grazed her cheek and she caught his male scent under his
cologne as they swayed to the music. She breathed him in
appreciatively. He stepped back momentarily, and they
looked at each other, acknowledging the growing attraction between them.

By the time he brought her back to the Villa Ivoire she
had agreed to go to Lyons with him for a day or two to see
the mills.

"You will stay at Charet-le-Roi, of course," he announced
in that commanding way he had which, strangely enough,
did not provoke her to instant rebellion. "My mother and
sisters are there to assure that the conventions are observed, as befits an American princess."

The last thing she wanted was to observe the conventions. She said, "You know more about princesses than I
do. I yield to your superior judgment."

"It is a woman's nature to yield," he said softly, then
kissed her hand, smiled slowly, and got back into his car.

♦

In his suite at the Hotel de Paris, Antoine de Sevignac lay
in bed staring into the darkness. He would marry Georgia
Brandon—he had decided it before they finished dinner—
and his reasons were eminently practical. But her exquisite face and figure confirmed the decision.

He pulled a soft square pillow to his side and rounded

it, his hand cupping and stroking it as if it were her body, that long-limbed, graceful body with its high, round breasts and flawless skin. He creased the pillow and slid his responsive penis reflectively into its satin folds.

She was such a curious mixture. Modern but majestic. Chic as a Parisienne but with a taste for jewelry in turn-of-the-century settings. Cool but decidedly erotic.

He wondered if she was still a virgin and decided that she could not be, not a female who radiated that much sensuality. She had probably fallen in love with some young puppy and yielded to his ignorant lovemaking. It would be a pleasure to show her what sex could be, to make her sob with passion in his arms.

Her father was the puzzle. Obviously the man had no control over his daughter or the marriage contract would have been signed by now. Of age, indeed! In France a woman of good family never came of age. His sisters, too plain to find husbands of their class among the war-depleted male population, lived at home with their mother.

In any case, Georgia's chastity was not an issue. A virgin bride for the propagation of de Sevignac heirs was no longer a necessity. His late wife, whose virtue had been proven with the traditional bloody towel on their wedding night, had persisted in her dreary fidelity long after she had borne him three sons. It was of no matter to him whether or not he had more children.

His mother was the only problem.

"Mongrels," she called the Americans. "Common colonials."

His mother was a model chauvinist: anyone who was not French, Catholic, and royalist was unacceptable in society. A partner in marriage must be of aristocratic lineage. The dowager marquise would be horrified.

"But you'll be a lot more horrified, *ma mère*," he muttered, "if the mills fail for want of money."

Antoine had no illusions about his business sense. In good times the Soieries Sevignac ran themselves. It was in times like these, when European markets kept dwindling, that the mills needed direction he had neither the skill nor the patience to provide.

Still, he had to survive, and to that end he had been selling off bits of his private art collection. Last year he had been forced to sell his favorite bronzes to a private collector. Had Georgia not turned up, the next thing to go on the block would have been the Château de Sevignac in the Loire, along with its vineyards and its highly respected label.

But his worries were over now. Georgia's fortune would keep the Soieries Sevignac in funds and Antoine in silk shirts, hand-turned shoes, and lively mistresses.

But the girl was not a fool. She would have to believe he loved her in the way romantic young women conceived of love, not merely in his way which, for him, was basic and physical. He knew he was congenitally incapable of fidelity and apparently they made a fuss about it in America. But he did not intend to live in America.

Having found the solution to his problems, he slept peacefully. In the morning he telephoned his mother and told her to send an invitation to Senator Brandon and to prepare a guest suite at Charet-le-Roi for his daughter.

◆

The house was a wide, square mansion of gray stone. It sat inside its formal gardens with an insolence conferred by age and nobility.

Georgia saw it in the sunset from one of the crested cars that had met them at the station, but the stone walls of Charet-le-Roi did not reflect the red light, as the rosy bricks and white pillars of Brandon Hall did, extending a glowing welcome to anyone who approached. A glaze of frost lay upon the vast grounds of Charet-le-Roi and shimmered on the naked plane trees that lined the avenue. The effect was one of austerity and rigorous adherence to tradition, in life as in architecture.

She knew that Antoine, sitting next to her in the back of the Bentley, was waiting for her reaction.

"It's very impressive," she said sincerely. "It has nobility and style." He had the same qualities himself; moreover, it pleased her to please him. "It's very large."

"Not really. Seventy rooms, only half of them with heat and electricity. The rest must be modernized." He fell silent, contemplating his domain; in the distance were stables, barns, flocks, and orchards.

For Georgia the train journey from Monte Carlo in his private railway car had sharpened the chemistry between them, even when he talked about his sons.

"They are all in their twenties and have married well," Tony said with more relief, it seemed to her, than paternal pride. "Antoine and Edouard have establishments in Lyons and are *sous-directeurs* of the mills. Henri, the youngest, runs the Château de Sevignac vineyards in the Loire."

Whatever he was saying, Tony de Sevignac generated a strong promise of physical fulfillment that made her slightly breathless. Sensual images crowded her thoughts. She had never met a man who could arouse her, as he did, with a glance of the eyes, and she wondered when he would find an opportunity for them to go to bed together. It could hardly happen at the château.

Quite aside from that attraction, she enjoyed his company. He was clever, witty and cultured, and his joie de vivre made him seem years younger than he was—only five years younger than Rhys.

"He's much too old for you," her father had said when the invitation arrived from the old marquise.

"I think he can manage to totter through his silk mills with me," Georgia had replied, not surprised that Rhys was objecting once again to a man she liked.

Her father seemed peevish but resigned. "I never knew you were so willful," he had sighed, "but have it your own way."

She intended to. Besides, the chance to have some of her designs translated into Sevignac silk was too tempting to pass up. In a different way, that was as exciting as the marquis.

◆

With a welcoming smile Antoine took her arm and they went up two wide, shallow stone steps under the portico. The door swung open on a vast, high-ceilinged hall with gleaming parquet floors and Oriental carpets creating pools of color.

In a stone fireplace ten feet high, a fire roared, its light dancing upon cathedral-back chairs upholstered in rich green velvet and upon the priceless Gobelin and Savonnerie and Beauvais tapestries covering the stone walls. Four huge chandeliers cast a dim electric light from the carved wood ceiling, but most of the illumination came from flickering gas lamps set on bronze sconces in the stone walls. It was at once lush and austere.

"It's splendid, Tony!" Georgia said, wondering what it was like to live in a museum.

A maid and butler took their coats. *"Madame la Marquise et les demoiselles vous attendent dans le petit salon, Monsieur le Marquis,"* the butler said, and Georgia went with Antoine through a door halfway down the entry hall to meet the dowager marquise and "the young ladies."

She felt as if she had walked into the nineteenth century. It was not only the furnishings—she was aware of marquetry and marble, of Aubusson and velvet, of ormolu clocks, porcelain lamps, and cloisonné vases in profusion—but the woman seated near the pink marble fireplace.

The Marquise de Sevignac was dressed in black crepe de Chine ruched in white at the throat and wrists. An abundance of pearls cascaded down her formidable bosom. Her white hair was dressed like the English Queen Mary's, swept high on her head into a crown of tiny curls. She was neither pretty nor homely. She was as handsome and as austere as the house, and she might have been wearing a court gown and a tiara as she sat there, waiting for her son and his guest to approach.

Tony bent to kiss her hand. "Madame," he said formally in French, "I have the honor to present Mademoiselle Georgia Brandon. Mademoiselle, this is my mother."

The marquise nodded, stretched the corners of her

mouth slightly, and offered her hand. With a movement of
her head she indicated the two girls seated opposite her.

"And these," Tony went on, "are my sisters, Eulalie and
Sidonie."

Georgia, turning, realized that *les demoiselles* were not
young ladies at all but women in their late thirties, totally
devoid of their brother's looks and charm and utterly
dominated by their mother. With as much grace as she
could muster, Georgia embarked upon an evening with
Antoine's family.

◆

"What would you like to see today?" Tony asked before
they got into the car.

"The mills, of course. That's what I came for." She
smiled, glad to be out of that oppressive house and its
three bleak women.

He gave the order to the chauffeur, then got in beside
her.

"I see you've brought some designs with you."

She nodded. "I just happened to pack them."

He smiled, and she handed them over and leaned back
as the car rolled smoothly toward the city, leaving the
estate behind. It was incredible to her that people still
lived as they did. She was accustomed to luxury; it was the
rigid formality that made Charet-le-Roi a museum, not a
home.

The suite she had been given had an enormous tester
bed draped in ivory shantung silk, with celadon green
brocade draperies and upholstery, and rose and cream silk
Chinese carpets, obviously loomed to order for rooms of
this size. It did not encourage relaxation.

It was obvious that the dowager marquise thoroughly
disapproved of Georgia, although she was rigorously polite. And the sisters had no choice but to follow suit.
Georgia smiled, imagining what Jillian would have said
about all three of them.

Tony gave a low whistle as he closed the folder. He was

looking at her with a different kind of admiration as he handed it back.

"These are superb," he said. "Really exquisite."

"You seem more surprised than you should be," she said.

"Talented women make me uncomfortable."

She laughed.

"No, really," he said, still watching her. After a moment he smiled. "After seeing these, I'm not sure I should disclose any of my secrets to you. Did you know that when China monopolized the culture of silk, the punishment for disclosure was death?"

"You're joking!"

"Not at all. Silk cloth had already come to the west— over the Great Silk Road across the Gobi Desert, then to Phoenicia, and then from Tyre to Imperial Rome—but only the fabric, not the secret of sericulture."

"How did the West discover the secret?"

"Legend has it—reliably, I think—that the Emperor Justinian sent two Persian monks who had lived in China for many years back there on a mission to procure silkworm eggs. Steal them, actually. The monks brought them out in the hollows of their bamboo staves with enough foliage to keep them alive. Most of our western silkworms are their descendants. We owe them a great deal."

"Your secrets are safe with me, Tony," she said. "I'm not a silk maker. And I want to sell you my designs, not pirate yours."

A typical Yankee! he thought. But such a beautiful one. He had come damn near an embarrassing erection again last night as they walked together. Then he had dreamed of rigid nipples and wet thighs and rocking hips. The girl was talented, but in bed she would want what all women wanted: to be carried away into submission.

He shook his head. "It still amazes me that an American heiress should be interested in business."

She laughed outright. "I might say the same of a French marquis."

"But my family was ennobled by Louis XIV as a result

of our contribution to the silk industry in France." He smiled lazily. "It was not only because my ancestor procured ladies for the king's pleasure, as small minds would have it. The first Marquis de Sevignac went right on weaving silk, as did his descendants after him—or at least the eldest son in each generation did. I thought I had escaped the burden—business is not my forte—until both my older brothers were killed in 1917."

"I'm very sorry," she said softly, thinking more charitably of the three black-clad women cloistered in the mansion. "I should have known."

"How could you?"

"Not many French families were untouched by the war."

"Brandons too?"

"No—but we lost a dear friend, a boy named Peter van Dorn. My sister still mourns him. She loved him very much."

They sat for a time without speaking as the wide, luxurious motor car approached the city then bowled along the avenues of Lyons. If Paris glitters, Georgia thought, this city glows. Paris was glamour and gaiety and art; Lyons was industry and quiet wealth and good living. It was the silk and culinary capital of France.

"I assume the sons take over for Brandons as well," he said.

She nodded. "But not the daughters. Unfortunately." She was practiced at maintaining an unruffled exterior, but this time her resentment came through. "My mother was the first woman in the family to take any interest in business, and I intend to follow her example."

"Mrs. Brandon?" He was astonished. He had met Constance several times at the Villa Ivoire.

"The present Mrs. Brandon is not my mother," Georgia said. "My mother died when I was born. Constance is her sister, but they have nothing in common. My mother was a woman of considerable business acumen at a time when that quality was neither expected nor admired in women."

It still wasn't, he thought, and turned his shrewd gaze upon her. She returned his look impassively, but he nodded as if he had grasped the nature of her relationship with her stepmother-aunt, and perhaps even the genuineness of her ambition.

"You're an unusual man," she said, but she did not elaborate and he, encouraged by the compliment, did not pursue it.

♦

The car stopped at the Soieries Sevignac and he helped her out. A uniformed guard, touching his cap, opened the heavy bronze doors of a building made of traditional Lyons limestone, and they were in a lofty, wood-paneled foyer. Georgia heard the distant sound of the looms and smiled in anticipation. Their coats were taken by a liveried footman, then Antoine escorted her to the waiting lift, his arm resting lightly around her waist.

His touch made her tingle. Her instinct insisted that he was an accomplished lover.

Then the lift stopped and her attention shifted to the gorgeous satins, damasks, brocades, georgettes, mousselines de soie, and taffetas, in colors so brilliant they took her breath away, being wound onto bolts and piled on tables. But it was the foulards that drew her closest scrutiny, those whisper-light silks used for men's ties, ascots, pajamas, and robes. The Sevignac designs were mainly the madder paisleys, beautiful but classic.

"Is your silk fiber imported?" she asked him.

"No. Except for raw silk, it is cultured here in the West, on silkworm farms. They are very delicate creatures, you know, as reclusive as lovers. The cocooneries must be quiet, clean, odor-free, and well ventilated so they can get on with their mating." He smiled at her. "Fortunately we are not so demanding."

"Go on," she said.

"The adult female lives only three days after she mates, and in that time she lays several hundred eggs. She has eyes but no mouth, since her purpose is solely to propagate. Her young have mouths but no eyes, since their purpose is to eat like gluttons. They consume about thirty meals a day of freshly chopped mulberry leaves. You can hear the rustle of their feeding at a silk farm. But they are tiny gluttons, only the diameter of a hair and about one-eighth-inch long when they hatch."

There was something at once tragic and repulsive to Georgia about this cycle of blind reproduction, death, and gluttony, and she was glad to be diverted by a table of the most exquisite brocade she had ever seen, in the rich, glowing red known as *rouge de Sevignac*.

Her hand passed over it gently, lovingly, appreciating the artistry that had gone into its spinning, dyeing, and weaving as only someone born to textiles could.

"It's wonderful," she said, and turned to find de Sevignac watching her with a look she had not seen before.

"What is it?" she asked.

He touched her cheek gently. "You're irresistible when you're like this."

"How am I?"

"Like *Alice aux pays des merveilles*."

"This *is* a little like Wonderland."

"And you are like a lovely child discovering happiness. I had hoped she was there, inside the serious artist."

It was as if he had taken her in his arms and kissed her. She was caught in the web of his charm, warmed by his perception of her hidden self. Then, remembering the workers all around them, she colored slightly and reminded him that he had been giving her a lesson in sericulture.

He went on. "In twenty to thirty days they begin to spin. The filament they secrete is called fibroin; serecin is the gum that holds it together. They attach themselves to the twigs provided for them and begin to enclose themselves in a silken shell." His hands described an enclosure, secret, soft, and intimate. "They work ceaselessly until the cocoon is complete—about twenty-four hours. Then the exhausted creature, now called a chrysalis, sleeps. It would reemerge from its cocoon in several weeks if we let it, but that would break the filament. So, except for those kept for breeding, we kill them in drying ovens and the silk is then reeled off in one continuous strand—from five to twelve hundred yards per cocoon on average."

She shuddered. "I didn't know they had to be killed."

His luminous eyes held hers. "Georgia, everything beautiful has its counterpart in evil, in ugliness."

They had come to the end of the vast hall, high-ceilinged to accommodate the great looms that silk weaving once required, and they stopped near one of the arched windows overlooking the city.

"I don't believe that," she said. "About beauty and evil."

"I hope you never will. If I had my way, I would protect you from ugliness forever." He took her hand. "Georgia Brandon," he said, "I think I have fallen in love with you."

She made a small gesture, warding off the danger of love. "I don't think love has anything to do with it yet."

He was nonplused by her candor. His voice dropped. "Georgia, when you and your family return to Paris, we can be together. I'll open my house."

She nodded and he raised her hand to his lips, turning her palm up, kissing it gently. She felt his mouth and the faint brush of his mustache. Then, once more asserting control over her rising desire for him, she returned to the business at hand.

"You've said nothing about using my designs."

He laughed aloud. "If it pleases you, we shall certainly make up a few." He spoke as if she were a whimsical child.

Alice in Wonderland, she thought. "I'm quite serious about this," she said. "If you aren't, please tell me."

He surveyed her carefully, saying nothing, and she knew exactly what he was thinking.

"One thing has nothing to do with the other," she assured him with a faint smile.

"You confuse me," he said. "That is how it would be with most women, a quid pro quo."

"But I'm not most women. I'm this one."

He shook his head. "I should say you are several women.

And I am in love with all of them. Come along, we'll talk to my chief technician."

The chief technician, Monsieur Gaillard, was encouraging. "These should render very well, Monsieur le Marquis," he said of the seven designs Antoine finally chose. "Of course, it will take some time to produce a sample of each of them."

"Take all the time you need, Gaillard." Tony thanked the man, then led Georgia down a shadowy corridor at the back of the building. He stopped in a doorway, took her in his arms, and kissed her, his mouth firm and tender against hers.

"I want you desperately," he said. "I love you."

"Yes," she said with surging desire for him. "Yes."

◆

"I think I'm going to marry him, Peggy," Georgia said on the day the family returned to Paris and she was dressing to meet him.

"Do you now?"

"Why not? He's charming, intelligent, and witty. Most of the men I've met are not."

"And they don't have his silk mills either."

"Those mills are already looming seven of my designs!"

"Saints preserve us, Miss Georgia! You'll not be marryin' a silk mill?"

"I loved him before I saw his mills."

"The same way you love that artist fellow?"

"No, Peggy, not only that way." She put her arms around her maid. "Be glad for me, please?"

"Aye, that I am, even though I don't hold with all this loverin' about before a girl marries." Peggy's round face flushed. "Still, I've never seen you look so happy. What will himself say when he gets back from America?"

"Oh, the usual things. That Tony's too old or too young or not good enough, or that he's more in love with my money than he is with me. But I'm going to marry Tony, Peggy, no matter what Father says."

28

◆

He was a more skillful lover than Breen, with an attention to detail that the artist had given only to his work. Tony de Sevignac went about lovemaking at an adagio pace. It made her so avid for consummation that there was no time for fantasy. It was as sensual as the silk he loomed. She might have been wrapped in a long, sleek swathe of satin.

At one point that night, in the darkened bedroom of his town house, she had the feeling that he was an observer at the feast, not part of it, but the impression was lost in a long, slow, intense climax that left her lying limp in his arms.

"Like a pair of exhausted silkworms," she said. "With no cocoon to show for it either."

"*Mais oui!*" he said. "We shall spin one together." He held her close to him, his lips against her hair. "My darling, will you marry me?"

There was no need to think. A married woman had freedom denied to young girls and spinsters, no matter what their wealth. And marriage to Tony promised exciting companionship as well as an outlet for her talent and a use for all that Rhys had taught her about textiles.

"Yes, I'll marry you."

"When?"

"Whenever you like. Tomorrow."

He laughed. "A future Marquise de Sevignac must be married properly."

"Is ritual so important to you?" But she knew it was. Whatever else he took lightly, Antoine de Sevignac prized his name and his heritage—and the traditional way of doing things.

"Of course it's important!" he said. "Isn't it to you?"

She thought of Rhys and knew that, regardless of his certain objection to this marriage, she wanted her father at her wedding. And Jillian too. And Malcolm and Uncle Adam and Peggy.

"Yes, you're right. It is to me too."

"Then I shall talk to your father as soon as he returns from America."

"Wait until my birthday and you won't have to talk to him at all."

"Will he disapprove?"

She put her arms around him. "Yes, but it doesn't matter. Because I do approve." She kissed him repeatedly. "I do. I do. I do."

♦

"It isn't fair!" Jillian wailed. "You'll be Madame la Marquise de Sevignac, and I'll be plain old Mrs. Whosis."

"Make up your mind, Jilly! You complained when I didn't get myself engaged and now you complain because I have. Anyway, what's wrong with being Mrs. Whosis?"

"Nothing, I guess. At least I'll know why Mr. Whosis marries *me*."

"Your fangs are showing. Now, not a word to the family. I'll tell Father when he returns." Rhys and Constance and the boys had arrived back in America in mid-January.

"I don't envy you that. But, Georgia, how *do* you know Tony loves you?" Jillian demanded. "Really loves you for yourself?"

"When it happens to you, you know."

"It happened to me once," Jillian said in that startling switch from brattishness to genuine bereavement that happened whenever she referred to Peter. It sometimes seemed to Georgia that her sister's only chance of happiness had died with that gentle boy, that he had touched the best part of Jillian and taken it with him when he went.

Georgia put an arm around her. "There are many kinds

of love, Jilly. You've had one sort, but your turn will come
to find another."

Jillian's head dropped to her sister's shoulder. "I hope
they aren't all taken before my turn comes."

♦

Georgia had never enjoyed Paris as she did now, with
Tony. They toured the city and its environs in his Isotta-
Fraschini, wearing fur dusters, goggles, and pigskin gloves.
She had never tasted such omelettes as they ate in country
inns, or such sandwiches of crusty bread and moist pink
ham spread with sharp Dijon mustard as they had in cafés
on the Left Bank, with strong hot coffee flavored with
chicory.

They had cocktails in the fashionable Bergère Bar, with
its walls lacquered in mauve, beige, and dark chocolate
brown, and dined in restaurants elegantly decorated in the
crimson velvet and gold leaf of the Belle Epoque. They
went walking by the Seine, a river designed for lovers,
under a winter sky as brilliantly blue as her eyes. Hour by
hour she abandoned caution for the heady wine of happiness.

She was not, however, completely adrift on a sea of
infatuation; she had lost her illusions very early in life. She
had seen signs of financial difficulty at the mills and at
Charet-le-Roi. But if Tony's interest in her was not purely
romantic, neither was hers in him. Their relationship was
based on something more mature than that: shared interests, shared tastes. What better use for her mother's money
than to restore Charet-le-Roi? Or to perpetuate a dynasty
that created an art form in its exquisite silks, provided
Georgia had a hand in their design?

She said nothing to Tony about that last condition, not
yet. After all, she did not require his approval or her
father's; she already had her mother's.

She was determined to learn everything she could about
the manufacture and sale of silk. Monsieur Gaillard was
eager to discuss his craft whenever she went to the mill in
Lyons, as eager to teach as she was to absorb. Tony let her
amuse herself. He indulged her as he would have kitten

playing with a skein of silk. He had other things on his mind.

"Doesn't it distress you," he asked when Rhys lingered on in America, "that your father will control your legacy even after you marry?"

"It would distress me if it were true. My uncle Adam is executor of my mother's estate and he has agreed to hand it over to me next month on my birthday." She glanced at him. "Does that make me more desirable?"

"As a woman, no. As a wife, decidedly. Would you believe me if I answered otherwise?"

"No. I want us to be honest with each other."

But she wished he had been just a little less honest.

Still, there was more between Tony and herself than mutual self-interest. It was in Tony's eyes when he looked at her, in his voice when he spoke. She felt it in her body when they made love. She craved a child by him, and she had never wanted a child by Samson Breen.

◆

She went to tell Samson Breen her news and promise him her continued financial help, only to find his studio occupied by a large, fierce-looking woman plastered to the elbows with papier-mâché and impatient to return to her work.

"Ask the concierge," she said, and closed the door.

"Monsieur left very suddenly on Christmas Day," the old man said. "Packed up all his canvases, paid his bills, and took himself off in two taxis."

"Was he in good spirits?"

"Merry as a grig."

"Did he leave a forwarding address or a message for me?"

No, Samson Breen had simply disappeared.

"I can't understand it," Georgia told Peggy. "Why would he go off without a word?"

"He's a man, isn't he?" Peggy snorted. "They're none of 'em to be trusted."

"You needn't worry, Peg. Tony will never jilt me."

She wondered briefly where Breen's portraits of her would surface—or if his sudden departure meant he had sold them privately. She felt vaguely uneasy—suppose Tony were to recognize her?—and then realized her uneasiness was on her father's account. He would be furious—as he would be about her engagement.

But there was nothing he could do. Her twenty-first birthday ball was only weeks away.

She was impatient for Rhys to return to France and make her engagement official—and astounded to read, in the Paris edition of the *Herald Tribune*, a week after she told Tony she would marry him, that Rhys had announced the engagement during a speech at a political dinner in New York.

"You told Father, didn't you?" she accused Jillian, brandishing the paper that carried three photographs: hers, Rhys's, and Tony's.

"Not a word!" Jillian swore. "Cross my heart and hope to die. I'll bet it was Tony."

"I couldn't wait another moment," Tony confessed. "I telephoned him the day you said yes."

"But Tony . . ."

"You thought he would object, my darling. How could I have waited?"

"What a way to give me his blessing!" Georgia said, both angry and hurt. "Third hand, via the press!"

"What does it matter how he did it?"

She knew Rhys was punishing her for becoming engaged without consulting him, for her approaching separation from him. It was a subtle punishment—he could always insist he meant it as a happy surprise—but her father was a wily man.

"I'd have married you without his consent," she insisted, and realized she had been looking forward to doing just that!

◆

"I never knew a man who attracted as much favorable publicity as you do," Martin van Reitjens said to Rhys in Washington, where Rhys spent nearly half his time now.

Van Reitjens preferred to keep out of the public eye. He had abandoned active practice of the law for political power broking. Most of his time was spent in meetings like this one, in private rooms at private clubs in the nation's capital. These five men often met for a drink before they dined or set off to visit their mistresses, who were either kept or hired for the night.

Senator Jonah Charles of New Hampshire, now chairman of the Senate Finance Committee, agreed with Martin, adding somewhat petulantly, "*My* daughter's engagement was a family affair, not a national event."

"Now, now, gentlemen," Ed Reedy admonished them jovially. "This kind of publicity's worth a fortune." He waved at the newspapers scattered on the floor at his feet.

The headlines—"Rhys Brandon's Daughter Affianced" "Brandon Beauty Engaged to French Aristocrat" "Brandon Textiles Heiress Will Be Marquise"—were accompanied by photographs of Rhys on the front pages and Georgia and her fiancé in the society columns.

Congressman Reedy, grown grossly obese and immensely powerful in reactionary circles, had clipped a fresh cigar, which he now moistened between his prominent pink lips, adding, "He'll be the best-known senator in the country."

"I assume the wedding will be in New York," John Anders said. Anders traveled between New York and Washington, a gray ghost without whose knowledge and advice nothing much happened in the nation's banking system.

"No," Rhys said. "At the de Sevignac estate. It's better that way. De Sevignac's Catholic."

"Unfortunate," Reedy commiserated.

"Then have a private Protestant service first, Rhys, and let the press know about it," Jonah Charles offered after a reflective pause.

"That's what I was thinking," Rhys said. "Anyone want a refill?"

He helped them all to another drink while they went on talking. They were more than his companions in adultery and politics. They had established a claim upon him with the promise of something for which he hungered as he had never hungered for any woman, even Georgianna.

They were going to make him president of the United States.

The only thing about Rhys that gave them pause was Crabtree. They still cited the pacifist movement and the international disarmament conferences organized to respond to a public outcry for peace, a worldwide outcry that had never before been equaled. There were peace marches and antiwar crusades. Women's groups sought to outlaw Armistice Day because it was a glorification of war.

His friends knew as well as Rhys that the conferences and the treaties were all show and no substance; arms traffic was too profitable.

"There are politicians aplenty," Rhys invariably reminded them, "who own large blocks of shares in munitions companies, all of you among them."

That was because the United States would soon be the third largest exporter of war materials in the world, after Britain and France, with foreign sales ballooning.

"Crabtree may be modest by comparison with giants like Du Pont and Remington and Bethlehem Steel," Rhys was fond of saying, "but it shows a healthy annual profit on domestic sales to the U.S. government alone."

So did hundreds of independent arms manufacturers. The government needed arms. American troops were sent all over the world to protect American interests. In addition to business enterprises in Nicaragua and Haiti, they were ready to protect the Panama Canal Zone. American warships had entered Chinese ports to succor American citizens should a threatened native rebellion erupt, and to protect, by their very presence, American-owned textile mills in China.

Armed forces had to be supplied with arms. So had the United States-supported governments of Cuba and Honduras, as well as—very secretly—the same insurgents the United States wanted those governments to subdue. The creed of the munitions maker was to sell to anyone who could afford to buy.

Rhys's supporters still grumbled about Crabtree, but now that de Sevignac had pulled off this engagement, Rhys would be able to bury his ownership of Crabtree deeply enough to satisfy everyone.

It was, in part, why Rhys had made the engagement public as soon as de Sevignac phoned him with the news. He couldn't risk having Georgia change her mind.

"Some of Rhys's luck seems to have rubbed off on his old friends the MacKenzies." Martin smacked his lips over his whiskey. "Enoch's political punch is gaining strength and Rhys's boy, Connor, is running an investment trust."

"Holy Christ, Rhys!" Reedy exclaimed. "Is your Mac-Kenzie the union man's son? I had no idea!"

"Ah, the penny finally drops," John Anders said, pressing his pale fingertips together. Reedy was useful, but the ascetic-looking Anders found him gross and avoided his company whenever possible.

"He isn't *my* MacKenzie," Rhys objected. "They're thorns in my flesh, the pair of them! But I won't have the father interfering with my mills. Something may have to be done about him."

"If he goes too far," Reedy replied, emitting clouds of blue cigar smoke, "something will be."

"I'm relieved to hear it," Rhys said. "It'll be a real comfort to Silas too."

"Real," murmured Jonah Charles, "but anonymous."

"Naturally," Rhys had assured them all.

Discretion was the better part of everything these men did. They trusted one another because they were bound together in a common cause: the presidency for Rhys and all that would flow from it for them. It would take a little time, but Rhys was only fifty. It would take money, too, but they had ways of getting money. It could be done.

"When do you sail?" Anders asked Rhys as the men went down to their waiting cars.

"Tonight at midnight. I'm meeting Constance and the boys in New York."

"Ah, yes, you must have the whole family together for Georgia's engagement party," Anders said.

"When's the wedding?" Martin asked.

"At Christmas." Rhys got into his car. "Soon enough." He waved good-bye and frowned as soon as the Bentley pulled away. "Not soon enough for me," he muttered to himself.

Georgia was relishing her independence too much. Rhys was impatient to have her safely married, as impatient as Tony would be to have her dowry. But haste would cause gossip. Furthermore, a wedding on a grand scale was de rigueur for their two families, and it required months of preparation.

Rhys fidgeted. Georgia was apparently enraptured with her fiancé now, but he wondered how long that would last.

♦

Georgia slipped into one of Tony's silk kimonos and got out of bed.

"Where are you going?"

"I have a fitting at Varnet—and some other crucial business besides. I want to show her those samples Gaillard sent up from Lyons."

Tony sat up. "Georgia, you can't continue designing after we're married!"

She looked down at him and decided it was as good a time as any to have it out. "Why not?"

"My dear girl, an American princess may work, but a French marquise does not."

She sat down on the bed. "We needn't advertise the fact that you're using my designs."

"*If* I use them," he interrupted, determined not to let control of their relationship pass from his hands to hers.

"But we both know you will!" She looked at him, waiting, and realized that the weight of her money was almost palpable there between them.

So this is how it feels to have power over my own life! she thought.

But she was using it for his happiness as much as for her own!

Tony thought carefully about laying down an ultimatum, but she would part with her money more easily if she had a personal stake in the success of his mills—and the designs were really too good to pass up. All it required was the discretion she had just promised. After a moment he made a gesture of compliance with his hands and smiled his assent.

"How can I refuse you anything?"

She leaned over and kissed him passionately. "You're a wonderful man, Tony, you really are."

He opened the kimono and his hands stroked her naked breasts while he watched her eyes close and her lips part.

"My God, you're beautiful," he said. "You *look* like a marquise."

She sighed. "Like this?"

"Most of all like this." He pulled her down beside him, his domination reasserted by her passionate response. She would have returned his caresses, but right now he wanted her passive, a woman thoroughly had, totally his.

"Don't move," he said, pressing her knees apart. "Lie still."

She felt like a flower being sipped at by a hummingbird, and soon she could not lie still. When her cries of passion had excited him beyond control, he took her.

This time he lay back on the pillows after she had disappeared into the bathroom. She was young and impulsive, but a baby or two would soon change that. The important thing was to marry her. Then he would have a husband's right to direct her behavior as well as first call on her fortune and total command of her delectable body.

La femme est menée par la verge, he reminded himself. When a woman was as sensual as Georgia, an upstanding cock was the rod most certain to control her—and she made him rise like a youth in his twenties.

He lit a cigarette and began thinking about his meeting

with her father when Rhys arrived at the end of the week.
It was high time he found out what else it was that
Brandon wanted of him.

♦

Georgia sat in Marie-Véronique Varnet's sumptuous office
overlooking the Rue St. Honoré and watched while the
famous couturière examined the flowing lengths of silk.

Varnet was a tiny blond woman of indefinable age and
brittle chic with a nose of wondrous proportions and the
self-assurance to match it. She wore heels so high she
seemed about to pitch forward on her thin, straight legs
as, birdlike, she tilted her head to appraise the silk streaming over chairs and settees—a king's ransom in antiques.

Georgia tried not to look as anxious as she felt.

"Magnifique!" Varnet said at last. "Absolutely splendid." She smiled at Georgia and went on speaking in brisk
French, occasionally tinged with an *accent Méridionale,*
for Marie-Véronique had worked her way up from a farm
in the south of France to the heights of Parisian couture.

"I can see these two for day or evening and the others
for resort wear, beach pajamas and such, as well as tea
gowns."

Georgia threw her head back, raised her arms, and
heaved a happy sigh. "That's the best thing I've heard in
ages."

"Surely not! The best thing was a proposal from the
most eligible man in France."

"This is different. I'm marrying Tony for myself, but
this is for my mother."

Marie-Véronique tilted her head inquisitively and listened while Georgia told her briefly about Georgianna's
legacy.

"When I was a child," Georgia finished, "I believed that
one day, when I'd finally done what she wanted me to do,
those painted eyes in her portrait would turn from the
distance and look straight at me."

Varnet shivered. "How positively spectral, *ma chère.*
But surely she is well satisfied with you now. Headlines

on both sides of the Atlantic, the *haut monde* already vying for invitations to the wedding, the society columns and *revues des modes* all a-twitter. *Le tout Paris* knew you were a beautiful girl, but now you're all the rage."

"I'm talking about success, not notoriety. You can understand that!"

"*Ma petite*," Marie-Véronique said patiently, "I became successful out of necessity. You were born that way. You have no need to do anything but marry well, dress splendidly, and chair a few charities."

Georgia shrugged, giving up explanations.

"Now, then," Marie-Véronique said. "Let's get on with your fitting."

"I've changed my mind," Georgia said. "That dress is too ingenue. I want something made out of this." She pointed to a length of her new fabric, a rich white satin splashed like a painter's palette with brilliant jewel tones of amethyst, sapphire, and turquoise.

Ah, Breen, Breen, she told herself happily, you'd be proud of me now!

Varnet raised her eyebrows as she went to her drawing board. "Am I to tell the fashion people the fabric design is yours?"

"Of course not! Tony would have a fit. Just say it's Sevignac silk. Not a word about me."

Not yet, anyway, she thought, and stood behind Varnet as the couturière's pencil flew.

"Tell me about the silk trade," Georgia said when tea was rolled in on a trolley. "Tell me everything you know."

"What are you planning? To put Tony's affairs to rights?"

"Why not?"

"You can't march in and run a huge company!"

"Why not? I could run Brandon Textiles with a little help. Is one business so different from the other?"

"You'd have to learn a lot!"

"I will. I am. You can help. I'd like to have a look at other silk mills—they don't have to know why—and you can get me into any factory on the continent."

"Ah, yes, but will Tony let you go?"

"Let me worry about Tony. Now tell me everything you know about silk!"

♦

"As I understand it," Tony said to Rhys, making no attempt to hide his satisfaction, "you have no control whatever over Georgia's money. Her uncle has, and will surrender it to her."

"How do you know that?" Rhys demanded.

"Georgia wrote to ask him. A wise course in my opinion." Tony watched Rhys's clear green eyes darken ominously at the manifold implications of that remark.

"I remind you that you have no rights over my daughter yet," Rhys snapped, "no matter how you gained her confidence. You agreed to a pre-nuptial contract."

"To protect *my* holdings, not hers." It was only half a lie. "And there remains the question of a dowry."

"A dowry? You're a greedy man, de Sevignac."

The two men glowered at each other. Then Antoine leaned back, scrutinizing his host carefully, and lit a cigarette. He was sure that Rhys would offer him a sizable settlement in the end, but his future father-in-law wanted more for it than a title.

Antoine felt on firmer ground. A man who wanted something was ready to bargain for it.

"What exactly do you want?" he asked.

Rhys examined his manicured nails. "Maybe I want to own part of a silk mill. To a textile man, your silk is as a masterpiece to a collector."

Antoine acknowledged the compliment but shook his head. "I don't believe your objective is a silk mill, nor do I have to part with mine. Georgia will provide whatever financial help the mills require to get them through a difficult period."

"My daughter may be generous, de Sevignac, but she is not foolhardy, especially not about her mother's legacy."

"She wants to design Sevignac silks," Antoine said, crossing his legs. "I see you appreciate how important that is to her. I have given my consent, provided she's discreet about it. So what, I repeat, do *you* want?"

Rhys gave up the cat-and-mouse game and stood, clasping his hands behind his back. "I need a European board chairman I can trust—and I am willing to pay him handsomely for taking on the responsibility. Call it a dowry if you wish." Rhys gave an indulgent smile. "In addition, there will be a substantial annual director's fee."

Tony nodded. Now they were getting somewhere.

"I have already formed a Swiss holding company for all the properties now grouped under Republic Industries," Rhys went on. "Switzerland is a more central location than New York for a multinational corporation."

He avoided mentioning at this point that he was heavily invested in Germany, where enormous amounts of American capital had been flowing for a year. The French were sensitive on the subject of a German industrial renaissance.

"I need a man who will execute my orders without question. In that way, I shall not appear to be actively involved."

"Very wise for a politician," Tony said, and Rhys shot him a quick glance. Unfortunately his prospective son-in-law was not entirely stupid.

"I've called it Eden. Its structure is the usual inverted pyramid. The same executives will continue to run my companies, but Republic's corporate control will be transferred to Eden with you as chairman of the board and putative owner."

It was a holding company within a holding company. Tony wondered what it was that Rhys wanted to bury so deeply, but this was not the moment to raise the issue.

"And the other directors?" he asked.

"The usual people." Rhys handed Antoine a list of names, men who made a career of directorships. They offered their prestige in return for generous stipends and caused no trouble. "You can choose from among them," Rhys said, and Tony nodded.

Rhys named the figure for the "dowry" and Tony, eminently satisfied with the negotiations, accepted. "But you must bring your influence to bear on the Senate Finance Committee to reduce import tariffs on my silk."

"My dear Antoine, I have no influence in the Senate or on its committees at present."

"But we both know you will soon have a great deal."

Rhys conceded that he would. "In any case, your silk can hardly be singled out for preferential treatment!"

"Grant it to the entire French industry, then. No one in the world can outsell my silks if they are offered at competitive prices."

"And bought by every woman who thinks they'll transform her into Georgia."

Tony crushed out his cigarette and leaned forward, his gold-flecked eyes crinkling in a smile. "The publicity will accrue to your benefit as well as mine. American infatuation with titles and with France is nothing short of phenomenal."

"Very well," Rhys said, "but it will take time."

"I'm aware of that."

Rhys glanced at his watch. "I hope you'll forgive me, but I have two more meetings scheduled."

They shook hands. It was obvious to Tony that Rhys, eager as he was for this marriage, disliked him thoroughly. It did not disturb him. That was the way of fathers with the men who married their daughters.

"I'm glad we understand each other," Rhys said, walking with him to the door.

"Perfectly," Tony returned. The relationship was founded on deception and held together by self-interest. Either was a more reliable bond than friendship.

29

♦

It was an enormous wedding, all the more festive because of the Christmas season, and was attended by members of the French elite in society, government, and the arts, all of whom looked down their noses at their American counterparts.

"Except for your papa," Marie-Véronique whispered to Georgia as the receiving line began to form in the great hall of the château. She adjusted the wedding gown of silver lace over white satin and fluffed out the veil, its first layer fashioned from Georgianna's shawl. "They all agree that he is absolutely *divine, ma chère*, an aristocrat to the core."

"What are *we*?" Jillian demanded. "Peasants?"

"I'm sure the dowager marquise thinks so," Marie-Véronique returned crisply. "There, Georgia, you are perfection. Just don't move an inch until everyone has seen this dress. It's my *chef d'oeuvre*! Here come your families. I must fly."

Tony spoke briefly to his mother before he left her in her wheelchair, flanked by his three sons and their wives and *les demoiselles*. Then he came to stand next to his bride while Rhys took his place on her other side.

"You are very beautiful, Georgia," Rhys said softly, "especially in that dress." It was the dress Georgianna had been painted in, copied by Varnet from the portrait.

"I call it morbid," Constance muttered just beyond him, but they both ignored her. On her wedding day Georgia's love for her father seemed as strong and unequivocal as it had ever been. She loved everyone today, especially the

410

people from Brandon's Gate: the John Anderses, the Martin van Reitjens, the Silas Cassadynes and their children, the girls among her twelve bridesmaids, and the boys among Tony's ushers.

Six hundred wedding guests began to file by, through the great hall and into the formal rooms of the château, which, like the food and the wine, the bride and the groom, were later described by the press as "storybook perfect."

◆

Jillian caught the bouquet and stood there holding it while the newlyweds departed under a shower of confetti and congratulations. She searched the crowd for a glimpse of Timothy Cassadyne, but it was Derek Anders who was at her side.

"Plan to do anything serious with that bouquet, Jillian?" he drawled.

"Do you?"

The direct question made Derek uncomfortable. "Me? I don't know. But all this wedding cheer is catching."

Jillian ignored him, virtually willing Tim to join her. She found him, got his attention with a wave of the bouquet, and when he arrived, she put her arm through his.

"Well," he said with an unconvincing jauntiness, "that's over. Who's next?"

"That's what I was just asking Jilly," Derek said. "Anyway, old man, be glad it wasn't you today."

"What about you?" Tim bristled. "You proposed to Georgia the night she came out."

"Puppy love, same as yours. It's no picnic, you know, being married to a goddess. Give me a real live girl any day." He raised his empty glass to Jillian. "I must go find a refill."

"God, that boy is a bore," Jillian said.

"Want a drink?" Timothy asked.

"I'll come with you to get it." They started across the

lawn. "Tim, you're coming to Antibes with us tomorrow, aren't you?"

The huge hazel eyes she turned on him were both sympathetic and admiring. She had been a real help since Georgia turned him down. Tim didn't know how he'd have gotten through all the wedding rehearsals and pre-nuptial parties without her. He'd thought of refusing to be part of the wedding party, of not watching Georgia throw herself away on that supercilious Frog. But people would have said he was sulking because Georgia had turned him down after all these years.

"Yes, I'm coming," he said to Jillian. "I could use some peace and quiet after this circus."

She smiled and took the glass of champagne he handed her. "We'll find a few quiet corners," she promised him.

◆

"You have nothing to reproach yourself for," Jillian said to Timothy one evening after dinner as they descended the stone steps from the Villa Ivoire to walk on the beach. She pulled her furs around her against the January air, cool even here on the Riviera.

Tim didn't reply, but he certainly agreed. It was Georgia who had behaved shamefully. He had begun to relax this past week, thanks to Jillian. She didn't mind listening when he blew off steam. She was sweet and understanding, and that wasn't easy, living with a family like hers. She deserved a lot better treatment than they gave her—as he had deserved better from Georgia.

He took Jillian's hand. "Tired?" he asked.

"Tired of walking in shoes and stockings." She stopped to take hers off, and his eyes followed her hands as they lifted her skirt and rolled down her stockings. "That's better," she said.

"Give me those, I'll put them in my pocket." He liked the feel of her silk stockings, still warm from her round thighs. Barefoot in January! Only Jillian would do that. He took her hand again. She was very pretty, with full breasts and a pouty mouth. He felt an erection begin and was glad she could not see it in the shadows, or see his hot blush when he said, "We could go and sit in the cabin for a while. There's enough moonlight to see by."

She nodded and they walked to the cabin the family used for changing out of wet swimsuits during warmer seasons. It had two small rooms, separated by a lounge with two canvas-covered divans. They sat down on one of them. Moonlight streamed through the windows and the surf whooshed softly at the shore. She dropped her furs and let them slide to the floor.

"So you're going to stay on in France after all," he said.

"Yes." She sighed. "Mama says she'll have no time to worry about me during the election campaign."

He put an arm around her. "I'll miss you," he said.

She gazed up at him, her eyes adoring. "I'm glad of that, Tim," she said softly. "I'll miss you too."

He bent his head and kissed her. It was the first time he had ever kissed her, and he liked the way she kissed him back, her soft mouth opening under the pressure of his lips and tongue. He turned her so that she lay across his lap.

"Oh, Tim," she whispered ardently, putting her arms around his neck. "I love you so much. I know I'm not supposed to say so, but I can't help it."

A surge of pride swept over him. It was something he needed to hear and in some inexplicable way it was doubly gratifying to hear it from Georgia's sister. He kissed her again and let his hand rest on her breast, then move to her bare thigh. She did not resist. Her legs parted when he slipped his hand inside her silk bloomers. She was warm and wet. He slid his finger inside her. He almost came then but he held on by thinking of what Rhys Brandon would say if he knew where Tim's hand was now. Rhys didn't like Tim, and the feeling was mutual.

"Jillian?" he said. "We'd better stop. . . ." It was more a question than a statement. But she didn't stop him. She wasn't cold, like Georgia; she loved him. He knew if he didn't stop he would marry Jillian, and that was all right too. That would show all of them. That would show *her*.

◆

Oh, God, don't let him stop, Jillian prayed, her eyes tightly closed as his fingers explored her. She was far too anxious to know whether she liked it or not. She pulled him closer, kissing him with parted lips. She thought she had lost when he took his hand away, but he was only unbuttoning his trousers. Then he pulled her bloomers off, lay on top of her, and prodded her insistently with his penis. It felt strange, soft and hard at once.

"Are you a virgin?" he mumbled.

"Of course," she said.

"Jillian, it may hurt."

"I don't care!" she whispered, trying not to tense her body. She had to make him go all the way or she might lose, even now. He pushed harder and she felt a sudden, sharp stab just before he erupted inside her with a long groan that sounded more like pain than pleasure.

She lay very still, waiting for what came next. It felt very wet down there and she was thankful her dress was pushed up way above her waist.

"Are you all right?" he whispered, still panting a little on her shoulder.

"That was wonderful," she answered, glad that it was over, amazed that this was all there was to the great mystery of sex. She took his handkerchief from his breast pocket and slid it down between her legs.

"Oh, Tim, I do love you," she whispered. Her head felt curiously disconnected from her body.

"And I love you," he said, and she knew she had won.

She wondered if he had liked it more with Georgia, but that was one question she would never, never ask.

◆

"It's quite a surprise," Silas said to Rhys on the flagstone terrace overlooking the garden, one night shortly before their return to America. Hastily he added, "A very welcome one, of course. But I always thought it would be Georgia, didn't you?"

Inwardly disdainful—he would never have allowed Georgia to throw herself away on Timothy Cassadyne—Rhys looked bemused and said that youth was unpredictable. "Timothy's a lucky man."

Silas thought that sounded patronizing.

"And Jillian's a lucky girl," he countered. "Tim's done a good job finding new markets for our cotton production, as well you know." It annoyed him to have to sing his son's praises, but fair was fair. Rhys might have had the idea to sell retail through the mail order catalogs that blanketed the country, but, damn it, Tim had made the plan work.

Silas watched Rhys loll back in his chair and put his long legs up on the veranda railing. He decided to get off the subject of Tim's worthiness.

"Where'll the wedding be, do you think?"

"New York."

"When?"

"Two months before the election. The wedding will create good publicity for my campaign."

"That means a long engagement," Silas observed. "A bit hard on them, isn't it?"

"They'll survive. To hear the women go on about it, it'll take that long to get Jillian's trousseau together."

"This engagement comes at a tricky time," Silas remarked, "with cotton prices collapsing. But between us we can set them up very nicely with a house in New York."

Silas could make damned sure Rhys gave his fair share, at least with respect to the several ventures to which he and Rhys were partners. He waited until Rhys nodded his agreement, then inquired, "How's Crabtree doing these days?"

The subject usually made Rhys mellow, but Silas knew the arms business had suddenly fallen on hard times. In England, Vickers and Armstrong had both been so close to bankruptcy that they had been forced to merge. Even the great Krupp, forbidden by the Versailles Treaty to manufacture his huge cannons, was in a slump.

"Well enough," Rhys replied complacently. "A forge is

versatile. It can make a variety of items. But there's a steady demand for machine guns and small arms."

"But we're taking the marines out of Nicaragua. Where will that leave our cotton holdings, never mind your munitions business?"

Rhys was unperturbed. "Our troops'll be back in Nicaragua by next year, mark my words. Don't worry about it."

Silas nodded, very willing to be soothed.

"I tell you, Silas," Rhys said with infinite satisfaction, "weapons are a fascinating business. They're the whores of the politicians, for sale to anyone who has the price." Rhys eyed his partner sympathetically. "It's human nature, much as you hate to admit it."

Silas let it pass. There was no use arguing with Rhys when he got on his high horse. He wasn't even a United States senator yet—although he was a certain winner—but he had influence in Washington. Last year he had supported a lobby to defeat the proposed tax on every bale of cotton brought to market. He had also encouraged the moratorium on German reparations payments and urged the subsequent loan of $2.5 billion to revive German industry. It was the Christian thing to do, everyone said.

"A fascinating business," Rhys was saying. "All sorts of people have popped up on my doorstep wanting to buy arms—including, once, Connor MacKenzie."

"The devil he did!" Silas laughed.

"You find that amusing?"

"I'll say I do! It puts you both in the same business, doesn't it?" Silas, awash in admiration for Connor's nerve, ignored Rhys's chilly expression. Silas still wondered how much Connor knew about that business with Dilys. There had been more to that last argument than a waltz with Georgia.

"Well, the boy always had enough moxie for three men," Silas said.

Rhys lit a cigarette and examined the smoke that curled from its tip. "You misunderstand, Silas. Connor was, and is, unaware that Crabtree belongs to me. He dealt with

Trask. I told Trask to agree to the sale and cancel it at the last minute."

"Why?".

"To teach the little bastard a lesson," Rhys said with a look on his face that made Silas shiver.

"From what I've heard of gunrunners, that could have been a very dangerous lesson," Silas said.

"He chose a dangerous line of work."

I'll be go to hell, Silas thought, if he wasn't trying to get that boy killed!

Silas felt decidedly uncomfortable at the turn the conversation had taken. He was a peaceable man, and physical violence, or the threat of it, unnerved him.

"I think you're exaggerating. What did Connor do, after all, except take you at your word? You were the one to give him big ideas—and he's done you proud. He got what he wanted."

"Not entirely," Rhys said, but he did not enlarge on that. He let his tilted chair come forward and got up to pour two more brandies.

He never changes, Silas thought, studying Rhys's physique and feeling painfully aware of his own more obvious advance through middle age. Rhys was as handsome as ever. He'd probably lost count of the women he'd had.

You're a real bastard, Silas thought. I've known you all my life and you've done some rotten things, but I never knew you were as mean as this.

"Enough about Connor." Rhys raised his glass with a happy smile. "Welcome to my family, Silas."

"Yes," said Silas glumly. "Thanks."

◆

"What on earth's the matter with you?" Susan Cassadyne demanded from her side of the bed. "You've been tossing for hours."

"Can't get to sleep," Silas muttered.

"Take some of my Veronal—or go sleep in one of the guest rooms. Constance and I have a million things to discuss tomorrow about the wedding."

"All right," Silas said wearily, turning back the covers and reaching for his robe. "I'll sleep down the hall." He stood up and knotted the cord around his expanding waist. "How do you feel about this engagement?"

"Delighted! How else should I feel?"

"You like Rhys, don't you?"

Her tone changed. "What do you mean?" Did he know about the fantasies she entertained of Rhys Brandon while she lay prone in the marital embrace, letting Silas pump away? She was sure Rhys did scandalous things in bed, things she could barely imagine and Silas certainly never attempted. "He's a fine man and everyone says he'll go far in politics."

"But what do you think of *him*?"

"Oh, Lord, Silas, you do pick the worst times to get philosophical! Our son is going to marry his daughter—the better girl of the two," she ran on rapidly. "As far as I'm concerned, Georgia's just like her mother. You can't do a thing with her." She drew a breath. "Rhys is our lifelong friend and your business partner. That's quite enough for me." And Susan flopped back on her pillows and pulled the sheet over her head.

Silas went downstairs, poured a shot of whiskey into a glass of milk, and drank it down. He shuddered, took the whiskey bottle, and climbed the stairs to the guest room, counting off on the treads the times he had been patronized by Rhys, or treated shabbily in their business deals together, or had his nose rubbed, as with Crabtree, in the fact that he often made the wrong decision.

There comes a time, Silas said to himself. There comes a time. . . .

But there was nothing he could do. His business interests were too closely bound up with Rhys's, and now their children were to marry.

"One thing's for sure," Silas muttered. "Rhys hates Connor MacKenzie worse than death, and when a man like Rhys has a hate on, better it be for Connor than for me."

♦

"But do you love him?" Georgia pleaded with her sister when the de Sevignacs' honeymoon culminated at a huge party given by Rhys at the Plaza Hotel in New York. The sisters had escaped to Georgia's suite, while downstairs Rhys's celebration for the newlyweds went merrily on.

"What do I know about love?" Jillian, looking chic in a gown of bronze satin, puffed rapidly on a cigarette.

"Enough."

"But anyone would be second best to Peter, so what does it matter? I'm marrying Tim no matter what Mama says. My engagement got me home from France, didn't it? Otherwise she'd have dumped me on your doorstep like a bag of laundry until you found me a husband."

"Jillian! You can't get married to spite Constance!"

Jillian's mouth set firmly in an expression familiar to her family. "You're angry because Tim got over you so quickly. I love Tim quite enough, thank you very much, and he loves me. I'm going to marry him and that's that." She glanced sidelong at Georgia. "Anyway, I have to."

Georgia closed her eyes for a moment, then looked at Jillian again. "You're not pregnant?" she asked finally.

"No, dear sister, but I *am* a fallen woman," Jillian said with satisfaction. "Sex is a messy business, though, isn't it? I've only ever done it once," she went on. "Mama's watched me like a hawk since we got engaged. But as I didn't much care for it, what's the difference?" Suddenly she burst into tears. "I just want something of my own. I want my own husband and my own house and my own life. I want to get away from Mama."

"Hush, Jilly, don't cry." Georgia stroked her hair. "I understand and I'm sorry I badgered you. Tim's a good man and he'll do his best to make you happy."

"Well, that's more like it," Jillian said. She stopped crying and powdered her nose before the girls went back downstairs to the party.

"Party!" Jillian sniffed. "It looks more like a nominating convention!"

♦

Tim watched the sisters enter the room together as he had
watched with Connor that night at Brandon's Gate. Georgia wore an inky black gown so simple it made Jillian look
overdressed.

Tim moistened his lips. Georgia was still the most beautiful woman he had ever seen. It was hard not to gape at
her breasts, upthrust under the clinging panne velvet of
that slip of a bodice. He had never touched her bare
breasts, never felt her nipples between his fingers. He
had been too goddamned noble for that, even though he
suspected she had a healthy appetite under her glossy
golden veneer. Well, she was getting it now; you could
tell by looking at her. Tim couldn't help imagining what
de Sevignac did to her in bed, things no decent man asked
of his wife.

With a certain pride at having deflowered her sister, he
looked at Jillian and realized, with a wave of pity, that she
was aware of the inevitable comparison people made between the sisters. Georgia was a woman who inspired
worship even as she aroused lust. Jillian was a pretty girl
who described herself accurately as almost, but not quite,
right.

Tim was suddenly relieved that she, and not Georgia,
would be his wife. Georgia would be impossible to satisfy,
sexually or any other way. Only an old roué with a title
was up to her requirements! Tim was impatient for the de
Sevignacs to go back to France, as if they so overshadowed
his own life that he couldn't begin to live until they were
gone.

He resented them fiercely and he was miserable in their
presence, but he was at Jillian's side when the family
gathered for a farewell dinner a few days later, and he
tried not to stare at Georgia.

♦

"Father's delirious about all the press coverage you and
Tony produced," Malcolm was saying to Georgia. He had

shot up at least two more inches since her wedding and he was broad but very thin, a boy with an angel's face, just struggling into manhood. "Does Tony mind being part of a political campaign?"

She laughed. "Tony needs publicity as much as Father does. Did you know that American sales of Sevignac silk increased fifteen percent since our engagement?"

"Marvelous. But are you happy, Rapunzel?"

"Yes, Malcolm, very. Doesn't it show?"

"I guess it does, but I don't like your living in France."

"I don't intend to, darling, not all year round."

"Does *he* know that?"

"He's agreed to it."

"I see," Malcolm said frostily. "Then he must need money badly."

"He does," Georgia returned calmly. "But he had plenty of chances to marry it before he chose me. We have a lot in common, you know. We like the same things. And we laugh together. I never really had much *fun* until I met Tony. And, Mal," she said eagerly, "I can't wait to get back to Lyons to have a go at those mills of his. Don't turn up your nose; they're as much art as industry. And I'm certain that within a year, I can—"

"Oh, for God's sake!" he muttered, shaking his head angrily. "So he didn't marry you for your money and you didn't marry him for his mills."

"Don't be glib, Malcolm," she said sadly. "Not with me."

"Just tell me why you married him!"

"To live with him. To enjoy him."

He hesitated. "But do you love him?"

"Yes, I do."

"Madly?"

"Madly? That kind of love is for children. I much prefer this kind."

"I wanted something more for you."

"An epic love? Like the stories I used to read to you?"

"Yes. To me you're still the heroine in every one of them."

She put an arm around him and hugged him close. "My beautiful baby brother. You're a hopeless romantic, and I adore you."

Tony, across the table, was surprised to see his dignified wife so demonstrative in public. Such goings-on would never be tolerated at Charet-le-Roi, but this was America, after all, and of all her family it was her youngest brother he disliked least.

♦

Georgia was eager to start reorganizing Sevignac Silks as soon as the newlyweds returned to Charet-le-Roi, but before she could even arrange a studio for herself at the mill, they went to the Château de Sevignac for a week that culminated in a grand dinner. That was followed by end-less weekends devoted to receiving relatives "who seem to multiply," Georgia remarked to her mother-in-law's hor-ror, "like the loaves and the fishes."

Then came at-homes with a stream of lesser relatives and family friends, women who might have been stamped out with a cookie cutter and men who had nothing to say to women beyond insipid gallantries.

Georgia put up with it until one autumn morning when Tony had left to visit his vineyards and she escaped to Paris. She telephoned Marie-Véronique Varnet, made an appointment for luncheon, and caught an early train. She carried with her a soft leather briefcase containing swatches of the designs she had given Monsieur Gaillard on her first visit to the Soieries Sevignac.

The perky blond couturière hooted with laughter over Georgia's description of her new relatives.

"Those country women are as dull as cows," she agreed. "But I'm sure you can add some spice to life."

"Not by gossiping," Georgia said, reaching for her brief-case and taking out the swatches. "I brought these for you to look at. The factory foreman made them up while we were on our honeymoon."

"*Quelle beauté!*" Varnet crowed, running the rich silk through her hands. Her fingers traced the bold designs in unorthodox color combinations: pink and red, orange and purple, turquoise and violet before she looked at Georgia admiringly. "You should be very proud. I shall take at least ten of them—*en exclusivité*, of course."

"That's a lot to ask," Georgia said. "You'll have the best of the line."

Varnet tapped her long red fingernails on the polished top of her desk. "You can't be suggesting that I take fewer?"

"Not at all. I'm suggesting you pay a royalty for the privilege of exclusivity."

Varnet cocked her head. "Are you? And where, *je vous prie*, did you learn about royalties?"

"From my father."

Varnet stopped tapping and gave a Gallic shrug. "Ah, the textile baron. He's taught you well. How much?"

Georgia named a figure.

"*D'accord*," Varnet said. "For all purchases over one hundred meters."

Georgia shook her head. "No. On the total *metrage* you purchase of each design."

"*Mon Dieu!* Is that all?"

"I would require that any fashion photographs you issue specify 'Sevignac Silk.'"

There was a brief silence, then Marie-Véronique threw back her head and laughed. "And I thought you were a novice in business! I wonder if Tony knows what manner of woman he has married."

"Are we agreed?" Georgia asked, extending her hand.

Marie-Véronique took it. "Absolutely. We shall both make a huge profit."

"Wait until you see my designs for summer. They're absolutely stunning."

"You must tell me everything! *Allons, chérie*, stay the night at my house. We can see a play and have dinner at Maxim's, just girls together. We can talk about the summer designs."

"What a marvelous idea!" Georgia telephoned and left a

message for Tony. She spent the afternoon at a small silk mill just outside Paris and the evening with Varnet.

"Keep the designs coming," Marie-Véronique said when they parted. "And give Antoine my love."

♦

Antoine was not amused when she returned to Lyons. She was not to go off to Paris alone without his permission, he scolded her in the privacy of their suite of rooms at Charet-le-Roi.

"I went to meet Marie-Véronique and I telephoned to let you know I was staying the night with her. It didn't require your permission! Good Lord, Tony, this is 1926!"

"But people still talk! *Madame ma mère* was incensed, and rightly so," he persisted.

"Your mother is a lady of the old school," Georgia said. "Don't expect me to live by her rules."

Tony drew a deep breath and retrieved his calm. "Georgia, it is *I* who expect you to behave like a noblewoman."

She put her arms around his neck. "Not always," she said.

He turned away. "I'm serious, Georgia."

"Then let's talk business. I showed the new samples to Varnet. Tony, she's mad about them! We're going to have the best season in years! You'll have to start up all but ten of your looms."

Tony, caught between gratification at the news and the nagging perception that she was escaping his suzerainty, forced himself to listen. In her visits to the mills and her talks with Gaillard, Georgia seemed to have grasped the problems of the silk trade. She was well on her way to reorganizing the workings of the Sevignac mills, suggesting procedures to save time and money that it would have been folly to reject.

She was talking now about better yardage yields per skein and sales projections based on Varnet's enthusiastic reaction. She even produced a preliminary breakdown of costs, worked out on her train trip back from Paris. That was the last straw!

Piqued, he pounced on one of the items. "Designer fees?" he asked.

"Yes, for me."

He lost his patience. "We agreed before we married that you would be discreet about that. Now you not only go running off to tell Varnet, who has the biggest mouth in Paris, but you propose that I pay you for your designs!"

"Varnet has known about it since our engagement and kept her promise to say nothing. I *am* discreet. But I will charge a fee for my designs, as any designer would. Why on earth not?"

"Because you're my *wife*, that's why. You belong to me and what you do belongs to me. It is my duty and my right to decide what use shall be made of your talent."

She shook her head, regarding him steadily.

"What does that mean?" he demanded hotly.

"I won't be controlled by anyone," she said simply. "Much less owned. My father tried to control me and I hated it."

"The rebellion of a foolish young girl!"

"No, Tony. It's how I am."

He knew he had been warned. But while independence in a mistress was exciting, it was unacceptable in a wife.

"It may be how you were," he said, bristling. "You're my wife now."

"What I do belongs to me! I want you to have it, but not by divine right."

He was unsettled by her quiet insistence. Most other women—even men—would have been shouting if they were as angry as she was, but only her eyes, darkened from their habitual vivid blue, showed it.

He knew she had a mind of her own, but not until this moment had he suspected that the passion in her nature extended to more than sex. Her graciousness, her composure, her self-possession were misleading. His wife, he realized with a sinking sensation, not only had a sharp mind for business, but a taste for power as well, and a temper all the more formidable because it was cold.

"I refuse to haggle over pennies," he said.

"We're discussing principles now."

"Not now. We must dress or we'll be late for dinner."

At dinner she was charming, describing the latest fashions for his unfashionable sisters and remaining impervious to his mother's censorious glances. But she went upstairs early; a headache, she said.

It was the usual female ploy, and he expected her to pretend she was asleep when he went up an hour later. To no avail, as she would realize if she tried such a thing! If he wanted her, he would have her.

His valet helped him to undress and he put on a robe and went into her bedroom. He had yet to sleep in his. To his surprise she sat up in bed reading. She held out her hand.

"Tony, don't let's argue."

She was beautiful. The skin of her face and arms was silvery, as if she were bathed in moonlight. He felt an erection begin.

"There is no reason to argue," he said, slipping out of his robe.

She smiled happily. "Then we agree?"

He got into bed and took her in his arms. "I'll show you how well we agree," he said, sliding his hands under the satin of her nightgown, drawing it up.

"This kind of agreement was never in doubt," she whispered.

◆

He stopped her with a kiss and made love to her with a vehemence that startled her, even as it aroused her. It was one of those nights when he wanted her responsive, but not active, when he orchestrated the encounter to last until she was thoroughly and repeatedly satisfied. It made her feel more like a toy than a wife, but she could not help responding to him physically.

"You're a fantastic woman," he said, still breathless, still lying over her, his head pillowed in the curve of her neck. "Do you love me?" he asked, still warm within her.

"Yes, Tony."

"Did I make you happy just now? Do I always?"

"Yes, you do."

"Then be the kind of wife I want you to be."

When she said nothing, he withdrew from her and raised himself on one arm to look down at her, silently demanding a reply.

"Tony, you don't own me, no matter how well you make love to me."

With an angry sound he flung his robe around him and left to spend the night in his own bedroom. When he awoke in the morning, his valet told him Madame had already left.

"To Lyons, sir," was Peggy's reply, pronounced as if the city were a pride of beasts. "Said she had some shoppin' to do."

Utter nonsense! Antoine raged to himself. But two could play at this game. She was to have accompanied him when he went to Zurich on business—she didn't know it was for her father's corporation, Eden—but he left that very morning without her and he stayed for ten days.

In Zurich he went to bed with a former mistress and an American divorcée. Aside from that, and the time he spent chairing a meeting of Eden's board, he brooded, not certain that this was the way to teach Georgia a lesson. The woman was stubborn as a mule!

When he returned to Lyons, his lawyer, Maître Mercier, insisted on rushing round to see him as soon as Antoine arrived at his office. It appeared that an American company called George-Art was the owner of certain of the designs Monsieur le Marquis was already producing for sale, and was pressing for its fees.

"Impossible," Antoine said, his hackles rising.

Maître Mercier cleared his throat and averted his eyes when he spoke again. "I believe the designs in question are the work of Madame la Marquise."

"They are," Tony said, placing his fingertips together precisely. "It amuses her to sketch."

"Ah, there you have it," Maître Mercier said delicately. "Some time ago she made George-Art sole owner of, and agent for, all her designs, past and future. I have seen the documents and all is in order." He cleared his throat. "Since your pre-nuptial contract provides for a clear division of property—"

"I know what it provides," Antoine cut him off.

"To clarify: what is George-Art's is hers, and what is hers is not, alas, yours."

"There is some misunderstanding. I shall clear it up and tell you what must be done."

"George-Art is pressing," the little lawyer whispered.

"Tell George-Art to go to hell! Good day, Maître Mercier." And Antoine rushed out of the office, determined to settle this once and for all.

30

♦

He took the stairs two at a time and burst into the sitting room of their suite. Georgia was lying on the Recamier couch watching the fire dance in the grate as he strode to her side.

"What the devil do you think you're doing?" he demanded savagely, hands on hips, his eyes glinting in the firelight.

"Protecting my rights," she flared back at him.

"Your rights! And what if I refuse to pay?"

"Then George-Art will issue a court order forcing you to stop production on my designs until you do pay. If you still refuse, I'll sue you. Then I'll sell them elsewhere."

He looked at her for a moment, then stalked to the window and stared out as dusk descended on his estate. He needed time to think. From the gold and onyx case she had given him he took a cigarette, tapped it twice, and lit it with a gold lighter. He puffed several times before he turned to confront her, very cool now.

"At this stage of production that would be ruinous and you know it, which means you would lose your entire investment in my mills. Since you're prepared to wrangle over the paltry sum your designs would fetch, I don't believe for a moment you would risk a much bigger loss."

It was his intention, Georgia knew now, to dominate her as completely as her father had! Aghast, she wondered why she had not seen that before she married him. But she had convinced herself that, as a married woman, she would have more freedom than she had had in her father's house.

The bitter truth was that money was the third partner in this marriage. Moreover, Tony neither admired her ambition nor supported it.

She leaned back on the curved arm of the couch, looking up at the dimpled cherubs painted on the ceiling, simpering in their innocence.

"Oh, Tony," she pleaded with more sadness than anger in her voice, "it isn't the money. It's more fundamental than that, more important." She tried once more. "I'm your wife, not your child. Part of my life belongs to me. If we're going to argue the point every other day, we'd have been better off apart."

His expression changed to shock. "Is that what you're suggesting?"

"No! Of course not! I was making a point."

Antoine, sulking, was nonetheless relieved. A separation would make the most horrendous scandal! And he wanted a tranquil marriage to ensure that her money financed the mills and left him free to restore his decaying properties and expand his art collection. Besides, there was no knowing what Rhys would do about the chairmanship of Eden if the marriage showed signs of strain.

And in two weeks they were sailing to New York for Jillian's wedding! What a rotten time for this to happen!

Besides, damn it all, he wanted *her*, no matter how

spoiled and stubborn she was! She had beauty and background and—unfortunately—brains. So he would let her
have her bloody fees! But he could not lose face, particularly after she had gone behind his back with this George-
Art nonsense. He needed a reason to capitulate, and he
stood there searching for one.

◆

She was dismayed by that, by his weighing and measuring, his calculation; she would have preferred honest anger.

He was not in the least interested in a principle she
believed vital to their happiness. He was concerned with
his pride and reputation and her money. But why wouldn't
he be? He had been brought up to believe he was the
center of the universe and those in his charge mere reflections of himself.

It struck her how like Rhys that was, and she wondered
anew why it had taken her so long to see it.

But they could not remain at an impasse. She was
pregnant, and her child was not going to live in the same
atmosphere Rhys and Constance had created. She did not
want to use her pregnancy to settle an argument, but she
saw no other way.

"Tony, it isn't for me," she lied, knowing the lie must
irrevocably alter their relationship. "It's so I can set up my
own trust for the baby."

His eyes widened, then swept over her body while a
triumphant expression appeared on his face. *I have you
now,* it said.

"A baby!" he said exultantly. "What wonderful news!"

She anticipated everything he did next, as if this were a
play she had seen before. He extinguished his cigarette
and came to kneel beside the couch. He stroked her hair
and kissed her forehead and asked why she hadn't told
him immediately. Of course she should have what she
wanted. He understood perfectly.

I see, Georgia thought wryly. Women in my condition
are slightly deranged and must be indulged.

"But this is truly marvelous!" he exclaimed, striding up

and down the room with his thumbs tucked into his vest pockets, fairly bursting with virility. "What do you want, a boy or a girl?"

"A girl," she said promptly.

He laughed and spread his arms wide. "It's like you, my dear wife, to know precisely what you want. But you shall have a daughter, since I am well provided with sons." He glanced at his watch. "Now I must pay my respects to *Madame ma mère*. She will be pleased to hear the news, and my sisters as well." He took her hand and kissed it. "Rest now. You're looking tired. Morning sickness?"

"It's too soon for that."

"Nevertheless, I shall order dry biscuits to be put by your bed and you must eat one the moment you open an eye in the morning." He smiled. "I shall take excellent care of you. I'm an old hand at pregnancies."

She smiled back, thinking that he could be the most delightful man in the world as long as he controlled it. When he had gone she placed her hands on her abdomen and communed with her baby.

"You'll be born in the spring," she said softly, "and I will never, never leave you, no matter what."

It was a serious promise to make, under the circumstances. Aside from their other differences, she had suspected for some time that Tony was having an affair, and now she was virtually certain of it.

◆

She invited Marie-Véronique Varnet to Charet-le-Roi and put the question to her.

"But of course he's having affairs. *Mon Dieu, ces Américaines!* Tell me, where is the harm, particularly when you will soon be swollen like a grape?"

"Sex isn't a toy, and he isn't a baby."

"Neither are you, *ma petite*, and I advise you not to behave like one. It's how Tony is."

"Have I the same license?"

"Certainly, if you want it, and provided you are discreet. Really, Georgia, you are the most fortunate of

women!" Marie-Véronique exclaimed. "You won't have to
wait until you've produced several unquestionably legitimate sons before you take a lover."

"I don't want a lover. I'm content with Tony."

"And he with you! You are married to a man who has all
the virtues. *Beau, riche, noble—un amant tres doué.* What
more do you want?"

"How do you know he's such a good lover?"

Varnet shrugged and cast her eyes to heaven. "I've
dressed many of his mistresses over the years. How else?"

"What's the point of marriage, I wonder."

"Marriage is for the perpetuation of a name and the
protection of property."

"And fidelity?"

"Fidelity is against nature, particularly in the male."
Marie-Véronique waved one scarlet-tipped hand, impatient at having to state the obvious. "And now, darling, do
please ring for tea. I'm famished."

It was not the situation itself that disturbed Georgia,
but her own equable acceptance of it. She was annoyed,
but not terribly upset, and that confused her. How could
she love Tony enough to live with him, sleep with him,
bear his child—and feel nothing more than mild annoyance when he was unfaithful to her?

But she *did* love him. It was not the epic love Malcolm
had imagined for her, but it was love enough for a life that
was going to be as full as hers.

She did what she had seen countless other women do:
she ignored his philandering, and her love, every untapped drop of it, was concentrated on her child.

◆

Listening to Jillian pronounce her marriage vows, Georgia
wondered how any woman could blithely promise to love,
honor, and obey a man before she had lived with him for
at least a year. She was still convinced that Jillian didn't
love Tim, nor he her. Yet, together, they had the self-
confidence each had lacked apart.

Maybe that was the point of marriage, to make one

whole of two imperfect halves. Tony was no angel, but then, in his opinion, neither was she.

It was a lovely ceremony, far less formal than hers had been. The church was more welcoming than a sixteenth-century stone chapel, and the guests were seated in flower-garlanded pews of polished mahogany upholstered in deep burgundy. Jillian wore white satin, and Georgia, as matron of honor, blush chiffon. The bridesmaids wore pale hyacinth silk and the ushers pearl-gray cutaways.

But the most important guest of all, Georgia thought, was inside her.

"Do I show?" she had asked Peggy that morning as she dressed.

"You're as flat as one of them French pancakes you like so much. You won't start showin' till your fourth month."

"I want to keep it secret for a while."

"You'll be tellin' Dilys, I hope, before we go back to France."

"Of course. I'll tell her at the church today."

"She won't be comin' to the church," Peggy said stiffly.

"Why not? She isn't ill again?" Influenza had kept Dilys from coming to New York the last time Georgia was in America, and Georgia had been too busy for a trip to Brandon's Gate.

"That she is," Peggy had said, bustling off downstairs.

Georgia's attention came back to her sister, now gazing up at Tim as he slipped the ring on her finger. Jillian looked radiant.

Be happy, Georgia commanded her sister fiercely. I want you to be happy!

". . . pronounce you man and wife," the Reverend Mr. Poole said. "You may kiss the bride."

The Mendelssohn recessional sounded, and Georgia handed Jillian her bouquet of white roses and lilies. Taking Derek Anders's arm, she followed the newlyweds up the aisle.

As she passed the family pew, Georgia heard Constance hiss, "What is that woman doing here?" Curious, her eyes swept the wedding guests and found Dilys at the back of the church.

"She's here!" Georgia said over her shoulder to one of the bridesmaids, Tim's sister, Clarissa Cassadyne, "Dilly is here!"

"Really, Georgia, you *are* the limit," Clarissa said from behind her, but Georgia was too shocked by Dilys's haggard appearance to notice the disapproving tone. Dilys *was* ill, seriously ill. Her drawn face lit up briefly at the sight of Georgia, but turned almost immediately, seeking someone else.

Georgia, borne along by the wedding party into the waiting limousines, was driven back to Rhys's three-story mansion on Sixty-eighth Street near Fifth Avenue. She waited impatiently, but Dilys did not appear at the reception when the other servants did, and as soon as Jillian and Tim had departed for a honeymoon in Bermuda aboard the Brandon yacht, Georgia went wearily upstairs to the suite she and Tony occupied.

"Dilys got right back on her train," Peggy explained. "Feelin' too peaky to stay, she said."

Tears filled Georgia's eyes. "I should have gone to her at the church," she said.

"No, Miss Georgia, you couldn't do that. There, now, you can go to the Gate to see her."

"See whom?" Tony came in from his dressing room, wearing pajamas and a silk robe. "What's wrong? Are you ill?" He came quickly to Georgia's side.

"It's Dilys who's ill," Georgia said. "She went straight back to Brandon's Gate."

"Hush now, darling," Tony said, signaling Peggy to leave them alone. "I'm sure she's in good hands."

"It's been years since I've seen her," Georgia wept. "I should have made the time."

"But you couldn't be in two places at once, *chérie*," Tony soothed her. "She understands that. Why not call her in the morning and fix up a visit while I'm in Washington?"

Georgia nodded. She dried her face with a handkerchief, but the tears kept forming and brimming over.

"*Allons, allons, ma petite.*" Tony made clucking noises and led her to the bed. He tucked her in and got in from the other side, holding her while she cried.

"Oh, Tony," she said when she was calmer. "Sometimes you can be so damned sweet."

"Is that a cause for hysterics?"

"I *do* love you," she murmured, half asleep.

"I am convinced of it," he answered, turning out the light.

She almost told him that she was not so convinced, that these occasional moments of tender solicitude, largely attributable to her pregnancy, did not make up for his tempers, his jealous claim to despotism in their marriage, or his infidelities, however random they were.

But tonight, with his arm around her and her child snug inside her, she fell asleep content.

In the morning she called Dilys and arranged to go to Brandon's Gate for a two-day visit.

"I can't wait to see you, Dilly," she said. "I love you so much."

"I love you, too, my darling child."

"Don't cry, Dilly, please, or I will too."

"No, you mustn't. Good-bye, my love, I'll see you on Monday."

◆

I can't, Dilys thought, putting down the phone. I can't pretend anymore.

It had always been hopeless, yet she had gone on hoping, all the more so every time she saw Rhys. Seeing him sapped her courage to leave this place, even when he had no time to hold her in his arms.

"I need you," he would tell her, even on the telephone. "You're the only woman in the world I trust."

How could she refuse him anything? He alone could make her heart soar because of his faith in her, his need of her. That was true love, more than sex. No one else

needed her, not Georgia, not Jillian, and not Connor.
Connor least of all, even though he called her once each
week and showered her with money she did not need and
gifts she could not use. She saw him seldom. It was
painful to be with her son because he hated her lover.

And now Rhys wouldn't want her either! He would be
furious. He had told her not to come, but how could she
stay away on Jillian's wedding day? It was bad enough to
have missed Georgia's. She loved those girls as if they
were her own. Georgia *was* hers, nourished by her body.
Hers and *his*. Almost from the beginning, when she was
falling in love with him, Dilys had thought of Georgia as
their child.

But Rhys had not even glanced in her direction yesterday, and that had torn her illusions to shreds.

She began to cry again. She cried often, lately, at the
most unexpected times and for no reason. But today she
had a reason. She wrenched up great sobs, but they gave
her no easement from the agony she felt. Constance would
force Rhys to dismiss her, and that would surely kill her.
She had to leave before he did that. She had just enough
pride left.

"But I can't," she moaned aloud in the lovely room that
had sheltered her and her sinful, shameful love for twenty
years.

Trembling, she reached for the bottle on her nightstand
and took a double dose of the nerve tonic Dr. van Dorn
had given her. She lay back, waiting for the blessed calm
it produced. Little by little it came, that altered state in
which all things seemed possible, even decisions.

Her hands unclenched and the muscles of her neck
relaxed. Courage that seemed real suffused her, and she
began to make plans. She vowed, as she drifted into a
doze, that she would not wait for that final, cruel farewell.
Before he could deliver it, she would be somewhere else.
She had all the money and securities Rhys had given her
over the years and every penny Connor had sent her. And
now she had the courage.

Courage?

Reality shattered her doze like ice water. She *had* no courage. She had only a vast, aching need inside her to be loved, an empty place that would never be filled.

Trembling, she tossed against the pillow, desperately seeking oblivion. Sleep! She must sleep or she would never be able to think, to plan, to escape from this place she loved. But sleep would not come.

She reached again for the bottle.

"This time," she whispered when the blissful languor began to steal over her. "This time I'll really do it."

◆

It was Peggy, her lips trembling, who brought Georgia the news.

"It's Dilys, Miss Georgia. She's in a coma. Dr. van Dorn says she's dyin'. I must go to her."

"She can't be dying!" Georgia insisted. "I won't let her die! I'm coming with you!"

Georgia ordered a car and scanned the train schedule while she dressed and put a few things into a bag. Then she went down to find her father, relieved that Tony was in Washington, meeting with the French commercial attaché.

She found Rhys and Constance in the drawing room, waiting for their luncheon guests to arrive.

"I'm going home," Georgia told her father. "Dr. van Dorn says Dilys is very ill, maybe dying."

Rhys shot out of his chair, his glance shifting momentarily to his wife. Constance remained impassive while one long, slender hand twisted a strand of the fringe on her dress.

"You mustn't go alone," Rhys said to Georgia.

"Peggy's coming with me."

"There'll be a lot to do, arrangements to be made," Rhys persisted.

Constance interrupted, her voice brittle. "If you leave this house tonight, I'll see that it costs you the election, so help me God."

Georgia did not even wonder why Constance was being hateful. She had always been hateful.

"Then come with me, Constance," Rhys said. "It's something we'd do for any of our people."

"Father," Georgia cut in. "Dilys may be *dying*! Are you coming or not?"

Rhys looked from Georgia to Constance, shook his head, and sat down, while Constance, lounging in her chair, lit a cigarette.

Georgia found Peggy waiting in the hall and together they left the house and got into the waiting car.

◆

She had come too late.

"An hour ago," Adam said.

"Oh, no," she whispered, sinking into a chair in the dust-sheeted drawing room at Brandon's Gate. "Not my sweet Dilly." She looked entreatingly at her uncle. "What happened?"

"Pneumonia, officially," he said. His eyes did not meet hers. "If you ask me, she died of loneliness."

A cry escaped Georgia and she bent forward in the chair. "How could I?" she moaned. "How could I have been so cruel?"

"My dear child." Adam came to comfort her. "It wasn't your fault."

"But it was, it was! She was the only mother I ever had—and all I gave her in return were good intentions and a letter every month. She brought me up to be better than that!"

Adam sat on the arm of her chair and took her hand. "It's time you knew you're not the one who could have cured her loneliness, Georgia, or Connor either."

She heard only the name. "Connor! Oh, God, poor Connor! Does he know?"

"He's upstairs with her."

So Connor was here, in this house, in the very room where they had spent so many hours together, and where a woman dear to both of them lay dead.

She shuddered. "Was he in time?"

"She'd been unconscious since Daisy found her and called the doctor and me. But he was with her when she died." His voice shook slightly.

"You look done in, Uncle Adam," she said, becoming aware of his fatigue.

"It's been a long day."

"You must go home and get some rest. I'll be all right here with Peggy and the maids. Is there anything I ought to do about the . . . the arrangements?"

"That's all been taken care of. The undertaker is on his way now. The funeral is day after tomorrow. Connor arranged it. He'll be staying with me."

"I'll go up to him," Georgia said, walking to the door with Adam and helping him on with his coat.

"Connor's very angry," Adam warned her. "Leave him alone for a while."

"No, not this time. I've always left him alone with his anger."

She kissed her uncle's cheek, and went slowly up the stairs, her heart beginning to pound.

◆

He was sitting on the edge of his mother's bed, one hand over her two clasped ones, the other holding on to the sleeve of her nightgown. There was a fire in the grate, and in the flickering light Dilys was young again, deep in a peaceful dream.

He looked up, his dark eyes full of anguish, and she went to put her arms around him, as if they had parted yesterday, not seven years earlier.

"Oh, Connor," she whispered, "how sorry I am."

He turned suddenly and his arms went around her. He pillowed his head against her body with an urgency born of love and pain.

I love you, she thought. You're the one I love.

But this was not the moment to tell him so. That moment might never come. Did he love her? Or was this only compassion, a need for shared tenderness?

"She was alone for so long," he said, and his shoulders shook. "She died alone."

"We should have been here, you and I," Georgia said, sharing his grief and his guilt. She rocked him, hearing him cry, crying with him. "Connor," she murmured, her love for him making her heart swell. "My Connor."

"Remember?" he said. "All the good times we had in this room."

"I remember. Just the four of us."

"It was even better before Jillian came, when I had you and Mother to myself."

"Come away now," she said, smoothing his hair. "Come sit by the fire with me."

With a long look at his mother he went with Georgia and they sat in silence, their hands clasped, until Peggy came in.

"Them funeral people have come for her," Peggy said with difficulty.

"Oh, my God!" Connor breathed.

"I'll see to it, Connor," Peggy offered.

"Yes, you mustn't stay here," Georgia said. "We'll wait downstairs." She held out her hand to him and he took it like an obedient child.

In the library she poured brandy into two snifters and handed him one. He drank it standing near the fireplace, intent on the flames. He looked very different, no longer the boy in sturdy country clothes, riding horses hell-for-leather and hunting game, sometimes in a black mood and sometimes dazzling people with that smile of his that seemed gone forever.

Now he was elegant and distant, and she might have dreamed that his arms had gone around her upstairs with a need for more than tenderness.

But whatever he felt for her, he was still her Connor, and she knew the roots of him better than anyone in the world could.

They sipped the cognac while the communion they had felt upstairs shrank into self-consciousness. She wanted to hold him again and feel him near her, but he was suddenly miles away, the gulf between them tenanted by her father, his mother, her husband, their separate lives.

There were muted voices on the stairs and then a thump in the hall that made them both flinch. Death was in the hall, in the house. Maybe that was why she longed so desperately to hold him. What better way than love for the living to vanquish death? Not romantic love, but love intensely physical, hot, of the flesh, crying out with life!

She watched him, wondering if he sensed her yearning for him, wondering how he could resist it, even in his grief.

When the noises stopped and the motor of the undertaker's car had dwindled away, he finished his drink and turned to her, gaunt and haggard, with an unfathomable look in his eyes.

Stay, she begged him silently. Stay with me. I need you. Come upstairs with me. Lie down and let me love you.

The tension between them grew.

"It's time I went along to Adam's," he said.

She felt suddenly hollow. "Yes, all right," she said, not looking at him. "And tomorrow?"

"I'll be over in the morning to go through her things," he said, obviously shrinking from the prospect.

"No," Georgia said, her voice low but emphatic. "You can do that tomorrow night. Tomorrow we're going riding, the way we used to. We'll take a picnic and make a day of it."

He almost smiled. "Once I was the general and you were the troops."

"I've changed as much as you have."

"You're still unreal," he said, gazing at her now. "You're still like the moon, as luminous—and as far." He stopped suddenly, collected himself, and made for the door. "I'll meet you at the stables at ten tomorrow morning. And, Georgia?" He turned back.

"Yes?"

"Thank you for coming."

She nodded and sank back in the chair, her mind racing

down several paths that finished at one inexorable truth: she was pregnant and her life was not her own. In point of fact, it never had been.

◆

They had ridden in silence for an hour and now she trailed him by a few feet, feeling the trickles of warm sun through the trees, smelling the green redolence of the woods, watching him.

His hips, like hers, moved forward and back with the movement of the horse. She imagined both of them naked, with nothing between them, moving like that together. She had imagined it for years after that moment when they danced together, perceiving the nature of ecstasy long before she experienced it.

It was not mere sensation she wanted. She wanted it from him, from those hands, from that body, her bridge to the depths of this man's soul. But for the first time in all their times together, she was not sure what *he* wanted.

And then, quite suddenly, he reined in his horse and turned to look at her. The ride, the picnic basket looped to his saddle, the checkered cloth and blanket rolled behind hers, were not the point of this expedition. It was all in those dark eyes of his, all in a look.

"The barn?" he said, and it was as if his mouth had brushed hers.

The silence was electric with their awareness of each other, not as friends now, not as children bereft of the same mother, but as lovers. It was as if they had been waiting all their lives for this day.

"The barn," she said, and, wheeling her horse, set off at a gallop. He passed her and was unstrapping the basket when she swung down from her horse.

They climbed up to the loft and spread the blanket. Connor opened the skylight and the balmy air of Indian summer poured in, mingling with the sweet smell of hay.

"Hungry?" he asked, looking down at her.

Only for you, she thought. "Not very," she said.

He nodded and took out the bottle of Burgundy and two

glasses, and they leaned back against a mound of hay, sipping the wine while, again, the tension grew.

"I never thought we'd do this again," he said.

"I knew we would."

He looked at her inquiringly.

"I don't know why," she said.

His dark eyes were probing and her heart raced faster.

"What happened, Georgia?" he asked softly. "What happened to us?"

The old hurt flickered inside her, the overwhelming sense of waste. "You left me without a word."

"I wrote to you! Why didn't you answer my letters?"

"Your letters never reached me." The hay rustled under the blanket as she sat up. "'And, of course, mine never reached you."

"Your father," he said, and knew with infinite sadness that it must have been his mother's doing too.

She nodded. "How naive I was! It never occurred to me he was capable of a thing like that."

"Of more than that! He threw me out that night because of you! I told him I'd come back to get you."

"But you didn't tell *me*!" Her temper flashed again and they were arguing. "Oh, Connor, why didn't you come for me?"

"I had nothing for months, not a penny! Then I made money doing something I couldn't talk about in public."

"What difference does that make to me?"

"You have no idea what poverty is, do you?" he said fiercely. "You think it's a charming little cottage in the country with kittens on the hearth. Well, it isn't! It's grime and vermin and stink. I had to have the money first."

"Money," she said scornfully. "It's always money."

"Spoken like a true Brandon."

"All right, then! I *don't* know what poverty is. Neither do you anymore. Why didn't you come when you had the money?"

"Because of how I made it," he replied, turning away.

"Tell me," she said, and he told her, his face averted.

He told her almost brutally, as if it gave him surcease to scourge himself, about the mercenaries, the gunrunning, the way he had used a woman to find out what he had to know about the Capitol merger.

She was astonished by the change in him, by the dark corners in him that were alien to her. But for all that, he was still her Connor, and there was nothing she could not forgive him.

"It doesn't matter," she said. "Did you think it would? I've been a schemer, too, haven't I? Worming my way into my father's affections, then marrying Tony just to escape from him!"

"That's different! You had no choice!" He shook his head, refusing to admit that her sins were as black as his, as vile as the next thing he told her: his heartless plan to marry someone like little Audrey Torrance for status. And finally he told her about Tirzah Kent and why he wouldn't marry a nightclub singer, not even Tirzah, who had mercifully said no five years before and still accepted their relationship the way it was.

"Five years?" Georgia whispered, overcome by a sexual jealousy she had never felt before. She had heard about his romance with a famous singer but she had no idea it had lasted so long.

"Do you love her?"

He nodded. "She's one of the few friends I have."

He loved the gorgeous Tirzah Kent! But what man would not, especially a man with Connor's voluptuous nature. How many women had he loved in the flesh while he loved Georgia only in her fantasies? Her own patrician blond beauty must seem pale and bloodless to him by comparison with Tirzah.

Again she doubted her perception of his feelings for her, of *his* reason for being here, until he said bitterly, "An admirable record to offer you, isn't it?"

New hope flooded her, and with it anger that he had made that judgment without her.

"Damn it, Connor! That was for me to decide, not you."

His temper wilted and, still not facing her, he asked, "Why? What would you have decided?"

"I'd have gone with you," she said hotly. "I loved you!"

He sat with his arms crossed on his knees, his head bent. "Sweet Jesus," he said at length very softly. "What have I done?"

Her anger turned to pity for them both, and she touched his shoulder, joining her own anguished regret to his. At her touch he turned swiftly and gathered her in his arms. Their mouths met with such a yearning passion that it made no difference where they were or what tragedy had brought them together again.

"And now," he whispered against her lips. "Do you love me now?"

"Yes, I love you! I'll always love you."

"Then nothing can keep us apart. I'm going to take you away with me tomorrow."

His arms went around her again and pulled her close. She was trembling with desire and felt him trembling too. She unbuttoned his shirt and bent to put her lips against the warm, smooth skin of his chest, tasting him with her tongue. She heard him gasp and felt his body preparing to possess her. There was a tremor between her thighs and an ache to feel him deep inside her.

She pulled her blouse open and pushed down the straps of her bra, brushing her bare breasts against the hair of his chest. His head came down and she felt his mouth at her nipples, and a wave of heat shot through the length of her body.

She was on the brink of something neither the earthy Breen nor Tony, so adeptly erotic, had ever given her. She craved it, as she craved Connor.

He opened her breeches and raised her hips to pull them off. Naked, she was lifted and held, cradled by those arms she knew so well and had never known like this. But she was not thinking then. She was afloat in bliss, grateful that she had a woman's body to tell him what words could not.

That very joy jolted her back to reality. With a moan she wrenched herself away from him.

"No!" she cried. "I could never leave you, then!"

He stilled beside her, mastering his desire, gazing at her in utter bewilderment.

"I must leave you, Connor, I must! I'm pregnant! I can never divorce Tony now."

She drew a long, sobbing breath. Then she fastened her bra and her blouse and pulled on her panties and breeches as if, by clothing passion, she could extinguish it.

He had turned away, his head again buried in his hands. She did not dare to touch him yet.

After a moment, he said, "It doesn't change anything, Georgia. Your baby will be as much mine as you are."

When she did not reply, he turned and grasped her shoulders. "Georgia, you *must* come with me. You must! You can't go on living with a man you don't love, not you!" He shook her. "It's the only honest thing to do."

"Yes," she said desolately. "It is. But Tony will never let me go. Or his child either."

"He'll have to. Rhys will use his influence."

"Not for you."

"No, he hates me as much as I hate him. But he'd do it for you."

"Not if I made a scandal that cost him the election."

"To hell with him, then. I'll manage Tony without him. Georgia, I love you! I won't leave you again. Say you'll come away with me tomorrow."

"Connor, I won't risk losing my baby, letting her grow up without me, not even for you." She hugged him fiercely. "You know why, better than anyone in the world!"

He felt her, frantic, in his arms. It was as if she and her baby were one, both to be denied a mother.

"I know, darling, I know. But I'll never let him take your child away from you. I swear it. Georgia! Please! For all we know, this is our last chance. We must take it! We can't say good-bye again."

He stroked her back and kissed the curve of her neck, and she clung to him, caught between need and panic,

love and the travesty it would have been to make love to
Connor with Tony's child inside her, only to say good-bye
to him forever. Yet, after these wild, unconsummated
moments, it would be torture to let him go.

"How can I?" she said from the depths of her anguish.
"How can I let you go?"

He was very still. "You can't. You must come with me
tomorrow."

"Oh, God, Connor, you know I want to!"

He rocked her against him. "We belong together, Georgia. I think we've always known that."

She kissed him, famished for him. "Yes," she whispered, "yes, we've always known it. There has to be a way
for us."

"If there isn't, I'll make one. I swear it."

She nodded, avid to believe that there was hope for
them, and lay back with him on the blanket, exhausted by
grief and remorse and passion denied. Soon they slept,
like lovers, in each other's arms.

It was early evening by the time they got back to
Brandon Hall, the understanding implicit between them
that until they had found a solution they must sleep apart.
Reluctantly Connor left her after supper and went upstairs
to his mother's apartment. And Georgia, missing him already, weeping afresh for Dilys, knowing a torment of
indecision that only Connor's presence could allay, tum-
bled into bed after a hot bath and sobbed herself to sleep
like a child.

She did not hear Connor slam out of the house a few
hours later, nor the growl of his car engine when he
charged away from Brandon Hall as if the Furies were
after him.

31

♦

A small party heard the service in the Presbyterian church at ten o'clock the next morning. Frail, white-haired Mary O'Brien was there in her wheelchair, pushed by Jeffers, just off the early train from New York with Cook. McGuire, the groom, now grizzled and weather-worn, was there with the small house staff. Daisy cried into one of the handkerchiefs Dilys had embroidered for her.

The mahogany coffin lay before them, its brass handles gleaming. It was incredible to Georgia that Dilys was locked away inside it, never to comfort a child again or share a cup of cocoa or sing a song in her high, clear voice.

Peggy slid into the pew beside Georgia, whispering, "Saints preserve us, his father's come. That's why he looks so fierce."

Georgia turned to see Enoch MacKenzie taking a seat at the back of the church. He was a rough draft of his son, not as tall, not as handsome, not as graceful. His face was tense and his eyes shadowed by shaggy brows.

Connor, who had entered through the vestry just before the service began, sat immobile between Adam and Dr. van Dorn.

"You'd think they was guardin' him," Peggy said, and Georgia nodded, puzzled.

She could barely see his profile, but he was not the man who had held her yesterday. Connor had been a beautiful boy, but the manly beauty he had now could turn cold as ice.

It was impossible! How could she cut herself and her

child off from family and friends? A pregnant woman who eloped with another man would never be received. And Tony would have her declared an unfit mother! Even if he let her go, she would be burdening the baby with an equivocal situation: two fathers, and a mother who was a social pariah.

It would be disastrous to go away with Connor today, but what had caution to do with this love, so old and yet so new? How much more of her life could she waste on a marriage such as hers? She would have to deal with Connor's volatility, even his hostility toward Rhys. If they were together, she could deal with anything, couldn't she?

Oh, Dilly, she yearned piteously, you always told me what was right. I wish you were here. I wish things were as simple now as they were then.

The church service ended and she watched Connor follow the coffin up the aisle. He looked at her, his face bleak with such anguish that she knew she would risk anything to be with him.

He made no objection when Enoch joined him behind the coffin.

"It isn't because his father's here," she said to Peggy. "Something terrible has happened."

◆

The mourners drove back to the private cemetery where Brandon retainers were buried. Georgianna lay in the family plot, half a mile away.

I've had two mothers, Georgia thought, and they were both too young to die.

"I am the resurrection and the life . . ." the minister began.

She glanced curiously at Enoch MacKenzie. His resemblance to Connor was disturbing. It should have drawn her to him, but he was guilty of that first desertion that had cost Connor so dear. Now Enoch stood protectively by his son, a brooding air about him.

He knows! Georgia felt suddenly certain. He knows why Connor is in such a colossal rage.

She shivered, and for a moment Enoch turned his head from Connor and looked at her, as if to warn her of something, as if they shared a despair beyond grief.

What, she wondered wildly. What is it?

"Man that is born of a woman," the minister said, "hath but a short time to live and is full of misery . . ."

The coffin was lowered. Connor dropped a handful of earth onto its lid and Georgia winced. It was a sound unlike any other and once heard could never be forgotten.

She watched Connor step back to stand beside his father, his eyes on the gaping hole in the green slope.

Look at me, she begged him. Tell me what it is that torments you so.

All heads turned as a car drew up at the cemetery's east gate and Rhys got out, followed by Constance and the three boys.

Georgia watched Rhys and Connor exchange a look. Enoch put a hand on his son's arm and Rhys turned swiftly to direct his wife and sons back into the car.

The boys obeyed him, but Constance did not. She was at his side when Rhys, avoiding Connor's furious stare, approached the grave, the sunlight glinting gaily, incongruously, on his blond hair. He waited until the last words were spoken; then he ordered the servants back to the house.

And Georgia, powerless, watched.

♦

"Get out of my sight!" Connor growled deep in his throat. But for Enoch's restraining arm, he would have leapt across the open grave to get to Rhys.

"For God's sake, Connor!" It was Adam. "This is his property!"

"Of course!" Connor's mouth curled with contempt. "Your property. Your daughter. Your *chattels*. Including my mother. It wasn't enough to seduce her. You're why she's dead, you miserable bastard. And you killed her long before she died. You made her a poor, pathetic creature with no spirit to resist you."

"Oh, my God," Georgia murmured. "Not Dilys! Not Dilys too."

"Not another word, Connor," Dr. van Dorn commanded. "Let her rest in peace."

"Give over, son," Enoch said. "She's at peace now."

"Pneumonia!" Connor's voice was like a pistol shot. "That's a lie! She took an overdose of Veronal."

Georgia gasped and Rhys's green eyes flickered to the doctor's face. The others stood in absolute silence, Enoch contemptuous, the minister aghast, Constance inscrutable.

She's glad, Georgia thought. She's always known about Dilys and she's glad.

"She didn't take it on purpose," Phillip van Dorn said haltingly. "Dilys wouldn't have done that."

"Don't lie to save his face!" Connor said. "It was a new bottle. She drank it all." He glowered at Rhys. "Why didn't you shoot her when you were finished with her the way you would a lame horse? But you needed someone to run this place, so you seduced her into staying on here all alone, waiting for a glimpse of you."

"It was what she wanted," Rhys said coldly. "All of it."

"By God, I *will* kill you," Connor said, struggling vainly to escape his father's grip.

"Conn, boy, don't. He isn't worth it!"

"Stop it!" Georgia screamed, sickened by the deceit, the murderous antipathy between the two men. "Connor! Stop it!"

Connor wheeled toward her as if she were a stranger. Then his eyes cleared and he looked at her with such despair that her heart ached for him.

"It's true, Georgia, all of it. I'm sorry you had to hear it like this. I'm sorry about a lot of things." They stood, separated by the grave, gazing at each other.

"I know," she whispered.

"Forgive me," he beseeched her.

"Yes, yes. I do."

"Come with me, then. It's time to go."

"Go where?" Rhys barked at her. "With *him*?"

"Yes," Connor said, his eyes fixed on Georgia. "With me."

There was a dumbfounded silence until Rhys wheeled around to his wife and commanded her to drive back to the house with the boys and the minister. Adam and Phillip van Dorn moved to go with them, at a glance from Rhys.

Adam and the doctor looked back anxiously, and Constance threw a vicious glance at Connor.

"Leave us, MacKenzie," Rhys snapped at Enoch.

"You bloody murdering snake," Enoch rumbled. "The only way I'll go is if Connor says so."

Connor nodded, and Enoch walked toward the cemetery's east gate, his footsteps inaudible on the soft grass.

"What madness is this?" Rhys demanded of his daughter, ignoring Connor.

"My own madness, Father," she said. "For once it has nothing to do with you."

"Everything he does has to do with me, don't you know that? Ask him why I threw him out of this house! Ask him why I sent you so far away!"

"He's already told me why."

"Georgia, you can't believe this man loves you!"

"I know he does. And I love him."

"You little fool!" her father said violently. "He's using you! He hated me enough to sleep with Constance and he wants you for the same kind of vengeance."

"Constance?" For a moment she could not take it in, and simply looked from one to the other of the two men. Then Connor's face told her it was true, both the motive and the act, and she recoiled from them, feeling dizzy and nauseated.

"Georgia, listen to me!" Connor implored her.

She shook her head, dumbfounded. "You hate him enough to make love to a woman you despise. And you"—she turned to her father—"hate Connor enough to tell me such a thing. What else will you do to each other? To me? I can't live with hate like yours. I'm not going to be your dueling ground, not anymore."

"Georgia," Connor pleaded. "Don't throw it away again! Don't do that to us. I love you!"

"Love? How can love survive such hatred?" She left them and walked slowly up to the west gate, exhausted by the heights and depths she had touched in three short days, craving only solitude and peace.

She heard Connor's voice as she walked.

"This isn't over, Rhys. If it takes me all of my life, I'll pay you back." Then there was silence, and one last time she turned to watch him. He walked down to where his father waited near the open door of his car, then disappeared into it. She heard the car door slam shut and winced as she turned away.

She walked on even when her father, striding rapidly, overtook her.

"Believe me, Georgia, it's for the best. It isn't love you feel for him. It's nostalgia. He isn't worth your tears."

"Why did you have to come here today?" she asked him dully.

"Be glad I did! I came because I cared for Dilys, no matter what lies he told you. She was my comfort, as she was yours."

Rhys's shoulders sagged and, as if by reflex or because she wanted to believe him, she told herself her father was not an evil man, only selfish and heedless of others.

Then he said, "So I had to come—and I had to bring Constance and the boys or there'd have been talk," and Georgia recoiled again. He would stop at nothing to get what he wanted, not even to using his sons for cover.

"My darling," he entreated her. "You must know what you mean to me."

"Yes, I know," she told him. "Now leave me alone, Father. Just leave me alone."

◆

In the third month of Georgia's pregnancy, a new apartment— consisting of a salon, a dining room, a kitchen, three bedrooms, four bathrooms, a night nursery, a day nursery, and a nanny's room—was being installed and decorated in the south wing of the mansion, leaving the center section to the dowager and her daughters.

A studio across from her present bedroom was rapidly completed for Georgia.

"So you need not travel to Lyons in winter weather," Tony had said.

"He wants to keep me home," she told Peggy privately, "where breeding women belong."

"Won't do you a bit of harm," Peggy said smartly with an anxious eye on Georgia.

At the moment Georgia was glad to stay at home. The nausea that had begun at Brandon's Gate was persistent.

"Crackers!" Peggy would grumble, holding Georgia's head with a cool cloth while she retched. "I'd give him crackers! There he goes, just like a man—off to Lyons just like always, and you heavin' fit to croak!"

The nausea usually slackened at mid-morning. Then Georgia dressed and rode sedately for an hour, glad of the bracing air and the exercise and the orderly calm all around her. It gave her a stronger purchase on her own deliberate calm, a bulwark against shock and sorrow and what might have been.

Charet-le-Roi had one hundred acres of garden but was without flowers or color or movement. It was a formal architectural garden with carefully clipped hedges and reflecting pools, designed by the man who had done Versailles, and her horse picked its way daintily along the gravel walks to reach the flat countryside. She longed for a gallop, but would not take the chance.

More than anything in the world, she wanted this baby. She wanted the trust and innocence and honesty of an infant.

When she returned to the house Peggy was waiting with a blue cablegram in her hand and a worried look on her face.

"They don't always bring bad news, Peg," Georgia reassured her, tearing the flap. She read the message and looked at Peggy. "It's from my father," she said. "He's been elected to the United States Senate by an over-whelming margin."

"Well," Peggy said, heaving a great sigh of relief. "That's all right, then. He's got what he wanted."

"He always gets what he wants," Georgia said. "That's the kind of man he is." She started up the stairs.

"You don't look like you enjoyed your ride very much," Peggy said, the anxious look reappearing on her broad face as she accompanied Georgia.

"That's because I have to be as regal and rigid and righteous as that garden." Georgia sighed. "I'll have to behave like an adult for the rest of my life." She shook her head desolately. "I must have been mad to suppose, even for a moment, that I could ever leave this place."

"We said we wouldn't speak of Connor, Miss Georgia. It doesn't do any good."

"What was he after, Peggy? Love or revenge?"

"Only the good Lord knows that," Peggy sniffed.

"You don't approve of me, do you?"

"You can't help it, most like. It's these modern ways has mucked up your life."

"Times have changed since you took care of Mother, Peggy." Georgia looked up at the portrait of Georgianna on her bedroom wall

"Some things never change, Miss Georgia. Marriage is marriage."

"No margin for error?"

"No. You have to live with your mistakes, the way your sainted mother did."

"Mistakes? What mistakes did she make?"

"Marryin' in the first place."

"Peggy, what are you talking about?"

Peggy flushed. "Mrs. Brandon hated bein' a wife. You know, the bed part of it. You ask me, it was why she lost all her babies but you, thanks be to God and all His saints for sparin' you."

"Hated it?" Georgia stared at Peggy.

"That she did! Never heard of a man hated it, but some women do. Your blessed mother couldn't wait to get into her tub afterward. I always ran her a bath while himself slept like the dead."

"But you said she wanted to marry him, Peggy!"

"Indeed she did! She had to marry someone, didn't she? I'm a workin' widow all these years and glad of it. Two years of marriage was enough for me! But young ladies of the gentry must marry."

"He says she was passionately in love with him!"

"He pretended she was! Night after night. She died of his pretendin', you ask me, all them miscarriages. But there, Miss Georgia, don't look like that. You're a married woman now and you ought to know there's a lot more goes on between men and women than's written in them story-books you young ladies read."

"Yes, Peggy, I know."

Georgia sat for a time staring at her mother's likeness, seeing in the averted head, the aloof posture, the distant attitude, something she had never seen before.

What manner of mother would this woman have been? Warm and loving, as Georgia had always believed she was, or as frigid as she had been with Rhys? She tried to see Georgianna's remote perfection through her father's eyes. A lascivious man and a woman who not only abjured his passion but was repelled by it! And they had been so widely envied! They had played their roles so expertly that only Peggy knew the truth—except, perhaps, for Constance, who had a sixth sense about sex.

And she, Georgia, had been called upon throughout most of her life to mitigate her father's tragedy, to worship him as Georgianna never had. No wonder Georgianna had not made Rhys executor of her will! He had been as much her jailer as he was Georgia's.

Leave me alone! Georgia protested to all the lies and all the liars. Even her own marriage had been a business arrangement, not the love match she had persuaded her-self it was. She had married to escape Rhys.

"Connor!" she moaned aloud, remembering Connor's face, the feel of his body, the taste of wine in his mouth and that other, headier wine she had not tasted and now never would.

What would she do about sex after the child was born? She and Tony had slept apart since Dilys died, with the pregnancy as an excuse, and he was drinking rather a lot lately. It made the prospect of sex less than inviting.

She pushed all the problems away and turned to the safe haven of the baby inside her.

♦

During the week Georgia lunched with the dowager and her sisters-in-law every day.

"Luncheon conversation," she told Marie-Véronique on the telephone, "is confined to the selection of a name, a nanny, and the decor of our new apartment."

"Safe subjects," Marie-Véronique approved.

"And the dowager has grown appreciably warmer toward me."

"She has obviously decided to endure what she cannot cure. How's Tony?"

"Utterly devoted. Whom have I to thank for that?"

"At the moment, there are two," Marie-Véronique said. "An Italian contessa and a Spanish dancer, both dark and sultry, you know the type. Musky. But you are the only blond in his life."

Georgia laughed shortly.

"I'm glad you're being sensible," Marie-Véronique said.

After luncheon each day, Georgia went to her studio to work. The only sound, other than the winter wind outside, was the clicking of Peggy's knitting needles making small sweaters and bonnets and leggings.

It was cozy in the studio. A fire crackled in the hearth, the blue velvet draperies kept the winter out, and a lavish tray arrived promptly at four o'clock with tea for Peggy, milk for Georgia, and an assortment of cakes and biscuits freshly baked by the pastry chef.

Pregnancy seemed to inspire Georgia. Ideas came to her faster than her fingers could fly across the slanted drawing board to get them down.

"Marvelous!" Tony always exclaimed when he came home to have his bath and dress for dinner. He would have said that even if the designs were dreadful, but they were superb, of that she was absolutely certain. Sevignac Silks bought all her designs; Tony didn't want anyone else to use the ones he wouldn't be producing.

"Your style," he told her, "is too distinctive. Exclusivity is essential in high fashion."

To Georgia it seemed foolish to let good designs languish, but she let the matter pass and life was peaceful at Charet-le-Roi, particularly when Tony was away on one of his frequent trips to Zurich.

"What is it this time?" she asked him with a show of wifely concern. She might better have asked, "Who?"

"A board of directors meeting," he said. "This one is particularly lucrative."

◆

Tony had discovered Crabtree's existence soon after he took over chairmanship of Eden's board.

Crabtree, he learned, had a reputation for designing, perfecting, and manufacturing new and experimental arms for itself and other munitions giants in which it held shares and to which it leased patents.

He understood at once the need for secrecy—and how useful his discovery might be if Rhys ever got out of hand. For the present Rhys's munitions fortune could only improve. Rearmament had quietly resumed in Britain and had never stopped in France and Italy.

"France has to stay strong," Tony declared to a basset-faced board member named Merrywell in the bar of the Hotel Baur-au-Lac. "England too," he added for Merrywell's sake, although Tony, along with the vast majority of his countrymen, detested the English on principle. "But I don't like these rumors about someday granting Germany military parity."

"Some say they need it for protection against the Russkis," Merrywell remarked, peering at Tony over his glass of port.

"And some of them say it's purely political, a serious attempt by the German government to undercut the radicals," Tony returned. "There are others, like this fellow Hitler, always ranting about what an insult the arms interdict is to German pride, and the government argues that parity will shut him up. Well, parity might sound harmless to the Yanks and the English, but not to the French! We've got the Bosch camped right on our borders."

"But don't you see, my dear chap," Merrywell interposed, wagging his head until his dewlaps trembled, "the Germans never really stopped making weapons. They're supplying quite a few countries, soon to include China and Japan."

"But they are forbidden by the Versailles Treaty to manufacture arms!" Tony objected.

"Ah, treaties," Merrywell said deprecatingly. "Krupp merely moved some of his operations to factories in Poland. Other German companies have warehoused machinery and equipment in Holland until times improve—meaning, until the world situation worsens again." Merrywell cocked his head and pursed his lips. "Some sources swear a war with Russia is inevitable and Germany ought to be rearmed for our own protection."

"That's like setting a fox to guard the chickens!"

"Not really. I don't like the Huns any better than you do, but the damned country *is* a natural buffer between us and the bloody Bolshies. Many a government would look the other way if Germany began to rearm."

"Not France!" Tony had bristled. He decided to look more deeply into French political opinion on the matter. The Soviets be damned! He didn't want the Germans in fighting form again. War had turned his life upside down once, and once was enough!

◆

In mid-May, Rhys arrived, uninvited, to be with his daughter during her confinement. The reporters, who had pursued him across the Atlantic for news of the handsome senator and the glamorous marquise, camped outside the mansion's gates. The dowager marquise noted, with shocked surprise, that Senator Brandon was not outraged and, what was worse, went out to chat with the reporters!

She was, nevertheless, quite taken with Rhys—"so elegant," she crowed, "*et tellement beau!*"—and was *très coquette* when they played cribbage in the evenings, listening attentively while he described the Senate chamber and its luminaries. Georgia, she had noticed, took scant interest in entertaining the dear man, and actually seemed to avoid him.

"I'm very worried," Rhys confided in a manner the dowager found *fort touchant*. "Georgia's mother died in childbirth, you see, and Georgia is so very like her."

"Nonsense," the dowager assured him. "Georgia is a strong, healthy young woman." She was moved to bestow a compliment. "A thoroughbred, like her papa."

"Madame is most kind," Rhys murmured with a winsome smile, and let her win the game.

It was not a pleasant time for Rhys. He flinched inwardly at the sight of Georgia's body bloated with another man's child, and he was impatient for the delivery.

Georgia was not. She was in no hurry to end the profound union she felt with her child. It was a union in which Tony had only an infinitesimal part; it was her body nourishing, protecting, breathing for the infant.

Her labor started at dawn on June fifth and went on into the afternoon. Her moans became cries as the hours passed.

"*Courage, madame,*" the doctor said, looking up from his book.

"Never you mind courage, Miss Georgia," said Peggy sharply, bending over her. "It's not him turnin' inside out. You yell your head off if you want to."

She clutched Peggy's hand as the afternoon light waned, panting as the pains became constant and the doctor rolled up his sleeves and washed his hands.

"I'm frightened, Peg."

"Whisht now, it'll be fine, Miss Georgia, dear, you'll see. And soon you'll have your wean in your arms."

"Just don't let me die, Peggy. I don't want her to grow up without me."

"Hush, my love, you aren't goin' to die."

"She did," Georgia gasped and cried as the fierce contraction took her. "I want her. I want my mother. I want Dilly."

"There, there, now, darlin'," Peggy crooned. "I'm here."

"*Un peu d'effort, madame*," the doctor instructed, and with a last wrenching push Georgia's daughter was born.

"Is she all right?"

"Perfect."

"Hear her cry, Miss Georgia! Louder than Master Malcolm did!"

She half slept while they kneaded her belly for the afterbirth, then fretted until the infant was placed in her arms.

She had loved the child for nine months, but the wave of feeling that suffused her now was beyond love. After all these months, she had dreaded the separation of this part of her flesh from the rest of her, but the ineffable bond was still there, unique among all other kinds of love in her experience. She was amazed by its power.

"My darling," she whispered, weak with bliss, and knew there was nothing she would not do for the happiness of this exquisite little creature.

She was named Georgianna Antoinette Marie Véronique Brandon de Sevignac, but her parents called her Gianna and her father was her devoted slave from the moment he held her in his arms.

Her christening was another grand affair in the de Sevignac chapel, attended by *le tout Paris*, with Malcolm and Tony's sister Eulalie as godparents. Jillian, well advanced in her own pregnancy, could not attend, but Constance did.

"She's dressing more decorously now than she did when you were married," Marie-Véronique remarked when she and Georgia retreated to the nursery for a moment's quiet.

"You know what they say about Caesar's wife," Georgia returned, leaning over the clouds of sheer white lawn, hand-embroidered with pink roses, that trimmed Gianna's bassinet.

"Everyone says your father has a great future in politics. It is difficult to know," Marie-Véronique went on, "who is the greater celebrity, you or the senator."

"Please don't let Tony hear that!" Georgia warned, touching the baby's cheek.

"We'll say it's *la petite Gianna* everyone wants to see."

"He won't mind that. He adores her. Look, Marie-Véronique, isn't she the most beautiful baby you ever saw?"

"*Absolument.* She'll sell more Sevignac silk than you have! *Mon Dieu,* Georgia, if looks could kill! I'm not suggesting you merchandise her. It will happen without your lifting a finger."

"And who told the press that I design for Sevignac Silks?" Georgia pressed her.

"Not I," the little blond woman said firmly, "but I'm glad someone did."

After the christening, quiet descended on Charet-le-Roi. In a few weeks a cablegram came from America with news that Jillian had given birth to a son she named Peter.

"They gave me something called twilight sleep," Jillian wrote later. "But now I feel as if the Baltimore & Ohio had gone through. Right now the baby's poor little face is all smashed in, but he'll look just like my Peter when his features revive. Tim is furious. He wanted a carrot-topped Cassadyne named for Silas."

"I'll survive," she closed the letter, "but I swear I'll never go through this again!"

Georgia put down the letter with concern. She wouldn't ask Jillian what was wrong with her marriage. Jillian might ask her the same thing.

◆

"Why do you let him do it?" Malcolm said to Georgia when they were alone on the terrace one day, except for Gianna, asleep in her pram. Malcolm had stayed on for the second week of his summer holiday before joining his family on the Riviera.

"Who?" Georgia asked. "Do what?"

"Father. Milk every occasion for all the publicity he can get, when you barely speak to him in private."

She shrugged. "An open feud would mean only more publicity."

Malcolm saw the logic of that. "Georgia, what happened between you and Connor at the Gate?"

"It was more what happened between Father and Connor. They despise each other more than ever."

"It's because of more than Father and Dilys, isn't it?"

She regretted his precociousness. He was only fourteen! "How long have you known about Dilys?"

"For years. Will and Richard told me."

"They would! Dirty little gossips." She watched him anxiously. "Do they trouble you?"

He shrugged, dismissing his brothers, and, after a moment's hesitation, asked in a rush, "Georgia, do you still care for Connor?"

She nodded. "A part of me always will."

"Oh, God! I knew it," he said. He stood and walked to the edge of the terrace and stared out at the gardens, his hands jammed into his pockets, a poignant mixture of boy and man. "How can you do it?" he asked hoarsely.

It was her physical intimacy with Tony that so revolted him, and she could not explain to him that sex was not motivated solely by romantic love.

You ask too much of your fairy princess, she thought. I'm only made of flesh and blood.

Yet she must console him somehow. Her problems were not his to bear. She could not let him know.

"Malcolm!" she said, softly persuasive. "It isn't a tragedy!"

"Isn't it?"

"Absolutely not. Tony and I understand each other. Yes," she insisted, "we do. He's a wonderful father. I have everything I want. I worry far more about what you intend to do with your life."

His bearing told her that he believed her because he

had to. It made her want to weep, that he had come so young to that universal deceit.

"Keep studying," he said at length. "At least until I'm twenty-one and he has no control over me. Then I'll decide." Suddenly he swung around to face her. "Georgia, are other families like ours, battling each other all the time? Are all fathers like him? He wants to keep us all in cages, like trained animals."

She went to his side and put her arm through his. "He's difficult, darling, I know. But he'll be too busy being a senator now to take much notice of us. Just stay out of his way."

"I'm damned if I'll campaign for him the next time he runs! And I'm going to take my degree in England when the time comes. I made Mother promise me that." He looked at her, his green eyes bleak. "Look at us, princess. We've had to put an ocean between them and us."

"When you go to school in England, we'll be near each other, and that's what matters to me."

Malcolm put his arms around her, holding her with a boy's awkwardness. He was almost as tall as Rhys and looked more eerily like his father every day, but their natures clashed so intensely that she dreaded a premature confrontation between father and son. Rhys would certainly prevail; Malcolm was still subject to his father's iron will even though he contrived to ignore it most of the time.

"I'm sorry, Rapunzel," he said finally, releasing her. "I didn't mean to add to your troubles."

"But I have no troubles," she said gaily, bending over the pram so he could not see her face. "And now I have Gianna. You can't imagine what a joy that is."

For the first time, she was not sorry to see Malcolm off on the train to Nice. Her brother's standards—those of an inexperienced boy for a sister he idolized—made her feel jaded and cynical as she waved to him from the platform. He made her feel ashamed that, very soon now, Tony would move back into her bed and the sexual relationship Malcolm deplored would continue.

But she did not deplore it. Tony was Gianna's father, for one thing, and Gianna was going to grow up in a happy home. For another, Georgia knew she was not ready to renounce sex for the rest of her life.

But before anything happened, she was fitted for a diaphragm by a gynecologist in Paris. Much as she loved Gianna, she wanted no more children of this marriage.

32

♦

It was good to have a man's arms around her, to share the release of physical tension. In the drowsy aftermath of lovemaking, it seemed to Georgia that her pessimism about her marriage had been excessive. But just then Tony spoke.

"You've changed," he said.

Her heart sank, because it was true. Tony was Tony, but she had changed, and the burden of the consequences was hers.

She was on the brink of telling him the truth—but to what purpose? There was no hope for her and Connor. There never had been. It would only hurt Tony for no reason.

"We're both different," she said. "We're parents now."

Tony decided not to pursue the matter aloud. She did not have a lover, of that he was certain: new mothers did not take lovers.

The change dated from months ago—the funeral at Brandon's Gate. She had come back to New York too desolate even to cry much less go posting off in search of sex. She had withdrawn instead.

Tony had become wary of disturbing her, a situation he did not relish. He began to sleep in his own room even before the doctor forbade sex for the rest of the pregnancy. He was well looked after elsewhere.

But tonight had convinced him that childbearing had nothing to do with it. It came to him that Georgia no longer loved him as she had.

He was an expert on how women behaved in bed. They could fake mounting passion and even orgasm—although Georgia's response tonight had been genuine—but they could not fake love. Georgia's love was centered on Gianna, and that left him oddly out in the cold, jealous and resentful no matter how much he loved his little girl.

And there was a wall around Georgia that aroused both his indignation and a resolve to breach it. He would start by giving her something she wanted, something that would keep her in France, where he preferred to be.

"I think you're restless" was his opening gambit.

"I am. And I'm worried. The mills keep losing money."

My money, was what she meant. He was spending it at a furious rate on projects better suited to his position than grubbing about in the silk mills that still mesmerized Georgia, motherhood notwithstanding. He had already spent most of Rhys's settlement and would soon need more capital. If the mills were her price for giving it to him, let her have them!

"The mills!" he groaned theatrically. "I loathe the mills."

"Then let me run them! Tony, you know I can! I've already told you how I'd cut costs."

He reached for a cigarette, as if he were considering his reply, but what she said was true. Thanks to her father, she had always known more about the textile industry than he did.

"Discretion's no longer the issue," she reminded him.

"Well, that's certainly true," he said resignedly. "Everyone knows that the Marquise de Sevignac herself designs Sevignac silks!"

Actually he had let it slip himself during a temporary slump in America, and the news made orders from overseas bound upward yet again—but to no avail. Increased production doubled his operating costs, something she insisted need not be the case.

"Your father won't like it," he said darkly, testing her allegiance to Rhys. For some time he had not been certain of its extent.

"He'll love the publicity," she said.

"I suppose so. To the Americans you'll be a national heroine."

And the French, who valued chic, sophisticated, talented women, however oddly they behaved, would throw up their hands and say Tony was a prince of a fellow to indulge his beautiful wife.

"If that's what you really want," he said finally, grudgingly, as if he had been reluctantly persuaded.

He expected a paroxysm of gratitude, emotional and sexual, but she only kissed his cheek and said, "You know it is, Tony."

He felt outmaneuvered. He needed a drink. "Then it's settled. I'll leave you to your rest," he said.

"Good night, Tony."

Good night, Tony! In the past she would have seduced him again, made love to him. She was enough to drive any man to drink.

♦

"It won't be easy," Georgia said to her stepsons in Tony's office after she had observed the mills at first hand for a few weeks.

Her stepsons—it was absurd to be stepmother to two men older than she was—were not involved in manufacture. Antoine supervised silk production and raw silk imports, and Edouard managed sales. It was Antoine, Tony's heir, who most objected to her new position. It would reflect badly on him if she managed to do what he had not.

"But can it be done?" he asked now, his eyes, as usual, shifting away as soon as she looked at him. Her sensuality disturbed him, but not as much as her control of the Soieries Sevignac did.

"Absolutely," she said.

Edouard smiled beatifically. "Well, that's welcome news. Things are in a rare mess if we can't show a profit on orders like these." He tapped the thick folder he'd brought to Tony's office, where Georgia now held sway.

Conasse! Antoine thought, the gross expletive venting his spleen somewhat.

"We soon will," she said, "and thank you in advance for your support." She stood, obliging them to stand, too, and thereby dismissing them without telling them how she planned to accomplish her miracle. Obviously they were not worthy of her confidence!

The two men said nothing until they reached Edouard's office.

"That woman's a menace," Antoine bristled as soon as the door closed behind him. "She doesn't know her place."

"I do," Edouard grinned. "She must be sensational in bed for Papa to let her do this."

"Don't be a fool!" Antoine snapped. "He did it because he hates doing it—and so she'll part more easily with her money."

"I'd like some of it," Edouard sighed. "And I don't mean her money."

"Idiot! We have to find a way to stop her."

"Nonsense. She'll trip herself up soon enough."

But Antoine was not so sure.

♦

The single large painting in the gallery window in Paris shouted "Breen" to Georgia before she was close enough to read his name on the canvas. She crossed the street and stopped to admire the lush landscape dominated by three native girls sunning themselves near a stream. She could almost smell the warm earth and the flowers.

His technique, always remarkable, had improved, but it was the man's *élan vital* that came through like a ray of sunshine. The painting fairly shone with light and Breen's untrammeled joy in living.

A card left propped on an easel announced *Vernissage, le 10 novembre 1927.* Last week. She had been too absorbed in her baby and the mills to notice any announcement in the papers of the opening.

"So you finally made it," Georgia said to herself with a happy smile, and walked into the gallery to find out if he had come back to Paris for the exhibit. A hasty look around revealed none of the Georgia paintings and, at once relieved and disappointed, she moved slowly from one new canvas to another, marveling at his talent.

"Georgia?"

She turned to see him in the doorway of the gallery director's office, still broad as a bear, with a scuffed leather jacket slung over his shoulder. He was dressed in denim pants and a flannel shirt, his beard longer than ever.

He dropped the jacket and held out his arms and she flew into them and was swept up. He smelled of pipe tobacco and a very expensive cologne, apparently his one concession to success.

"Oh, Sam, you'll never know how glad I am to see you."

"I thought I'd be in the doghouse for staying away so long," he said when he had put her down. "Then I heard you got married, so I knew just how much I meant to you."

"But you were the one who went away! Where did you get the money?"

He was startled. "I thought it was from you! I thought you were sending me away to get famous enough to marry— and then changed your mind."

"No, Sam!" She laughed. "I know you're not the marrying kind."

"Well, I'll be damned! Come and have a drink and we'll talk about it."

They found a café and ordered coffee and Calvados, but the identity of his benefactor remained a mystery.

"Where did you go?" she asked, her eyes sparkling with pleasure just to look at him.

"The South Sea islands, just like old Gauguin."

"Except that you're not a tortured soul. I think that's why I missed you so much."

"Hell, Georgia, you've been too busy to miss me. I read the magazines." He took her hand. "You made it, too, didn't you, princess?"

"Oh, yes," she said. "I made it."

He leaned forward. "But?"

"The 'but' is a long story, Sam."

"I've got plenty of time."

She glanced at her watch. "I haven't, not today. I'm in Paris on business."

He winked. "What kind of business?"

"Not that kind."

"In love with this count you married?"

"He's a marquis—and I thought you didn't believe in love."

"I believe in a quiet little dinner at my place next time you're in town, with plenty of time for us to get caught up and maybe a slap and a tickle for auld lang syne."

She smiled, shaking her head. "It isn't an affair I need right now, Breen. It's a friend."

"Okay," he assured her, his broad face almost serious. "But I owe you a lot more than friendship. Those portraits of you made me a lot of money."

"Who bought them?"

He shrugged. "Damned if I know. My agent sold them off, one by one, to private buyers. You could be hanging in a royal palace or on the wall of some cathouse in Istanbul."

"But you kept your promise about naming them?"

"Yeah," he said, embarrassed by his own gallantry. "They're all called 'Woman.' That's what you are: the essential female."

"I'm not so sure of that. When were they sold?"

"About a year ago. Took me almost that long to tear myself away from Papeete after I got the money. But here I am, about to become a household word."

"No one deserves it more than you do."

They met at his apartment two weeks later, and he listened without comment while she told him all of it: Rhys, Dilys, Connor, Constance. And about her marriage, her baby, and her work with the mills.

"But it isn't enough," she finished.

Breen stroked her arm. "This Connor gets to the heart of you, doesn't he? A place no other man has ever reached. I wonder what it does to Tony."

"He resents me. He doesn't know why. He thinks it's only because of the mills."

"What are you going to do?"

"Nothing. I made my bed, quite literally."

Breen shook his head. "I guess I'm lucky. I never loved anyone like that." He glanced at her. "Except maybe you."

"You're sweet, Sam. But it's the woman in your paintings you love, and I'm not made of oil on canvas."

"I noticed," he said ruefully.

But her mind was elsewhere. "Tony's sons can't stand the sight of me," she went on. "They object to everything I do."

"Why don't you bring in someone you can trust?"

"I would if I could find someone."

Breen pulled at his beard. "I know a man who might be persuaded, but not unless he likes what you're doing."

"Who is he? What does he do?"

"Now he paints. Once he manufactured textiles in China. Made a fortune. He retired when he turned sixty and came to France to be an artist." He shrugged. "He's not much of a painter. You ask me, he's itching to get back in harness. Let me see what I can do."

Breen sent her Michael Hatton, a spare, gray, taciturn man with an air of perpetual gloom about him, until he handled silk. Then his face lit up like a child's when the birthday cake comes in. He nodded his appreciation of the fabrics she showed him.

"Fine stuff," he said with an appreciative nod, "but you ought to chuck those looms."

"It'll cost a fortune to replace them, and this is a bad time."

"It's always a bad time for new equipment."

"I can finance it, but the de Sevignac brothers will object."

He shrugged. "Who's running these mills?"

"I am."

"Then run them!"

"I'll need your help."

"For a while," he said.

"I was thinking of a five-year contract."

He shook his head. "I won't tie myself down for longer than two. But by then you'll know as much about the silk industry as I do."

"If you can teach, I can learn."

He held out his hand and she took it to seal the bargain. "The principle's the same," he said, "whether you're making teapots or dusters or silk. What you need is a marginally better product and the common sense to produce it for less than the competition can. That's what your father did."

She was surprised. "Do you know him?"

"A little. You're nothing like him."

"No, I'm not."

"He had a cozy setup in China."

"I'm going to have a cozier one right here."

♦

Looking back on those days, Georgia could not honestly call them unhappy. In less than a year Mike Hatton had helped her to reorganize, trimming waste, saving time and money on production methods, producing almost a fifth more yardage with a minimal increase in costs. The Soieries Sevignac showed a small profit in 1928 and would show a much bigger one in 1929.

Gianna was healthy and happy, and although Tony seemed increasingly disgruntled about Georgia's success with his mills, she decided to ignore it. When they attended the opera, the races, balls, and dinner parties, they appeared to be a united couple. In Gianna's presence they were even loving.

And then Georgia was forced into a showdown with Antoine at the mill. It was because of something Hatton had discovered.

"I'll come right to the point," she told Antoine in her office. "I know you've been circulating rumors about my hopeless incompetence and our imminent collapse. I want you to stop."

He did not deny it. He sat there in his dark, vested suit, wearing a tie of her design and sniffing at the carnation in his buttonhole.

"I want an undertaking from you right now," she went on, "that you will stop."

His eyes glittered balefully. "Then get the hell out of our mills," he said. "I should be sitting in that chair, not you!"

"Possibly, but that is not the issue. And your father didn't think so."

He smiled thinly. "He thinks so now. The rumors were my father's idea." His smile broadened at her visible shock. "He knows he acted too hastily by putting you in charge. It seems he wants you home, where you belong, not conspiring with your American renegade."

"Because I'm doing the job I set out to do? Is he fool enough to lose a fortune just to keep me at home? If that was what he wanted, he'd have told me himself."

Or would he? Tony was in a perpetual sulk and drunk, too, more often than not.

Antoine said nothing.

"I want it stopped," Georgia repeated, holding on to her aplomb. "Or I'll charge you publicly with larceny. You can't tell me *that* was on your father's instructions!"

His indolent air vanished. "How dare you?" he challenged her.

"Oh, stop pretending, Antoine! You've been diverting company money to your private bank account for years. I have all the proof I need. Don't make me use it."

He wet his lips nervously. "What do you want?" he demanded, and she knew her bluff had succeeded.

"Your resignation—unless you stop sabotaging everything I'm doing, everything you failed to do over the past years! You could have taken over from Tony at any time. He'd have welcomed it."

"The devil he would! My father is very jealous of his prerogatives, whether or not he exercises them." Antoine sneered, his eyes raking over her body. "You're a fine piece, *belle-mère*, but you're not very clever about men, except for Hatton, your Machiavelli, if he isn't something more!"

She ignored the insolence, taking another tack. "What I've accomplished is for your benefit, Antoine! The mills are entailed to you and your sons, not to me! I haven't interfered in any way with your silk production."

"I simply do not like taking orders from a woman," he muttered.

"You don't have to like it. Just stay out of my way, or I'll start a few rumors myself about the future Marquis de Sevignac stealing from his own father."

"I knew you were hard as nails," he said finally, "but I thought you had some sense of family loyalty!"

"Ha!" she erupted scornfully. "You're hardly the one to lecture me about loyalty! I want your word that you'll stop maligning me and the Sevignac mills—without telling your father about this conversation—or I'll make your embezzlement public. Don't underestimate me, Antoine. I mean what I say."

"All right." He spat the words. "And I don't underestimate you. You're an unnatural woman."

"I didn't ask you here to discuss my character."

"How are you going to blackmail my father into letting you stay?" he demanded, once again examining her body attentively. "In the usual way?"

"That's my concern, not yours. Good morning."

After he had gone she sat quietly for a while, her head propped in her hands, getting control of herself. She had known for a long time that Tony was jealous, but not venomously so.

An unnatural woman. Was she? For wanting to do what she did well? For needing something more than a failed marriage that would never go smoothly unless she lived it on Tony's terms—as a docile, decorative society matron, with nothing to fill her days but Mah-Jongg, gossip, and charity committees.

Antoine was a snake, but he *had* acted on Tony's orders, she was convinced of it.

Tony was her mistake, as Rhys had been Georgianna's.

It was always dangerous to act in anger. Now that Antoine had been silenced, it was better to wait and see what to do about Tony.

♦

Until now her days had flown by. Lunch, followed by a siesta, was at least a two-hour affair among the gourmets of Lyons, and Georgia always drove home to lunch with Gianna, now almost two. When her evenings and weekends were not taken up by social functions or business dinners, she spent them in the nursery, playing games and reading stories until Gianna's bedtime.

And when she could, she went to Paris to see Samson Breen, who had suddenly become the artistic darling of society. He was the only person she knew with whom she could be herself.

Her unrest sharpened when she and Tony dined at home under her mother-in-law's jaundiced eye. The dowager's frigid disapproval of Georgia's career cast a pall over everyone but Tony, who clearly enjoyed it.

"For God's sake, Tony," Georgia had told him often enough in private, "you're not a schoolboy anymore. You're the head of this family."

"Am I?" was his sour reply. "I thought I'd ceded that position to you."

Tonight, on their way downstairs, he asked slyly how the lady tycoon was doing, and she almost slapped him.

"Damn it, Tony, you ought to be proud of what I've

done. In another year those mills will be back on top,
where they belong, more than solvent, and turning away
customers."

"You have the soul of a rug merchant," he said haughtily.

"That's because you've had three too many drinks
already."

She always knew when Tony had spent the afternoon in
bed with a mistress. This had been one of them, and she
observed him with disgust as the family sat in the drawing
room after dinner. Mother and son talked politics, *les
demoiselles* sat in meek silence, and Tony, drinking steadily, smoked the hand-rolled cigars he ordered from Havana.

"I've never known you to be so fervent about anything
before," the dowager said with a meaningful glance at
Georgia. Her son was not as madly in love as this wayward
daughter-in-law supposed.

Georgia remained silent, thinking bitterly how distinguished Tony's silver hair made him look, and what an
attractive man he would be without the alcohol-induced
puffiness that had crept in around his eyes and jawline and
was beginning to thicken his waist. Attractive? He was
nothing short of contemptible for trying to destroy her
success in such an underhand way.

"I am fervent only about my lady wife," Tony said airily,
"whose revered father is not the only man in this family
with a political future."

"*Mon cher fils.*" His mother beamed. "Then you have
decided on public office!"

"*Government* office, *ma mère,*" he corrected her, speaking with the inebriate's careful emphasis on each syllable.
"I, for one, would never stoop to run in an election. No,
what France needs is men of impeccable lineage, working
quietly behind the scenes."

"Whatever happened to the Revolution?" Georgia said.

"In their hearts my countrymen are monarchists," the
dowager rebuked her.

"Quite right, *ma mère.* The whole world wants a leader,
no matter what title they give him: king, emperor, *duce,*
prime minister, president."

"France isn't the whole world," Georgia remarked. "But even in France I'm sure they prefer their officials sober."

Sidonie and Eulalie gasped.

"It is not a wife's place to criticize her husband," the dowager snapped.

"It's not a husband's place to patronize his wife. Now, if you'll excuse me, I'm going up to bed." She bade the two sisters good night.

She sat down to think when she was in her bedroom. The entire nature of her relationship with Tony had altered considerably. Over the past year he had made love to her as eagerly as ever, and she had let her body respond automatically. But several weeks earlier he had exhausted her in his frantic attempt to recapture a lost erection.

"Tony, please. It doesn't have to be tonight," she'd said.

"Keep trying," he gasped, pushing her head down to his groin again.

She had redoubled her efforts, her own superficial excitement fading into revulsion.

"Wait until morning," she had said finally, humiliated for both of them.

"It's your fault," he railed at her.

"No, it isn't. It's because you drink too much."

"Don't preach to me!" he had shouted, storming off to his own room.

He had come to her the next morning, sober and apologetic, and they had made love with an echo of their old feeling for each other. But from then on he had begun to fail more often: alcohol sparked his desire and at the same time stopped him from satisfying it.

At first she resented him, but tonight she despised him, and she knew she could not embark again upon another session of arid, degrading lust.

She whirled to face him when, without knocking, he opened her bedroom door.

"Did you think a closed door would keep me out?" he demanded, striding toward her.

"Keep away from me!" she cried angrily. "Don't touch me. You reek of whiskey."

His eyes flashed ominously. "What a complete bitch you are! You're a mother and a manufacturer, but you're not a wife."

Her control deserted her. "I know how you've been trying to get me out of the mills," she accused him. "I want to know why."

He was shocked into sobriety. "Who told you?"

"What does it matter? It was a despicable thing to do."

"It was my prerogative as your husband."

She shook her head disdainfully. "You make such a claim to honor, but you haven't any. Why didn't you tell me what you wanted instead of going behind my back? What is it you *do* want?"

"I want to feel I'm first in command. You make me feel like a poor second."

"If you feel like a poor second, you've done it to yourself, Tony!"

He glared at her in silence for a moment. Then he said, "You have a lover, haven't you?"

"No, that's your special talent! You couldn't be faithful for more than a few months after we were married."

"Aha! You're jealous!" he announced triumphantly, pointing an accusing finger at her.

She sighed hopelessly. "Yes, all right, I'm jealous. Now leave me alone."

"And if I refuse?" He took her arm, his fingers pressing into her flesh. "You are still my wife."

"That's a condition I can easily rectify!"

"Just try it!" he snapped. "But remember that this is France, where a father's rights over his children are absolute. *And* over his wife. You will not divorce me, but make no mistake, even if you did, Gianna would stay with me."

She stared at him, her eyes blazing. "Don't you dare use that baby as a bargaining chip! You're even lower than I thought you were. We'd break her heart by fighting over her—and you say you love her!"

"I do," he muttered, caught between villainy and conscience.

"You're beneath contempt." She broke away from him. "Get out of my sight."

He went out, slamming the door behind him. She locked it, sliding the bolt home with a sharp crack.

Her hands were shaking when she went into the bathroom to splash water on her face. It was the first time they had alluded to divorce but, far more disturbing, it was the first time he had openly threatened to use the baby to keep Georgia where, now, she would be hard put to stay.

She lay awake most of the night, slowly regaining her self-control, aware that, for Gianna's sake, she must find some way to live with him peacefully, some way that was neither marriage nor divorce.

He had left the house before she was dressed in the morning, and she went on to the mills, her body aching as if it had been battered. There were roses waiting for her when she came home at lunchtime and a *rivière* bracelet of diamonds and sapphires arrived in the evening.

Tony offered her a constrained apology, more form than substance, and she accepted it in the same spirit.

"If you want me out of the mills," she added quietly, "say so. But don't expect me to sit here and do nothing."

"You can do as you like about the mills," he said. "I won't stand in your way."

"We can't be at each other's throats anymore. We mustn't put Gianna through that."

"I am as concerned for my child's happiness as you are."

They remained aloof from each other in private. Tony devoted himself to politics, and in public they were still a serenely happy couple, the way Rhys and Georgianna had been, although Georgianna had never been able to lock her bedroom door, a circumstance that filled Georgia with pity and frustrated rage for her mother.

Now Georgia had to lock that door for her, just as she had to succeed to prove herself worthy of her mother's legacy. More often, though, her frustration was for herself.

Now Charet-le-Roi became a meeting place for the men

who ran France, and Georgia was its gracious, charming hostess. As if to return the favor, Tony limited himself to wine with dinner and waited for some indication that he could approach her again.

She did not give it.

"Sometimes he's his old charming self," she told Sam Breen. "But I can't." She shook her head helplessly.

"What are you going to do?"

"Have the usual sort of marriage, I suppose."

"You ought to leave him."

"You know I can't do that. Gianna loves him. Her little face lights up whenever she sees him."

Breen put an arm around her.

"He loves her too," Georgia went on. "I think she's the one unselfish love in his life." She sighed. "This whole disaster is half my doing anyway. He knew exactly what he wanted when we married. I only thought I did. He's not a fool; he knows I don't love him anymore and he resents me for that. Sometimes I think I ought to tell him about Connor. He might feel better, knowing it can't come to anything." She closed her eyes. "Oh, God, Sam, what a mess I've made of it. I have everything I thought I wanted—but it's all wrong."

In the end she and Tony settled for estrangement. They were considerate of each other, even affectionate when Gianna was around, but it was pretense all the same, and the pretense ended as soon as they entered their separate apartments for the night.

And one day, lying with her head in Sam Breen's lap, she made no protest when he kissed her gently. She did not object when he undressed her or when she felt the tickle of his beard against her belly once more and his mouth on her breasts. She lay curled in his arms for a long time, letting him soothe her with tenderness before they made love.

"You love Connor that much?" Sam asked her an hour later through the smoke of two cigarettes.

"I love him that much."

"Then damn it, Georgia, go get him! Take what you want for once in your life!"

"You make it sound so simple! No woman in her right mind would want to be a pawn in the battle between my father and Connor."

"What's to say Connor hasn't learned as much as you have? Why not take a chance on him?"

She turned suddenly to pillow her cheek against his broad chest. "It's all I think about anymore."

"Listen, princess, this life is not a dress rehearsal. It's for real. One performance and the lights go out forever."

She wondered, on her way back to Charet-le-Roi, how long she could stay in the wings, waiting to go on.

BOOK IV

◆

1931–1939

33

♦

"They can't let Germany collapse," Connor said to Guthrie Torrance on a broiling hot Saturday morning in July. "Chase and the Guaranty Trust would go under with her—not to mention the one and a half billion invested by America's private sector. Whatever you have in Germany is safe."

"Well, you've just come back from there, so you're in a good position to know," Torrance said with a sigh, moving restlessly in his chair in Connor's office.

"The only problem I can foresee is the present majority party. If Hitler pursues the policy outlined in *Mein Kampf*, it could mean war. I won't support German rearmament."

"Not even if the arms were trained on Russia?" Torrance asked testily. "But we can cross that bridge if we come to it."

Guthrie Torrance was not a happy man. Two years after what was now universally called the Crash, Torrance's houses in Palm Beach and Newport were closed, his yacht was in dry dock, and four of his cars were up on blocks. In the past he would have spent the entire summer in Newport with his family. Now they would have to be content with one month on Cape Cod.

It took more charity than Torrance possessed not to resent the amazing luck of the man sitting opposite him, particularly in view of the offer he had come to put to Connor.

"You, apparently, continue to prosper," Torrance said sourly.

Connor shrugged. "I'm not the only one who got out of the market in time."

"You're one of the very few. But what I want to know is what you got into!" Torrance's efforts to pry the information out of Barney Abbott, his former employee, had proved fruitless. Abbott had laughed at him!

"Sorry, Guthrie. That information comes at a price."

Connor had closed down the Hemisphere Investment Trust five months before the Crash, avoiding the ruin that befell investment trusts when the value of their paper holdings plunged. Connor's market transactions were still handled by his own Hemisphere Investments, although he collaborated with TD&D and other firms on deals too big for him to take on alone.

A second company, Northern Light, managed the utilities he had acquired since Black Thursday, and a third, Clarion Radio, manufactured radio sets. It also owned the thirty-odd radio stations—most of them in the nation's heartland—that he and Barney Abbott had picked up between his trips to California to see the Blankenships and Tirzah. And then, there was AirShip.

He had a stock answer for people who asked where he was putting his money.

"Where my intuition leads me," he always said. He watched the older man, who was sunk in gloom, and thanked the gods for his intuition.

♦

It had warned him to get out of equities entirely in the fall of '29, even before he went to California to see Racey's first son, Alexander Martin, eight pounds, one ounce, and the image of his mother.

"You hold a baby like an expert," Belinda told him.

"I should. I had five to practice on when I was a kid."

"How about one of your own?"

Connor made no reply, but he was thinking seriously about marriage, if not fatherhood. Solitude, absolutely essential to him when he was laying a financial base and building his companies, had become onerous. He felt excluded, a loner in a world of couples. And he had reached a time of life when compromise was acceptable.

When the two men were alone, he told Racey that he had also taken the Blankenships and Tirzah, whose portfolios he managed, out of stocks.

"Fine, if you say so. But why now, with the market still soaring?"

"Because equities are grossly inflated. Stock prices reflect a kind of gambling euphoria, not the real worth of the companies behind them."

"The English papers are calling Wall Street the financial capital of the world."

"I know. And people on the Street think I'm seeing goblins under the bed. But I trust my intuition."

"So do I," Racey said. "It's made a lot of money for all of us."

"It also tells me that if you still want to buy that aeronautics company, I'll put up the bulk of the capital."

"You're kidding!" Racey said, but his smile glowed.

And so they had formed AirShip to buy and expand a company involved in the design—and eventual manufacture—of bigger, safer passenger aircraft. TranShip, Racey's thriving transport and local passenger line, became an independent affiliate.

Racey had called him after Black Thursday, with a whistle of admiration.

"Your instinct was always worth a fortune!"

"Not without the money to back it up."

"Then I'm glad you made a pile, for my sake if not for yours."

"Why not mine?"

"Because you don't enjoy it! You live like a hermit. Sure, you dress like a duke, you go to Europe whenever you choose, you've got that showplace on Long Island and almost any woman you want—but you can't get a kick out of life without someone to share it."

Racey, who knew all about Georgia, also knew it was wiser not to mention her name to Connor.

"I'll consider it," Connor said.

He *was* considering it. He was considering Audrey Torrance.

◆

Guthrie Torrance, oblivious to his daughter's unmaidenly lust for Connor and to Connor's plans for her, now stirred from his melancholy reflections and pursed his wide, deeply bowed mouth.

"Would you care to put your 'intuition' to work for TD&D?"

"In what capacity?" Connor asked. He lounged in his chair, smoking lazily, but every muscle in his body was taut. This day had been a long time coming.

"As a consultant."

Connor shook his head.

Torrance hesitated another moment before he took the final plunge. Torrance, DeVries, and Deventer had never made this offer to a man of obscure background. It was unheard of, but so was the economic disaster that had struck the country.

More bank failures and bankruptcies every day; steel production dropping steadily; automobile production virtually at a standstill. There were a million used cars on secondhand lots and fewer and fewer people who could afford to run the cars they owned, much less buy new ones. Cotton prices were so low that the third-largest crop in the South had been plowed under.

And those fools in Washington had crippled foreign trade by passing the highest tariff in history! With retaliatory tariffs abroad and anti-American quotas and embargos, the future looked black.

Torrance took a deep breath and capitulated. "As a partner and V.P. in the firm, then."

"Provided," Connor said, his voice calm but his spirits soaring, "I'm a member of the board as well."

Torrance nodded, resigned to it. He had dealt out the offer piece by piece, but he had warned his partners, particularly Lin DeVries, that MacKenzie would demand the whole ball of wax. Still, if they were to keep their heads above water, they needed Connor's genius for investment in this kind of market. His reputation alone would bring in badly needed business.

Torrance had never seen MacKenzie smile in quite this way before. It made him look boyish even if he was rising thirty-five! He was a brilliant man, however remote. What matter if he was not exactly the right sort? He looked and spoke and dressed like a gentleman. These days a man didn't have to *be* one if he had several million dollars.

Lord in heaven, Guthrie lamented, what has the world come to?

Connor, exultant over his triumph, was damned if he'd let it show. "I presume you'll want to discuss this with the senior partners," he said.

"I already have," Torrance said, rising and extending his hand. "Consider it a fait accompli. Welcome aboard, Connor."

"Thank you, Guthrie."

"We'll have a partners' luncheon in September, but you and I must have a drink on it. I'm meeting Mrs. Torrance at the Plaza. Join us."

Two plums in one day! The partnership *and* an invitation into the presence of Grace Torrance, a priestess of the old guard, a committeewoman, a sponsor of debutantes. Connor was certain this meeting had been arranged so that she could look him over.

She knew Audrey was "seeing" him, but she had no suspicion that Connor and her daughter were intimate. It was the only way Connor could describe what went on between them whenever they were alone: Audrey, ravenous for orgasm, flinging herself onto Connor's lap, pantiless, her slender legs akimbo—and Connor obliging her one way or another. He had avoided penetration and, technically, Audrey was a virgin, a condition she was desperate to change.

Connor and Torrance went downstairs and hailed a cab. Brokers who could still afford chauffeured limousines did not bring them to the Street. A bitter citizenry was blaming the brokers and speculators for the incredible reversal of their country's fortunes.

"You get a smaller share of the blame," Audrey had told Connor the day before as she sat reading the Sunday papers on his living room couch.

"They're more indulgent to a self-made man."

"No, it's because you don't fit the standard caricature of a greedy Wall Street player. You don't have a paunch or jowls or beady little eyes."

She came to him and, facing him, straddled his legs, grinding herself against his groin.

"Behave yourself, Audrey. Mills is here."

She nibbled on his ear. "Elope with me, Connor. Then we can lock the door and do terrible things to each other."

"Your father would be furious."

"Who cares?"

"I do. I can't antagonize the man if I want a seat on his board."

Well, now he *had* the seat! Connor sat in the taxi quietly, exhibiting none of the elation of a man who had just achieved a lifelong goal. He had made it a rule never to show his joys or his sorrows except to a few carefully chosen people, and Guthrie Torrance would never be one of them. Neither would Audrey.

But he had made it to the castle keep! He was inside the Establishment and, if he married Audrey, he would be part of the social elite as well.

His spirits plummeted as the taxi drew away. He should have been sharing this with Georgia, as he had shared his dreams with her. That impulse would never change, no matter what he achieved. It darkened everything he did.

He stared out the window. The memory of her stricken face, the sight of her trust in him dying in her eyes, still haunted him.

◆

Those twenty-four hours would never leave him. Right now, in a taxi in New York City, it was Georgia's face he saw. It was his father's voice he heard as their car pulled away from the little cemetery at Brandon's Gate. He could still feel the anguish that had choked him then, like earth being shoveled over his own grave.

"Where to, Conn?" Enoch's voice resonated in his head.

"New York," he said.

He knew he would turn forever on this skewer of pain, all the more agonizing because some of it was self-inflicted.

Constance! Sweet Jesus! He would have given his soul to wash that madness away.

"I'll come with you." Enoch was tentative, expecting a rebuff.

Poor bastard, Connor thought. You're twenty-two years late, but you're here.

"Suit yourself."

"It's a sorry business," Enoch said mournfully. "I can't believe Dilys took her life."

"Beyond a doubt."

My mother's dead, Connor told himself dully. My lonely, pathetic, melancholy mother is dead and I did nothing to save her.

"Over him?"

"Yes. Her diary was among her papers." So were all of his own untransmitted letters to Georgia. Dilys had betrayed him long before he betrayed himself.

"She was a braw lass." Enoch sighed. "I tried to help her get away, but she didn't want to leave the place—or him, either, the smarmy bugger."

Connor listened while Enoch told him about the bank draft.

"I suppose you think that cancels out everything," Connor said.

"Ah, give over, Connor, for Christ's sake! I know what I did! Do you think I don't curse the day I left you? I was young and hotheaded. I was stupid. I thought it was the only way to do what I had to do."

"Then we're guilty of the same sin," Connor muttered without elaborating.

For a moment he was quiet, his head resting on the cab's upholstered seat. Then, "My God, my *God*!" he groaned, the words erupting. "I wish I'd never met her!" He had come so close to paradise! He could still feel her in his arms.

"Aye, lad," Enoch said. "She'll break your heart if you let her."

"She already has—and I hers. But we love each other, that's what I know. We always will. There'll never be another woman for me, not in a lifetime of other women."

And Enoch had sat in silence, with only dumb comfort to offer for this incurable anguish.

♦

There were signs of the times everywhere as the cab proceeded up Fifth Avenue through the stifling heat. Apple sellers were not so abundant as they had been a while before—more fortunate New Yorkers had insisted that the shabby men be restricted to certain areas—but there were plenty of men in worn business suits, too proud to get on a breadline, who still came to the city every day to hunt for jobs. In the spring those men in business suits had worked in the parks, turning up earth and seeding grass with their soft, office-workers' hands.

Now signs announced that there were no jobs available, even for men who would rather dig ditches than take charity or for women who accepted very low wages. A top New York stenographer's salary had dropped from thirty-five dollars a week to eighteen.

In the big department stores, where salesclerks now earned as little as five or ten dollars a week, there were fewer lights and they were not turned on until absolutely necessary. New York City was dim. Some hotels had closed off several floors and some—but not the new Waldorf-Astoria—had dispensed with room telephones to save monthly connection charges.

"My God, this city's dreary," Guthrie said.

"It's the same everywhere," Connor agreed.

A pall of hopelessness had descended over the country, despair and apathy replacing the stubborn optimism that had immediately followed the Crash. In America, a man who had no work was assumed to be a drunk or a vagrant. Now it was not only the lazy who were idle, but respectable middle-class men as well, who had worked hard all their lives and been contemptuous of those who did not.

They were turning the contempt inward, on themselves.

"Thank heaven Raskob put up his Empire State Building," Torrance sighed as they passed the new skyscraper on Thirty-fourth Street. "It's a reminder of better days."

"There's still big money around," Connor said.

"Afraid to show its face!"

"Tact," Connor suggested skeptically. The rich had never been tactful before. Part of their present restraint was a response to whispers of revolution if the situation did not improve.

The taxi turned left off Fifth Avenue and dropped them at the Plaza. They went up the shallow steps and past the lobby to the Palm Court, where Grace Torrance, a dainty woman with a queenly carriage, waited for them at a table. To Connor's surprise, Audrey was with her.

Mother and daughter wore light summer suits of pastel silk shantung—the long skirts still looked awkward to Connor after so many years of seeing legs on display—and small, pastel straw hats. It was considered vulgar to dress to the nines, even if one had the money to do so; simplicity was in fashion now.

Audrey was a pretty girl with hair the color and texture of cornsilk and a delicate complexion. She smiled, showing the small, even white teeth that frequently nipped at Connor. She had Guthrie's bowed mouth, odd on Guthrie but appealing on her, and big blue eyes.

"Grace, may I present Connor MacKenzie? Audrey already knows him." Guthrie's opinion of the acquaintance was in the way he said it.

Grace Torrance offered her gloved hand, and Connor took it and smiled at her in the way that invariably made women want to mother him. Her answering smile was very warm. She was so utterly ladylike that he had a wicked impulse to lift her out of her chair and whirl her around the skirted tables of the Palm Court.

"Hello, Connor," Audrey said in her whispery voice.

"Audrey," he replied, and sat down between Audrey and her father.

The men ordered drinks and Connor, ignoring Audrey's hand on his thigh, found himself being gently pumped by Grace Torrance who, failing to extract from him anything about his background, soon changed the subject to his house on Long Island.

"Colonial?" Mrs. Torrance inquired. "Or Georgian?"

"Oh, Mummy, it's modern! It's been in all the magazines."

Connor described his glass and redwood house while Audrey's hand wandered in the direction of his crotch. He had not copied Brandon Hall. He would own it someday and the mills along with it.

The only real punishment was to take from a man what he cherished most. Rhys had done that to him, not once, but repeatedly; he would be repaid in kind. Connor bought up every share of Brandon Textiles that came on the market, but the family still held a majority of the stock.

"It sounds most unusual," Mrs. Torrance was saying dubiously.

"You must come and see it." Connor glanced at his watch. "I have a luncheon appointment. Will you excuse me, Mrs. Torrance?"

She returned his smile. "Perhaps you'll come to dinner when we're back in New York."

"I'd be delighted," Connor said.

"So would I," Audrey agreed in the whisper that became a shriek when she climaxed.

Connor shook hands with Guthrie. "Enjoy your holiday."

"I'll see you first thing in September," Torrance said. "The lawyers will have done their work and we'll be interested to hear what you have to suggest."

I'm sure you will, Connor thought.

He left the Plaza, then doubled back to the Oak Room by the side entrance. He was early, but he wanted another drink and some time to absorb the fact of this latest good fortune.

It was obvious that Torrance had chosen to make the

offer on the first Saturday in August because half the Street was away and there would be less publicity about it.

Connor smiled. Publicity had a way of finding *him* and this time he would tell Barney Abbott, who guarded Connor's privacy with the same devotion he gave to Connor's business interests, to provide a wide trail for the reporters to follow.

He took a table, ordered a Pimm's Number One, and lit a cigarette, trying to decide what his next move should be.

Probably the defloration of Audrey, to be followed by their engagement. Torrance could hardly withhold his consent from one of his own partners!

◆

"You look like a cat with a dish of cream."

Oliver Petrie had quietly rolled his chair close to the table and now stretched out a hand. Connor rose and clasped it, and the two men regarded each other carefully, as they always did at their all too infrequent meetings.

Oliver spent most of his time in the House of Representatives in Washington and Connor, when he wasn't inspecting his investments in Europe, had interests that kept him flying to cities all over America.

"Tell me what you're gloating over," Oliver demanded impatiently.

"As of this morning I'm a partner at Torrance, DeVries, and Deventer—and a member of the board."

"That's great news! But they're the ones to be congratulated."

"And what's happening in your life, Congressman?"

"I must be successful. Too many of the best people wish I'd never been elected."

"Anne?" Connor immediately regretted having trespassed on private territory, but Oliver, lighting a cigarette, did not appear upset.

It was odd, how each man was reluctant to discuss his private nemesis. For Oliver, it was his relationship with his wife. For Connor, it was Brandon's Gate and everyone who was part of it.

Except Enoch. Everyone talked about Enoch. Since Dilys died, it was with his father that Connor maintained a cautious link, largely by telephone, occasionally over a meal. Enoch's pride in his son made Connor uncomfortable; exactly why he could not say.

"On the contrary," Oliver replied finally. "Anne likes being a congressman's wife. No, I meant the pacifists in both chambers. According to them, no one in this country wanted to go to war—and without opening my mouth I'm a painful reminder that the country enthusiastically sent Johnny marching off to France and that he got killed over there—or worse."

"I don't have to ask who's leading the opposition."

"Senator Brandon, that noblest pacifist of them all. He's making excellent political capital of it: he wants the presidency and he may get the nomination if the Depression ends before the next election."

Oliver looked questioningly at Connor, who shook his head.

"My ambition," Oliver went on, "is more modest. All I want is a fair deal for the veterans. Do you remember that Bonus Bill Congress passed in twenty-four?"

"An endowment policy for veterans, wasn't it?"

"Yes, to mature in 1945. But some of the men are in desperate need of that money right now, and we'd like to get it for them." He shook his head. "Hoover's given us the Veterans' Administration and disability benefits, so to him we're a privileged group already."

"Hoover wasn't on the Western Front," Connor said. "And Brandon's tack?"

"Same as the President's. But Brandon makes it sound as if supporting war veterans is equivalent to advocating war. Since he wants to be president, he doesn't dare get on the country's hate list along with the market speculators and the munitions makers."

"Market speculators like me?"

Oliver laughed. "But it wasn't illegal when you were doing it. Anyway, is there anything left to manipulate?"

"No, but there are still good investments if you're prepared to wait for your profit."

Oliver raised his glass. "Happy days, Connor—and I'll buy lunch, to celebrate your latest success."

They ordered asparagus, cold lobster, and potato salad, and over lunch the conversation, inevitably, returned to hard times and politics. Oliver had sold his rubber plants to Firestone before automobile production ground to a virtual halt, and expanded the company's food and pharmaceutical divisions. Since his election, his cousins had been running his business.

"It's obvious you thrive on politics," Connor said.

An almost imperceptible shadow crossed Oliver's face. "It keeps me out of trouble," he said enigmatically.

Bitch! Connor fumed silently. So Anne Petrie was still in firm possession of her husband's heart. Why did he go on loving the damned woman? They didn't make love, Connor was sure of that now. He wondered again if Oliver could—and even if he could, if he was too ashamed of his withered legs to do anything about it. He wanted desperately to help, but all he could do was listen, and Oliver was not ready to talk.

"Do you expect a big fight with Brandon?" Connor asked.

"Oh, yes. The man's a born politician. And that voice of his! If he takes to broadcasting against the bonus, we've had it."

"Unless you broadcast too." Connor grinned gleefully.

Oliver returned the grin. "Are you offering to sell me time on your radio stations?"

"At the lowest rate consistent with regulations—provided the public doesn't know about it. I want to get your bill through, but I'm not interested in politics."

"Maybe you should be. At any rate, I accept the offer and the conditions." Oliver chuckled. "Brandon will come sniffing around to know how we're paying for the broadcasts."

"You mean you talk to each other?" Connor offered his cigarette case and they ordered coffee.

"Often. He'd never be churlish to a veterans' advocate, particularly a crippled one. He has to keep our relationship friendly, in case the tide should turn."

"Yes, that sounds like him," Connor said contemptuously. The venom was not lost on Oliver. "You know him?"

Connor regarded Oliver for a moment before he answered. "I grew up in his house, that big house on the hill I told you about."

Oliver nodded. It was his first acknowledgment that he remembered every word they had exchanged that night, both his own deeply personal confidences and what little there had been of Connor's. Both men were aware that the admission had deepened their friendship.

"So he's your Judas!" Oliver said softly. "I'll be damned."

"Be careful of him, Oliver. He's not what he seems."

"I will be. Do you have any contact with him?"

"No! I despise him—and the feeling's mutual."

"You must have been devoted to each other."

Connor looked at him sharply.

Oliver nodded insistently. "Yes, yes. If there was no love lost, you'd have forgotten it long ago."

But this was as far as Connor was prepared to go today, and that was clear to the perceptive man in the wheelchair who sat opposite him.

◆

"Hello, Congressman," said a soft voice, interrupting their silence.

"Sondra!" Oliver shook hands with the woman standing near his wheelchair. "How nice to see you again!"

Connor got to his feet and was introduced to Mrs. Overholt, who refused Oliver's invitation to join them, gesturing toward her escort a few tables away by way of explanation. She was a very attractive woman of indeterminate age, and she looked cool and pretty in navy blue linen iced with white. A crisp white straw hat half covered her softly waved dark hair. She was the kind of woman men called feminine.

She stayed for only a few minutes, her brown eyes straying to Connor from time to time before she said good-bye and left them.

"That's Arthur Overholt's widow," Oliver explained.

"The press lord?"

"The very same. She's been driving the conservatives crazy over the fate of the publishing empire Arthur left her."

"Yes, I've read about it."

"Who hasn't? If you ask me, she's rather enjoying it."

"What's she like?"

"One of those women who needs taking care of. Arthur was almost thirty years older and he doted on her. She handled the social side of Arthur's life expertly—and it was demanding, let me tell you. Apparently her interest in his publishing empire didn't stop there. But she can't run it, so she has to sell it. The question is, to whom?"

"Power," Connor said.

"I beg your pardon?"

"She's had a small taste of power and doesn't want to let go. It's heady stuff. I've been amassing money for years, but as a lifework it palls beside the getting of power. I'll tell you something, Oliver. Communications will determine who has it in the future."

"Go on," Oliver said.

"Even the financial potential of radio, which is enormous, doesn't compare with its power potential. Radio can reach everyone in this country simultaneously, as no newspaper can. And it's a better base than politics because it doesn't depend on constituents."

"But it depends on advertisers, who can withhold revenue if a newspaper backs an unpopular issue."

Connor smiled. "That wouldn't matter if the paper had enough money to weather any storms."

"And you'd have enough!" Oliver laughed aloud. "Do your inspirations always arrive like this, like a bolt from the blue?"

"Not always. But I think I'll have a talk with Mrs. Overholt about her late husband's empire."

Oliver paid the check and Connor walked beside the wheelchair into the lobby. Oliver always refused to be pushed.

"Are you on schedule?"

Oliver looked at his watch. "Just. I only have to collect Max and my bags." Max was his attendant and they were on a swing around the country, addressing veterans' groups.

"Call me when you get back to Washington," Connor said. "We'll arrange those broadcasts."

They shook hands and Oliver rolled his chair backward into the elevator, a white-haired man with a young face and old eyes.

"Soon," Connor said, frustrated because there was so little he could do to help this singular man.

Oliver nodded and the elevator doors closed.

◆

"He protects himself by denying anything is wrong," Connor told Tirzah on the telephone that night.

"I always said you two have a lot in common," she returned dryly.

"Touché," he said, smiling. She knew him too well.

Tirzah was one of the constants in his life. With the advent of talking pictures, she had gone beyond Tin Pan Alley recognition to national fame, but she hadn't changed.

"What would you say," he asked her, "if I bought a chain of newspapers?"

"I'd say what's in it for me." She laughed. "But what do you want with newspapers?"

"A voice in making national policy."

"Like the senator?"

"No, not like him! Like me."

She was silent for a moment. "Will you ever stop running?" she asked.

"No. Will you?"

"Probably not. Which newspapers?"

"The Overholt chain."

She whistled. "The one the little widow's been making such a stink about selling?"

"The very same."

"That's big stuff. Will she sell to you?"

"I plan to put the question to her tomorrow."

Tirzah's hearty laugh boomed over the wire.

"What's the joke?"

"You'd be wiser to put something else to her. Sounds like the little lady's been basking in the limelight, but if you ask me, what she really wants is a good bang."

"Come on, Tirzah! How the hell would you know that?"

"Just a feeling. Let me know if I'm wrong. When are you coming out? I need to see you."

"Anything wrong?" he asked quickly.

"No, you fool! I just need *you*! Your wit, your smile, your glorious cock."

It was his turn to laugh. "Okay, okay. I'll fly the whole lot out in a few weeks."

After they said good-bye, he got the Overholt number from information. Mrs. Overholt was at home, the butler said, and in a moment she picked up the extension.

Connor put aside the bawdy humor of his conversation with Tirzah and asked decorously if she remembered having met him that afternoon.

"Of course," she said, her voice low and sweet.

"Well enough to have dinner with me?"

"Possibly," she said. "Is this about the newspapers?"

"Not entirely."

"Perhaps you'd better see my lawyers," she said, crisply now.

"I'd rather look at you."

She laughed, not Tirzah's belly laugh but a breathy laugh, almost girlish, giving in.

She would be free on Friday, and he arranged to call for her at seven.

34

♦

Sondra hooked her stockings to her girdle, put on a pair of satin briefs and a matching bra, pulled on her slip, and sat down at her dressing table.

She peered anxiously into the mirror. She had applied her makeup carefully, but there were some things makeup could not hide. Sondra was forty-five and the man she was dining with tonight was more than ten years younger.

What a stunning man he was!

Sondra hugged herself, thinking about him. Those dark eyes, that handsome face, that tall, powerful body. What would it be like to go to bed with a man like him after twenty-five years of marriage to darling Arthur?

Arthur had loved her just as much as dearest Daddy had, but although he was only forty-seven when they married, he had been as conservative in bed as he was in politics—or so Sondra had been forced to conclude until she found his secret collection of pornography.

Arthur would have been horrified to know that she pored over the pictures at every opportunity. It made her feel hot all over to see what some people did in bed.

Arthur had never thrust his head between her thighs or asked her to take his penis in her mouth. Arthur never used a fake *thing* that was much bigger than his was. . . .

The telephone rang and she answered it before the butler could.

"What's all this about you and Connor MacKenzie?" Letty Pemberton's voice drawled over the line.

"How did you . . ." Sondra began, and then said, "Lester, of course." Lester Pemberton was one of her attorneys. "Hasn't your husband heard about privileged information?"

"Don't be silly, Sondra. You and I were in diapers together. Now tell me all about it."

"There's nothing to tell. He's interested in buying the chain, so he's taking me to dinner to talk about it."

"You wouldn't sell to him!"

"Why not?"

"He isn't quite the thing, my pet, gorgeous as he may be."

"Letty, you're the most awful snob!"

"And you, of course, are not! But I suppose it isn't business *you* have in mind. Take care, Sondra. MacKenzie's not dear old Arthur, who was more or less content to dandle you on his knee. This man has more sex appeal than Rudolph Valentino."

"Ugh! I'll never know what women saw in that greasy Italian."

"Promise," Letty yawned. "A promise of ecstasy. Those smoldering eyes! You must be sure to tell me all about MacKenzie's technique."

"For God's sake, Letty! I hardly know the man! And I have to finish dressing."

Sondra put the receiver in its cradle and looked at herself in the mirror again. She was blushing furiously, but her eyes were sparkling and she looked younger, definitely younger. She had always looked a good ten years less than she was. Arthur said it was because she had been cherished, as the good Lord intended for women of her class.

Her hands slid down to cup her breasts. They were nice breasts, firm, neither too large nor too small. She was as slim as the day she married Arthur. Her belly was flat and her legs shapely. She looked down at herself, then rose suddenly, unhooked her stockings, removed her girdle, and replaced it with a garter belt and wide-legged tap pants.

Feeling young and very naughty, she rang for her maid

and was buttoned into a pale yellow chiffon dress that set off her dark hair, mercifully still unsmirched by gray.

"Lovely, madame," the maid said. "The pearls or the citrines?"

"The citrines," Sondra said just as the bell rang downstairs. She fastened her earrings, took the bag and gloves her maid held out to her, and ran lightly down the staircase.

Connor was in the small drawing room, and she watched him for a moment through the open door. She didn't want him to cherish her! She wanted him to want her, to put his hands all over her, to do every shocking thing in Arthur's pictures. She trembled. Lust, long sublimated, rose to take command of her.

♦

She pretended to ponder the sale for a week. It was the perfect excuse to see him every day, even though she would have given him the damned newspapers if she thought it would make him marry her.

"Of course you're not thinking of marriage!" the omniscient Letty warned her. "He's not the marrying kind, and even if he were, he isn't *our* kind."

"So you are at constant pains to remind me, Letty. A lot of our kind are in the cart since the Crash, but he isn't. And TD&D made him a partner."

"That was by necessity, not choice. I'm your friend and I have to tell you that people are talking about you."

"There's nothing to talk about!"

That was true enough, much as it pained Sondra to admit it. Connor was a perfect gentleman. Everything about him was perfect, from his Savile Row suits to the Bugatti 41 Royale he drove. He knew a lot of people in café society and the entertainment world—"from his notorious connection with that sex-mad Tirzah Kent," Letty reminded her ominously—but he was, after all, a broker, a member of the stock exchange, and as much sought after by the press as a matinee idol. No wonder!

And he had the right amount of money, enough to buy the Overholt empire. It included, among its newspaper dailies, the *New York Messenger,* the *Philadelphia Morning Courier,* the *Chicago Clarion,* the *St. Louis Sentinel,* the *Boston Bulletin,* and the *Detroit Compass.* It published several influential quarterlies, five women's glossies, four screen magazines, and a host of less prestigious "rags," as Lester Pemberton called the bawdier slicks of the Overholt press.

"I'm flatly against selling to him," Lester told her firmly.

"I haven't decided yet," Sondra replied, her passion lending her courage.

"Arthur must be turning over in his grave! He was a lifelong conservative, and God alone knows what this MacKenzie's political affiliations are."

"Arthur was somewhere to the right of the Emperor Tiberias."

"A remark like that has to be straight out of MacKenzie's mouth, Sondra, not yours. Let me make it perfectly clear: Enoch MacKenzie's son cannot be trusted with the power those publications represent!"

"Connor's a roaring capitalist, no matter what his father does!"

"We can't be sure of that!"

"You see a Bolshevik behind every tree, Lester! But they're my publications and I'll sell them to whomever I please."

"Then be prepared to take the consequences. You can't thumb your nose at your own class with impunity."

But she was heedless, caught in the grip of something even stronger than social pressure. She had to have Connor for herself. All her life she had got whatever she wanted, but she had never wanted anything as wildly, as wantonly, as she wanted him.

Still, she knew she had to dissimulate to get him, not go slavering after him like a bitch in heat or cling like the proverbial vine. He appeared to like independent women, some of them infra dig like that nymphomaniac Tirzah Kent. And he had been seen often enough with little Audrey Torrance—so loathesomely young, so fortunately away for the remainder of the summer—so he must like ingenues too.

Sondra had to strike just the right note between woman and girl, between virtue and unconscious vice.

◆

She almost fainted when, at last, he kissed her good night during the second week of their acquaintance. She had never been kissed like that before.

"Come to Sands Point for a few days," he whispered, his lips against her cheek, his arms pressing her body close to his.

She accepted, knowing from the moment she stepped into his car for the long drive out to Long Island that she would have no control over what happened there. She had abandoned all the familiar securities of her life—her house, her position, her connections—to step into another world alone with him.

Out of the corner of her eye she watched him handle the Bugatti as if it were a woman, coaxing it to its best performance. She watched his strong, graceful hands on the wheel and saw, with incredible excitement, the strain of his thighs against the fabric of his slacks.

She had always been someone's little girl, and right now she felt like a virgin. He was utterly, overwhelmingly male, and the men she knew were not.

When they arrived at the enormous cantilevered glass-and-redwood house, she hardly saw the vast rooms, the unusual mix of modern and antique Chinese pieces, the furniture made to order for a big man, the two pools, one indoors and one out—even while she pretended to admire it all.

At dinner he was entertaining, as always, but she was too excited over what was coming to eat. It was in the way he looked at her. Her legs felt weak.

She talked easily, out of long practice, even when they went into the living room for coffee and liqueurs, but she was wildly aware of him sitting next to her. She stopped in mid-sentence when he took her glass and put it on a table with his own. He leaned forward and kissed her.

Her hands came up to frame his face and her lips parted hungrily. She made a small, eager sound of passion.

"Come to bed," he said, and she nodded and went with him up the stairs to his bedroom, not looking at him, her face flushed, her breathing quick.

She closed her eyes while he undressed her and began to tremble when his fingertips roved over her, brushed her breasts, stroked her navel, opened the cleft hidden by her pubic hair. She was embarrassed to be so wet, but he seemed to like that.

He put her on the bed and shed his clothes. He had a body like the statues she had seen in Florence, from the spread of his shoulders to his narrow waist to the curved, resting penis nestled between his long legs.

She was shaking when he got on the bed beside her. She felt the play of his mouth on her nipples, felt his lips open the petals between her thighs, and when she reached for him, he was no longer at rest but hard and hot and ready.

She had never burned for sex like this, never pulled up her knees and opened herself with such absolute abandon, never felt a sensation as exquisite as his mouth coaxing her to a violent climax.

Then she was in a feverish haste to feel him inside her. She heard herself moan with bliss. Her body arched and her hips rolled toward a second peak when she felt him come with her.

She drifted back to the feel of his body and the smell of his skin and kissed him lingeringly, knowing that she had to have him for always no matter what she had to do to get him.

◆

"How did you meet Oliver?" she asked on their last day while he lay in the sun and she sat under a fringed parasol near the pool.

He told her, knowing she was sounding out his politics.

He didn't mind. Sondra was endearing. She was a charming, elegant woman who was involved in a business deal that was way over her head. She had a lonely quality, like an untenanted house. It moved him, even as her sexual naiveté excited him.

He wanted to take care of her and her newspapers, but it seemed that marriage was her price.

And why not? She was an infinitely wiser choice than Audrey Torrance. And she was just as social. Of course there would be no children, but that did not trouble him. He could marry in order to fill an empty corner of his life—while he advanced its central aim—but he had never considered children.

He reached for a bottle of suntan oil, reluctant to commit himself before she agreed to the sale.

Sondra watched those hands—God! how they made her body sing—rub oil on his broad chest, where just enough dark hair curled, on his muscular arms and flat belly, on his legs. His black woolen trunks outlined the mound between his thighs. She moistened her lips. She was drenched with desire, just looking at him.

"You never talk about yourself," she said.

"No need. It's all been printed in the Overholt press."

She blushed. She had pored over back issues of Arthur's newspapers, searching for every mention of him. She was fascinated by his many romances, but that was in the past. Now she wanted him to herself.

"You've never been involved in politics," she ventured again, Lester's warning ringing in her ears.

He sat up and looked at her. "Is that what's worrying you? I'll tell you right now, if I had any politics, they'd be different from your husband's."

"I don't care about that!" Her hands moved nervously and she averted her face. "If you want the truth, Connor, what worries me is that I'm in love with you. So much that I don't know what I'll do if you're not in love with me too."

She looked at him helplessly. He was moved by her vulnerability.

The obvious solution vibrated between them. But she was in love with him and he was not in love with her—or with any other woman but Georgia. Still, he did care for her. He had grown fond of her. It was good having someone at his side morning and night who loved him, only him, as devotedly as Sondra did. Why not marry this woman, who was intelligent, charming, and chic?

More than that, she was his chance to go beyond the Social Register, to challenge Rhys from a position outside society or politics. A communications empire like Overholt's was not built in a day. It would take Connor years to develop one of his own. He could have all that power ready-made, waiting to be used. By the provisions of Arthur's will, Sondra would retain a twenty percent share, but that was not a problem.

He had only to say he loved her—but he could not shoulder that responsibility.

"Sondra, I feel a great affection for you, but it may not be what you want."

"Is there someone else?" she whispered, rigid with fear.

"No, not in the way you mean. There's no one else I could marry."

She sparkled with joy. "That's wonderful! You can marry me!"

He smiled, that rare, wonderful smile of his. "I will if you'll sell me the Overholt press at a fair price."

"Yes, whatever you want, yes!" Her heart was too light to be troubled by the warning he had given her, the bargain they had just made. There was no other woman he could marry! That was all she heard. She knew she could make him love her as madly as she loved him.

To her surprise, he picked up the telephone, asked for a number, waited a moment, then spoke. "All right, Barney. Get started on it." He hung up and smiled at her.

"Aren't you going to kiss me?" she asked plaintively.

"I'm going to do more than that," he said, rubbing the

oil off with a towel. He walked to her and lifted her off
the lounge.

He was beautiful. He was virile. He was hers.

"Hurry," she whispered. "Hurry!"

♦

Connor told Audrey the news, safely separated from her
by a table at Sherry's, as soon as she came back from the
Cape.

"You *can't* be serious," she said, her pink mouth quiver-
ing. "She's old enough to be your *mother*."

"Not unless she had me well before puberty. But I'd
have made you unhappy, Audrey, and your whole family
as well. I can't take domestic squabbling."

"Everyone has a family!" she snapped. "Are widows and
orphans the only women safe enough for you to marry?"

Then she wept a little, but carefully, without smudging
her mascara. "You'll get tired of her," she warned him
when he put her into a cab. "And then you'll come back to
me. But I won't be a virgin when you do."

"Come on, Audrey, don't do anything foolish. You're
too good to throw yourself away."

"You did!" was her parting salvo.

Connor's friends were divided. Tirzah, who came to
New York to appear in a benefit and met Sondra briefly,
thought Connor was mad.

"Never mind the sweet voice and the dainty ways! That
rose has thorns."

"You shouldn't have, Tirzah," Belinda Blankenship
scolded her when she heard about it. "Connor's human.
He needs someone."

"There's only one woman that man wants, and we all
know it. What's the point of getting himself tied to another one?"

"I think, Madame Spitfire," Belinda said, "with a loaded
look at Racey, that you'd like to keep him for yourself."

"Okay, all right! At least I don't cling the way that aging
debutante does. She's so jealous she'll drive him nuts!"

But the Blankenships and Oliver Petrie, who approved, held their peace.

Sondra was besieged on all sides.

"Go to the devil!" she told her women friends. "You just wish you could get your claws on him!" And she refused to listen to Arthur's business cronies' dire predictions. "A bunch of old fussbudgets," she called them, laughing heartily with Connor.

There were only four guests at the civil ceremony in Connor's apartment on the first Monday in September: Racey and Belinda, who flew in with Tirzah for the wedding, and Oliver, who gave the bride away.

Sondra, in beige silk surrah and a small, veiled hat, had made no objection to Tirzah's presence, however much she resented it, but she was determined to put a stop to *that* now that they were married. Her own friends, she explained, were still out of town for the summer and it would have been pointless to plan a big wedding.

They all knew she feared that many of them would have refused the invitation. They all knew she counted on secrecy and the Labor Day holiday to keep the wedding off the front pages until she and Connor returned from the long European honeymoon he had promised her. The strategy worked.

But the women's pages soon picked the story up, to a collective gasp of prurient interest across the country. People whispered and snickered and laughed, but at Sondra, not at him.

"It's humiliating to see a woman take the vows with a younger man!" Letty told her friends with a keen eye on Constance Brandon. "It has to be for sex."

"These days it might be money," Edith Phipps suggested.

"No, they both have their fortunes intact," Constance snapped. "It was a tradeoff. He wanted those newspapers and she wanted a stud."

"She's no fit mate for a man like that," Edith remarked, rolling her eyes.

"There has to be something lewd about the woman," Constance scoffed. "Little lady Sondra has been hiding

her light under a bushel. But I don't care what he's doing
to her in bed. I give that marriage no more than a year."

The gossip had died down by the time the Connor
MacKenzies returned from their honeymoon. The day
after that, Connor left with Barney Abbott for a more
thorough inspection of his newly acquired property and
Sondra, enraptured by her new husband, forgave all the
women who came rushing to welcome her home, their
shock no match for their avid curiosity.

The men, however, among them Linton DeVries and
Lester Pemberton, agreed to watch every move MacKenzie made with the Overholt press.

♦

"Old Arthur ran a tight ship," Connor said to Barney
Abbott in Philadelphia, the last stop on their way home.

Barney nodded. "From every point of view. Are you
going to adhere to his political line?"

"What do you think?" Connor asked.

Abbott laughed. "You'll be starting out with a real blast,
supporting the veterans' Bonus Bill. Those papers have
been rock solid conservative for decades. They never once
advocated giving labor an extra penny in wages or bonuses."

"Every dog has its day," Connor said with satisfaction.
"And now I have to shower and change. I'm having dinner
with a Democratic boss of this fair city."

"And so it begins," Barney said.

"It begins very well."

In the course of the trip Connor had dined with at least
two dozen political potentates who were eager to see
which way the Overholt press would jump. In Philadelphia this evening his host was Austin Craely.

"You'll lose half your subscribers if you espouse a Democratic way of thinking," Craely sounded him out.

"I'd count on picking up more than that in your wards,"
Connor said. "This is going to be a hotly contested election. I might help you if you were prepared to help me."

"What about your father?"

"What about him?"

"Well, you know our party's pro-Labor, but John L. Lewis is a staunch Republican."

"Lewis doesn't cast my father's vote."

Craely shrugged. "You could look at it that way."

"I do. I run my own show and he runs his. I don't know which way he'll go and, frankly, I don't care."

"Okay, okay. I just wondered."

It was something everyone wondered about. The inevitable question annoyed Connor and put a strain on his still-tenuous relationship with Enoch.

◆

"Come on, laddie," his father had boomed the last time they spoke on the telephone. "It's none of my doing, them putting us together. I never breathe a word about you to the papers. I wouldn't talk about that wedding I wasn't invited to."

"Did you expect to be?"

"I guess not. What's she like, your wife?"

"Elegant. Charming. Very social."

"So I heard. No use for labor leaders, has she?"

"No more than you have for her class."

"I could answer that better if I met her."

"Sometime, maybe." The last thing Sondra wanted was an introduction to a burly proletarian with piercing eyes and a loud voice. She simply ignored her husband's connection to Enoch.

"So my son's a press lord now! What are you going to do with your new toys?"

"Get that Bonus Bill passed, for one thing."

"We're on the same side of the fence on that one. And then?"

"Put a Democrat in the White House next year."

"What the hell for? This country needs good solid business interests in the White House, and that means a Republican. It's new factories that make jobs, not a lot of Bolshevik theorizing about who owns the means of production."

"How about a fair share of the profits? How about minimum wages and maximum hours?"

"We don't need a Democratic president for that. That's what I'm here for."

"I hate to tell you this, but nobody lives forever, not even you!"

"You're a stubborn bastard, Conn." Enoch had said it proudly.

"I come by it honestly."

That made his father laugh heartily and the conversation had ended, as it usually did, abruptly.

They were not overtly friends, but Connor's grudging respect for his father's position of power had become reluctant affection.

Enoch had been at Connor's side during the most humiliating, agonizing hours of his adult life. It was impossible to stand so emotionally naked before another human being without forming a tie to him, however imperiled it was by the past.

◆

"You may be a city slicker," Austin Craely told him now, lighting up a cigar after their dinner in a restaurant that called itself French. "But when it comes to whores, our Rita is prime beef and guess what? Tonight she's reserved for you."

Connor hesitated. Whores were not his style. On the other hand, it would be tactless to refuse a man whose cooperation he wanted. Craely drove them to a large frame house outside Philadelphia that looked sedate enough from the street but was hung with red velvet and gold tassels inside.

Connor was escorted upstairs by a black girl in a short, sheer uniform, complete with a cap and a tiny apron that stopped just above her naked, smoothly shaven pubis. She smiled as she opened the bedroom door for him, then hurried back downstairs.

Inside the dimly lit room he saw a woman lying on the

ed, her face obscured by big feather pillows while she
moked a cigarette in a long holder.

"Come on in, honey," she said. Her voice sounded
amiliar—or perhaps it was the words. He crossed the
oom.

Her face was still hidden in the depths of the pillows,
but not her body. She wore only a silk shift which she now
pulled slowly up to her waist, exposing a great bush of
black pubic hair. That, and a mole on her right thigh,
made him certain.

"Rhoda?" he asked softly, and she sat up abruptly and
peered at him in the dimly lit room.

"Connor MacKenzie!" she breathed in disbelief.

"What in hell are you doing here?" he demanded.

She gave a crooked smile. "What's it look like?"

"But why?"

"Because I like it, that's why. I always liked it." She
ground out her cigarette and dropped the holder on the
bedside table. "Here I get it regularly and the pay's better
than secretarial." She switched on the bedside lamp and
scrutinized him. "Holy cow, you're even bigger than I
remember, but not any better-looking." She grinned. "Why
are you paying for it?"

He sat down on the bed. "Tell me about you first," he
said.

She said she had decided not to work behind a desk,
waiting around to marry the only kind of second-rate guy
who would want to marry *her*.

"I had nothing to offer but snatch," she said wryly, "and
once they got it, the nice guys weren't going to marry me
for it."

She had left home to offer her talents to several establishments in the big cities, but this one paid best. She was
saving for a place of her own, where she would make a
fortune and service only the customers she liked.

She raised a cynical brow. "If you hadn't dropped out of
sight the way you did, I might have made enough on the
market to have my own house by now."

"I'm sorry about that," he said. "Life got hectic."

"Yeah, I know. You got rich and famous and I go screwed." She said it without rancor.

"Where are you planning to open this house of yours?"

"Washington, D.C.," she said. "New York's got plenty of places, but not Washington. I figure all those senators need a really classy place to go, something that'll make them think they're in Paris. Not to mention all the foreign ambassadors." She leaned forward to let him light another cigarette for her and one for himself. "It'd be a real fancy place," she said dreamily, "with gorgeous furniture and the best booze in town. I'd charge even higher rates for the fancy fucking and hire girls who like the nasty stuff. Some men are nauseating in bed." She shook her head incredulous at the men's demands and the women who liked them.

He flinched. Dilys's diary had hinted that some of Rhys' sexual tastes, too embarrassing for his mother to describe were obnoxious to her. He had destroyed the diary, but the thought was burned into his brain, another reason that he would destroy Rhys, no matter how long it took and without implicating Georgia or his mother.

He smoked silently, remembering his visit to the attorney whose name he had found among his mother's papers and his astonishment at the size of the trust fund Rhys had set up for her in 1913. In addition to the substantial amounts Rhys had paid into it over the next thirteen years, Dilys had deposited every penny Connor had ever sent her and the bank draft from Enoch. She had left it all to Connor, a mixed legacy of Brandon blood money and MacKenzie conscience money, and he had kept it separate, like a leprous growth he could neither live with nor cut out.

What better way to use that money than to let other women choose the men they went to bed with and the manner of the coupling?

"I'll put up the money for you, Rhoda," he said.

She stared at him, her head tilted to one side, until she saw that he meant it.

"A partnership?" she asked.

"No. It'll be all yours."

Again she weighed his intent. "'What do you want from me?"

"Nothing. I owe it to you."

She chewed her lip. "Yeah, you do. But you must want something for it!"

"Hell, I don't know." He thought a minute. "Men tend to talk in relaxed surroundings. From time to time I might like to hear what certain politicians are saying."

"You'd bankroll a whorehouse to know *that*?"

He shrugged. "Any source of information is worth tapping. Rhoda, I *do* owe you. I got started in big trading thanks to you. I want to pay my debt."

"I don't believe it's that simple, but I'm gonna let you do it!" she said excitedly. "But, Connor, it'll take a pile of money for the kind of place I want. I might have to buy land and build the house myself. It's for sure I'll have to pay off all the public do-gooders who can't wait to drop their pants in private."

"Whatever you need," he said.

She put a pillow over her face and screamed with delight, kicking her legs. Emerging flushed and happy, she said, "It takes a smart man to know when he can trust a woman."

"You forget I knew you when," he said.

"Once."

"Once was enough."

"How about twice?"

He shook his head. "Not in this place," he said. "I'm here because it wasn't diplomatic to refuse. Another time, maybe."

"Sure. The place I'm going to run will be a palace."

But they both knew it was unlikely they would ever climb into bed together. They exchanged telephone numbers and talked about financial arrangements. He would give her bearer bonds, untraceable to him, and she would be on her own after she cashed them in. She was free to call him in New York if she needed advice or more money. Somehow he didn't think she would need either. She was smart and tough and single-minded, like him, like Tirzah. She knew what she wanted. And she had no illusions about herself or anyone else. He was drawn to people like that.

When sufficient time had elapsed, he kissed her cheek, shook her hand, and went downstairs to drive back to town with Boss Craely. The next day he and Barney Abbott flew back to New York.

It was good to find Sondra waiting at home in place of those silent, empty rooms. It was good to make love to a rapturous, all-adoring woman. And it was good to hear her tell him afterward that they had been invited to a New Year's Eve party, the kind of invitation that very definitely meant he had made it over the wall.

♦

Rhys, watching Connor's climb, waiting to see what his political direction would be now that he owned a formidable press empire, had graver problems on his mind. As 1932 advanced with a worsening economy, his colleagues were gloomy.

"The country won't vote Republican," Senator Jonah Charles prophesied despondently as they descended the broad Capitol steps. "Not while they call those squatter slums Hoovervilles! If the voters don't blame Hoover for the Depression, they blame big business."

"Who have the Democrats got?" Rhys demanded. "Only Franklin, a millionaire like the rest of us when the very word is anathema to the public."

"Don't count Franklin out," another senator chimed in. "His 'forgotten man' speech was political magic."

"Don't count me out either," Rhys returned.

"What I want to know," Jonah Charles said, "is what those MacKenzies are going to do with Arthur's publications. Mark my words, he's going to help push that damned Bonus Bill through the Congress."

"The Senate will vote against it. And I had a call this morning from Les Pemberton," Rhys said. "We're meeting with some other publishers to plan how to deal with the problem as soon as I get back from Europe."

"High time," the other senator said.

But Rhys had a more immediate problem. Cotton had fallen to five cents a pound, no matter what measures he had successfully sponsored to prop it up. His fortune was more than large enough to withstand any slump, but this one was lasting a long time and meant he had to use large sums of Crabtree money, which had to be washed through his other companies.

He debated whether to take Tony into his confidence, get him more involved in Eden than in the parlous state of French politics that was absorbing his attention lately. France was rearming. Germany was getting ready to rearm, Versailles Treaty or not. Rhys was coining money, and his first love, after the presidency, was Brandon Textiles. The size of his inventories made him anxious.

His other love was still Georgia, more exquisite than ever but as unforgiving as her mother had been. She would not accept that he had told the truth at that ghastly funeral to save her. Only in Gianna's presence—the child adored her grandfather—did Georgia even look at him. Rhys was hoping for a grandson—he never thought of Jillian's Peter in that context—to strengthen the ties of family, but there were no signs of that. In fact, the couple rarely saw each other long enough to mate—a circumstance that, paradoxically, did not entirely displease Rhys.

"Where are you going?" Constance asked when she came home to find Rhys and his baggage in the hall of their house in Georgetown.

"To Switzerland. I have urgent business there."

"You might have asked me along!"

"It was a last-minute decision."

"My eye!"

"I haven't time to argue."

"You don't have a leg to stand on is what you mean."

"Good-bye, dear wife," Rhys said sarcastically. "Parting is such sweet sorrow. I'll be back in time to sink the Bonus Bill in the Senate."

"Maybe your ship will sink first," Constance returned, and went up the stairs to vent her spleen by breaking a lamp and a perfume flacon, neither of which she liked.

Then she considered the evening before her. There were a few men she could call, men who could fill in, literally and figuratively, for Rhys when he was away. But none of them excited her.

"Bastard," she hissed, thinking of Connor, who did. "Treacly bitch," she added for Sondra's benefit. It infuriated Constance that Connor had married a woman only a little younger than herself. The sight of him, when they ran into each other at big parties and in the better nightclubs, made her want to stab him.

His marriage, despite her dire predictions, was nine months old and showed no signs of disintegrating. But Connor's recent membership in the exclusive club of high society was in danger.

"If he thinks he can rape the Overholt press and get away with it," she had raged to Letty Pemberton, "he's riding for a fall."

"Calm yourself, darling. One would think you wanted to change places with a string of newspapers."

Constance decided to stay at home and read *Sanctuary* tonight. Now, there was a rape! The substitution of a corncob pipe for a penis had to be amusing. Besides, she had her reputation to protect, for her sons as well as for her husband.

Will had just graduated from Harvard, as Richard would next June. Malcolm, the odious little beast, no matter that he was the spit of Rhys, would enter Oxford University in the fall. It was just as well; no one could live with him—no one but Georgia, the lady tycoon, of whose dominion over the French silk industry Constance must pretend to be proud. Jillian, as usual, was unhappy and nervous as a cat. Small comfort for Constance, the core of whose life was still Rhys.

Sometimes, when they were making their angry kind of love together, she could pretend she had him, really had him.

But he was not her only ambition. There was no sacrifice Constance would not make to be First Lady. She had a lot of eyes to spit in, first among them Connor MacKenzie's!

35

♦

Connor could always tell when his wife was upset over something. Her mouth narrowed, her shoulders stiffened, and when she spoke her voice was an octave higher.

"Cheer up, Sondra," he said as they approached Washington in his new plane, more lavishly fitted out than the old Handley-Page. "It wasn't much of a wedding."

"It was *the* wedding of the year, and we shouldn't have missed it."

"You could have gone without me."

She looked daggers at him. "And have everyone talking."

"Let them."

She was silent.

"Sondra," he said persuasively—or was it resignedly? "Oliver put everything he had into getting the Bonus Bill through the House. He's one of my best friends and I have to be with him when the Senate votes tonight."

"That bill won't get through the Senate and there's nothing you or the Overholt press can do about it."

"The MacKenzie press," he reminded her. "All the more reason why Oliver will need my support—and I'll need yours."

That was not true, but he said it to elicit the little smile of surrender that always marked the end of their arguments. They were minor arguments, at worst, mainly because Sondra objected to having Connor out of her sight. She went with him almost everywhere, even though she was petrified of flying. There was a fully staffed mansion in each of "our cities," as she persisted in calling locations where Arthur's papers circulated, and she had only to call ahead to have the house opened and dinner invitations sent to everyone who was anyone.

Lately, though, with the MacKenzie press clearly on the side of the Bonus Marchers, the new wages-and-hours laws, and Franklin Delano Roosevelt's candidacy, not everyone accepted—and some of those who did were clearly undesirable. Democratic senators, bankers, and industrialists were not as objectionable to Sondra as Democratic party bosses and ward heelers. It irked her to play hostess to such as they, but she had managed to ignore it—until today.

Today they should have been at that wedding, she and Connor together, among the right people, showing everyone how happy they were.

But he had just said he needed her—and that was food and drink to Sondra, the only kind she craved.

Connor, now circling over the capital during his descent, pointed downward to the scattered shantytowns the Bonus Marchers had built.

"There hasn't been anything like this since the Continental soldiers besieged the new Congress in Philadelphia."

Sondra made a moue of disapproval. "What did *they* want?"

"Their pay for winning the Revolution." He leaned forward in the cockpit. "Give 'em hell, guys," he shouted, unaware that Sondra winced.

He wondered if any of the men from the Lost Battalion were among the squatters below.

◆

A month before, in mid-May, three hundred veterans, starting in Portland, Oregon, had made their way across the country, first by foot, then by freight car, picking up ex-servicemen along the way. Their intention was to get the Patman Bill, authorizing immediate payment of their bonuses, out of committee and put to a vote.

"Will it work?" Connor had asked Oliver then.

"Who knows? Local vets are giving them help and the National Guard units, too, but only to get them out of their states in a hurry. They want no part of this problem."

The "problem," calling itself the Bonus Expeditionary Force, arrived in Washington fifteen thousand strong and growing. They had been organized along military lines, under the command of the former field artillery sergeant who had started the march.

They set up twenty-seven encampments with shacks and lean-tos made of cardboard and burlap and bits of blanket, the largest of them on the mud flats along the Anacostia River. Some sent for their wives and children.

"They are quiet and orderly," Connor's newspapers and radio stations reported, "and, in their dire need, a blot on the honor of this nation."

The poor sent them nickels and dimes; wealthy sympathizers began to donate food.

For a while sympathy ran high for the men, if not their cause, but as the Patman Bill approached its House vote on June fifteenth, the marchers and the kind of pressure they represented had become unpopular with most of the press and the Congress. Patman himself would have nothing to do with the marchers. But Oliver Petrie appeared often at their rallies. He was photographed in their midst, on one occasion with Connor at his side.

"'The Wall Street buccaneer turned press lord,'" Oliver read from a conservative newspaper, "'is not qualified to talk of honor.'" He shook his head. "They don't know anything about you, do they?"

"Maybe I'm not helping your cause, Oliver."

"The hell you aren't!"

It was when the marchers gathered on the steps of the

Capitol while the House was voting that their ragged presence seemed to become ominous and Washington turned uneasy.

"Disgraceful!" Senator Brandon declared to reporters after the affirmative vote in the House. "This is legislation by the mob!"

"The senator forgets that these are *American* soldiers," Connor insisted in an interview. "They're in Washington out of desperation, to petition, not to threaten."

The reporters, sensing a feud between the senator and the press baron, trailed both men like hounds at a fox hunt.

Now it remained to be seen what the Senate would do tonight. Connor landed the plane and he and Sondra got into a waiting Packard to drive to the Overholt house in Georgetown.

♦

Sondra was in the bath when Connor picked up the telephone in his study and gave the operator an unlisted number in nearby Virginia.

"Hello?" Her voice was always low and welcoming when she answered her private line.

"Rhoda? It's Connor. I'm in Washington."

She chuckled with pleasure. "When'd you blow in?"

"An hour ago. How are you?"

"Terrific. Business is booming. I'll be making you a payment on this love palace before you know it."

"Damn it, I don't want your money!"

"Okay, okay! What's biting you?"

"Are you busy tonight?"

Her voice changed to a suggestive purr. "Never too busy to fit *you* in." She laughed. "Pardon the pun."

"Thanks, but I'm calling for a friend of mine." He paused. "How would you feel about a man who can't walk?"

"Fine, unless he wants to fuck me with his foot."

"Rhoda!"

"Okay, okay. I'm listening. Who is he?"

He told her about Oliver. "I wasn't even sure he could function until we tied one on a few weeks ago and he told me he can. But he hasn't had a woman since the war. He's ashamed of his legs and his wife's no help."

"The poor bastard," Rhoda clucked. "Why does he stay with her?"

"They have a son—and he loves her, don't ask me why. Maybe it's because he thinks there's still a hope of sex. I'm not even sure he's ready for you yet, but if he is . . ."

"You want to bring him out here."

"Yes, but it'll be late. We're having some people in tonight while the Senate votes on the Bonus Bill."

"They're going to defeat it," she said. "I had a whole bunch of senators out here last night and they're going to defeat it for sure."

"Yes, I know." Connor sighed. "Damn it! He worked so hard. So many people did."

"Well, he might want my kind of comfort. I'll be here, whatever time you come."

"Thanks, lady. You're a peach."

He hung up, unaware that Sondra, in her bath, had quietly picked up the phone—a habit she had when Connor was talking—just as Rhoda was saying "my kind of comfort."

"Oh, my God," she murmured, leaning against the cold tiles of the bathroom. "Oh, my God."

◆

When the news came that the Senate had defeated the bill by a vote of sixty-two to eighteen, conversation in Oliver's suite at the Willard stilled.

Oliver was still on the telephone. "How'd they take it?" he asked. He listened for a moment, then hung up.

"The men were quiet at first," he told the roomful of people. "Then a murmur began."

"A murmur multiplied by ten thousand," Connor said, "must have sounded like a roar."

Oliver nodded and pressed his lips together for a moment before he spoke to his friends.

"Well," he said dejectedly, "we can be noble in defeat."

There were words of praise and encouragement, but the mood was somber and in half an hour the room had emptied. Oliver rolled his chair to the window and sat there, looking out.

"I can't bear to see him like this," Connor whispered to Sondra. "I'm going to take him out for a spin."

"I'll come with you," she offered immediately.

"No, Sondra, not tonight."

"Why?" Her voice was climbing, even in a whisper. "Where are you going?"

He looked down at her, his face impassive. "I don't feel obliged to tell you that."

"He's only an excuse!" she snapped at him. "I know you're going to see a woman. A 'peach' of a lady."

His expression did not change. "How long have you been listening to my telephone conversations?"

She flushed. "I have a right," she whispered, trembling.

He shook his head slowly, deliberately. "Neither of us has the right to spy on the other. This is a marriage, Sondra, not a war."

"Call it what you like. I'm going home!"

She ran from the room and he went out with Oliver, down in the elevator and out into the balmy night, where Oliver's devoted man, Max, waited with the Rolls. Oliver let Max lift him to the backseat of the car. The chair was folded and put into the trunk.

"Where to?" Max asked.

"The Forum, in Alexandria," Connor said. "Do you know where it is?"

"Yes, sir."

"It has the best bar in Virginia," Connor said, "quite apart from its other attractions. Okay?"

Oliver hesitated, then nodded, and the two men sat in silence for a time.

"Bad luck," Connor said when Oliver finally stirred. "I'm sorry, for you as well as for them."

"You'd think I'd have learned to accept failure by now," Oliver said, his gaze turned on the passing scenery. "It's crazy, but I felt as if winning for them would work some kind of miracle for me."

Lord, Connor thought, he needs some kind of miracle. Let it be this one for the moment.

He knew it was not sex for its own sake Oliver needed. He needed an approximation of love. Barring the real thing, a facsimile would serve. It was the same for everyone, for Connor, for Sondra, for Georgia.

I love you, he told her silently. I want you. Come back to me.

They said nothing more until the car crossed the line into Virginia.

"Maybe this isn't such a good idea," Oliver said.

Connor put a hand on his arm. "I come out here often for a drink and to listen to some good piano music, that's all. The lady of the house is an old friend of mine."

Oliver smiled. "You know the damnedest people."

"Remind me to tell you how I met Rhoda."

The Rolls stopped and the chair was deployed. The two men went up the path to the private entrance Connor always used, where Rhoda was waiting.

"Hello, Connor. Welcome, Connor's friend. Come in."

Her makeup was minimal and her dress, black chiffon over silk, had a white satin collar. She looked like a company wife presiding over a cocktail party as she led them to a table in the softly lit bar.

A bottle of cognac with a siphon and two snifters stood on the table, next to a centerpiece of fresh flowers and a selection of cigarettes and cigars. A young man in white tie and tails played expertly on a baby grand piano.

"Very nice," Oliver said, relaxing a little.

"Thank you. I'm sorry you lost, Congressman." Rhoda poured brandy into the snifters. "Better luck next time."

"Join us," Oliver invited.

A waitress brought another glass and Rhoda sat down. With an ease born of her long experience with men, she guided the conversation. She was a rabid baseball fan, among other things, and she loved the opera as much as Oliver did.

She was amusing and appealing and somehow she made it clear to Oliver that she was available without being vulgar about it. If she wasn't genuinely attracted to Oliver Petrie, Connor reflected with admiration, then she was giving the best performance he had ever seen.

After a while Oliver went with her to see the club rooms designed for clients who preferred to drink and talk in private. An hour later a maid appeared in the bar with a note for Connor.

Feel free to go whenever you're ready. Take Max—I'll get a cab in the morning. Thank you for this, Connor. I'll remember you in my prayers.

Connor smiled broadly, tipped the maid and the piano player fifty dollars each, and went home.

Sondra was waiting for him, tear-streaked and penitent.

"I'm sorry," she wept. "I've been a bad girl, I know, but it's only because I love you so much."

"Don't cry," he said, picking her up as if she were a child. He felt pity for her, pity that killed desire.

"I'll never listen in again, I swear it. But I have to know the truth. Are you having an affair?"

He mastered his impatience. "No, Sondra. I haven't touched another woman since we were married."

It was the absolute truth. So was the emptiness of his every waking hour. So was the desperate way he wanted Georgia, the reason he worked constantly and furiously to forget what was past forgetting.

In his arms Sondra sighed with relief. "I couldn't live without you, you know," she said, her head against his shoulder.

"Don't talk rot. Now it's time we went to bed."

Her arms tightened around his neck. "Oh, yes, my darling. Love me, love me, make love to me."

Somehow, he did.

◆

They were in Newport for a house party when Oliver called from Washington. Connor took off an hour later.

"Two men dead and a policeman badly injured since I

phoned you," Oliver Petrie said. He had been waiting in his Rolls for Connor's plane to land. "It started where some of them were living, at those old buildings on Pennsylvania Avenue scheduled for demolition months ago." The car pulled away immediately.

"What happened?"

"Hoover ordered the army to get the squatters out since the police couldn't. The goddamn cavalry charged with fixed bayonets! Like Teddy Roosevelt going up San Juan Hill! Except that their targets were American army veterans. Except that a seven-year-old kid was stabbed in the leg for moving too slowly! The soldiers had tear gas to open the way and five tanks to back them up! Tanks! Can you believe it?"

Connor shook his head. "Hoover just lost the election."

"If it *was* Hoover! There's talk that General MacArthur disobeyed Hoover's orders when he authorized weapons."

"Where are we going?"

"To the Anacostia flats, where the marchers retreated. Maybe I can persuade them to clear out quietly. They have nothing to gain by staying. Not until after the elections, anyway."

Connor nodded. He had known he would have to leave Sondra in Newport as soon as he heard the tension in Oliver's voice on the telephone, but now he wondered what the hell good he could do here. He was on the marchers' side; he still championed their cause. But he was not one of them, as Oliver seemed to think he was.

Twenty minutes later he was gazing in shocked disgust at the squalor of the camp. Dwellings, most of them no better than hovels, were crammed together, grimy even in the gathering dark. The smells of unwashed bodies and open cooking fires were pungent in the July heat.

The men who crowded around the car to welcome Oliver were ragged, and dazed from the morning's events. They shouted their dismay to Oliver, and their mingled breath, rank with malnourishment and rotting teeth, poured into the car.

Connor felt uneasy here on the river flats. He had never

known poverty like this, but he remembered vividly his paralyzing fear of it after his father deserted him and his mother. And here, as there, there were stately houses in the distance, on a hill. A pinpoint of his carefully controlled anger flared out of control within him and began to burn.

"You shouldn't stay here, Major, sir," one of the men said to Oliver. "There might be trouble. Look, the army's just there, on the other side of the bridge."

They peered through the deepening dark at the movement on Virginia Avenue. The threat hung in the torpid air, even at this remove.

"I swear I seen General MacArthur there, the Chief of Staff," someone said. "He was over to Pennsy Avenue this afternoon."

Max turned from the driver's seat, a worried frown on his face. "I think we'd better go, sir."

"*No!* If anything happens, I want to be here to see it. No one will believe *them*." Oliver gestured toward the marchers.

"Okay," Connor said. "But watch from a safer distance. You'll be no use to them dead. Let's go, Max."

"In a minute." Oliver opened the door and leaned out of the car as far as he could. Connor gripped him around the waist to keep him from falling.

"You men listen to me—and pass the word! Retreat to the far side of the camp. If they come across that bridge, don't resist, for God's sake! Don't even *look* like you want a fight. Just fall back. Then clear out and go home. We may have lost a battle, but I promise you we'll win *our* war the way we won theirs for them. Now go! That's an order."

"Yes, sir, Major!"

Connor pulled the door closed and tapped Max on the shoulder. The car backed along the river to the far perimeter of the camp.

They watched when the soldiers came across the Anacostia Bridge, firing tear gas in all directions. They saw the shacks being torn down and set ablaze and the men shuffling backward in a cringing retreat as the fires lit up the summer night.

The sight of the shabby, dispirited men made Connor's chest swell with rage. There they were, patriotic lambs who had gone bravely to a slaughter staged for profit and territorial gain. All they asked in return was work and, if the country had no work to give them, then they wanted a small piece of the pie they had fought to protect.

"If they can't have what's coming to them," he said suddenly to Oliver, "at least they don't have to leave here beaten!" Connor sprang out of the car and set off at a run. "Come on!" he shouted to the startled men as he passed them. "If this camp's going to be leveled, let's do it ourselves!"

The men took up the cry, instinct urging that this was the only autonomous act left to them. They followed Connor, kicking and shoving at the flimsy walls of the shanties, punching with their fists, venting their frustration, their misery, the bitterness of their betrayal.

And Connor, lashing out at his own loss and his own betrayal, lunged savagely, flattening one shack after the other with his fists and feet while, around him, the fire spread.

"Hey, get outta the fire, buddy!" one of the marchers yelled to him from outside a low circle of flames, but he punched on until three of them came in and pulled him away.

He stood there, his fists still clenched, gasping for breath, watching a man run from the camp. Suddenly the man fell in the slow motion of exhaustion, first to his knees, then onto all fours, and finally flat in the dirt, where he lay still near the licking flames.

Connor raced to pick him up. As he did, a light flashed once, then again, and he looked up, momentarily blinded by the flashbulb.

"Get the hell out of my way," he snarled. He carried his burden to the car, followed by the reporter. Max had opened the front door and he put the emaciated man on the seat.

"MacKenzie?" the reporter shouted at Connor, poking his head into the car. "What the hell are *you* doing here?"

"None of your goddamn business," Connor said, tapping the unconscious man's face gently to bring him around.

"Oh, yeah? Well, I'll quote you on that, mister! Hey, this must be my lucky day," he said, spotting Oliver in the backseat. "Got a statement for me, Congressman?"

"Isn't *that* statement enough for you?" Oliver asked with contempt, pointing at the burning camp.

"On the Hill they say these marchers were organized by the Communists," the reporter said.

"You stupid bastard," Connor shouted at him, seizing his tie, shaking him. "What kind of reporter *are* you anyway? Do you have to believe everything *they* say? Can't you find out the truth for yourself?" He pushed the man away. "Get the hell out of here! This man needs a doctor."

They dropped their charge at the nearest hospital. Connor would stay the night at the Willard. A hush fell in the lobby as they entered and went to the elevators, Oliver in his wheelchair and Connor filthy, his face blackened from smoke, his shirt and pants torn. Upstairs they exchanged a look and parted for the night. There was nothing much to say.

◆

The next day the Bonus Army was gone, but smoke from its camps still hung over the capital like a mourning ghost as the two friends waited for breakfast to be served in Connor's suite.

"I never knew there was that much rage inside you," Oliver said, watching the black cloud of smoke.

Connor made a gesture of incomprehension, amazed by the violent surge of feeling that had breached his defenses.

He called, "Come in," to the knock at the door, and the breakfast table was wheeled into the room, followed almost immediately by Sondra, who ran to Connor's side.

"I came as soon as I heard." She looked at his bruised, swollen hands. "Darling, you're hurt!"

He touched her cheek, grateful for her concern. "Not seriously."

"Oh, Connor, why do you do such things?" She remained kneeling by his chair, uncomprehending.

"He's all right, Sondra," Oliver told her.

"There's something for you, Mr. MacKenzie," the waiter said. He handed Connor a folded newspaper and an envelope before he left.

Connor opened the flap of the envelope and read aloud the note inside.

"I'll show you what kind of reporter I am, MacKenzie. I'm going to find out what else you've been keeping quiet for so long." Connor looked up at Oliver. "Who's Paul Gilbert?"

"That reporter who was on the Flats last night," Oliver said.

Connor opened the paper. The huge photograph on the front page was of Connor, dirty and disheveled, with the exhausted veteran in his arms and fury on his face. The headline read "Medal of Honor Winner Rescues Brother-in-Arms—Again."

"The Congressional Medal?" Sondra breathed. "You never told me that."

"He got it saving my life," Oliver told her.

"He doesn't tell me anything," Sondra said.

There was a loud knock on the door, which then opened without invitation. Enoch strode in, carrying the same paper, with a smile that sat oddly on his craggy face.

"Well done, laddie," Enoch boomed. "Damned if you haven't joined us underdogs." His burr was particularly pronounced when he was elated.

"This is a private apartment," Sondra said, "not Grand Central Station."

"My wife, Sondra," Connor said, and, with a faint smile, watched his wife and his father square off for their first meeting.

"Glad to know you, daughter," said Enoch, shrewdly choosing the salutation most certain to infuriate her. "And honored to meet a hero's wife." He turned back to Connor. "They can't get to you now, Conn."

"What *is* he talking about?" Sondra demanded of Connor. "Who can't get to you?"

"There's a campaign being mounted against the Mac-Kenzie press," Enoch said to the two men. "They were about to organize a 'We Don't Read MacKenzie' movement because they don't like your politics." He shook his head. "But they'll not succeed this time. Americans cherish their heroes. They have precious few of them, God knows."

"Who's behind it?" Oliver asked.

"The usual bunch. Some politicians." Enoch glanced briefly at Sondra. "The industrial mucky-mucks. The men who'd rather risk a revolution than see Roosevelt in the White House."

"Including John L. Lewis," Oliver said.

"But not me," Enoch returned. "Not anymore."

"Who told you about this?" Connor asked.

"No matter." Enoch never talked about his vast network of voluntary informers.

"Sit down and have some coffee," Connor offered.

Enoch beamed. "Sure, son." He pulled a chair up to the table.

"I'm going to change," Sondra said. "Connor, we're expected for dinner at eight this evening. We'd better leave right after lunch. Good-bye, Oliver. Take good care of yourself." She barely acknowledged Enoch as she left.

"Tell me," Connor commanded.

"Rhys Brandon and Jonah Charles head up the politicans in the Senate," Enoch said, ladling six spoons of sugar into his cup just as he had done in the cottage years before. "Along with Reedy in the House and some of the power brokers, including those grandees from Brandon's Gate, van Reitjens and Anders. They've joined forces with people the Overholt press always supported before you put the old man's newspapers in the enemy camp. In New York there's a fella name of Pemberton, your wife's attorney, and your partner, Linton DeVries."

"The bastards," Oliver said.

"What do they know about me?" Connor asked.

"Nothing much, but they're looking, now you've put a crimp in their 1932 plans. But if Franklin gets himself elected, they'll be out for blood in thirty-six. They'll sink anyone they have to."

"Thanks for the tip."

"Hell, boy, don't thank me," Enoch said. "What's a father for?"

The remark, unanswered by his son, made Enoch shake Oliver's hand and depart as abruptly as he had come.

"There goes an honest man," Oliver said.

"You think so? He's wily as they come."

"One doesn't preclude the other. What's in your past that was so bad?"

Connor lit a cigarette before he answered, facing Oliver squarely. "You're not going to like this. I recruited mercenaries and I sold guns, some of them illegally. I should have told you."

Oliver nodded. "Yes, you should have."

"But knowing how you hate guns and armies, this 'hero' lacked the courage. It was long over by the time we became real friends." Connor lowered his head into his hands, rubbing his temples. "Now that they're after me, you're at risk too. If they find out, it could finish you in politics."

"I'll have to take that chance. I owe you so much, Connor!"

"You owe me nothing! Do what you have to do. It's the way of the world."

"Not my way."

"Thank God for that," Connor said, his voice husky.

"Your father," Sondra said when they were airborne that afternoon, returning to New York, "is not a nice man."

"No, he isn't, not in the way you mean."

"Then why do you have anything to do with him?"

"He's a mine of information. For example, did you

know that Lester Pemberton is one of the men who's out to get me?"

"No, I didn't," she said, genuinely startled. "But you can't blame people for being offended by some of the things you print."

"Do I offend you?"

"I don't read anything but the society pages. But I wish you'd be more circumspect. I don't think you care as much about what you're *for* as about what you're *against*—whatever that is. I still don't know."

He took her hand. It was the most perceptive remark she had ever made. But Connor, who would never tell her what he was against, was beginning to know what he was for, even if it had taken a nightmare like the Anacostia flats to tell him.

"The irony," Racey pointed out the next time Connor was in California, "is that you finally became a member of the Establishment only to champion virtually every cause it opposes."

"I feel sorry for Sondra," Belinda said. "She's caught in the middle."

"I told her where I stood before we were married," he said.

"Oh, Connor, she's so in love with you she doesn't hear any of that."

In November, after the election swept the Democrats to power, Sondra's apprehension deepened. Connor went all out to support the New Deal programs designed to breathe life back into the stagnant economy.

There were angry protests from business and industry against the measures—and outrage against the patrician president, Franklin Delano Roosevelt. "That traitor in the White House" his former friends and schoolmates called him. But the new president's confidence was contagious and the public's faith in him enormous. The opposition, as Enoch had predicted, backed off to retrench for elections that were only four years away.

"I thought you'd spend more time with me after that man got elected," Sondra said ruefully.

"I'll only be away for two nights," he told her, kissing her briefly before he hurried out the door, bound for a conference in Detroit with his radio station managers.

She was desperately afraid that he was sleeping with other women, but she could not accuse him without proof. She knew it annoyed him when she complained, but some devil drove her to it.

She led the life of a New York society woman, serving on committees, chairing teas and benefits, giving parties and going to them. She spent hours at fittings and whole days having beauty treatments to stave off the insidious portents of age.

That kind of life had been enough when she was Arthur's wife, but now everything was flat and dull unless she was with Connor. It was torture when he was away. Her days were tedious and her sleepless nights seemed endless.

Those nights gave her time to contemplate her failure. Connor did not love her as she loved him. He was attentive and affectionate and wonderful in bed, and when she was in his arms she believed he was faithful. But it was not enough. Her soul clamored for him, even more than her body did. She had not lost the habit of getting what she wanted.

What if he left her for some woman half Sondra's age?

"But I'll never let him go," she would mutter as she paced the floor alone at night. "I'd die without him. And they'd all laugh at me! Dear God, how they'd laugh!"

36

♦

In one of The Forum's richly furnished private salons, Connor and Abbott were trying to draw out their guest over coffee and liqueurs.

David Delaney, a spare, soft-spoken man with agate eyes behind his rimless glasses, was one of the mainstay insiders of the Democratic Party, a political tactician who looked like a college professor.

"According to Rhoda, he humps like a goat," Barney Abbott had remarked when he extended the invitation that, it was understood, included sex with any girl of Delaney's choice, at Connor's expense, when their discussion was over.

"Not our concern" was Connor's response. "I want to know if FDR thinks radio is a monopoly, and Delaney can tell me."

Now the three men were comfortably ensconced in wing chairs of softest black leather. Daylight filtered through sheer silk curtains under gold satin draperies. There was a well-stocked bar in the corner and porcelain dishes of petit fours on the side table with the Georgian silver coffee service and an engraved humidor.

They might have been in a private home, except for the masterpieces of erotica that hung on the gold-brocaded walls. Rhoda Bonner had an eye for art. One portrait, of a man and two girls, variously joined, particularly drew Delaney's attention.

"We all know radio programming's completely controlled by the ad agencies," Barney Abbott said, reclaiming Delaney's attention, "and the agencies are cut from the same cloth as the sponsors. There are over fifteen million unemployed in this country, but radio never heard of the Depression."

"They program ex-vaudeville comedians, mysteries, music, or romantic dramas," Connor said. "That's it. And in those dramas everyone's white and working. Nobody ever heard of bread lines! You know as well as I do that it's designed to make the voters believe they don't need FDR!"

Delaney nodded. "But it's a free country. The Liberty League Crusaders and the Forum of Liberty can attack FDR's causes, like unemployment insurance, surplus profits taxes, and so on, to their hearts' content." He squinted at Connor. "They might even attack you for defending the New Deal so vigorously."

"I trust the right people will come to my defense," Connor said pointedly.

"As you will come to theirs in thirty-six," Delaney said.

"That's a given."

"In politics, MacKenzie, the only given is that nothing is a given. But I'll tell you what else radio needs," Delaney went on. "More news. What news broadcasts there are come after peak time and last no longer than five minutes."

"The wire services won't furnish news to us. If they do, the newspapers will cancel their contracts. We've spent weeks trying to convince liberal newspaper publishers that radio news won't kill print news, that each serves a different purpose."

"Any luck?"

"No. The newspapers are already losing advertising revenues to radio."

"Yes, I heard you'd bought up a dozen or so papers cheap."

"Better me than the opposition. Anyway, some papers have even stopped publishing radio program logs and started to shout 'monopoly.' Yet, to protect themselves, more and more newspapers have applied for broadcast licenses."

"Monopoly could be a problem," Delaney said. "Hearst, for example, is big enough to control both the press *and* the airwaves in certain cities."

"So am I."

"Unfortunately, there are as many Hearsts as there are MacKenzies. More."

Connor fixed him with an uncompromising stare. "I want to know if my stations will be declared a monopoly."

Delaney shook his head.

Connor and Abbott smiled at each other, relieved.

"The trouble is," Barney summed up, "big business is thoroughly entrenched in communications, and we know what big business thinks of the New Deal."

"Big business," said Delaney, "sees a Communist behind every federal program. According to them, providing jobs is the responsibility of private enterprise, not government, even in a constipated economy like this one." Delaney finished his drink.

"I like you, MacKenzie," he went on, "and I appreciate your support. So does the President. Maybe you ought to consider a larger role in politics."

"Thanks, but I don't care for blood sports. I like where I am and what I'm doing."

Delaney stood and smoothed his lapels. "Well, gentlemen, I think our business is concluded. You know what they say about all work and no play." He pressed the button on the wall to summon an escort to one of the establishment's twenty-five opulent bedrooms. His eyes strayed back to the painting. "Pussy, anyone?"

"Not today," Connor said. "I'll be in touch soon." He waited until Delaney had gone before asking Abbott, "Are you indulging?"

"Why not? After all, this *is* the classiest bordello in the Western Hemisphere." He chewed his lip. "Connor, you know whom you're up against, don't you? Both the Crusaders and the Forum of Liberty are backed by the biggest companies in America: Quaker Oats, Armour, Du Pont,

General Mills, Swift, Standard Oil, Brandon Textiles.
Scratch a radio sponsor or a big ad agency like Lord and
Thomas, and you'll find a company that is not answerable
to the voters, yet has enormous power to influence this
country through radio programming. If people want radio,
and they do, they're going to absorb the ideas provided for
them."

"You mean radio has become a Pandora's box?"

"I do—unless there's more than one opinion being
expressed."

"That's where I come in."

Abbott nodded. "Loud and often, I hope. This is a huge
country, but 'rugged individualism' is on its way out already. People are absorbing the same opinions, standards,
and ambitions whether they realize it or not. I think
there's great potential danger in that." Abbott pressed the
bell. "End of speech. I need a different kind of exercise."

When his escort, attired in a transparent maid's uniform, arrived, Abbott said good-bye, not asking if Connor
was staying on for sex. Connor never did.

♦

Connor left the salon and made his way to Rhoda's office.
There was no reply when he knocked, and he let himself
in with the key she had given him. Oliver had one as well.
Rhoda and Oliver saw each other regularly. They had
become fast friends as well as lovers.

Connor felt restless, at loose ends. Sondra was in New
York, but he was not in the mood for Sondra and her
petulant disapproval of his politics, her constant suspicion
of him.

In bed she exploded into a frantic sexuality that was
more draining than fulfilling. Sex was the only proof he
could offer that he was faithful. And he was. He did not
consider his occasional nights with Tirzah an infidelity.

"Sondra would never understand this," Tirzah had told
him the first time they went to bed together after his
marriage.

"No, she's too conventional."

"Wrong, wrong, wrong! She's crazy about you."

"Aren't you?"

"Sure, but I'm crazier about me. How long can you take her tantrums?"

"Indefinitely I suppose. After all, I married her."

"Right! But you didn't abduct her! She married you too."

He needed the liberating kind of sex he had with Tirzah, sex that didn't have to prove anything, that just was; as, once in a while, he needed a clever, down-to-earth woman friend like Rhoda Bonner.

He sat down, extracted a cigarette from his case, and had just lit it when he noticed the new painting of a nude hanging above Rhoda's mantel.

He sat absolutely still, transfixed by it, and the cigarette burned unnoticed between his fingers. His eyes drank in the naked woman who seemed three-dimensional, so remarkable was the technique of the artist.

She was lying on a chaise longue, her graceful arms lifted above her head with its fall of golden hair. Her face was hidden, but her body gleamed, as luscious as the red velvet on which she lay. He wanted to touch her in the same way he had touched Georgia, had cradled her naked body against him that day in the barn. This woman was so familiar to him, she might have been Georgia.

At this very moment Georgia was in New York. It was why he had left town. He could not risk a chance meeting; it would have undone him completely to see her when he could not touch her, claim her, love her.

He usually knew where she was: international society editors and fashion magazines were always hot on her trail, as well as news reporters. She was photographed with her lovely little girl, or wearing a gown of her own silk at a gala, or at resorts like Deauville and Monte Carlo and Gstaad. And the American press, who called her the American princess, never failed to mention her in connection with her illustrious father.

With a low groan Connor got out of the chair, searching the depths of the portrait to catch a glimpse of Georgia's face. He could almost feel the warmth of her that day, smell the sweetness of the hay and the perfume of her hair. For a magical instant he was living in those enchanted moments.

He stared, his eyes blurring, bereft of the person he had loved and trusted from the marrow of his bones since he was a small child. He missed her. Time had not softened the ache of her absence or eroded the wall of circumstance between them. He knew by now it never would.

Rhoda's voice startled him out of his communion.

"Is she like that?" she asked.

"Who?"

"The woman you love." She put a hand on his arm. "I've known a lot of men in my life, Connor, but never one as lonely for one woman as you are." She took the burnt-down cigarette from his fingers and crushed it out.

"I want that painting, Rhoda."

"Hey! That's a Samson Breen! Do you know how seldom his paintings come on the market?"

"Rhoda, please! I'll pay you anything you want for it and I'll buy you whatever you choose to replace it."

She folded her arms and looked at him, shaking her head. "Why the hell can't I ever say no to you? All right, you can have it. But I'll want a Manet to replace it if I can't find another Breen."

"Anything."

She contemplated her briefly held prize. "That's the damnedest painting, isn't it? It doesn't belong in a whorehouse—that's why I kept it in here—but it's so erotic it makes you crazy."

He nodded.

"Where are you going to hang it? No wife would let you put that in her living room, least of all Sondra."

"I'll find a place for it."

He already had a place. Unknown to Sondra, he had converted the penthouse suite in one of his New York City office buildings into a three-bedroom apartment. It was his escape from the perpetual tandem of marriage. Only Racey, Oliver, Barney Abbott, and Tirzah knew where it was—and Mills, his valet, who went almost everywhere with him.

Like so many people who finally get what they want, Connor found high society disappointing. Once the initial challenge of charming them into acceptance had passed, he was bored by the same people who gathered in the same places to say the same things, migrating with the seasons to one body of water or another, like seals or salmon.

"There are only two hundred people in New York," he told Sondra. "It seems like there are more only because they keep changing their clothes."

He went to the penthouse to think, plan, or read without interruption, even though his absence gave Sondra jealous fits. But he couldn't have her at his side constantly, alternately criticizing and adoring him, waiting for him to prove he loved her by taking her to bed.

He hugged Rhoda and kissed her cheek. "I'll send for it in a day or two. And thanks, lady."

"Yeah, I know. I'm a peach. Are you ever gonna take a bite out of me?"

He hugged her again. "I don't want to ruin a perfect friendship."

She saw him to the door, closed it behind him, and leaned against it, looking at the painting.

"Why couldn't I have been you?" she asked the woman. Then she gave herself a little shake and walked resolutely to her desk.

◆

In one of the luxurious bedrooms upstairs Rhys Brandon lay quietly, waiting for the girl's mouth to excite him to erection, but he could not seem to give himself over to her efforts. A procession of irrelevant details filed through his head, diverting him from the girl's soft, sucking sounds. What was her name? Mitzie? No, that one was long gone. Was her hair blond? He opened his eyes and looked down. It was brown. Maybe that was the trouble. She did not fit his fantasy.

He closed his eyes and the procession inside his head resumed. What was Connor going to do and how much longer would he wait before he did it?

Connor had made no extraordinary moves as yet to prejudice Rhys's career. His were not the only newspapers that were against Senator Brandon's ultraconservative policies.

So what was he planning? Rhys had entertained no doubt whatever, since Dilys's death, that Connor was planning something. Was Enoch involved? Rhys fought against every labor bill that came up and had helped to scuttle a few before Franklin moved into the White House.

Connor would certainly strike before the next election. It was a sword of Damocles hanging over Rhys's head.

The irony was that Connor was Rhys's creation. Again Rhys felt that odd mixture of resentment and unwilling pride that Connor's incredible success always inspired in him. After all, it was Rhys who had seen Connor's potential in the first place, no one else! It was Rhys who had created this wealthy, powerful Frankenstein's monster.

The girl stopped her ministrations and lay back on the pillow at his side. He looked down at his groin again and a different kind of panic seized him at the sight of his lolling penis. Impotent? At scarcely sixty? He turned his head to his companion, as if she had the answer.

"It happens," she said in the flat tone of an oft-repeated remark.

"Not to me," he said. He put his hand between her legs and slipped a finger inside the folds.

"Oh, no!" she said, rolling away. "If I let all my customers do that, it'd be worn away in a week." She got up and put on her robe. "Don't worry," she said without conviction. "You'll be fine next time."

She left, and he washed and dressed, trying and failing to ignore the incident. It worried him the same way Connor worried him, both reminders of his fleeing youth and challenges to his preeminence. For a moment he felt panic, as if he would lose everything—his mills, his Senate seat, the presidency, and his virility—if he didn't get Connor before Connor got him.

Then he pulled himself up sharply. Connor knew nothing about Crabtree, but it was Crabtree that kept the Rhys faction from exposing Connor's sleazy past: they felt the connection was too close for comfort and that Connor might find out and respond in kind. But they could abandon the past and examine Connor's present more closely. No man led such an exemplary life as Connor appeared to do.

As for sex . . . Suddenly Rhys thought of Constance, a far more subtle voluptuary than any whore, and not at all concerned over the possible erosion of her private parts. In fact, she liked to display them, spread on a bed wearing a black garter belt and sheer silk stockings. Just thinking of that spectacle stirred him.

He smoothed his tie, shot his cuffs, and went downstairs. He settled his bill and took a cab back to his office on the Hill.

"I won't be joining you tonight," Rhys told Ed Reedy on the telephone. "There's something else I must do." He paused. "But I think it's time to start that investigation we discussed."

"High time," Reedy agreed. "Better to be safe than sorry. I'll put some men on it."

"On both of them," Rhys said. "The old bastard is trying to unionize my southern mills."

Reedy laughed and hung up.

Rhys's next call was to Constance to say he would be free that evening after all.

"How about a quiet dinner at home? Just the two of us."

She laughed, a sultry, promising laugh. "Why not? I had nothing exciting planned, except what I'll be wearing."

She knew what he wanted in bed and she was eager to give it to him. It was one of her few virtues. Another was that, in thirty stormy years of marriage, although she infuriated him regularly, she had never bored him.

He stopped at his jeweler and selected a necklace and bracelet of blood coral for her. He gave them to her after they had been to bed. She deserved it.

◆

It was late one evening, when Connor was having a drink in the Willard's Peacock Alley, that he saw Jillian emerge from the hotel's Crystal Room. Jillian was—what?—twenty-nine now, but he knew her immediately. The sulky expression was the same, the glossy hair and the large hazel eyes.

She stood alone for a moment behind a marble column, looking distraught, in a flowing dress of embroidered apricot chiffon. She was a stylish, bosomy young woman who was very pretty except for a pout that, to any man who didn't know about her moodiness, might have seemed sultry.

She turned nervously when he approached her, then gasped and, with a small shriek of delighted recognition, threw her arms around his neck.

"Connor! Where did you spring from?"

"Fourth table on the left. Come and have a drink with me." He saw her glance at the doors of the Crystal Room with a little smile.

"That's right, Jilly, they can get along without you for a little while, whoever they are."

She went with him to his table. He ordered a champagne cocktail for her and another whiskey for himself, then sat back and contemplated her with unvarnished pleasure.

"How are you, Jilly? As good as you look, I hope."

"I'm pretty much the same. Nothing changes for me."

"That's not so. You have a son. How old is he now?"

"Going on eight, the same as Gianna." She watched him carefully, but there was no reaction. "He's a wonderful little boy. He even looks like Peter."

They were both silent for a moment, remembering the young man they had both loved.

"But aside from him," she went on, "nothing's changed.

I still don't belong in my family. Any more than you did,"
she added.

"You have your own family now."

She blinked in surprise. "I do, don't I? I wonder why I
never think of it that way. I just go on trying to be one of
the Brandons and fighting with them instead. It makes
Tim furious. He has to get along with Papa because of the
mills."

"Is Tim in there?"

"Everyone is. Georgia too. It's Richard's engagement."

He didn't hear the last sentence. "It was good to see
you, Jillian," he said, rising abruptly, "but I don't like
drinking in public places. If you'll excuse me now, I'll
retire to my own bottle."

"I'll go with you," Jillian said, aware of his discomfiture.
"I haven't talked to you in years."

He did not argue, eager to get away from those doors
and the people on the other side of them.

"But only for a while," he said, striding rapidly to the
elevators with Jillian hurrying along beside him. "I have
some calls to make—and you don't want to worry Tim."

She wanted to worry all of them, Tim in particular. She
smiled at several people she knew as they walked to the
elevators, hoping someone would tell Tim she had gone
upstairs with the scandalous Connor MacKenzie. She hoped
someone would tell Clarissa and Blanche and Cecily too.
They'd think all kinds of terrible things. Most delicious of
all was what Georgia would think.

In the living room of the suite where he still preferred
to stay in Washington when Sondra wasn't with him, she
kicked off her shoes and tucked her feet up on the couch,
watching him put out a bottle of whiskey and two glasses.
He poured, then swallowed his drink at a gulp. Jillian
followed suit, and he refilled the glasses before he sat
down on the couch next to her.

Lord, what an exciting man he was! And he had had the
wildest reputation before he married the Widow Overholt,
as Mama persisted in calling Sondra MacKenzie behind
her back. Jillian found it impossible to think of him as

plain old Connor, who had carried her around, encouraged her to walk, and read stories to her and Georgia under the big oak at Brandon's Gate.

"You really hate Papa, don't you?" Jillian said, curling up contentedly, feeling the neat whiskey warm her all the way down to there. She turned her head on the cushions to watch his profile, admiring his straight nose and his thick wavy hair, not a mop of red ringlets like Tim's, and free of the tonic and brilliantine other men affected. "Well, I hate him too. He never cared a damn about me the way he did about Georgia—and you, once. You were lucky to escape when you did. I had to get married."

He smiled bleakly. "I didn't escape, I was thrown out. But I think you *have* changed, Jillian." He looked at her appreciatively. Her baby fat was gone and her eyes looked enormous in her oval face. She had a generous mouth and creamy skin like her mother's. "For one thing, you're not a child anymore. You're a woman, a lovely young woman."

"That means a lot, coming from you. You're said to be a great connoisseur of women." Her face flushed as an idea took more graphic shape in her mind, and she finished the second whiskey quickly, imagining him bringing her to unimaginable ecstasies. The liquor fired that warmth inside her that Timothy sometimes aroused but never satisfied. She felt relaxed and uninhibited.

Why don't I? she thought. He would know how to calm the inner nervousness that made her hands unsteady and her laughter humorless and uncontrollable. Anyway, it wasn't *fair*! A woman was entitled to sexual fulfillment. Margaret Sanger said so. Tears of deprivation welled up in Jillian's eyes and she sniffed.

He turned to her. "What's wrong?"

"Me. I'm all wrong. Being married to Timothy is no bed of roses." She glanced at him from under her lashes. "Particularly not in bed." She brushed her tears away but more accumulated and rolled down her cheeks.

He handed her a handkerchief. "Tell me, Jilly." The same caring words he had said to her so often in childhood made her eyes fill again.

"Everything! Especially *that*! He's still in love with Georgia, and when he makes love to me he pretends it's her the way it used to be."

Connor shook his head slowly, his mouth curling down in utter rejection of that. "He never made love to Georgia," he said.

She would not believe him; she had based her life on the conviction that she was inferior to her sister in the eyes of her parents, her husband, and the whole rotten, implacable world. The emotional structure of her life—however warped, it was the only one she had—required that as an injustice for her to rail against, to hate, and to blame for all of her unhappiness.

"Were you lovers, you and Georgia?" she blurted out.

"No," he said, his black eyes gazing at her so steadily that she had to believe him. She put her head on his shoulder. How would Georgia feel about being upstaged for once by her little sister?

"Connor?"

"Yes?"

"Make love to me."

♦

The invitation was so devoid of sexual passion that he almost laughed, but he cared too much for her to add another brutal rejection to the hundred she had experienced and the thousand she had only imagined.

He took her hand and kissed it. "I'm tempted, but no, Jilly. It would be a big mistake."

"Why? *They* always get what they want!"

"And the bed would be crowded with them: Rhys and Constance, Tim and Georgia—even the ghost of Peter van Dorn. We could never be friends again."

"Oh, God," she said, hiding her face with her hands. "I'm so mortified."

"Why? It's only me."

She gave a strangled little laugh, cried for a while longer, then accepted a cigarette and let him dry her face with the handkerchief.

"Tell the truth, Jilly," he said. "Is it all Tim's fault?"

She shook her head, glad to confess it to someone. "I hold back to get even with him. He's not a bad man, and he's a wonderful father. He's just—ordinary."

Connor agreed, but this was not the moment to say so.

"Why don't you give him a chance? It can't be a picnic for him either."

She made no reply, and after a few moments he said, "I think it's time for you to fix your face and go back downstairs."

He waited for her on the couch, sad for her unhappiness and the way she invariably hurt herself by trying to get even with life. He hoped she would find a lover; he didn't doubt she needed one.

Jillian, freshly made up, came out of the bathroom.

"Shall I take you down?" he asked, his reluctance apparent.

"No. You don't want to bump into Georgia." She touched his cheek gently. "You're still in love with her, aren't you?"

He nodded.

"Thank you for trusting me enough to tell me." She held out her hand. "Good-bye, Connor."

He wanted to hug her, but it would have shaken her dignity and she needed all she had. He walked her to the door.

"Don't let them grind you down, Jilly."

And Jillian, going back to the reception, decided that it wasn't what had happened between them that mattered, but only what people would *think* had happened. She didn't need to say a word.

I've been alone in a hotel room with Connor MacKenzie! she told herself. Let them put *that* in their pipes and smoke it!

She sailed into the ballroom, her head held high.

"Where the devil have you been?" Timothy demanded, and Jillian smiled.

◆

Upstairs, Connor locked the door, turned out the lights, and went back to the couch to drink seriously, but after another shot of whiskey he put the bottle down.

Georgia was downstairs. He had only to walk into that ballroom to see her.

And he could not do it! He didn't care about making a fool of himself, even before the people whose inner circle he had fought so long and hard to penetrate, but he could not brook another rejection from her.

He rang for Mills. "Call the airport and tell them to get my plane ready for takeoff in an hour. Charts for Los Angeles."

"Very good, sir," the valet said. "Will I be going?"

"No, you're needed to arrange shipment of a painting to the penthouse, and I want you there to receive it. I'll give you the details later."

Connor's next call was to Sondra.

"It was a long meeting," he said.

"Where are you?" Her voice was sharp, suspicious.

"At the Willard. But I have to fly to Detroit tomorrow."

"Really, Connor, this is too much! For how long this time?"

"Only a day or two. Then we can go to Bermuda and have a few days alone."

"All right," she said, still truculent.

"Good. I'll call you tomorrow."

He hung up and put in a call to California, wondering why it had seemed like a good idea to marry Sondra. He still cared about her, but they were as different as chalk and cheese, she totally dependent, he unwilling to be bound.

He did not feel like a husband, and Sondra's voracious love for him made him uncomfortable. The marriage had become a limited partnership whose principals were apart more than they were together.

Yet she was physically obsessed by him, and sex was the one thing that sweetened her disposition. In bed his gently reared society wife—who, more and more, objected to his show-business friends and his political opinions—erupted into gutter language and a frenzied, clutching sexuality that dampened his desire for her.

He had needed someone, yes, but it would have been better for both of them if he had gone on alone. His responsibility to her weighed heavily on him now—but what would be the point of divorce?

The call came through.

"Tirzah! Thank God I caught you."

"What's wrong?"

"I have to get away from here. Where will you be at dawn tomorrow?"

"I can cancel my studio call, but this had better be good."

"It's just me."

"That's good enough."

She was waiting for him when he reached her sprawling mansion in the Hollywood hills and, without saying very much, they went upstairs to bed.

He slept until late morning, swam hard in the pool for an hour, and sat down to lunch with her on the terrace.

"Better?" she asked.

"Much."

"It's Sondra, isn't it? I told you the rose had thorns."

"The rose is a vine, Tirzah, demanding constant attention."

"Any woman with half an eye would know you hate that. Why doesn't she? She's not a child."

"That's precisely what she is."

"At—what is it?—fifty?"

"Almost. That's another thing. I don't give a damn how old she is, but she thinks I do, and it scares the hell out of her."

"Out of most women."

"Then they're fools. There's more to a woman than her age or how she looks."

Tirzah smiled. "'You never *did* fit the pattern, did you? But if you ask me, almost forty is scaring the hell out of *you!*"

He nodded. "Forty's the time when all the lonely places

yawn open, and you see the things you haven't been and done. Forty's when you realize you won't live forever."

Tirzah's expression changed as she understood what had happened to bring him here. "You've seen her again, haven't you?"

"No, but she was right there, at a party at the Willard." He shook his head. "I thought time healed everything."

"Only if you let it." She sensed the longing in him. She could see it in his eyes. "Sooner or later, you have to let her go, honey. And her rotten father with her."

"How can I let her go? She's part of me."

Tirzah made no reply, and they sat on the terrace in silence, watching the breeze ruffle the trees like a restless spirit.

37

♦

"**Y**ou're against amending the Neutrality Act, Senator Brandon," Connor said. Arms crossed, apparently relaxed, he leaned back against a marble console in the crowded reception rooms of the French ambassador's Washington residence and surveyed Rhys. "Even though your stand will stop weapons shipments to the Republicans in Spain?"

"To either side of that tragic civil war," Rhys amended. "I am, and will remain, a dedicated pacifist."

"I'm not sure that peace is where your primary dedication lies."

There was a buzz of whispers from the group of onlookers who were waiting for the sparks to fly, as they usually did when the right-wing senator and the liberal publishing ycoon squared off. They were outwardly civil, even glib, but there was an inner tension about them that fascinated people, as of a volcano rumbling and possibly about to erupt.

"For example," Connor went on, "I wonder why your pacificism doesn't extend to the Far East. The Japanese are pillaging Peking, Shanghai, and Nanking, but neither they nor the Chinese are classified as belligerents, and therefore arms sales to them remain legal. I suspect your primary consideration is the protection of your textile mills."

Rhys appeared unruffled. "The political implications of the two cases are entirely different."

"Of course. You don't own any textile mills in Spain."

There was a chuckle from the spectators and Rhys's smile deserted him.

"I take exception to that, MacKenzie. American property must be protected wherever it is."

"In Nicaragua, too, you say. And I suppose your concern has nothing to do with your cotton and sugar plantations there."

"Pure coincidence," Rhys maintained, his face betraying nothing of the outrage Connor knew he felt.

"Tell me, Senator," Connor went on, gathering steam. "Shouldn't we protect democracy as ardently as we do your business interests?"

"Spain again, MacKenzie?"

"Yes, Spain, one of the few democracies left in Europe. A duly elected government, a republic like ours, is under Fascist attack."

"It is not our concern."

"Italy's annexed Ethiopia and Germany's reoccupied the Rhineland. The coups in Greece and Nicaragua have put two more dictators into power, Metaxas and Somoza. Isn't that our concern?"

"You have a warrior's lust for battle, MacKenzie," Rhys said with patronizing forbearance. "But I intend to fight against American entanglement in foreign wars."

"How? By rolling up the oceans like carpets?"

Rhys shrugged, hands held palm upward as at a stubborn child, and turned away.

"You got to him this time, MacKenzie," one of the onlookers said, and began arguing the case with several other guests who had witnessed the exchange.

Connor made his way to the bar, thinking that it had been a draw; thinking, too, that some benevolent fairy must have blessed Rhys with eternal youth. He still stood straight as a poplar, and his hair, mixed blond and argent, was like a crown. But there was a barely discernible hesitation in his movements that made Connor reflect, for the first time, that his nemesis was not immortal.

He wondered what would goad his ambition when Rhys was gone. He had attained the wealth and influence he had always wanted, but the need to avenge himself still smoldered, ready to burst into flame at the first opportunity.

If he couldn't have Georgia, at least there was that.

Connor still bought up every share of Brandon Textiles stock that came on the market, but he knew a takeover would be impossible without the shares of at least one of the family members. Since the bequest forbade sales outside the family, there was as much chance of his getting control of the mills as there was of a cold day in hell.

On the other hand, over the past two years Connor had become chief gadfly to the pacifist/protectionist/isolationist faction Rhys represented. He had marshaled the MacKenzie newspapers and radio stations for the feud—a reporter's dream—and had sworn privately that Rhys would never get to the White House.

Defeat was precisely the punishment Rhys deserved, but it would never ease Connor's hunger for Georgia. Sometimes, when he was alone with that painting, like a miser with his cold, inanimate gold, his desolation was immense. Without Georgia even a victory over Rhys was meaningless. Everything was.

He scanned the room for Sondra but, as always when he was having a verbal duel with Rhys, she had vanished. Connor made his way through the crush looking for her, impatient to leave now that the highlight of his evening was over.

And then he turned and, amid that crowd of people, saw Georgia watching him, no more than five feet away.

They did not move, except for an inner leaning apparent only to the two of them. Her face told him that whatever else there was between them, there still was love.

In one stride he was beside her, taking her hand.

"Are you real?" he asked softly.

"Now I am," she whispered. "I haven't been for a very long time."

"Nor have I, not for more than ten years."

She glanced around quickly, gave him a bright social smile, and resumed their sotto voce exchange, rapidly, almost breathlessly, charged with feelings that they could not speak, not here, not now.

"I thought I could forget you," she said. She shook her head. "Next year maybe I will. Some year. But not yet."

"I must talk to you," he said. "I must see you alone. Tomorrow at three?"

"Where?"

He gave her the address of a neighborhood bar in Alexandria. "No one you know goes there."

She nodded briefly and he looked at her with his heart in his eyes. She reached out to touch him; then she remembered where they were and turned and left him.

He watched her retreat with a feeling of panic that it might be years before he saw her again, that once more life would hold no joy for him. He watched her disappear into the crowd, and wondered how he would endure the hours until three o'clock the next afternoon.

When he lit a cigarette, his hands were shaking and he waited until he had them under control before he went to find his wife.

◆

"Why must it be Senator Brandon?" Sondra demanded querulously on their way home to her house in Georgetown.

"What?" he said, miles and hours away.

"Why can't you argue with someone else?"

He made no answer.

"Arthur admired him," she said, her perfect little nose uptilted.

Connor struggled back to the present. "It's been reliably reported that Arthur died some time ago."

"You know what I mean!"

"No, I don't, but I'm sure you'll tell me."

"You should see how you look when you're arguing with him!"

"Probably like a happy man."

"It's the only time you *are* happy, having a duel to the death with a gentleman. It's vulgar and rude and embarrassing, the sort of thing your father would do." She stopped abruptly. Oh, my God, she thought, why did I say that?

"You can't stand the sight of him, can you?" Connor observed without heat.

"Neither can you."

"That isn't so. I just don't want to have the word 'labor' tied to everything I say."

"At least you never see him, thank heaven!"

"I see him."

She was shaken by that. What else did he hide from her?

"He frightens you," Connor said. "It's as if his class bore the mark of Cain and work clothes hid cloven hooves and a tail."

Again, she was swept away by temper. "Oh, Connor, really! The man's uncouth! And I didn't marry him. I married you."

"How do you deal with the fact that I come from the same class he does?"

"I try not to think about it!"

"But your friends remind you, don't they?"

Alarmed now, she clutched his arm. "Connor, they're just waiting for an issue they can fight you on and win."

"They?"

"Pemberton and his crowd."

"And Brandon and his."

"And you make it worse by irritating one of the finest gentlemen in this country!"

He raised an eyebrow. "Implying that I am not a gentleman?"

"No," she whispered. "I didn't mean that."

"Yes, you did. I prefer it when you're honest." He turned to look at her, his expression remote. "Poor Sondra," he said.

"Why do you say that?" she demanded, her lips going white under her makeup.

"I've made a mess of your life, haven't I?"

"Yes, you have!"

"I'm sorry," he said. "I should have considered what all this would do to you."

"Oh, Connor," she cried, "we could be so happy if only—" She broke off, shaking her head, turning away.

He didn't ask her what she meant. He knew. *If only* he loved her more than she loved him.

They drove home without speaking. At the top of the stairs she turned to him.

"Don't leave me alone tonight. Come to bed and I'll make you forget we ever quarreled."

All he wanted was to surrender to his dream of bliss.

"I've forgotten it already," he said. "And I have some work to do. Sleep well, Sondra."

He felt her watching him until he reached his room. He shut the door behind him and leaned against it, his eyes closed in a fever of anticipation.

◆

He held Georgia's hands across the table, and the current crackled between them like electricity in a storm. Each was aware of the other's urgency, the conviction that this was a moment to be seized or lost forever.

He had never expected his love for her to come tumbling out in a bar with rough, uncovered flooring, over a pitted table stained with bottle rings.

"I have to explain about Constance," he said.

"No, you don't. I'm not so fainthearted now as I was then."

"Has it been bad for you?" He seized on it, sorry and glad at once that her existence had been as flawed as his.

"It was what I deserved, no more, no less. And you?"

"The same. Georgia, anything good I've ever done is for you, to show you that I'm better than you know. The rest is the devil inside me."

"I've known that for a long time. You're still my Connor, devil or not."

He was caught between the power of love and the magnitude of their loss. His voice grew suddenly harsh.

"Jesus, the years we've wasted!"

"Do you think I don't know that?" Her face was anguished. "But what else could I have done?"

"We'd have beaten Tony! There's nothing we can't do together. I'm glad you haven't had a moment's happiness."

"No more than you have," she cried stormily, still clinging to his hands. "Oh, Connor, why did I let you go? Why wasn't I stronger than you had been?"

He longed to put his arms around her. "It was too much for you," he defended her. "Your father. My mother—"

"That was *their* doing," she cut in, "not ours."

Their fingers were laced together. She was trembling and he wanted desperately to hold her, just to hold her. His raison d'être since he was seven years old had been to make her happy, and he could not bear what his monumental stupidity over Constance had done to her, what it had cost them both.

"I love you," he said. "It can't be wrong when I love you so much."

"I don't care if it's wrong!"

"Is there any hope for us?" he pleaded.

"There has to be! We'll find a way to be together someday."

"Now!" he said. "I want you now!"

"Yes," she whispered. "I love you."

"Even after what I did?"

"Even after what *I* did."

"When?" he urged. "Where?"

"I'll be in New York all of next week. Can you get away?"

They arranged to meet the following Monday night at his private penthouse, and he watched her climb into her car and drive away with the feeling that he had been severed from half of himself.

◆

He was waiting downstairs when her taxi drew up on Monday night. He walked her quickly past the night watchman into the deserted building, instantly aware of the tension between them.

"Any trouble?" he asked in the elevator, in dread that it was over before it had begun.

"No trouble," she said.

They looked at each other in silence. They were approaching an intimacy that, for vastly different reasons, was as illicit now as it had been when they were children.

There had been that surge of eroticism in the barn, but they had both lived through years that made the interlude seem a dream they had shared, not the lusty heat of reality.

Inside the apartment she dropped her handbag on a chair, crossed to the windows, and stood gazing at the brilliant panorama thirty-nine floors below.

"It's better without the lights," he said, switching them off.

"It's magnificent. We might be on some other planet."

He waited at a little distance, sensing that he must not touch her yet.

"I wish we were," he said.

"It would be easier."

"Georgia, what is it? Are you going to tell me you're leaving me again?" he asked, his voice hollow.

She shook her head, still facing the city, her arms crossed, hugging herself. "No! How could I? But I can't leave Tony either. Not yet. That's what I have to tell you."

It was because of Gianna. No one understood better than he what Georgia felt about a daughter's need for her mother.

"I know that," he said.

"Then you know this is all we can have for a while, Connor. And not even this for months at a time."

"I'll accept anything—except losing you again."

She turned to him. "I'll never leave you, Connor. I love you. But I'm afraid of love. It never brought me anything but grief."

"Or me," he said.

"I've always held back with everyone but you." She walked toward him, the shape of her long legs visible against the thin fabric of her dress. "Remember once, when I was little, how I wasn't afraid to drop out of a pear tree because you were there to catch me? Connor, catch me now."

He put his arms around her, his senses ravished just by her nearness. He held her for a long moment before he kissed her, and then it was as if they had invented love—tasting the sweetness of her mouth, feeling the shape of her emerge and mold itself against him. He undressed her where she stood by the multicolored lights of the city, felt her round breasts and the patch of velvet hair between her legs. Then his own clothes were tossed aside and they were lying in his bed and she was real now, not imagined, impatient to have him inside her, opening like a sea of softness for his seeking body. He began that long, exquisite glide into the liquid heat of her and knew that, this time, with this woman, while he took her body, what he wanted was her heart.

"My Connor," she whispered, enclosing him.

"Say it," he implored her. "Tell me again."

She said it to the rhythm of passion, and if any trace of sorrow lingered in him once they had passed the peak, it was for the lost years they could never relive, and for her divided heart.

"My darling, you must believe me." Her mouth was

moving against his, speaking to his thoughts as she had always done. "You're the only man I've ever loved."

With a rapture that was almost pain, he took her to him and, with her, all the joy and anguish of his life.

◆

In the window seat of her bedroom in Georgetown, Sondra stared out of the window as if the hot tongs of jealousy that tortured her could reach New York and burn him too.

She went over every word they had said to each other the day before. They had been in the breakfast room of the Overholt mansion—after six years of marriage to Connor, she knew people still called it that. It was a pleasant room, especially at this season when the scent of roses wafted in from the garden.

"Something's come up," Connor had started, pushing his waffle around on his plate. "I'll be tied up all weekend, maybe longer."

"You said you couldn't miss the Senate today under any circumstances."

He had taken a deep breath before he spoke and suddenly she hadn't smelled the roses, only the brimstone of her wild, impotent rage. "Sondra, I have something to tell you."

"No! I don't want to hear it."

"You must. What's the point of our going on this way?"

"You're my husband! That's point enough."

"It will never solve our differences."

She had crumbled her toast, unaware her fingers were writhing like snakes.

"Are you telling me you want a divorce?"

"I think it would be better for both of us."

"Is there someone else?"

He had nodded and started to speak, but her hand had shot out, upsetting her glass. It cracked with a small tinkle and she had stared down at it in disbelief before she looked at him again.

"No!" She had said it through clenched teeth. "No divorce."

"I don't understand. Why not? You're infuriated by everything I do."

"Do you think I'm going to be ridiculed by all of New York and Washington, with everyone saying I couldn't hold a man ten years younger than I am?"

"Oh, for God's sake, Sondra. This has nothing to do with how old we are."

"She's younger than I am, isn't she?"

"Yes, but it can't be reduced to anything so absurd. She's—"

"Shut up! I don't want to know who she is or anything about her. Go on and fuck her if you want to, like you do that Tirzah tart, and be damned to you! But tell her I'll never divorce you and I'll never give you grounds to divorce me."

They had stared at each other in silence before she rose from the table and walked swiftly from the room.

Now she sat by the window, wondering who the woman was, imagining him doing to some nameless, faceless girl what he had once done to her. Her body ached for him even as she hated him.

The worst of it was that she was powerless to hold him, even after all she had given him—the newspapers, a place in society, her love for him! He had never loved her as she loved him, body and soul!

She flushed, her desire for him as hot as her rage.

To add insult to injury, all her old friends were avoiding her because of Connor and Connor's horrible father and Connor's politics and Connor's obvious boredom with the people who mattered!

Unable to bear the silence, she reached for the telephone and poured it all out to Letty Pemberton.

"I've been warning you that people wouldn't stand for it indefinitely, Sondra," Letty declared with more self-righteousness than sympathy. "Lester warned you too. Guthrie Torrance is half crazy, trying to get your husband off his board. And it might get worse. If this Depression goes on, there's bound to be a Republican president in

1940, probably Rhys Brandon, and then you'll *really* be out on your derrière."

"What can I *do* about it?"

"Divorce him and come back to the fold. Lester will figure out what to do about the papers after that."

"*Divorce* Connor?"

"You have that Tirzah Kent bitch as grounds. I must say, Sondra, that at your age it's ludicrous to be so lovestruck. Husbands are only escorts after the honeymoon's over. And you're well preserved. We'll soon find you someone else to marry."

"I want Connor!" Sondra wailed.

Letty clucked with patronizing impatience. "He may be the best lover you've ever had, but be reasonable, darling. You don't spend all your life in bed."

"What would you know about it, sleeping with that poor excuse for a man you married?" Sondra hung up.

"I won't let him go," she muttered to herself. "I'll just be patient until he's had his fill of his floozie and then he'll come back home. Men always do."

She snatched at the telephone when it rang again, eager to vent more wrath on Letty, and heard Enoch's voice asking for Connor.

"He's out," she said curtly.

"And a good morning to you too," Enoch replied.

"Is there anything else?"

"Yes. I'd like to know why you hate the sight of me."

"Because you're a Communist boor and a bad influence on Connor."

He grunted. "Then you don't know your husband at all, little lady. No one has any influence on Connor."

Again Sondra slammed down the receiver and went to examine herself in the three-way mirror on her dressing table. She was past fifty and Connor never seemed to age at all.

Nothing to do with how old she was! Like hell!

On the all too infrequent occasions lately when he did come to her bedroom, she never let him see her naked until she was lying down; she was afraid that he would notice the slackening of her breasts and thighs, the suspiciously dark pubic hair she had dyed as regularly as the hair on her head. She hated Sands Point in the summer because he liked to make love in the woods, in the glare of a merciless sun that revealed every wrinkle and blotch on her skin.

But she wanted him! God, how she wanted him.

She had always had her way until she met him. She cursed that day now. She cursed everything and everybody. Most of all, she cursed Connor.

She grabbed her manicure scissors and began to shred a handkerchief. The metal points of the scissors screeched as she drew them across the glass top of the dressing table, like fingernails on slate.

"Damn you, Arthur!" she shouted. "You promised you'd always take care of your little girl!"

◆

"Was that his missus on the phone?" Neeley Mack asked.

Enoch nodded. "Hates me like the plagues of Egypt."

"You got no love for her neither."

"I tell you, Neeley, she's a nasty piece of work, for all her fancy ways."

"Yeah, she ain't like them society wimmin who're always after you to fuck 'em."

Enoch laughed. "They think I'm an old bull elephant. One of them said the rumor is I have one ball of coal, the other of steel, and a cock as big as the Empire State Building."

Neeley guffawed, but Enoch's smile had already faded. "That Sondra's out to gobble his soul."

"He married her to get them papers, din he?"

"Hell, she went for him ass over teakettle. He could have had her *and* the papers without a wedding. But he was looking for something. He was almost happy for a while there. It wasn't what you'd call the grand passion, but he liked having her around." Enoch shook his head. "Until he found out what she's like."

Enoch squinted at Neely. "Brandon's spies still trailing him?"

"Yeah, but he ain't done nothin' terrible."

"He still goes to California to see that singer, doesn't he?"

"Yeah, but that's old news."

"Just keep an eye on him," Enoch said. He looked at his pocket watch and hoisted his large body from its chair. "Time for me to go," he said, and went, curiously light on his feet for a man of his height and breadth.

Like his son, he had become a political force to be reckoned with, a doughty leader of labor's ranks. Two years earlier he had supported John L. Lewis's new Committee for Industrial Organizations to unionize mass-production workers along industrial lines rather than by trades, a daring innovation.

Through last winter and this spring, he had helped to captain a half million men in sitdown strikes, strikes that led to bloody battles in the streets and ended in a defeat for labor, not only in "little steel" but in the southern textile mills, to Rhys Brandon's infinite satisfaction.

"Not only has that hooligan failed to organize the southern mills," Rhys announced gleefully to the press, "he's had to accept a wage reduction!"

Enoch had been forced to beat a temporary retreat in the field, but the fight for a wages-and-hours law went on in the Congress, and he was on his way to the Senate debate today. Connor would be there, but Enoch never approached his son in public and refused to discuss him with the press.

"He goes his way, I go mine," he maintained gruffly when Paul Gilbert, the reporter who had trailed after Connor ever since the veterans' riot at the Anacostia flats, questioned him.

But he would have given a lot to have Connor confide in him as he had done in the car bearing them both away from Dilys's funeral and the one woman Connor loved. Enoch would have given anything to make up for the misery he had caused by making one impetuous decision when he was too young to see the long-term consequences of his act. None of it would have happened if he hadn't left his wife and son to fend for themselves.

"The sins of the fathers," he sighed morosely in the back of his chauffeured black sedan, and his heavy brows deepened the shadows in his dark eyes.

♦

Jack Dickinson, as pink-cheeked as the day Connor had first met him in Boston, but much stouter, accepted a drink and a cigar when he arrived at the penthouse late the next night. He crouched on the edge of his chair while he talked. He was buying arms for the Loyalists in Spain and he needed help.

"I had a hard time tracking you down," he told Connor. "Thanks for calling me back."

"Jack, I haven't been in the arms trade for years."

"I know that. I didn't come for guns," Dickinson said, studying his drink. "I came for money."

"I see."

Dickinson flushed. "Honest to God, Connor, I'm not making a penny on this deal. I've given them all I could raise, or I wouldn't be here."

"It isn't the money," Connor said. "Do you know what the penalty is for shipping arms to Spain? A ten-thousand-dollar fine and five years in prison."

"Sure, I know. I read your papers. And I'd rather not get myself arrested either. But you won't have anything to do with the merchandise." Dickinson drained his glass. "Look, have I ever bothered you since you got out of the business? Have I ever shot off my mouth that I even knew you? No one'd ever hear about this."

Connor got up to refill the glasses. "I trust you, Jack. But I'm curious. Didn't you always tell me you were your only charity?"

Dickinson nodded. "Until I went over there and saw for myself."

"You've been to Spain?" Connor spun around, fascinated.

"Yeah, south from Paris and over the Pyrenees. It's a

rotten deal, Connor. I never gave a shit which side I supplied, but this time it's different. It's not a Communist war, like they try to make it out. The Russians are sending these poor bastards propaganda and blankets instead of guns, while Franco's got the krauts and the eye-ties on his side, practicing aerial bombing for the main event." He gestured with his beefy arm. "C'mon, Connor, you don't think Hitler rearmed to hold parades, do you? He's already making eyes at Austria and the Czechs."

Connor agreed. Germany was clearly gearing up for another war, just as Hitler had promised in *Mein Kampf*. Hitler had said he would bring France to her knees and then England, establish German hegemony over all of Europe, and colonize the "inferior" Slavic peoples. He was preparing to do just that.

Connor had cut back on his investments in Germany in 1935, when the anti-Semitic Nuremberg Laws were announced, but his partners at TD&D, along with a large sector of American investors, had not. The time was not far away, Connor believed, when a stand would have to be made, either for or against Hitler, by countries, governments, and, ultimately, individuals.

"You'll make a fortune in military aircraft if there's a war," Dickinson was saying. "And that guy you hate will make another one."

"Who?"

"The senator. Brandon. The owner of Crabtree."

"Wait a minute, Jack! Are you sure of that?"

"Sure I'm sure. I bought stuff off that company for years, through a guy named Ed Trask. No one talks about it, but some of the dealers know it's Brandon's company."

"I can't believe no one's ever gone public with it!"

"Hell, they ain't gonna dry up a prime source by tellin'. I still get the best prices from Crabtree."

"Did Brandon own the company when that cancellation nearly got me killed?"

Dickinson nodded.

Connor thought furiously, remembering Ed Trask and his nervous, unconvincing excuses for reneging on the delivery . . . feeling the point of a knife and a trickle of blood down his neck on a Baltimore pier.

"Christ!" he said. "The bastard wanted to get me murdered."

"I thought that was why you hated his guts like you do."

"My God," Connor said softly. He was motionless for several moments before he realized that Jack was waiting, his pale-lashed eyes fixed on Connor's face.

"All right, Jack, I'll give you the money, but cash-and-carry only and no mention of me in your little black book."

A broad smile creased Dickinson's face. "Hot dog! I knew I could count on you, Connor."

"Wait here a minute."

He went to the wall safe in the bedroom, withdrew almost everything he had in it, and came back to Jack. "Here," he said. "This should help."

"Jeez, Connor," Dickinson said, his eyes widening when he saw how much there was. "Thanks."

"Just keep it under your hat."

"Wild horses," Dickinson said, making a cross over his heart.

"Don't get yourself killed," Connor said, accompanying him to the door.

Dickinson shook his head. "I can't go over there and fight," he said mournfully. "They want me to do this here stuff." He brightened. "But you could go. They need fliers."

"If you need more money," Connor said, scribbling something on a card before Jack waddled into the elevator, "call Barney Abbott at this number. I move around a lot, but he can always find me."

When he was alone, he began to pace, pounding his right fist into the palm of his left hand. For some reason the extent of Rhys's hatred shocked him. Rhys had actually put Connor's life in jeopardy! What would Rhys do to punish Georgia?

Connor had just been handed priceless information—the great pacifist was a munitions maker!—but how could he use it to its best advantage? Timing was everything in politics. Released too long before the election, it would be stale news in 1940, explained away by Rhys if there was a war in Europe.

Not if. When.

Did everything, even Adolf Hitler, redound to Rhys's advantage?

Jack was right. When war came, Rhys would make another stupendous fortune. Everyone would, Connor and Racey included, in everything from war material to comic books. Connor was convinced the market was headed for another break; if the shaky economy collapsed again, the Neutrality Act arms embargo would go by the boards overnight: America would reopen its factories and put its people back to work making weapons for both sides.

Or would Rhys, that supreme dictator of other people's lives, urge Congress to support only his fellow Fascists? If Rhys won the presidency, would the Congress listen to him?

Connor had to know more about Crabtree without appearing to look. He called Barney Abbott.

"You're kidding!" Barney said, shocked out of his sleep by what Connor told him.

"No. He'll never get into the White House now."

"Stalin would have a better chance."

"Put some good people on it right away. Start in Europe; he goes there too often, even for a fond father."

As soon as he put down the telephone, Connor's mind shifted, in the silence of the penthouse, from the political to the personal, to Rhys as a jealous father who tyrannized his children, and he put his head back against the chair cushion, in the grip of the same frustrated rage that had darkened his life since adolescence. Hamlet was right. A man could smile and smile and be a villain.

He was in a position to ruin Rhys at last, but would he do it now that there was Georgia to consider?

Georgia.

Memory and anticipation suffused him, obliterating everything else. What an extraordinary woman she was! She was not embittered from having lived in her own hell; it had made her forgive him his.

He walked into his bedroom and stood looking at the bed where they had made love. *That* was love, that exquisite blend of passion and tenderness he had felt for the first time last night, that hunger to possess and yet to protect, to give more than he took. The few hours until he was with her again would be achingly empty. He wanted to look up and see her. He wanted to watch her walk across the room. He missed the sound of her voice.

He turned to the painting, feeling a communion with it both sensual and sublime. He had dealers hunting for the five other Breen canvases called "Woman" that Georgia had told him about. He wanted them for himself as he wanted her, as somehow, someday, he must have her.

He put out the lamp and lay down in the dark, gazing at the spotlighted painting, intoxicated by the remembered touch of her. He knew every detail of that body now, but a thousand times, in his mind, he had lifted her down from its frame and held her as he had held her last night, in that rhapsody of desire and consummation, his dream and reality become one. Last night Georgia had cast an ineffable spell upon his body as, long ago, she had left an indelible mark upon his soul.

38

♦

Tony, drowsing after a late night, reached for Georgia and encountered only empty space. He came fully awake and contemplated the space and the fact of his rampant penis. His wife—his famous, elegant, successful wife—had not shared his bed for years.

He bathed and dressed and knocked at her door. Peggy, starched and silent, let him in with her usual air of disapproval, which, if anything, became even haughtier during these interminable stays with Georgia's family—in Rhys Brandon's house, no less.

"Thank you, Peggy," Georgia said. "I can finish." The maid withdrew.

Georgia was at her dressing table, putting on pearl earrings. She wore a black crepe dress and a triple strand of priceless pearls. Her hair was pulled into a chignon under a white fedora.

Bon Dieu, he thought, what a gorgeous woman she is! Georgia had never been a *cool* blond.

"You're dressed already," he said, for something to say. "Where are you going?"

"I'm taking Gianna to hear my father speak in the Senate, remember?"

"Ah, yes, of course," he said. "You look very beautiful."

She made no reply, putting some subtle finishing touches to her maquillage. She was like a ripe peach, more seductive now than she had ever been. It was unjust that he should be denied his own wife!

"Georgia," he burst out, "this situation is ridiculous! We can't go on this way."

"What way?"

She always made it difficult for him!

"You know perfectly well what I mean," he said. He waited, but there was no reply. "What do you expect me to do if you won't sleep with me?"

She raised an eyebrow. "The same thing you did when I *was* sleeping with you."

He regarded her, apparently at a loss. Then he said, as confidingly as a small child, "You never bored me."

"Then what were your other women in aid of?"

"I don't know," he said with an air of wonder. "I never really thought about it. Having a mistress is the done thing."

She sighed. It was as difficult to hate him as to love him. "I'm delighted to know I never bored you."

"A man can change, Georgia! Let me prove it!"

"Your mistresses mean nothing to you?"

"Less than nothing!" he asserted, taking heart from her apparent appreciation of the position.

"Then you debase them as well as yourself." She turned to dab Arpège on her wrists and behind her ears. "I won't allow you to debase me."

He bristled. "That's no way to speak to your husband! Whenever we come to this house you behave like a fishwife."

"We come to give Gianna a sense of family—and so you can hatch political plots at the embassy. You won't have to endure it for too long." She looked in the mirror and dabbed her perfect nose with a small puff. "Unless there's a war."

He brushed that aside. "We come because you still worship your father, with all his vices."

"Tell me, Tony, do you think Gianna will drop *you* when she discovers *your* vices?"

"By God, this *is* your father's doing! He'd like nothing better than to see us divorce, but I warn you, Georgia, I will never agree to that."

"Oh, spare me, Tony!" she said hotly, her vehemence startling him. Lately she was apt to explode when he least expected it. She had also acquired the unfortunate habit of saying precisely what she thought.

"I've lived with you all these years for Gianna's sake!" she went on. "But I won't prostitute myself by going to bed with you, not even for her." Then she turned away and picked up her bag and gloves. "I'll be late," she said, under control again.

He was always more jealous when they were in America. At heart she was still a Yankee, with a Yankee's admiration for the kind of men crossbreeding produced, apparently virile but not in the least *raffinés*. By all reports they were like the Italians: rabbits in bed.

"How late?" he asked.

"Late. I have a dinner engagement. Miss Giles will bring Gianna back from the Senate in time for tea. Lean

on the French commercial attaché today, Tony. The boy-
cott on Japanese silk has to mean more business for us,
and we need it."

When she had gone, he sat down at her dressing table,
touching her hairbrush and her crystal scent bottles. He
picked up a linen handkerchief and held it to his lips,
wondering what he was going to do.

He had been building another profession for himself.
Several years ago he had joined Croix de Feu, a decidedly
fascist paramilitary organization dedicated to preserving
France from Socialists, Communists, and others of their
ilk, by which was meant the lower orders. Leaving Croix
de Feu before it was banned, he eventually joined its
successor, Colonel de la Rocque's Parti Social Français.
His friends were all affiliated with right-wing movements,
in which Tony had become a person of consequence,
although, for the moment, discretion was essential.

The Parti Social Français, while giving lip service to *la
gloire et l'honneur,* was nevertheless not prepared to let
France be bled dry in another war, regardless of mutual
assistance pacts with the British.

His wife, a political infant, thought that was contemptible.

"It's a matter of survival," Tony insisted. "Let the British offer up another generation of young men to be slaughtered. We can't afford to. Do you know how many
Frenchwomen never married because all the young men
were dead? Do you know that France is one of the most
underpopulated countries in Europe because so many were
killed? Do you know what we have lost in property and
productivity? If it comes to war, we will make some honorable arrangement with Hitler."

"How can you make an honorable arrangement with the
devil? I thought you detested the Germans."

"I detest the Communists more. And Hitler is anti-
Communist."

"And rabidly anti-Semitic too. Anti everything that isn't
pure Aryan and perfect except, of course, for that little
monster, Goebbels. The Nazis make me sick. Look, Tony,

I'll be hostess to your fascist friends, but don't expect me to share their opinions—or yours."

But whatever Tony's new prominence, it had not protected him from a catastrophe far worse, he considered, than the German occupation of Austria two months earlier. He had realized he was in love with his wife! He was as ridiculous as that provincial clod in *Madame Bovary*. Tony knew Georgia had lovers—any man would have known it just by looking at her—and for the first time in his life he was unbearably jealous. Of his wife, *grand Dieu*, of his own wife!

He sighed and got up to follow her downstairs.

♦

From the stairway Georgia heard Gianna and her cousins asking questions and Rhys patiently answering them. She smiled, feeling a burst of love for her child, only eleven but already so confident. Georgianna would have been proud of her.

Gianna adored Rhys, as did all his grandchildren: Will's two, Richard's two, and Jillian's Peter. It was said that a man couldn't be all bad if children loved him. Maybe so, but Georgia knew too much about her father's duplicity, and last year she had learned from Connor about his political hypocrisy in the matter of Crabtree.

She felt a quickening inside her when she thought of Connor. She would be in Connor's arms again in just a few hours, in the house he had bought for them in Alexandria.

She *loved* him. It was a pale description of how she felt, but she could find no other words. To watch him, to hear him speak, to simply *be* in the same space with him made her heart sing.

He gave her what neither Samson Breen nor Tony ever could. It was love fulfilled with nothing held back, a far headier wine than fantasy and so much more than sex.

She could not bear to be apart from him too long. After a month or two she would find some reason to come to America, almost always bringing Gianna, almost always accompanied by Tony. It was increasingly difficult to behave, for Gianna's sake, with her customary serenity, but she managed to put it on now like a cloak before she walked into the small drawing room.

"Good morning," she said, blowing a kiss to the children.

Gianna, dressed, on this spring day, in primrose yellow voile with a matching bow in her dark, curly hair, leaned against Rhys's chair, with solemn Peter Cassadyne, her favorite cousin, at her side. Will's little girl and Richard's daughter were whispering in a corner, and the other two boys sat cross-legged on the carpet playing cat's cradle.

Constance stood near the open French windows, dressed and hatted for the Senate, looking out at the garden and smoking a cigarette in a long ivory holder. She turned her head slightly by way of greeting.

Rhys watched Georgia move across the room, unsettled as always by the sight of her luscious beauty. She walked like a goddess. It was impossible not to worship her, although she rarely spoke to him and never smiled except when they were being photographed together, an invariable boost for his career and her silk mills.

My glorious darling, he thought. Someday you'll realize what I did for you and be grateful to me.

"This child is as bright as a new penny," he said, trying and failing to catch Georgia's eye. "It's in the blood." He turned back to his granddaughter. "You must be very quiet in the Senate today and listen to what I say so we can discuss it afterward. Now go to Miss Giles and put on your hat. It's almost time to leave." He kissed Gianna's cheek.

"Come on, Peter," Gianna said to her cousin, but he shook his head and moved closer to Rhys in a bid for his attention that reminded Georgia of Jillian.

Gianna, her tilted de Sevignac eyes shining with excitement, shrugged at his refusal, called a vague good-bye to Constance, who never answered to any form of "Grandmother," and stopped to give her father a resounding kiss and a hug as he appeared. The others acknowledged Tony's arrival with more restraint.

"Everyone will talk about *this* speech," Constance said.

"I devoutly hope so," Rhys replied, smoothing his silver-gilt hair. Barring some unforeseen catastrophe before the 1940 elections, Rhys had an excellent chance at the nomination and the presidency. The market collapse of late 1937 had been faster and more brutal than the Crash of '29, with all the gains so hard won since 1935 wiped out and starvation once more threatening millions.

If the New Deal can't cure the Depression, people were beginning to mutter, let the Republicans try!

"It's Connor who worries me," Constance went on, her rancor not lost on Rhys and Georgia, who glanced briefly in each other's direction. "Don't pretend he isn't making trouble for us." She looked at Georgia. "Your hero has turned out to be a menace," she charged with acid reproach.

"I'm not responsible for what Connor does," Georgia said impassively.

"Who is?" Rhys said. "Except, possibly, the Overholt woman."

"That marriage is a farce," Constance snapped. "A matter of convenience."

Tony had followed the exchange with delight, all the while observing his wife out of the corner of his eye. The childhood ties between Georgia and Connor MacKenzie were part of Brandon tribal lore, but he had never seen her display any interest in the handsome brute. Tony, who knew Connor only through press coverage of him, found him *sympathique* because he ridiculed Rhys. But MacKenzie was, after all, a servant's son and far beneath Georgia's notice.

"Convenience is a practical basis for marriage," Tony said, adding pointedly, "It's a great risk to marry for love."

"Some women do," Constance said derisively. "To their infinite sorrow."

"That doesn't apply to you, my dear," Rhys told his wife ambiguously.

"Not at all!" Tony smiled. "You're a devoted couple."

"Devoted to the presidency!" Constance said.

Rhys, unflappable, unfolded his tall body. "I must go," he said. "Georgia?"

"I'll take my own car." She collected Gianna and her governess in the hall, and went out, counting the hours now.

◆

She arrived at the house in Alexandria before he did and let herself in. There were vases of fresh flowers everywhere and she smiled when she saw the dining room table. It had been set with candles and a bowl of yellow roses, Royal Doulton china, and Waterford crystal. He loved beautiful things.

"You're an incurable romantic, my darling," she said, smiling to herself. "Like me."

The house, where he often came alone when she was in France, reminded her of Connor. It had unexpected corners. It was not exactly severe, but it had no superfluous ornament, nor did *he* require any.

She stopped at the new phonograph, one of the latest models produced by Clarion Electronics. Connor was very proud of it. It changed several records automatically, so he could sit in the dark and listen for hours.

He's alone too much, she thought. I ought to be here with him.

There were books everywhere, and she leafed through a few, reading the notes he had penciled in the margins. He never stopped studying, and his business trips to Europe had kept his languages fluent. Several issues of German newspapers were on the table near his oversized chair, and she could imagine his grave expression when he read them.

Hitler angered him. Anyone did, whose purpose was to control others. It was one of the many traits they shared.

"He's a dangerous man," Connor fumed. "And all that interests this country is the Lambeth Walk and who's going to play Scarlett O'Hara!"

"The things you've been involved in," she told him, marveling at it, "have nothing to do with your contemplative side. Mercenaries and guns, planes and radios and newspapers! You'd have made a wonderful teacher, as Malcolm has."

"I'd like to see him again."

"He'd like to see you too. Arrange it, why don't you, the next time you're in England."

"He knows about us?"

"He's always known, even as a boy."

Connor had reached out to touch her cheek. "You love him very much, don't you?"

"I adore him. I want him to be happy. He loves teaching in England—he's always been an Anglophile—and he seems to have found some serenity at last."

Now she sighed. There was very little serenity in Connor, except when they were alone together. Even though he swore that political differences were behind his fight with her father now, she was sure a part of Connor was still bent on retribution.

He loved her, she knew that, but he relished her all the more because she was Rhys's daughter.

She was not surprised to learn how much Brandon Textiles stock Connor had accumulated over the years under various names. She had refused his offer to turn everything over to her.

"Connor, I'd sell my stock on the open market if the family were free to. I want no more to do with running Brandon Textiles than Malcolm does. It's the Sevignac mills that interest me."

"Rhys must hate knowing that."

Rhys. It was always Rhys.

Then she shook her head, refusing to let that endless struggle blight this evening.

Or her worry over how long Connor could wait for her and she for him.

Feeling dusty, she went through to the bedroom, undressed, and got into the shower. The warm water poured through her hair and caressed her skin like sable. She smoothed the cake of lavender soap over her body, taking sensuous pleasure in the creamy lather, imagining it was

Connor's touch all over her. Aroused, she let the water sluice over her, luxuriating, anticipating.

She didn't hear Connor come in and undress. When he got into the shower with her she laughed with pure pleasure and put her arms around him. She kissed him, tasting him and the water, feeling him and the heat.

"Here," she said, taking the soap. "Let me." Her hands moved over his body slowly, expertly, thoroughly.

"Georgia," he whispered when she had finished and the lather was in bubbles at their feet. "I want you so much."

"Have me then."

He slid his hands under her and lifted her. Her arms and legs went around him, taking him in, while the water flooded over them and their sounds of passion echoed. They were deep in their own Eden, bathed in bliss.

◆

He toweled her dry and wrapped her hair in a terry-cloth turban before they sat down to supper in their robes.

"I found another Breen last week," he said.

"Which one?"

"You're brushing your hair."

"Ah, yes. That's one of the best."

"That leaves two still at large."

"That apartment looks like a gallery."

"Those paintings are all I have when you're away. I imagine I'm talking to you, touching you, even turning your head so I can see your face." His dark eyes roved over her face. "I've come to feel very close to Breen because of those paintings. If anyone else but me had to know you so well, I'm glad it was an artist of his caliber."

There were tears in her eyes. "I love you, Connor, for the way you are. You're the best man I ever knew, the only one I want."

She went to sit on his lap, her cheek pressed to his.

"Marry me," he said.

"Oh, darling, it's what I want, too, you know that, but we must wait a little longer. I wish Gianna hated her father, or was indifferent to him, but she isn't. She adores him."

"Then let me come to Lyons to see you. These long separations drive me mad."

"No!" She sat up and held his face between her hands. "Lyons is a small town and Tony is going to make a lot of trouble as it is. I can't give him any grounds for taking my baby away from me. Connor, promise me you'll stay away from Lyons!"

"All right, darling. I promise." He rocked her against him, soothing her. "I wonder where we'll live when we're married."

"Brandon's Gate?"

They looked at each other.

"If it's what you want," he said, "I'll get it for you."

♦

It was almost midnight when Constance, deep in Daphne du Maurier's *Rebecca*, heard the butler tap on Rhys's door and then Rhys's sleepy response. She put the book down.

"Telephone, Senator," the butler said. The bedroom telephones were turned off at night. "It's Mr. Reedy. He says it's urgent."

With a talent born of long practice, Constance lifted the receiver, holding the cradle down until a few seconds had elapsed.

". . . just had a call," Ed Reedy was saying when she eased it up.

"Yes?"

"Pay dirt! One of MacKenzie's regular callers, here and in New York, turns out to be Jack Dickinson, a known gunrunner who also recruits volunteers for Spain!"

"Then we've got him!" Rhys said, fully awake.

"Almost. Next time we'll pick up Dickinson right outside the door with the money in his pocket. Even that's only circumstantial, but it's all we'll need in the court of public opinion."

"Then why all this urgency?"

Reedy cleared his throat. "The detective identified another regular visitor too."

"Who is it?"

"Now, don't get your bowels in an uproar, Rhys," Reedy said.

"I will if you don't get on with it! It's the middle of the goddamn night!"

"Your daughter," Reedy said.

Constance gasped, and pressed her hand tightly over the mouthpiece.

"Which one?" Rhys demanded, a glimmer of desperate hope in his voice.

"Georgia," Reedy said.

Constance clutched her midriff as if she were in pain.

"There's some mistake," Rhys said.

"I'm afraid not. I thought I'd better tell you."

"Why would Georgia go to see him?" Rhys asked blankly.

"Come on, Rhys! The usual reason. They're lovers."

"Don't say it!" Rhys gasped. "I'll kill him for this."

"Well, I know how you feel, Rhys, but the rest of us have better ways and other reasons for getting rid of him. He's starting to make a fool of you, in case you hadn't noticed!"

"Reedy, you're an old friend. Don't tell the others about her."

"Well, of course not," Reedy said. "It has no bearing. I'll see you tomorrow."

"God in heaven!" Rhys said, and hung up.

Constance replaced the receiver and sat staring at the door as if it were a movie screen. Georgia in bed with Connor. Georgia held by him, touched, tasted, entered, made to shudder in one exquisite climax after another.

Constance, breathing rapidly, twisted a lock of her hair and bit her lower lip in absolute fury. She had always suspected it! There had been something between those two from the time they were children, when Connor used to glare at Constance with those fierce black eyes of his! He had probably had Georgia at Brandon's Gate when he was still a boy and the maids were swooning over him.

Sensual. People had whispered it of Georgia, too, from her earliest adolescence. With good reason!

But did Connor love her? No, Constance decided, Connor was incapable of loving anyone. He was doing this for the same reason he had seduced Constance: to get even with Rhys. Georgia must be told the facts of life, including every detail of Constance's affair with Connor.

She threw the book across the room, breaking its spine against the door, wishing it were that easy to deal with him.

But right now she had to keep Rhys from doing something stupid. She snatched at her robe, pulled it on, and went quickly out of her room and into her husband's. The bedside light was still on, and he lay staring at the ceiling.

"I heard," she said, going to sit on the edge of his bed. "I listened in."

He glared at her.

"Well, what did you expect?" she demanded. "I always said he got to her when she was still a girl. Maybe he knew about Dilys. He'd have done anything to avenge his mother. People of his class worship their mothers. Nothing's changed for him since then, believe me. The question is, what are you going to do about it?"

"Finish him," Rhys said.

"It's about time! But you can't do it yourself and you can't drag *her* into it without being tarred by the same brush. You'll have to make do with his gunrunner friend. And let that pig, Reedy, release it to the press."

"You're enjoying this," he snarled. "I want to kill the bastard, and you're enjoying it!"

"Really, Rhys! He didn't rape her. She spread her legs willingly. And she'll drop him soon enough when she finds out about me."

"She knows about you. I told her at Dilys's funeral, to keep her from running off with him then."

Constance took a deep breath and blew it out sharply. "Well, I can't say much for your precious daughter's ethics."

"*Ethics?*" Rhys shouted. "*You?* Are you insane?" He motioned her away with his fist. "Don't you realize what he's done? He's seduced *my* daughter! He's violated my name and my honor. He threatened to do it years ago, when he came back from the war, and now he's done it! I'm the one he defiles every time he has her. I ought to kill him. I ought to kill them both!"

"Yes, but that's not the way to get into the White House." She stood to fire her parting shot. "Look here, Rhys, you can mourn about Georgia all you like, but you'll get no sympathy from me. After all, the apple hasn't rolled far from the tree. You both adored Connor from the start, and neither of you is a model of fidelity. So stop whining and get on with it."

She left him and he lay motionless, jealousy burning like acid, deep in his vitals. His adored child, Georgianna's child, debased! She had betrayed him, her own father, to become Connor's mistress. For how long, he wondered. Constance said since Brandon's Gate. He covered his face and groaned at the thought.

Finally he reached for a bottle of sleeping pills on the night table, poured water from a carafe, and swallowed two tablets. He put out the light and presently he slept, but toward morning he was plagued by dreams of Connor making love to Georgia at Brandon's Gate. No! It was Georgianna in the bed, his frigid wife, consumed with lust for the dark-haired youth as she had never been for Rhys.

In his dream Rhys advanced on the rutting couple in the bed, bent on murder, and knew that the woman was Georgia after all, and the man with her was himself.

He awoke with a start, drenched with sweat. It was seven o'clock, but he could not get back to sleep. Finally he rang for his valet to draw a bath. He wanted to be out of the house before Constance was up. As for Georgia, he could not bring himself to look at her, knowing this. It was fortunate that she avoided him now.

◆

A little after midnight Connor let himself into the house in Georgetown, half of him still with Georgia, the other half panicked by yet another parting as her long visit came to an end. They were to meet in two days, but he was always afraid he would never see her again.

He climbed the stairs to his bedroom, undressed, and put on a robe. He was fixing a whiskey and water at the small bar in the bookcase when Sondra opened the door.

"I thought you were in New York," he said.

"I was, but this is where I belong," she said in a tight, dry little voice. "I'm your wife, in case you'd forgotten."

"For God's sake, Sondra," he sighed. "I'd rather not argue it tonight."

"I don't care *what* you'd rather," she said furiously. "I've put up with your insults long enough."

"Insults?"

"You come and go like a boarder. You hardly look at me. You haven't made love to me for a year! Yes, I call that insulting. I'm your wife, and you promised to love *me*, not some slut who poses naked!"

He looked at her in shock.

"Oh, yes, I found out about your love nest, and today I got inside and saw your pornographic pictures. You're obscene!"

He was shaken by the idea that she had penetrated his privacy. His hands grasped the bookshelves, his knuckles white. "Sondra, I asked you months ago . . ."

"To divorce you, I remember. But until then we had a marriage. Now all we have is your nasty little affair with that tart, whoever she is."

"Oh, come off it, Sondra," he said impatiently. "You said you didn't care what I did. You wouldn't let me tell you about her. In my book that's acceptance."

"All *right*! I've been a fool to let it go on like this, but I thought it would pass. And it must, before someone finds out about it! I won't have everyone laughing at me, whispering that I couldn't hold you. Unless we live as husband and wife again, I *will* get a divorce."

He was very still. "On what grounds?" he asked.

"You want to protect her, don't you? God, how I hate you!" she screamed suddenly. "You never wanted me, you wanted Arthur's papers. And I gave them to you." She broke off with a little sob, then mastered herself and once more regarded him stonily. "But I can take them away from you, and if we divorce, I will."

He gazed at her, wondering how it was that one woman could share his soul and the other merely furnish his life.

"I'm sorry, Sondra," he said softly. "I thought we understood each other. I didn't set out to hurt you, believe me, but she—"

"I don't want to hear about her!" she shrieked, putting her hands over her ears.

"Don't be a child!"

She shook her head violently. "I don't want to know! I don't need to know, or anyone else either. I'm going to charge you with fraud."

"Fraud?"

"You married me under false pretenses. I wouldn't have sold you those papers if I'd known you were going to destroy Arthur's lifework and profane his memory and alienate me from my friends and everything I was brought up to believe."

She took a deep breath, expecting him to concede, to beg her not to take his precious papers away from him. When he said nothing, her body seemed to cave in. Then another expression crossed her face and she moved swiftly to where he stood.

For a moment he thought she was going to strike him, but she reached up and kissed his mouth avidly, with little grunts of passion.

"Show me what she does in bed that I don't do," she said in a strangled voice. "Come on, show me!"

"Sondra, stop it." He pulled away and held her at arm's length. "It isn't as simplistic as that. Believe me, I don't regret the years I've spent with you. I owe you a great deal. Can't we part friends?"

"I don't want your gratitude. I want *you*." She gave a little sigh. "But if you really want us to part friends, then make love to me, just once more, for old time's sake."

"Sondra," he began, talking softly, affectionately, trying to calm her if he could; but she tore at the straps of her gown and when it fell around her feet she pushed his robe open and reached to fondle him, cupping his testicles, gripping his penis.

For the first time in his life he was unresponsive to an ardent woman.

She looked up at him, horror congealing on her face. With a strangled cry she reached for her gown, wrapped it around her, and fled, slamming the door behind her.

Her hands shaking, she found Lester Pemberton's number and gave it to the operator. The Pembertons' butler, accustomed to hysterical calls at all hours from Mr. Pemberton's nervous clients, roused him.

"Sondra, what the hell ails you?" Lester demanded grumpily. "I was fast asleep!"

"Do it, Lester," she almost screamed into the telephone.

"Calm down, Sondra. Do what?"

"Get me a divorce!" She drew a ragged breath. "Use fraud. Use anything but adultery. But get me a divorce and get back control of those papers."

"With pleasure," Pemberton said.

39

♦

Guthrie Torrance, avoiding Connor's eyes, slid the letter of resignation across his desk.

"Under the circumstances," he said, "we have no choice, whatever my personal regret."

"You're such a bad actor, Guthrie," Connor said, signing it. "You could have asked for this years ago, when I first started to affront your conservative sensibilities."

But of course Guthrie had preferred to wait until Con-

nor was under investigation by the House Committee on
Un-American Activities for giving aid to Spain and by the
Justice Department for possible violation of the Neutrality
Laws, not to mention his involvement in a highly publi-
cized divorce.

"Fight for your papers, Connor," Georgia told him before she sailed for France again in October. "You've worked
too hard to give them up."

"I'd gladly give them up if only you'd stay here, where
it's safe. Georgia, think! There's going to be a war. The
Munich Pact is only a way to give the Allies time to
prepare. Hitler's in the Sudetenland already. Czechoslo-
vakia is next and France isn't far down on his list of
conquests."

"Tony doesn't think France will fight. And Gianna's
with Tony. I'm going over to bring her back as soon as I
can."

"Thank God! But let me come with you and we'll bring
her back together."

She shook her head. "That's not the way to deal with
Tony. You'll have to trust this part of it to me."

"How long?"

But she had no way of knowing, and he was alone in the
penthouse on the day she sailed, feeling as if his life were
ebbing away with the tide that took her out.

♦

The *Normandie* was bustling with passengers and visitors
and the gaiety of a sailing. A crowd of people spilled over
from the living room of the de Sevignac suite on the
Promenade Deck and into its private dining room, where
the bar was set up. The heady scent of flowers blended
with hot canapes and the women's perfumes. Flashbulbs
from a dozen cameras popped along with the champagne
corks, and laughter rose and fell.

There was reason to rejoice.

"If Brandon's letting the marquise go back to France,"
Senator Charles assured a roomful of guests, "it's proof
there'll be no war in Europe. There'll be 'peace in our

time,' just as Prime Minister Chamberlain promised after Munich."

"Some people called it appeasement, Senator." It was Paul Gilbert, pencil and pad in hand, his assistant now charged with the camera.

"Some people are warmongers," Charles replied. "We need a president who isn't."

"And a vice president who agrees with him?" Gilbert prodded.

Charles looked coy and the people around him laughed. Brandon and Charles! What a ticket that would make!

But, while it had nothing to do with America, Hitler's madness had stretched its tentacles across the Atlantic. Some people were saying already that if Europe went to war, America would be pulled in, too, just like the last time.

But not the people gathered here today. They were politicians and clergymen, industrialists and bankers and society people, all of them publicly pacifist and isolationist. They had a keen instinct for winners and they wanted to be seen with the next president and his family. They buzzed eagerly about Connor MacKenzie's fascinating legal problems, but Senator Brandon had refused any questions from reporters, remarking only that he was not at all surprised at the turn things had taken.

"I may comment later, but this is a family occasion," Rhys said with one of his winning smiles.

Inside, though, he was in ferment.

He had found it difficult to look at Georgia since Ed Reedy's call, but Constance had organized this bon voyage party and insisted he attend.

"It's priceless publicity and no one has to know you can't stand the sight of each other," Constance said with a look of infinite satisfaction. "Just don't think about the other thing."

But Rhys, as he approached Georgia with the remnants of his public smile still clinging to his lips, thought he might explode because of the other thing.

"I'd like a word with you in private," he said to Georgia

and, after a moment's hesitation, she nodded and led the way through a field of reporters to one of the empty bedrooms. Her expression, when he had closed the door, was as hostile as his.

"What do you want?" she demanded. "If you've come to gloat over what's happening to Connor, you've chosen the wrong person."

"Of course! He blames me for it! That's just like him." Rhys imagined them together and avoided her eyes.

"But it *is* you. You're hiding behind Reedy and the FBI."

"It was my duty to give them the information! He broke the law!"

"So have you, in a hundred different ways, in your mills and on your plantations. Connor's honest. He doesn't preach one thing and do another."

He ignored that, his eyes probing hers. "I hope you know where your loyalties lie," he said, "even if you behave like a strumpet. Couldn't you have found a more suitable lover?"

"So you know that too," she said.

"Anyone who'd taken the trouble to have him followed could have found you out."

"I love him," she said, her voice breaking. "I always will. You must know that."

"Is that your definition of love?" he said scornfully.

"What's yours? The way you used my mother?"

"How dare you?" he said, aghast. "Your mother loved me!"

"She couldn't stand to have you touch her!"

His face flushed. "God alone knows what lies he's fed you from the servants' hall!" Rhys thundered.

"What a hypocrite you are," she said, turning to go.

He regained control of himself. "One thing more." She looked at him and he raised his arm, pointing toward the door. "There are mobs of reporters out there. I want you to make it clear you're loyal to me."

"No!" she said. "Absolutely not."

He took her arm, but she wrenched it away.

"I'm *not* loyal to you," she said icily. "And I won't pander for you."

"Because of him? He's nothing but the same grasping upstart who came between us in the first place."

"*He* didn't come between us. You did! I loved you long after Connor knew the truth about you, but all you've ever loved is your own ambition, never mine or anyone else's." Her eyes were dark with pain. "How you must have hated me, Father, when you told me about Connor and Constance. I'll never forgive you for it."

She opened the door and left him.

♦

"You're white as a sheet!" Jillian was at her side when Georgia crossed quickly to the bar and asked for a brandy. "What's going on between you and Father?"

"He wants me to show the press I'm his loyal daughter," Georgia whispered, biting off the words, "no matter what he's done to Connor."

"Then Father *is* behind it! Tim said so right away. Well? Will you do it?"

Georgia shook her head.

Concerned for her distress, Jillian plucked the brandy glass from her sister's hand and led her back into the empty bedroom. Georgia, whatever jealousy she inspired, had always been Jillian's rock. It was frightening to see her like this.

"Sit," Jillian ordered, pointing at the bed. "And drink the brandy right down."

She waited until a faint tinge of pink appeared in Georgia's pale cheeks. Then Jillian said, "You and Connor are lovers, aren't you?"

Georgia regarded her sister, a fashionable young matron who had starved her plumpness away and feasted instead on gossip, sentimental novels, and romantic movies. But Jillian was faithful to Tim, and her veiled complaints about their sexual incompatibility had stopped. It was romance Jillian craved, not the marital felicity she had, and Timothy was not a romantic man.

Connor was. He had everything a man should have, except control over his own life.

"Yes," Georgia said at length. "We are."

"How long has it been going on?"

"For over a year."

"Lord," Jillian breathed. "Does Father know?"

"He just found out. He doesn't give a damn about the Neutrality Law; you know that as well as I do. He's out to get two things: the White House and Connor's head on a plate. Mine too, now."

"You know, I asked Connor to take me to bed once," Jillian reminisced, glad to see she was diverting Georgia. "I ran into him the night of Richard's engagement party. Things didn't seem so rosy for him, either, so I suggested we share our misery. He told me there'd be too many people in bed with us and to go home and stop punishing Tim for being Tim."

"You obviously took his advice."

Jillian shrugged. "Why not? It wasn't the first time, was it? Anyway, what happens now? Are you going to marry Connor?"

"As soon as I bring Gianna to this country."

"And Tony?"

"He'll try to keep her, but he'll have a tough time doing that once I've got her in America."

Jillian sat beside her on the bed and put an arm around her. "They all want you—Connor, Tony, Father. That's what comes of being a goddess. You ought to be an ordinary female like me."

"You're not ordinary," Georgia said.

"Well, I *am* extraordinarily pregnant," Jillian agreed with a smile.

"I'm happy for you, Jilly." She did not remind her sister how adamant Jilly had once been that she'd never go through another delivery.

"Yes, although it's been fun trying for four years. I hope Peter won't mind. But just think, I can eat for two and get round as an igloo."

"When are you due?"

"Late April. Will you be back?"

"I don't know if I can arrange it by then. I'll try."

A gong sounded in the corridors to send all visitors ashore. "That's for me," Jillian said. "Good luck, Georgia."

They embraced. "I love you, Jilly," Georgia said, and Jillian said, "Me too," wondering why it was so hard for her to declare love when she could so easily convey ridicule, anger, and passion. She was sorry for her sister for the first time in her life.

♦

"For the love of heaven, Connor," Oliver Petrie pleaded, "go somewhere and let your lawyers prepare your defense. I'll give my personal pledge to the FBI that you'll return."

"That's what I've been telling him," Barney Abbott said.

"You have my vote," Racey put in. "The man thinks his empire will collapse without him. But AirShip is my province, and Barney can see to the rest."

"And I'll watch Sondra like a hawk," Enoch promised.

The four men sat in Connor's suite at the Willard, watching their host pace. Outside, the snow fell, promising a white Christmas, but there was no cheer in the atmosphere, only strain.

"I get the distinct feeling I'm expendable," Connor said.

"Don't be a horse's ass," Enoch rumbled. "But you're driving your attorneys crazy. Go to Europe, why don't you? See what's really going on."

Connor stopped his pacing. "That's an idea," he said. "I might as well earn my punishment."

"What do you mean?" Oliver asked.

"I'll go to Spain."

"Damn it, son!" Enoch exploded. "That's not where I meant."

"I'll go as an accredited member of the press," Connor said. "While I still own a press."

It was how Connor came to board the *Île de France*, with the feeling that he could not simply sit still until his cases came to trial, not while Georgia's letters held little hope of her early departure from Lyons.

In Paris he tracked down Jack Dickinson's contacts and was smuggled across the border at Perpignan and into the midst of General Franco's offensive against northern Spain and the last Republican strongholds.

"Another early bird!" a ragged, one-eyed Loyalist general sneered at him when he arrived in Barcelona. "You took your bloody time getting here!"

"Never mind that. Just give me something to fly."

"I thought you were a reporter."

"Do I look like a reporter?"

He was assigned a J-15, powered by a Wright-Cyclone engine, built in Russia under American license.

He was part of an army facing almost certain defeat, short of every conceivable necessity but spirit. From the air he looked down on a panorama of destruction, of indiscriminate bombing by the German Condor Legion's planes, whether or not a town had any strategic value or harbored any fighting men. It was a landscape of rubble, to which the Loyalist forces added each time a Stuka was shot down, or one of their own perished in an explosion of orange heat with purple at its burning human core.

On the ground Connor smelled death and ate whatever came to hand—a few times he suspected there was rat meat in the communal stewpot. The men washed it down with *grappa* laced with ether and sang marching songs and talked with crudity and reverence of women. It was better to be here, fighting Germans, until he could fight to keep his press empire and stay out of prison.

Until he could deal with Rhys.

Until he could marry Georgia.

Two months later Madrid fell and the Spanish Republic died.

A new terror has begun, Connor wired out in the first story his papers had received from him in weeks. *Franco is executing thousands of Loyalists and imprisoning thousands more. He has sworn to restore Spain's feudal, Catholic, and agrarian society and, to that end, he has closed*

Spain's borders and withdrawn from Europe while Europe inches closer to war.

If any confusion remains about the generalissimo's politics, just remember that F stands for Franco, for the Spanish 'falange,' and for fascism, no matter what its nationality.

In April, Connor, with not enough fuel to fly out of Spain, abandoned his plane south of the Pyrenees and slipped across the French border to Le Perthus with the last of the refugees, as weary, smelly, and bedraggled as they were.

He wangled his way out of the internment camp with his press credentials and went to Paris to book passage for America and the legal marathon that awaited him there. It was spring, the most glorious season of all, but he was too stunned by his experiences in Spain to notice, too preoccupied by memories of the friends he had made so quickly and as quickly lost to death or defeat.

He was painfully aware that bombs would almost certainly rain on Paris as they had on Barcelona and Madrid, on Bilbao and Durango and Guernica. The size of a city was irrelevant. What mattered was that the Germans were ready, even eager, to bomb civilians.

The sidewalk cafés were crowded and the chestnut trees ready to burst into bloom, but the government, in a different rite of spring, had strengthened France's army and lengthened work hours in its defense plants.

Unwilling to linger in Paris, forbidden by Georgia to go to Lyons, Connor crossed the Channel to England and drove to Malcolm's school in Devon.

◆

"I only *look* like him," Malcolm said, smiling his father's lazy smile as he stood in the doorway of his flat. At twenty-six, he was more like his father than ever. "Come on in, Connor."

Malcolm waved him to a chair near the grate. "Take a pew. Tea's almost ready—unless you prefer something stronger?"

"Tea's fine. You gave me a start. The last time I saw you, you were—what?—three or four years old. And now you're the spit of your father when I first set eyes on him."

Malcolm had gone into his kitchen. "I thought Georgia warned you," he called out.

"She did." He hadn't seen her for six months. He had one more day to wait.

Malcolm came back with the tea tray and a long fork. "Let it draw while I toast you a scone," he said.

It was a welcoming room, with hand-turned beams and leaded windows, furnished with large, comfortably shabby armchairs and light-faded carpets. Books filled the shelves and were piled on a large desk near the window. Spacious as it was, it seemed too small for the two very tall men who occupied it.

"I'm sorry this took so long to happen," Connor said. "Georgia was always in favor of our getting together."

"So was I, but the pater would have objected when I was too young to overrule his objections—and then I came away to England."

"And you don't care about his objections now."

"I didn't care then. It just wasn't convenient—and I didn't know where you were or what you were up to. No good, by all reports." He smiled.

Connor smiled back. "I'm about to have my day in court."

Malcolm served the scones with butter and jam. The aroma of the tea cake brought back to Connor the nursery fire, and Dilys, with a sharp, unexpected pang.

"You'll go to jail for helping to buy those guns if my father has anything to say about it," Malcolm said, pouring tea. "He's still spouting pacifism as if Spain never happened."

"I'll have to get around him."

"Rhys is not to be got round so easily," Malcolm said. "I had to come all this way to do it."

"Georgia says you're a changeling, like her."

Malcolm shook his head. "She's right, but it's worse for me. I was cursed with both his name *and* his image." His frosty smile did not reach his eyes.

"Never mind Rhys. I want to hear about you."

"Nothing spectacular to tell. I write a little, but it's never as good as what I read. Still, most of the boys understand what I'm trying to teach them and that's something. It's a good life. But not for long, I'm afraid."

Connor nodded, his expression grave.

"It's incredible," the younger man said, his demeanor changing. "Half the people in this country are blind as bats—and too long in the driver's seat. They wouldn't let us begin to prepare on any scale at all, so we still have horse cavalry to fight tanks! They're reluctant to sign a mutual assistance pact with France and the Bolsheviks. I agree, Stalin's a butcher, but Russia's the key to whether or not war comes before we're ready for it. It'll be a vicious, filthy war, and a lot of my boys will be dead before it's over. I might be dead myself, but not without a fight."

"Are you sure you want to fight? It's not all bugles and glory."

"Have you been to Germany recently?" Malcolm asked.

"Not recently. But I have business to wind up there after I've seen Georgia."

"I spent Christmas there with a few of my students. It's no place for children, I can tell you. Bristling with guns and parades and screaming propaganda. Jews forced to wear six-pointed stars, beaten and humiliated by bully boys swaggering round the streets with truncheons and swastika armbands. I don't want Hitler to bring that kind of thing here."

"Hitler swears he doesn't want war with England."

"Provided England lets him take all he wants."

"Will she?"

Malcolm shook his head. "No, not in the final event."

"Even though she betrayed the Loyalists by refusing to help them? Germany sent arms *and* the Condor Legion to help Franco."

"You're right, of course. To our eternal shame. But when Hitler goes too far, England will fight. I know this sounds ridiculous, but there's still such a thing as honor."

"It doesn't sound ridiculous. But I've heard it before."

"Yes, of course. Your lot were supposed to make the world safe for democracy—which wasn't the real reason for that war. Ironically, it *is* the reason for the one that's coming, even if no one believes that yet. Hitler wants Poland now."

"From where I sit, he's going to get it."

"I've been taking flying lessons," Malcolm said. "To judge by Spain, this will be an air war. You were clever to keep up your flying."

Connor nodded. "I shuttle between Washington, New York, and California. And I race on occasion."

"What's in California?" Malcolm smiled. "Aside from the films?"

"Airplane factories. I own several with a partner, the fellow I went to France with to join the Lafayette Escadrille."

Malcolm's green eyes studied him. "Do you make passenger or military craft?"

"Passenger, but converting to war planes is simple enough."

"War planes for sale to whom?"

"Not to Germany."

"Why not?" Malcolm raised a skeptical brow.

"I know this sounds ridiculous," Connor said, "but there's such a thing as honor."

Malcolm laughed. "I'm glad I like you, Connor."

"So am I."

"Georgia loves you," Malcolm said.

Connor stood up, his hands jammed into his pockets. "I wish she'd get the hell out of France for good," he said grimly. "The situation is more dangerous every day."

"I know." Malcolm shook his head in sympathy. "How about a walk around the grounds?" he suggested. "It might burn off some of that tension."

They walked over the peaceful green countryside for an hour, talking about Brandon's Gate and the family and the things Adam had taught them both. They had a drink at a pub and parted amicably, promising to keep in touch.

Connor drove to a hotel in Sidmouth, almost deserted at this time of year, where Georgia met him, a ray of sunshine in the fine, soft mist of Devon.

♦

He was too happy the first two days to raise a contentious subject. On their third and last day they drove to Cornwall and stopped at Bude to sit on the soaring heights overlooking the sea. They looked down at the broad beach and listened to the cries of the swooping gulls, like omens of what was coming. A bracing wind polished their faces and tugged at her hair.

"Georgia," he asked. "How long?"

"With Hitler's help, not much longer."

"You're not going to wait until he invades France!"

"No. Only until his next aggressive move."

"I don't like having our lives dependent on Adolf Hitler."

"Neither do I, but I can take Gianna home the moment he moves. Tony won't stop me then. I'll get a divorce in Reno."

"He could contest it. Are you willing to take that chance?"

She kissed him. "Yes. Are you?"

"You know I am. Frankly, I'm more concerned with Gianna's reaction to me than Tony's."

"She'll love you—and you'll love her. She's so many things I wasn't."

"What things?"

"Spontaneous. I was controlled. She's sure of herself. I was always plotting to make Father love me and protect myself from Constance. Gianna just lives. I don't want her to go through the kind of court battle Gloria Vanderbilt did. It would change her forever."

For the first time he truly saw her, not solely as the abiding love of his life, but as she saw herself: a mother who was herself forever motherless. She was all he had, but she had a prior obligation and its significance dismayed him.

"What is it?" she asked.

"Just that I love you more than I can ever say."

"You don't have to say. I know."

"I want to give you everything. I want to take care of you."

"Do you want a child?"

"Yes," he said. "God, yes!"

♦

When they parted he went on to Germany to see the dye works he had bought soon after he had formed Hemisphere, and the automobile plant in which he was one of several partners. He was not permitted inside either place.

"Renovations," he was told by otherwise cordial, beaming Germans.

Like hell, he thought. Poison gas was probably being manufactured in the dye works and tanks in the auto plant.

Berlin disturbed him, even after Malcolm's warning. There was a strange undercurrent, a barely controlled violence, as of men who felt it was their turn now and were eager to take it.

Connor stayed long enough to select several cases of Deutsche Grammophon recordings, finding it difficult to equate German culture and technology with Nazi brutality. He sailed from Bremen, having decided to sever his last ties to German industry.

♦

"I'm glad that's over," Barney Abbott said as he and Connor left the courthouse in lower Manhattan. "Is your freedom worth two million?"

Connor mopped his face with a handkerchief. It was a warm, moist day in August, with showers threatening.

"It is. I'd have given her more to get this divorce."

"But not the papers!"

"This is America! A difference of opinion does not constitute fraud." But, in fact, Sondra had settled when Connor threatened to say his affair with Tirzah was her real reason for divorcing him.

"Now back to Washington for a waltz with the Justice Department," Barney said.

"And a possible five years in the clink."

"I don't think so. Germany and Russia have signed a nonaggression pact in Moscow."

Connor stopped walking abruptly and turned to Barney. "Are you serious?"

"Yes. I had a chance to look at the newspapers while you were signing away your money in court."

"Jesus," Connor swore. "The Communists and the arch anti-Communist."

"Stalin isn't ready to fight anyone yet, least of all Germany."

"And Hitler avoids fighting on two fronts. Then the war will start soon." He resumed walking again, eager to get back to his office and possible word from Georgia.

"France and England are mobilizing," Barney agreed. "I hate to say this, but the timing couldn't be better for you. I don't think anyone will be very hard on a man who just fought the Fascists in Spain. This country's already ashamed of its do-nothing policy there."

"But is the House Un-American Activities Committee?"

"I think so."

"And the pacifists?"

"Ah," Barney said, "they're another kettle of fish entirely. It's one thing to approve a faraway cause and quite another to go to war over it."

Abbott was prophetic. Connor was fined the full ten thousand allowed by law, but he was spared prison.

"You don't seem as jubilant as you should be," Oliver said when they met for a drink afterward.

"I'll be jubilant when I hear from Georgia, not before."

"I have a message for you from someone at State," Oliver said. "Fellow named Benton Daly."

"What about?"

"He didn't say, but meet him, Connor. It'll help pass the time while you're waiting."

◆

He met with Benton Daly that afternoon in a tacky office near the Treasury Building, apparently chosen because it was discreet. Daly was a youngish, balding man of medium height, wearing a pinstripe suit and a Harvard tie, with a diamond pinky ring on his right hand and a wedding band he constantly twisted on his left. He was one of Roosevelt's "brain trust"—and yet, Connor reflected, all the king's men had not been able to put the American economy back together. It was a war in Europe that would create jobs for the ten million Americans still unemployed.

"Sit down," Daly said briskly, taking the executive side of a battered gray metal desk. "I'll come right to the point. There's a great deal we'd like to know about the situation in Europe which, I'm told, is where you've spent a lot of time. We need people with fluent French who can help gather intelligence."

"Why from the French?" Connor asked, nonplused. "We have nothing to fear from them!"

Daly pursed his lips doubtfully. "Not directly. But they don't want a war, not over Poland, and that's where Hitler will go next. In July some of them said, 'Why die for Danzig?' Maybe they'll ask 'Why die for Britain?' too. After all, France is all that stands between England and Germany, and England's dangerously unprepared. No one knows for certain what will happen when push comes to shove."

"Are you saying the French might not fight?"

Daly nodded. "It's a possibility. France was decimated in the last war and the army the Germans can field is awesome, to say nothing of the German Air Force."

"*Die Luftwaffe*," Connor said.

"Yes, Oliver told me you speak German too." Daly looked pleased.

"What about the Maginot Line?" Connor asked.

Daly shrugged. "It was designed when trench warfare was still in style. It might not hold against those motorized German divisions. If the Germans can't get past the Maginot Line, they'll go around it. We're afraid Hitler might go through France like a hot knife through butter—or that

France will capitulate to save lives and property. If that happens, Hitler can charge across the Channel that much sooner."

"And come knocking on our door after he's finished off England? That seems unlikely."

"So did the German-Soviet Pact. The boss is really worried about the French fleet. If Hitler should get his hands on it, along with his own fleet and Italy's, he'd control the Atlantic." Daly twisted his wedding band in the opposite direction. "That ocean seems to shrink more every day and we're no better prepared than Britain is. So we can't risk a German victory over England until we're ready to defend ourselves if we have to. The question remains: will France fight and for how long?"

"How the devil could I tell you that?"

"By working with intelligence in England. They're already receiving information from the anti-Fascist French."

"Most of whom are Communists and therefore considered a threat by the powers-that-be in France."

Daly nodded. "But all Communists aren't Bolsheviks, as your papers were the first to point out. So. Will you go to England?"

Connor nodded. Georgia would be coming to England. "But I can't say for how long," he told Daly. "I had no idea you were looking for a spy."

"We might need quite a few before this is over. We haven't even got a centralized agency for foreign intelligence, only the FBI, and Hoover is dead set against foreign entanglements. He watches FDR like a hawk, so we have to move cautiously. For the moment we need observers to see how the English operate their intelligence community." Daly stood and reached across the desk to shake Connor's hand. "The boss will appreciate this," he said with a meaningful smile.

They separated, and Connor went back to the Willard to tell Oliver.

"Tirzah would call this a bad part in a B movie," Connor said while Mills packed his bags.

"I think it's right up your street," Oliver said.

"That's beside the point. I want to be in England when Georgia gets out."

He took Pan American's 314-class Yankee Clipper to Southampton. The giant flying boat that, for want of sufficient airports, took off and landed on great pontoons fascinated him. It had two decks, an upper one for the flight crew, mail, and navigation, and a lower one for passengers, as spacious and luxurious as a first-class hotel. The Clipper had deluxe compartments, each furnished with a love seat, an occasional chair, a dressing table, and private washstand. It had a bar and a galley with a steam table, and a dining salon that offered several sittings.

Connor kept mostly to his compartment. He had no wish to discuss his overpublicized difficulties with curiosity seekers. He wanted to think about Georgia.

He managed to sleep fitfully in his pull-down berth for a few hours of the long night and only heard in the morning, when the steward brought his breakfast, that Germany had invaded Poland. He was in London when war was declared two days later.

BOOK V

♦

1939–1944

40

◆

Georgia made a search of the rented house on the outskirts of Reno before she saw Gianna sitting on a shady bench in the garden with her favorite teddy bear. The bear had been abandoned for more sophisticated things, but Gianna had retrieved it from the nursery the day war was declared and had not relinquished it since.

Georgia stood looking at her twelve-year-old daughter intently and felt a pang of loss along with her pride.

The teddy bear notwithstanding, Gianna was no longer a little girl who believed her mother was infallible. There was a new tension about her long-legged, burgeoning young body. It was time for her to use the self-assurance Georgia had tried so hard to give her, time for her to start flying free. It was a difficult time for a mother and daughter under the best of circumstances—and these circumstances were far from good.

There had been a painful departure from France without Tony, and then a brief stay in London, a blacked-out city pocked with trenches and braced to defend itself against invasion by this new and terrible warfare called Blitzkreig.

Even Malcolm, Gianna's dearly loved uncle, had not assuaged her terror. Malcolm was wearing the blue uniform of the Royal Air Force.

"He'll be killed," Gianna whispered, trembling in Georgia's arms. "And Papa and *Grand-mère* and the aunts as well."

"Darling, you mustn't dwell on death like that. There's been no fighting since England and France declared war.

Papa said Hitler was more surprised by the declaration than anyone, and there might not even *be* a war."

Gianna's eyes looked suddenly old. "Papa doesn't really believe that and neither do I."

In London, Gianna had said very little to Connor, who was always with them.

"But she knows," Peggy warned Georgia as they prepared to fly home.

"How could she know?"

"Anyone would know! She sees your face when you look at him and his when he looks at you. It's time you told her the truth."

But Georgia clasped the truth to herself as rapturously as she had clasped Connor in her arms during those few chaotic, wonderful hours they had managed to spend alone together, making love and making plans for him to stay in London until her divorce, as secret as she could make it, was final. Their wedding would take place after a decent interval had elapsed, for Gianna's sake.

Her wedding to Connor! Provided, of course, that Tony had no idea it was imminent. She wanted to treasure her plans until the last possible moment.

The moment came when she and Gianna were in their private compartment on the Pan American Clipper to New York.

◆

"I hate him," Gianna shouted as she stared at Georgia with reddened, angry eyes.

"That isn't fair. You hardly know him."

"I don't care! I hate him anyway!" Gianna's voice rose dangerously and her hands curled into fists and pummeled Georgia's shoulders. "You can't marry anyone!" she sobbed. "You're Papa's wife!"

Georgia stilled the fists and held Gianna close to her. "Gianna, listen to me," she said gently, her own face wet with tears. "You're old enough to understand the human side of this. I care for your papa and I always will, but I

don't love him the way a woman should love her husband.
I haven't loved him in that way for a very long time."

Gianna colored, the red flush staining her cheeks and
her neck. Sex was not a mystery to her, but she contrived
to ignore sex between her parents. Now she drew herself
up, ramrod straight, and moved away from her mother.

"That's a lie! You want to marry that man, Connor."

"Yes, I do. But your father and I were estranged long
before Connor came back into my life. That's the truth,
Gianna, I swear it on your uncle Malcolm's life."

Gianna's honey-colored eyes opened wide at that assurance, absorbed its gravity, and fell before its weight. She
had to believe it.

"Did you ever love Papa at all?" she asked, still sullen
and accusing.

"Oh, yes, I did," Georgia replied, thinking it was only
half a lie. What had she known of love then? Who had
ever shown her what real love could be? "I wanted to
marry your father the day I met him. He was so handsome
and clever."

"He still is!" Gianna burst out. "He is! He is!"

"Yes, Gianna, he is, but that isn't enough for love."

"I don't understand why not," Gianna had said mournfully.

"Why do you always want Paddington Bear when things
go wrong?" Georgia said, stroking the animal's plush head,
worn bare with loving. "Why not Tommy Tiger or Ermengard
the Seal?"

"Because Paddington makes me feel better," Gianna
said in a small voice.

"Because you love him in a different way from the
others, even though you love them too."

"And that's how you love Connor?"

Georgia nodded. "He was my Paddington Bear when I
was little and wanted my mother. I promise you, Gianna,
someday you'll understand all of this, but for now you
must trust me, darling, please trust me."

What else can she do? Georgia agonized. She needs me
in order to survive, even if survival means abandoning her

father. God forgive me, I never meant to do this, not to her.

Gianna had made no reply and they said nothing more during the long journey to Nevada or the long week after they arrived.

♦

"It's lovely, isn't it?" Georgia exclaimed when the lawyer who was to handle her divorce had left them in the large two-story house of white brick, furnished in the colors and patterns of the Southwest. It was here they would live while Georgia established the residency requirement for her divorce.

"Pretty enough," sniffed Peggy, peering under a couch for dust puffs, "but not what you're used to."

"There's a fine stable nearby," Georgia continued brightly, hoping for some reaction from Gianna, but there was none.

"I expected this," Georgia told Peggy anxiously that night. "She's bereft of her father, her home, her grandmother, and her doting aunts. She's frightened half to death of the war."

"This is nothing to do with the war, Miss Georgia! She doesn't want you to marry Connor any more than you liked your father being married to Constance."

"My God, Peggy, are you saying I'll have to choose between Connor and my child?"

"It may come to that," Peggy said grimly.

"But I can't give him up," Georgia cried wildly. "I can't. We belong together. Peggy!"

"I know, my love, I know."

♦

Still hesitating on the shaded terrace, Georgia now contemplated her once-bright, ebullient, almost invariably sunny child. Gianna had turned as silent and withdrawn as a little ghost. Her last two nights at Charet-le-Roi had been torn by nightmares, her screams piercing the quiet of the mansion, bringing the household running to calm a terror that could not be calmed, not even by her parents.

But now there was more to Gianna's misery than either divorce or terror, and Georgia was determined to find out what it was before another day went by, thickening the wall between them.

Reluctantly Georgia went into the garden, where the breeze played over the flower beds and the fountain tinkled as merrily as if hearts never broke and good intentions never paved the road to hell. A delicious odor of sun-warmed earth and greenery infused the pure air. Such a lovely place. Such an incongruous setting for emotional turmoil.

Georgia sat down on the bench and stroked her daughter's glossy curls.

"Darling, you must talk to me," Georgia said. "You know you can tell me anything, anything at all. Is it that Papa is still in France—or that I want to marry Connor?"

Suddenly Gianna collapsed in the circle of her mother's arm. "It's all my fault," she wept wildly. "If I'd been braver, we could have stayed at Charet-le-Roi until Papa was ready to come away with us."

"Darling, no! Papa and I decided months ago to send you to America the moment war came."

"You mean you *argued* about it!" Gianna broke into fresh sobs. "And now you're going to divorce Papa because of the arguments. Over *me*! It's all my fault!"

"It isn't! It's no one's fault. It happened all by itself. You must believe me. It had nothing to do with you." She held Gianna until the sobbing stopped.

"Do you hate Papa?" Gianna breathed, her anger wilting, yielding, while she clung to the one parent she had left, as Georgia had.

I'll be better than Rhys, Georgia swore silently. Even if I have to live without my Connor.

"No, I don't hate Tony. He and I will always be friends, no matter what happens."

"And I can see him whenever I want to?"

"Whenever you want and for as long as you like as soon

as the war's over. Or before that, if he decides to leave France."

"He won't leave!" Gianna said proudly. "Not as long as France needs him. A de Sevignac believes in noblesse oblige."

In a moment she spoke again, warily negotiating the best bargain she could.

"Will I have to call *him* Papa?"

"No. Tony's your father."

"Do I have to *like* him?"

"No. But you must be polite to him, as a de Sevignac is expected to be."

Gianna nodded. "Will I stay a de Sevignac?"

"Yes, until you marry."

"I'll never marry," Gianna sighed.

"Then we'll be together always."

Gianna drew a long, shuddering breath and touched her mother's anxious, caring face. "I love you, Mama, but I love Papa too."

"I know you do, my darling. He needs your love as much as I do."

They sat on for a while in silence. Gianna nestled close inside her mother's arms, but even in that ultimate sanctuary she was buffeted by forces she could neither comprehend nor control.

Georgia held her, exhausted by all that had happened and all that was yet to happen before she and Connor were home free.

She couldn't be totally candid with Gianna until she was older. She would probably never tell her how rotten Tony was when he thought his pride was at stake, or that he would certainly contest this divorce as soon as he heard about it.

◆

"I just wanted to say good night," he had said, coming into her bedroom at Charet-le-Roi after seeing the doctor out.

He had crossed to the bedside to take her hand tenderly. "Gianna's sleeping peacefully now," he said.

"My poor baby," Georgia sighed, patting his hand, glad of his presence. "I never want to hear her scream like that again."

Tony nodded, his face still pale with worry, but his expression changed when he noticed Georgia's half-packed vanity case.

"I see you've made up your mind to go," he said stiffly.

"Tony! After the past two nights, you know Gianna must leave!"

His face had lapsed into the sly look it always wore when he was searching for an advantage, and she was on her guard again.

"I cannot desert my country in time of war," he began.

"You're not suggesting Gianna stay here with you?"

"I haven't decided," he said. "It isn't easy for me to let her go. I love her as much as you do."

Georgia's voice softened. "I know you do. But it won't be forever, Tony. Everything's in chaos now, but you may see your way clear to follow much sooner than you think."

"Would your door be open to me if I did?"

"Tony, you're Gianna's father. That will never change. But right now you must let her go—and for her sake you must do it gracefully. It'll be hard enough for her to leave you as it is."

"And the mills?"

"Everything's in order. If you decide to switch back to full dress-silk production, the technicians know exactly what to do. The Germans, no doubt, will want Sevignac dress silks."

They looked at each other.

"I love you," he said suddenly. "I discovered it too late, but it's a true love all the same. I wish you could believe that."

"Oh, Tony, I'm so sorry." She was unexpectedly touched by him. "I do care about you, no matter what's happened."

He sat down on the bed and put his arms around her and she let him, her heart heavy with regret, her need for tenderness enormous in the chaos all around them.

"Georgia," he whispered, "pretend you love me, just once more?"

"Oh, Tony, what's the point? It won't change anything." She drew away from him.

His hand closed viciously around her arm. "You can't wait to get away from me, can you?"

She said nothing.

"What will you do, divorce me as soon as you get to America?"

"What if I do? Tony, you're hurting me."

He squeezed her arm. "I'll contest it."

She shrugged. "Then the divorce won't be granted."

"Damn right it won't." He relaxed his grip. "As to your plan for immediate departure, you'll have to persuade me to agree to it." He raised her hand and kissed its palm.

"Really?" Her flesh crept. "How?"

He no longer smiled. "I want to make love to you. It's my right, damn it!"

"And if I agree, you'll let me take Gianna to safety without breaking her heart, is that it? Otherwise this child, whom you say you love, must take her chances in air raids or an invasion by your Nazi friends that will terrify her to death."

She threw back the covers and slid down onto her back, thrusting her long legs apart. Her body glistened through the sheer silk of her nightgown. "All right then, come on. Do it and get it over with. Gianna's life is worth it!"

He had left the bed and was watching her face, aghast, his lips trembling. "Georgia, is that how you think of me?"

"Yes, damn you, yes!" She sat up, trying to control the trembling of her hands and her voice.

"I'll tell you something, Tony. When you first came in here tonight I half wanted you to stay, out of some sentiment I don't understand myself. Maybe because I'm leaving you in danger. Maybe because we loved each other once and each of us has much to forgive the other. But look at us now! Oh, Tony, there *is* good in you, but you bury it. Why can't you be a man in any other way than this?" She gestured toward her body, then swept the quilt up and covered herself.

He stood for a moment, his anger gone, a look of shame and defeat on his face. Then he turned and left her.

In the morning he had been tender with Gianna, gallant with Georgia, and he had let them go as if the decision were entirely his.

So, Georgia had reflected as she and Gianna and Peggy drove to Geneva and took a privately chartered plane to London, it *was* Adolf Hitler who was ultimately responsible for her departure from France. But no one, she reminded herself now, listening to the fountain play, not even the Führer, could protect her from Tony.

She smoothed the curly head of Tony's child and comforted Gianna and told her a little about how marriages are made and broken and how illusions almost always die.

◆

But not always. They had been in Reno for a month when Georgia knew she was pregnant, that those enchanted hours in London had led to this.

"Oh, God, Peggy, think of it!" she exulted in a whisper so that no one in the sleeping house should hear. "Connor's baby! I'm going to give my Connor something of his own."

"Holy saints, Miss Georgia!"

"Yes, I know what you're thinking." She beamed, whirling Peggy around the bedroom. "But I'll ask Connor to come back and marry me right away. He was going to stay in England until the divorce was final. Then we were going to wait six months, maybe a year, before we were married. We were going to be discreet." She laughed richly, joyously.

"Discreet?" Peggy hooted. "And you in the family way already! Whose idea was it? That great gaby's, I'll be bound."

"No, Peg, it was mine. I couldn't not. I wanted him so much, all of him, without anything between us." She paused, her hands clasped in wonder. "It was never like that before! I never felt such bliss, never in my whole life. I thought there would be a child of it every time he touched me. I was like Molly Bloom. 'Yes I said yes I will Yes.'"

"There, my love." Peggy blushed, averting her eyes from Georgia's radiant face, from her naked delight. "You mustn't be tellin' me secret things like that, about yourself or Molly Bloom."

"It's no secret! I love him, Peggy. I love him. I love him."

"But who'll be the wean's legal father?"

That stilled her. It changed her from a rapturous woman to the efficient executive who had made a flourishing corporation out of some foundering silk mills.

"This divorce must be granted immediately," she told Peggy with authority, "never mind what the laws about residence are. It must be granted before Tony has time to hear about it and contest it, and Connor and I must be married at once." She looked at Peggy. "I know one man with enough influence to arrange all of that quietly."

"He never will!" Peggy gasped. "Not the way he hates Connor."

"I'll make him do it," Georgia said, sitting down at her writing table. "Start packing for Washington, Peggy. I'm going to write to Connor."

"Better cable," Peggy advised.

"No. A cable's too public."

Her hands shook with excitement, but she steadied herself and, thinking hurriedly but clearly, she began to write.

◆

"You must be mad!" Rhys ranted, shaken by what she had just told him.

All the austere dignity of his study—the American flag and the flag of New York State flanking his chair, the framed photographs of Rhys with luminaries from every country and every profession, the awards and honors and medals and honorary degrees—could not protect him from this cool, blunt, exquisite beauty who had once been his little girl, his sweet princess in the first blush of her womanhood, his Galatea, his other unattainable goddess.

"I'm quite sane," she said. "I've arranged to get this far without publicity because everyone's intent on the war. But I must get to the altar before Tony finds out that's where I'm bound."

"Why should I do it?" Rhys demanded, his cheeks purple with rage. "Why should I help you to marry a man who's bent on destroying me, a man I loathe?"

"Because you want to be president."

Crabtree was a more persuasive reason, but it was Connor's weapon, not hers.

"How do you suppose a divorced daughter will advance my cause?" he said venomously.

"Will a bastard grandchild improve your chances?"

"A bastard?" He glared at her until he understood what she meant. "You wouldn't!"

"Oh, yes, I would," she said coldly. "I will."

"No. You'll stay married to your husband, by God! Let him be the legal father. He's not going to tell anyone the truth."

"A solution worthy of you, Father! But I don't want any part of it. If this child is not a MacKenzie, it'll be a Brandon—and a bastard. 'Father unknown' the birth certificate will say. Think how that will look on the front pages."

He sat staring at her in horrified disbelief. "I never knew you were like this."

She shrugged. "You never really knew me at all."

"You were so perfect, so pure."

"Was I?" Her blue eyes glinted strangely. "Too pure to be the object of any man's carnal lust but yours? Especially if the man were Connor! I should have been married to him long ago."

He cleared his throat, glaring at her. "You Lilith," he muttered. "You devil."

"Yes, yes. But I had two excellent teachers, you and Constance. Well, then, what's it to be? You can save me any further adulterous gestation by getting the divorce put through immediately. Connor and I will be married as soon as he can get here. It'll be a very quiet wedding. No one will know until months from now—and by then, I'm sure, your Mr. Reedy will have backdated the marriage license to conform to a legitimate nine-month pregnancy."

"When is this abomination to be born?" he whispered.

"Abomination?" A chill swept through her, but she was not to be diverted. "In June," she said.

He paled. "In June?"

The Republican convention was scheduled for June and she was well aware that three very substantial opponents stood between Rhys and the nomination: Thomas Dewey, the popular New York district attorney on whom Humphrey Bogart's role in *Marked Woman* had been based; Senator Robert Taft of Ohio, whose family tree boasted one president already; and Wendell Willkie, a recent convert to the Republican cause who had caught the imagination of the public as well as the party.

It was his craving to prevail over these formidable men that would decide him, not any concern for his prospective grandchild.

"I'll deal with it," he said shortly. "Now leave me."

She sat looking at him for another moment, amazed that she had ever loved him, yet wrenched with sorrow that she loved him no longer.

Had he set out, all those years ago, to cherish and protect her, as she herself had sworn to cherish Gianna, only to have circumstances lead him to hurt her?

It's loving you that I miss, Papa, she mourned, walking away from him toward the door. I miss being your princess. Will that longing never end? How can it be that I'm thirty-five years old and I still want my daddy?

She turned. "Father?" she said softly.

But he was already on the telephone, and either he did not hear her or he chose not to reply.

◆

"Russia was the key," Merrywell was saying to Connor in London at the moment Georgia met with her father. He lit his pipe while coffee and cognac were brought to the lounge of the Connaught. War or not—and people had begun calling this strange period of nonbelligerency the "phony war"—they had dined well on spring lamb, pink and running with juice, garnished with tiny peas, baby carrots, and new potatoes, followed by Camembert cheese and a green salad, with a soufflé Grand Marnier for dessert.

"If we'd done a deal with that old butcher, Stalin," Merrywell continued when his pipe was going, "there'd have been no war. Not even the bloody Boches can fight on two bloody fronts."

Connor nodded, but it was not second guesses about the war he wanted. It was incontrovertible evidence linking Rhys and Crabtree, and Barney Abbott had told him Merrywell, who was on the board of Rhys's Eden Corporation, was the man to supply it for the right price.

Merrywell shook his head, deep in melancholy. "It's a mug's game," he grumbled. "Fancy our having to choose between the Nazis and the Reds. Either way we'll come a cropper. Totally unprepared, you know. Be invaded the minute the Huns move their arses and finish off the bloody French."

Merrywell cocked an eye at Connor. "Switzerland's the place to be. So much money banked there, no one dares touch the place. Might burn up the records or open a can of worms and show who's in bed with whom."

"For example?" Connor probed, interested in the conversation now.

"Hitler isn't being financed entirely by Germans, my dear chap! Your fellow, Raymond Swing, said it years ago: each of these Fascist states has a leader who first moved toward socialism and then came to terms with the finance capitalists in his own country and elsewhere."

Get on with it! Connor thought impatiently. Tell me what you want.

"There's money to be made in this, and we're all going to make it: England, France, America, Japan. They'll sell each other weapons, too, the way they did the last time. The French *poilus* will be killed by guns made in France and the Tommies by stuff out of Vickers, mark my words."

"And you would like to establish residence in Switzerland," Connor said, getting to the point himself.

"Indeed I would, but one needs a packet to acquire a *permis de séjour*. The Swiss don't want anyone becoming a charge on the state. And one's expected to contribute substantially to the public weal: a library, a courthouse, that sort of thing."

They agreed upon a price, and a few days later Merrywell supplied Connor with papers documenting the intricate thread that led from Crabtree, through Eden's interlocking directorates, back to Republic Industries, and straight to Rhys Brandon.

◆

Colonel Lord Edward Fairleigh, Connor's superior at the Special Intelligence Service, set out two glasses and a bottle of whiskey. No ice, no siphon, Connor noted, but he had become accustomed to sipping fine Scotch whiskey neat, as the British did.

He accepted the glass and drank, still in the breeches and leather jacket he had worn to fly a Westland Lysander to yet another clandestine meeting with a fledgling underground network in northern France. The war was almost moribund for want of fighting, but in France, as in England, they were getting ready.

"How did it go?" Lord Fairleigh inquired.

"The Resistance is eager to fight now. How they'll react when push comes to shove is anyone's guess. The Nazis are not famous for obeying the rules of war."

"There were atrocity stories in the last show," the colonel remarked.

"We know for a fact that this time they burned civilians alive in Poland, sir, most of them Jews, many of them women and children."

The colonel sighed, peering into his glass. "Civilization hasn't caught up with them yet."

Connor leaned back in his chair. The Lysander was a far cry from this luxurious square room, walled by books, its lamps abloom in the early November dusk.

He always met with Fairleigh here at the colonel's home in London because his connection to British Intelligence had to be secret. There were powerful forces intent on keeping America out of this war, supported by a citizenry that, however hostile to Hitler, was still dealing with the Depression. There were ten million workers jobless despite gradually reopening defense plants, and the country had firmly turned its back on Europe. The President himself had sworn to keep the country out of war.

But what would happen, every man in England wondered, if France fell—or capitulated—before the mighty German army that had just pulverized Poland? The British Isles would certainly be invaded forthwith—and they had only a meager supply of arms to defend themselves. The cream of the British Army, the British Expeditionary Force, was already in France.

"So," the colonel roused himself, half sitting on the corner of his desk. "Will France hold?"

"If we're to believe the men I spoke to, no, sir. The Resistance will fight on, but France will capitulate."

"Damn!" the colonel swore.

Connor looked grim. "It may be pure speculation," he offered.

"It comes from too many sources to be speculation." The colonel rose from his perch, a compact man with pale brown hair, an engaging face, and the assurance of the English aristocrat. He was a quiet man with the devotion to duty that had made Britain a world power. Even if that power, in Connor's opinion, had at times been misdirected, the spirit behind it would save England—if anything could.

"Well, then," Fairleigh was saying, "it's our job to keep these networks alive and feeding us information. Where are those lists and the maps?"

The two men were still leaning over the desk when a

knock at the door preceded Lady Rowena Fairleigh, the earl's daughter, and Malcolm Brandon.

Rowena kissed her father affectionately. She had his fresh complexion and his elegance, but her mouth was fuller and her wide eyes sparkled with fun under the visor of her Women's Auxiliary cap. The uniform did little to hide her well-curved body. She radiated excitement whenever she was near Malcolm.

Envy washed over Connor. He wondered what in hell he was doing here, so far away from Georgia.

"Sorry to interrupt you and Connor, Daddy," Rowena said, the delicate color deepening in her cheeks, "but this news couldn't wait. Malcolm's asked me to marry him and I've said yes!"

Her father smiled down at her, then at Malcolm. "I can't pretend I'm surprised."

"Neither can I," Connor said. "Congratulations to you both."

"For once I'm speechless," Malcolm said, his handsome face aglow. "I hope you know, Colonel, that I'll love her all my life."

The colonel extended his hand, nodding.

The three of them burst into talk, making plans, laughing, hugging each other, and Connor, watching, envied them anew.

"Connor," Malcolm said, "there was a letter for you in the pouch. From the princess. I brought it along."

"Excuse me for a moment." Connor took the letter and withdrew across the room to read it. When he had finished, he stood staring at it, transfixed.

"Connor?" It was Malcolm at his side. "Is anything wrong?"

Connor shook his head. "Hell, no. We're having a baby," he said softly.

"That's great news!"

"I'm going back so we can be married immediately, or the child will be de Sevignac's legally."

"God forbid. And the divorce?"

"Georgia says she'll have the final decree by the time I get there. I wonder how she did it."

Malcolm beamed. "My sister is an extraordinary woman."

Connor put the letter in his pocket. "Not a word to anyone, Mal, until we're married. We can't risk Tony's finding out."

"Of course not, old man. We'll miss you at our wedding though." Malcolm's glow faded a little. "I counted on you to stand up for me."

"Get married by Friday and I will."

Malcolm smiled broadly. "Rowena?" he said, crossing the room. "I have the most marvelous idea. All we need is a special license."

They were married at St. Margaret's, both of them in uniform, Rowena carrying a bouquet of orchids and roses rushed up to London from the Fairleigh greenhouses.

"Be happy," Connor said, embracing Malcolm before he left.

"And you. I always wanted you for a brother, and now it's happened."

"Sometimes you get to choose your relatives. But be careful, Malcolm. There's a war on."

"You could have fooled me."

Colonel Fairleigh was sorry to see him go. "I wish you'd chosen a moment somewhat less fraught. Your Resistance people like their *Corbeau*." Raven was Connor's code name, chosen because he was dark and quiet and traveled by air.

"Emergencies don't stand upon the moment, sir," Connor replied.

"I wish you well, whatever it is."

"And I you. Good-bye, Colonel, it's been a pleasure."

He boarded his plane, still barely able to believe that in a few days he would be married to Georgia. He thought of her through the long hours of the flight, of having and holding her for the rest of his life, of the child inside her.

It was difficult to describe what he was feeling, until he

realized that he had never before had absolutely everything he wanted, and he was fearful that it might be snatched away from him.

◆

He was walking up the long path to the house in Alexandria when the door opened and Georgia came out. He ran the rest of the way, swooped her up in his arms, and carried her inside.

"My wife!" he laughed, spinning with her. "My wife," he whispered, kissing her. "I can't believe it. I won't believe it until we can tell everyone."

He put her down and she traced his mouth with her fingers, then laid them lightly on his lips before she turned and started up the stairs. His hands were on her waist and he felt the sway of her hips while his desire for her surged.

"No one must know except Malcolm—and Jillian, of course—not until the baby's born," she said, and her voice told him she was as ravenous for him as he was for her. "Everyone thinks I'm still in France, so I've been hiding behind veils and sunglasses. I feel like a different woman, new and mysterious."

She stopped on the stairs and turned to look down at him, her beautiful face luminous in the half light, her gilt hair rich and loose around her face. She was wearing a gossamer silk wrapper that barely veiled her superb body, that body he knew so well and would never know well enough to satisfy his hunger. He sank to his knees on the stairs below her, his head pillowed on her belly, his arms holding her, passion rising in him against the heat of her body. He loosened the sash of the wrapper with his teeth and it parted, exposing the tangle of blond hair between her legs.

His hands on her breasts, he teased at the hidden cleft with his tongue, heard her gasp, and felt her legs part.

"Not here," he whispered, and with an easy motion he picked her up again and carried her up the stairs.

He put her on the bed and dropped his clothes.

"You're so beautiful," she said, touching the muscles of his stomach and legs, stroking the erect, demanding penis.

"Now," she said. "I want my heaven now."

He kissed her, excited anew by the soft moist silk of her mouth and the way her tongue brushed his. She reached for him and made a sheath for him, first between her breasts, then with her mouth, until he pulled back and moved down to tease at the magic petals, fleshy, steamy, delicate, and hot.

"Connor!" she cried in an ecstasy so intense it was almost pain. He felt her taking him, clasping him with those velvet ridges deep inside her, and they were catapulted to the other side of themselves, where they were all there was.

◆

"What time is it?" she asked him an hour later.

"Does it matter?"

"No. Gianna's away at school. A convent school in Montreal." Georgia sighed. "She chose it because it's far away and French."

"Does she like it?"

"As much as she likes anything at the moment. Poor baby, she has to like me because I'm all she's got." She moved closer to him. "I can remember how that feels."

"It's not the same for her as it was for you," he reminded her. "You've been her mother in every good sense of the word. I'm the trouble, but I'll make her like me."

"You will," she murmured, her lips against his chest. "You're irresistible."

"Georgia, how did you manage this?" he asked.

"I persuaded my father to cut through the red tape."

He was silent for a moment. "That couldn't have been easy."

"No, but I told him this baby would either be a MacKenzie or a Brandon bastard, not a de Sevignac."

"You'd have done that?" he asked, astonished. "Made a bastard of our child?"

"Yes! Or maybe not! Connor, I don't know! He believed

I would, so it's academic now. I'd rather forget I had to go to him."

Always attuned to her, he realized she would be forever wary of becoming again the third leg of that triangle: Connor, Georgia, Rhys.

He put his arms around her and held her close, blotting out everything else.

"This is all that matters," he said. "And this." He slid down to press his face against her body where the baby nested. "This is the only thing that's real."

♦

They were married in Maryland the next day, Georgia in a large hat with a heavily spotted veil, Connor in a modest ready-made suit. They were one eloping couple among many. Then they flew to Canada to spend several polite and awkward hours with Gianna, saying nothing about the baby, before they returned to the house at Sands Point.

"You might have called me before this!" Jillian said tartly when Georgia telephoned her. "I'd never have told anyone! And here I was, worried to death because I thought you were still in France with your mad husband, and all the time you were getting pregnant and then married in some awful place in Maryland. You haven't even seen the baby!"

"Alexandra Seena. She's a lovely baby. I'm looking at her picture now. Seven pounds, seven ounces."

"That was eight months ago."

"Is she a Brandon or a Cassadyne?"

"All Cassadyne," Jillian said. "But gorgeous—as you'd know if you'd bothered to see her."

"Jilly, darling, don't be hurt. We couldn't tell anyone or risk being seen because of Tony, as well as for Gianna's sake."

"I guess you couldn't," Jillian conceded, mollified. "How's Gianna taking the divorce?"

"Like a de Sevignac. She is not amused. And she wants to spend Christmas with you and Peter and the baby, not with us."

"She's welcome—and don't sound so worried. She'll get over being mad as soon as she spends some time in New York. Half the people in society are divorced. Now tell me about this marriage. Are you bored with a man you've known since the day you were born?"

"Bored? With Connor?"

"No, I suppose not. Well, after all this, are you happy?"

"Ecstatic, except for Gianna. Need you ask?"

"I keep thinking of what Oscar Wilde said about there being only two tragedies in this world. One is not getting what you want and the other is getting it."

"I've tried the first tragedy long enough, Jillian. I'm ready for the second."

♦

They seemed to live in the same dream at Sands Point, through the snows of February and on into the first signs of spring, as if the seasons were keeping pace with this pregnancy and would not bring forth until Georgia did.

"It's as if we were children again," Connor said one day. They sat on a wooded hill about a mile from the house with new buds all around them.

"Yes," she agreed. "You even look like that boy. You had a smile that broke my heart. And when you were angry the sun went behind a cloud for me."

"I was never angry at you."

She nodded. "Remember how I wanted us to make a blood pact of friendship."

He turned to her, his hands resting on the dome of her belly. "We've made one now."

She put her arms around him, holding him as tightly as she could. "I love you," she crooned. "I love having your child growing inside me. Oh, Connor, tell me it's all right for me to be as happy as this, as much in love as this, that nothing will take it away from me."

"Nothing will, my love, my darling. I won't let it."

At Easter, Gianna came home and for several days kept her eyes averted from her mother's body.

"I didn't want to tell you on the telephone," Georgia

said finally, "but the baby won't go away, so we might as well talk about it."

"Does Papa know?"

"I don't think so. I didn't tell him because it isn't his child."

"But I am!" Gianna burst out. "And I don't want you to die."

"Darling, I won't die!"

"Your mother did!"

"She was delicate. I suppose it was fashionable for ladies to be delicate in those days. But I'm not! I ride and I swim and play tennis. And I had you with no trouble at all."

Gianna appeared comforted by that. Then she stole a look at her mother. "Papa is an adulterer, isn't he?"

Georgia was startled. "Who on earth told you that?"

Gianna shrugged. "I heard it."

"I suppose they thought it was *très gallant* of him."

Gianna nodded. "Did you?"

"No. At first I was very hurt."

"And then?"

"Then I tried not to think about it. But that never works, does it?"

"Are you happy now?"

"Oh, yes. Because of you and Connor."

"And your baby," Gianna said accusingly.

"Yours, too, Gianna. I won't love you any less, if that's what you're worried about. Aunt Jilly didn't stop loving Peter when Alexandra was born. It's a special talent mothers have." She held out her arms to Gianna. "Come on, darling, let yourself be happy. It's your nature. You always filled the house with sunshine for your papa and me."

"Oh, Mama," Gianna said, curling up close to Georgia. "Why do things have to change?"

"It's called life, honey. There'll be times when you'll pray for a change."

"I've had all I want," Gianna said.

◆

"I think it's going to be all right," Georgia told Connor that night.

"And I think you need a day and night alone with her."

"You know, you're right! Lord, what a marvelous man you are. You always understand these things."

"One day and one night," he repeated. "I can't be away from you longer than that."

Since their marriage he had left her infrequently, to attend to business he couldn't deal with by telephone. The rest of the time they were together on rides and walks around the estate and frequent spins in Connor's plane.

As the presidential nominating conventions drew near, it was inevitable for them to speak of Rhys, whom *Life* had called the certain Republican nominee until Wendell Willkie appeared on the scene.

"It worries me that Crabtree was shipping guns to the Fascists while Rhys was against repeal of the embargo *and* against 'cash-and-carry' arms purchases by the British." He eyed Georgia uncertainly. "Is he anti-Communist or pro-Hitler?"

"Rhys has never been pro anything but himself."

Connor frowned. "Still, he's not the kind of man we need in the White House at a time like this. Roosevelt's the only man who can keep the Democrats in power, but Roosevelt will be up against a major precedent if he runs for a third term. Emotions will be running high. Even my father's switching back to a Republican vote. He'd join forces with the devil to keep us out of the war."

"I'd like to meet your father sometime."

"Later, maybe. Where he goes, a gaggle of reporters is never far behind." He returned to what was troubling him. "If the country doesn't want to give FDR a third term, someone will have to stop Rhys. I'm not sure Wendell Willkie can."

"It's your decision, Connor. Do what you have to do."

"But how can I involve you in a scandal like that? Not to mention Gianna and Jilly and her children—and our child?"

"We've already involved them in a bigger scandal. We'll all survive."

But Connor was not so sure.

41

♦

"It's a boy," Georgia decided early in May, when she was in her eighth month.

"A boy?" He smiled delightedly. "How can you tell?"

"Just a feeling."

"I wouldn't argue with any of your feelings."

She laughed. "I'm not the oracle at Delphi."

"You are to me."

They had just set out on a walk that morning when they heard Mills calling Connor through the sweet spring air. They looked at each other, the contentment dashed from their faces by apprehension.

"I'll see what he wants," Connor said.

"I'm coming with you."

"Over here, Mills," Connor called, waving to the man as they came out of the trees.

They heard Mills call, "Germany's invaded Holland and Belgium," and looked at each other again, feeling their dream splinter around them while the bees buzzed on, indifferent to the holocaust about to engulf the world.

Scandinavia had been invaded in April. Now they watched with the rest of the world, incredulous, as the Nazi armies, in a feat unparalleled in history, swept across the

Low Countries and into the Ardennes, then drove west to the sea, splitting the Allied forces in half and driving the British Expeditionary Force out of Belgium and back to the English Channel.

Holland surrendered on May 15 and the Belgians thirteen days later. On June 9, Norway capitulated. At the end of May there began the rescue of Allied troops from the beach at Dunkirk by an armada of British pleasure boats under an umbrella of RAF fighter planes.

Malcolm was flying air cover over Dunkirk.

In the midst of their worry about him, they moved to a new town house in New York City to be close to the hospital for the birth and to welcome Gianna, who arrived after her school broke for the summer. She was very subdued, fearful for her father and Malcolm, quietly frantic about Georgia.

"I wish she'd let me comfort her," Connor said.

"She wants to, I can tell by the way she watches you, but it's not something we can force."

They had no choice but to wait.

"Is Mama all right?" Gianna asked Peggy a dozen times a day.

"Land sakes!" Peggy exclaimed. "You've only to look at her, Miss Gianna, to see she's in fine fettle."

"I wish Connor were having the baby, not Mama."

Peggy looked sour. "The Lord in His wisdom decided otherwise."

"But He made men bigger and stronger."

"Hmph! It only looks that way. There'd be no babies at all if men had the bearin' of them! Now you stop frettin', my girl. She had you, didn't she, and never even minded the pains 'cause she wanted you so much."

"Did she really?" Gianna breathed, warmed.

"I was right there the whole time," Peggy affirmed. "All she wanted after that last big push was to have you in her arms. The happiest day of her life, it was."

Gianna stayed close to Georgia, both of them following the news of the German Army's progress toward Paris in the first days of June. When they were sure Malcolm had survived Dunkirk, it remained to be seen what would happen to Tony.

"If the Germans get too close to Paris, Pétain will declare it an open city and sue for peace."

Georgia leaned over the map in the upstairs sitting room, the sheer curtains streaming in the June breeze, and tried to reassure Gianna even as the German juggernaut swept implacably south.

"Tony told me that was Pétain's plan. And Paris is a long way from Lyons—"

She stopped speaking suddenly, bent forward, and clapped both hands to her back with a little grunting sound.

"Mama?" Gianna cried. "Mama?" She saw a sheen of perspiration form on her mother's face and screamed for Connor.

He came, taking the stairs three at a time, and bent over Georgia. "Has it started?"

"Yes," she gasped. Then she smiled reassuringly and stretched out a hand to Gianna. "Baby, don't cry. It always hurts a little, but I'm going to be fine."

"Oh, please, Connor," Gianna wept, "don't let my mother die. I won't be mean to you anymore if you'll just not let her die."

Connor put an arm around the frantic girl and spoke with an easy assurance he did not feel.

"Do you think I'd let anything happen to either of you? Now go find Peggy and tell her we're ready to go to the hospital."

He sat with Georgia in the small cubicle called a labor room for as long as they would let him, holding her hand, flinching every time she did. Inside himself he was as frightened for her as Gianna was. He was remembering Dilys giving birth, the cruel forceps, the sickly-sweet smell of chloroform, the dead blue baby lying on newspapers spread on the floor. He remembered his fear and his rage and the terrible need for his mother, for that one perfect, unqualified love.

He was petrified that by his very love for Georgia, by

his passion, he himself might be the author of his greatest loss, the one he could not bear.

When they took Georgia to the delivery room, he went down the hall to where Gianna and Peggy waited.

"They say it'll be very soon now," he said hoarsely.

"Is she going to die?" a tear-streaked Gianna beseeched him.

He picked her up and set her on his lap. "No, baby," he said, rocking her with an intolerable ache in his throat. "She won't die. I love her so much, Gianna. I don't know what I was doing all those years without her, but I wasn't living."

They looked at each other, and the child was touched by the man's truth, by his love. Her arms tightened around his neck and she put her head on his shoulder in the first gesture of trust she had ever shown him. They stayed that way, with Peggy beside them, until the doctor came to tell them that Georgia had given birth to a healthy boy, and mother and child were fast asleep.

It was June 14, 1940, the day the German Army entered Paris.

◆

"We thought we'd make an occasion of it," Jillian said. "All Brandon's Gate girls together."

"I'm glad you did." Georgia smiled around the circle of faces—Clarissa, Blanche, and Cecily had come to the hospital with Jillian—thinking that they were no longer "the girls."

Tim's sister, Clarissa, was stout and round-cheeked now, with threads of gray in her red Cassadyne curls. She had four children.

"But God knows how," Jillian had giggled before "the girls" arrived. "She's such a prude. I think she makes Tibby do it through a sheet."

Blanche and Cecily had two children each, were very chic, and, according to Jillian, enchanted by matinee idols and movie stars.

"For enchanted"—Jillian winked—"read screwed, as often and as vigorously as possible."

Tea had been sent over to the hospital by Sherry's and the four visitors, after viewing Brandon Malcolm MacKenzie and pronouncing him the image of his handsome father, had settled down to pastries and gossip in the bedroom.

"What a sly boots you are, Georgia," Blanche said archly. "Sitting on Connor's nest when everyone thought you were in France with Tony."

"She was far too clever to stay in France with Tony," Jillian said, rushing to her sister's defense. "For all we know, he's a prisoner of war."

"No," Georgia said. "The terms of the surrender put a demarcation line across France, and Lyons is south of it. The south is unoccupied. Tony's safe."

"He's part of the new government at Vichy, isn't he?" Clarissa said pointedly.

"Unfortunately, yes."

"Then you did well to divorce him, for your father's sake as well as yours," Cecily put in. "Who'd have believed the French would surrender! The Vichy French are no better than traitors."

They talked on while Georgia, on the bed, drifted in and out of the conversation, dozing from time to time.

Rhys had not come to see her, nor had she expected him. He had kept his part of the bargain: her marriage license to Connor had been predated to September, and Brandon was not only healthy and beautiful but legitimate—barring a challenge from Tony. There had been no word from him yet, but then, there hadn't been much time since the story became public.

She glanced at the newspapers on her bedside table.

"Sweet Georgia Brandon de Sevignac MacKenzie Does It—Again."

The sexual implication had infuriated Connor, but Georgia only laughed.

"They'll find someone else to insult in a few days," she said.

Rhys's quotes made it sound as if she had divorced Tony because of his Nazi sympathies, virtually ignoring her marriage to Connor and saying generously that his differences with his new son-in-law had always been purely political.

So, she thought, Hitler's conquest of six countries in ten weeks was threatening even to Rhys. The shock of that massive onslaught was chipping away at American indifference to the war, but not yet at the determination to stay out of it.

"Somewhere in the not too distant future we might not have any choice but to defend ourselves," she had read that morning in one of Connor's editorials. "Hitler decides whom next to attack, not his victims."

"Hitler has no designs on the Western Hemisphere," Senator Brandon was quoted in a campaign speech when the Republican Convention was only days away.

"Hitler claimed he had no designs on England either," Connor's editorial riposted, "but the British are bracing for an invasion they'll have to resist with pike staves, broomsticks, and the seventy thousand rifles the British Expeditionary Force managed to bring home from Dunkirk. Will America find herself in a similar position someday?"

Georgia reflected that it could have been a clean debate on a vitally important issue—except that nothing between her husband and her father was clean. Everything was furred over by the moss of the past.

There was a stir in the sitting room, and she opened her eyes to see Jillian coming back in from the parlor of the hospital suite and her friends watching her intently.

"You have a visitor in the sitting room," Jillian said. "Enoch MacKenzie."

"Who does that dreadful man think he is?" Clarissa demanded with an angry flush. "Barging in here as if this were one of his dreadful mines!"

"Maybe we'll be in the papers tomorrow," Blanche said in happy anticipation. "Were there reporters?"

Cecily smoothed her hair. "Let me go out and send him

away for you, Georgia. I've always wanted to say boo to that old villain."

They all looked expectantly at Georgia.

"Ask him to come in," she said. "If you don't mind waiting in the sitting room."

"Is this wise?" Clarissa cautioned.

"Definitely," Georgia said. "I'm as curious about him as he is about me."

♦

He was carrying a stuffed panda as large as a three-year-old child. In his rumpled suit he seemed to overflow the severe, angular, sanitized room. She knew from the newspapers that he was a few years younger than Rhys, but he looked older, and there was something touching in the way he regarded her, like a man who was unwelcome more often than not, wherever he went.

"Now that you're out of hiding," he said in his gruff voice, "I thought we could meet."

"High time," she said. "Have you seen your grandson?"

He nodded, a smile lifting the sagging lines of his face. "A braw laddie. The spit of Connor.'" His face expanded still more with pride. "Connor's mighty pleased with fatherhood."

"Oh, yes, he's a born father. And he's in love with Brandon."

"Brandon? He's going to call him Brandon?" Enoch pleated his shaggy brows. "What the hell's got into him?"

"Nothing." She laughed, feeling a sudden kinship with him. "It's customary."

He grunted. "To you, maybe. Not to him. Except, of course, he always wanted to be one of you."

"No. First he wanted to be yours, Mr. MacKenzie," she said gently. "But he thought you didn't want him."

He accepted that. "Yes," he said heavily, more to himself than to her. "What I wouldn't give to have him trust me again." Then he roused himself abruptly. "Well, and where shall I put this beastie?" Enoch was still holding the panda.

"Anywhere. There, in the corner. And thank you very much for bringing it."

Tenderly, he deposited the stuffed animal, then turned back to her. "You're a rare bonny woman. Looking at you, I mind your mother when she would come down to the flats at Brandon's Gate in her carriage."

"Did you know her?" Georgia asked eagerly.

"Not to speak to—workers didn't converse with owners' wives in those days—but I saw her often enough. Like a queen she was, but a good queen."

"Peggy—my maid, who was her maid too—says she did a lot of good for the workers."

"She and I were out for the same thing, however our reasons may have differed."

"I've wondered if she didn't insist upon a lot of things simply because *he* didn't want to do them."

He nodded. "The senator was never civic-minded."

"It's very strange," she said, "but you're the only person I've ever met—except Connor, of course—to whom I can say exactly what I think."

They smiled at each other.

"You must come to see your grandson often, Mr. MacKenzie."

"Enoch. I will, and I thank you. I suppose your father won't."

She shook her head.

He watched her intently with Connor's eyes, a stranger yet not a stranger. "You're always in the middle, aren't you?" he said shrewdly. "Between Connor and him."

"Not anymore."

He nodded approvingly. "You're clever," he said. "Most beautiful women aren't."

"Enoch, I don't think you're a very good judge of women, but I'm very glad you came."

He surveyed her again for a moment, then with a little nod he turned and left with as little ceremony as he had come. She heard the door to the corridor close in the next room and then her friends poured back.

"No one will believe this!" Cecily said. "The badman of

the unions bearing a great plush animal like a burnt offering!"

"What did he want?"

"To be a grandfather."

"How do you feel about that?" Jillian wanted to know.

"I like it. I like him."

"Really, Georgia!" Clarissa said.

♦

"I wondered if you were ready to come back to work," Benton Daly told Connor, minutes after they met.

"That depends on what you have in mind."

"Nothing specific at the moment, but we're going to lay the groundwork for an intelligence organization, just in case."

"Come on, Benton, you know how this country feels about intelligence organizations. And I've already drawn J. Edgar Hoover's beady eye over the Spanish Loyalists. I'd be something less than an asset to you."

"Unless we get into the war."

"Any chance of that?"

"Not much. Not yet. But the situation in Washington is untenable. Countries are falling in Europe like dominoes and most of our intelligence is gathered at cocktail parties. We have no idea whether Britain will survive when the Wehrmacht crosses the Channel. Old Joe Kennedy insists she can't possibly, but the boss doesn't think the ambassador's opinions are holy writ. Still, whether we get drawn into this war or not—and I sure as hell hope not!—we ought to know what's going on." Daly leaned forward. "We have a man in England already, working with their Special Intelligence Service on a wider administrative scale than you did."

After a moment Connor shook his head. "It's a job that needs doing, Benton, but I can't go back to England now. I'm not going to leave my son."

Daly offered belated congratulations. "Will you help to get the boss reelected to a third term?"

"Yes," Connor said. "I plan to do that." He glanced at

his watch. "You'll have to excuse me, Benton. I have an appointment." He stood, extending his hand. "I know you'll keep in touch."

"One of these days I'll persuade you," Daly said.

Connor shook his head, waved, and set off down the walk, a striking man with a touch of gray at his temples and, at this moment, a set look about his face. He walked to a taxi rank, got into the first cab, and gave an address in Georgetown.

When he arrived at the Brandon house he paid the driver and sent him away before ringing the bell. A butler let him in and conducted him to a small parlor. Constance, chic and soignée in a wide-shouldered gray silk crepe draped and stitched at bosom and hips, sat down and waved him to a chair as soon as the butler withdrew.

"Well, well, well," she purred. "Alone at last. And what could you possibly want with me?" Despite herself, she had pulled in her flat stomach and arched her back to pull her breasts taut.

But he was intent on something else.

"I want you to make Rhys withdraw from the race for the Republican nomination," he said. "I wouldn't bother you, but he flatly refuses to see me."

She laughed shortly. "If I'd known what you wanted, so would I."

"If he doesn't withdraw," Connor said, "I'll make Crabtree public."

"Crabtree?"

"Rhys's munitions firm, one of the biggest." He watched her eyes turn saucerlike. "He's owned it for years. I'm ready to print everything about it, even to the way he won those first foundries in Troy, playing cards in a whorehouse."

"You're lying," she whispered.

"I assure you I'm not. I have the proof." He took a sheaf of papers from his breast pocket. "These are copies."

She looked through them, her agitation growing. "Even so, you wouldn't involve Georgia and Jillian and their children in such a scandal. Georgia would never forgive you."

"This doesn't concern her."

Constance shot to her feet. "You'll never make me believe that. She and Rhys have their differences, but he's still her father. Who did she ask to get her out of the mess you put her in? She would never help to destroy Rhys, not even for you."

"She's left the decision entirely to me."

Constance flared her nostrils in disgust. "What a pair the two of you are! You seduced her when she was only a child! How else would you have such influence on that stubborn, spoiled bitch?"

Connor flushed. "Don't talk rot, Constance! Just listen to me! Rhys will jeopardize the future security of this country by turning his back on the British when they're hanging on by their thumbs. I'm going to see that he doesn't get the chance. If this weren't a third term for Roosevelt, Rhys wouldn't worry me. But Rhys is popular, God help us. He just might be elected. That's a greater risk than I care to run."

Connor rose from his chair. "That's all I came to say. Tell him to take his name out of nomination by midnight tomorrow, or there won't be a voter in this country who doesn't know he's a munitions man by the early editions."

Constance looked up at him from under her lids, her eyes fixed on Connor's as if to read his mind.

"Do you expect me to believe your only motive is patriotism?" she said scornfully. "Do you expect anyone— even your wife—to believe that? You've been waiting for twenty years to get back at Rhys and me, but you'll lose your wife and son if you do."

"Will you persuade him to withdraw or won't you?"

"Go to the devil," Constance said.

They exchanged a long, bitter look before Connor left. As soon as she was alone, Constance paced up and down, clasping her hands.

"He won't," she repeated. "He wouldn't dare. I won't say a word to Rhys. He might do something stupid if I do."

It was just as well, though, that they were going to

Southampton today. Connor might still try to get to Rhys—or he might try blackmailing the children! She picked up the telephone and gave orders to her secretary.

"Call my children, all of them, and tell them to be in Southampton by tomorrow afternoon at the latest."

♦

Connor put down the telephone and turned to Georgia in the small sitting room of their house in Alexandria. "It's almost midnight and there's been no statement from him yet."

She looked at him over Brandon's head, resting on her shoulder. The baby was fast asleep.

"I think this is the most delicious feeling in the world," she said, pressing her lips gently to her son's head. "I had forgotten how overwhelming a baby's trust is."

Connor looked at her in supplication.

"No, Connor, I want no part in this either way," she said gravely.

"Constance says I want revenge, pure and simple."

"Do you?"

"God, Georgia, how am I to know? Does a man know when he's come full circle? Or only think he knows? I feel as if I don't have the time to hate him anymore. There's no room for anyone but you and Brandon and Gianna. But can I be sure?"

She shook her head, at a loss, wondering how *she* could be sure.

"Why don't you sit here with Brandon for a while before you decide?"

He sat down and she put the baby in his arms and left the room. He looked at Brandon, deep in peaceful sleep, and joy overcame him, so intense that it brought tears to his eyes.

"I love you, my son," he whispered. "I never knew I could love anyone the way I love you and your mother."

He closed his eyes and searched himself for the hatred he had worn like a hair shirt since he was a boy. He listed Rhys's infamies one by one, but the litany had lost its power to infuriate him. He truly did not care what became of Rhys personally, only what became of Georgia and Brandon and Gianna, of Enoch, his own little family.

Brandon stirred, yawned mightily, and opened his eyes.

"What do you think, Brandon?" Connor asked softly. "Suppose Rhys were totally unrelated to us by blood and tears and circumstance. Suppose he were just another politician, a liar with possible Fascist sympathies. Would I fight him?"

Brandon followed the sound of his father's voice with unfocused eyes. He waved a chubby fist that grazed Connor's nose.

"Yes, I would, Brandon, with whatever weapon I could find. Crabtree's the only weapon strong enough to stop him now."

The baby's delicate lids, veined with tiny threads of blue, blinked twice and once more enclosed him into his infant dreams.

Shifting Brandon to his shoulder, Connor went to the telephone and called Barney Abbott.

"Not a peep out of him," Barney said.

"Then do it."

"It's the right thing, Connor."

"Maybe not, but it's the only thing."

He turned out the lights in the little sitting room and went slowly up the stairs to Georgia.

◆

"Be quiet!" Rhys ordered, striding down the hall of his house in Southampton. "I have to think."

"How could you have been so stupid?" Constance shouted, slamming the library door shut behind her. "Didn't you have enough money without making popguns?"

"It wasn't money, you ridiculous woman! It was power. Women don't understand that." Rhys flung himself into a chair.

Constance stood over him, hands on her hips. "You owed me the White House, Rhys. After all I've put up with since the day I married you, you owed me that. I had no idea about any of this."

She waved the headlines at him. PACIFIST SENATOR MADE MILLIONS IN WEAPONS.

He did not answer her. Soon there would be a crowd of reporters clamoring outside the gates, and he had to consider what to say to them.

At least his wretched sons were sequestered from the press. Fortuitous, Constance's having invited them to Southampton, or God alone knew what a clever reporter might have made them say! They had been huddled upstairs like frightened sheep in a storm ever since the telephones started ringing at six this morning.

Rhys had been on the phone for hours, with Constance glued to his side, while his erstwhile supporters told him how much he owed them, how they had warned him, and what he had lost. He didn't want to hear any more of it. He wanted to think.

He wondered briefly if something had happened to his star, but he couldn't accept that. He had never failed to get what he wanted—except the two things he wanted most: Georgianna and the presidency. Well, she was dead, but he wasn't, and there had to be a way to salvage his political career.

And after he had done that he must deal once and for all with the mill worker's son who had become his nemesis. Unbearable that Rhys himself had nurtured the seed of his own destruction. He must find a way to crush Connor and the MacKenzie press, and if Georgia went with him, so be it. It was no better than she deserved.

But not yet. He could not give vent to his ferocious wrath yet.

"What did your buddies say about the Senate?" Constance demanded.

"Nothing."

"Oh, God," she moaned. "If the Senate censures you, I'll never be able to hold up my head in Washington—or anywhere in this country! And there's no decent place to live abroad because of this goddamn war!"

"They won't dare censure me! Half of them own stock in munitions companies, including Crabtree, and they know I know it."

Then he was deep in thought again. A pulse was visible at his temple and she watched him, holding her tongue for the moment, not daring to tell him that she had been warned and had made the wrong judgment. He would kill her if she ever told him that!

Connor! She had suffered enough at his hands. She had laughed with the others when the widow Overholt took him for a fortune, but now Washington would be laughing at *her*.

"The war could save everything for me," Rhys said suddenly.

"What do you mean?"

"They'll need munitions makers if we get into this war. They've turned to us already, to build up the country's defenses. They lifted the arms embargo to get production rolling."

"You haven't been listening to yourself, Rhys! We're not going to get into this war!"

He ignored her. "My Senate seat's safe until 1944. A lot can happen by then." He stood and thrust his hands into the pockets of his velvet smoking jacket. "The isolationists won't want my support after today, but if Hitler keeps rolling or we get into the war, they'll be the ones on the wrong side of the fence." He got to his feet. "Get packed," he said to his wife. "You and I are going on an inspection tour of my plantations in Central America."

"Rhys, I'm not going anywhere near those pestholes of yours. Have you lost your mind?"

"Constance, listen carefully. I've lost the White House this time, but there's always 1944. Right now I have to get out of the limelight. When I come back I'll support Roosevelt's move to build up our defenses. Eventually, kicking and screaming, I'll support our entrance into the war. It's inevitable anyway. They'll need me then, and whom America needeth she doth not chastise overmuch. Do you understand?"

After a moment she nodded slowly. "You have more gall than any man I've ever met," she said, admiration in her eyes. "But what are you going to tell the reporters when they descend?"

"That I believe in peace and neutrality, as I've always said; that I'm still opposed to the President's initiatives for large offensive weapons—to keep Senators Nye and Borah off my back for the moment—and that most of Crabtree's production is small arms, the kind the Constitution gives us the right to carry. I'll apologize, without specifying for what." The pulse in his temple had stopped. "The public thrives on apologies, provided a man doesn't grovel excessively."

She almost smiled. He would do it, too, with that sincerity that fooled almost everyone. And they would forgive him because for them, as for her, it was better to have a clay-footed idol than no idol at all.

He was still working it out, chewing his lip. "I promise you this, Constance," he said finally. "The minute America's security appears to be threatened, I'll be home free. Now I must telephone Jonah Charles. Go and pack—and tell the children to go home, we're closing the house."

Constance left him, a curious excitement in her, as if she had fallen in love all over again. She went up the stairs and into the second-floor sitting room, where Will and Richard and their wives were talking with Jillian and Tim. They looked up.

"Well?" Tim demanded, bristling like a turkey cock.

Constance gave him a look of derision. "Go home, all of you," she said. "We're closing the house."

"Come on, Mother," Will insisted. "Tell us what he's going to do."

"Ride it out," she said.

"He lies for twenty years and he thinks he can ride it out?" Richard gave a short, ugly laugh. "Not this time. This time they've got him."

"You'd like that, wouldn't you?" Constance said. "You'd like to see him lose, no matter what it might cost you. Well, I'll tell you something. He's not going to lose. He's worth ten of all of you put together. So just keep your mouths shut and let us get on with it."

She started out of the room, then turned back to survey them all. "The trouble with you," she said, her lustrous eyes stopping on each of the three men, "is that you haven't got the balls God gave a newt!"

She tossed her head at their astonished gasp and sailed out of the room, thinking, how could any woman resist a man like Rhys? Nothing stopped him. By next year Washington might be laughing out of the other side of its face.

42

♦

"I don't think anything will ever surprise me again," Georgia said to Connor at the breakfast table on a Sunday morning. She spoke over the chatter of Gianna and Brandon, who was eighteen months old and often unintelligible to anyone but his half sister.

"You mean the Russian offensive?" Connor said. "I didn't think they had it in them either, not after the beating Hitler gave them. But what do I know? I didn't believe the French would surrender or the RAF could beat the Luftwaffe. I didn't think Hitler would turn and invade Russia as soon as he did. And I'm damned if I know what the Japanese are up to, except no good."

In a moment Connor emerged again from behind the *New York Times* and glanced around the table. "What's everyone doing today?"

"I'm going ice skating with some friends," Gianna said.

"Me, me!" Brandon crowed, clapping his hands.

Gianna looked pained.

"Nanny will take him," Georgia soothed. Gianna loved her baby brother, but there were limits to her devotion.

Georgia looked lovingly at her son. Brandon was going to be tall, and he already had Connor's beautiful face, but no dark clouds drifted across the sun of that personality—not yet, anyway. Maybe they never would.

"Where would you like to go, Brandon?" she asked him seriously. "You're still too little to skate."

"Onna buff," Brandon said.

"He'd like to live on the top deck of a Fifth Avenue bus." Georgia smiled. "How could I deny such a glorious infant?"

"You could say no," Gianna said tartly, but Brandon gave her such an adoring smile that she relented and jumped up to kiss him.

When Brandon was taken off for a nap by his nanny, quiet descended while the family riffled through the few dozen newspapers that were delivered daily to the town house. The large, square living room in New York, extremely elegant in silks and velvets when Brandon was born, had recently been redecorated in childproof chintz. A fire in the grate competed with the crackle of newsprint: with only fifteen shopping days until Christmas, the Sunday editions bulged with advertising.

Gianna, very aware of fashion at fourteen, noted that skirts were short and, because of a shortage of imported fabrics, would probably stay that way. But peplums were in style, and those huge Joan Crawford shoulders were beginning to shrink. Gianna wished mightily that she didn't have to dress like a baby, in knee socks and oxfords, a gray skirt, white shirt, and school blazer. On weekends she wore plaid skirts, sweaters that showed her pretty bosom, bobby socks, and saddle shoes.

Connor was checking on his companies' ads for new products. A Clarion television set was about to be put on the market. Clarion's FM radio had been introduced a few months before and was widely accepted.

The Great Depression was not completely over; statistics stubbornly revealed that over five million workers still could not find work, even though many others were employed at defense plants, AirShip among them.

In the comics things were no longer comical, nor were they absolutely neutral. While Dick Tracy was hot on the trail of lawbreakers, Joe Palooka had joined the army and Don Winslow of the Navy was looking for a saboteur.

America's one active involvement in the war had been virtually ignored by a country bent on neutrality: pilots of America's Eagle Squadron had flown with the RAF throughout the great air battle that saved England from invasion.

"I can't go," Racey had said, looking glum last year while the London Blitz was at its height. "Not if we're going to turn out the number of planes the army wants, let alone what England needs. Anyway, I'm too old for combat. If I put one of these new fighters into a dive, I'd black out. So would you." When there was no reply from Connor, he repeated it. "So would you!"

"Hell, I'm not too old. I didn't black out diving those J-15s."

Racey, still thin as a wire and looking, as always, much younger than he was, had stopped to stare.

"You're not going?" he demanded of Connor.

"No, I'm not going. I'm staying right here with my family, where I belong. Anyway, the army needs radio and electronic gear as much as it needs aircraft."

Racey, relieved, had contemplated his friend. "You're a contented man, aren't you? I never thought I'd live to see it."

A very contented man, Connor thought now with a glance at Georgia. It was quiet times like these he loved most, when he could believe that what he had was his to keep: his wife, his son, his daughter. Gianna was the biggest surprise of all, this bright, sensitive child of a mistaken marriage. Connor never referred to her as his daughter, nor did she allude to him as her father, but a loving bond had existed between them since the day Brandon was born.

Don't let anything change, Connor thought, looking at

Georgia and Gianna. I've waited so long for this. I only want to keep it.

"Let's take Brandon on the 'buff' ourselves," he said to Georgia. "It'll give Nanny a break."

"It'll give you a treat, is what you mean! Yes, let's take him."

"It'll have to be after lunch," Connor said. "I have to call Barney about some figures this morning."

It was not long after they were seated on the upper deck of a bus that afternoon that they noticed people running in the streets, calling to each other. Then small knots of excited Sunday window-shoppers gathered, ignoring the Christmas displays and stopping to talk to one another at corners.

"Something's happened," Connor said. "Let's find out what it is." He carried Brandon down the stairs and they got off the bus at the next stop.

"What's happened?" Connor called to a dour-looking man.

"The Japs have attacked Pearl Harbor, wherever the hell that is."

"Hawaii," Connor said, looking at Georgia in alarm. "Our Pacific fleet's based there."

"Well, I bet it ain't anymore, not all in one piece, anyway. Treacherous little bastards—beggin' yer pardon, ma'am." He went off down the street, where the holiday windows seemed suddenly dimmer.

"Buff!" Brandon yelled, waving his arms.

"Quiet, Brandon," Connor said, and the child subsided immediately, responding to his father's tone.

"Well, we're in it now," Connor said grimly, thinking how badly prepared the country was for war. "I wonder what the damage was. Let's find a place where we can get some news."

At Rumpelmayer's they found a crowd of people gathered around a radio lent by the chef, but since the first announcement at 2:25 P.M., there had been no further news, only repeat bulletins.

"Can we hold out until we're ready to fight back?"

Georgia asked him, sipping chocolate with Brandon on her lap.

"We'll have to. But if they got through our defenses to Pearl Harbor, they can get through to Alaska and the West Coast as well."

At home that evening the radio carried news of the anxious crowd gathered outside the White House, very like the crowds, Eric Sevareid was to remark, who had waited outside 10 Downing Street and the Quai d'Orsay in 1939, hoping for words of encouragement, since there was no longer hope of peace.

The next day sixty million people listened wherever there was a radio—turned up loud at corner candy stores or in parked cars in the streets, or hooked up to high school loudspeakers and company public address systems—while President Roosevelt delivered a brief message to the Congress. The United States was at war.

"Damned treachery!" Enoch thundered to the press. "An undeclared attack while their ambassadors were conferring in Washington. We'll show them what American labor can produce when its back is up."

"I never wanted to see another war," Congressman Oliver Petrie said from his office in Washington. "But this is one that must be fought."

An embarrassed silence prevailed among pacifists, isolationists, and America Firsters. The possibility of bombs falling on American cities had become chillingly real. With barrage balloons floating over Los Angeles and submarine watches being organized off New York, there was nothing they could say.

"They've folded their tents this time," Benton Daly told Connor on the phone from Washington. "We're shifting into high gear."

"I'm moving my family to Alexandria," Connor said. "Georgia and I both think we can do more to help there. Do you still want me?"

"We want you."

"Then I'll call you as soon as we've settled in." Connor

hung up and turned to Georgia. "Office of the Coordinator of Information," he said.

"I know I can be useful somewhere," she said. "Textiles are priority items and no one can get more yardage out of a loom than I can." She sighed. "It wasn't how I'd hoped to get back into the industry."

Four days after Pearl Harbor, Germany declared war on the United States.

"I've been doubly vindicated!" a jubilant Rhys declared to Constance, and within the week he was photographed between two sons in uniform. He had ordered Will to join the navy as a procurement officer; Richard was a lieutenant (j.g.) who would eventually serve aboard a destroyer.

Three weeks later the senator requested, and received, special permission from the White House to go to England on government business. The front pages soon carried a three-column photograph of the handsome legislator flanked by his look-alike pilot son and his visibly pregnant English daughter-in-law.

"He's diabolic!" Georgia told Jillian. "Will and Richard weren't enough for him. He had to use Malcolm too! He's worked his way back into the country's good graces already."

"Well, the country needs guns. Rowena's really pretty, isn't she?" Jillian said.

"It makes me angry," Georgia went on. "He virtually disowned Malcolm for joining the RAF and suddenly Malcolm's his fair-haired boy. What's he up to?"

"Well, well! You sound jealous."

"Only to you."

"Don't bark at *me*! Anyway, those boys make marvelous publicity after the Crabtree fiasco. Who can resist a politician who's part of the arsenal of democracy and has three fighting sons in the bargain? He's sure to keep his Senate seat in forty-four."

"Jilly, he still wants to be president!"

"Let him try! I'm sure you and Connor will find a way to stop him. Now I must run. I have a Bundles for Britain meeting. Come spend the weekend soon and we'll have a real chat!"

But soon they were all too busy for chatting, drawn into the hard work, the worry, and the excitement of a vast nation gearing up for total war. For years the United States had tried to stay out of the war. In the months that followed it was all anyone could think about.

♦

Georgia put on a terry-cloth robe and, rubbing her wet hair with a towel, walked into the bedroom of the Alexandria house.

Gianna looked up from the bed, where she was sprawled with a book. "Shall I do your shoulders?" Gianna asked.

"Oh, would you?" Georgia sat down at her dressing table, still drying her hair.

"Here, let me," Gianna said. She toweled her mother's hair vigorously, then took a wide-toothed comb from the dressing table and carefully combed out the tangles before she began kneading Georgia's shoulders. "Was it a bad day?" she asked presently.

"It was a silly day," Georgia replied, describing her meetings with the War Production Board. "The hosiery industry is afraid women will get into the habit of going barelegged and advises leg makeup and drawing seams on with an eyebrow pencil if the stores are temporarily out of nylons. That way they won't lose the habit. The girdle manufacturers can't get enough rubber to 'support' women in their war work. It was like the Mad Hatter's tea party."

Gianna laughed softly, and Georgia, watching her in the mirror, smiled. What an extraordinary creature her daughter was! Gianna was fifteen now, but she might have been thirty. She seemed to have left childhood behind in New York and taken up her own set of war responsibilities: day school, scrap drives, selling war stamps, helping Peggy keep house, and writing letters to Malcolm in England and the family at Charet-le-Roi.

"For their morale," she said. It was uncertain which of the letters to France got through. She had a few brief notes from Tony, saying little about his life but reminding her that he loved her.

Gianna had pinned a huge map of the world on one wall of her room, where she plotted the war and her three uncles' movements in it. Will and Richard, Georgia suspected, had been included out of family loyalty, but Malcolm was Gianna's second love, marked by a flag with a lion's crest. "Like the Lion Heart," she said. There was a second, smaller flag for Malcolm's son, Malcolm George Connor Fairleigh Brandon, born in June 1942. A large fleur-de-lis, the royal insignia of France, was planted firmly at Lyons for her father.

Now Georgia smiled at her. "Thanks for the massage, darling. It helped. What did you do today?"

"I went to *Grand-père*'s office and helped stuff envelopes. New York is falling behind in scrap drives."

Gianna maintained her relationship with Rhys without comment from Georgia. She did not question the chasm that existed now between her mother and her grandfather.

"Maybe she thinks all families are that way," Connor suggested.

"Whatever she thinks, she won't give up her right to whatever family she has left."

"There's no reason why she should."

Gianna was a busy teenager, an ardent salvager of rubber, tin, aluminum, and paper. The shortages were multiplying every day: no new cars had been produced since war was declared, and items such as hair curlers, stockings, sugar, gin, tea, rubber baby pants, appliances, new radios, metal office furniture, washers, sewing machines, and vacuum cleaners were hard to find.

"I'm starving and Connor's late," Gianna said, and they turned to the more mundane matter of what there was for dinner on one of the meatless days of the week.

◆

"Why me?" Connor demanded of Benton Daly.

"Something to do with the French Resistance. We've been expecting it since Torch."

Torch was the code name for the American landings in French North Africa a month earlier, in November 1942.

There had been opposition from France's Vichy Army—
which saw the landings as invasion, not liberation—but
the attack had also sent the Germans south across the
demarcation line to occupy all of France, including Lyons.

"If the Resistance is going to survive until we invade the
Continent," Daly went on, "they need all the support we
can give them."

"But anyone over there could go in my place!"

Daly shrugged. "For some reason they're insisting on
you. I'm sorry, Connor, but orders are orders."

There was no arguing with the Office of Stategic Services. He had known that before he accepted assignment
to the OSS when it replaced the COI and several other
groups hastily created to deal with intelligence after Pearl
Harbor.

Connor called home to say he'd miss dinner and stayed
to put his files in order. He was due at the airport early
the next morning.

♦

Georgia was upstairs reading to Brandon when Connor got
home, but Gianna was waiting for him. He kissed her,
glad of her presence. She had grown too quiet lately,
preoccupied with confusion about her father.

"The girls say he's a collaborator," she had told Connor
angrily, her eyes bright with tears.

"Then to hell with the girls!" he had advised her. "I'm
sure your father acted in the best interests of his country,
as he saw them. It isn't easy to stick it out during an
occupation, you know. Even if there are German troops
occupying two thirds of the country, the French at Vichy
control civil administration for the whole country. That's
better than letting Nazis do it."

He had spoken with far more conviction than he felt.
Vichy was a blot on French honor that it would take a long
time to expunge. As for Tony, he hated the very idea of
him.

But if the Vichy government had been excoriated before
the Germans spread southward, it was anathema now,

even in France. The Vichy Milice was actively helping the Gestapo in their roundups and mass deportations to the east, not only of refugee Jews and Jewish citizens of France, but—and this was the last straw!—of able-bodied Frenchmen as well.

Connor knew from the reports that came across his desk that there was suspicion in France about the ultimate fate of the resettled Jews—what use, after all, were old people, babies, and children in labor camps?—but that Frenchmen should be shipped off to work in German fields and factories was intolerable. Incensed by what they called the "real deportations," Frenchmen fled to the underground, some bursting to fight the Nazis, some solely to escape the voyage east.

Who spoke for France, then? was the question many Americans were asking. Vichy and Laval, who collaborated, they claimed, to keep France French—or de Gaulle's London-based government-in-exile which had never surrendered?

The more important the Resistance grew, the more Gianna questioned where Tony stood in this hateful combat by Frenchmen against their own people.

But tonight she was watching Connor, aware that he was troubled, and panicked by a sign of mortal weakness in a man of infallible strength.

"Is anything wrong?" she asked him.

"I'm going away for a while," he said.

"Going where?" It was Georgia, from the doorway, and he turned to her.

"London first. I don't know after that."

Georgia paled, but said nothing.

"Will you see Uncle Malcolm?" Gianna asked.

"If he's there." But Connor's eyes were on Georgia.

"Can you take him the scarf I made for him?"

"Sure, honey, go on up and put it in our bedroom. I'll pack it tonight."

Georgia, still in the doorway, waited until Gianna had gone, then shook her head. "I don't want you to go, Connor. I don't care if that's not the patriotic thing to say."

He went to put his arms around her. "God, how I love you," he said, his lips against her cheek. "Why are those words so banal? Why aren't there better words for what I feel for you?"

"Hold me," she said. "Just hold me."

♦

In London, Colonel Lord Edward Fairleigh was as perplexed as Connor.

"I don't know why, but they will meet with 'Corbeau' or no one. Coming after Torch, we had to agree." He shrugged. "You met a lot of Resistance people in thirty-nine and forty. It could be any one of them."

"Whoever it is, he's taken his bloody time since Torch! And can we trust him?"

"That's what I must decide, based on what you say after your meeting with him."

"When is it?"

"About a week, no more."

"So long?"

"The network's arranging to get him to your landing point. As soon as they do, you're off. You can get caught up on the picture here while you're waiting. And see my daughter. She could do with a little cheering up."

Connor called Rowena, and they met for dinner at one of her favorite restaurants. She was already seated, wearing her Women's Auxiliary Air Force uniform with that same spanking neatness he had noticed about her from the first. She stood when she saw him and they hugged each other.

"How are you, Ro?"

"I'll do," she said. "And you?"

"Going quietly mad," he admitted. "I never planned to be here."

"So I gathered from Daddy." They sat down and looked at each other. Something had changed her since that day when she announced her engagement to Malcolm; she was love rapt, riding her personal wave of happiness, feeling immortal. Now she had that strained look so many women wore these days, in their constant wait for news of destruction and death.

"Where's Malcolm?"

"I'm not sure," she said, and her mouth trembled. She looked at Connor with haunted eyes.

"I'll find out where he is," he offered.

"Daddy offered to do the same thing, but it's better not to know." She gave herself a brisk little shake. "Now let's talk about happier things and then I'll take you home to see Malcolm George Connor Fairleigh Brandon."

The little boy was six months old, with his mother's delicate coloring and Malcolm's vivid green eyes.

"He's wonderful," Connor said, holding him. "Why do I feel so proud?"

"Because you love his father and his father loves you."

His heart went out to her. "I never had much of a family, Ro, but it's expanding every day." He kissed the baby and put him back in his crib. "Come on, let's brave the blackout and go to hear some good music. We might even dance."

Rowena smiled. "I'm glad you're here, Connor, even if you'd rather not have come. All right, let's go dancing."

They went to The 400 and were caught up in the frantic gaiety of wartime London. The people in the nightclub had survived the Blitz and, for the moment, the war. They were warm bodies and they laughed and drank and fell in love to songs that said "I'll Be Seeing You" and "We'll Meet Again" with more hope than certainty.

♦

Five days later Connor was piloting a Lysander across the Channel, still pondering the identity of the man he was going to meet. There were any number of men in the Armée de l'Air who would have preferred to deal with him. The scornful British still resented France's lightning capitulation two years before.

The mission bore a heavy responsibility: to decide whether the man, whoever he was, could be trusted, and if the information he had to offer was worth the risk of plugging him into any part of the Resistance network.

The rendezvous tonight was in a field east of Rouen, and when he was over the general area he made two passes, buzzing his motor each time, before three lights leapt out of the pitch darkness, marking the ends of the runway. It was a short landing span even for the incredible Lizzie. He made another turn, cut his speed, dropped steeply over the trees, and bumped down onto the clearing. The Lizzie stopped obediently at the other end, where almost any other aircraft would have crashed into the trees.

"Good girl," he said appreciatively to the Lysander.

The signal lights went out. Connor cut his engine, slid back the hatch, jumped down, and waited, his revolver in his hand, until a low-pitched voice gave him the right greeting and he returned it.

"Where is he?" he asked, still in French, holstering his gun.

"Over there, in the trees with my partner." The man offered him a small bottle of brandy and waited while Connor took a swig and handed it back. "You can talk to him while we unload. I hope you brought plenty of Stens."

Connor nodded and pointed to the canvas-wrapped guns strapped to the Lysander's stub wings. "Ammunition in the other seat," he said, and followed his guide across the makeshift runway and into a grove of poplars.

The figures of two men emerged from the gloom and Connor, in a beam from one of the flashlights, saw Tony de Sevignac.

"I should have guessed," Connor said.

"Here's the flashlight," the Resistance man said.

"Turn it off. I'd rather not look at him," Connor replied shortly.

"Just signal with it when you've finished." The two men moved away and Connor turned to Tony.

"We don't have much time," he said. "What do you want?"

Tony was brief. He was offering to provide information from inside the Vichy government.

"The United States is not at war with France," Connor said.

"Among other things, it's information on my German friends I'm offering," Tony said.

"I see. Do you include Klaus Barbie among your friends?" Barbie was the notorious Gestapo chief of Lyons.

"No. Not him. He reeks of blood. But I'm in the confidence of several Germans in Berlin and I'm prepared to tell you everything they tell me," Tony replied.

"You can start now," Connor said, and listened intently to what Tony told him, committing it to memory.

"You've taken your time about doing this," Connor said when Tony had finished.

"It would have been dangerous to come to you as soon as the Germans crossed the demarcation line and swallowed the rest of France. They were looking for disgruntled Vichy men. I'd have ended up in Montluc," Tony said, referring to the prison in Lyons where Barbie conducted his tortures.

"And if Von Runstedt hadn't taken the south? Would you still be a Vichy supporter?"

"Your government was quick enough to recognize Vichy!"

"We didn't anticipate it would collaborate with the Nazis to the extent it has!"

"Well, neither did I!" Tony shot back. "Look, MacKenzie, I didn't make this world, I only live in it."

"With your new militia! They're as brutal as the Nazis are."

"The Milice and the Nazis won't win this war. The Allies will. And when you do, some collaborators will be shot and some will be persona non grata—for a while."

Connor made himself suppress his contempt for the man and concentrate on the essentials.

"De Sevignac, most of what you've told me I can get from the Resistance."

"I offered it 'among other things.'"

"I'm waiting."

Tony leaned against a tree. "For a man who knew Rhys Brandon had to be kept out of the White House, MacKenzie, you are politically naive. Don't you know that your leaders fear the French Communists as much as Vichy does and that the Resistance is riddled with them? There are two things vital to Pétain: that France remain French—which is why he made a deal with Hitler to let Vichy administer the country, occupied or not—and that the Communist threat be destroyed. Better Germans than French Bolsheviks who'll be puppets for Moscow."

"And where do you fit into this scenario?"

Tony leaned forward. "I can tell you what Vichy intends to do when the Allies finally invade France, as invade they must. If Pétain should convince the French people not to cooperate with the Allies, no invasion can succeed. You may see Pétain as a traitor, but to the French he is still the hero of Verdun, still 'Mon Général.' A proclamation from him still carries weight. Why do you think the Germans take such excellent care of him?"

"So you're offering political espionage."

"And help in keeping France out of Communist hands after the war. You're going to need men like me, take my word for it."

"And what do you want in return?"

"Protection from the excess of patriotic zeal that will be turned against collaborators when France is liberated. I expect you to get me out before that day. That's my proposition. Take it or leave it."

"We'll take it," Connor decided, "provided the information you gave me tonight proves out. We'll arrange to get your material out by courier." He paused. "Tell the truth, de Sevignac. You could have made this deal with anyone. Why did you ask for me?"

"Not because I enjoy talking to my wife's lover. But you know I can be trusted."

"Do I? You refer to me as Georgia's lover when we've been married for two years. If I get you out, do you plan to charge her with bigamy?"

"I could have done that at any time, regardless of the

war. But give me your word that I won't be branded a collaborator, and I won't contest the divorce now."

"God!" Connor said, brimming with contempt.

"Nothing personal," Tony went on. "A mere matter of life and death. Well? Have I your word on it?"

"No. If it weren't for Gianna, I'd let you hang for treason. Let's say my ultimate decision will depend on the quality of your information."

"Now I know why Rhys hates you so much," Tony said sarcastically. "You're as ruthless as he is." He paused. "I had another reason for wanting to see you. Tell me about my little girl."

"What're you offering in exchange for her?" Connor asked disdainfully.

"Please," Tony said, his longing in his voice. "Tell me."

Yielding, Connor told him about Gianna, speaking rapidly, incongruously, in this deserted field, about a young girl's health, her friends, and her progress in school.

"Is she ashamed of me?"

"Yes."

"Will you tell her you saw me tonight?"

"No. It could endanger too many lives if she ever let it slip, yours being the least of them."

"Have it your way, but my Gianna would never let it slip. She's a de Sevignac." Tony sighed heavily. "I can see you care for her and that's all that matters to me right now. Is Georgia well?"

"She's fine," Connor said.

"And your son?"

So he knew about Brandon!

"I prefer not to discuss my son with you."

"As you like, but since you have a child of your own, you will perhaps grant me one last request without conditions. If the Nazis discover me, tell my Gianna I tried, will you?"

"Of course I will!" The words burst from Connor, out of his unexpected compassion for this unpredictable man. He could never tell Gianna what happened if Tony were discovered and killed, only that her father was a man of courage, never mind his motives.

There was a short silence, then Connor went on rapidly. "You'll be contacted by another man, code name Gulliver, who never saw either of us. Don't respond to anyone else. Your code name is Cassius."

Tony accepted without comment the name of a man Caesar distrusted. "Contacted where?"

"Wherever it suits the underground. The mills, your house, possibly Paris. Espionage is a slow, painstaking process. Don't expect to see the results of your efforts for a long time, if ever."

"Don't lecture me, MacKenzie. Signal your men. I have to get back to Paris."

"Pleasure trip?" Connor inquired, flashing the light.

"I still sell silk to the couture for fashionable Nazi *herren und frauen*. It allows me a certain freedom of movement. When I travel to Berlin I hear interesting things. Goering is a great connoisseur of silk."

The two Resistance men approached and flanked Tony. "Do we kill him or not?" one of them demanded.

Tony's shock was almost palpable.

"Nothing personal," Connor told him. "A simple matter of life and death. No, don't kill him. Take him wherever he wants to go. I've finished here."

The taller of the two men accompanied Connor to the plane, shook hands, and went to rekindle the light at the far end of the field. There was no wind. Connor climbed aboard, started his engine, and swung the plane around. He waited for the light to appear, wondering how much of Tony's offer sprang from the desire to protect himself and how much from his need to repair his image in Gianna's eyes.

Either motive was more to be trusted than a sudden burst of patriotism.

Connor gunned the motor when the light flared. The plane leapt forward, surged up, and was airborne in one hundred and seventy yards, its undercarriage almost skimming the treetops. Connor patted the Lysander affectionately.

He would be back in London tomorrow and, with any luck, back in Washington within a week.

He thought of Tony. *There's good in him,* Georgia insisted. Maybe there was, just a little.

"Damn the man!" Connor swore, realizing that he had promised to get Tony out in time. Well, someone else would have to do that.

♦

Colonel Fairleigh nodded soberly when Connor reported the relevant portions of the conversation. He was far too much an English gentleman to comment on the obvious reason for de Sevignac's insistence that he would talk to no one but Connor.

"He's right about the political situation," the colonel said. "There are dozens of Communist groups in France. If they ever formed a coalition, the country would fall into their hands like a ripe apple. That is to be prevented at all costs."

"All costs?"

Fairleigh nodded soberly. "Even if it means a military occupation of France following the liberation. We'll have to make concessions to the Russians in Central Europe. We can't afford to give them any undue influence in France."

"And de Gaulle?"

"A voice crying in the wilderness."

"Sir, that voice—and the message it carries—is getting through to large groups of resistants."

"But will the Communists among them be loyal to us, or to him, or to the Party at the end of the day? And before we even get that far, will Vichy support or sabotage an invasion? That's what we have to know and that's what de Sevignac and his kind can tell us." He scrutinized Connor carefully. "Can we trust him?"

"Yes," Connor said, and hoped to God he was right. After a moment he asked, "Am I free to go back to the States, sir?"

"You will be in a day or two. There are quite a few

people in Whitehall and the SOE who want to talk to you." He smiled. "I'll do my best to keep you happy while you wait."

◆

"Where've you been this time, you old reprobate?" Malcolm said, opening the door to the Fairleighs' London residence.

"Malcolm! What a surprise!" Connor hugged him. "When did you get in?"

"Yesterday. I have thirteen days more."

He needed them, Connor thought, noticing Malcolm's gaunt face, his tight jaw.

"I hope you're not going to spend them in London," Connor said.

"No, we only stayed to see you. We're going to the manor in Kent. And you?"

Connor smiled. "Back to the manor in Alexandria."

"Still living in your old love nest? Isn't it time you built the princess a respectable castle?"

Connor handed his coat to the butler. "I will when the war and the shortages are over."

"Come and have a drink. There's something I'd like you to take back for me."

It was actually for Georgia, a proxy allowing her to vote Malcolm's shares of Brandon Textiles stock.

"I can't be bothered with that kind of thing in my line of work," Malcolm said. "I hope you don't mind."

"Why should I?"

"It puts her back into a relationship with Father."

Connor shook his head. "Your proxy—or my approval— won't influence her one way or another."

"That's all right, then," Malcolm said. He frowned again. "He's given me Brandon's Gate."

If Connor felt anything at all aside from disappointment for Georgia, it was a sense of relief.

"When?" he asked.

"He told me he was going to before Mal was born, and I've just now received the deeds. It was a gift, he said."

Malcolm smiled thinly. "Of course, it was more in the nature of a bribe. You know, so Ro and Mal and I will smile for the camera during his next campaign."

"Will you?"

"No. I agreed to a family photograph last year and you know what he did with it!" Malcolm looked at Connor almost defiantly. "But I wanted Brandon's Gate like the very devil, and I took it and to hell with his expectations!"

"Well, it was the right thing to do. You love the place."

"So do you and Georgia."

"Yes, but we can visit you there."

Malcolm nodded. "Well, I'm glad to see the rancor's gone, though I'm damned if I understand where."

"Neither do I, Malcolm. Maybe it's because so many other things matter more to me than Rhys, among them seeing you get safely through this war."

Again he was aware of Malcolm's restless eyes, his nervous chain-smoking, his inability to remain long in repose. But for that agitation, as he sat there with his long legs stretched out and crossed at the ankle, he might have been the indolent young Rhys Brandon, a bit thinner but all the same a golden boy.

But Rhys was fool's gold and Malcolm was the real thing.

"I'm feeling a bit ragged," Malcolm conceded. For him it was a significant admission.

"What is it, Mal?"

"The usual. It seems to be creeping closer," Malcolm said, gazing into his own distance, reluctant to say *death*. "And I have so much more to lose now, Rowena and my son and the life we want to live together. Maybe I've been too lucky too long." His eyes came back to Connor, waiting for his reaction.

"Don't you believe that," Connor said. "Tirzah once told me that luck isn't something that happens, it's something you make. I'm living proof. I've come through some dangerous patches on the luck I made for myself, and so will you."

A smile lit up Malcolm's face, as if Connor were the

Sibyl of Cumae and had just delivered a certain promise of life.

"Thanks, old man," he said softly. "I guess I needed to tell someone how frightened I am. Scared blue every time we scramble, if you want to know. It's hard to be a hero all the time."

"I'll take you as you are and so will Rowena. Malcolm, you don't have to prove your courage to anyone. You just have to keep your head and do your job."

Malcolm's blond head fell forward into his hands and he nodded. His shoulders dropped as some of the tension eased out of them. "God, I'm glad you came," he said softly through his hands. "You're the closest thing to a real brother I ever had."

"I wish I'd found you sooner," Connor said.

"Never mind, you're here now."

After several moments Malcolm tossed his head back, ran his fingers through his hair, and pushed his tall body out of the chair.

"Come on, let's go upstairs and see my son. Rowena says he liked his uncle Connor on sight."

♦

When he returned to America, Georgia's reaction to the news about Brandon's Gate was the same as Connor's.

"I'm sure his generosity will find its way into the newspapers," she said. "I'm glad Malcolm realizes why he did it."

"Don't you wish he'd attempted to bribe you instead of Malcolm?"

"No, Malcolm's a long way away. I wouldn't want to deal with Rhys at such close quarters, not about Brandon's Gate." She smiled. "Maybe Malcolm will want me to take care of it for him until he comes home."

Connor nodded, both relieved and apprehensive. He had once promised to get Brandon's Gate for her if she wanted it, but he had become increasingly reluctant to return to the place, lovely as it was. Still, if it made her

happy to take care of it for Malcolm, the least he could do
was help.

Connor had brought with him a photograph of the Malcolm Brandons: Rowena as fair as summer, Malcolm looking like an RAF poster, and the baby with his enormous
eyes and an expression as solemn as Malcolm's had been
at his age.

"Who's that?" Brandon asked, pointing to the baby.

"That's your cousin Malcolm."

"He's a baby!" Brandon said.

"So were you," Georgia said, wishing he still were.

"He's gorgeous," Gianna sighed. "I wish I could see
them all."

"You will, darling."

"I know, 'when the war's over.' But this war will never
end!"

◆

It began to seem that way. The war raged on, although the
tide had turned. In the Pacific, the long road back that
began at Midway would transform obscure islands and
atolls—Guadalcanal, Bougainville, Tarawa, Makin, Iwo Jima,
Wake—into historic battle sites. In the west, Italy would
surrender within the year and the RAF Lancasters and
American Flying Fortresses would bomb deeper into Germany every day.

It was the other news coming out of Germany that
appalled her when Connor told her some of it.

"Because I have to tell someone," he said. He was sick
at heart over the reports that crossed his desk about the
death camps in Eastern Germany and Poland, about accelerated transports of Jews, in unbelievably cruel conditions, to wholesale murder at the end of the line.

"It can't be true," she cried. "Why would the Germans
do such things?" And then, persuaded that they *were*
doing them, with the fabled precision and force of German
intellect, she asked, "What are we doing to save them?"

"There was discussion about bombing the rail lines to
the camps—or bombing the camps themselves. Many would

die, but it would be a cleaner death than the kind the
Germans inflict on them. In the end it was decided that it
would be politically unwise to make an issue of it." He bit
off the next words with acid mockery. "This must not be
seen as a war to save the Jews."

"My God," she whispered. "What are people made of?"

"Nothing admirable," he said bleakly.

"You are. Malcolm is. Brandon will be."

"It's all bloodlust, Georgia! It always has been, since
men started walking upright—and probably long before
that. It makes me wonder if any man knows what enormi-
ties he's capable of once the killing starts."

She took him in her arms. "Ask a woman. Ask me. I
know you through and through. You aren't capable of
infamy. You're not responsible for it and right now there's
nothing you can do about it."

"But someone must, and soon," he said grimly, and it
was then that she began to fear she might lose him to this
war.

43

♦

"The D-Day invasion will be a massive action, but
our little group will coordinate with the French,"
Benton Daly told Connor, pointing to a map of France.

Daly looked ill at ease in a colonel's uniform and Connor noticed that more than two years into the war, he still
twisted his wedding ring whenever he was nervous.

"You mean with the Free French?" Connor asked.

"And the French Resistance in general. Except for Cassius. He must be brought out. We need everything he can

tell us about the political climate inside France, and he's decided to clam up until he's out of danger. He's your special assignment."

"Damn it, Benton! Action in the field wasn't part of this deal."

"I did my best, Connor, but Cassius won't come out with anyone but you. You've been given the assignment. And a commission as major, U.S. Army. Your volunteer days are over."

"What do I want with a commission?" Connor demanded—and then he knew. Rank would offer some protection if he were captured behind the German lines, but only if the Germans chose to honor the Geneva Convention on the rules of civilized warfare.

Civilized warfare? The terms were mutually exclusive.

"When does the balloon go up?" he asked.

"D-Day? No idea. Winston and the boss are still fighting about where and when. Maybe never."

It was what Connor told Georgia a few days later when they were preparing for bed.

"I thought you'd do all your spying in civilian clothes," she said, eyeing the uniform on its hanger as if it were alive and deadly. "Can you refuse?"

He almost told her the worst of it—that he was going in for Tony at Tony's insistence.

"Would you want me to refuse?" he said, taking refuge in a cliché because he could not tell her the truth.

"Yes!" she cried, almost running toward him. "Yes! You've done all you could to help win this war and so have I. Why can't they leave us alone?"

"Georgia, I won't be in the fighting. I'm an intelligence officer, not a combatant. And it may never happen."

"Don't say that! It always happens." She held him, her hands moving over him as if she were trying to touch all of him at once, to gather him into herself, where he would be safe.

"Why do they do it?" she implored him. "What drives men to fight?"

"I don't know," he said with a great sadness in him.

"I see it in Brandon. Gianna was strong, even willful, but he's aggressive, like a bantam cock." She held him closer. "I hate you for it, do you know that? You think women are proud of you for bludgeoning one another to death, but they're not. They want live heroes, but they always hate the dead ones for leaving them behind to mourn. Why do you make me hate you when I love you so?"

He had no answer for her. He was speechless by the depth of her anguish.

"I want to make love to you," she whispered suddenly, frantically. "It's the only way I ever really have you to myself."

She unfastened the robe he wore and let her own peignoir ripple off her body to fall in a pool of silk. Naked, she kissed his mouth avidly, then let her body slide down the length of his until her cheek was pillowed in his groin. Her hands gripped his buttocks and her mouth enveloped him, but strangely, as in an atavistic ritual, at once a testimony to his maleness and a reminder of his human vulnerability.

He pulled her up and took her to the bed. He had seen her in many moods of passion, but she had never been like this, so violently possessive, as if she would subsume him and so save him from himself. She was astride him, covering him, her perfect hips grinding frenetically in pursuit of something she could not attain, her round breasts full in his hands, her closed eyes raining tears until he stopped her and pulled her down beside him, soothing her, loving her gently until her sobs were sounds of passion and her anger had become resignation.

"Forgive me," he pleaded. "I never meant to leave you."

"I know," she said, speaking rapidly, her words tumbling out like stones, falling one over the other. "But I'm so frightened for you. You mustn't die without me in some lonely place, no, you must wait for me and I'll come and die with you, because I won't live without you, not ever again, because I can't."

"I'm not going to die," he said, trying to believe what he said. "You're not going to mourn for me."

♦

His orders came in April, and he was ready except for a few last things.

One was a meeting with his father in the same bar in Alexandria where he and Georgia had risked everything to start down a new road together. It was different now: brighter, livelier, sharply at variance with Connor's mood.

Enoch was waiting for him, smoking a pipe and sipping Scotch whiskey in a booth in the rear. Connor bought himself a brandy at the bar and slid into the seat opposite him.

Enoch was only a few years away from seventy now. His hair was grizzled and age had blurred the contours of his face, but he was a striking man still, with the piercing dark eyes he had bequeathed to Connor.

"What's wrong?" he demanded.

"Is it that obvious?"

"It is to me, son."

Connor's voice dropped. "I have to go away for a while."

Enoch sucked his breath in. "Sweet Jesus."

"I want you to take care of Georgia and the children for me."

"Ah, Conn, did you think you had to ask me that?"

Connor shook his head. "No. I wanted to see you before I went."

Enoch cleared his throat. "When will that be?"

"That's top secret. I could be shot for even telling you I was going."

"I'd have shot you myself if you hadn't. You'll make it, Conn. You're like me. They try and they try, but we win in the end."

Connor nodded, then looked more closely at his father. "How are you? Your health, I mean?"

"I'm like Moses. I'll live to one hundred and nineteen, then I'll give a heave and coast into one hundred and twenty."

"I'll bet you will at that," Connor said. "When Mum used to read me Bible tales, I always thought of you as Moses. You're still a little like him, handing down the law."

"Your mother would say it's blasphemy you're talking," Enoch said, and suddenly they were remembering, and Connor was a child again, riding high on his father's great shoulders, hearing Enoch's booming laugh and feeling safe, safe, safe.

When it was time to go, he slid out of the booth reluctantly. "I wish we had more time to talk," he said. "But I've got a million things to go over with Georgia tonight."

His father stood with him, never quite as tall as Connor remembered.

"Anything else, Conn?" Enoch was waiting.

He's been waiting for years, Connor thought, and so have I. He put his arms around his father.

"Good-bye, Dad," he said. "Look after yourself."

"And you, my braw laddie."

Connor left without looking back, and Enoch sat down heavily in the booth, staring at his hands, spotted with age but carefully manicured.

"Dad," he said incredulously. "He hasn't called me that in forty years."

◆

"It's the invasion, isn't it?" Georgia said. "Tell me, Connor!"

He nodded. The invasion itself was no secret. It had been the obvious road back since Dunkirk, although the projected place and the date of the landings had shifted with the fortunes of war and the rise and fall of generals. Now, though, the time and place had been decided and that *was* top secret. Not more than fifty men in the world knew the details. It was devoutly hoped that none of them was German.

"When will you leave?" she asked him.

"Tomorrow."

"How long will you be gone?"

He shook his head. "I don't know, darling."

"Sometimes," she breathed, "I think we were fated never to live together. It took years for us to find our way back to each other, and still it doesn't work for us. No wonder I've always been afraid of love."

"It works for us," he said, his dark eyes pleading with her. "Don't be afraid of that."

She bit her lip, nodding. "I wish I could behave like those brave little wives in the movies, waving their men off with chins up and no tears until the train pulls out." She got up, feeling cold inside. "I need a drink, don't you?"

She poured two cognacs at the bar near the window and came to join him. They sat close together, their arms around each other.

He knew she was suffering and there was nothing he could do to help her. It was like watching her suffer labor pains; he had the same frustrated feeling of guilt and helplessness.

He held her, stroking her hair for a while. Then he said, "Georgia, there are some business matters I must go over with you."

"All right," she said, and the leaden weight inside her doubled. He had never done this before.

He reached for the stack of files on the desk, each a summary of one of his companies. Clarion's plant had been converted when the production of civilian radio sets was banned for the duration, but its broadcast and newspaper divisions were prospering, although he had sold several stations recently.

The Northern Light utilities companies had expanded near several military installations. Hemisphere Investments posted modest but consistent growth and profit in real estate and brokerage. AirShip, like every defense industry, was booming, and Connor's stock portfolio, still concentrated in technology and defense, was strong.

But the MacKenzie press, she knew, was his pride. It gave him a platform from which to air his views. It gave him the influence and power he had dreamed of in the hayloft at Brandon's Gate.

"I'll be interested to see what you do with them." He smiled, tapping an envelope. "These are my powers of attorney in case you need them."

She took the envelope he handed her. It had taken several weeks, at least, to prepare all this. Why hadn't he told her before tonight?

Because he knew I'd hate it, she decided. He knew I'd behave the way I'm behaving now.

She thought again what a terrible risk it was to love anyone. They would all leave you eventually, one way or another.

She watched him as he spoke, her eyes moving from his face to his body. It seemed impossible that something as small as a bullet could cut down that magnificent body forever, just blow his life out like a candle. Or maybe it would be a tiny, haphazard piece of shrapnel, shrieking through the air. She saw him lying in some muddy field in France, his restless energy stilled forever, with so much yet for them to feel and say and do together.

She made herself listen.

"Abbott will do the real work. If you could poke your beautiful nose into things whenever the spirit moves you, I'd appreciate it."

Why weren't they sending Barney Abbott overseas to be killed? Because Barney Abbott hadn't volunteered his services and Connor had, not in one war, but in three! But she didn't love Barney Abbott. She loved Connor precisely because he fought back.

He opened a folder labeled BRANDON and put it into her hands. "This is a running list of my acquisitions of Brandon Textiles stock," he said. "Hemisphere will continue to buy whatever comes on the market."

The number of shares he had acquired since their marriage startled her. She reopened the Clarion and Hemisphere folders and compared some dates.

"Connor, you've been selling property and radio stations to buy Brandon stock!"

"I have. More precisely, to buy a controlling interest in the mills for you."

"For me?"

"You want them," he said. "You've always wanted them."

"No," she protested. "Why would I want the mills?"

"Because he locked you out of them."

"You think that's the reason for my quarrel with my father?"

"Part of it."

She rejected that with a decided shake of her head. "In any case, you'd have to mortgage your holdings to the hilt, including the newspapers, to get control of those mills!"

"I'm prepared to do that."

Again she rejected it. She was thinking of him, not herself. Didn't he see that the mills and Rhys were one and the same? It was still Rhys he was after, always Rhys, even though he loved her. That would never change, that shadow standing between them, not even after Rhys was dead and gone.

After a moment she took refuge in small actions: the lighting of a cigarette, the pouring of two more cognacs. She came back to the couch and reluctantly took the thick, folded document he handed her.

He put the Brandon folder away. "There's only this," he said. "Then we'll have finished."

She knew it was his will, and she unfolded it, the heavy paper crackling in her hands, and made herself read its provisions. Apart from minor bequests to friends and a trust fund for Gianna, everything was hers, most of it in trust for Brandon, whose education he left entirely to her discretion.

Remorse assailed her. He trusted her absolutely with everything he had: his beloved son and the hard-won achievements of a lifetime.

She nodded, accepting responsibility for everything he had built, ready to defend that abandoned seven-year-old boy who had blundered into her life so long ago looking for someone to love him truly, faithfully, for always.

"I love you," she whispered. "You're the best man I ever knew. You deserve to have everything you want."

"You," he said. "You're all I want."

◆

"The wags insist," Colonel Fairleigh told Connor in London, "that only the barrage balloons are keeping this particular British Isle from sinking."

Connor nodded, reading the list of matériel now accumulating in the south of England for the invasion, in addition to three million Allied troops. The armada of five thousand ships included landing craft, transports, cargo vessels, coasters, minesweepers, and almost nine hundred war ships, among them miniature submarines to guide the assault craft through the darkness to the beaches.

The armada would take on board trucks, tanks and bulldozers, artillery, antiaircraft guns and ambulances, locomotives, field kitchens, hospitals, and laundries. For security purposes, the Allied invasion troops were already being cordoned off behind barbed wire and guarded by two thousand counterintelligence agents.

The intelligence people were sending in special tripartisan Jedburgh teams—American, British, and Free French—to prepare and coordinate Resistance attacks from the rear of the German forces.

"But what do the Germans know?" Connor asked.

It was not impossible to find out. The British had broken the German Enigma code early in the war and were privy to all the Nazi High Command's radio exchanges. The information gathered this way was invaluable, although the Allies were forced to act on it with great care, lest the Germans realize they had it.

"Ay, there's the rub." Fairleigh frowned, pulling the lobe of his right ear. "So far they haven't mentioned it on their radio calls. The Resistance is leaving false trails to convince them the landings will be at the Pas de Calais."

He handed another thick dossier to Connor. "Operation Fortitude is part of the deception, a fake army installation we've set up. We have acres of uninhabited tents, smoke from dummy field kitchens, cardboard tanks, false radio traffic, the lot—right across from the Pas de Calais to make the Germans concentrate their defenses there. But our job, yours and mine, is the French Resistance—or, rather, keeping all those splinter groups quiet until H-hour."

"What about Anvil?" It was the code name for the projected landings on the French Riviera.

"Postponed. They need every craft they have for Overlord."

"The Resistance will be disappointed," Connor said.

"Vichy, however, will be delighted. Cassius says Pétain has promised a proclamation in case of invasion: no aid to the invaders and no attacks on German occupation troops. So far, Cassius has been bang on in his predictions."

Connor, who had cursed Tony all the way across the Atlantic, nodded. "Will Anvil be canceled altogether?"

"That remains to be seen. Churchill is violently anti, Eisenhower is pro. FDR will decide."

There was a note in Fairleigh's voice that Connor had heard before. The Supreme Allied Commander, General Dwight David Eisenhower, wielded more power in England than had been held by a foreigner since the Norman invasion in 1066, and the British didn't like it. Nor did they like having the whole show directed by Yanks after they'd endured the Blitz alone and defended the west until their American cousins were forced into the battle. They treated the Yanks like naughty children: they were fond of them but appalled by their rude behavior.

Fairleigh glanced at his watch. It was 23:30 hours, time for the nightly BBC broadcast of Resistance messages. Fairleigh switched on the radio.

A series of apparently aimless remarks began, read in impeccable Parisian accents by one of the Free French.

"The molasses will turn into cognac."

"John has a long mustache."

"There are ashes in the soup."

These messages might signal the dispatch of a boat to a specific point on the coast to collect a downed RAF pilot, or the imminent arrival of three aircraft with an arms drop over a field in a *département* of France.

The broadcast lasted about five minutes and Connor

switched the radio off when it was over. "What's the signal for the invasion?"

"The first line of a Verlaine poem—*Les sanglots long des violins d'automne*—will alert them that invasion is imminent. The second line—*Blessent mon coeur d'une longueur monotone*—will mean the landings will come within forty-eight hours."

"Paul Verlaine will be turning in his grave."

◆

"Now that he's out of the country," Constance said, "the timing's perfect."

"I haven't the faintest idea what you're talking about," Sondra replied.

Constance snapped at a piece of celery and began crunching. "Your ex-husband, who else? God, but I'm sick of rabbit food!" She studied Sondra's face. "You don't diet, but you're too thin, you know. Regardless of the Duchess of Windsor's opinion, it is possible for a woman to be too thin. What you want is a nice dish of vengeance, properly chilled."

Sondra speared the olive from her dry martini. "I'm listening," she said.

Constance described a classic takeover. All Sondra needed to do was line up enough conservative money to add to her twenty-percent share of the former Overholt press and present Rhys with the means for a hostile takeover.

"Why Rhys?" Sondra demanded.

"Because it's almost nominating time again. Think what those papers could do for a Republican campaign!"

Sondra nodded.

"Of course, everyone loves a hero," Constance went on, "and Connor's been back in the public's good graces for some time now. But so has Rhys. Connor's enemies will go along if they're told Rhys is behind the takeover."

"Is he? What would Rhys want with a lot of newspapers?"

"That's beside the point. I don't intend to tell Rhys until it's a fait almost accompli." Constance decapitated a scalion. "Well, what do you say? Isn't it time that scoundrel vas forced to lose more than money?"

Sondra nodded. "High time."

"That's settled, then! Now we must hope Connor doesn't get himself killed before he's lost what he loves most."

"That isn't the newspapers," Sondra said, her face an igly red. "It's his wife. Did you know she posed for a series of nudes by Samson Breen?"

"So I've heard," Constance said. "But Rhys certainly wouldn't like it noised about."

"Connor bought up every one of those damned paintings. He had them hung in a room in that penthouse of his in New York. I saw them when Lester took me there. Walking into that room was like reading a dirty book."

"Fascinating," Constance said. "But we can't use it. Just get your friends together and Connor won't know what hit aim."

"I hope he does know," Sondra said. "I hope it kills aim!"

♦

"It's about time you came to New York," Jillian said. "Better than sitting in Alexandria, just waiting. I've invited Silas to dinner tonight. You were always fond of Silas."

Georgia nodded, listening to the voices of the children in the next room. Peter and Gianna were having a serious discussion about the war and Brandon and Alexandra were playing house.

Jillian's artificially bright tone softened. "He'll be all right, Georgia. I know he will."

"Women always say that to each other, but you don't know it and neither do I. I'm scared to death."

Jillian flew to her side. "Don't cry, Georgia, please don't. It frightens me. It's like the end of the world."

"I never knew you felt like that about me," Georgia said, controlling herself.

"Oh, yes. You were always brave and strong. Nothing

frightened you, not even Mama. You never batted an eyelash, no matter what she said. I envied you that."

"And I admired you for rebelling, even when it got us into trouble."

"I had no idea you admired me at all."

"Jilly, you know I love you."

"Love is not the same thing as admiration."

"No, but I *do* admire you! Your humor and courage and stubbornness."

Jillian hesitated. "There's something I've always wanted to ask you."

"Go ahead."

"All right, I will." Jillian took a deep breath. "Were you and Tim ever lovers?"

"No," Georgia said. "We never even came close."

"Well, I'll be damned. I'd have sworn you were."

"Does it change anything?"

Jillian considered that for a moment. "No. I didn't love Tim when I married him, but how could I? I resented him too much for wanting you. But I love him now and he loves me, and now is what counts, isn't it? Come on, it's no good moping around here. Let's go to the Plaza for tea."

◆

"Is Will certain of this?" Silas Cassadyne demanded of Timothy. They were alone in Silas's office at the Republic Industries building in New York.

"Will's seen the reports, Pa! They charge Brandon Textiles with shipping substandard merchandise: cheap dyes that run, canvas that doesn't keep the rain out, hammocks that shred, shirting and knit goods that fall apart in the first washing."

"God almighty, with a war on! That's what comes of letting strangers run his mills while he's in hot pursuit of the White House." Silas looked at his son. "This is not our fault. I told him we couldn't deal with the northern mills. We had enough to handle with all the others. I warned him. But he wouldn't listen."

"When did he ever listen?" Tim said disgustedly.

"But this time we'll be ruined along with him. Did you talk to him? What did he say?"

"I haven't been able to reach him yet." Tim's lip curled with contempt. "The senator is on a train bound for a speech in Boise."

Silas thought hard, his ruddy face stitched into angry lines. "I'll get through to his campaign manager and speak to Rhys as soon as he arrives in Boise," he said. "He'll have to get his political pals to keep that report out of the newspapers. In the meantime I'll call Procurement, army and navy both, and pretend we discovered it ourselves. I'll say we've already fired the men responsible and are starting to make restitution. That *must* be done before the report officially reaches us. You'll have to get to Brandon's Gate right away, Tim, and have a writ sworn out against those crooks. We'll not only fire them, we'll send them to jail!"

Two hours later Silas was repeating it all to Rhys on the telephone.

"So you'd better forget your patriotic speeches," he concluded hotly, "and get back to Washington. I'll meet you there tonight. I've done all I can, but if the press gets hold of this, I wouldn't give you two cents for a share of Brandon stock or Cassadyne either."

"Don't be an old woman, Silas," Rhys said, rattled but reluctant to praise his partner's quick thinking.

"That's easy for you to say! You've got Crabtree to take up the slack, but all I've got is my reputation as a textile man. I don't want it ruined by your stupidity."

"Get off the phone, Silas. I haven't got time to listen to you moan."

Rhys's hands were shaking when he hung up, and he was breathing rapidly. The room whirled for a second or two. Closing his eyes only made the vertigo worse.

This was bad. It was far worse than the Crabtree thing because there was no justification for it, none in the world. Anyone who shortchanged American fighting men would be pilloried. For a politician, it was the one crime as bad as illicit sex.

He opened the door of the small office that had been put at his disposal. "Cancel my speech," he told his secretary. "And get me on a plane back to Washington right now. Charter a plane. Buy one if you have to."

He went back to the desk, still slightly dizzy and utterly bereft, with no one to help him. He had sacrificed his sons to the war effort—although Will was still sitting on his behind in San Diego. He felt a mighty rage against Will and, consulting a small black notebook, he put in a call to his son, fuming while he waited for the operator to ring him back, pouncing on the phone when she did.

"Commander Brandon," Will's voice said.

"You useless little bastard!" Rhys said. "Why didn't you tell me?"

"I couldn't find you!" Will protested. "What are you going to do?"

"I wouldn't have to do anything if you'd been smart enough to find those reports and destroy them."

"Destroy them? I could be court-martialed and shot just for telling you about them!"

"If you want the truth, Will, it's time you did something to justify your existence, because up to now you've been absolutely worthless to me."

"Worthless?" Will shouted. "I've tried all my life to please you. Malcolm never did, and you gave *him* Brandon's Gate."

"After this last performance of yours, I ought to give him Brandon Textiles too!"

"I hate you!" Will shouted. "Do you hear me, you miserable bastard? I've always hated you!"

Rhys hung up on him.

44

♦

Georgia watched the anxious faces gathered in Jillian's living room the following night, knowing her decision was already firm in her mind. It was two in the morning and everyone but Silas, who had just arrived from Washington, wore nightclothes and robes. The atmosphere betrayed the serious nature of the discussion.

"I'd never have believed it," Silas repeated, shaking his head. "Those bastards—pardon me, girls—have been riding on his coattails for years, and they turned him down cold. But they were my friends too! If they wouldn't do it for Rhys, you'd think they'd have done it for me."

"Maybe they couldn't resist an opportunity to get Rhys out of their hair," Tim said. "He'll have to stop running for president—at last."

Silas gnawed his lip, staring at Georgia. "Do you have any ideas?" he asked tentatively. Georgia had a fine reputation in textiles, but she was a female, after all, and that made her perpetually a girl in his eyes.

"What you and Tim did today was brilliant," she said, "but under the circumstances it isn't enough. You and Father were the owners of record while that substandard stuff was being made, and you still are."

"So?" Tim said. For the first time in his life he was seeing Georgia in a nightgown and a robe, and there was nothing on his mind but business.

"You'll have to make some changes," Georgia said, "before they're made for you. The government doesn't even have to bring charges. The War Production Board has the power to limit your production or stop it altogether—or to cut off your raw materials, which amounts to the same thing. I've worked with those people for years and I'm sure I can convince them this wasn't your doing, even though it remains your responsibility. Then you'll have to persuade military procurement not to take its orders elsewhere and—"

"The WPB can't keep the story away from the press!"

"No, and Brandon stock is bound to plummet. But the report will lose impact if Brandon Textiles has a new chairman before the report and the story are even published."

"Impossible," Silas declared. "Rhys will never step down!"

Georgia took a moment to reply. It had become clear to her over the course of this long afternoon that Connor was right: she had coveted her father's mills for a long time.

It wasn't Connor who was still tied to Rhys. It was herself.

She clasped her hands in her lap. "He will step down for me," she said, looking around the table. "And if he refuses, I'll force him out, provided you give me control of enough stock."

"You'd do that to Father?" Jillian exclaimed.

Again Georgia looked around the circle. "I need your shares. I'm offering to buy them at sixty-five percent of market, which is all they're going to be worth for a while. As soon as—"

"Seventy," Silas interrupted her, and after a moment Georgia nodded.

"That's still highway robbery!" Tim objected furiously. "I'm not going to hand over my share of the Brandon mills to you! I've swallowed too much of my pride to earn it."

"Let me finish, Tim. I'll undertake to sell a portion back to you at the same price as soon as this blows over. I'll retain only what's necessary to guarantee my position as chairman of the board."

And what Rhys should have given to my son on the day he was born, she added mentally.

"You'll be taking an enormous risk," Silas said. "Suppose the government prosecutes? Suppose the military suspends orders to our mills? And the scandal—suppose you can't get past that?"

"I *can* and I *will*," Georgia said firmly. "But I need the power to do it." She paused. "Nothing will change. We'll be partners in the mills that you and Father own jointly and we already agree on how they should be run." Her eyes met Silas's, then Tim's.

"You want the mills for Connor!" Tim blurted out suddenly, his face an ugly red.

"No," Georgia said. "I want them for myself."

"I don't believe that," Tim said.

"I do," Jillian said. "She's always wanted them."

There was a momentary silence.

"But the money's Connor's," Tim insisted.

"Some of it." Most of it, but she couldn't tell Tim that.

"So he'll be running the mills when he comes back."

"He'll have to take them away from me first," Georgia said.

"You've always given him anything he wanted," Tim said with a loaded look that made his meaning clear. "But I for one am not ready to get into bed with Connor MacKenzie."

"Well, I am, if it comes to that!" Silas said, thumping the table. "I always liked that boy. He has gumption." He turned to Tim. "Son, you'll have to bury your old grudges or we might lose our shirts."

"But why should we dump an empire in *her* lap? Why not in mine? I wasn't an owner of record."

"Then by all means take over, Tim," Georgia said, briefly apprehensive that he might do just that. But Tim had never been a gambler. She added, "Provided you have the influence and are willing to risk that much of your own capital."

Tim's jaw moved as he clenched his teeth. He stared, narrow-eyed, at Georgia. "If Connor were here, I'd swear he'd paid off those windbags in Washington to withdraw support from Rhys."

"Malarkey!" his father said. "Why would Connor sabotage something he wants? I'm not going to look a gift horse in the mouth. I'll sell you my shares, Georgia. Tim, what about yours and the children's?"

Tim nodded shortly, avoiding Georgia's eyes.

"Jillian?"

"Why not? It'll serve Papa right."

Silas was making notes. "Georgia, you've got your stock and Gianna's. Plus ours. What else?"

"Connor's—"

"There!" Tim exploded. "I knew it!"

Georgia went on. "And every share I can buy. And Malcolm's proxy. And Will's, unless he changes his mind before he goes on active duty."

"Active duty?" Tim echoed. "Will?"

"He called me today. He doesn't give a damn about the mills anymore. He and Father had a terrible argument and he's asked to be transferred."

"If everyone in this family went to war after an argument with Father," Jillian said, "we'd all be in the front lines." She yawned. "I'm going to bed. Silas, your room's ready if you want to stay."

"I do. There are details to be ironed out in the morning."

♦

The press had the story two days later and Georgia began to buy Brandon stock as it was dumped on the market to begin its precipitous slide. Washington buzzed with yet another Brandon scandal, but the attention of the general public was riveted on Brandon's glamorous new board chairwoman.

The war had put thousands of American women to work for the first time in their lives, without their having to suffer clucks of sympathy for lacking a provider, or disdain for losing their femininity. They liked their new independence.

Eighty-five thousand were in women's branches of the army, navy, coast guard, and marine corps. There were women running small family businesses and vital volunteer services, driving trucks and ambulances, staffing and directing the United Service Organizations to provide entertainment for the troops. The idea of a woman running a

mammoth corporation did not shock most of them, particularly when the woman was Georgia MacKenzie, whose
exciting career they had followed since she was the "American princess."

Georgia chose a dress of vivid royal blue silk, high-
necked and long-sleeved, to chair her first meeting. Her
hair, under a matching fedora, was pulled into a chignon
low on her neck, the style she most preferred.

"That color's a bit festive for the occasion, don't you
think?" Jillian whispered, peering through a crack in the
door at the crowd of well-barbered and tailored men gathered in the boardroom.

"*Vogue* doesn't think so," Georgia said. "Neither does
Time. There was a photo session this morning. The board,
of course, is expecting docile black with pearls and humility. This will put them off their stroke."

"I should have guessed," her sister said. "Humility was
never your strong suit. Shall we go in?"

"You go ahead. I'll come in when everyone's seated."

"A dramatic entrance?"

"Yes. I want them to stand up for the new chairman of
the board."

"Father won't be here."

"I know." Rhys, in fact, had not been seen in public for
several days.

"He's not sick," Jillian said. "It's frustrated ambition.
Mama says his political buddies not only refused to quash
that report, they told him he was a political dodo doomed
to extinction after serving out this Senate term."

"That would kill him."

"Would you care?"

But Georgia, adjusting her hat in the mirror, knew
suddenly that she *did* care. The game was hardly worth
the candle if her father wasn't there to see it.

"I must say, that avalanche of paper seems to agree with
you," Jillian said, looking at Georgia's reflection. "It's been
raining instructions, affidavits, transfers, and I don't know
what else for two weeks."

"It's like running the de Sevignac mills again," Georgia

said. "But these mills are mine, and the feeling of power that gives me is astounding."

"*You* astound me," Jillian returned. "You always have. You've got a face and figure most women dream of, but that's never been enough for you. This is what you want! Control of some dreary mills and power. Father's power! You're as bad as Connor."

"No," Georgia said. "I'm worse than Connor because he's past it and I'm not."

There was a knock at the door and Jillian, with a final gesture of incomprehension, gave her hair a last pat and left the room. Georgia, with no time to think about her motives now, prepared to follow.

◆

It *is* a dramatic entrance, Jillian thought minutes later when Georgia walked into the boardroom. Her sister had always combined absolute poise with sensuality and never more so than now, in that all-concealing, all-revealing dress, its electric color reflected in her cool blue eyes and the flashing diamond earrings she wore.

There was a rustle as the men around Jillian rose.

I'll bet more than their legs are standing up, Jillian thought, smothering a wild little laugh.

So there they stood, out of deference to a woman who didn't give a damn for that empty kind of deference. They had obviously come prepared to help the little lady along, but as the meeting progressed, there was no doubt that she was firmly in control without any help.

Rhys, as expected, was not present. He had refused to see Georgia at all since she forced him to step down, although he pretended to be proud of her for the benefit of the press.

"Glad he didn't turn up today," the board members whispered to one another with the universal glee accorded the fall of a titan. "Shoddy goods to our boys! It's worse than the munitions thing!"

But the consequences of a Brandon mills failure made them shudder. They did not enjoy being directed by a woman—particularly one who aroused more than their business instincts—but she had a solid reputation in textiles and was, moreover, a favorite of the press. The company needed all the good publicity it could muster.

"Better a Brandon in the driver's seat than a stranger," they had all agreed, "provided the Brandon isn't Rhys."

"He'll instruct her from behind the scenes until her brothers come back to take over," one of the less perspicacious directors told Timothy Cassadyne when the meeting was over.

"No man can instruct that woman," Tim said, grimacing. "I wouldn't give you a nickel for Will's chances, or Richard's either, of ever running those mills again."

The board member recalled that exchange with a shudder when Will Brandon was killed in the Pacific.

♦

"Where is he?" Georgia asked Constance when the memorial service was over and the guests were leaving Rhys's Georgetown house.

"In the loggia, but he doesn't want to see you," Constance snapped.

"Then he can tell me that himself."

She walked the length of the loggia until she found Rhys sitting in one of the chintz-upholstered wicker chairs, in an attitude long familiar to her.

"Hello, Father," she said.

Rhys, his face pinched, his eyes bleak, looked back at her.

Oh, my God, she thought, can I still feel compassion for him?

"Will and I argued the last time I spoke to him," Rhys said hoarsely.

"I know."

"He told you about that? Did he tell you what I said?"

"Does it matter? You and Will were always arguing."

"Not like that! I told him he was worthless." He looked up at her, inviting a rebuke, almost needing one. "That's why he's dead."

She sat down in the chair next to his.

"Do your godlike powers extend to matters of life and death? Then save Connor for me. Save Tony for Gianna. Save Malcolm for all of us. Save the whole benighted world."

Rhys turned away. "I don't understand you. I never understood any of my children. Except for Malcolm, I don't much admire them." His glance flickered toward her, then away. "But at least they didn't take control of my company away from me! You did that."

"Better I than someone else, surely."

"I'd agree if that were true, but you took it for Connor!"

"No. That's what I came to tell you. I took it for myself."

He regarded her suspiciously. "Why?"

"To show you that I could!" she said, angry again. "To show you I wasn't part of your collection—or Tony's, or anyone's! As soon as I've put things in order, you can have your damned mills back. All I want is the share in them that you denied my son. I don't want him to wonder why he was the only Brandon whose birth was unmarked by a traditional gift of stock. I don't want him wondering why he was singled out for exclusion. Children wound easily. But you've always known that."

He remained silent and she looked at him, her anger flowing away, diluted by something akin to pity. Rhys had always been the god of his own creation, and now he was faced with a dilemma. He was a self-infatuated man whose glory had suddenly evaporated. There was nothing left for him to worship and no one who would worship him.

"I want to see my grandson," he said suddenly.

"Why?"

He seemed startled. "Because he's mine!"

"Yours? You called him an abomination before he was born."

"For God's sake, Georgia, must I be accountable for every word I've ever spoken in anger?"

"That went beyond the bounds of anger, and yes, you are accountable." She looked at him in silence for a few moments before she said, "All right, for his sake, because

he deserves to know his family, I'll bring him to see you.
But I'll stay with him while he's here."

He was astounded. "Do you suppose I'd harm the child?"

"You'd try to *mold* him, to *form* him, the way you tried
to form me and Malcolm and Connor. You'd try to turn
him against his father. You love tinkering with children
when they're young. That's why you gave Brandon's Gate
to Malcolm, to get him back so you could create little Mal
in your own image! Don't you think Malcolm knows that?"

He pressed his lips together, his hands trembling slightly.
Her heart turned over again, and she struggled to see him
objectively, as she knew she must. He was like a wounded
lion shorn of his power over the pride. He was apparently
defeated, but not dead, and he was still capable of maim-
ing anyone who got too close to him.

Rhys turned to her, a gleam in his green eyes. "But
Malcolm accepted it, didn't he?"

"Of course he did. He loves it! *It*, Father, not you. He
loves the years we lived there with Dilys and Jilly and
Uncle Adam, and the memory of love before we were old
enough to know the price of it. He loves what I love."

"Are you suggesting I should have given it to you?"

She sighed. "It was never your property I wanted,
Father. It was you." She got up suddenly, overwhelmed
by the hopelessness of it. "I'll bring Brandon in a few
days. I must go home now."

She left him, feeling free of him, as Connor had been
for years now, had her own vision been clear enough to
see that.

Come home, she pleaded silently to Connor. Come
home so I can tell you I'm the one who was shackled to
him, long after you had let him go.

◆

"Brandon, this is your grandfather."

"How do you do, Grandfather?" Brandon, his thick
shock of dark hair brushed, his face shining, his expression
expectant, offered his hand.

Rhys took it, thinking that the child's dark eyes seemed to peer into his heart. He cleared his throat.

"You're a tall fellow for your age."

"My father is very tall," Brandon confided. "He's in the war," he added, concern clearly mixing with his pride.

"I know your father. I met him when he was a few years older than you are. He'll be back, don't you worry, if only to plague me." Rhys lapsed into a momentary silence. "Well, now, I have something for you out on the loggia. Do you want to see it?"

Brandon looked at his mother for approval. "Yes, sir," he said. "Can I take it home with me?"

"It's too complicated to transport, Brandon. I think you'd better come here to play with it. That way we'll see more of each other." Rhys glanced at Georgia and rose from his chair. "Shall we find out what it is?"

"Yes, please," Brandon said, looking up at Rhys's height. "You're tall too." He turned to his mother, nodded as if pleased with this adventure and, tucking his hand into Rhys's, skipped along beside him.

"A touching sight," said Constance's voice behind her.

"I think so," Georgia said.

"What a hypocrite you are! You've taken everything from him."

"I intend to keep only what is mine and Brandon's."

"But Connor took the White House from him. Do you suppose Brandon can make up for that?"

"Brandon's not a pawn in this game any more than Gianna was. Rhys is Brandon's grandfather. They have a right to find out if they like each other." She started for the loggia while, behind her, Constance demanded, "And what will Connor have to say about that?"

But Georgia had no way of knowing, only the conviction, while she waited for word from Connor, that she had done the right thing.

In addition to her job at the War Production Board, she worked incessantly to make the mills produce. She watched the price of Brandon stock stop sliding, then slowly, painfully, begin to inch its way up in the direction of the price she had paid for it.

The press, which had come out screaming for Brandon blood, had turned more benign recently because she made good copy even without a scandal. She was often photographed, wearing black for Will, looking beautiful, capable, and calm. Inside she was shivering with apprehension lest the black be for Connor.

And then, not long after Will's funeral, the Brandons were swept off the front pages by the Allied invasion of Normandy, and she knew where Connor was and why he hadn't written.

In the sitting room in Alexandria, Georgia watched Gianna update her maps. Will's flag, with a gold star on it, remained in the Pacific where his ship had gone down, but Gianna was moving Connor's and Malcolm's from London to the Normandy beaches, where Operation Overlord was in bloody progress. Then she came to curl up on the couch beside Georgia, and they sat in the fading light of a June evening, staring at the map as if it could reveal where Malcolm was flying, where Connor had landed in Normandy.

◆

But Connor was not in Normandy. He had been sent to the south of France soon after D-Day.

"The southern Resistance," Colonel Fairleigh had recapitulated for him before Connor left England, "is already sabotaging rail lines and roads throughout the area to keep German reinforcements in the south from reaching Normandy. I'm afraid some of the resistants still think Anvil is part of D-Day."

"But if they rise, they'll be slaughtered by the Germans!"

"Most of them have been warned," Fairleigh replied. "Not all, I fear. Do your best. There must be no risings yet."

Fairleigh paused for a moment, his face grave, then went on. "In addition, it's essential to arrange that arms and ammunition drops, when and if we make them, do not fall into the hands of the Communist Resistance."

"Politics again," Connor said. "At a time like this!"

"Politics indeed. Much as Churchill and Roosevelt detest de Gaulle—and we're all agreed he's an arrogant bastard who believes he *is* France—they'll let him head a provisional government just to keep the Communists out of power. So we cannot arm the Communist resistants, and we must control the other splinter groups of the underground as well, or there could be civil war in France after the liberation."

"I thought we were fighting Nazis," Connor said. "But Cassius once told me I was politically naive."

The colonel looked up. "We're going to need men like Cassius in postwar France. Thus far he's been clever enough to stay off the Gestapo's list of suspects, but his luck can't hold much longer. He's in danger from both sides and he must be fetched out of Lyons before he's executed as a collaborator by the Resistance. You ought to be back in London with him in two weeks at the outside."

Connor was flown aboard a Royal Air Force Halifax from Tempsford to Clermont-Ferrand, a Resistance center some hundred miles west of Lyons. He was met by French agents of the OSS network whose hostility he sensed the minute they picked him up. They had been waiting four years to fight Germans in the open, and the chance had been denied them again.

The chief of this Resistance cell was waiting for Connor in the curtained, candlelit kitchen of a farmhouse on the road to Clermont-Ferrand. The smells of cheese and sausage blended with that of an oil used to lubricate guns. A vat of laundry boiled on the stove and the odor of wet muslin made him think of laundry day at Brandon's Gate.

He knew something about the man he faced. Codenamed Claude, the chief had heavily lashed brown eyes and a baby face that belied both his age and his proven talent for sabotage and espionage. Before the war Claude had been a philosopher of repute, but to judge from the hard intensity of his eyes, contemplation of man and the universe gave him far more pain than comfort now.

He was still a teacher by profession. A clubfoot had

spared him from conscription by the French, and his profession from deportation by the Germans. He smoked constantly, the cigarette pinched between fingers stained deep gold.

The farmhouse itself was crammed with OSS equipment, principally radio sets, grenades, M-1 rifles, and rounds of ammunition. After a brief exchange of news Claude opened a cabinet stacked with boxes of the potassium cyanide capsules made by Squibb for the OSS.

"We're not dealing with men," Claude said dryly, handing a capsule to Connor. "The SS are beasts. Or, if you prefer, butchers, like the one in Lyons."

Connor put the capsule in his wallet, uneasy at holding his own death in his hands.

"You probably think it an excessive precaution," Claude declared, scrutinizing him. "Even melodramatic."

"No," Connor said. "I'm surprised you haven't had to use them more often." He paused, reluctant to ask the next question. "How do you protect your network from infiltration by collaborators?"

"Ah, yes, the collaborators," Claude said bitterly. He sucked the smoke of his cigarette deep into his lungs. "I accept only men with a personal score to settle, preferably those who've had a father or brother killed or transported." His mouth twisted. "Macabre credentials for a job, aren't they?"

Connor nodded. "It's a macabre world. I'm authorized to tell you that one of our most valuable agents in Lyons is in the Vichy government and I must get to him before the Resistance does."

"Who is he?"

"The Marquis de Sevignac."

Claude whistled. "That Fascist rat? Then he's fooled a lot of people, including me."

"The Communists call him a capitalist rat, but he's been giving us prime intelligence for over a year."

"To save his skin, no doubt. After the liberation, everyone in France will claim he was in the Resistance."

"Not everyone in the Resistance is completely pure

either. At any rate, I'm not here to question de Sevignac's motives. My orders are to bring him out."

They went to Lyons a week after the Normandy invasion to meet with a Resistance chief at the Café des Beaux-Arts. De Sevignac, the man told them, was in Berlin. Connor would have to wait.

♦

"There's noise someone's out to buy up the MacKenzie press," Enoch said, proceeding carefully.

"How do you know?" Georgia asked him, alarmed.

"The usual way. An exchange of favors."

They had been walking toward a park some distance from the WPB and now they sat side by side on a shaded bench. He hated to worry her. He was very fond of her and she had enough on her plate already, since she had been dividing her time between Washington and New York, working for the War Production Board and running the mills.

"It couldn't come at a worse time," Georgia said. "A lot of Connor's money is tied up in Brandon stock and that hasn't recovered enough for me to borrow against it."

"Borrow?"

"Whoever's behind this will offer the stockholders more per share, and the only recourse is for me to match it."

Enoch crossed his bulky arms and chewed his lip. "You may not have to," he said. "The takeover was started by the ex-Mrs. MacKenzie and your stepmother."

"That's different!" Relieved, Georgia shook her head, her shoulder-length blond hair swinging. "They scheme and plot but they know nothing about business."

He nodded. "Aye, but they do! They've been lining up the money. The thing is, the money told them flat that it's no deal if the Overholt woman's in the driver's seat again, and she told *them* that Rhys Brandon's behind the whole thing."

"Father!"

Enoch nodded. "It might not be true."

"Why not? He's done worse! He doesn't believe I'll give up the mills and he's doing this to pay me back!"

"You must leave him to me," Enoch offered.

"It's Connor and me he's after, Enoch! And this time he might get Connor's papers because I made a terrible mistake in judgment! I thought we'd reached a kind of understanding." Her face betrayed her pain. "Not love or trust, it could never be that, but at least an armed truce."

"There, now," he said, ready to defend her against dragons. He took her hand. "Georgia, do you trust me?"

She focused her attention on him, her affection for him plain to see. "You know I do."

"Then I'll see to it."

It took him two days to get through to Rhys on the telephone.

"I have something to say to you, Brandon," he announced.

"Then say it and be quick about it."

"It's to be said in person. I'll come to you."

"Out of the question."

"It concerns my son, Brandon. He's got his life on the line, never mind he's your girl's husband and Brandon's dad. If you knife him in the back now, you'll have to resign from the Senate."

"I don't know what you're talking about."

"There's only one way to find out."

Enoch was shown into the Georgetown study late that evening. Rhys did not invite him to sit down, nor did he sit himself. They stood, Rhys as finely drawn as a Picasso and Enoch as broad as a stevedore, while Enoch outlined the proposed takeover of the MacKenzie press.

"Organized by those two females," he finished.

Rhys looked genuinely astonished. "I had nothing to do with it," he protested.

"Maybe. But who'll believe your wife wasn't acting on your instructions?"

A red stain of anger darkened Rhys's cheeks as he considered all the implications.

"I'll put a stop to it," he said. "You have my promise."

"Your word's not fit to shovel dung," Enoch said.

Rhys stiffened. "Get out of here, you peasant!" he ordered. "I don't want to lay eyes on you again as long as I live."

"You will though," Enoch said on his way to the door, "unless I can tell Georgia you've pulled the plug on this scheme."

"You must tell her I had nothing to do with it!"

"I might even do that," Enoch said over his shoulder, "if the humor is on me."

When he had gone, Rhys strode to the study door, flung it open, and went upstairs to his wife's room.

"Do you know who's been here?" he fumed from the doorway. "Enoch MacKenzie!"

"Why?" she demanded, amazed.

"He came about *my* part in the proposed buyout of the MacKenzie press."

She blinked a few times, then tossed her book aside. "Damn the man! I wanted to tell you myself," she said. Her satisfied smile faded as he approached her chaise longue.

"Are you out of your mind?" Rhys roared. "What possessed you to lend my name to such a harebrained scheme?"

"Why not?" Constance shouted back. "I've already organized almost all the backing you'll need to take those newspapers away from him."

"You ought to be locked up! I'll have to put an end to this myself."

"It's that brat of his, isn't it? You've gone sentimental over him in your dotage, just the way you did over his father. I warned you then, Rhys! I warned you."

"You meddlesome bitch! Don't you understand that I'm in no position to act against him now? We're at war. He's a man on a mission, for the OSS no less. God knows what else he's found out about me."

"You mean there's *more*?"

He waved an arm, too angry to speak.

"What am I supposed to tell your prospective backers?" she demanded.

"I'll tell them myself," he rapped. "You're a stupid woman with delusions of grandeur."

"And you're a fool!" she said. "I'm the one who should

be carrying on because you lost us your last chance at the White House. But am I? No! I arranged a brilliant maneuver for you—and you haven't the guts to go through with it. Or maybe you're still in love with your daughter."

"That's *enough!*" he whispered savagely.

She recoiled from the look on his face and he left the room. She watched him go, as furious with him as she had always been but for vastly different reasons.

Now she always knew where he was. So elusive for years, Rhys was constantly underfoot, waiting for calls to glory that would never come because he had been dumped by the people who made presidents. He was counting on reelection to the Senate in November, but she was not at all certain he would win.

There were a hundred other schemes he could have been involved in, but he wanted the kind of spotlight that was found only in the political arena. He gloried in the title and the special treatment, the deference. If he lost the Senate, he would be like an actor without a stage. Even his precious mills wouldn't make up for that, provided, of course, that his bitch of a daughter really gave them back.

Except for his sexual pursuit of the fountain of youth, she had him to herself now, but fate had played another dirty trick on her. She had him, but she didn't want him, and she was stuck with him until she died. Or he did.

Disgusted, needing to talk to someone, she telephoned Sondra.

"Call off your dogs," she said. "Rhys doesn't want the papers."

"Why not?" Sondra gasped.

Constance told her. "It's Georgia's fault. She's been using her whelp to play on his sympathies."

"I always said it was Georgia we should have gone after."

Constance's eyes lit up gleefully. "Let's have a drink and talk it over," she said.

◆

Connor waited past the end of June, when Anvil—
rechristened Dragoon—was officially resurrected and landings on the Riviera scheduled for August 15. He waited
through July while one hundred thousand canisters of
arms and ammunition were air-dropped to the Free French
in Provence. He could do nothing when the *maquisards* of
the Vercors, a natural fortress in the French Alps, came
out of the bush to fight as an army. They were now
besieged in their mountain fastness by superior numbers
of German occupation troops.

He stayed in the loft of the farmhouse barn in Clermont-
Ferrand during the day, out of the way of the couple who
owned it. His companions, on his night missions to receive and disperse weapons, were the two agents who had
come for him when he arrived—a squat, pudgy, red-
cheeked baker called Mercure, and a huge, ugly ironmon-
ger called Beau—and Claude.

Claude brought him books to pass the long, dull hours
of the day, and Connor was soon awash in French, dipping
into the great novelists as if this were a perpetual Sunday
at Brandon's Gate long ago, when he munched apples and
read his assignments for Adam and dreamed of making
Rhys proud of him.

Three times he and Claude went stealthily to Lyons for
news of Tony. Twice they saw a roundup of Jews, most of
them women and children.

"For 'resettlement' in the east," Claude muttered, his
face wiped clean of all expression. They watched with a
crowd of equally blank-faced bystanders, as if what they
were watching weren't really happening. "They send them
to a detention center in Drancy and from there to
Auschwitz."

"I know," Connor said. "We've known about it for some
time."

"They sent a huge transport out on D-Day," Claude
said. "I hear they've stepped up operations all over Europe since then, to get the job done. Do you still want to
rescue de Sevignac?"

"He was never part of this," Connor said. Then he

caught sight of a slim, fair-haired woman carrying a small boy, and his muscles gathered involuntarily to move him forward. Claude put a restraining hand on his arm and they turned away.

"What can we *do*?" Connor whispered as they walked along the winding streets of the weavers' quarter.

"Nothing. Not yet." Claude paused to light a cigarette. "Listen, hero." He looked up, his eyes burning with anger. "*You* read the reports about it. *We* stood by and watched it. *They* did it. Which is worse, do you think?"

"Are you saying we're as guilty as they are?"

"Maybe we are," Claude said wretchedly. "But that can't be, because if everyone is responsible, then no one is." He stopped and stood staring down the empty street. "I'm saying that 'all that walks in the guise of man is not human,' and the knowledge terrifies me."

They looked at each other, hoping for comfort, finding none.

"Come on," Claude said. "Let's get out of here."

The first week in August they got word that Tony was back in Lyons.

45

♦

It was eerie to creep silently by night across lawns and hedges he knew well by description but had never seen before. It was like a waking dream to come upon the square stone mansion where Georgia had lived. Charet-le-

Roi lay at peace under the starlit sky, but it was secured like a fortress, the gates chained, the windows barred.

Mercure and Beau had just killed the two French militia men who patrolled the house, killed them with a dispatch that raised the hairs on Connor's neck. There was something chilling about the impersonality of the act. A throat, a blade, a swift slash: death.

"Too savage for you?" Claude whispered while the men wiped the blades of their knives on the soft grass and crept forward to look for a way into the house. "Why? They were traitors to their own people. They didn't deserve to live. You've fought in wars before. You've done your share of it."

"Agreed, but mostly from the air," Connor said softly.

"Is it cleaner up there?" Claude's eyes remained fixed on the house and the figures of his men melting into its shadows.

"I thought so until now. But killing is killing, no matter where you do it."

"Not so," the teacher said softly. "For example, there's the latest news from the Vercors. When the *maquisards* had to retreat to the forests, the SS ran amok in the villages. They killed everything that moved. Cats, dogs, and livestock as well as infants, doctors, nurses. What kind of men wreak vengeance like that? The people were hacked to pieces and impaled on meat hooks in the butcher shops. The Vercors is a morgue, the way Central Europe will be a Jewish burial ground long after they find those concentration camps. So, for me, all killing is not the same. How it is done matters, and why." Once more Claude peered through the darkness. "Come on. They've found a way in."

Silently they slid into the vast cellars of the mansion, then through the kitchens to the grand entrance hall and up the palatial stairs to the bedrooms. There was a dim light under one of the doors, and Connor opened it noiselessly to confront a very old lady propped up on lace-trimmed pillows, her white braids streaming down the bodice of her high-necked satin nightdress.

"Our apologies, Madame la Marquise," Connor said in French. "We have come to rescue your son."

The marquise eyed him with exquisite contempt. "My son is not at home," she said.

Ignoring that, Connor told the other three where Tony was likely to be: in the apartment he had occupied with Georgia and Gianna.

"I'll stay with Madame," Connor said. There was no doubt in his mind that she would call the police if he left her.

"You are not French born," she declared. "Who are you?"

"I'm not at liberty to say, but I know Tony very well."

"Liar! You are from the Resistance. My son does not consort with Communist gangsters."

He turned and crossed to the window. The curtains were drawn and he had moved the heavy damask to look out over the park when he heard the unmistakable sound of a trigger being cocked.

He whirled, going for his revolver as she raised the gun and shot him.

He was aware of a scuffle at the door, then of a familiar voice shouting, "For God's sake, *ma mère*, what have you done?"

◆

Nothing in Georgia's social experience had prepared her for a meeting with the only other important woman in Connor's life.

"I'm on my way overseas with a USO troupe," Tirzah had explained on the telephone in her famous voice. "If I run into Connor, I know he'll want firsthand news of you."

Georgia had agreed, and now she and Tirzah sat in the small parlor, sipping iced coffee and waiting for Brandon to wake from his nap. The quiet pressed in on them, interrupted only by two angry birds squawking at each other in the garden and the whir of an electric fan.

"Will you actually go to France?" Georgia offered the plate of cake.

Tirzah refused the cake. "Yes. Close to the line, they said. But it looks like the guys have moved far enough inland to keep me from singing in the surf."

"I wish I were a singer."

"No, you don't," Tirzah said flatly. "You like being exactly who you are, including the part that's Mrs. Connor MacKenzie."

And there it was, spread out between them like a deck of cards.

"Wouldn't you have liked it?" Georgia said.

"Yes and no. Connor's a demanding man."

"He said your career always came first with you."

"It does. It did. Maybe it was because you always came first with him. When it came to Connor, I was never sure what I wanted." Tirzah raised her shoulders. "There was no fighting you, lady. He couldn't—and I wasn't about to climb in the ring with the two of you."

"He was fighting a lot more than me."

Tirzah, lighting a cigarette, made no comment. She had said enough already, perhaps too much. They were both relieved when Brandon came in.

"You're just like Connor!" Tirzah said, startled.

Everyone told Brandon that and he was still too young to resent it. "Do you know my daddy?" was his invariable response.

"Oh, yes, we're old friends. I'm going overseas to sing for the troops, and if I see your dad, I'll tell him I met you."

"My sister's in boarding school," Brandon said, very impressed by it. "So you can't meet her. Maybe you can see my cousin, the baby Malcolm, in London. That's overseas."

"I'll try," Tirzah said, wondering how a Gypsy's daughter would go over in an earl's house.

"Or my two grandfathers."

Tirzah glanced quizzically at Georgia. "Really? Tell me about them."

"I have Grandpa Enoch and Grandfather Brandon. I have a grandmother, too, but she doesn't like children."

"Why not?" Tirzah urged, dying to hear what else this perceptive child had to say about his family.

But Brandon had moved to his mother's side and was asking for a piece of cake.

"Peggy has some for you with your milk."

He left them after a brief squeeze of Tirzah's hand that moved her oddly. She had never felt at home with children, but this one, Connor's flesh and blood, with Connor's eyes and Connor's stance, was different.

"Time for me to go," she said to Georgia, standing now and uninhibitedly smoothing the tiny diagonal tucks of her dress over her lush body. She reached for her handbag and glanced up to find Georgia watching her. They looked at each other without speaking, then moved down the hall to the front door.

"You don't want us to meet again," Tirzah observed.

"No. Nothing personal, you understand."

Tirzah chuckled. "You're right. We'd be pushing our luck. Good-bye, Georgia MacKenzie." Tirzah got into her waiting limousine.

"Good luck over there."

Georgia watched the car pull away, then went back into the house. The meeting with Tirzah had given her something to anticipate. Now worry settled over her again like a pall

Was security so tight in Europe that even an OSS officer couldn't get a message through? Where was he? What was happening to him?

It was Oliver Petrie who called to tell her.

◆

"We have another visitor," the nursing sister said, speaking in the first person plural like Brandon's nanny. "Are we up to it, Colonel?"

"Who is it?" Connor asked.

"That American singer, Tirzah Kent," the nurse said, smoothing his sheets. "Such a trail of lords and ladies as have come to see us," she clucked. "Not to mention the marquis. The staff is in a rare tizzy. I'll go down and fetch her."

He closed his eyes while he waited. They had put him in a private room because he was OSS and might have said too much in his delirium. And they had made him a lieutenant colonel.

Tirzah, wearing a khaki uniform and a soft-crowned cap with a visor, watched him silently from the doorway for a moment before she stepped into the room.

Had Georgia guessed that she still sang most of her songs to Connor? Tirzah was known for blatantly sexy performances, but it was no act. All she had to do was think of him.

He felt her presence and opened his eyes.

"Hi, honey," she said, advancing to the bed. "You don't look so hot."

"Neither do you in that getup. What are you meant to be?"

She smiled broadly and tapped the USO badge on her sleeve. "A girl singer off to entertain the troops. They get coffee and doughnuts and me! Maybe they'd rather have gin and Rita Hayworth, but this is war." She leaned over to kiss him. "I wanted to wear some jazzy clothes, but they wouldn't let me."

"The uniform can't hide it all. You're still dynamite." He smiled.

She laughed her deep, rich laugh. "I see your watch is still ticking. How are you?"

"Like a cat on a hot tin roof." He glanced down at his torso, bandaged from midriff to navel.

"The amazing thing is that the old lady had the strength to pick up the gun and fire it."

"A lioness protecting her cub. Who told you?"

"Oliver. He swore me to secrecy. It was just after I'd been to see your wife and son. Oliver told me the lion cub was feeling like the back end of a horse, and now your wife thinks there's such a thing as too much contrition."

"I enjoy Tony's contrition," Connor said. "He signed

every legal document my lawyers sent over. He'd have signed away his title if I'd asked him to."

"Where is he?"

"In Paris with de Gaulle's new government. One of these days he'll head a ministry."

"His daughter's impatient to see him."

He nodded. "She'll have to wait until the rest of Europe is liberated."

Tirzah looked pensive. "It must be something for a girl to love a father so much."

"Or a boy," he said. He glanced at her speculatively. "So you and Georgia finally met."

"Yeah. That's some woman you married. Now I know why the columnists call her a princess."

"Did you like each other?"

She shook her head. "Women who've been involved with the same man never really *like* each other. Let's say we respect each other. Cigarette?" She lit one for him and placed an ashtray on his chest. "How long will they keep you here?"

"God knows."

"Well, I'll be back and forth to see you. That oughta make you feel better."

He reached for her hand. "You always make me feel better."

"Do I?" she said softly, but now she knew for sure that they would never make love again.

"You know it. I hate to think what my life would have been without you."

"Me too. Well, I'm off to sing my heart out to those GIs before they march off to Berlin. I'll see you in a few weeks."

He was hoping to be home by then, but it would have been ungracious to say so. He put out the cigarette and drifted into a doze. He saw himself lying on the floor at Charet-le-Roi, shot through his midsection with a Walther PBK, helpless for the first time in his life. It was of Oliver Petrie he was thinking in that moment before he lost consciousness, thinking that Oliver should give up politics, divorce Anne, marry Rhoda, and *live*!

When he came to he was in the cellar of the chateau, eager for the morphia supplied by Claude and monitored by the de Sevignacs' family doctor, who was tending him secretly during his daily call on the old marquise. Each time it wore off, Connor groaned from the throbbing pain and the high fever that made the doctor look grave.

"He must be taken to a hospital," he grumbled on the second day.

"Hospital? They'd give him to Barbie and Barbie would torture him to death," Tony argued, changing the cloth on Connor's forehead. "We must wait for the plane. It's his only chance."

"And yours," Claude interjected sharply.

"Given the choice," Tony shot back, "I'd rather live."

"Shut up, both of you," Connor had complained through the morphia that did not so much obliterate pain as make him mind it less. "I can't hear myself think."

"You don't have to think," Tony said. "I'll think for you."

"Think about the worry you're causing my wife! Think about not contesting that divorce."

"I gave you my word. I won't contest it. Our wife has nothing to worry about."

"Not ours! Mine."

"All right, yours. But I love her too. I knew it too late, but it's a real love even so."

"Is that why your mother shot me?"

"For God's sake, MacKenzie!" Tony's woe was almost comical. "You know I had nothing to do with that!"

And Connor, with a grimace, had drifted off. He stayed in a fuzzy state until the third night when movement jarred him awake. He realized that he was being carried toward the rear of the darkened house on a makeshift stretcher and every step sent stabs of hot pain shooting through his middle.

He groaned.

"Quiet!" Claude's voice warned in his ear. "They've posted new guards out front."

They picked their way silently to a waiting farm truck and placed the stretcher on a pile of straw redolent of poultry manure. The smell made him retch and he tried to drag himself up. Hands restrained him and he fought feebly, cursing at the top of his voice and producing only a murmur.

He remembered their alarm, their whispered consultation, the feel of another needle in his arm, then nothing. Tony told him later that he had been driven to a Resistance airfield to meet an incoming bomber that missed its first rendezvous, leaving them to wait through another day in a sun-drenched field, the reek of the camouflaged poultry truck mixing with the scent of hay and field flowers while they fanned flies away from Connor's bandages. He remembered waking up and shouting again in his delirium, then of warning himself to be quiet lest the Germans hear him, of thinking he was Major Oliver Petrie and that one of the anxious men around him was Captain Connor MacKenzie. He remembered shouting for water, a cascade of water, a flood of cool, sweet water—and being given only a sip of tepid liquid, all the doctor had allowed with a wound like his.

"He looks bad," he heard someone say at dusk on that endless arid day.

"He's strong." That voice was Tony's. "I won't let him die. I could never face my daughter if I let him die."

"*Écoutez!*" Beau said, holding up a finger. "Is that a motor?"

They had left him in the tall grass while they lit three flares, and then he was carried to the bomber. His stretcher was laid upon an inflated rubber raft and he was given another shot by the army medic sent to attend him.

He woke only once on that flight to England, to feel Tony's hand holding his, as he would have held a sick child's.

"Tony?" he murmured now as someone took his hand.

"No, it's Malcolm."

♦

Malcolm's left arm was in a sling, and there was a bandage around his head.

"Very fetching," Connor said as casually as he could. Malcolm was like London: battered but still jaunty.

Connor had come to share Malcolm's admiration for the English. London carried on, business as usual, in a land-scape of burnt-out rubble. The whole country had en-dured onerous rationing, blackouts, and the ravages of war for five years, but it was a severe blow to morale when unmanned rocket bombs—Hitler's secret weapon—began hurtling across the Channel, raining random death at any hour of the night or day.

Malcolm was like the nation he had adopted. He had character and spirit and a lot of heart. Connor loved him protectively, as he loved Brandon.

"Sit down," Connor invited. "Is it anything serious?"

"No. The bandages are largely for effect while I'm on leave." Malcolm sat down in a hospital chair too small for him. "I just read my mail. You've got control of the mills at last."

"Georgia has, not I."

Malcolm brushed that aside. "To Father it amounts to the same thing. I'm afraid it will make the situation worse between you."

"Nothing could make it worse," Connor said. "Come on, Mal! You didn't suppose we would ever shake hands and make up, did you? We have the habit of hostility. It's like a drug."

"I often wonder what it was like between you before the hostility. My father has never seemed exactly beneficent to me."

"That's the point. He only *seemed* that way to me. I couldn't forgive myself for letting him dupe me so completely."

"You had other good reasons," Malcolm said.

"Fuel for a fire that was already burning brightly."

"And this sudden friendship Georgia's allowed between Brandon and Rhys?"

"I'm not going to deprive Brandon of a grandfather even if Rhys and I have nothing to say to each other." Connor stirred restlessly. "Damn it, I want to get home!"

"I can see that."

"Make the earl pull some strings, will you? He won't listen to me."

"Consider it done."

Malcolm was as good as his word. Connor's orders to fly back to Washington came through a week later.

◆

Connor felt every thrum of the B-17's motors as Bomber Ferry Command crossed the Atlantic, but he was glad to be awake. He wanted to think about his life with Georgia and his son now that the fighting was over for him.

The war raged on. France was free, but it would be a hard fight to reach Berlin before the Russians did, as some politicians insisted they must.

Connor would return to his desk at the OSS after a few weeks' leave. He and Georgia would live in Alexandria until the war ended and then return to a new house in New York. He had his companies to run and she had Brandon Textiles.

He wondered if controlling the mills had changed anything for her.

He dozed off finally, and the sound of the motors made him dream he was in the old Number One mill, working the mule while a smiling Georgia, in white organdy trimmed with blue ribbons, watched and applauded, and he loved her so much he thought his heart would burst with it. Then his dream faded and he slept until the plane landed at Matthews Air Force Base.

She was waiting for him behind the link fence on the dimly lit tarmac. It seemed like an eternity before he had his arms around her, and they held each other for a long moment without speaking.

"Promise me," she whispered.

"Anything."

"Don't ever leave me again."

"I swear it."

She was trembling violently, and he straightened to study her face. Even in the dim light he could see that her eyes were red, the lids swollen from hours of weeping.

"Tell me!" he said in cold dread. "Tell me what's happened, Georgia!"

"Malcolm and Rowena," she said like a sleepwalker. "The restaurant they were in was hit by a rocket."

"No!" he moaned while she collapsed against him and clutched him as if he could cancel it out. He could barely see her through a blur of tears, and he said nothing. What was there to say?

He held her for what seemed a long time, stroking her hair while she sobbed, feeling utterly bereft and helpless, in his own mute and crushing grief, to help her bear hers.

"Come on, darling," he finally whispered. "Let me take you home."

◆

"What are we doing here?" Jillian wept. "I don't want to hear Malcolm's will read. I don't care what he did with his money. It's his baby I care about."

They were seated around the table in Rhys's formal dining room in Georgetown, Jillian with Tim on her left and Georgia on her right, and Connor seated next to Georgia. At a little distance, the space between them accentuated by empty chairs, were Will's widow and his two children, Richard with his family and, finally, at the head of the table, Rhys and Constance, both unusually quiet.

The Fairleighs' legal representative, Mr. Pennyworth, cleared his throat.

"If everyone is ready," he said in an upper-class British accent untainted by his many years in America, "I shall skip over the small bequests," he announced. "The major bequest, since Mrs. Brandon died with the Squadron Commander, is to his infant son, Malcolm George Connor

Fairleigh Brandon, just two years old. He entrusts joint
guardianship of the child to his sister, Georgia Brandon
MacKenzie, and her husband, Connor MacKenzie, and
appoints the same couple to be joint executors of his son's
estate, including the infant's shares in Brandon Textiles
and also the estate known as Brandon's Gate, until said
child attains the age of twenty-one."

There was a momentary silence in an atmosphere thick
with emotion.

"I'll be damned," Tim Cassadyne said.

"I'll fight it," Rhys said with a black look at Connor.
"You'll never get Brandon's Gate."

"For God's sake, Rhys," Connor said.

A taut silence descended on the room as Rhys shot to
his feet.

"You presumptuous bastard! Who are you to reprimand
me?" His long body arched over the table toward Connor.
"You've been a thorn in my flesh since the day I set eyes
on you. I took you in. I raised you. I educated you. And in
return you robbed me of what I valued most. You married
into my family and then, at the height of my political
career, you attacked me! It wasn't enough for you to take
away the presidency. You meant to destroy my reputation
as well!"

Connor glanced at Constance. So she had never told
Rhys he could have spared himself the Crabtree disclosure
simply by withdrawing from the nomination! She glowered at Connor now, her eyes sullen under red, puffy lids,
and suddenly he realized that he had never known Constance to cry, not once in all these years. He was momentarily touched because her grief was for Malcolm, because
something in her flinty heart had stirred to mourn her
youngest son. But she was still despicable. She and Rhys
had earned each other. He turned back to Rhys.

"I'd do it again," he said quietly. "You'd have been a
menace in the White House."

"What makes you think you're qualified to judge?" Rhys's
tone became insinuating as his gaze flickered between
Georgia and Connor. "Did you really believe you could

make yourself over in my image merely by fornicating with a Brandon?"

Georgia put a hand on Connor's arm, then withdrew it and sat motionless in her chair.

A look of disgust crossed Connor's face and for a moment his body tensed. Then he shook his head. "No, Rhys. I haven't wanted to be you since I was twelve years old."

"You were perfidious even then! God knows what went on between you and Georgia when she was still a little girl."

"You're beneath contempt," Connor said, rising, anger in his dark eyes.

"I? You alienated the affections of my daughter and my son. Why else did she marry you? Why else did Malcolm make such an appalling will?"

"Because he trusted me! That's what you can't abide." Connor sat down, his hand flung out in a gesture of repudiation. "Christ, Rhys, aren't you tired of it? Haven't you had enough?"

His green eyes glittering, Rhys resumed his seat, pulled a cigar from his breast pocket, bit off the end, and spat it out with exquisite contempt. He struck a match and puffed small jets of smoke.

"You're the one who wants more, MacKenzie. You couldn't rest until you had my daughter and now, to make your vengeance complete, you want to have her in *my house!*"

"It's Malcolm's house," Connor said. "In nineteen years it'll belong to his son."

"I'll make sure of that," Rhys said, "if I have to come back from the grave to do it."

"You can spare yourself the journey, Rhys," Constance said in a hollow voice. "Now that Malcolm's dead, no one gives a rap who owns the damned place."

"It's my ancestral home," Rhys replied pompously.

"Then why did you give it to Malcolm?" Richard asked curtly.

"Because he deserved it," Rhys returned.

"More than Will and I did?" Richard shouted at him. "You can go to hell! I hope you do! Come on," he ordered his own family. "We're getting out of here." He ushered Will's widow and children out with him.

"When will the child be sent here?" Rhys asked Pennyworth, who had not turned a hair at the ugly scene.

"As soon as his guardians so direct."

"What about the earl? Has he no objections to losing his grandson?"

"Lord Fairleigh was very fond of his son-in-law—and, I might say, of Major MacKenzie. His Lordship knew and approved the provisions of the Squadron Commander's will. He feels his grandson should take up his new life as soon as possible. When the war is over, he trusts arrangements will be made for the boy to visit England frequently."

Pennyworth looked at Connor, who nodded, his expression bleak.

"If that's all, Mr. Pennyworth," Georgia said, "we must go. We have arrangements to make." She bent to kiss Jillian's cheek. "I'm going to need your help," she said, and left with Connor. Pennyworth packed up his papers and followed.

"He didn't consider me at all," Rhys said when Pennyworth had gone. "I'm young Malcolm's grandfather."

"What if you are?" Constance demanded. "You've alienated the only son I have left. And who would want the responsibility of raising a two-year-old child?"

"I would," Jillian said.

Tim took her hand. "Malcolm and Georgia were very close."

"But I loved him just as much!"

"I know you did, honey, but Malcolm hardly knew me," Tim said.

There was another sad silence.

"Well, Father?" Jillian demanded. "What mischief are you going to do now?"

"There's nothing I can do," Rhys said heavily. "Absolutely nothing."

◆

"Benton Daly can't understand you," Oliver said in his suite at the Willard. "He thinks business is boring."

"Business has its moments and I've had enough espionage to last me a lifetime."

Oliver glanced at his friend, fully aware that the issue of working with the OSS was not at the core of Connor's deep melancholy, and determined to make him say what was.

"Is this a pacifist I see before me?" Oliver asked.

"Not exactly," Connor said. "But three wars are enough for any man, wouldn't you say?"

"That, unfortunately, has never been left for each of us to decide independently. But the OSS only wants you for Research and Analysis."

"I can't analyze Russia. I know nothing about it."

"What does anyone know? Churchill called it a riddle wrapped in a mystery inside an enigma." Oliver sighed again, searching for a way into Connor's mood and finding none.

"What about you? You and Rhoda?"

"We'll go on as we are."

"Oliver, is that good enough?"

"It's the best we can do. You can imagine the kind of publicity there'd be if I divorced Anne and married Rhoda. And maybe it's selfish, but I want to stay in the House. It's been my life."

Connor nodded. "Have it your way, then, Oliver. I'd be the last person to call it selfish."

They smoked in silence for a few moments before Connor put out his cigarette and rubbed his eyes.

"Someday," he said, "I'll have to explain to young Malcolm why his mother and father died."

"And why you didn't."

Connor nodded.

"There's no explanation for either," Oliver said firmly. "In your heart you know it, and so will he when the time comes to talk about it. When does he arrive?"

"Next week."

"Georgia said you'd be spending Thanksgiving at Brandon's Gate. That ought to brighten your spirits considerably."

"Not really."

"Why not? You love the place."

"It doesn't seem important anymore."

"What's changed it for you?"

"I'm haunted by things a Resistance chief told me. 'All that walks in the guise of man is not human,' he said. It's true. It's the essence of this century, brutalized by violence and hungering for more. I don't want any part of it."

"Connor, you can't change a horror by refusing to accept it." Oliver leaned forward in his wheelchair to put a hand on Connor's arm. His thin face, no longer too young for his white hair, was compassionate and grave. "You—especially you—must do something about it. Above all, you must take your joy wherever you can find it."

It was what Oliver had done all these years, but for himself, Connor reflected when he left the Willard, it was not enough.

How could he take any joy in Malcolm's house when Malcolm was dead?

◆

"I see it, I see it!" Brandon jumped up and down expectantly, the only one of them whose joy in the moment was undimmed.

Georgia, Connor, Gianna, and Brandon waited at Mathews Air Force Base for the same kind of Bomber Ferry Command B-17 that had brought Connor home such a short time ago. They had been waiting for almost an hour behind the wire gate before they sighted the plane.

"It's coming in," Gianna said. "He's safe at last."

The khaki-colored plane with its white markings landed with a rumble, a roar, and a squeal of its tires. A long, narrow flight of stairs was wheeled up to it, the door opened, and an officer peered out. Connor waved and the officer nodded and turned to help out a woman in a caped blue coat and hat, the immaculacy of her white gloves apparent even at this distance.

"That's Malcolm's nanny," Brandon said out of long experience with English nannies.

And then, clutching the woman's hand, a small boy appeared, dressed in short pants, a jacket, and knee socks. A shock of platinum hair was visible under his cap, and he clutched a stuffed animal under one arm.

To the family waiting for him, there was something unbearably pathetic about the way he took the stairs one at a time, planting both feet firmly on each one and looking around before he went on, as if to test the stability of this alien world.

"It's a Paddington Bear," Connor said. "Like yours, Gianna."

Gianna nodded. "Poor baby."

"He's awfully little," Brandon said.

"That's why you must be very kind to him," Gianna said to Brandon, drying her eyes.

"Why is everyone crying?"

"Because Uncle Malcolm and Aunt Rowena are dead."

"Oh," Brandon said, but he had never met his aunt and uncle and he didn't understand about death, not really, except that it made grown-ups cry, even his father.

"Can I go out to meet him?" Brandon asked. "Please?"

"Yes, you and Gianna."

They raced across the tarmac toward the trio descending from the plane.

Georgia leaned against Connor. "I want my brother back."

"Yes," he said, putting an arm around her.

"I need a moment more. I can't let that baby see me like this. He'll think I'm sorry he came." She shook her head. "Maybe I am. I never wanted to see him this way."

"He's so utterly defenseless," Connor said.

"So were we, and we survived."

"We had each other."

"Yes, we did. But I want to do it over. I want to change

—myself, the way things were, the way things are. You're
ne only thing I wouldn't change."

"I love you," he said. "Sometimes I can't believe you're
eal."

He watched her fix her tear-streaked face, wondering if
neir future was ineluctably determined by their past, no
natter how far he had come from Brandon's Gate. Even
oung Malcolm, coming toward them on his stout little
egs, bound them to the past.

"Georgia," he said earnestly. "I don't think we should
ve at Brandon's Gate."

She was silent for a moment, watching him.

"All right," she said finally. "We won't go there to live.
ut I'd like to take little Malcolm there for Thanksgiving,
ist to see it, just for a few days. Malcolm would have
ked that."

"For a few days then." He looked up. "They're here.
re you ready?"

"Ready," she said.

◆

: was raining on the night they arrived at Brandon's Gate
a caravan of cars, Gianna and the boys with their
annies in one, Georgia and Connor in a second, Peggy
d Mills with the luggage in a third.

Even rainswept, the house looked welcoming to Connor
; they drove up the drive. It was one of the few places in
e world that had never seemed smaller each time he
turned to it.

But inside, even in the flurry of getting two small boys
 bed, Connor felt uneasy. There were ghosts in Brandon
all, living and dead.

He and Georgia occupied her old bedroom, avoiding
e master suite by tacit agreement.

"It would have been better to have the house com-
letely redecorated," Georgia said when they got into
ed.

"Even then," he said doubtfully.

"Don't think about that now." She held out her arms.

"Make love to me. I used to lie in this bed, a lusty virgin and wonder how it would be."

"Like this," he said, holding her. "And this."

"Oh, yes," she said eagerly. "Like that."

The rain was still lashing at the windows when they fell asleep, but by morning the weather had cleared and they had their coffee on the terrace under a sparkling autumn sun and watched the two little boys play with a kitten on the lawn.

It had been some time since Connor was aware of anything as simple as sunshine on a broad, green lawn.

"I'd forgotten how beautiful it is here," he said.

"But you still don't want to live here."

"No. We've lived here all our lives. It's time we move on."

"Connor, we can't drop the past as if it were excess baggage."

"Did you see that?" Gianna's voice interrupted them and they turned to watch her cross the terrace, dressed in the plaid skirt, cashmere sweater, and saddle shoes that was the uniform of girls her age. "Malcolm's let go of his teddy bear for the first time since he arrived!"

Gianna was seventeen now, and planning to major in psychology when she started college. She was unmistakably de Sevignac—"Except for her clothes," Georgia remarked. "Tony will be scandalized!"—but she had Georgia's height, Georgia's grace, and Georgia's voice. She was fiercely proud of her father and eager to go to France as soon as he could send for her. She loved Connor, but it was Tony she longed for.

"Yes, you're right," Georgia said, turning back to the children.

"That's very significant," Gianna explained seriously. "It means he's beginning to feel secure with us. And I'd better rescue that kitten before they kill it with kindness." She ran down the terrace steps and across the lawn.

Georgia sighed. "I might be looking at Malcolm when he was two."

"That's the trouble," Connor said. "There are too many memories here."

"They'd come with us no matter where we went."

He looked up at the unclouded blue of the sky. "Maybe I don't feel entitled to it," he said.

She took his hand and held it to her cheek. "I thought that was it. But it was Malcolm's to give."

"I don't know if I can take his gift."

"You haven't had much practice, my darling. No one ever gave you anything you really wanted, not even me, not without a struggle."

But he was reluctant to discuss the matter, even with her. His love for her might make him yield when, for both their sakes, he should not. Paradise was not for everyone. He got up.

"I have some calls to make," he said, bending down to kiss her. "I won't be long."

He crossed the terrace and went through the French windows into the drawing room. He stopped, as if the room held him with its familiar, half-forgotten furnishings. It needed a lot of work, but it was clean and quiet and orderly, as if Dilys were still presiding over its antiquated splendor, preserving it intact to the smallest detail.

How he loved this house, and how bitterly he had coveted it! Now, at an agonizing cost, it was his to cherish for a time—but perhaps the risk to him and Georgia was as great as the cost.

He moved across the drawing room to the piano and bent to look at the photograph of Rhys and Constance and the three boys, amazed that they had ever been so young.

Those boys look terribly stupid. That was Jillian.

Malcolm's not bad. That was Georgia.

Malcolm. His friend, his not-quite son, so well beloved and so sorely mourned.

I'm glad I like you, Connor. You're the nearest thing to a real brother I ever had.

And Malcolm's son, with his father's platinum hair and clear green eyes and a look of Rowena about him. Connor's now, to love and protect as he did Brandon and, finally, to set free in a perilous world where heartache waited.

Who gave you permission to dance? Who the hell do you think you are? I'll kill you if you come anywhere near her.

Unalterable.

She loves me, you fool. She always has and there's not a damned thing you can do about it!

And that, too, was unalterable. That was the saving grace.

Connor, let's make a pact of friendship—in blood!

Do we really need a blood pact?

No. You'll always be my best friend.

"Yes." He said it to Georgia and to the rustling voices in this house, acknowledging the bitter and the sweet of his life, the things he could change and those he could not, the things he would never have and that sense of self no one could ever take away from him again.

He had to carry the past with him, but he would live in the present, no matter where he was.

He looked around the square, high-ceilinged room, accepting Malcolm's gift, before he went out to the terrace to tell Georgia.

Acknowledgments

♦

In the extensive research required for this novel, the following books were particularly helpful:

McElvaine, Robert S. *The Great Depression—America 1929–1941*. New York: Times Books, 1984.

Perrett, Geoffrey. *America in the Twenties—a History*. New York: Simon & Schuster, 1982.

Thomas, Gordon and Max Morgan-Witts. *The Day the Bubble Burst*. New York: Doubleday & Company, 1979.

Schachtman, Tom. *The Day America Crashed*. New York: G. P. Putnam's Sons, 1979.

Galbraith, John Kenneth. *The Great Crash of 1929*. New York: Time Incorporated, 1962.

Dixon, Wecter. *The Age of the Great Depression, 1929–1941*. New York: Macmillan, 1958.

Schoenbrun, David. *Soldiers of the Night—The Story of the French Resistance*. New York: E. P. Dutton, 1980.

Above and Beyond—A History of the Medal of Honor from the Civil War to Vietnam. Boston: Boston Publishing Company, 1985.

Hall, Carolyn. *The Twenties in VOGUE*. New York: Harmony Books, 1983.

Hall, Carolyn. *The Thirties in VOGUE*. New York: Harmony Books, 1985.

Woolman, Mary Schenck and Ellen Beers McGowan. *Textiles*. New York: Macmillan, 1946.

Engelbrecht, H. C. and F. C. Hanighen. *Merchants of Death*, New York: Dodd Mead & Company, 1934.

Sampson, Anthony. *The Arms Bazaar—From Lebanon to Lockheed*. New York: The Viking Press, 1977.

Dubofsky, Melvyn and Warren Van Tine. *John L. Lewis* (abridged edition). University of Illinois Press, 1986.

Barnouw, Erik. *A Tower in Babel*. New York: Oxford University Press, 1966.

Walkowitz, Daniel J. *Worker City, Company Town*. University of Illinois Press, 1981.

Horn, Pamela. *Rise and Fall of the Victorian Servant*. New York: St. Martin's Press, 1975.

ABOUT THE AUTHOR

LEONA BLAIR was educated both in the United States and abroad. A former newspaper editor, she is the author of *A Woman's Place*, *With This Ring*, and *Privilege*. She lives in New York, where she is at work on a new novel.